PULP FICTION: THE

Edited by Otto Penzler
Introduction by Laura Lippman

PULP FICTION:
THE DAMES

Edited by Otto Penzler
Introduction by Laura Lippman

Quercus

(*keithdeutsch@comcast.net*; *www.blackmaskmagazine.com*) proprietor and conservator of the respective copyrights, and successor-in-interest to Popular Publications, Inc.

'Kindly Omit Flowers' by Stewart Sterling from *Black Mask Magazine*, March 1942. Copyright © 1942 by Pro-Distributors, Incorporated; renewed 1970 by Popular Publications, Inc. Reprinted by special arrangement with Keith Alan Deutsch (*keithdeutsch@comcast.net*; *www.blackmaskmagazine.com*) proprietor and conservator of the respective copyrights, and successor-in-interest to Popular Publications, Inc.

A CIP catalogue record for this book is available from the British Library.

ISBN (HB) 1-84724-231-6
ISBN-13 978-1-84724-231-0
ISBN (TPB) 1-84724-232-4
ISBN-13 978-1-84724-232-7

10 9 8 7 6 5 4 3 2 1

Typeset by Deltatype Ltd, Birkenhead, Merseyside
Printed and bound in Great Britain by
Clays Ltd, St Ives plc.

CONTENTS

PREFACE

The first female detective to appear in a series of stories was not published until sixteen years after the issue of Edgar Allan Poe's groundbreaking *Tales* in 1845, in which M. Auguste Dupin starred. It was in *Experiences of a Lady Detective* by 'Anonyma' that Mrs. Paschal was forced to accept the offer of a 'strange, exciting and mysterious' career as a detective when her husband suddenly died, leaving her impoverished.

Many women followed in her footsteps, usually making a single appearance but often proving interesting or popular enough to gain the status of a series character. Since women in real life were rarities as members of a police force or as private detectives, the majority of female literary sleuths were either nosey old maids, curious and perky reporters, amateurs who stumbled upon a corpse and thought it either their duty or a bit of fun to find the murderer, or, frequently, a sidekick to a male detective, much as Hastings was to Poirot and Watson was to Holmes.

Women were not significant in the early years of the pulp magazines. Hulbert Footner's Rosika Storey was a successful character in the pages of *Argosy*, eventually appearing as the prime figure in six books beginning in the late 1920s, but she had little company. *Black Mask*, the greatest of all pulp magazines, seldom used stories in which women were featured, rarely bought stories by women writers, and never had a female series character. The major authors didn't mind at all writing about women; they merely wrote about them, sometimes with great prominence, as the catalyst for all the ensuing action. Also, in more cases than not, they were the victims, either innocents or bad girls who got what was coming to them (according to the murderer).

As the detective pulps began to lean more and more toward the hard-boiled private eye, females as central figures slipped even further into the background. This is less surprising than it may seem at first blush. The vast majority of readers of the major detective pulp magazines (*Black Mask, Detective Fiction Weekly, Dime Detective*) were young males. Teenagers and those unsophisticated men who were a bit older loved the notion of the lone gun, the modern knight, the two-fisted private eye who fearlessly battled villains of every type, even whole gangs, in the quest for justice and, not incidentally, the slim blonde who marveled at his courage and resourcefulness.

When girls (and they were usually called girls, or dolls, or, heaven help us, frails, or some term of endearment like honey or sugar or baby or cutie) took the role of detective, they tended to be acceptable to male readers mainly when they were assistants, girl friends, or professional sidekicks, such as reporters. Their roles were predictable in most stories. If they weren't present as comic relief, they needed to be rescued. It would be impossible to calculate the number of pretty young things who were kidnaped or held hostage until our hero burst through a door on the last page to save her – often from a fate worse than death. One needs only to look at the colorful cover paintings that adorned the magazines for evidence of this cliché. It is a rare cover indeed that does not display a buxom beauty in a low-cut dress or sweater, frequently in tatters, being menaced by a thug or gang of thugs.

Some of the lesser pulps, those that paid even less than the standard penny a word, began to feature women in the second decade of the detective pulps, the 1930s, while those that sought an audience with racier material, such as *Gun Molls*, *Saucy Stories* and *Spicy Detective*, had even more ample reason to feature them. In these pages, opportunities for placing luscious young beauties in grave peril of violation were rampant, providing titillation to young male readers who hid their ten-cent purchases inside newspapers or more respectable journals.

Unlike previous books in this series (*Pulp Fiction: The Crimefighters* and *Pulp Fiction: The Villains*), there is no full-length novel between the covers for the good reason that not one of the female characters found herein, nor any others of significance (with one exception) ever appeared in a full-length book. The one exception is Rosika Storey, Hulbert Footner's creation, whose adventures are so tedious that readers would be tempted to hunt me down and stone me if one of them were foisted upon them. If you have read any in the past, you know what I mean; if you haven't, just be grateful.

One area in crime fiction in which woman have been featured with some regularity is as criminals. Among the most accomplished are Madame Koluchy, a master thief in *The Brotherhood of the Seven Kings* by L.T. Meade and Robert Eustace (published in 1899; Eustace later collaborated with Dorothy L. Sayers on *The Documents in the Case* in 1930) and Madame Sara, a criminal whose activities included murder, in *The Sorceress of the Strand* by L.T. Meade, published in 1903.

The pages of the pulps are rich with female jewel thieves of a certain elegance who seem always to be in formal attire at a country house party or a penthouse soirée. They function largely in the same manner as such male counterparts as A. J. Raffles, though they are often required to use their seductive beauty to escape capture. Tough broads appeared in later pulps, either as out-and-out hoodlums or, more frequently but no less dangerously, as gun molls for their gangster boyfriends.

All types of female detectives and crooks who first saw the light of day in pulp magazines appear in these pages – the largest such compilation in the history of publishing. There are independent private investigators, assistants, rogues, victims, molls, police officers and innocent bystanders. They are young and old, good looking and not, funny and dour, brave and timid, violent and gentle, honest and crooked. In short, very much like their male counterparts.

Otto Penzler
New York, January 2007

INTRODUCTION

Lately, it seems to me, there is a lot of hand-wringing about the lack of suitable role models for young people. Apparently, there was some halcyon period in U.S. history when everyone was good and pure, a time when rosy-cheeked boys and girls ate sandwiches made from Wonder Bread while choosing among an embarrassment of heroic riches. They were told that they could grow up to be presidents or astronauts or surgeons or firefighters. Now our young people watch something called celebutantes in homemade sex tapes on YouTube, and we are all going to hell in a handbasket. Or so I've heard. My Internet connection is too slow to watch videos.

At any rate, I simply cannot work myself into the requisite tizzy. You see, I actually came of age as feminism was dawning and what I remember is a dearth of female role models, good or bad. We were advised that any *boy* could grow up to be president; a girl had to set her sights on First Lady. A boy might train to be an astronaut, but a girl could aim no higher than stewardess – and, yes, that was the only term used at the time. If you scanned the textbooks of my grade-school days, virtually the only females you would find would be Pocahontas, Sacagawea and Amelia Earhart. Granted, Earhart really did break the mold. But the mistakes she made in her final journey didn't do much to change all those jokes about women and their sense of direction.

The pop culture of the 1960s did not act as a corrective to the academic void. In the comics, we had Betty or Veronica fighting over the dubious prize of Archie Andrews. At the movies, all I remember is Julie Andrews, who seemed to find fulfillment in tending to others' children. On television, the highlight of the week was the June Taylor Dancers, spreading their legs in synch. (That's not a double entrendre, but a perfectly literal description of the geometric patterns the dancers made when the camera switched to an overhead shot.) I thought it was marvelous, but I doubted I could ever perform such feats. Even then, I knew I wasn't a team player.

How desperate was I for a role model? Desperate enough to fixate on Lois Lane, as played by Noel Neill in all but one season of the *Superman* television series with George Reeve. As I parsed it out, an extremely lucky girl might grow up to be a lady reporter and, occasionally, someone would kidnap her and gag her, and then Superman would show up. Also, one would wear a lot of hats. Fated, perhaps, by my double-L initials, like Lois, I did become a reporter, but a hatless one, and Superman never once put in an appearance.

The point is, I might have been better off with a steady diet of the pulps. Certainly, I wouldn't have been any worse. True, the pulps of the early 20th century will never be mistaken for proto-feminist documents. As Otto Penzler notes in his foreword, the motif of rescue is as prevalent here as it was in any *Superman* episode. Still, even if women seldom take the lead in these stories, there is just enough kink in these archetypes of girlfriend/hussy/sociopath to hint at broader possibilities for the female of the species.

Take Polly Knight in Randolph Barr's 'The Girl Who Knew Too Much.' She seems to be little more than a gang girl Pocahantas, offering to sacrifice her rosy flesh – and we are frequently reminded of its pink perfection – for the sake of the newspaperman she has met by chance. Polly, as it turns out, is not quite the damsel in distress that she appears to be.

Creamy skin, along with jaw-dropping beauty, is a frequent motif in these stories, as are gray eyes, most notably in Dashiell Hammett's 'The Girl with the Silver Eyes.' Here, the Continental Op comes face to face with an old nemesis, and marvels at the effect this chameleon has on every man she meets. 'Porky Grout, whose yellowness was notorious from Seattle to San Diego, standing rigidly in the path of a charging metal monster, with an inadequate pistol in each hand. . . . she had done that to Porky Grout and he hadn't even been human!' The story is vintage Hammett – and provides a lovely inside joke, the red herring of a Baltimore address only a few blocks south from where Hammett lived as a boy.

Raymond Chandler's story here is also vintage, albeit an immature one, if you will. One doesn't need to be a Chandler scholar to spot some *very* familiar elements – an unsavory book dealer with a penchant for kinky photos, a wild-eyed thumb-sucker named Carmen, and a dead chauffeur. 'Killer in the Rain' should be taught in college creative writing courses, if only as an object lesson in how a disciplined writer can reshape material, deepening its themes and expanding its possibilities.

The most dynamic female in these stories, for my money, is the avenging 'Angel Face' in Cornell Woolrich's 'One Night in New York.' Although she requires a timely rescue in the end, her resourcefulness and bravery is beyond question. For the love of her brother, she withstands torture and risks death. But, as she tells us in the story's first paragraph, when she refers to her makeup as war paint, she's being quite literal.

Of course, the reader inclined to pick up this volume is probably already steeped in the work of Chandler, Hammett and Woolrich. But even for the pulp cognoscenti, there are multiple treasures to be unearthed, the style ranging from a little campy to downright classic. Your mileage may vary, as the kids say now, but I was particularly taken by Dizzy Malone in 'The Jane from Hell's Kitchen,' piloting her plane above the Atlantic Ocean and surviving a fusillade of bullets. (Take *that*, Amelia Earhart!) And I feel as if I found a new friend in the acerbic, absurdly competent Sarah Watson, featured in D. B. McCandless's 'He Got What He Asked For.'

Around the time that I read this anthology, the United States was titillated – there is no other word – by the story of an astronaut who drove cross-country to confront a romantic rival. Determined to make good time on the 800-mile-plus journey, the astronaut wore an adult diaper. The items packed for the trip included a BB gun, a four-inch folding *buck knife*, a new steel mallet, black gloves, rubber tubing, and plastic garbage bags. We may never know exactly what was planned, for the intended victim foiled the attack and the assailant was arrested and charged with attempted murder.

The big twist was that the astronaut was a woman. But then, so was the quick-thinking victim. One could argue that this is progress of a sort, women seizing the initiative and taking action, with no men at all at in the climactic confrontation. Or one could conclude that feminism is still a little spotty when women decide that eliminating other women is the way to resolve a romantic triangle. All I know is that I prefer the company of the dames within these pages, who parade before us in impeccable suits, filmy negligees, torn evening dresses and – in the memorable case of Sarah Watson – a voluminous purple kimono worn over a corset. But not a diaper, never a diaper, thank God. Even the most venal among them have more class than that.

Laura Lippman
February 2007

ANGEL FACE

CORNELL WOOLRICH

In 1935, Cornell Woolrich (1903–1968) submitted a story titled 'Angel Face' to *Dime Detective* which published it as 'Murder in Wax' in its March 1, 1935, issue. A couple of years later, he sold a similar story about an avenging angel to *Black Mask*, published it as 'Face Work.' This story has been reprinted often as the title Woolrich clearly wanted for it, 'Angel Face,' finally given to it by Frederic Dannay when he reprinted it in *Ellery Queen's Mystery Magazine* for December 1946. While it has the usual number of plot inconsistencies one expects from the great poet of darkness, it is quintessential Woolrich in all its noir glory. Both 'Face Work' and 'Murder in Wax' were the basis for one of the seven great novels in his memorable 'Black' series, *The Black Angel* (1943).

In addition to its frequent reprints, 'Face Work' enjoyed other incarnations. It was bought for the movies soon after publication – the first of numerous Woolrich stories to be filmed. Columbia made it into a weak 54-minute B movie titled *Convicted* in 1938. Although it starred a young Rita Hayworth and meticulously followed the story, even lifting much of the original dialogue, it is neither a noir film nor a memorable one. Twelve years later, it was aired as 'Angel Face' on radio's famous *Suspense* series (May 19, 1950) with Claire Trevor as the good-hearted stripper who tries to save her brother from being convicted of a murder.

'Face Work' was first published in the October 1937 issue of *Black Mask*.

ANGEL FACE
CORNELL WOOLRICH

I had on my best hat and my warpaint when I dug into her bell. You've heard make-up called that a thousand times, but this is one time it rated it; it was just that – warpaint.

I caught Ruby Rose Reading at breakfast time – hers, not mine. Quarter to three in the afternoon. Breakfast was a pink soda-fountain mess, a tomato-and-lettuce, both untouched, and an empty glass of Bromo Seltzer, which had evidently had first claim on her. There were a pair of swell ski slides under her eyes; she was reading Gladys Glad's beauty column to try to figure out how to get rid of them before she went out that night and got a couple more. A Negro maid had opened the door, and given me a yellowed optic.

'Yes ma'am, who do you wish to see?'

'I see her already,' I said, 'so skip the Morse Code.' I went in up to Ruby Rose's ten-yard line. 'Wheeler's the name,' I said. 'Does it mean anything to you?'

'Should it?' She was dark and Salome-ish. She was mean. She was bad medicine. I could see his finish right there, in her eyes. And it hadn't been any fun to dance at Texas Guinan's or Larry Fay's when I was sixteen, to keep him out of the orphan asylum or the reformatory. I hadn't spent most of my young girlhood in a tinseled G-string to have her take apart what I'd built up, just to see what made him tick.

I said, 'I don't mind coming right out with it in front of your maid – if you don't.'

But evidently she did. Maybe Mandy was on a few other payrolls beside her own. She hit hcr with the tomato-and-lettuce in the left eye as preamble to the request: 'Whaddo I pay you for, anyway? Take Foo-Too around the block a couple of times!'

'I tuk him once already, and he was a good boy,' was the weather report she got on this.

'Well, take him again. Maybe you can kid him it's tomorrow already.'

Mandy fastened something that looked like the business-end of a floor mop to a leash, went out shaking her head. 'You sho didn't enjoy yo'self last night. That Sto'k Club never do agree with you.'

As soon as the gallery was out of the way I said, 'You lay off my brother!'

She lit a cigarette, nosed the smoke at me. 'Well, Gracie Allen, you've come to the wrong place looking for your brother. And, just for the record, what am I supposed to have done to him, cured him of wiping his nose on his sleeve or something?'

'He's been spending dough like wild, dough that doesn't come out of his salary.'

'Then where does it come from?' she asked.

'I haven't found out. I hope his firm never does, either.' I shifted gears, went into low – like when I used to sing 'Poor Butterfly' for the customers – but money couldn't have dragged this performance out of me, it came from the heart, without pay. 'There's a little girl on our street, oh not much to look at, thinks twelve o'clock's the middle of the night and storks leave babies, but she's ready to take up where I leave off, pinch pennies and squeeze nickels along with him, build him into something, get him somewhere, not spread him all over the landscape. He's just a man, doesn't know what's good for him, doesn't know his bass from his oboe. I can't stand by and watch her chew her heart up. Give her a break, and him, and me. Pick on someone your size, someone that can take it. Have your fun and more power to you – but not with all I've got!'

She banged her cigarette to death against a tray. 'O.K., is the screen test about over? Now, will you get out of here, you ham-actress, and lemme get my massage?' She went over and got the door ready for me. Gave a traffic-cop signal over her shoulder with one thumb. 'I've heard of wives pulling this act, and even mothers, and in a pitcher I saw only lately, Camilly it was called, it was the old man. Now it's a sister!' She gave the ceiling the once-over. 'What'll they think of next? Send grandma around tomorrow – next week East Lynne. Come on, make it snappy!' she invited, and hitched her elbow at me. If she'd touched me, I think I'd have murdered her.

'If you feel I'm poison, why don't you put it up to your brother?' she signed off. And very low, just before she walloped the door after me: 'And see how far you get!'

She was right. I said, 'Chick, you're not going to chuck your job, you're not going to Chicago with that dame, are you?'

He looked at me funny and he said, 'How did you know?'

'I saw your valise all packed, when I wanted to send one of your suits to the cleaners.'

'You ought to be a detective,' he said, and he wasn't pally. 'O.K.,' he said, 'now that you mention it,' and he went in and he got it to show me – the back of it going out the door. But I got over there to the door before he did, and pulled a Custer's Last Stand. I skipped the verse and went into the patter chorus. And boy did I sell it, without a spot and without a muted trumpet solo either! At the El-Fay in the old days they would have all been crying into their gin and wiring home to mother.

'I'm not asking anything for myself. I'm older than you, Chick, and when a girl says that you've got her down to bedrock. I've been around plenty, and "around" wasn't pretty. Maybe you think it was fun wrestling my way home each morning at five, and no holds barred, just so – so. . . . Oh, I didn't know why myself sometimes; just so you wouldn't turn out to be another corner lizard, a sharpshooter, a bum like the rest of them. Chick, you're just a punk of twenty-four, but as far as I'm concerned the sun rises and sets across your shoulders. Me and little Mary Allen, we've been rooting for you all along; what's the matter with her, Chick? Just because her face don't come out of boxes and she doesn't know the right grips, don't pass her by for something that ought to be shampooed out of your hair with gasoline.'

But he didn't have an ear for music; the siren song had got to him like Ulysses. And once they hear that. . . . 'Get away from the door,' he said, way down low. 'I never raised a hand to you in my life, I don't want to now.'

The last I saw of him he was passing the back of his hand slowly up and down his side, like he was ashamed of it; the valise was in the other one. I picked myself up from the opposite side of the foyer where he'd sent me, the place all buckling around me like seen through a sheet of water. I called out after him through the open door: 'Don't go, Chick! You're heading straight for the eight-ball! Don't go to her, Chick!' The acoustics were swell. Every door in the hall opened to get an earful.

He just stood there a split-second without looking back at me, yellow light gushing out at him through the port-hole of the elevator.

He straightened his hat, which my chin against his duke had dislodged – and no more Chick.

At about four that morning I was still snivelling into the gin he'd left behind him, and talking to him across the table from me – without getting any answer – when the door-bell rang. I thought it was him for a minute, but it was two other guys. They didn't ask if they could come in, they just went 'way around to the other side of me and then showed me a couple of tin-heeled palms. So I did the coming-in – after them; I lived there, after all.

They looked the place over like they were prospective tenants being shown an apartment. I didn't go for that; detectives belong in the books you read in bed, not in your apartment at four bells, big as life. 'Three closets,' I mentioned, 'and you get a month's concession. I'm not keeping you gentlemen up, am I?'

One of them was kind of pash looking; I mean he'd washed his face lately, and if he'd been the last man in the world, well, all right, maybe I could have overlooked the fact he was a bloodhound on two legs. The other one had a face like one of those cobblestones they dug up off Eighth Avenue when they removed the trolley tracks.

'You're Jerry Wheeler, aren't you?' the first one told me.

'I've known that for twenty-seven years,' I said. 'What brought the subject up?'

5

Cobblestone-face said, 'Chick Wheeler's sister, that right?'

'I've got a brother and I call him Chick,' I consented. 'Any ordinance against that?'

The younger one said, 'Don't be so hard to handle. You're going to talk to us and like it.' He sat down in a chair, cushioned his hands behind his dome. He said, 'What time'd he leave here this evening?'

Something warned me, 'don't answer that.' I said, 'I really couldn't say. I'm not a train-despatcher.'

'He was going to Chicago with a dame named Ruby Rose Reading; you knew that, didn't you?'

I thought, 'I hit the nail on the head, he did help himself to his firm's money. Wonder how much he took? Well, I guess I'll have to go back to work again at one of the hotspots; maybe I can square it for him, pay back a little each week.' I kept my face steady. I said, 'Now, why would he go anywhere with anyone with a name like that? It sounds like it came off a bottle of nail-polish. Come to the point, gentlemen. What's he supposed to have done?'

'There's no supposition about what he's done. He went to the Alcazar Arms at eight-fifteen tonight and throttled Ruby Rose Reading to death, Angel Face.'

And that was the first time I heard myself called that. I also heard the good-looking one remonstrate: 'Aw, don't give it to her that sudden, Coley, she's a girl after all,' but it came from 'way far away. I was down around their feet somewhere sniffling into the carpet.

The good-looking one picked me up and straightened me out in a chair. Cobblestone said, 'Don't let her fool you, Burnsie, they all pull that collapsible concertina act when they wanna get out of answering questions.' He went into the bedroom and I could hear him pulling out bureau drawers and rummaging around.

I got up on one elbow. I said, 'Burns, he didn't do it! Please, he didn't do it! All right, I did know about her. He was sold on her. That's why he couldn't have done it. Don't you see, you don't kill the thing you love?'

He just kind of looked at me. 'You go to bat for the thing you love too,' he murmured. He said, 'I've been on the squad eight years now. We never in all that time caught a guy as dead to rights as your brother. He showed up with his valise in the foyer of the Alcazar at exactly twelve minutes past eight tonight. He said to the doorman, 'What time is it? Did Miss Reading send her baggage down yet? We've got to make a train.' Well, she had sent her baggage down and then she'd changed her mind, she'd had it all taken back upstairs again. There's your motive right there. The doorman rang her apartment and said through the announcer, "Mr. Wheeler's here." And she gave a dirty laugh and sang out, "I can hardly wait."

'So at thirteen past eight she was still alive. He went up, and he'd no sooner got there than her apartment began to signal the doorman frantically. No one answered his hail over the announcer, so he chased up, and he found your brother crouched over her, shaking her, and she was dead. At fifteen minutes past eight o'clock. Is that a case or is that a case?'

I said, 'How do you know somebody else wasn't in that apartment and strangled her just before Chick showed up? It's got to be that!'

He said, 'What d'you suppose they're paying that door-man seventy-five a month for? The only other caller she had that whole day was you yourself, at three that afternoon, five full hours before. And she'd only been dead fifteen to twenty minutes by the time the assistant medical examiner got to her.'

I said, 'Does Chick say he did it?'

'When you've been in this business as long as I have, you'd have their heads examined if any of them ever admitted doing anything. Oh, no-o, of course he didn't do it. He says he was crouched over her, shaking her, trying to restore her!'

I took a deep breath. I said, 'Gimme a swallow of that gin. Thanks.' I put the tumbler down again. I looked him right in the eye. 'All right, I did it! Now how d'ye like that? I begged him not to throw his life away on her. When he walked out anyway, I beat him up to her place in a taxi, got there first, gave her one last chance to lay off him. She wouldn't take it. She was all soft and squashy and I just took a grip and pushed hard.'

'And the doorman?' he said with a smile.

'His back was turned. He was out at the curb seeing some people into a cab. When I left, I took the stairs down. When Chick signaled from her apartment and the doorman left his post, I just walked out. It was a pushover.'

His smile was a grin. 'Well, if you killed her, you killed her.' He called in to the other room, 'Hey, Coley, she says she killed her!' Coley came back, flapped his hand at me disgustedly, said, 'Come on, let's get out of here. There's nothing doing around here.'

He opened the door, went out into the hall. I said, 'Well, aren't you going to take me with you? Aren't you going to let him go and hold me instead?'

'Who the hell wants you?' came back through the open door.

Burns, as he got up to follow him, said off-handedly, 'And what was she wearing when you killed her?' But he kept walking to the door, without waiting for the answer.

They'd had a train to make. I swallowed hard. 'Well, I – I was too steamed-up to notice colors or anything, but she had on her coat and hat, ready to leave.'

He turned around at the door and looked at me. His grin was sort of sympathetic, understanding. 'Sure,' he said softly. 'I guess she took 'em off, though, after she found out she was dead and wasn't going anywhere after all. We found her in pajamas. Write us a nice long letter about it tomorrow, Angel Face. We'll see you at the trial, no doubt.'

There was a glass cigarette-box at my elbow. I grabbed it and heaved, beserk. 'You rotten, lowdown – detective, you! Going around snooping, framing innocent people to death! Get out of here! I hope I never see your face again!'

It missed his head, crashed and tinkled against the door-frame to one side of him. He didn't cringe, I liked that about him, sore as I was. He just gave a long drawn-out whistle. 'Maybe you did do it at that,' he said. 'Maybe I'm underestimating you,' and he touched his hatbrim and closed the door after him.

The courtroom was so unnaturally still that the ticking of my heart sounded like a cheap alarm-clock in the silence. I kept wondering how it was they didn't put me out for letting it make so much noise. A big blue fly was buzzing on the inside of the windowpane nearest me, trying to find its way out. The jurists came filing in like ghosts, and slowly filled the double row of chairs in the box. All you could hear was a slight rustle of clothing as they seated themselves. I kept thinking of the Inquisition, and wondered why they didn't have black hoods over their heads.

'Will the foreman of the jury please stand?'

I spaded both my hands down past my hips and grabbed the edges of my seat. My handkerchief fell on the floor and the man next to me picked it up and handed it back to me. I tried to say 'Thanks' but my jaws wouldn't unlock.

'Gentlemen of the jury, have you reached a verdict?'

I told myself, 'He won't be able to hear it, if my heart doesn't shut up.' It was going bangetty-bangetty-bang!

'We have, your honor.'

'Gentlemen of the jury, what is your verdict?'

The banging stopped; my heart wasn't going at all now. Even the fly stopped buzzing. The whole works stood still.

'We find the defendant guilty of murder in the first degree.'

Some woman screamed out 'No!' at the top of her lungs. It must have been me, they were all turning their heads to look around at me. The next thing I knew, I was outside in the corridor and a whole lot of people were standing around me. Everything looked blurred. A voice said, 'Give her air, stand back.' Another voice said, 'His sister. She was on the stand earlier in the week.' Ammonia fumes kept tickling the membranes of my nostrils. The first voice said, 'Take her home. Where does she live? Anybody know where she lives?'

'I know where she lives. I'll take care of her.'

Somebody put an arm around my waist and walked me to the creaky courthouse elevator, led me out to the street, got in a taxi after me. I looked, and it was that dick, Burns. I climbed up into the corner of the cab, put my feet on the seat, shuffled them at him. I said, 'Get away from me, you devil! You railroaded him, you butcher!'

'Attagirl,' he said gently. 'Feeling better already, aren't you?' He gave the old address, where Chick and I had lived. The cab started and I couldn't get him out of it. I felt too low even to fight any more.

'Not there,' I said sullenly. 'I'm holed up in a cheap furnished room now, off Second Avenue. I've hocked everything I own, down to my vaccination mark! How d'you suppose I got that lawyer Schlesinger for him? And a lot of good it did him! What a wash-out he turned out to be!'

'Don't blame him,' he said. 'He couldn't buck that case we turned over to the State; Darrow himself couldn't have. What he should have done was let him plead guilty to second-degree, then he wouldn't be in line for short-circuiting. That was his big mistake.'

'No!' I shrilled at him. 'He wanted us to do that, but neither Chick nor I would hear of it! Why should he plead guilty to anything, even if it was only housebreaking, when he's innocent? That's a guilty man's dodge, not an innocent man's. He hasn't got half-an-hour's detention rightfully coming to him! Why should he lie down and accept twenty years? He didn't lay a hand on Ruby Reading.'

'Eleven million people, the mighty State of New York, say that he did.'

I got out, went in the grubby entrance, between a delicatessen and a Chinese laundry. 'Don't come in with me, I don't want to see any more of you!' I spat over my shoulder at him. 'If I was a man I'd knock you down and beat the living hell out of you!'

He came on, though, and upstairs he closed the door behind him, pushing me out of the way to get in. He said, 'You need help Angel Face, and I'm crying to give it to you.'

'Oh, biting the hand that feeds you, turning into a double-crosser, a turncoat!'

'No,' he said, 'no,' and sort of held out his hands as if asking me for something. 'Sell me, won't you?' he almost pleaded. 'Sell me that he's innocent, and I'll work my fingers raw to back you up! I didn't frame your brother. I only did my job. I was sent there by my superiors in answer to the patrolman's call that night, questioned Chick, put him under arrest. You heard me answering their questions on the stand. Did I distort the facts any? All I told them was what I saw with my own eyes, what I found when I got to Reading's apartment. Don't hold that against me, Angel Face. Sell me, convince me that he didn't do it, and I'm with you up to the hilt.'

'Why?' I said cynically. 'Why this sudden yearning to undo the damage you've already done?'

He opened the door to go. 'Look in the mirror sometime and find out,' was all he said. 'You can reach me at Centre Street, Nick Burns.' He held out his hand uncertainly, probably expecting me to slap it aside.

I took it instead. 'O.K., flatfoot,' I sighed wearily. 'No use holding it against you that you're a detective. You probably don't know any better. Before you go, gimme the address of that maid of hers, Mandy Leroy. I've got an idea she didn't tell all she knew.'

9

'She went home at five that day. How can she help you?'

'I bet she was greased plenty to softpedal the one right name that belongs in this case. She mayn't have been there, but she knew who to expect around. She may have even tipped him off that Ruby Rose was throwing him over. It takes a woman to see through a woman.'

'Better watch yourself going up there alone,' he warned me. He took out a notebook. 'Here it is, One Hundred Eighteenth, just off Lenox.' I jotted it down. 'If she was paid off like you think, how you going to restore her memory? It'll take heavy sugar. . . .' He fumbled in his pocket, looked at me like he was a little scared of me, finally took out something and shoved it out of sight on the bureau. 'Try your luck with that,' he said. 'Use it where it'll do the most good. Try a little intimidation with it, it may work.'

I grabbed it up and he ducked out in a hurry, the big coward. A hundred and fifty bucks. I ran out to the stairs after him. 'Hey!' I yelled, 'aren't you married or anything?'

'Naw,' he called back, 'I can always get it back, anyway, if it does the trick.' And then he added, 'I always did want to have something on you, Angel Face.'

I went back into my cubbyhole again. 'Why, the big rummy!' I said hotly. I hadn't cried in court when Chick got the ax, just yelled out. But now my eyes got all wet.

'Mandy doan live her no mo'e,' the colored janitor of the 118th Street tenement told me.

'Where'd she go? And don't tell me you don't know, because it won't work.'

'She done move to a mighty presumptuous neighborhood, doan know how come all of a sudden. She gone to Edgecomb Avenue.'

Edgecomb Avenue is the Park Avenue of New York's darktown. Mandy had mentioned on the stand, without being asked, that Reading had died owing her two months' wages. Yet she moves to the coloured Gold Coast right on top of it. She hadn't been paid off – not much!

Edgecomb Avenue is nothing to be ashamed of in any man's town. Every one of the trim modern apartment buildings had a glossy private car or two parked in front of the door. I tackled the address he'd given me, and thought they were having a housewarming at first. They were singing inside and it sounded like a revival meeting.

A fat old lady came to the door, in a black silk dress, tears streaming down her cheeks. 'I'se her mother, honey,' she said softly in answer to what I told her, 'and you done come at an evil hour. My lamb was run over on the street, right outside this building, only yesterday, first day we moved here! She's in there daid now, honey. The Lawd give and the Lawd has took away again.'

I did a little thinking.

Why just her, and nobody else, when she held the key to the Reading murder? 'How did it happen to her? Did they tell you?'

'Two white men in a car,' she mourned. ''Peared almost like they run her down purposely. She was walking along the sidewalk, folks tell me, wasn't even in the gutter at all. And it swung right up on the sidewalk aftah her, go ovah her, then loop out in the middle again and light away, without nevah stopping!'

I went away saying to myself, 'That girl was murdered as sure as I'm born, to shut her mouth. First she was bribed, then when the trial was safely over she was put out of the way for good!'

Somebody big was behind all this. And what did I have to fight that somebody with? A borrowed hundred and fifty bucks, an offer of cooperation from a susceptible detective, and a face.

I went around to the building Ruby Rose had lived in, and struck the wrong shift. 'Charlie Baker doesn't come on until six, eh?' I told the doorman. 'Where does he live? I want to talk to him.'

'He don't come on at all any more. He quit his job, as soon as that—' he tilted his head to the ceiling, 'mess we had upstairs was over with, and he didn't have to appear in court no more.'

'Well, where's he working now?'

'He ain't working at all, lady. He don't have to any more. I understand a relative of his died in the old country, left him quite a bit, and him and his wife and his three kids have gone back to England to live.'

So he'd been paid off heavily too. It looked like I was up against Wall Street itself. No wonder everything had gone so smoothly.

No wonder even a man like Schlesinger hadn't been able to make a dent in the case.

'But I'm not licked yet,' I said to myself, back in my room. 'I've still got this face. It ought to be good for something. If I only knew where to push it, who to flash it on!'

Burns showed up that night, to find out how I was making out.

'Here's your hundred and fifty back,' I told him bitterly. 'I'm up against a stone wall every way I turn. But is it a coincidence that the minute the case is in the bag, their two chief witnesses are permanently disposed of, one by exportation, the other by hit-and-run? They're not taking any chances on anything backfiring later.'

He said, 'You're beginning to sell me. It smells like rain.'

I sat down on the floor (there was only one chair in the dump) and took a dejected half-Nelson around my own ankles. 'Look, it goes like this. Some guy did it. Some guy that was sold on her. Plenty of names were spilled by Mandy and Baker, but not the right one. The ones that were brought out didn't lead anywhere, you saw that yourself. The mechanics of the thing don't trouble me a bit, the how and why could be cleared up easy enough – even by you.'

'Thanks,' he said.

'It's the who that has me baffaloed. There's a gap there. I can't jump across to the other side. From there on, I could handle it beautifully. But I've got to close that gap, that who, or I might as well put in the order for Chick's headstone right now.'

He took out a folded newspaper and whacked himself disgustedly across the shins with it. 'Tough going, kid,' he agreed.

'I'll make it,' I said. 'You can't keep a good girl down. The right guy is in this town. And so am I in this town. I'll connect with him yet, if I've got to use a ouija board!'

He said, 'You haven't got all winter. He comes up for sentence Wednesday.' He opened the door. 'I'm on your side,' he let me know in that quiet way of his.

He left the paper behind him on the chair. I sat down and opened it. I wasn't going to do any reading, but I wanted to think behind it. And then I saw her name. The papers had been full of her name for weeks, but this was different; this was just a little boxed ad off at the side.

AUCTION SALE

Jewelry, personal effects and
furniture belonging to the late
Ruby Rose Reading
Monarch Galleries Saturday A.M.

I dove at the window, rammed it up, leaned halfway out. I caught him just coming out of the door.

'Burns!' I screeched at the top of my voice. 'Hey, Burns! Bring that hundred and fifty back up here! I've changed my mind!'

The place was jammed to the gills with curiosity-mongers and bargain-hunters, and probably professional dealers too, although they were supposed to be excluded. There were about two dozen of those 100-watt blue-white bulbs in the ceiling that auction rooms go in for and the bleach of light was intolerable, worse than on a sunny beach at high noon.

I was down front, in the second row on the aisle; I'd got there early. I wasn't interested in her diamonds or her furs or her thissas or her thattas. I was hoping something would come up that would give me some kind of a clue, but what I expected it to be, I didn't know myself. An inscription on a cigarette case maybe. I knew how little chance there was of anything like that. The D.A.'s office had sifted through her things pretty thoroughly before Chick's trial, and what they'd turned up hadn't amounted to a row of pins. She'd been pretty cagy that way, hadn't left much around. All bills had been addressed to her personally, just like she'd paid her rent with her own personal checks, and fed the account herself. Where the funds originated in the first place was never explained. I suppose she took in washing.

They started off with minor articles first, to warm the customers up. A cocktail shaker that played a tune, a make-up mirror with a light behind it, a ship's model, things like that. They got around to her clothes next, and the women customers started 'ohing' and 'ahing' and foaming at the mouth. By the looks of most of them that was probably the closest they'd ever get to real sin, bidding for its hand-me-downs.

The furniture came next, and they started to talk real money now. This out of the way, her ice came on. Brother, she'd made them say it with diamonds, and they'd all spoken above a whisper too! When the last of it went, that washed up the sale; there was nothing else left to dispose of but the little rosewood jewel-case she'd kept them in. About ten by twelve by ten inches deep, with a little gilt key and lock; not worth a damn but there it was. However, if you think an auctioneer passes up anything, you don't know your auctioneers.

'What am I offered for this?' he said almost apologetically. 'Lovely little trinket box, give it to your best girl or your wife or your mother, to keep her ornaments in or old love letters.' He knocked the veneer with his knuckles, held it outward to show us the satin lining. Nothing in it, like in a vaudeville magician's act. 'Do I hear fifty cents, just to clear the stand?'

Most of them were getting up and going already. An over-dressed guy in my same row, across the aisle, spoke up. 'You hear a buck.'

I took a look at him, and I took a look at the box. 'If you want it, I want it, too,' I decided suddenly. 'A guy splurged up like you don't hand a plain wooden box like that to any woman that he knows.' I opened my mouth for the first time since I'd come in the place. 'You hear a dollar and a quarter.'

'Dollar-fifty.'

'Two dollars.'

'Five.' The way he snapped it out, he meant business.

I'd never had such a strong hunch in my life before but now I wanted that box, had to have it, I felt it would do me some good. Maybe this overdressed monkey had given it to her, maybe Burns could trace where it had been bought. . . .

'Seven-fifty.'

'Ten.'

'Twelve.'

The auctioneer was in seventh heaven. 'You're giving yourself away, brother, you're giving yourself away!' I warned my competitor silently.

We leaned forward out of our seats and sized each other up. If he was giving himself away, I suppose I was too. I could see a sort of shrewd speculation in his snaky eyes, they screwed up into slits, seeming to say, 'What's your racket?' Something cold went down my back, hot as it was under all those mazdas.

'Twenty-five dollars,' he said inexorably.

I thought: 'I'm going to get that thing if I spend every cent of the money Burns loaned me!'

'Thirty,' I said.

With that, to my surprise, he stood up, flopped his hand at it disgustedly, and walked out.

When I came out five minutes later with the box wrapped up under my arm, I saw him sitting in a young dreadnaught with another man, a few yards down the street.

'So I'm going to be followed home,' I said to myself, 'to find out who I am.' That didn't worry me any; I'd rented my room under my old stage name of Honey Sebastian (my idea of a classy tag at sixteen) to escape the notoriety attendant on Chick's trial. I turned up the other way and hopped down into the subway, which is about the best bet when the following is to be done from a car. As far as I could make out, no one came after me.

I watched the street from a corner of the window after I got home, and no one going by stopped or looked at the house or did anything but mind his own business. And if it had been that flashy guy on my tail, you could have heard him coming from a block away. I turned to the wrapped box and broke the string.

Burns' knock at my door at five that afternoon was a tattoo of anxious impatience. 'God, you took long to get here!' I blurted out. 'I phoned you three times since noon.'

'Lady,' he protested, 'I've been busy, I was out on something else, only just got back to Headquarters ten minutes ago. Boy, you threw a fright into me.'

I didn't stoop to asking him why he should be so worried something had happened to me; he might have given me the right answer. 'Well,' I said, 'I've got him,' and I passed him the rosewood jewel case.

'Got who?'

'The guy that Chick's been made a patsy for.'

He opened it, looked in, looked under it. 'What's this?'

'Hers. I had a hunch, and I bought it. He must have had a hunch too – only his agent – and it must have been his agent, he wouldn't show up himself – didn't follow it through, wasn't sure enough. Stick your thumb under the little lock. Not over it, down below it, and press hard on the wood.' Something clicked, and the satin bottom flapped up, like it had with me.

'Fake bottom, eh?' he said.

'Don't be an echo. Read that top letter out loud. That was the last one she got, the very day it happened.'

' "You know, baby," ' Burns read. ' "I think too much of you to ever let you go. And if you ever tired of me and tried to leave me, I'd kill you first, and then you could go wherever you want. They tell me you've been seen going around a lot lately with some young punk. Now, baby, I hope for his sake, and yours too, that when I come back day after tomorrow I find it isn't so, just some more of my boys' lies. They like to rib me sometimes, see if I can take it or not." '

'He gave her a bum steer there on purpose,' I pointed out. 'He came back "tomorrow" and not "day after," and caught her with the goods.'

'Milt,' Burns read from the bottom of the page. And then he looked at me, and didn't see me for once.

'Militis, of course,' I said, 'the Greek night-club king. Milton, as he calls himself. Everyone on Broadway knows him. And yet, d'you notice how that name stayed out of the trial? Not a whisper from beginning to end! That's the missing name all right!'

'It reads that way, I know,' he said undecidedly, 'but there's this: She knew her traffic signals. Why would she chuck away the banana and hang onto the skin? In other words, Milton spells real dough, your brother wasn't even carfare.'

'But Militis had her branded—'

'Sure, but—'

'No, I'm not talking slang now. I mean actually, physically; it's mentioned in one of these letters. The autopsy report had it too, remember? Only they mistook it for an operation scar or scald. Well, when a guy does that, anyone would have looked good to her, and Chick was probably a godsend. The branding was probably not the half of it, either. It's fairly well known that Milton likes to play rough with his women.'

'All right, kid,' he said, 'but I've got bad news for you. This evidence isn't strong enough to have the verdict set aside and a new trial called. A clever mouthpiece could blow this whole pack of letters out the window with one breath. Ardent Greek temperament, and that kind of thing, you know. You remember how Schlesinger dragged it out of Mandy that she'd overheard more than one guy make the same kind of jealous threats. Did it do any good?'

'This is the McCoy, though. He came through, this one, Militis.'

'But, baby, you're telling it to me and I convince easy, from you. You're not telling it to the Grand Jury.'

I shoved the letters at him. 'Just the same, you chase out, have 'em photostated, every last one of them, and put 'em in a cool, dry place. I'm going to dig something a little more convincing to go with them, if that's what's needed. What clubs does he own?'

'What clubs doesn't he? There's Hell's Bells—' He stopped short, looked at me. 'You stay out of there.'

'One word from you. . . .' I purred, and closed the door after him.

'A little higher,' the manager said. 'Don't be afraid. We've seen it all before.'

I took another hitch in my hoisted skirt, gave him a look. 'If it's my appendix you want to size up, say so. It's easier to uncover the other way around, from up to down. I just sing and dance. I don't bathe for the customers.'

'I like 'em like that,' he nodded approvingly to his yes-man. 'Give her a chord, Mike,' he said to his pianist.

'The Man I Love,' I said. 'I do dusties, not new ones.'

> *'And he'll be big and strong,*
> *The man I love—'*

'Good tonsils,' he said. 'Give her a dance chorus, Mike.'

Mike said disgustedly, 'Why d'ya wanna waste your time? Even if she was paralyzed from the waist down and had a voice like a frog, ain't you got eyes? Get a load of her face, will you?'

'You're in,' the manager said. 'Thirty-five, and buy yourself some up-to-date lyrics. Come around at eight and get fitted for some duds. What's your name?'

'Bill me as Angel Face,' I said, 'and have your electrician give me an amber spot. They take the padlocks off their wallets when I come out in an amber spot.'

He shook his head, almost sorrowfully. 'Hang onto that face, girlie. It ain't gonna happen again in a long time!'

Burns was holding up my locked room-door with one shoulder when I got back. 'Here's your letters back; I've got the photostats tucked away in a safe place. Where'd you disappear to?'

'I've landed a job at Hell's Bells. I'm going to get that guy and get him good! If that's the way I've got to get the evidence, that's the way. After all, if he was sold on her, *I'll* have him cutting out paper dolls before two weeks are out. What'd she have that I haven't got? Now, stay out of there. Somebody might know your face, and you'll only queer everything.'

'Watch yourself, will you, Angel Face? You're playing a dangerous game. That Milton is nobody's fool. If you need me in a hurry, you know where to reach me. I'm right at your shoulder, all the way through.'

I went in and stuck the letters back in the fake bottom of the case. I had an idea I was going to have a visitor fairly soon, and wasn't going to tip my hand.

I stood it on the dresser-top and threw in a few pins and glass beads for luck.

The timing was eerie. The knock came inside of ten minutes. I'd known it was due, but not that quick. It was my competitor from the auction room, flashy as ever; he'd changed flowers, that was all.

'Miss Sebastian,' he said, 'isn't it? I'd like very much to buy that jewel case you got.'

'I noticed that this morning.'

He went over and squinted into it.

'That all you wanted it for, just to keep junk like that in?'

'What'd you expect to find, the Hope diamond?'

'You seemed willing to pay a good deal.'

'I lose my head easy in auction rooms. But, for that matter, you seemed to be willing to go pretty high yourself.'

'I still am,' he said. He turned it over, emptied my stuff out, tucked it under his arm, put something down on the dresser. 'There's a hundred dollars. Buy yourself a real good one.'

Through the window I watched the dreadnaught drift away again. 'Just a little bit too late in getting here,' I smiled after it. 'The cat's out of the bag now and a bulldog will probably chase it.'

The silver dress fitted me like a wet compress. It was one of those things that break up homes. The manager flagged me in the passageway leading back. 'Did you notice that man all by himself at a ringside table? You know who he is, don't you?'

If I hadn't, why had I bothered turning on all my current his way? 'No,' I said, round-eyed, 'who?'

'Milton. He owns the works. The reason I'm telling you is this: You've got a date with a bottle of champagne at his table, starting in right now. Get on in there.'

We walked on back.

'Mr. Milton, this is Angel Face,' the manager said. 'She won't give us her right name, just walked in off Fifty-second Street last Tuesday.'

'And I waited until tonight to drop around here!' he laughed. 'What you paying her, Berger?' Then before the other guy could get a word out, 'Triple it! And now get out of here.'

The night ticked on. He'd look at me then he'd suddenly throw up his hands as though to ward off a dazzling glare. 'Turn it off, it hurts my eyes.'

I smiled a little and took out my mirror. I saw my eyes in it, and in each iris there was a little electric chair with Chick sitting strapped in it. Three weeks from now, sometime during that week. Boy, how they were rushing him! It made it a lot easier to go ahead.

I went back to what we'd been talking about – and what are any two people talking about, more or less, in a nightclub at four in the morning? 'Maybe,' I said, 'who can tell? Some night I might just feel like changing the scenery around me, but I couldn't tell you about it, I'm not that kind.'

'You wouldn't have to,' he said. He fooled with something below table-level, then passed his hand to me. I took it and knotted my handkerchief around the latch-key he'd left in it. Burns had been right. I was a dangerous game, and bridges were blazing and collapsing behind me.

The doorman covered a yawn with a white kid glove, said, 'Who shall I announce?'

'That's all been taken care of,' I said, 'so you can go back to your beauty sleep.'

He caught on, said insinuatingly, 'It's Mr. Milton, isn't it? He's out of town tonight.'

'You're telling me!' I thought. I'd sent him the wire that fixed that, signed the name of the manager of his Philly club. 'You've been reading my mail,' I said, and closed the elevator in his face.

The key worked, and the light switch worked, and his Filipino had the night off, so the rest was up to me. The clock in his two-story living room said four-fifteen. I went to the second floor of his penthouse and started in on the bedroom. He was using Ruby Rose Reading's jewel case to hold his collar buttons in, hadn't thrown it out. I opened the fake bottom to see if he'd found what he was after, and the letters were gone, probably burned.

I located his wall safe but couldn't crack it. While I was still working at it, the phone downstairs started to ring. I jumped as though a pin had been stuck into me, and started shaking like I was still doing one of my routines at the club. He had two phones, one downstairs, one in the bedroom, which was an unlisted number. I snapped out the lights, ran downstairs, picked it up. I didn't answer, just held it.

Burns' voice said, 'Angel Face?' in my ear.

'Gee, you sure frightened me!' I exhaled.

'Better get out of there. He just came back, must have tumbled to the wire. A spotter at Hell's Bells tipped me off he was just there asking for you.'

'I can't, now,' I wailed. 'I woke his damn doorman up getting in just now, and I'm in that silver dress I do my number in! He'll tell him I was here. I'll have to play it dumb.'

'D'ja get anything?'

'Nothing, only that jewel case! I couldn't get the safe open but he's probably burned everything connecting him to her long ago.'

'Please get out of there, kid,' he pleaded. 'You don't know that guy. He's going to pin you down on the mat if he finds you there.'

'I'm staying,' I said. 'I've got to break him down tonight. It's my last chance. Chick eats chicken and ice-cream tomorrow night at six. Oh, Burns, pray for me, will you?'

'I'm going to do more than that,' he growled. 'I'm going to give a wrong-number call there in half an hour. It's four-thirty now. Five that'll be. If you're doing all right, I'll lie low. If not, I'm not going to wait, I'll break in with some of the guys, and we'll use the little we have, the photostats of the letters, and the jewel case. I think Schlesinger can at least get Chick a reprieve on them, if not a new trial. If we can't get Milton, we can't get him, that's all.'

'We've got to get him,' I said, 'and we're going to! He's even been close to breaking down and admitting it to me, at times, when we're alone together. Then at the last minute he gets leery. I'm convinced in my own mind he's guilty. So help me, if I lose Chick tomorrow night, I'm going to shoot Milton with my own hands!'

'Remember, half an hour. If everything's under control, cough. If you can get anywhere near the phone, cough! If I don't hear you cough, I'm pulling the place.'

I hung up, ran up the stairs tearing at the silver cloth. I jerked open a closet door, found the cobwebby negligee he'd always told me was waiting for me there whenever I felt like breaking it in. I chased downstairs again in it, more like Godiva than anyone else, grabbed up a cigarette, flopped back full length on the handiest divan and did a Cleopatra – just as the outside door opened and he and two other guys came in.

Milton had a face full of storm clouds – until he saw me. Then it cleared and the sun came up in it. 'Finally!' he crooned. 'Finally you wanted a change of scenery! And just tonight somebody had to play a practical joke on me, start me on a fool's errand to Philly! Have you been here long?'

I couldn't answer right away because I was still trying to get my breath back after the quick-change act I'd just pulled. I managed a vampish smile.

He turned to the two guys. 'Get out, you two. Can't you see I have company?'

I'd recognized the one who'd contacted me for the jewel case, and knew what was coming. I figured I could handle it. 'Why that's the dame I told you about, Milt,' he blurted out, 'that walked off with that little box the other day!'

'Oh, hello,' I sang out innocently. 'I didn't know that you knew Mr. Milton.'

Milton flared, 'You, Rocco! Don't call my lady friends dames!' and slapped him backhand across the mouth. 'Now scar-ram! You think we need four for bridge?'

'All right, boss, all right,' he said soothingly. But he went over to a framed 'still' of me, that Milton had brought home from Hell's Bells, and stood thoughtfully in front of it for a minute. Then he and the other guy left. It was only after the elevator light had flashed out that I looked over and saw the frame was empty.

'Hey!' I complained. 'That Rocco swiped my picture, right under your nose!'

He thought he saw a bowl of cream in front of him; nothing could get his back up. 'Who can blame him? You're so lovely to look at.'

He spent some time working on the theory that I'd finally found him irresistible. After what seemed years of that, I sidestepped him neatly, got off the divan just in time.

He got good and peeved finally.

'Are you giving me the runaround? What did you come here for anyway?'

'Because she's doublecrossing you!' a voice said from the foyer. 'Because she came here to frame you, chief, and I know it!'

The other two had come back. Rocco pulled my picture out of his pocket. 'I traced that dummy wire you got, sending you to Philly. The clerk at the telegraph office identified her as the sender, from this picture. Ask her why she wanted to get you out of town, and then come up here and case your lay-out! Ask her why she was willing to pay thirty bucks for a little wood box, when she was living in a seven-buck furnished room! Ask her who she is! You weren't at the Reading trial, were you? Well, I was! You're riding for a fall, chief, by having her around you. She's a stoolie!'

He turned on me. 'Who are you? What does he mean?'

What was the good of answering? It was five to five on the clock. I needed Burns bad.

The other one snarled, 'She's the patsy's sister. Chick Wheeler's sister. I saw her on the stand with my own eyes.'

Milton's face screwed up into a sort of despairing agony; I'd never seen anything like it before. He whimpered, 'And you're so beautiful to have to be killed!'

I hugged the negligee around me tight and loked down at the floor. 'Then don't have me killed,' I said softly. It was two to five, now.

He said with comic sadness, 'I got to if you're that guy's sister.'

'I say I'm nobody's sister, just Angel Face that dances at your club. I say I only came here 'cause – I like soft carpets.'

'Why did you send that fake telegram to get me out of town?'

He had me there. I thought fast. 'If I'm a stoolie I get killed, right? But what happens if I'm the other kind of a doublecrosser, a two-timer, do I still get killed?'

'No,' he said, 'because you were still a free-lance; your option hadn't been taken up yet.'

'That's the answer, then. I was going to use your place to meet my steady, that's why I sent the queer wire.'

Rocco's voice was as cracked as a megaphone after a football rally.

'She's Wheeler's sister, chief. Don't let her ki—'

'Shut up!' Milton said.

Rocco just smiled a wise smile, shrugged, lit a cigarette. 'You'll find out.'

The phone rang. 'Get that,' Milton ordered. 'That's her guy now. Keep him on the wire.' He turned and went running up the stairs to the floor above, where the other phone was.

Rocco took out a gun, fanned it vaguely in my direction, sauntered over.

'Don't try nothing, now, while that line's open. You may be fooling Milton, you're not fooling us any. He was always a sucker for a twist.'

Rocco's buddy said, 'Hello?'

Rocco, still holding the gun on me, took a lopsided drag on his cigarette with his left hand and blew smoke vertically. Some of it caught in his throat, and he started to cough like a seal. You could hear it all over the place.

I could feel all the blood draining out of my face.

The third guy was purring, 'No, you tell me what number you want first, then I'll tell you what number this is. That's the way it's done, pal.' He turned a blank face. 'Hung up on me!'

Rocco was still hacking away. I felt sick all over. Sold out by my own signal that everything was under control!

There was a sound like dry leaves on the stairs and Milton came whisking down again. 'Some guy wanted an all night delicatess—' the spokesman started to say.

Milton cut his hand at him viciously. 'That was Centre Street, police headquarters. I had it traced! Put some clothes on her. She's going to her funeral!'

They forced me back into the silver sheath between them. Milton came over with a flagon of brandy and dashed it all over me from head to foot. 'If she lets out a peep, she's fighting drunk. Won't be the first stewed dame carried outa here!'

They had to hold me up between them, my heels just clear of the ground, to get me to move at all. Rocco had his gun buried in the silver folds of my dress. The other had a big handkerchief spread out in his hand held under my face, as though I were nauseated – in reality to squelch any scream.

Milton came behind us. 'You shouldn't mix your drinks,' he was saying, 'and especially you shouldn't help yourself to people's private stock without permission.'

But the doorman was asleep again on his bench, like when I'd come in the first time. This time he didn't wake up. His eyelids just flickered a little as the four of us went by.

They saw to it that I got in the car first, like a lady should. The ride was one of those things you take to your grave with you. My whole past life came before me, in slow motion. I didn't mind dying so terribly much, but I hated to go without being able to do anything for Chick. But it was the way the cards had fallen, that was all.

'Maybe it's better this way,' I said to myself, 'than growing into an old lady and no one looks at your face any more.' I took out my mirror and I powdered my nose, and then I threw the compact away. I'd show them a lady could die like a gentleman!

The house was on the Sound. Milton evidently lived in it quite a bit, by the looks of it. His Filipino let us in.

'Build a fire, Juan, it's chilly,' he grinned. And to me, 'Sit down, Angel Face, and let me look at you before you go.' The other two threw me into a corner of a big sofa, and I just stayed that way, limp like a rag doll. He just stared and stared. 'Gosh, you're swell!' he said.

Rocco said, 'What're we waiting for? It's broad daylight already.'

Milton was idly holding something into the fire, a long poker of some kind. 'She's going,' he said, 'but she's going as my property. Show the other angels this, when you get up there, so they'll know who you belong to.' He came

21

over to me with the end of the thing glowing dull red. It was flattened into some kind of an ornamental design or cipher. 'Knock her out,' he said, 'I'm not that much of a brute.'

Something exploded off the side of my head, and I lost my senses. Then he was wiping my mouth with a handkerchief soaked in whiskey, and my side burned, just above the hip, where they'd found that mark on Ruby Rose Reading.

'All right, Rocco,' Milton said.

Rocco took out his gun again, but he shoved it at the third guy hilt first. The third one held it level at me, took the safety off. His face was sort of green and wet with sweat. I looked him straight in the eyes. The gun went down like a drooping lily. 'I can't, boss, she's too beautiful!' he groaned. 'She's got the face of an angel. How can you shoot anything like that?'

Milton pulled it away from him. 'She doublecrossed me just like Reading did. Any dame that doublecrosses me gets what I gave Reading.'

A voice said softly, 'That's all I wanted to know.'

The gun went off, and I wondered why I didn't feel anything. Then I saw that the smoke was coming from the doorway and not from Milton's gun at all. He went down at my feet, like he wanted to apologize for what he'd done to me, but he didn't say anything and he didn't get up any more. There was blood running down the part of his hair in back.

Burns was in the room with more guys than I'd ever seen ouside of a police parade. One of them was the doorman from Milton's place, or at least the dick that Burns had substituted for him to keep an eye on me while I was up there. Burns told me about that later and about how they followed Milt's little party but hadn't been able to get in in time to keep me from getting branded. Rocco and the other guy went down into hamburger under a battery of heavy fists.

I sat there holding my side and sucking in my breath. 'It was a swell trick-finish,' I panted to Burns, 'but what'd you drill him for? Now we'll never get the proof that'll save Chick.'

He was at the phone asking to be put through to Schlesinger in the city. 'We've got it already, Angel Face,' he said ruefully. 'It's right on you, where you're holding your side. Just where it was on Reading. We all heard what he said before he nose-dived anyway. I only wish I hadn't shot him,' he glowered, 'then I'd have the pleasure of doing it all over again, more slowly.'

CHOSEN TO DIE
LESLIE T. WHITE

Leslie Turner White (1901–1967) was born in Ottawa, then moved to California, where he became a lifelong member of the law enforcement community. He became a largely self-taught expert in fingerprinting, electronic eavesdropping, photography, trailing suspects and other nascent tools of crime fighters.

He had headline-making experiences in the tong wars, battles with communists and numerous other major criminal activities in California, all recounted in his autobiography and fictionalized in such novels as *Homicide* (1937), *The River of No Return* (1941) and his most important book, *Harness Bull* (1937), which included a four-page glossary of 'S'language' – terms used among members of law enforcement organizations. The novel served as the basis for the famous motion picture *Vice Squad* (1953), released in Great Britain as *The Girl in Room 17*, directed by Arnold Laven with a screenplay by Lawrence Roman; it starred Edward G. Robinson.

In 'Chosen to Die,' private investigator Duke Martindel is married to Phyllis, a smart lawyer who he met while she was a law student and he was still a member of the police department. They got married the day she passed her bar exams. Phyllis, though still young, has largely retired, mainly taking on a case only when her husband gets in trouble.

'Chosen to Die' was first published in the December 1, 1934 issue of *Detective Fiction Weekly*.

CHOSEN TO DIE

LESLIE T. WHITE

CHAPTER ONE

Robbers' Plea

Phyllis Martindel was jerked from the depths of a sound sleep with an abruptness that left her breathless and moist with perspiration. She cocked her head, listening, but the apartment seemed all too silent, like a morgue peopled with the dead. Propped upon one elbow, she sought to force her eyes to pierce the darkness but the tarnished silvery glow that seeped through the single window mellowed into opaque shadows before it reached the bedroom door. She leaned over and touched the broad shoulders of her husband and seemed to absorb some of his great strength from the contact. Her heart ceased its mad fluttering as she tried to recall what had awakened her.

Then she felt, rather than heard, the door swing open!

The limp hand suddenly became a bony talon that tightened on her husband's flesh. 'Hey! What's the idea?' he grumbled thickly.

She shrank against him. 'Duke! There is – there is someone in the apartment!'

He gave her a playful bunt with his head and then his lazy voice drawled out of the darkness beside her. 'Say, Phyl, just because you're married to a detective don't be so damn suspicious. Oh, well, if there's anyone here tell 'em to g'wan away and come back at a decent—' He stopped abruptly as the sudden glare of a flash blinded him.

'Keep your hands away from that pillow, Duke!' a tense voice commanded from the shadows behind the source of light. 'Get 'em in plain sight on top the covers!'

Duke Martindel arched his neck and blinked into the beam. Very slowly he spread his big hands on top of the counterpane, then shot a sidelong glance at his wife. 'Darling,' he grinned wryly, 'is this guy calling on you or me?'

A shadow moved across the wan light of the window. The shades were carefully drawn, then a wall-switch clicked and the room was flooded with light. Martindel pushed himself erect and stared at his guests.

They both had guns on him, but there the similarity ceased. The big man at the foot of the bed had apparently dressed hurriedly for his visit, for even the up-turned collar of his black topcoat failed to hide the fact that he wore no tie. Close-cropped gray hair bristled from the brim of a derby that shaded his tiny close-set eyes – eyes that reminded Martindel of twin bullet holes in a cantaloupe. His square jaw and heavy jowls were tinted a deep purple by a stubble of beard and he carried a scar that coursed upward from the corner of his thin mouth to the criss-crossed sack under his right eye. It was the first time Duke Martindel had ever seen stark fear in Sam Skuro's eyes.

'Get up Duke!' growled Skuro. 'You're goin' places.'

Martindel felt the convulsive clutch of his wife. He turned his head and looked at the man who had drawn the window shade.

'Well, Gus Nuene! Since when have you and Sam gone into the kidnaping racket?'

The man addressed as Nuene gave his neck a nervous jerk. He was very tall and very thin like a giant crane and the angled bridge of his hooked nose made it seem as though he were perpetually sighting a shotgun. He was all straight lines and angles.

'This isn't a snatch, Duke,' he announced. 'We got a job for you.'

Martindel chuckled without pleasantry. 'I maintain an office, boys.'

Sam Skuro made an impatient gesture with his gun. 'Pile out, Duke,' he growled. 'We're in one hell of a hurry. This is on the level.'

Duke Martindel glanced at his wife and a thrill of pride suffused him. She looked very young and very cool lying there with her round blue eyes fastened on Skuro's gun muzzle. Brown hair tumbling around her bare shoulders made her look like a school girl rather than a clever lawyer and the wife of a well known detective. Duke grinned in spite of himself.

'Phyl,' he said in an audible stage-whisper, 'you're the legal brains of the family. What would you advise in a situation like this?'

Phyllis Martindel was scared – Duke could tell that by the way the nostrils on her little turned-up nose quivered – but she prided herself that she could match her husband's cool wit, so she tried it now. 'Darling, they seem to be clients of yours.'

The detective's quick laughter brought a dark scowl to the swarthy features of Sam Skuro. 'Listen, Duke, this is no time for wise-crackin'. There's big dough in this for you.'

Nuene took a step nearer the bed. 'Ten gran', Duke! That's more than you private dicks can make in a year on a straight job.'

Martindel chuckled. 'Straight job? Now that's a word I didn't think you boys included in your vocabulary; you, Gus Nuene, the slickest con-man in town, and Sam Skuro the veteran peterman! Why, Sam, you must be well over fifty! You were cracking cribs when I was in short pants.'

Skuro leaned over the foot of the bed. 'Duke, you got a reputation in this town. Everybody that knows you at all knows you left the police department and went into private practice because the department went crooked.'

'Part of it did,' Martindel admitted.

Skuro nodded vigorously. 'All right, then, part of it; the biggest part. Well, you wouldn't sit by an' see them frame an innocent man, frame an' hang him, would you?'

The detective drew up his knees and locked his hands around them. 'Sam, you old fraud, you couldn't be innocent of anything.'

Nuene said: 'You know Harry Washburn, Duke?'

Martindel nodded. 'Sure. He's the grand jury investigator. We teamed on the force when I was in harness.'

Sam Skuro's gun sagged. 'Listen, Duke, before my God, I didn't kill Washburn!'

The detective stiffened slightly. 'Well, who said you did?'

Skuro opened his mouth as if to say something, apparently changed his mind and swivelling, walked over to a small radio near the bed. With trembling fingers he rotated the dial. Then he stepped back and listened as the cool, impersonal voice of the police announcer droned out of the instrument.

'. . . railway stations, apartments, rooming houses and small hotels. Repeating general order to all cars. Description of wanted men as follows: Sam Skuro, age fifty, six foot one, two ten, gray, close-clipped hair, bullet head, dark complection, scar running from right corner of mouth to right cheek-bone. Skuro is a three-time loser, dangerous criminal. Gus Nuene, confederate, probably holed up together. Nuene five eleven, thirty-eight, gaunt and angular, dark and sleek, well dressed, thin hawk-face, cold gray eyes. Take no chances in arresting these men as they are wanted for murdering investigator Harry Washburn. All cars will patrol their . . .'

Sam Skuro switched off the instrument. Both men kept their eyes on Martindel's sober features.

Duke spat: 'Cop-killers!'

Skuro caught the bed post. 'We didn't, Duke! I'm tough, I've cracked a lot of cribs in my day, slugged a lotta guys, but before my God, Duke, I never drilled a guy.' He paused and amended the statement by adding, 'I never drilled a guy in the back!'

Martindel's voice was cold. 'What did you come to me for?'

'We're bein' framed, Duke. With our records any jury in the world would sink us. We're innocent, we need help.'

Martindel gave a dry laugh that lacked mirth. 'What you birds need is a lawyer, not a detective. You better speak to my wife.'

Nuene shook his head. 'No, Duke, a lawyer can't help us out of this spot.'

'Have you got an alibi?' Martindel asked.

The two visitors exchanged glances. Nuene answered through tightened lips. 'We can't use it, Duke.'

Nuene shot another glance at Sam Skuro. The latter gave his head a perceptible nod. Nuene turned back to the detective.

'Duke, we'll lay our cards on the table – cold. But first we want your word that under no circumstances will you tell the law.'

Martindel shook his head. 'I can't give my word on that. If they subpoena me into court, I'll have to talk.' He smiled sardonically. 'However, if you boys hired a good lawyer and told her your troubles, she would be able to protect your confidences by the laws of privileged communications.'

Phyllis swung around. 'Darling! I don't want—'

'Go on, boys,' Duke interrupted. 'Tell the attorney your troubles.'

Nuene nodded to Sam Skuro; Sam began to talk. 'Harry Washburn was diggin' up a lot of graft dope—'

'Skip it,' Duke cut in. 'We know all about Washburn's activities.'

'Well, he knew too much so he got bumped at five minutes after twelve.'

'Ask him who bumped him?' Duke suggested to his wife.

Skuro answered before Phyllis had a chance to repeat the query. 'I don't know that. It was framed to look like Gus an' me did it.'

'How do you mean – framed?' asked Phyllis.

Skuro shrugged helplessly. 'Phoney evidence – I don't know just what. A friendly stoolie tipped me off just in time to the raid or we'd have been—' He ended with a shudder.

'They want us – dead,' contributed Nuene.

'Where were you at five minutes after twelve?' Phyllis Martindel wanted to know.

Both men hesitated, then Sam Skuro heaved his shoulders. 'In the main vault of the County and Suburban Bank!'

Martindel laughed harshly. His wife gasped.

'They were cracking the bank, darling,' the detective told her drily, 'when Washburn was murdered.'

'Couldn't you prove that?' Phyllis asked. 'It would be better than being charged with murder!'

'Not much better,' Duke put in. 'Sam and Gus are both old offenders, if memory serves me right they each have three convictions behind them.'

'That's right,' Nuene admitted wearily.

'And that means they'll get life even if convicted for cracking the bank.'

'It means,' Nuene corrected drily, 'that unless you prove us innocent we'll both be killed by the cops. We heard they don't aim to make any arrests in this case; they don't want to chance it to a jury in case anything slips up. It's a frame, I tell you, Duke!'

'But how,' protested the charming lawyer, 'can we prove you innocent when you are guilty of something else?'

Skuro bit his lip. 'Your husband will know how to handle that, ma'm.'

'You tell me,' suggested Martindel.

Nuene spoke: 'For ten gran', Duke, we want you to frame us innocent!'

Duke Martindel whistled softly and dropped his feet over the edge of the bed. 'That's a new one,' he mused aloud. 'They are guilty of one crime and want to be framed innocent on one they did not commit.' He shook his head. 'I don't want any part of it, boys. You're a couple of bad eggs that should be frying up in the big house.'

His wife caught his arm. 'But, Duke, if they didn't kill Washburn, you wouldn't want to see them—' She stopped, embarrassed.

'They robbed a bank,' he reminded her. 'I'll be compounding a felony if I monkey with that or try to cover it up.'

Nuene interrupted. 'We thought of that, Duke, so we got a counter proposition. Suppose we give you the dough we got out of that crib – fifty thousand, it was – and you go and make a deal with the manager. It's a small, independent bank and I don't think the manager would want any publicity about the job if he could recover his dough on the quiet.'

'Any damage done?'

Nuene shook his head. 'Not much. We stuck up the watchman and gagged him with tape. Sam opened the vault like it was a can of sardines.' He glanced at his wrist watch. 'It's not three yet. If you beat it out to the manager's house, offer to return the dough and pay for any damages, I think he'll listen to reason. We're on the level about this, Duke, we don't want to dangle for something we didn't do.'

Skuro contributed: 'The manager's name is Mayhew Henderson. He lives at Two Sixty Carthay Circle. He's home tonight – we checked all those angles.'

'The money?' Duke asked.

'We'll leave it on your back door step.'

'Where will you boys be?'

Skuro shook his head decisively. 'You don't need to know that, Duke. We'll get in touch with our' – he gave Phyllis Martindel a glance – 'our attorney when the time comes.'

'How do you know I won't run out on you with the money?'

'Two reasons,' Nuene replied. 'First, you're a square dick; second, you'll want to know who knocked off Washburn by shooting him in the back.'

Sam had already backed out of the room and now Gus Nuene followed. As the door closed, Martindel grinned at his wife.

'Well, Mrs. Martindel, how would you like to go to Europe on sixty thousand—'

'No thank you, Mr. Martindel. Now will you be on your way to Carthay Circle.' She placed a tiny foot in the small of his back and prodded him out of the bed.

29

CHAPTER TWO

Murder Frame

Duke Martindel brought his roadster to a stop diagonally across the street from a large, brick mansion. He turned the beam of his spotlight onto the white numerals painted on the curb, saw they were 260. Then he climbed out and approached the darkened house.

It took considerable argument to convince the sleepy butler who answered the door that the matter was of sufficient importance to disturb the slumber of his master. But the sounds of the verbal exchange succeeded where the reasoning had failed, for a stubby little man appeared at the head of the stairs and demanded to know what the trouble was. Before the servant could speak, Martindel cut in.

'Mr. Henderson, I am a detective. I have some very urgent business to discuss with you relative to your bank.'

Henderson gave an astonished grunt and padded down the stairs, his slippers clap-clapping on the polished surface. He dismissed the butler with an imperious wave of his hand, tightened his robe around his full figure and led the way into a small reception room off the hallway. Without sitting down, he faced the detective.

'Now, sir,' he demanded. 'What business have you to discuss?'

Martindel let his eyes sweep the banker in a cold, appraising stare. To him, every man was a subject to be dealt with differently and he wondered how best to approach the rather delicate matter he had to discuss. Henderson, he readily surmised, was not a man that would have any sympathy for others; there was a tightness around his small, thin mouth, set as it was in his chubby face, that suggested cruelty. He stared at his visitor with a haughty frown, but Duke saw a tremor of fear in the depths of his eyes and it heartened him. He made his approach accordingly.

'Mr. Henderson, if your bank was burglarized, your vault rifled, it would be rather awkward from a business point of view, would it not?'

The banker's eyes bulged. 'Burglarized? Why what are you trying to say?'

'Your bank was burglarized last night. The vault was cleaned!'

Henderson collapsed into a chair. 'Are you from the police?' he gasped.

Martindel shook his head. 'No, I am a private detective.'

'You represent the insurance?'

'I,' the detective put in flatly, 'represent the burglars.'

Henderson gave a startled grunt, then groped for the telephone. Before he could lift the receiver, Martindel pinned his hand down.

'Wait a minute,' he suggested quietly. 'You would do well to hear me out.'

'You can't blackmail me!' blustered the banker.

'I'm not trying to blackmail you. I have with me the entire amount stolen and enough extra to make good any damages incurred by the entry. It is a most unusual circumstance, but I want to return the money on behalf of the criminals on the one condition that you make no report of the incident. I believe, if you will consider the matter from all angles, you would be well advised to agree. If your clients knew that your vault could be opened like' – he grinned as he recalled Gus Nuene's apt simile – 'like a can of sardines, you would lose a lot of business.'

Henderson hesitated and his hand slowly came away from the instrument. 'What about Chris Foy, the watchman?' he queried huskily.

'Foy is all right, so I understand,' Duke assured him. 'I'm confident he will keep his mouth shut under he circumstances. He is now bound and gagged at the bank.'

'You have the money with you?'

'In my car. I suggest that you dress and come with me. We will liberate the watchman, return the money to the vault and let the matter drop.'

Henderson squinted at Martindel. 'I don't understand why you are doing this. Do you expect a reward?'

'No. I expect nothing – from you. My reasons, on the other hand, are no concern of yours. Are you going to come, or not?'

Henderson ran a chubby hand across his moist forehead as though the matter was too much for his comprehension.

'How do I know this isn't some trick to get me to open the bank?' he asked defensively.

Martindel shrugged. 'You don't know, but you cannot afford to take a chance that I might be right. If someone discovers the burglary before we get this money back, you know what will happen to your depositors. They'll walk out on you. I'd suggest that you pile into some clothes and make it snappy.'

Henderson nodded. 'I'll be ready in five minutes,' he promised and hurried from the room.

He was ready in six minutes by Martindel's watch. He came into the room dressed in a conventional serge suit, but a too obvious bulge in his right coat pocket warned the detective that he was armed. Duke frowned impatiently. It irritated him when untrained men carried guns. With a curt nod, he led the way out of the house and across the street to his roadster.

Henderson hesitated before entering. 'Where is the money?' he demanded.

Martindel swore softly, walked to the rear of the machine and unlocked the turtleback. He opened the portmanteau and held the beam of a small pocket flashlight on the contents. It was bulging with currency and negotiable bonds.

'Satisfied?' he growled.

Henderson bobbed his head, edged into the seat and sat warily in one corner. The detective stretched his lanky frame under the steering wheel, depressed the starter and tooled the machine into motion.

31

The ride was made in silence. The banker crouched on the extreme end of the seat and it was quite apparent that he did not trust his companion. But Duke Martindel was indifferent to that. There was nothing he had to discuss with Mayhew Henderson and he wanted time to mull over the strange situation in which he found himself.

Perhaps he was a plain damn fool. He knew he could trust neither Gus Nuene or Sam Skuro as far as he could throw them with a broken wrist; he was too experienced a veteran to believe that quaint old fairy tale about honor among thieves; that was plain hooey. He sought to mentally marshal his facts, slim as they were. First, Nuene and Skuro were scared – they had to be plenty terrified to return fifty thousand in loot. Both men were veteran criminals, but they were the old-time craftsmen, not the modern, back-shooting assassin of today. Duke nodded to himself – yes, he was inclined to believe the precious pair when they said they did not kill Washburn. If they had killed Washburn in looting the bank – they would hardly be willing to return the loot. It would appear logical for them to use the money in making a get-away.

But Harry Washburn was dead! Duke had heard that officially from the police broadcast, and Skuro and Nuene were accused and suspected of the crime. Yet it was easy to find a motive why certain people and factions might want the relentless investigator out of the way. Duke had worked with Harry Washburn back in the days when he was in harness and even then, Washburn was a cold-blooded, tenacious man-hunter. There was something about the way he tore into a case that chilled even his co-workers. But he was a smart dick, uncompromisingly honest, and he had risen rapidly, although cordially disliked by his associates, and when the grand jury picked him out of the entire force to investigate certain underworld activities in the city, dislike turned to fear.

Duke knew what it was to be feared and disliked. He had chucked the police force when things became too raw for his taste and opened a private bureau. He had made good on several well paying cases and wisely invested his surplus. Honest coppers, like old 'Skipper' Dombey, grizzled pilot of the detective bureau, favored him, gave him tips and did what they could to help him along. But the department was under the thumb of Inspector Egan of the uniformed men. Egan hated two things – Duke Martindel was both of them.

A cheerful grin stole over Duke's tanned features as he recalled Phyllis booting him out of the bed. What a girl! Even after some three years of marriage, Duke continued to marvel at his luck in winning her. They had met when she visited the police department as a member of a law class studying criminal procedure. The day she passed her bar examination they were married. Since that time, she had only practiced law when it was necessary to extricate her adventurous husband from some escapade. Yet Duke invariably insisted that she was the real business head of the family and that he merely worked for her. It tickled him immensely when she begged him to quit the detective business, with its attendant dangers, and then the first case that looked as though some innocent party might be in trouble, she insisted that he take it and straighten it out.

The sudden looming up of the County and Suburban Bank before him broke up his reverie. He stopped the car at the curb in front of the building and switched off the engine.

'All right,' he grunted at Henderson. 'Let's go.'

The other hesitated, moistening his lips. 'I warn you,' he jerked huskily. 'If anything is—'

'Don't be a damn fool!' cut in Martindel. He opened the door and stepped to the sidewalk.

Henderson followed reluctantly. He paused, glanced suspiciously up and down the deserted street, then hurried across the sidewalk and keyed open the front door. He started to enter, changed his mind and stepped aside for the detective to proceed him.

Duke gave an impatient snort, knuckled open the big door and strode inside. The foyer was dimly illumined by a night-light that bathed the empty cages in pale shadows. The thick marble pillars, cold and stark, reminded Duke of a mausoleum. Some strange unfamiliar dread began to come over him. He glanced around but could see no sign of the watchman. Casting a quick look over his shoulder, he found Henderson watching him through narrowed eyes.

'Where's the vault?' he asked.

The banker jerked his head toward the rotunda. As Duke passed the end of the cages, he saw the vault door ajar. He pushed aside a brass rail and strode over. He shot another glance at Henderson, then gripped the big handle and swung the door outward. He jumped backward with an unwitting gasp of surprise.

For the trussed-up body of a man tumbled out of the dark recess of the vault and fell at his feet!

Martindel rasped a curse, whipped out his flash and turned the light on the features of the man on the tiled floor. One quick glance was sufficient; the man was dead.

'Foy!' choked Henderson.

Martindel dropped to one knee beside the corpse. The watchman had been beaten about the head until it was but a pulpy mass. Ropes wrapped around his body held him mummy-like and the dirty strips of adhesive tape across his dead lips added a grim touch to the horror of it all. The detective's jaw tightened and the veins along his temples swelled. He pushed slowly erect and turned to Henderson.

'I don't understand—' he began, then stopped abruptly as he found himself staring into the tremulous muzzle of the banker's gun.

'You dirty crook!' rasped Henderson. 'Don't move or I'll kill you!' His rotund little body was doubled into a half-crouch as he backed toward a desk.

Martindel stiffened. 'Be careful of that gun,' he suggested drily. 'It might go off.'

'It will go off if you move before the police get here!' promised Henderson. He put his left hand behind him and patted the desk as he searched for the instrument.

Duke Martindel bit his lip. He was in probably the worst predicament of his eventful career. If the police caught him now – he shuddered. He turned his attention to Henderson. The latter was just picking up the receiver.

Duke gauged his distance. Henderson stood about ten feet away. The gun was aimed in the general direction of the detective's broad chest but the muzzle wavered in a restless arc. Duke heard the receiver make metallic noises, saw Henderson open his mouth to speak, then he jumped—

He went feet first like a player sliding for a base. The gun roared over his head – the marble foyer amplifying the sound. Then his feet struck Henderson's legs and with a terrified bleat, the banker flopped on top of him.

Duke's powerful arm closed around Henderson's throat, choking the cry before it was born. He rolled over, came to his knees then releasing his strangle hold, he caught the other by the tie and jerked him into a sitting position. Henderson made one futile attempt to cry out just as Duke's fist reached his jaw. The bleat turned into an indifferent *whoosh* as the air left the tubby body and Mayhew Henderson cradled his head on the mosaic floor and temporarily lost all interest in the encounter.

Martindel combed his fingers through his hair and stood up. The telephone lay on its side, the receiver squawking imperiously. With a soft oath, he pronged the thing and recovered his crush felt. He jammed it on the back of his head, carefully wiped the handle of the vault door so as to eradicate any fingerprints, and moved swiftly toward the front of the bank.

He was directly in the middle of the foyer when the barred front door suddenly swung inward and three blue-coated figures barged inside. The pale moonlight glinted on blued steel. A cold, venomous voice knifed the stillness.

'Hold it. Martindel!'

Duke Martindel froze immobile. He rasped the one word: 'Egan—' and made a run for it.

A gun belched in his face. His head exploded and he went down – cold.

CHAPTER THREE

French Leave

Daybreak filtering through the grimy little window of the headquaters' interrogation room, fell in wan splashes on the weary features of Duke

Martindel. With clothing disheveled, his shirt front stiff with dried blood and a turban of bandages crowning the upper portion of his head, he sprawled in a hard-backed chair in the center of the battered room. There were four other men present, but Martindel's eyes were focused unwaveringly on the tall, gaunt figure that stood before him, silhouetted by the tiny window.

Inspector Egan was a thinnish man whose gauntness was deceptive. Like a puma, his muscles were so evenly divided over his frame as to be unnoticeable. His face was long and narrow and the features sharp, fox-like, and his salt-and-pepper brows, when he frowned, formed a straight unbroken line across the upper part of his face. This tended to thrust his colorless eyes into a pocket of shadow and give to them a metallic luster that was disconcertingly impersonal. No man on the department had ever seen him smile. He was shrewd and intuitive; he seemed to smell a situation before it was possible to know by any other means. Few men liked him personally, but he had the knack of winning the respect and blind obedience of his men. It was rumored that he was the real power behind the city government, but such rumors were always whispered furtively, for Wyatt Egan was not the type of man to oppose unless one was prepared to prove his accusation.

'Talk?' he asked Martindel.

Duke shrugged. 'Sure. I didn't kill Chris Foy.'

Egan tugged at his nose. It seemed to lengthen in his hand. 'It was a two-man job – who was your partner.'

'I didn't have a partner, Egan; I didn't need one.'

'That your story?'

'Part of it.'

'What's the rest of it?'

'I didn't crack that vault.'

One of the other cops laughed. Egan rocked on his heels meditatively. When he spoke, his voice was low, controlled as though he were holding himself back.

'You killed Chris Foy, Martindel, then tried to put one over on Henderson. Don't forget, we found fifty thousand bucks in the turtle-back of your roadster. How do you explain that?'

Duke shook his head. 'I'm not going to try,' he said wearily.

'You had ten thousand dollars in your pocket,' Egan went on. 'You know where that came from, don't you?'

'Sure, but you don't.'

'Wrong,' corrected Egan drily. 'We checked the serial numbers of those bills and found they were part of the loot stolen from the Seaside National Bank last month. Talk yourself out of that one.'

Duke Martindel swore softly and covered his chagrin by gingerly patting the bandage around his head. From the neck up he was just one big ache; a slug from Egan's gun had creased his skull and come, literally, within a hair's-breadth of killing him. And now, with throbbing head, he found the predicament almost too much for him. The evidence was damning – he could not dispute that fact.

He tried to reason it out in his mind. Although satisfied that Sam Skuro and Gus Nuene had deliberately framed him for the burglary and the murder of the watchman, Foy, he could see no point in explaining the matter to Inspector Egan. In the first place, he had been caught red-handed and would be, in any case, considered an accomplice of Skuro and Nuene. As such, his testimony would be worthless in court and he would be regarded equally guilty with the other pair. Then, too, the police were perfectly satisfied that Skuro and Nuene were the murderers of Washburn; they neither would be, nor could be, induced to change that theory.

A sharp commotion in the corridor outside broke in on his musing. Egan scowled and started across the floor when the door swung open and a woman darted into the room. Her eyes settled for an instant on the group, then with a little cry, she ran to the prisoner and threw her arms around him.

'Duke! Are you hurt, darling?' she whimpered.

Martindel jumped to his feet. 'Phyllis!' Then he grinned ruefully. 'No, Phyl, Egan shot me in the head where it couldn't do any damage.' He cast a glance over his shoulder where the inspector was growling at a desk sergeant.

The latter was fuming embarrassedly. 'I couldn't stop her, Inspector!' he apologised. 'She walked right past me an' headed for this room.'

Egan swung around. 'You'll have to get out, Mrs. Martindel,' he snapped.

Phyllis Martindel drew herself up to her full five feet. 'I will not!' she retorted.

'The hell she does, Egan,' put in Duke. 'She's my attorney, in case you don't know.'

Phyllis slapped a folded document on the table. 'Here is a writ for Duke's release.'

Egan pushed it away from him. 'You keep a supply of those damn things all filled out.'

The girl gave him an icy stare. 'I think you will find it in perfect order.'

Egan picked it up. Without unfolding it, he turned to Martindel. 'Duke, I happen to know that you had two visitors earlier this morning; Sam Skuro and Gus Nuene. We want those two. Where are they?'

'Haven't the slightest idea,' Duke told him.

Egan tugged at his nose. 'We know definitely that they came to see you. After they left, you went out. Now I want to know what business they had with you that prompted that. You're in a bad spot, Duke, so you better talk. In any case, I can take you before a magistrate, put you under oath and either force you to talk or put you in the position of an accomplice, because the only excuse you could give for not talking is that it might tend to incriminate you.'

Martindel grinned maliciously. 'I'm only a dumb private dick, Egan; I work for my lawyer. Skuro and Nuene came up to see her because she's their attorney as well as mine. They didn't tell me a damn thing.'

The inspector's eyes retreated into a deeper socket of shadow. 'I'll make her talk,' he growled.

Phyllis shook her head. 'I don't think you will!' she challenged him testily. 'If you know anything about legal procedure at all, you know that an attorney cannot be forced to testify to any conversation with a client. That is a privileged communication, you murdering old crook!'

Egan sniffed; it was the nearest he ever came to laughter. 'You make a fine pair – a shyster mouthpiece in skirts and a crooked, double-crossing, gum-shoe. That's like marrying a jackal and a skunk.'

Duke smiled thinly. 'You're well up on zoology, Egan, but then, that's natural. Now, how about this writ?'

Inspector Egan turned slowly and walked over to the window where he stood straddle-legged, his hands behind him, staring into the street below. Finally, after a moody silence that lasted for nearly five minutes, he swung around and shook the crumpled writ at he Martindels.

'You win this round,' he growled. 'I'm not ready to tip my hand yet. This case has a lot of angles and if I resisted this writ, I'd have to go into court and show my evidence right now. When I'm ready, I'll have you picked up, Duke, but in the meantime, don't either of you try to leave town. You can beat it now.'

Phyllis sniffed disdainfully and proffered a pack of cigarettes to her husband. Duke came slowly to his feet, paused with irritating nonchalance to light his smoke, then with a cynical grin for the somber-faced coppers, he turned and limped out of the room.

They tramped down the dingy stairs in silence. At the front door of the station-house, she gave his arm a squeeze.

'Drive, darling?'

Duke grinned, shook his head. 'You drive, Phyl. I want to think.' He crossed the sidewalk and opened the door of his wife's coupé.

Phyllis slid under the wheel and Duke lolled beside her, his head resting against the top of the cushion. As his wife tooled the little car into the early-morning traffic, she laughed.

'I'll bet you're thinking what a smart little wife you have,' she chided. 'I don't know what you would do if I didn't keep yanking you out of tight spots all the time, you big baby.'

Duke grinned. 'It would be mighty dull, Phyl. You invariably yank me out of one spot, all right, but you drop me into the middle of a tighter one.'

'Meaning—'

Duke tried a smoke ring – and failed. 'Darling,' he asked, 'Do you look good in black?'

'Hideous! Why?'

'Then you better watch your step unless you want to be wearing a widow's garment.'

A tinge of terror crept into Phyllis' voice. 'What do you mean, Duke?'

'I mean that something's up,' he told her drily. 'Why do you suppose Egan turned me loose?'

She hesitated. 'Why, the writ—'

'Nope, darling, wrong. Old Egan could beat that writ without half trying. All he had to do was to show to any magistrate that I was captured in a bank in the wee morning hours with a dead man and fifty thousand bucks in my car and—' he made an eloquent gesture with his hands.

'Then why did he turn you loose?' she protested.

Duke shrugged. 'Egan tried to kill me; he wants me – dead. Perhaps it is just his personal animosity, perhaps it is something else.'

'You think he knows you had nothing to do with the bank robbery—'

Martindel sighed. 'I'm not sure. Did you hear from Skuro or Nuene?'

'Sam Skuro called; he left a number where we could reach him in an emergency.' She fished a slip of paper out of a pocket and handed it to him.

'When was that?'

'Just before I left for the station.'

Duke flipped his cigarette stub into the street. 'By the way, how did you know I was down at headquarters?'

'Somebody telephoned. They told me you were in a jam and needed an attorney – they should have said a nurse. I didn't recognize the voice.' Anxiety crept into her tone. 'You didn't tell me why Egan turned you free, Duke.'

Duke pushed himself erect in his seat. 'I can't answer yet, except to say that there must be a damn good reason, otherwise he wouldn't have done it. Don't underestimate old Egan, he makes a fox look like a moron by comparison.' He reached up and adjusted the rear-view mirror so that he could see behind without turning his head.

'Don't drive so fast, darling,' he suggested.

'Why—' Phyllis asked, startled. 'I always drive—'

'Because you're making it tough for those dog-faced flatfeet of Egan's to stay on our tail.'

She whistled softly. 'You mean they are following us, Duke? Shall I lose them?'

'*Uh-uh*. I know a better way. We don't want them cluttering up our own apartment, so drive to Chelsea Street. I know a nice quiet family hotel. You remember it, darlink; I took you there for a couple of days right after I gave you that nice mink coat.'

Phyllis shot him a malicious glance. 'You know very well I never had a mink coat.'

Duke chuckled. 'Pardon me. I got us confused with two other people.'

Phyllis Martindel brought the coupé to a stop before a small hotel that was sandwiched in between two austere apartment houses. A bell-hop ran across the sidewalk and yanked open the door.

Duke handed him a dollar. 'Put this bus in a safe place, son. We don't want it for several hours; I need some sleep.' He left the hop in charge of the coupé and crossed the sidewalk. As he pushed open the door of the hotel, he glanced over his shoulder and saw a sedan drift slowly past.

'I don't understand how you can talk of sleep at a time like this,' sighed his wife. 'I never felt less like sleeping in my life.'

Duke chuckled. 'Well, Phyl, keep it a secret then,' he whispered as they approached the desk.

After exchanging the usual greetings with the hotel clerk, Duke picked up the pen and wrote *Mr. and Mrs. Duke Martindel* in bold letters across the registry card. 'And now,' he told the clerk, 'we want a room with a southern exposure. I am very particular about rooms.'

The clerk picked up a key ring. He signaled to an assistant to take his place and then he circled the counter. 'The only rooms we have with a southern exposure, Mr. Martindel, face on an alley at the rear,' he said doubtfully. 'I'll be glad to show you what we have.' He led the way to the elevator. As the lift started to rise, he told the operator to stop at the sixth floor.

Duke interrupted him. 'That's too high. My wife has a very poor heart; she likes something nearer the ground than that. Don't you, darling?'

Phyllis gave him a quick grimace. 'Of course,' she acquiesced.

At the clerk's command, the elevator paused at the second floor and they got out. The clerk showed them a room on the southwest side.

'How do you like this, Mrs. Martindel,' he inquired.

Before Phyllis could reply, Duke cut in. 'No, this won't do. How about something on the other side of the hall.'

The clerk shrugged and led the way across the hall. As they passed through the door, Phyllis whispered: 'Have you gone completely crazy?'

Duke winked. 'Don't forget, I was shot in the head.'

The next room seemed to please the detective, although it appeared identical with the other one. But the clerk was used to cranky customers, so he politely inquired if there was anything else they wanted.

Duke nodded. 'Yes, I want perfect quiet.' He tapped his bandaged head significantly. 'I had a slight accident and I intend to get a little rest. Please put a *Do Not Disturb* sign on the door and a plug in the phone. Under no circumstances do I wish to be bothered. If there are any visitors or phone messages, kindly get the name or numbers. Is that plain?'

'Certainly, sir,' agreed the clerk. 'I will see that you are not interrupted.'

Duke handed him a bill. 'Since we had no baggage, I will pay in advance for the room. Put the receipt in my mail box.' He dismissed the clerk with a wave of his hand.

As the door closed, Phyllis sank on the bed and made a weary little gesture with her hands. 'Crazy! Crazy as a loon! A murder charge hanging over your head, the police trying to kill you and you come to a respectable hotel and act like an old maid on her honeymoon.'

'No such thing,' he corrected her, 'as an old maid on a honeymoon.'

'Be serious, Duke,' Phyllis begged. 'What in the world made you do this. Why, you said yourself that the police were following you. They will be sitting down in the street waiting for you.'

'Exactly, darling. That's what I'm counting on. Do you know why I didn't take that room across the hall? Well, this room has a fire escape, the other did not. I am very timid about fires, you know.'

Phyllis grimaced. 'Oh, you fool! I see it now. You went to all the trouble of renting this room and telling those monstrous lies, just to sneak out of here and lose the police. I could have lost them in five minutes.'

He kissed her. 'Remarkable, Watson! But I don't want to lose them; I want them sitting out front and I want head-quarters to believe I'm holed up here asleep. You can bet your sweet little life that right this very minute, a scared desk-clerk is repeating my orders to a couple of Egan's bloodhounds.'

'So what?'

'So I take French leave through that window and get in touch with that double-crossing Sam Skuro. After that, well, who knows.'

Duke hurried into the bathroom. He carefully unwound the bandage and found that the wound had caked over. He gingerly adjusted his hat and came back into the bedroom. Phyllis still sat on the edge of the bed looking very crestfallen.

'Oh Duke, why did you get mixed up in this terrible affair. Let's take a boat to Europe, or someplace.'

'I offered you that, Mrs. Martindel,' he reminded her with a grin, 'but you chased me into this, literally kicked me headlong into it. Now I've got to get out of it. Bye.' He brushed her cheek with his lips, crossed the room and raised the sash.

The alley appeared deserted. The fire escape was the type that descends with weight, so Duke eased his bulk through the window and turning, blew a kiss to his wife. 'I'm glad you have a weak heart, darling. Hope it's over me.'

Phyllis wrinkled up her pert little nose at him. 'Conceited idiot!' she jeered as he softly closed the window behind him and disappeared.

Once on the alley level, Duke swung west. At the first street that intersected the alley, he turned south until he located a drug store. Inside, he found a phone booth, dialed headquarters and asked for Captain Dombey. When he finally heard the low, quiet voice of the veteran detective on the wire, he said: 'Hello, Skipper. This is Martindel.'

Dombey grunted in surprise. 'I wasn't expectin' a call from you, Duke.'

'I imagine not. Are you working on the Washburn case, Skipper?'

'We're all workin' on it, in a way,' Dombey replied cautiously. 'The dragnet's out for Skuro an' Nuene.'

'Preferably dead, eh?'

Dombey gave another noncommittal grunt. 'I heard somethin' like that,' he admitted drily.

From his pocket, Duke fished out the memo his wife had given him. 'I think I can locate that pair, Skipper,' he said, 'but I have reasons for wanting them taken alive. How about it?'

The copper agreed. 'That's all right with me, Duke. What's the angle?'

'Call the telephone company and get the address on this telephone number.' He tilted the slip of paper so that the light fell across it. 'Hempstead Two-four-two-o-six. Then pick up an extra gun for me and meet me alone.'

'Where?'

'Drive down Market. Go slowly after you pass Glendale Avenue. I'll hop aboard if everything is O.K.'

'I'll be there in twenty minutes,' the copper promised and hung up.

CHAPTER FOUR

Trap For Rats

Captain Dombey looked just what he was – a straight cop. Nature had molded him for the task; years in harness had sculptured his character in deep, seamed lines. He was broad and strong, built close to the ground, with powerful neck and ham-like fists, the better to fight when the going was rough. His crag of a jaw might represent bull-headed aggressiveness, or perhaps just strength of character.

Time had mellowed nature's work by carving deep channels along his leathery old face, by crowning his massive head with thick silvery hair, and by giving to his voice a low richness that stirred the listener. Through twenty years of departmental intrigue, of crime, of hatred and tragedy, old Skipper Dombey had gone his quiet, sure way, doing his work as best he could, sticking, helping, fighting.

As Duke Martindel swung onto the running board of the Skipper's machine, he felt all those things in one quick rush of confidence.

Dombey wasted no words in idle greeting. 'That number you gave me – it's a roomin' house on Chester Street. Want to go there?'

Martindel slipped into the seat, nodded. 'Who killed Washburn, Skipper?'

Dombey grunted. 'I'll bite. It was supposed to be Sam Skuro an' Gus Nuene.'

'Couldn't have been. They got an alibi.'

41

Dombey glanced sideways. 'How do you know, Duke? You were supposed to be robbin' a bank.'

Martindel nodded grimly. 'Sam and Gus framed me on that, Skipper.' He briefly recounted the series of events that had transpired since the moment he was awakened to find Skuro and Nuene in his room.

Dombey remained silent. At length he shook his head deliberately. 'Nuene might pull that, but it don't sound like Sam Skuro. Sam has slugged too many men to make a mess of it like you say Foy was.'

'That's the rub,' Duke growled. 'Foy was either beaten to death and then gagged, which would be silly, because any fool could have seen he was finished, or else he was bound and gagged and then battered, which would be needless brutality.'

'That's what I can't figger,' Dombey contributed. He took a gun out of his coat pocket and pushed it toward his companion. 'I don't think you'll need this; I've pinched Sam a dozen times an' never had to use one.'

Duke tested the balance of the revolver, flipped open the cylinder and checked the load, then shoved it into his pocket. He was about to speak, when Dombey suddenly slowed the machine.

'What's this?' he growled. 'There's the dead wagon in front of the roomin' house I was headin' for.'

Duke felt a queer, unfamiliar tightening around his diaphragm as he glanced through the windshield. A crowd stood in a great semi-circle around the coroner's small black truck and uniformed policemen were seeking to clear a path for traffic.

'Looks like we was late,' Dombey commented morosely. He pulled over to the curb and stopped. 'You wait here, Duke. I'll mosey over an' prowl the joint.' He slipped out to the sidewalk and melted into the excited throng.

Duke slumped in his seat, jerked his hat down until the brim rested on the bridge of his nose and lighted a cigarette. Intuitively he knew the answer, but when Dombey came back to the car five minutes later, he verified it.

'Sam an' Gus got it,' he grunted laconically. 'Resistin' arrest.'

Duke felt a little sick. It came to him suddenly that he had not eaten since the day before. As though the veteran read his mind, Dombey suggested:

'Let's get a cup of coffee, kid.' Without waiting for a reply, he piloted the car around the first corner and drove until he came to a small, counter lunchroom.

Coffee warmed him, stirred him out of his apathy. 'I counted on Sam,' Duke mused glumly. 'He was my one alibi. Now Egan's got a fine set-up; he cleans up the Washburn killing by fastening it onto Skuro and Nuene and then bumping them off. I'm the goat on the murder of Chris Foy.'

'It's bad,' Dombey admitted.

'Bad, hell!' Duke retorted with a rueful grin. 'It's terrible. Now I see why

Egan turned me loose; he wanted me to lead him to Skuro. With them out of the way, I'll be next. They'll try to knock me off for resisting arrest!'

Dombey shook his head slowly. 'Listen, Duke, nobody'll knock you off while you're with me.'

'Thanks, Skipper, but you can't be with me always.'

'That's what I was thinkin', Duke,' Dombey said quietly. 'The safest place for you right now is in jail as my prisoner. Why not let me book you on suspicion, then take over the case an' have my boys prove you didn't do it.'

Duke laughed without pleasantry. 'Skuro and Nuene tried to let some one prove them innocent, Skipper. They got a free ride in the official meatwagon. No, I'll go it alone for—' He stopped as the waiter paused in front of him.

'Say, mister,' said the waiter, 'you're wanted on the phone.'

Duke frowned. 'You must have made a mistake. No one knows I am here. What name did they ask for?'

The waiter shrugged. 'It's a dame. She didn't ask for you by name. She said there was a tall, good-looking young guy sittin' in here with a cop.'

Dombey sniffed. 'G'wan, Duke, that must be for you.'

Martindel rose, walked to the rear of the lunchroom and picked up the receiver that dangled from a wall phone. Clapping it to his ear, he growled: 'Hello?'

'It's your shyster mouthpiece,' came the familiar voice of his wife. 'I just thought you might be interested to know that two men have been following you.'

Duke started. 'Where are you, Phyl?'

'Across the street, in a drug store, you idiot. Knowing you need a wet nurse, I followed you after you left the hotel. This pair picked you up when you met Captain Dombey.'

'Cops!'

'I don't think so, darling. They are young and sleek-looking. One – the tall one – walks with a limp in his left leg. The other is squat and tubby. He seems to walk on his heels.'

'Where are they now?'

'Sitting in a green sedan halfway down the block. Now, you fool, will you go to Europe with me?'

Duke grinned wryly. 'Can't just now, darling, I've got a business engagement, but will you please go home and quit playing detective!'

'Who is your engagement with, Mr. Martindel?'

'Two mugs in a green sedan, Mrs. Martindel,' said Duke, as he pronged the receiver.

Duke's first impulse was to repeat to Dombey what Phyllis had told him, but by the time he reached his stool, he changed his mind. The copper gave him a quizzical, sidelong glance.

'Someone you know?' he inquired.

43

Duke shrugged. 'A dame who saw us enter. She tried to date me up. Called from the drug store across the street.'

'That's the hell of bein' good-lookin',' grunted Dombey, then changed the subject by asking: 'Well, what did you decide to do?'

Duke lighted a cigarette before answering, finally gave his decision. 'I'm not going to risk my life in a courtroom, Skipper; I'll take my chances outside where I can do my own fighting. As it stands right now, I'm framed for a bank job and a murder, neither of which I committed. I know that Sam Skuro and Gus Nuene didn't kill Washburn. They're a pair of crooks, I'll admit, and they're better off dead, perhaps, but they did not murder Washburn.'

'All of which doesn't help you,' Dombey put in drily.

'Admittedly, but it does explain things. For instance, I committed a crime – compounded a felony when I sought to square that bank job by returning the money. Even a regular city cop has to break the law many times in order to get around some legal red tape in settling a more serious offense, but when a private dick gets tripped up, he's in a jam.'

'You haven't any evidence as to who did kill Washburn,' Dombey pointed out.

Duke shook his head. 'Not yet.'

'That "yet" is the trouble,' Dombey grunted. 'If your hypothesis is correct, if the reason they released you was so you would lead 'em to Skuro and Nuene, then you've served your purpose an' your number is up about now. You won't have a chance even to get started, Duke. No you better come in with me.'

Martindel grinned, but shook his head. 'By the way, Skipper, do you know a couple of mugs, one tall – that walks with a limp in his left leg, the other short, squat and gives the impression of walking on his heels?'

Dombey frowned, massaged his forehead with gnarled fingers. 'Sounds like Louis Nagel an' Tubby Arnison. Nagel's a tall flashy-lookin' wop from St. Louis. Arnison used to be a stoolie for Egan before he graduated into the money rackets.'

'Arnison still stool?'

Dombey snorted. 'You tell me, kid.'

'Guns?'

'Yeah – Nagel anyhow. Tubby's just a dirty little rat that started out snatchin' purses.'

Duke pushed to his feet, jockeyed a coin down the counter and faced the copper. 'Thanks, Skipper. My appreciation and all that. I'll be seeing you.'

The old man shoved erect. 'Wait a minute, kid, I'll tag along a while.'

Duke gave his head a decisive shake. 'Thanks, but I'd prefer to go it alone. There's a lot of angles to this and there's no use of you risking your pension on a losing bet. You can do me one favor though – if the breaks go against me, keep an eye on Phyl.'

Dombey grunted. 'I'll marry her myself the day she's a widder.' He gave the younger man a friendly punch on the chest. 'You're just a headstrong damn fool, Duke.'

Martindel grinned, swung around, and leaving Dombey staring after him, barged outside. He cast a quick glance across the street, but could see no sign of Phyllis. A whimsical smile twitched the corner of his mouth, then he let his gaze wander casually down the block. The green sedan was parked within a hundred yards of where he stood. His smile vanished. His hand brushed against the hard lump in his pocket where the gun reposed and he felt the impulse to run amuck. He felt stifled, as though a great unseen web were slowly tightening around him. The sacrificial goat! But why? What was back of it all? Why were these mugs tailing him? How did they know where to pick him up? No one knew that but Dombey and himself. For a brief moment he felt the urge to charge the green sedan and gun out the pair, but almost immediately reason prevailed. That would be suicide and get him no place, except, perhaps, the morgue.

A cruising cab offered a chance to meditate. The driver caught his signal and a moment later he was comfortably ensconced in the tonneau. Up until the moment that the driver asked him where he wanted to go, Duke had been undecided, but when the question was suddenly propounded, he gave directions for reaching a small cottage in the mountains just back of the city. As the driver turned back to his task of piloting the swaying cab, Duke risked a hasty glance out the rear window. The green sedan had swung in line behind.

He had no plan. The tiny cottage suggested itself because of its isolation; he wanted to get these two hoods alone someplace where he was not likely to be disturbed. It was situated on the edge of a small lake; Duke and Phyllis had spent their honeymoon there.

He wanted, first to know why these men were tailing him and who sent them. He fished a cigarette out of his pocket and tapped it musefully against the window. Abruptly the possible answer came to him: Egan! Egan had released him on a writ when he might well have been held; Egan had sent his flat-feet to follow him, and now two hoods magically appear on his tail. That was too coincidental especially since one of the pair was a stoolie of Egan's. There was only one possible explanation – Egan, knowing that Duke was friendly with Dombey and often called when he was in trouble, had tapped the wires on all the Skipper's calls. That would explain the appearance of the two mugs at the rendezvous.

A grim, cynical smile twisted the corner of Martindel's mouth. He could use more direct methods in dealing with two known criminals than with the police. His fingers slipped into his coat pocket and massaged the checkered butt of the gun Dombey had given him. Perhaps Tubby Arnison could be induced to wag his tongue.

The cab suddenly swung into a clearing and stopped before the little cottage. Duke stepped out and handed the driver a bill.

'Want I should wait, mister?' asked the man at the wheel.

Martindel grinned, shook his head. 'No. I'm expecting friends.' He waved the cab away amd mounted the steps to the wide veranda that encircled three sides of the little cabin. He opened the front door, walked swiftly through the dust-covered living room and let himself out a rear door. A short run brought him to the fringe of trees that formed a hedge around the cottage. He took out his gun and padded in a great arc until he came to a spot where he commanded a view of the front of the cabin.

CHAPTER FIVE

Duke Makes A Killing

The cab was gone. For a few moments he could see no sign of human life, then his sharp eyes picked up the outline of a man standing in the shadow of a tall tree. Even as Duke watched him, a second man – a short, fat fellow – eased out of the brush and joined his taller companion.

They held a whispered consultation, but their words did not reach the detective. However, their meaning was obvious, for both drew guns, examined them briefly and slipped them into convenient pockets.

Duke sized them up. The tall one – Nagel, if Dombey was correct – was swarthy, and vicious-looking. His close-set eyes, thin mouth and the way he carried his head low, like a bull, suggested that he would be a tough nut to crack. His squat companion, on the contrary, had a moon-face that looked soft and flabby. He had eyes that could easily cradle fear. Coupled with a killer of Nagel's type, Tubby Arnison might conceivably commit murder, but if left to his own devices, Duke surmised that he would slide into rackets that carried with them a lesser chance of physical liability.

Nagel suddenly stepped into the clearing and approached the cottage; Arnison drew his gun, braced it against the tree and covered the veranda.

Duke's teeth bared in a cold smile. So that was it? Nagel was going to lure him out while Arnison shot him from ambush! He melted back into the trees and silently made his way to a spot directly back of the stubby little gunman. Then he eased forward—

Tubby Arnison's first indication of misfortune came when Duke pressed the cold muzzle of his revolver against his well-rolled neck.

'Not a sound!' Martindel reached forward and removed the gun from the tremulous fingers. 'Now call to your partner and tell him to come back here!' He increased the pressure of the gun on Arnison's neck. 'Any tricks, mug, and I'll part your hair from the inside!'

Arnison nodded, terror-stricken. He lifted his voice and jerked huskily, 'Hey, Louis, come here a minute!'

Nagel glanced back, hesitated and then started to retrace his steps. When he reached a point about halfway across the clearing, he suddenly jerked to a stop. Perhaps some animalistic instinct warned him of danger, for his hand suddenly streaked toward his pocket.

Martindel saw it coming. He took a quick swing at Arnison's head with one gun. As the squat hood toppled into the brush with a squeal of pain and terror, he jumped into the open.

'Don't try it, Nagel!' he warned.

The St. Louis gunman flung a curse at him and brought his gun up shooting. Duke's first shot was high. Before he got in a second, a slug from Nagel's gun tore into his leg, turned him halfway around and dropped him on his hands and knees. He rolled over, braced one elbow on the ground and fired twice in quick succession.

Nagel was dead before he hit the ground!

Duke rolled over hastily, expecting trouble from Arnison, but the tubby little assassin was clinging groggily to a tree, trying to wipe the blood out of his eyes. Duke inched over to a sapling, pulled himself erect and tested his leg. It was numb now and refused to hold his weight.

He dropped Arnison's gun into his pocket, picked up his own, and turned the muzzle on the fat man. 'Snap out of it, Tubby,' he rasped harshly. 'Amble out there and grab hold of your boy friend. Drag him into the bushes here. We may be having company. Step lively.'

Arnison wavered, wet his thick lips and looked at the gun. Duke let his thumb toy with the hammer. That decided the gunman. He mumbled something unintelligible and swayed across the clearing. He hesitated a long time before he could bring himself to touch his dead confederate, but at last he caught Nagel by the ankles and dragged him into the surrounding trees.

'Now,' commanded Duke, 'we'll go into the house where we can have a nice, quiet chat. Get going, mug!'

Arnison moved with surprising alacrity. Duke broke off a branch to serve as a walking cane and hobbled after him. It was painful work limping up the four steps to the veranda for he had to keep his eyes fastened on the waddling bulk of his prisoner. But at last he made it and pushing into the cottage for the second time since his arrival, dropped into a chair near the door. He let his eyes settle musefully on the other's flabby features.

Arnison stood with his back to a small table in the center of the room. He was a man close to forty with watery eyes that shifted constantly. His red, bulbous nose was criss-crossed with little purple veins and his puffy cheeks seemed to drag down the skin under his eyes like a St. Bernard's. Periodically he opened his mouth as if to speak, but no words came.

It was Martindel that broke the stillness.

'Arnison, I'm not going to fool with you. I'm going to ask you some questions and I want smart answers. First, who sent you after me to make this kill?'

The prisoner wagged his head. 'We weren't goin' to bop you, fella. You got us all wrong. This was just a heist, see! We saw you pass down the state highway an' tailed you—'

The roar of Martindel's gun drowned his words. He gave a shrill bleat of terror, clawed at the fleshy part of his leg and toppled on his face.

Duke's voice was chilled. 'That didn't hurt you much, Arnison, but it's a sample of what you can expect if you keep on with those lies. Now I happen to know you picked up my trail down in the city about the time I met Captain Dombey. Who sent you after me, Arnison?'

The hood sobbed, dragged himself to his hands and knees and crawled toward the detective like a cur dog. 'S'help me, I don't know,' he whined. 'Nagel got the orders from somebody, but I don't know who. Nagel's dead now an'—'

Duke leaned forward. He cupped the gun in the palm of his hand and struck the hood across the side of the head. Arnison yelped and fell on his face, grovelling.

Martindel straightened. 'I know different, Tubby. Talk, or I'll shred you to ribbons. I've no compunction about killing you; none whatever. For the last time – who sent you two guns after me?'

Arnison slowly lifted his head and stared at Duke through a veil of blood. 'I can't, s'help me! He'd kill me—'

Duke raised his gun to the level with the other's battered countenance. 'O.K., Tubby, if you'd rather have it now.' He thumbed back the hammer.

Arnison hesitated until he heard the second click of the gun, then terror seized him. 'Wait!' he bleated. 'I'll talk!' His head fell forward into his arms and he sobbed out the name so huskily that Martindel had to lean forward to catch it.

'Egan—'

Duke's mouth contracted. 'Why?' he rasped.

'He wanted you dead for the bank job!' choked Arnison.

Duke grunted, leaned back and contemplated the man on the floor. So his guess was correct – Egan had made a deal with these two rats to remove him. His scowl deepened. What good was this information? If he returned Arnison to the city, the stool-pigeon would deny his accusation the moment he was under the protection of the police. Even if he didn't, it would be the word of a known criminal against a police official; Duke knew he could not get to court with anything as slim as that.

Duke pulled himself erect, hobbled across the room and picked up a telephone. He pulled it as far as the cord would allow, then placed it on the floor.

'Tubby,' he commanded grimly. 'I want you to make a call, a very important call.'

Arnison lifted his head and stared. The detective canted his head toward the instrument. 'Crawl over to it, Tubby. Call Inspector Egan, tell him Nagel shot me, but that he got it as well. Suggest that you found something of vital importance and ask him to come out here. The idea is, Tubby, that unless Egan comes to this cottage, you're going out the hard way.'

Arnison choked. 'You want me to lure Egan here? My God, guy, you don't know what you're askin'!'

Duke squinted along the barrel of his gun. 'Have you ever seen what happens when they take you to the morgue, Tubby? How they rip you open down the middle, stick a water-hose into you to wash out your insides. If I shoot you in the head, for instance, they'll cut off your skull to see where the bullet went. They'll—'

'Cut it!' screamed the gunman. 'Cut it, I tell you!'

'There's the phone, Tubby,' Duke suggested drily.

Arnison inched toward the instrument on his stomach. His tremulous fingers fumbled with the receiver as he sought to remove it.

'Easy, Tubby, easy,' cautioned Martindel. 'I'll hold you responsible if Egan doesn't show up, so don't let him smell a rat.'

Arnison sobbed aloud, shuddered convulsively, then took down the receiver. In broken sentences he jerked out the number of headquarters, but by the time he got the inspector on the wire, his voice was reasonably cool.

'Arnison, chief. I don't want to talk over the phone, see, but can you come up here right away?' He shot a sidelong glance at Duke, then shut his eyes as though to blot out the vision of the gun muzzle. 'We – Nagel got him, chief, but you better come. I found somethin', see. I – yeah, we're up in a cottage on Bear Mountain.' He choked out the directions for reaching the cabin, then slowly cradled the receiver.

Duke grinned cynically. 'He's coming?'

Arnison shuddered. 'He's comin'!' he sobbed and dropped his head in his arms.

When the noise of a car reached the cabin about a half hour later, the stage was set. Duke Martindel stood back of the entrance door, leaning on the top of a chair. Tubby Arnison, still trembling with terror, crouched on another straight-backed chair beside the center table, facing the front door. Brakes ground outside, then the motor died. A car door slammed.

Arnison mumbled something. Duke wagged the gun. 'Easy, Tubby,' he whispered. 'Easy.'

Steps pounded up across the veranda, paused a moment then the door swung open. Egan strode into the room.

'Well, Arnison, where is he?' demanded the inspector. Duke reached out and slapped the door shut with his free hand. 'Right here, Egan! No, don't reach for that gun. You can't make it!'

The uniformed man swiveled like a cornered hobo. For a brief instant he seemed undecided whether to go for his gun, then he slowly elevated his hands.

'What is this?' he snapped.

'This,' Duke told him drily, 'is a show-down. Arnison here has been telling me some interesting things, Inspector, things that corroborate some old-time suspicions of mine.'

Egan flashed a venomous glance at the quaking stoolie, then turned back to Martindel. 'You're a damn fool, Duke!' he commented. 'Put down that gun!'

'You're right, Egan, I am a damn fool.' Duke admitted. 'But I'm not going to put down this gun until we settle a few points of interest. First, I'd like to know what excuse you have for putting a couple of hoods on me!'

Egan shrugged. 'You're crazy. You can't prove a thing.'

'Who said anything about proving it? I'm curious, that's all, damn curious. For instance, I'm curious to know how it happened that Harry Washburn was murdered at the exact moment that Skuro and Nuene were cracking the County and Suburban Bank, how you appeared at the bank just as I was leaving.' His mocking smile vanished into a scowl. 'And, lastly, Egan, I'd like to know why you deliberately shot at my head.'

'We don't take bank robbers alive,' growled Egan, 'not after they kill a watchman.'

Duke sniffed. 'But you weren't supposed to know that Foy was dead when you walked in there. That's another point I'd like cleared up, Egan – the killing of Foy. Sam and Gus didn't kill him, I didn't, so who did?'

'You can't talk your way out of this mess,' Egan threatened.

Duke grinned sardonically. 'I'm not going to do the talking, Inspector. Tubby here, for instance, knows a lot of interesting things.'

Egan ponderously swung his head. Arnison winced before the cold glitter of those colorless eyes. 'S'help me, chief, I ain't—' he choked to a stop.

Duke hefted his gun. 'Well, Tubby, make up your mind. Don't be bashful – this is a nice, chummy get-together. Now what do you know about this business?'

Arnison pulled himself erect, his fingers tightened around the back of his chair. 'My God, you wouldn't murder a man in cold blood?'

'Don't be a fool!' rasped Egan. 'He's bluffing you.'

Duke smiled, but said nothing. His thumb dragged back the hammer of his revolver and in the silence of the dusty room, two distinct clicks were audible. Arnison's voice rose to a shriek.

'Bluffin' hell! I ain't gonna die, I ain't, I tell ya.'

Martindel had hoped to provoke an argument between his two captives and thus glean some of the truth back of the tangled mess. He well knew

Egan's vicious temper and he counted on Arnison's fear of death to form a verbal explosion of some sort. But he was hardly prepared for what followed.

Arnison was trembling from head to foot. 'You got me into this, Egan!' he shrilled. 'He'll shoot me down like a dog. I won't die – s'help me, I won't, I tell ya—'

Duke swung his eyes to Egan to see how the latter was taking it, when Arnison flung the chair!

With one leg injured and unable to bear his weight, Duke had propped himself against the chair in front of him. Arnison's wild fling struck the chair, knocked it from under him and he fell headlong to the floor. As he went down, he tried to swing his gun, but Egan kicked it from his hand and it bounced across the room.

Duke cursed his own carelessness, rolled over and tried to drag himself erect. Then he paused. He saw Arnison swing and pounce toward the revolver. Just as the crook reached it, a gun roared. Arnison gave a startled yelp, pirouetted once and sprawled in a corner.

Duke jerked his eyes away, brought them back to Egan. The inspector was lowering his own service revolver and a faint dribble of smoke curled from the muzzle.

'There goes a perfectly good witness,' Duke drawled cynically.

Egan turned. 'You won't need any witnesses,' he growled. 'Not where you're going.'

Duke gave up trying to pull himself to his feet. He sat back on the floor and looked into the relentless features of the policeman. 'So it's like that, Egan?'

The inspector nodded. 'Just like that.' He stepped sideways so that he could get a clear, unobstructed shot at the man on the floor.

Duke sighed. 'Just one question. Why was I framed on that bank job?'

Egan drew back the hammer of his gun. 'You can ask Arnison that when you meet him in hell.'

Abruptly a gun thundered into the silence. Duke's first impression was that Egan had fired. The inspector stood with his arm still outstretched, but now his gun had vanished and his hand was dripping blood.

Duke called on his waning strength to drag himself erect. He jerked around to face the hoodlum, but Arnison still lay inert where he had fallen.

Then a door opened and Captain Dombey and Phyllis came into the room. Dombey covered Egan. Phyllis gave a little whimper and ran toward Duke, arms outstretched. He swayed forward to meet her. The floor rose suddenly. He went out.

Duke recovered consciousness in the hospital to find Phyllis sitting on the edge of the bed, holding his hand. 'Take it easy, darling,' she whispered, and he saw that she smiled through her tears.

'How'd I get here?' Duke wanted to know.

A familiar voice answered from the foot of the bed. 'They started to put you in the meat wagon,' Dombey growled, 'but your wife wouldn't stand for it. Was afraid they'd get their loads mixed, I guess, so you made the trip in an ambulance.'

Duke winced as he tried to move his leg. 'Say, where's Egan? Did you kill him?'

'Naw,' grumbled Dombey. 'We're savin' him to hang. I'll try to get passes for us all – we can make a day of it.'

Phyllis shuddered. 'Not the Martindels,' she assured the grinning copper. 'They are going to Europe.'

Duke groaned. 'They can't hang him without more evidence than we got. Gosh, what a lousy shame you didn't show up before Arnison was killed.' He frowned at them both. 'Say, how did you two happen to show up?'

Dombey chuckled. 'Well, it's a long story, but I figured as long as you didn't want the date with the swell-lookin' jane in the drug store, I'd mosey over. I dated her up myself an' we ambled up here. By a strange coincidence, you was here.'

Duke scowled at his wife. 'So,' he sneered, 'you don't trust me? You follow me—'

'Oh, shut up!' Phyllis said.

'About Arnison,' Dombey butted in, 'he ain't dead. Egan's slug creased his skull, but it didn't do him no damage. However, me'n the doc made him think he was slated for the long trail. Did he talk? Ha!'

'Plenty. First, he says—' Dombey stopped as a physician motioned him to silence.

'Our patient has had enough, I'm afraid, Captain,' the doctor said firmly. 'The details can wait until—'

'The hell they can!' shouted Duke. 'I want to know why Egan framed me?'

Dombey turned at the door. 'O.K. You was in the way. Egan wanted a goat for the Washburn kill, so his stoolies tipped him off to the fact that Sam Skuro an' Gus Nuene were set to crack the bank at midnight. Egan set a watch on the bank job and sent Arnison an' Nagel out to bump Washburn. According to Arnison, Nagel did the actual kill. Egan had Skuro and Nuene followed so that they couldn't establish an alibi, but somebody tipped Sam off by telephone and he an' Gus beat it over to your place.'

'*Humph!*' grunted Duke thoughtfully. 'I'm beginning to see through it. Who killed Foy?'

'Egan. They followed you to Henderson's home, guessed what you was goin' to do, so Egan figgured it a good chance to frame you proper an' so have a sucker for the bank job. He gave Foy the works. Arnison saw him do it. Egan began to get restless when he knew you was working against him, so he decided to let the boys polish you off. Well, so long.' He closed the door.

The doctor took Phyllis by the arm and gently propelled her to the door. 'No more questions for this young man,' he announced firmly.

'Just one,' shouted Duke. 'Just one, Doc.'
'And that is—'
'How soon can a guy travel to Europe with a leg like this?'

A PINCH OF SNUFF

ERIC TAYLOR

Eric Taylor was a frequent, though not prolific, contributor to various pulps in the 1920s and 1930s, notably to *Black Mask*, *Dime Detective* and the lower-paying *Clues*.

While the seal of approval that came with being published in the Golden Age of *Black Mask*, in the years in which it was publishing Hammett, Whitfield, Cain, Nebel and its other major stars, would normally have given an author greater opportunity for success, this seems to have eluded Taylor. He never published a novel and never even had a single short story collected in an anthology.

Some of this may be due to the fact that he eschewed the traditional path of most pulp fiction writers, which was to produce a series detective. In the seven stories published in *Black Mask*, for example, three were about different detectives and three were about thieves, including the story collected here.

Another reason that Taylor may not have enjoyed the financial and critical success of many of his fellow pulpsters is his melodramatic style. The impossibly pitiful early years of the heroine of 'A Pinch of Snuff' would have been an embarrassment to producers of stage plays at the turn of the last century, at which audiences were encouraged to hiss at the villain as he twirled his moustache while throwing a waif out of her home to freeze in the winter snow.

'A Pinch of Snuff' was originally published in the June 1929 issue of *Black Mask*.

A PINCH OF SNUFF

ERIC TAYLOR

In Montreal they like to show you the view from the top of Mont Royal. To the south, church spires like gracile mile posts guide the eye to the green St. Lawrence, panting here from its fierce flight over the Lachine Rapids, widening for its majestic march to the sea. Beyond the river lies a great plain that meets the sky near the hills along the American border. To the north, the Laurentian Mountains hide uncountable lakes that lie like verde antiques, cool and inscrutable as they await a sportsman's rod. To the west, gay red roofs peer through the verdant screen of maples, while to the east. . . . But Montreal might prefer that you didn't look to the east.

A family of five brooded in a single room apartment in an East End flat. The room was hot, steaming, fetid with the snow that melted on Armand's coat and the baby wash that hung on a length of twine.

Armand sat sullen, his right hand stroking a nearly-empty bottle. He glanced across the room toward his youngest brat and thought it droll that the gin and milk should end simultaneously. His eyes wandered over to Gabrielle. He saw the ugly lines that poverty had etched across the fragile beauty of youth. She had cheated him, he thought. Bony, hollow-chested, with bent shoulders, reproachful eyes, and mute lips – a hag at thirty! Could this be the dancing-eyed, cream-skinned beauty he had wed thirteen years ago?

Irène moved across the room toward the table. Armand scowled. A doctor down at the clinic had informed Armand that Irène was undernourished. A thin arm crossed Armand's vision and raised the cover of a thin metal box. A savage blasphemy burst from Armand's lips. His hand struck out. One of Irène's pale cheeks flushed crimson as she jumped back. Gabrielle turned with a furious protest on her lips. But something she saw in her husband's eyes choked back the words.

'She knows there is no bread in the box.' Armand said after a minute.

At nine o'clock Armand went out. At a corner grocery, where his credit had been stopped, Armand halted to beg an empty sack. With this beneath an arm he struck south to a district of small wholesale produce merchants.

Before a window, Armand stood in deep thought for a long time. The flakes of snow that were falling grew larger. A few drops of rain fell, and Armand's decision was made. This mild winter was starving the poor. Mid-January and the river was still unfrozen despite the supplications of a thousand women who prayed for cold that their men might work at the ice-cutting.

Armand broke the window and crawled into a small warehouse. A few minutes later Armand thrust the filled sack through the window he had broken. He dropped to the street and raised the sack to his shoulder.

But recently there had been other raids on the wholesale provision houses. A keen-eyed detective with a reputation to make was watching the district.

At the detective's first cry to halt, Armand threw down the sack and ran. Armand was lean and fleet, and the detective had less at stake. At the detective's third cry, Armand's heart lifted. He was escaping the law. Then the detective fired. Something reached up from behind and gripped Armand's leg. He staggered forward painfully, dragging this leg that seemed to be caught in a trap. He turned down an alley. His leg felt free now, but very heavy. He climbed a fence, fell to the ground and lurched forward. Twenty minutes later he reached his room weak and panting.

Gabrielle cried out her fear when she saw him. She ran to lock the door. Irène raised a small head from a heap of blankets that lay on the floor. Panic stifled her crying as a heavy pounding shook the door.

Armand glanced down and saw the blood that dripped from his soaked trousers. The hammering on the door increased. Gabrielle was holding him close. She was sobbing her anguish and kissing him. He must not leave her. For God's sake, no! She and the little ones – they would starve!

The soft wood door seemed to bellow inward. Armand kissed her once. He bent for an instant to drop a tear on the face of Irène. Then he seized an empty gin bottle and slid to the door.

The door crashed and Armand struck. The bottle shattered. The detective fell forward into Armand's arms. Armand's fingers closed on the man's throat. The detective tried to speak, but Armand choked back his words. And then a great blast shook the room. The low jet of gas was blown out.

The room was heavy with rancid smoke and escaping gas. Someone came in who shut off the gas and later lighted it. There were two men on the floor. One of them, the detective, rose slowly.

Gabrielle crossed the floor to her man. She stood above him – ominously calm, immobile. Then a long-drawn scream echoed the anguish of the woman in despair. She clutched at her breast and pitched forward across the body of Armand.

Neighbors and strangers swarmed into the room. Irène's frail little body shook with the chill of terror. The detective, with a gun in his hand, shouted fierce orders.

Irène crept from her blankets. The detective angrily waved back the intruders pressing in the doorway. The child slipped into the throng and was pushed with the rest from the room.

She stood in the doorway watching when the ambulance attendants brought stretchers into the room. She saw the doctor bend over her mother and heard him pronounce her dead. She saw him turn from her father and shake his head hopelessly. She was jostled roughly out of the way when the stretchers were carried from the room.

Irène shrank back further as a giant policeman carried her two baby sisters, one in each arm, from the room.

The dark hall was a swirling vortex of the morbidly curious. Men and women swarmed the place and fought for a glimpse into the room of tragedy. Police threw them back roughly. Children clung to their mothers' skirts crying out their fear. Irène shrank from sight in a corner.

In time the police herded the neighbors into their own quarters and quiet reclaimed the building.

Irène crept fearfully down the hall. A policemen guarded the door to Armand's room. Irène stood there for a minute gazing dully, dry-eyed, at the door. The policeman waved an enormous nightstick and ordered her to be gone.

Irène walked slowly to the street door. She flung a last startled glance over her shoulder and fled down the street. Her spindling legs revealed amazing fortitude and carried her miles from that East End flat.

That night she fell in with a crippled beggar. Outcast, nearly helpless, the discovery of a bit of humanity more wretched than himself was flattering. The beggar took Irène to a basement. She made peasoup for him, and he rewarded her with two blankets.

Irène told him her story and the beggar reciprocated with the tale of a thrilling flight from a crime that had ended when a freight train ground off his two legs. He told her further tales of glorious days and nights in the underworld. He promised to learn the name of the detective who had killed Armand and murder him.

Irène took courage from his brave tales. '*Non!*' she exclaimed passionately, 'you find the name, and I will kill him!'

There were no truant officers to evade. Irène cooked peasoup for 'Sticks' Grady until he died of acute alcoholism three years later.

Irène was sixteen, but looked twenty. She was tall, too thin, but pretty in a hard way. Her eyes were smoldering bits of repressed hate. Her cheek bones were too prominent, and her lips were thin and straight. Sticks Grady had trained her well, and Irène was ready for crime.

She experimented with shop-lifting, snatching purses, and picking pockets, then tried burglary and found it most profitable. She could move through a house with the fleet grace of a shadow. Against the hazards of capture she carried a small stiletto – a weapon essentially feminine, but with the deadly possibilities of a cobra. The blade was a scant three inches in length and came to the point of a needle. Irène meant one day to strike that point to the heart of a detective named Jean Duret, who, Sticks Grady had informed her, was the slayer of her father.

In time her life drew Irène into contact with other thieves. She was cunning and ambitious and organized a band. Irène lived with her companions in an old three-story stone building on St. Paul Street. The house was two hundred years old and ran back to an ancient cobbled street named St. Amable. The windows were few and narrow. They had originally been protected with thick iron shutters to withstand the arrows and bullets of the Iroquois. Fragments of these shutters still clung to rusted hinges.

Irène rented the two upper floors and professed to run a lodging house for sailors. For fifty years the ground floor had been occupied by a snuff manufacturer, but now that part of the building stood vacant, giving Irène's band the run of the whole place. The cellar was a deep, dark pit that smelled foully of the river. A small section of the flagged floor of the cellar was a trapdoor that opened down into a tunnel which Irène had heard was once part of the early fortifications of the city. Irène marked that tunnel for the tomb of the detective, Jean Duret.

Her band of thieves held up ships' officers on the dimly-lighted streets leading to the river. They occasionally lured drunken seamen to the grim, iron-shuttered house on St. Amable; robbed them, and threw their senseless bodies into deserted alleyways or abandoned warehouses. With one or two of the more skillful, Irène swept uptown on forays on the rich. She was surprisingly lucky, and the gang prospered.

It was on a night that Irène sat in her room weaving mental webs to ensnare the detective, Jean Duret, that a stranger hammered on the St. Amable Street door.

Irène's eyes peered through the perforations in a rust-eaten iron shutter. She saw a big man, wide of shoulders, but not stout. He was dressed in a pair of cord trousers and a blue flannel shirt. She could not see his face.

A frown of perplexity crossed Irène's forehead. It was not some fool thinking to rent a room, because the only lodging sign was an inconspicuous one on the St. Paul Street side of the house. The knocking on the door persisted. Irène was alone. She drew the stiletto from her breast and swiftly descended the foot-worn stairs.

'Who is there?' she demanded.

'It is I, Le Loup. I come from Desfarges!'

' "Le Loup," ' Irène repeated. 'I don't know you.'

'You know Desfarges. Desfarges, of the Black Water Tavern?'

'Yes.'

'Then open this cursed door! Is it not enough that Desfarges has sent me?'

Irène opened the door doubtfully. The tall stranger entered and closed and locked the door. 'My card, miss!'

Irène looked deep into the man's eyes. Her glance dropped uncomfortably.

The lines of that long, lean face were ruthlessly hard. A knife slash that began near the right ear ended at the fellow's mouth. There was a sardonic twist to the other side of his mouth. Thick cords stood out upon his neck. His cleft chin was outthrust in swagging bravado. 'My card, miss!' he repeated with a distorted grin.

Irène reached forward and accepted a sheet of folded paper. She opened the paper slowly, her eyes still more upon her curious visitor than upon what he had offered as his card.

'Read,' the man laughed.

Irène's eyes dropped to the paper. She drew back startled, then a smile flitted across her lips. He was droll, this Apache. What he offered as his card was a police bulletin from Paris bearing his photograph, his fingerprint classification, and his Bertillon measurements. Beneath these details was the printed information that Emil Desjardins, alias Le Loup, was wanted for the savage murder of an old woman.

Irène glanced from the photograph to the man. 'The scar?' she asked.

'It was acquired since that episode,' Le Loup laughed.

'And what do you want of me?' Irène demanded.

'Desfarges told me that I could trust you – else I would not have offered my *card*. I have placed my life in your hands. I want shelter. The police may be looking for me here; though I got clean away from France.' He leaned close to Irène. 'Desfarges told me of your cellar; he told me, too, of the old tunnel that leads to the fortifications. I want shelter, protection, Miss, and a chance to escape if necessary. But I expect to earn it!'

Desfarges was the gang's fence. Irène was under obligations to him. She dared not send this Apache away.

She took Le Loup through the house. She showed him the two-foot thickness of the stone walls. With a flashlight she guided him to the cellar and showed him the trap in the flagged floor that opened into the tunnel.

Le Loup and Irène stood silent while the Apache gazed approvingly at the closed trap. There was not a sound in the cellar but their breathing. Then from beneath their feet came the faint squeal of rats.

Le Loup grinned, but Irène drew back with a shudder. 'The tunnel is alive with them,' she explained. 'New wharves of cement are being built and the rats have been driven back from the waterfront. They have little chance to find food now, and Jules, one of my men, tells me they will eat each other until none but a few remain. It is not a nice place, down there, but it it better than the gallows, or the guillotine, eh! And there is small danger that you will have to use it.'

At first Irène's band received Le Loup with suspicion. But he was a spectacular figure and his endless bragging caught the fancy of these unimaginative rouges. By day the Apache amused himself in the practice of knife-throwing in the old quarters of the snuff manufacturer. He appeared to be a careless braggart, but Irène noticed he was always careful to wipe away the particles of dust or snuff that might have clung to his knife during this sport. At night Le Loup drank enormous quantities of gin and talked. He swaggered about the hideout, voicing opinions and offering advice in a manner that alarmed Irène.

A night when he and Irène happened to be alone in the house, Le Loup threw open her door without knocking.

Irène jumped to her feet and faced the Apache. He stood on the threshold, his great body filling the doorway. His eyes glittered menace; his torn mouth was distorted in a grin.

Irène struck a hand to her breast. 'Get to your quarters!' she cried.

Le Loup stepped toward her. A stiletto flashed into Irène's hand. Her arm swept downward and struck. But Le Loup was swifter. His hand shot forward. Blood spurted from his palm, but he held Irène's wrist. Le Loup laughed hysterically. His teeth ground in a frenzy. Irène felt an enormous pressure on her wrist. Her arm was bending at the elbow. The stiletto came up in her hand guided by the powerful arm of Le Loup. Irène's eyes dilated with horror. Her face was a mask of fear. But she uttered no cry.

Le Loup forced her wrist backward until the stiletto was a scant inch from her throat. Irène's left hand shot forward and her nails clawed at Le Loup's eyes. The Apache grinned and gripped that wrist in his left hand. Irène retreated until her back was pressed hard against the wall. Still the stiletto drew nearer. She felt its sharp point graze on her flesh. Her skin was pierced, Irène screamed when she felt a short, hot flash in her throat. Le Loup laughed and dropped her wrist.

'Another time, my vixen, it will not be a scratch!'

He reached down and tore a great piece of silk from her dress. This he bound around his bleeding palm.

Irène stood silent, the stiletto dangling from her limp hand. Le Loup looked contemptuously from the dagger to Irène's eyes. But Irène had forgotten the stiletto. She was looking at Le Loup with new interest. For in the Apache, Irène suddenly saw the weapon with which she would destroy Jean Duret, the killer of her father.

Two of the band entered the house and the tension was broken. Le Loup walked from her room and Irène closed and locked her door.

She could hear Le Loup and the others laughing in another room. Their talk grew boisterous and Irène knew they were drinking. A loud scraping of chairs reached Irène's ears, then came the clump of heavy feet descending the stairs. Le Loup had gone out for the first time since his arrival.

It was hours later when Irène was awakened by a soft rap on her door.

'Who is there?' she called quietly.

'Joe.'

Irène arose and opened the door. A pale, trembling wretch slid into her room.

'*Mon Dieu*, Joe, what is it?'

'Le Loup,' Joe whispered hoarsely. 'Godin and I drank with him. We went out at midnight. There was a lone sailor on St. Paul Street. We crept into a doorway. When he passed, I stepped out with my gun. He raised his hands and Godin emptied his pockets. Le Loup stepped forward and counted the haul. "Here, young fellow," Le Loup shouted, "let this be a warning to you to carry a fuller pocket in the next world!" With that he struck the sailor to the heart. It was awful. Then as we came home, the madman boasted that he kills on every job. We must flee, Irène, or he will hang us all!'

Irène laughed softly. 'You are upset, Joe. Here is money. Take Godin and go to the country for a rest. Stay away for some weeks, and when you return go to Desfarges before you come here. Where did you leave this sailor?'

'We dragged him into the passage by Dionne's warehouse.'

Irène dressed quickly, then waited in her room until she heard Godin and Joe steal down the stairs. She slipped on a pair of kid gloves and stepped into the hall. She paused at Le Loup's door and heard him deep in an alcoholic sleep. Irène laughed softly and went downstairs.

She paused in the old snuff factory long enough to scoop up a pinch of dust from a corner, then she stepped out into St. Amable Street. The narrow, cobbled street was silent and deserted. Irène skirted the block and came to St. Paul Street. The old stone buildings, old as the city, and once the homes of early adventurers from Old France, loomed up in great black shadows. Irène moved swiftly under the protecting shield of the darkness. Soon she came to the passage by Dionne's warehouse. She listened for a full minute, then crept toward the victim of Le Loup's knife.

They had placed him in a doorway and he sat with knees drawn up and head thrown forward. He looked like a drunken man asleep, but the flesh on his face was cold to the touch.

Irène bent over him and found the wound where his coat was wet. She opened his coat, then drew her stiletto and dipped its point into the pinch of dust she had taken from the snuff factory. She threw a startled glance along the passage. Her breath came in short gasps. The stiletto point sank easily into the open wound. Irène withdrew the blade and wiped it carefully on the man's coat. Again she dipped its point in the dust in her gloved hand, and this time touched the blade lightly along the rent Le Loup's knife had made in the sailor's coat.

Half an hour later the dagger was washed clean, the gloves were destroyed, and Irène was back in her room.

In the morning she told her band singly of Le Loup's killing and warned them to scatter.

It was noon when Le Loup, sullen and dishevelled, came from his room. 'Where are the others?' he demanded abruptly.

'Pah!' Irène exclaimed in disgust, 'the cowards have run! They are fools. This is the safest place in the city – in the country, for that matter. What detective would look for a murderer within a hundred yards of the murder?'

Le Loup winced at the word murderer. He seemed to have lost some of his bravado. 'What about this detective Duret? Joe was telling me something of him.'

Irène laughed lightly. '*Mon brave* you are nervous this morning. Does Le Loup fear Duret? Come have a drink!'

'I fear no one!' Le Loup blustered, 'but they tell me. . . .'

'I will tell you of Duret,' Irène said quickly. 'He is gun-shy. There was an episode years ago. Duret killed an innocent. Since that day he has been gun-shy. When he gets into a tight corner, he will draw his pistol, but he will hesitate and hold his fire. I tell you Duret is not to be feared. He is ambitious. He has been on homicides for three years now. When he can, Duret will work alone to gather all the glory. And other detectives do not care about working with him because in a corner, he is uncertain. Why are you afraid? Last night you were so strong – so heroic.'

Le Loup's face broke into a smirk. Like a mask removed the fear was struck from his countenance.

'But come,' Irène said. 'I must watch at the windows so that if Duret should come you will have time to hide.'

Irène left Le Loup with a bottle of gin and spent the afternoon moving between the windows on St. Amable and St. Paul Streets.

As five o'clock drew near Irène's vigilance increased. The body of the sailor she knew, must have been discovered at seven o'clock when Dionne's warehouse was opened. At nine it would have been placed in the hands of the coroner. Before that time the enterprising Duret would be engaged on the case. Duret and the coroner would discover the dust in and about the dead man's wound. Dr. Leclaire the famous *medicin-legiste*, would take the dust to his laboratory. Some hours later he would pronounce the dust to be snuff.

Duret's theory would be that the murderer was addicted to snuff. But then the clever Leclaire would point out that from the depth and width of the wound it was obvious that the weapon was too large to be a clasp knife therefore it was improbable that the knife was carried in a pocket. Leclaire would offer the suggestion that the murder was committed in some place where there was a large quantity of snuff, and that later the body was carried to the passage where it was found. From that point it would be a matter of minutes until Duret appeared at the old snuff factory. And Irène knew that Duret would make his first investigation of the old stone house alone.

It would have been simpler for Irène to have lured Duret to the house with a telephone call notifying him of the whereabouts of Le Loup. But then Duret would have descended on the place in force.

At twenty minutes to six Irène's heart quickened as she glimpsed the familiar figure of the man who had killed her father. The detective was on the opposite side of St. Paul Street. A shadow crossed Irène's face as she saw Duret walk casually down the block without a side glance. In a moment he had passed beyond her vision and Irène regretted that she had not made some signal to attract him. But then he might have called for help before entering the place.

When Duret disappeared, Irène crossed the building and watched through the perforations of a rusy iron shutter on St. Amable Street.

In a few minutes the detective loomed into sight. Irène's face glowed. Duret had stopped. A bell jangled noisily.

'Le Loup! Le Loup!' Irène called quickly, 'to the cellar and into the tunnel! Duret has come. He is alone! You can work the trap?'

'Yes.' Le Loup answered, as he stole down the stairs.

The bell rang again. Irène descended the stairs and opened the street door. Duret, tall, handsome, well-fed, stood upon the threshold. Irène's eyes met his. She swayed uncertainly for an instant while a little room fetid with the smell of drying clothes swam before her eyes. She saw Armand her father limp into that room, his foot dripping blood. She saw this man who stood before her burst in and grapple with her father. She heard again the screams of her mother. Her ears seemed to burst with the crash of gunfire. Then her nostrils were drenched with the stench of powder and the room was dark.

As though through a mist she saw Duret again. She recovered with a start.

Duret was gripping her arm; he was searching deep into her eyes. He relinquished his hold slowly. 'Pardon, madame, I thought you were about to faint.'

Irène smiled weakly. 'You remind me of my father!' she said.

Duret bowed gravely and said nothing.

'What do you wish. It cannot be that you want one of my rooms,' Irène said, glancing significantly at Duret's well-fitting clothes.

'No, madame, I came to look over this factory, but the doors are locked. I thought perhaps there might be an entrance from your hall.'

'There is,' Irène admitted readily, 'and it is open because I have permission to use the cellar beneath to store my lodgers' boxes. You have seen the agent?'

'Of course, madame.'

'Then come in.'

Irène opened the door that lead into the old snuff factory. Duret stepped into the large room. His eyes searched into dark corners and satisfaction glowed on his face. He turned abruptly to Irène. 'I understood the place has not been used for some time yet upon the floor I see signs of recent occupancy.'

'It is my lodgers, m'sieu. Some of them have been with me for years and they keep their boxes in the cellar. They have to pass through here to reach the cellar stairs.'

'What do your lodgers do madame?'

'They work on the docks – that is all but one!' Irène leaned toward Duret and her voice grew guarded. 'That one is a strange fellow. I have considered mentioning the matter to the police. He has been with me only a week. He does not work and he does not leave the house – at least during the day. Today, whenever the bell rang, he went to the cellar before I had time to open the door. Do you think I should report him to the police, *m'sieu*?'

Duret looked shrewdly into Irène's eyes. She returned his gaze evenly.

'Listen, madame, I come from the police. Where is this fellow now?'

'You are a detective?' Irène asked with awe in her voice. 'Come, *m'sieu*, I will show you. He went down the cellar as I came to answer your ring.'

Irène lead the detective across the snuff factory to the cellar door. She descended the stairs boldly. Duret thought for a second that perhaps he should call for assistance. But this woman went so coolly, he drew his revolver and flashlight and followed.

They saw no one in the cellar. Duret peered behind rubbish-filled packing cases and small trunks. The detective noticed a piece of strange mechanism. He was about to speak of it when Irène gestured toward a mark on the flagged floor. 'See, *m'sieu*, is that not a footprint?'

Duret stepped forward. He reached the spot on the floor Irène had indicated. He turned suddenly as he heard a subdued laugh behind him. Then the floor dropped beneath his feet and Duret was plunging through space.

Irène ran to the edge of the trap. She flashed a torch into the black pit. The detective was on his feet now, groping for the torch he had dropped in falling.

The dark shape of Le Loup appeared suddenly in the zone of light. Irène switched off the torch and left them in darkness. A red glow flashed from the tunnel three times and the floor rocked with the concussion of shots. Irène heard a sharp scream that did not come from Le Loup. She knew then that the Apache's knife had found its mark in the dark. 'Papa! Papa!' she cried hysterically.

The killer of her father was dead! But Irène was reminded suddenly of the second object of her vengeance. She ran forward to the short lever that controlled the trapdoor. Her moment of ecstasy over Duret's scream had cost her dear. The lever stuck in her hands when the trap was half closed. Irène threw her weight wildly against the iron bar. A gasp of exhaustion escaped her lips. Suddenly the lever moved freely. Irène jammed it home with a cry of exhaltation. And then she heard the mocking laugh of Le Loup at her side.

His right arm wound around Irène's side, binding her arms as he drew her against his body with the strength of a boa constrictor. Le Loup's left hand manipulated the trap lever. He turned swiftly, raised Irène in his two arms and tossed her into the tunnel.

Irène struck hard on the tunnel floor. She lay stunned for an instant but came to quickly with Le Loup's mad laughter in her ears. She looked up and light dazzled her eyes. Le Loup had found the flashlight Irène had dropped. Irène was conscious of a writhing movement at her feet. She glanced down and saw Duret clutching at a knife that was buried in his thigh. The knife came from the wound and Le Loup backed from the edge of the trap. The detective arose on one knee.

Irène saw the head and shoulders of Le Loup as he bent over the lever to close the trap. She screamed and grasped frantically at the edge of the lifting door. The trap was closing. With horror in her heart Irène saw she would be pinned by her hands between the closed trap and the cellar floor. She released her hold and dropped back into the tunnel. As she fell a faint breath of air struck her gently on the cheek. Something that gleamed bright whizzed past her head. Scream after scream came from Le Loup above. Then the trapdoor dropped. The tunnel was in utter darkness and the cries from Le Loup came faintly as from a great distance.

Irène stood listening. Slowly the cries of Le Loup receded into silence. Irène could see nothing. But now she could hear the sharp squealing of many rats.

'Duret! Duret! You killed him?'

The detective did not answer.

Panic seized Irène and she crawled about the tunnel groping for the detective. Her hand struck something and she heard a soft moan.

'Duret! Duret!'

She wondered fearfully if the detective were dead. Her hands went into his pockets and at last found a box of matches. She struck one and looked into the detective's face. He was ghastly in the wan light of the match. She clutched at his wrist and cried out her joy when she felt the beat of life. The match end burnt her fingers and she struck another. Off to one side Irène caught a gleam of nickel. She reached out and found the flashlight the detective had dropped.

Irène switched on the light and looked at the detective's leg. She ripped off lengths of her skirt and fastened a tourniquet above the wound. Then she bound the wound itself. She worked over the detective with frenzied solicitude. The ironic thought that this was the man she had sought to kill did not cross her mind. She knew only that she was in terror of being alone. When she had bound Duret's wound, Irène sat down beside him.

She thought of the flashlight battery. That must be conserved.

Hours later, it seemed, Duret recovered consciousness and asked for water. Irène recalled him to their predicament.

The detective looked at her strangely, but said nothing. He ran a hand to his bandaged leg and looked more mystified than before. 'Tell me,' he said at last, 'is there a way to raise the trap from below?'

Irène shook her head hopelessly. 'No. The trap can be worked only from above. Once open, it may be set to close itself, but there is no way to raise it. One of my – my lodgers told me that arrangement was a precaution against thieves or an enemy getting into the tunnel. The tunnel is as old as Montreal. Most of it has been blocked up and built over. I suppose there was once some central place where the trap could be worked from below. I have never been down here before, but I understand there is only a small section of the tunnel now in existence.'

'Then come,' Duret said 'we will investigate. I can walk on one foot if you will permit me to lean a little upon your shoulder.'

They moved slowly down the littered passage. Rats scuttled beyond the range of their flashlight. As the light advanced, the squealing of the rats increased. Then in a few more minutes, they heard no more of the rats and the tunnel ended abruptly against a cement wall.

Duret stood in deep thought. 'The rats have gone,' he said slowly. 'And they did not pass through this wall of cement!'

The detective lowered himself to the ground and crawled back along the tunnel, examining the walls. The rats had dug many galleries, but they were nothing more than black holes.

He was nearly halfway back to the trapdoor beneath the stone house when he shouted to Irène.

She ran forward and dropped to her knees beside him.

'Look!' he cried.

Irène peered through a rat hole and saw twilight ahead. The detective put his mouth to the hole and shouted for help. He called until he was exhausted. But there was no answering cry from the world beyond.

Irène drew the detective aside. 'It is nearly night,' she said, 'there is no one about these streets. It can be only a short distance. I can dig.'

Irène went to work on the wall with her stiletto. The earth flew back from the rapid knife thrusts, but it was tedious work and at the end of an hour, though her fingers were raw from tearing away the loosened earth, she had progressed only a short distance.

Duret lapsed into unconsciousness after his violent shouting for help and Irène toiled on alone. She stopped from time to time for a brief rest, and during one of these intervals tightened the tourniquet and replaced the sodden bandage on Duret's leg.

At last the wall before her crumbled and the dislodged earth fell outward. A great rush of fresh air nearly overwhelmed Irène. She widened the opening quickly and crawled through.

The sky was lightening in the east and Irène saw that she was in the excavation for a new building that was being erected two blocks from the house on St. Amable Street.

She was free. And with her safety her mind recalled the motive that had led up to this adventure in the tunnel. The primitive tourniquet and bandage she had wrapped around Duret's wound would not stanch the flow of blood much longer. She had only to abandon him and her vengeance would be complete.

Strangely enough, the thought gave Irène little satisfaction. Some subtle change had come over her in those first moments of terror in the tunnel. She recalled suddenly the throb of joy that had pulsed through her when she felt the feeble stirring of life in Duret's wrist when she had believed him dead.

Her mind reverted across the years to that night in the East End flat. For the first time she saw clearly the inevitability of the whole affair. Duret, her father, and her mother, all toys of the same malignant fate. Her father wrought up to insane resistance by the hysterical fears of her mother. Duret, entering the house to make a simple arrest suddenly struck upon the head and seized in a death grip. With amazing clarity she saw the ruin the lust for vengeance had made of her own life. And now that it lay within the hollow of her hand what an empty mockery that vengeance was.

Irène dropped slowly to her knees and crawled back through the hole. She tried to arouse Duret. Failing this, she began to drag him through the narrow passage. The pain of movement, or the rush of fresh air to his lungs, aroused the detective to consciousness as Irène drew him clear of the hole.

Duret looked about him in surprise. His eyes turned up to look deep into Irène's. Her gaze dropped.

'You came back for me,' he said tenderly. His tone changed. 'Listen, go to the cellar. And go with caution. See if Le Loup is there. Put on a coat to cover your torn dress, then come back to me.'

Irène ran up the ramp to the sidewalk and went swiftly to the hideout. She climbed the stairs and procured a coat and flashlight from her room. Back downstairs, she crept into the cellar. She saw Le Loup doubled over the lever by the trap-door, the handle of his own great knife protruding from his stomach.

Irène ran back to Duret. The detective seemed surprised, and smiled at her return.

'He is dead!' she said quietly.

The detective nodded. He lifted his eyes whimsically. 'Now tell me, why did you do that thing to me?'

She flushed and turned away.

'And why did you later save my life?' he added.

Irène laughed harshly. Words surged from her heart and she told him of her band of thieves. She told him, too, of her identity, of the pinch of snuff, and of her plot to kill him.

'Then why did you not let me bleed to death?' Duret demanded.

'Ah, give me no credit for that. Alone I would have gone mad in that place!'

'Why did you wander off from your father's room that night?' Duret asked.

She shrugged her shoulders. 'My mother was dead; my father was dead; the police took away my two baby sisters, and I was afraid they would come back and take me. I went far that night. I was in St. Henri shivering on a corner when a crippled beggar came upon me. He took me to his cellar. Later this beggar told me it was a detective named Duret who had shot my father. I swore to kill this Duret.'

Duret's face blazed with anger. 'This beggar, what did he want of you?'

'Nothing. He was kind to me. He provided me with food, shelter, and clothes, and he taught me the tricks of the underworld. I cooked for him. He was old, and I relieved his loneliness.'

'He did you an awful wrong!' Duret said fiercely. 'There is a pencil and notebook in my pocket. Thank you.'

Duret wrote rapidly. 'Go now to the hotel in the market-place and telephone for help to be sent me. Then go to this address. There you will find your father and your sisters. He was not killed, but dangerously wounded that night. . . .'

A convulsive sob shook Irène. She cried, 'Papa! Papa!' and swayed upon her feet.

Duret looked alarmed. 'Get help for me quickly!' he said in a sharp voice. Irène steadied, and Duret continued. 'Later, we found your father steady work; he is well and prosperous. We combed the city for you at that time, but your beggar had hid you well!

'Stay with your father and say nothing of this business. The police will not question you. My report will deal only with the snuff factory and the cellar. Later I shall come to see you and we may discuss your future. Now leave me and send help quickly. I am weak and tired.'

'And you mean, Duret, that you do not arrest me?'

Duret smiled whimsically. 'Arrest you over a trifling pinch of snuff? Hardly!'

KILLER IN THE RAIN
RAYMOND CHANDLER

The fourth short story published by Raymond Chandler (1889–1959), 'Killer in the Rain' was never reprinted during his lifetime. As with 'Curtain,' which had its magazine appearance the following year, Chandler had 'cannibalized' the story for his first novel, *The Big Sleep*. Six characters and much of eleven chapters in the novel, were lifted in whole or in part from 'Killer in the Rain,' generally being fleshed out to provide more fully-developed characters.

Names were changed. None of Chandler's short stories featured Philip Marlowe, the hero of all seven of his novels, though whether named Carmody, Dalmas, Malvern, Mallory or remained unnamed, as in the present story, they were interchangeable with his famous creation.

The wild young woman who is the catalyst for all that transpires in both the novel and this story, is named Carmen Dravec here but Carmen Sternwood in *The Big Sleep*. Drug-addicted, alcoholic, perhaps a bit dim, almost certainly a sociopath, the beautiful Carmen was played by the now-forgotten Martha Vickers in the 1946 Warner Brothers movie that starred Humphrey Bogart as Marlowe. The novel added a sister who tried to protect the reputation of her younger sibling by getting the detective to end his investigation.

'Killer in the Rain' was originally published as a novelette in the January 1935 issue of *Black Mask*.

KILLER IN THE RAIN
RAYMOND CHANDLER

I

W e were sitting in a room at the Berglund. I was on the side of the bed, and Dravec was in the easy chair. It was my room.

Rain beat very hard against the windows. They were shut tight and it was hot in the room and I had a little fan going on the table. The breeze from it hit Dravec's face high up, lifted his heavy black hair, moved the longer bristles in the fat path of eyebrow that went across his face in a solid line. He looked like a bouncer who had come into money.

He showed me some of his gold teeth and said:

'What you got on me?'

He said it importantly, as if anyone who knew anything would know quite a lot about him.

'Nothing,' I said. 'You're clean, as far as I know.'

He lifted a large hairy hand and stared at it solidly for a minute.

'You don't get me. A feller named M'Gee sent me here. Violets M'Gee.'

'Fine. How is Violets these days?' Violets M'Gee was a homicide dick in the sheriff's office.

He looked at his large hand and frowned. 'No – you still don't get it. I got a job for you.'

'I don't go out much any more,' I said. 'I'm getting kind of frail.'

He looked around the room carefully, bluffing a bit, like a man not naturally observant.

'Maybe it's money,' he said.

'Maybe it is,' I said.

He had a belted suede raincoat on. He tore it open carelessly and got out a wallet that was not quite as big as a bale of hay. Currency stuck out of it at careless angles. When he slapped it down on his knee it made a fat sound that was pleasant to the ear. He shook money out of it, selected a few bills from the bunch, stuffed the rest back, dropped the wallet on the floor and let it lie, arranged five century notes like a tight poker hand and put them under the base of the fan on the table.

That was a lot of work. It made him grunt.

'I got lots of sugar,' he said.

'So I see. What do I do for that, if I get it?'

'You know me now, huh?'

'A little better.'

I got an envelope out of an inside pocket and read to him loud from some scribbling on the back.

'Dravec, Anton or Tony. Former Pittsburgh steelworker, truck guard, all-round muscle stiff. Made a wrong pass and got shut up. Left town, came West. Worked on an avocado ranch at El Seguro. Came up with a ranch of his own. Sat right on the dome when the El Seguro oil boom burst. Got rich. Lost a lot of it buying into other people's dusters. Still has enough. Serbian by birth, six feet, two hundred and forty, one daughter, never known to have had a wife. No police record of any consequence. None at all since Pittsburgh.'

I lit a pipe.

'Jeeze,' he said. 'Where you promote all that?'

'Connections. What's the angle?'

He picked the wallet off the floor and moused around inside it with a couple of square fingers for a while, with his tongue sticking out between his thick lips. He finally got out a slim brown card and some crumpled slips of paper. He pushed them at me.

The card was in gold type, very delicately done. It said: 'Mr. Harold Hardwicke Steiner', and very small in the corner, 'Rare Books and De Luxe Editions'. No address or phone number.

The white slips, three in number, were simple I.O.U.s for a thousand dollars each, signed: 'Carmen Dravec' in a sprawling, moronic handwriting.

I gave it all back to him and said: 'Blackmail?'

He shook his head slowly and something gentle came into his face that hadn't been there before.

'It's my little girl – Carmen. This Steiner, he bothers her. She goes to his joint all the time, makes whoopee. He makes love to her, I guess. I don't like it.'

I nodded. 'How about the notes?'

'I don't care nothin' about the dough. She plays games with him. The hell with that. She's what you call man-crazy. You go tell this Steiner to lay off Carmen. I break his neck with my hands. See?'

All this in a rush, with deep breathing. His eyes got small and round, and furious. His teeth almost chattered.

I said: 'Why have me tell him? Why not tell him yourself?'

'Maybe I get mad and kill the——!' he yelled.

I picked a match out of my pocket and prodded the loose ash in the bowl of my pipe. I looked at him carefully for a moment, getting hold of an idea.

'Nerts, you're scared to,' I told him.

Both big fists came up. He held them shoulder high and shook them, great knots of bone and muscle. He lowered them slowly, heaved a deep honest sigh, and said:

'Yeah. I'm scared to. I dunno how to handle her. All the time some new guy and all the time a punk. A while back I gave a guy called Joe Marty five grand to lay off her. She's still mad at me.'

I stared at the window, watched the rain hit it, flatten out, and slide down in a thick wave, like melted gelatine. It was too early in the fall for that kind of rain.

'Giving them sugar doesn't get you anywhere,' I said. 'You could be doing that all your life. So you figure you'd like to have me get rough with this one, Steiner.'

'Tell him I break his neck!'

'I wouldn't bother,' I said. 'I know Steiner. I'd break his neck for you myself, if it would do any good.'

He leaned forward and grabbed my hand. His eyes got childish. A grey tear floated in each of them.

'Listen, M'Gee says you're a good guy. I tell you something I ain't told nobody – ever. Carmen – she's not my kid at all. I just picked her up in Smoky, a little baby in the street. She didn't have nobody. I guess maybe I steal her, huh?'

'Sounds like it,' I said, and had to fight to get my hand loose. I rubbed feeling back into it with the other one. The man had a grip that would crack a telephone pole.

'I go straight then,' he said grimly, and yet tenderly. 'I come out here and make good. She grows up. I love her.'

I said: 'Uh-huh. That's natural.'

'You don't get me. I wanta marry her.'

I stared at him.

'She gets older, get some sense. Maybe she marry me, huh?'

His voice implored me, as if I had the settling of that.

'Ever ask her?'

'I'm scared to,' he said humbly.

'She soft on Steiner, do you think?'

He nodded. 'But that don't mean nothin'.'

I could believe that. I got off the bed, threw a window up and let the rain hit my face for a minute.

'Let's get this straight,' I said, lowering the window again and going back to the bed. 'I can take Steiner off your back. That's easy. I just don't see what it buys you.'

He grabbed for my hand again, but I was a little too quick for him this time.

'You came in here a little tough, flashing your wad,' I said. 'You're going out soft. Not from anything I've said. You knew it already. I'm not Dorothy Dix, and I'm only partly a prune. But I'll take Steiner off you, if you really want that.'

He stood up clumsily, swung his hat and stared down at my feet.

'You take him off my back, like you said. He ain't her sort, anyway.'

'It might hurt your back a little.'

'That's okay. That's what it's for,' he said.

He buttoned himself up, dumped his hat on his big shaggy head, and rolled on out. He shut the door carefully, as if he was going out of a sick-room.

I thought he was as crazy as a pair of waltzing mice, but I liked him.

I put his goldbacks in a safe place, mixed myself a long drink, and sat down in the chair that was still warm from him.

While I played with the drink I wondered if he had any idea what Steiner's racket was.

Steiner had a collection of rare and half-rare smut books which he loaned out as high as ten dollars a day – to the right people.

II

It rained all the next day. Late in the afternoon I sat parked in a blue Chryler roadster, diagonally across the Boulevard from a narrow store front, over which a green neon sign in script letters said: 'H. H. Steiner.'

The rain splashed knee-high off the sidewalks, filled the gutters, and big cops in slickers that shone like gun barrels had a lot of fun carrying little girls in silk stockings and cute little rubber boots across the bad places, with a lot of squeezing.

The rain drummed on the hood of the Chrysler, beat and tore at the taut material of the top, leaked in at the buttoned places, and made a pool on the floorboards for me to keep my feet in.

I had a big flask of Scotch with me. I used it often enough to keep interested.

Steiner did business, even in that weather; perhaps especially in that weather. Very nice cars stopped in front of his store, and very nice people dodged in, then dodged out again with wrapped parcels under their arms. Of course they could have been buying rare books and de luxe editions.

At five-thirty a pimply-faced kid in a leather windbreaker came out of the store and sloped up the side street at a fast trot. He came back with a neat cream-and-grey coupé. Steiner came out and got into the coupé. He wore a dark green leather raincoat, a cigarette in an amber holder, no hat. I couldn't see his glass eye at that distance but I knew he had one. The kid in the windbreaker held an umbrella over him across the sidewalk, then shut it up and handed it into the coupé.

Steiner drove west on the Boulevard. I drove west on the Boulevard. Past the business district, at Pepper Canyon, he turned north, and I tailed him easily from a block back. I was pretty sure he was going home, which was natural.

He left Pepper Drive and took a curving ribbon of wet cement called La

Verne Terrace, climbed up it almost to the top. It was a narrow road with a high bank on one side and a few well-spaced cabin-like houses built down the steep slope on the other side. Their roofs were not much above road level. The fronts of them were masked by shrubs. Sodden trees dripped all over the landscape.

Steiner's hideaway had a square box hedge in front of it, more than window-high. The entrance was a sort of maze, and the house door was not visible from the road. Steiner put his grey-and-cream coupé in a small garage, locked up, went through the maze with his umbrella up, and light went on in the house.

While he was doing this I had passed him and gone to the top of the hill. I turned around there and went back and parked in front of the next house above his. It seemed to be closed up or empty, but had no signs on it. I went into a conference with my flask of Scotch, and then just sat.

At six-fifteen lights bobbed up the hill. It was quite dark by then. A car stopped in front of Steiner's hedge. A slim, tall girl in a slicker got out of it. Enough light filtered out through the hedge for me to see that she was dark-haired and possibly pretty.

Voices drifted on the rain and a door shut. I got out of the Chrysler and strolled down the hill, put a pencil flash into the car. It was a dark maroon or brown Packard convertible. Its licence read to Carmen Dravec, 3596 Lucerene Avenue. I went back to my heap.

A solid, slow-moving hour crawled by. No more cars came up or down the hill. It seemed to be a very quiet neighbourhood.

Then a single flash of hard white light leaked out of Steiner's house, like a flash of summer lightning. As the darkness fell again a thin tinkling scream trickled down the darkness and echoed faintly among the wet trees. I was out of the Chrysler and on my way before the last echo of it died.

There was no fear in the scream. It held the note of a half-pleasurable shock, an accent of drunkenness, and a touch of pure idiocy.

The Steiner mansion was perfectly silent when I hit the gap in the hedge, dodged around the elbow that masked the front door, and put my hand up to bang on the door.

At that exact moment, as if somebody had been waiting for it, three shots racketed close together behind the door. After that there was a long, harsh sigh, a soft thump, rapid steps, going away into the back of the house.

I wasted time hitting the door with my shoulder, without enough start. It threw me back like a kick from an army mule.

The door fronted on a narrow runway, like a small bridge, that led from the banked road. There was no side porch, no way to get at the windows in a hurry. There was no way around to the back except through the house or up a long flight of wooden steps that went up to the back door from the alley-like street below. On these steps I now heard a clatter of feet.

77

That gave me the impulse and I hit the door again, from the feet up. It gave at the lock and I pitched down two steps into a big, dim, cluttered room. I didn't see much of what was in the room then. I wandered through to the back of the house.

I was pretty sure there was death in it.

A car throbbed in the street below as I reached the back porch. The car went away fast, without lights. That was that. I went back to the living-room.

III

That room reached all the way across the front of the house and had a low, beamed ceiling, walls painted brown. Strips of tapestry hung all around the walls. Books filled low shelves. There was a thick, pinkish rug on which some light fell from two standing lamps with pale green shades. In the middle of the rug there was a big, low desk and a black chair with a yellow satin cushion at it. There were books all over the desk.

On a sort of dais near one end wall there was a teakwood chair with arms and a high back. A dark-haired girl was sitting in the chair, on a fringed red shawl.

She sat very straight, with her hands on the arms of the chair, her knees close together, her body stiffly erect, her chin level. Her eyes were wide open and mad and had no pupils.

She looked unconscious of what was going on, but she didn't have the pose of unconsciousness. She had a pose as if she was doing something very important and making a lot of it.

Out of her mouth came a tinny chuckling noise, which didn't change her expression or move her lips. She didn't seem to see me at all.

She was wearing a pair of long jade ear-rings, and apart from those she was stark naked.

I looked away from her to the other end of the room.

Steiner was on his back on the floor, just beyond the edge of the pink rug, and in front of a thing that looked like a small totem pole. It had a round open mouth in which the lens of a camera showed. The lens seemed to be aimed a the girl in the teakwood chair.

There was a flash-bulb apparatus on the floor beside Steiner's out-flung hand in a loose silk sleeve. The cord of the flash-bulb went behind the totem pole thing.

Steiner was wearing Chinese slippers with thick white felt soles. His legs were in black satin pyjamas and the upper part of him in an embroidered Chinese coat. The front of it was mostly blood. His glass eye shone brightly and was the most lifelike thing about him. At a glance none of the three shots had missed.

The flash-bulb was the sheet lightning I had seen leak out of the house and the half-giggling scream was the doped and naked girl's reaction to that. The three shots had been somebody else's idea of how the proceedings ought to be punctuated. Presumably the idea of the lad who had gone very fast down the back steps.

I could see something in his point of view. At that stage I thought it was a good idea to shut the front door and fasten it with the short chain that was on it. The lock had been spoiled by my violent entrance.

A couple of thin purple glasses stood on a red lacquer tray on one end of the desk. Also a potbellied flagon of something brown. The glasses smelled of ether and laudanum, a mixture I had never tried, but it seemed to fit the scene pretty well.

I found the girl's clothes on a divan in the corner, picked up a brown, sleeved dress to begin with, and went over to her. She smelled of ether also, at a distance of several feet.

The tinny chuckling was still going on and a little froth was oozing down her chin. I slapped her face, not very hard. I didn't want to bring her out of whatever kind of trance she was in, into a screaming fit.

'Come on,' I said brightly. 'Let's be nice. Let's get dressed.'

She said: 'G-g-go – ter – ell,' without any emotion that I could notice.

I slapped her a little more. She didn't mind the slaps, so I went to work getting the dress on her.

She didn't mind the dress either. She let me hold her arms up but she spread her fingers wide, as if that was very cute. It made me do a lot of finagling with the sleeves. I finally got the dress on. I got her stockings on, and her shoes, and then got her up on her feet.

'Let's take a little walk,' I said. 'Let's take a nice little walk.'

We walked. Part of the time her ear-rings banged against my chest and part of the time we looked like a couple of adagio dancers doing the splits. We walked over to Steiner's body and back. She didn't pay any attention to Steiner and his bright glass eye.

She found it amusing that she couldn't walk and tried to tell me about it, but only bubbled. I put her on the divan while I wadded her underclothes up and shoved them into a deep pocket of my raincoat, put her handbag in my other deep pocket. I went through Steiner's desk and found a little blue notebook written in code that looked interesting. I put that in my pocket, too.

Then I tried to get at the back of the camera in the totem pole, to get the plate, but couldn't find the catch right away. I was getting nervous, and I figured I could build up a better excuse if I ran into the law when I came back later to look for it than any reason I could give if caught there now.

I went back to the girl and got her slicker on her, nosed around to see if anything else of hers was there, wiped away a lot of fingerprints I probably hadn't made, and at least some of those Miss Dravec must have made. I opened the door and put out both the lamps.

I got my left arm around her again and we struggled out into the rain and piled into her Packard. I didn't like leaving my own bus there very well, but that had to be. Her keys were in her car. We drifted off down the hill.

Nothing happened on the way to Lucerne Avenue except that Carmen stopped bubbling and giggling and went to snoring. I couldn't keep her head off my shoulder. It was all I could do to keep it out of my lap. I had to drive rather slowly and it was a long way anyhow, clear over to the west edge of the city.

The Dravec home was a large old-fashioned brick house in large grounds with a wall around them. A grey composition driveway went through iron gates and up a slope past flower-beds and lawns to a big front door with narrow leaded panels on each side of it. There was dim light behind the panels as if nobody much was home.

I pushed Carmen's head into the corner and shed her belongings in the seat, and got out.

A maid opened the door. She said Mister Dravec wasn't in and she didn't know where he was. Downtown somewhere. She had a long, yellowish, gentle face, a long nose, no chin and large wet eyes. She looked like a nice old horse that had been turned out to pasture after long service, and as if she would do the right thing by Carmen.

I pointed into the Packard and growled: 'Better get her to bed. She's lucky we don't throw her in the can – drivin' around with a tool like that on her.'

She smiled sadly and I went away.

I had to walk five blocks in the rain before a narrow apartment house let me into its lobby to use a phone. Then I had to wait another twenty-five minutes for a taxi. While I waited I began to worry about what I hadn't completed.

I had yet to get the used plate out of Steiner's camera.

IV

I paid the taxi off on Pepper Drive, in front of a house where there was company, and walked back up the curving hill of La Verne Terrace to Steiner's house behind its shrubbery.

Nothing looked any different. I went in through the gap in the hedge, pushed the door open gently, and smelled cigarette smoke.

It hadn't been there before. There had been a complicated set of smells, including the sharp memory of smokeless powder. But cigarette smoke hadn't stood out from the mixture.

I closed the door and slipped down on one knee and listened, holding my breath. I didn't hear anything but the sound of the rain on the roof. I tried throwing the beam of my pencil flash along the floor. Nobody shot at me.

I straightened up, found the dangling tassel of one of the lamps and made light in the room.

The first thing I noticed was that a couple of strips of tapestry were gone from the wall. I hadn't counted them, but the spaces where they had hung caught my eye.

Then I saw Steiner's body was gone from in front of the totem pole thing with the camera eye in its mouth. On the floor below, beyond the margin of the pink rug, somebody had spread down a rug over the place where Steiner's body had been. I didn't have to lift the rug to know why it had been put there.

I lit a cigarette and stood there in the middle of the dimly lighted room and thought about it. After a while I went to the camera in the totem pole. I found the catch this time. There wasn't any plate-holder in the camera.

My hand went towards the mulberry-coloured phone on Steiner's low desk, but didn't take hold of it.

I crossed into the little hallway beyond the living-room and poked into a fussy-looking bedroom that looked like a woman's room more than a man's. The bed had a long cover with a flounced edge. I lifted that and shot my flash under the bed.

Steiner wasn't under the bed. He wasn't anywhere in the house. Somebody had taken him away. He couldn't very well have gone by himself.

It wasn't the law, or somebody would have been there still. It was only an hour and a half since Carmen and I left the place. And there was none of the mess police photographers and fingerprint men would have made.

I went back to the living-room, pushed the flash-bulb apparatus around the back of the totem pole with my foot, switched off the lamp, left the house, got into my rain-soaked car and choked it to life.

It was all right with me if somebody wanted to keep the Steiner kill hush-hush for a while. It gave me a chance to find out whether I could tell it leaving Carmen Dravec and the nude photo angle out.

It was after ten when I got back to the Berglund and put my heap away and went upstairs to the apartment. I stood under a shower, then put pyjamas on and mixed up a batch of hot grog. I looked at the phone a couple of times, thought about calling to see if Dravec was home yet, thought it might be a good idea to let him alone until the next day.

I filled a pipe and sat down with my hot grog and Steiner's little blue notebook. It was in code, but the arrangement of the entries and the indented leaves made it a list of names and addresses. There were over four hundred and fifty of them. If this was Steiner's sucker list, he had a gold mine – quite apart from the blackmail angles.

Any name on the list might be a prospect as the killer. I didn't envy the cops their job when it was handed to them.

I drank too much whisky trying to crack the code. About midnight I went to bed, and dreamed about a man in a Chinese coat with blood all over the front who chased a naked girl with long jade ear-rings while I tried to photograph the scene with a camera that didn't have any plate in it.

V

Violets M'Gee called me up in the morning, before I was dressed, but after I had seen the paper and not found anything about Steiner in it. His voice had the cheerful sound of a man who had slept well and didn't owe too much money.

'Well, how's the boy?' he began.

I said I was all right except that I was having a little trouble with my Third Reader. He laughed a little absently, and then his voice got too casual.

'This guy Dravec that I sent over to see you – done anything for him yet?'

'Too much rain,' I answered, if that was an answer.

'Uh-huh. He seems to be a guy that things happen to. A car belongin' to him is washin' about in the surf off Lido fish pier.'

I didn't say anything. I held the telephone very tightly.

'Yeah,' M'Gee went on cheerfully. 'A nice new Cad all messed up with sand and sea-water. . . . Oh, I forgot. There's a guy inside it.'

I let my breath out slowly, very slowly. 'Dravec?' I whispered.

'Naw. A young kid. I ain't told Dravec yet. It's under the fedora. Wanta run down and look at it with me?'

I said I would like to do that.

'Snap it up. I'll be in my hutch,' M'Gee told me and hung up.

Shaved, dressed and lightly breakfasted I was at the County Building in half an hour or so. I found M'Gee staring at a yellow wall and sitting at a little yellow desk on which there was nothing but M'Gee's hat and one of the M'Gee feet. He took both of them off the desk and we went down to the official parking lot and got into a small black sedan.

The rain had stopped during the night and the morning was all blue and gold. There was enough snap in the air to make life simple and sweet, if you didn't have too much on your mind. I had.

It was thirty miles to Lido, the first ten of them through city traffic. M'Gee made it in three-quarters of an hour. At the end of that time we skidded to a stop in front of a stucco arch beyond which a long black pier extended. I took my feet out of the floorboards and we got out.

There were a few cars and people in front of the arch. A motor-cycle officer was keeping the people off the pier. M'Gee showed him a bronze star and we went out along the pier, into a loud smell that even two days' rain had failed to wash away.

'There she is – on the tug,' M'Gee said.

A low black tug crouched off the end of the pier. Something large and green and nickelled was on its deck in front of the wheelhouse. Men stood around it.

We went down slimy steps to the deck of the tug.

M'Gee said hello to a deputy in green khaki and another man in plainclothes. The tug crew of three moved over to the wheelhouse, and set their backs against it, watching us.

We looked at the car. The front bumper was bent, and one headlight and the radiator shell. The paint and the nickel were scratched up by sand and the upholstery was sodden and black. Otherwise the car wasn't much the worse for wear. It was a big job in two tones of green, with a wine-coloured stripe and trimming.

M'Gee and I looked into the front part of it. A slim, dark-haired kid who had been good-looking was draped around the steering post, with his head at a peculiar angle to the rest of his body. His face was bluish-white. His eyes were a faint dull gleam under the lowered lids. His open mouth had sand in it. There were traces of blood on the side of his head which the sea-water hadn't quite washed away.

M'Gee backed away slowly, made a noise in his throat and began to chew on a couple of the violet-scented breath purifiers that gave him his nickname.

'What's the story?' he asked quietly.

The uniformed deputy pointed up to the end of the pier. Dirty white railings made of two-by-fours had been broken through in a wide space and the broken wood showed up yellow and bright.

'Went through there. Must have hit pretty hard, too. The rain stopped early down here, about nine, and the broken wood is dry inside. That puts it after the rain stopped. That's all we know except she fell in plenty of water not to be banged up worse; at least half-tide, I'd say. That would be right after the rain stopped. She showed under the water when the boys came down to fish this morning. We got the tug to lift her out. Then we find the dead guy.'

The other deputy scuffed at the deck with the toe of his shoe. M'Gee looked sideways at me with foxy little eyes. I looked blank and didn't say anything.

'Pretty drunk that lad,' M'Gee said gently. 'Showin' off all alone in the rain. I guess he must have been fond of driving. Yeah – pretty drunk.'

'Drunk, hell,' the plain-clothes deputy said. 'The hand throttle's set half-way down and the guy's been sapped on the side of the head. Ask me and I'll call it murder.'

M'Gee looked at him politely, then at the uniformed man. 'What you think?'

'It could be suicide, I guess. His neck's broke and he could have hurt his head in the fall. And his hand could have knocked the throttle down. I kind of like murder myself, though.'

M'Gee nodded, said: 'Frisked him? Know who he is?'

The two deputies looked at me, then at the tug crew.

'Okay. Save that part,' M'Gee said. 'I *know* who he is.'

A small man with glasses and a tired face and a black bag came slowly along the pier and down the slimy steps. He picked out a fairly clean place on the deck and put his bag down. He took his hat off and rubbed the back of his neck and smiled wearily.

''Lo, Doc. There's your patient,' M'Gee told him. 'Took a dive off the pier last night. That's all we know now.'

The medical examiner looked in at the dead man morosely. He fingered the head, moved it around a little, felt the man's ribs. He lifted one lax hand and stared at the fingernails. He let it fall, stepped back and picked his bag up again.

'About twelve hours,' he said. 'Broken neck, of course. I doubt if there's any water in him. Better get him out of there before he starts to get stiff on us. I'll tell you the rest when I get him on a table.'

He nodded around, went back up the steps and along the pier. An ambulance was backing into position beside the stucco arch at the pier head.

The two deputies grunted and tugged to get the dead man out of the car and lay him down on the deck, on the side of the car away from the beach.

'Let's go,' M'Gee told me. 'That ends this part of the show.'

We said good-bye and M'Gee told the deputies to keep their chins buttoned until they heard from him. We went back along the pier and got into the small black sedan and drove back towards the city along a white highway washed clean by the rain, past low rolling hills of yellow-white sand terraced with moss. A few gulls wheeled and swooped over something in the surf. Far out to sea a couple of white yachts on the horizon looked as if they were suspended in the sky.

We laid a few miles behind us without saying anything to each other. Then M'Gee cocked his chin at me and said:

'Got ideas?'

'Loosen up,' I said. 'I never saw the guy before. Who is he?'

'Hell, I thought you was going to tell me about it.'

'Loosen up, Violets,' I said.

He growled, shrugged, and we nearly went off the road into the loose sand.

'Dravec's chauffeur. A kid named Carl Owen. How do I know? We had him in the cooler a year ago on a Mann Act rap. He run Dravec's hotcha daughter off to Yuma. Dravec went after them and brought them back and had the guy heaved in the goldfish bowl. Then the girl gets to him, and next morning the old man steams downtown and begs the guy off. Says the kid meant to marry her, only she wouldn't. Then, by heck, the kid goes back to work for him and been there ever since. What you think of that?'

'It sounds just like Dravec,' I said.

'Yeah – but the kid could have had a relapse.'

M'Gee had silvery hair and a knobby chin and a little pouting mouth made to kiss babies with. I looked at his face sideways, and suddenly I got his idea. I laughed.

'You think maybe Dravec killed him?' I asked.

'Why not? The kid makes another pass at the girl and Dravec cracks down at him too hard. He's a big guy and could break a neck easy. Then he's scared. He runs the car down to Lido in the rain and lets it slide off the end of the pier. Thinks it won't show. Maybe don't think at all. Just rattled.'

'It's a kick in the pants,' I said. 'Then all he had to do was walk home thirty miles in the rain.'

'Go on. Kid me.'

'Dravec killed him, sure,' I said. 'But they were playing leap-frog. Dravec fell on him.'

'Okay, pal. Some day you'll want to play with *my* catnip mouse.'

'Listen, Violets,' I said seriously. 'If the kid was murdered – and you're not sure it's murder at all – it's not Dravec's kind of crime. He might kill a man in a temper – but he'd let him lay. He wouldn't go to all that fuss.'

We shuttled back and forth across the road while M'Gee thought about that.

'What a pal,' he complained. 'I have me a swell theory and look what you done to it. I wish the hell I hadn't brought you. Hell with you. I'm goin' after Dravec just the same.'

'Sure,' I agreed. 'You'd have to do that. But Dravec never killed that boy. He's too soft inside to cover up on it.'

It was noon when we got back to town. I hadn't had any dinner but whisky the night before and very little breakfast that morning. I got off on the Boulevard and let M'Gee go on alone to see Dravec.

I was interested in what had happened to Carl Owen; but I wasn't interested in the thought that Dravec might have murdered him.

I ate lunch at a counter and looked casually at an early afternoon paper. I didn't expect to see anything about Steiner in it, and I didn't.

After lunch I walked along the Boulevard six blocks to have a look at Steiner's store.

VI

It was a half-store frontage, the other half being occupied by a credit jeweller. The jeweller was standing in his entrance, a big, white-haired, black-eyed Jew with about nine carats of diamond on his hand. A faint, knowing smile curved his lips as I went past him into Steiner's.

A thick blue rug paved Steiner's from wall to wall. There were blue leather easy-chairs with smoke stands beside them. A few sets of tooled leather books were put out on narrow tables. The rest of the stock was behind glass. A panelled partition with a single door in it cut off a back part of the store, and in the corner by this a woman sat behind a small desk with a hooded lamp on it.

She got up and came towards me, swinging lean thighs in a tight dress of some black material that didn't reflect any light. She was an ash-blonde, with greenish eyes under heavily mascaraed lashes. There were large jet buttons in the lobes of her ears; her hair waved back smoothly from behind them. Her fingernails were silvered.

She gave me what she thought was a smile of welcome, but what I thought was a grimace of strain.

'Was it something?'

I pulled my hat low over my eyes and fidgeted. I said:

'Steiner?'

'He won't be in today. May I show you—'

'I'm selling,' I said. 'Something he's wanted for a long time.'

The silvered fingernails touched the hair over one ear. 'Oh, a salesman. . . . Well, you might come in tomorrow.'

'He sick? I could go up to the house,' I suggested hopefully. 'He'd want to see what I have.'

That jarred her. She had to fight for her breath for a minute. But her voice was smooth enough when it came.

'That – that wouldn't be any use. He's out of town today.'

I nodded, looked properly disappointed, touched my hat and started to turn away when the pimply-faced kid of the night before stuck his head through the door in the panelling. He went back as soon as he saw me, but not before I saw some loosely packed cases of books behind him on the floor of the back room.

The cases were small and open and packed any old way. A man in very new overalls was fussing with them. Some of Steiner's stock was being moved out.

I left the store and walked down to the corner, then back to the alley. Behind Steiner's stood a small black truck with wire sides. It didn't have any lettering on it. Boxes showed through the wire sides and, as I watched, the man in overalls came out with another one and heaved it up.

I went back to the Boulevard. Half a block on, a fresh-faced kid was reading a magazine in a parked Green Top. I showed him money and said:

'Tail job?'

He looked me over, swung his door open, and stuck his magazine behind the rear-vision mirror.

'My meat, boss,' he said brightly.

We went around to the end of the alley and waited beside a fire-plug.

There were about a dozen boxes on the truck when the man in the very new overalls got up in front and gunned his motor. He went down the alley fast and turned left on the street at the end. My driver did the same. The truck went north to Garfield, then east. It went very fast and there was a lot of traffic on Garfield. My driver tailed from too far back.

I was telling him about that when the truck turned north off Garfield again. The street at which it turned was called Brittany. When we got to Brittany there wasn't any truck.

The fresh-faced kid who was driving me made comforting sounds through the glass panel of the cab and we went up Brittany at four miles an hour looking for the truck behind bushes. I refused to be comforted.

Brittany bore a little to the east two blocks up and met the next street, Randall Place, in a tongue of land on which there was a white apartment house with its front on Randall Place and its basement garage entrance on Brittany, a storey lower. We were going past that and my driver was telling me the truck couldn't be very far away when I saw it in the garage.

We went around to the front of the apartment house and I got out and went into the lobby.

There was no switchboard. A desk was pushed back against the wall, as if it wasn't used any more. Above it names were on a panel of gilt mail-boxes.

The name that went with Apartment 405 was Joesph Marty. Joe Marty was the name of the man who played with Carmen Dravec until her papa gave him five thousand dollars to go away and play with some other girl. It could be the same Joe Marty.

I went down steps and pushed through a door with a wired glass panel into the dimness of the garage. The man in the very new overalls was stacking boxes in the automatic elevator.

I stood near him and lit a cigarette and watched him. He didn't like it very well, but he didn't say anything. After a while I said:

'Watch the weight, buddy. She's only tested for half a ton. Where's it goin'?'

'Marty, four-o-five,' he said, and then looked as if he was sorry he had said it.

'Fine,' I told him. 'It looks like a nice lot of reading.'

I went back up the steps and out of the building, got into my Green Top again.

We drove back downtown to the building where I have an office. I gave the driver too much money and he gave me a dirty card which I dropped into the brass spittoon beside the elevators.

Dravec was holding up the wall outside the door of my office.

VII

After the rain, it was warm and bright but he still had the belted suede raincoat on. It was open down the front, as were his coat, and vest underneath. His tie was under one ear. His face looked like a mask of grey putty with a black stubble on the lower part of it.

He looked awful.

I unlocked the door and patted his shoulder and pushed him in and got him into a chair. He breathed hard but didn't say anything. I got a bottle of rye out of the desk and poured a couple of ponies. He drank both of them without a word. Then he slumped in the chair and blinked his eyes and groaned and took a square white envelope out of an inner pocket. He put it down on the desk top and held his big hairy hand over it.

'Tough about Carl,' I said. 'I was with M'Gee this morning.'

He looked at me emptily. After a little while he said:

'Yeah. Carl was a good kid. I ain't told you about him much.'

I waited, looking at the envelope under his hand. He looked down at it himself.

'I gotta let you see it,' he mumbled. He pushed it slowly across the desk and lifted his hand off it as if with the movement he was giving up most everything that made life worth living. Two tears welled up in his eyes and slid down his unshaven cheeks.

I lifted the square envelope and looked at it. It was addressed to him at his house, in neat pen-and-ink printing, and bore a Special Delivery stamp. I opened it and looked at the shiny photograph that was inside.

Carmen Dravec sat in Steiner's teakwood chair, wearing her jade earrings. Her eyes looked crazier, if anything, than as I had seen them. I looked at the back of the photo, saw that it was blank, and put the thing face down on my desk.

'Tell me about it,' I said carefully.

Dravec wiped the tears off his face with his sleeve, put his hands flat on the desk and stared down at the dirty nails. His fingers trembled on the desk.

'A guy called me,' he said in a dead voice. 'Ten grand for the plate and the prints. The deal's got to be closed tonight, or they give the stuff to some scandal sheet.'

'That's a lot of hooey,' I said. 'A scandal sheet couldn't use it, except to back up a story. What's the story?'

He lifted his eyes slowly, as if they were very heavy. 'That ain't all. The guy say there's a jam to it. I better come through fast, or I'd find my girl in the cooler.'

'What's the story?' I asked again, filling my pipe. 'What does Carmen say?'

He shook his big shaggy head. 'I ain't asked her. I ain't got the heart. Poor little girl. No clothes on her. . . . No, I ain't got the heart. . . . You ain't done nothin' on Steiner yet, I guess.'

'I didn't have to,' I told him. 'Somebody beat me to it.'

He stared at me open-mouthed, uncomprehending. It was obvious he knew nothing about the night before.

'Did Carmen go out at all last night?' I asked carelessly.

He was still staring with his mouth open, groping in his mind.

'No. She's sick. She's sick in bed when I get home. She don't go out at all. . . . What you mean – about Steiner?'

I reached for the bottle of rye and poured us each a drink. Then I lit my pipe.

'Steiner's dead,' I said. 'Somebody got tired of his tricks and shot him full of holes. Last night, in the rain.'

'Jeeze,' he said wonderingly. 'You was there?'

I shook my head. 'Not me. Carmen was there. That's the jam your man spoke of. She didn't do the shooting, of course.'

Dravec's face got red and angry. He balled his fists. His breath made a harsh sound and a pulse beat visibly in the side of his neck.

'That ain't true! She's sick. She don't go out at all. She's sick in bed when I get home!'

'You told me that,' I said. '*That's* not true. I brought Carmen home myself. The maid knows, only she's trying to be decent about it. Carmen was at Steiner's house and I was watching outside. A gun went off and someone ran away. I didn't see him. Carmen was too drunk to see him. That's why she's sick.'

His eyes tried to focus on my face, but they were vague and empty, as if the light behind them had died. He took hold of the arms of the chair. His big knuckles strained and got white.

'She don't tell me,' he whispered. 'She don't tell me. Me, that would do anything for her.' There was no emotion in his voice; just the dead exhaustion of despair.

He pushed his chair back a little. 'I go get the dough,' he said. 'The ten grand. Maybe the guy don't talk.'

Then he broke. His big rough head came down on the desk and sobs shook his whole body. I stood up and went around the desk and patted his shoulder, kept on patting it, not saying anything. After a while he lifted his face smeared with tears and grabbed for my hand.

'Jeeze, you're a good guy,' he sobbed.

'You don't know the half of it.'

I pulled my hand away from him and got a drink into his paw, helped him lift it and down it. Then I took the empty glass out of his hand and put it back on the desk. I sat down again.

'You've got to brace up,' I told him grimly. 'The law doesn't know about Steiner yet. I brought Carmen home and kept my mouth shut. I wanted to give you and Carmen a break. That puts me in a jam. You've got to do your part.'

He nodded slowly, heavily. 'Yeah, I do what you say – anything you say.'

'Get the money,' I said. 'Have it ready for the call. I've got ideas and you may not have to use it. But it's no time to get foxy. . . . Get the money and sit tight and keep your mouth shut. Leave the rest to me. Can you do that?'

'Yeah,' he said. 'Jeeze, you're a good guy.'

'Don't talk to Carmen,' I said. 'The less she remembers out of her drunk, the better. This picture—' I touched the back of the photo on the desk '—shows somebody was working with Steiner. We've got to get him and get him quick – even if it costs ten grand to do it.'

He stood up slowly. 'That's nothin'. That's just dough. I go get it now. Then I go home. You do it like you want to. Me, I do just like you say.'

He grabbed for my hand again, shook it, and went slowly out of the office. I heard his heavy steps drag down the hall.

I drank a couple of drinks fast and mopped my face.

VIII

I drove my Chrysler slowly up La Verne Terrace towards Steiner's house.

In the daylight, I could see the steep drop of the hill and the flight of wooden steps down which the killer had made his escape. The street below was almost as narrow as an alley. Two small houses fronted on it, not very near Steiner's place. With the noise the rain had been making, it was doubtful if anyone in them had paid much attention to the shots.

Steiner's looked peaceful under the afternoon sun. The unpainted shingles of the roof were still damp from the rain. The trees on the other side of the street had new leaves on them. There were no cars on the street.

Something moved behind the square growth of box hedge that screened Steiner's front door.

Carmen Dravec, in a green and white checkered coat and no hat, came out through the opening, stopped suddenly, looked at me wild-eyed, as if she hadn't heard the car. She went back quickly behind the hedge. I drove on and parked in front of the empty house.

I got out and walked back. In the sunlight it felt like an exposed and dangerous thing to do.

I went in through the hedge and the girl stood there very straight and silent against the half-open house door. One hand went slowly to her mouth, and her teeth bit at a funny-looking thumb that was like an extra finger. There were deep purple-black smudges under her frightened eyes.

I pushed her back into the house without saying anything, shut the door. We stood looking at each other inside. She dropped her hand slowly and tried to smile. Then all expression went out of her white face and it looked as intelligent as the bottom of a shoe box.

I got gentleness into my voice and said:

'Take it easy. I'm pals. Sit down in that chair by the desk. I'm a friend of your father's. Don't get panicky.'

She went and sat down on the yellow cushion in the black chair at Steiner's desk.

The place looked decadent and off-colour by daylight. It still stank of the ether.

Carmen licked the corners of her mouth with the tip of a whitish tongue. Her dark eyes were stupid and stunned rather than scared now. I rolled a cigarette around in my fingers and pushed some books out of the way to sit on the edge of the desk. I lit my cigarette, puffed it slowly for a moment, then asked:

'What are you doing here?'

She picked at the material of her coat, didn't answer. I tried again.

'How much do you remember about last night?'

She answered that. 'Remember what? I was sick last night – at home.' Her voice was a cautious, throaty sound that only just reached my ears.

'Before that,' I said. 'Before I brought you home. Here.'

A slow flush crept up her throat and her eyes widened. 'You – you were the one?' she breathed, and began to chew on her funny thumb again.

'Yeah, I was the one. How much of it all stays with you?'

She said: 'Are you the police?'

'No. I told you I was a friend of your father's.'

'You're not the police?'

'No.'

It finally registered. She let out a long sigh. 'What – what do you want?'

'Who killed him?'

Her shoulders jerked in the checkered coat, but nothing changed much in her face. Her eyes slowly got furtive.

'Who – who else knows?'

'About Steiner? I don't know. Not the police, or someone would be here. Maybe Marty.'

It was just a stab in the dark, but it got a sudden, sharp cry out of her. 'Marty!'

We were both silent for a minute. I puffed on my cigarette and she chewed on her thumb.

'Don't get clever,' I said. 'Did Marty kill him?'

Her chin came down an inch. 'Yes.'

'Why did he do it?'

'I – I don't know,' very dully.

'Seen much of him lately?'

Her hands clenched. 'Just once or twice.'

'Know where he lives?'

'Yes!' She spat it at me.

'What's the matter? I thought you liked Marty.'

'I hate him!' she almost yelled.

'Then you'd like him for the spot,' I said.

She was blank to that. I had to explain it. 'I mean, are you willing to tell the police it was Marty?'

Sudden panic flamed in her eyes.

'If I kill the nude photo angle,' I said soothingly.

She giggled.

That gave me a nasty feeling. If she had screeched, or turned white, or even keeled over, that would have been fairly natural. But she just giggled.

I began to hate the sight of her. Just looking at her made me feel dopey.

Her giggles went on, ran around the room like rats. They gradually got hysterical. I got off the desk, took a step towards her, and slapped her face.

'Just like last night,' I said.

The giggling stopped at once and the thumb-chewing started again. She still didn't mind my slaps apparently. I sat on the end of the desk once more.

'You came here to look for the camera plate – for the birthday suit photo.' I told her.

Her chin went up and down again.

'Too late. I looked for it last night. It was gone then. Probably Marty has it. You're not kidding me about Marty?'

She shook her head vigorously. She got out of the chair slowly. Her eyes were narrow and sloe-black and as shallow as an oyster shell.

'I'm going now,' she said, as if we had been having a cup of tea.

She went over to the door and was reaching out to open it when a car came up the hill and stopped outside the house. Somebody got out of the car.

She turned and stared at me, horrified.

The door opened casually and a man looked in at us.

IX

He was a hatchet-faced man in a brown suit and a black felt hat. The cuff of his left sleeve was folded under and pinned to the side of his coat with a big black safety-pin.

He took his hat off, closed the door by pushing it with his shoulder, looked at Carmen with a nice smile. He had close-cropped black hair and a bony skull. He fitted his clothes well. He didn't look tough.

'I'm Guy Slade,' he said. 'Excuse the casual entrance. The bell didn't work. Is Steiner around?'

He hadn't tried the bell. Carmen looked at him blankly, then at me, then back at Slade. She licked her lips but didn't say anything.

I said: 'Steiner isn't here, Mister Slade. We don't know just where he is.'

He nodded and touched his long chin with the brim of his hat.

'You friends of his?'

'We just dropped by for a book,' I said, and gave him back his smile. 'The door was half open. We knocked, then stepped inside. Just like you.'

'I see,' Slade said thoughtfully. 'Very simple.'

I didn't say anything. Carmen didn't say anything. She was staring fixedly at his empty sleeve.

'A book, eh?' Slade went on. The way he said it told me things. He knew about Steiner's racket, maybe.

I moved over towards the door. 'Only *you* didn't knock,' I said.

He smiled with faint embarrassment. 'That's right. I ought to have knocked. Sorry.'

'We'll trot along now,' I said carelessly. I took hold of Carmen's arm.

'Any message – if Steiner comes back?' Slade asked softly.

'We won't bother you.'

'That's too bad,' he said, with too much meaning.

I let go of Carmen's arm and took a slow step away from her. Slade still had his hat in his hand. He didn't move. His deep-set eyes twinkled pleasantly.

I opened the door again.

Slade said: 'The girl can go. But I'd like to talk to you a little.'

I stared at him, trying to look very blank.

'Kidder, eh?' Slade said nicely.

Carmen made a sudden sound at my side and ran out through the door. In a moment I heard her steps going down the hill. I hadn't seen her car, but I guessed it was around somewhere.

I began to say: 'What the hell—'

'Save it,' Slade interrupted coldly. 'There's something wrong here. I'll just find out what it is.'

He began to walk around the room carelessly – too carelessly. He was frowning, not paying much attention to me. That made me thoughtful. I took a quick glance out of the window, but I couldn't see anything but the top of his car above the hedge.

Slade found the potbellied flagon and the two thin purple glasses on the desk. He sniffed at one of them. A disgusted smile wrinkled his thin lips.

'The lousy pimp,' he said tonelessly.

He looked at the books on the desk, touched one or two of them, went on around the back of the desk and was in front of the totem pole thing. He stared at that. Then his eyes went down to the floor, to the thin rug that was over the place where Steiner's body had been. Slade moved the rug with his foot and suddenly tensed, staring down.

It was a good act – or else Slade had a nose I could have used in my business. I wasn't sure which – yet, but I was giving it a lot of thought.

He went slowly down to the floor on one knee. The desk partly hid him from me.

I slipped a gun out from under my arm and put both hands behind my body and leaned against the wall.

There was a sharp, swift exclamation, then Slade shot to his feet. His arm flashed up. A long, black Luger slid into it expertly. I didn't move. Slade held the Luger in long, pale fingers, not pointing it at me, not pointing it at anything in particular.

'Blood,' he said quietly, grimly, his deep-set eyes black and hard now. 'Blood on the floor there, under a rug. A lot of blood.'

I grinned at him. 'I noticed it,' I said. 'It's old blood. Dried blood.'

He slid sideways into the black chair behind Steiner's desk and raked the telephone towards him by putting the Luger around it. He frowned at the telephone, then frowned at me.

'I think we'll have some law,' he said.

'Suits me.'

Slade's eyes were narrow and as hard as jet. He didn't like my agreeing with him. The veneer had flaked off him, leaving a well-dressed hard boy with a Luger. Looking as if he could use it.

'Just who the hell are you?' he growled.

'A shamus. The name doesn't matter. The girl is my client. Steiner's been riding her with some blackmail dirt. We came to talk to him. He wasn't here.'

'Just walk in, huh?'

'Correct. So what? Think we gunned Steiner, Mister Slade?'

He smiled slightly, thinly, but said nothing.

'Or do you think Steiner gunned somebody and ran away?' I suggested.

'Steiner didn't gun anybody,' Slade said. 'Steiner didn't have the guts of a sick cat.'

I said: 'You don't see anybody here, do you? Maybe Steiner had chicken for dinner, and liked to kill his chickens in the parlour.'

'I don't get it. I don't get your game.'

I grinned again. 'Go ahead and call your friends downtown. Only you won't like the reaction you'll get.'

He thought that over without moving a muscle. His lips went back against his teeth.

'Why not?' he asked finally, in a careful voice.

I said: 'I know you, Mister Slade. You run the Aladdin Club down on the Palisades. Flash gambling. Soft lights and evening clothes and a buffet supper on the side. You know Steiner well enough to walk into his house without knocking. Steiner's racket needed a little protection now and then. You could be that.'

Slade's finger tightened on the Luger, then relaxed. He put the Luger down on the desk, kept his fingers on it. His mouth became a hard white grimace.

'Somebody got to Steiner,' he said softly, his voice and the expression on his face seeming to belong to two different people. 'He didn't show at the store today. He didn't answer his phone. I came up to see about it.'

'Glad to hear you didn't gun Steiner yourself,' I said.

The Luger swept up again and made a target of my chest. I said:

'Put it down, Slade. You don't know enough to pop off yet. Not being bullet-proof is an idea I've had to get used to. Put it down. I'll tell you something – if you don't know it. Somebody moved Steiner's books out of his store today – the books he did his real business with.'

Slade put his gun down on the desk for the second time. He leaned back and wrestled an amiable expression on to his face.

'I'm listening,' he said.

'I think somebody got to Steiner too,' I told him. 'I think that blood is his blood. The books being moved out from Steiner's store gives us a reason for moving his body away from here. Somebody is taking over the racket and doesn't want Steiner found till he's all set. Whoever it was ought to have cleaned up the blood. He didn't.'

Slade listened silently. The peaks of his eyebrows made sharp angles against the white skin of his indoor forehead. I went on:

'Killing Steiner to grab his racket was a dumb trick, and I'm not sure it happened that way. But I *am* sure that whoever took the books knows about it, and that the blonde down in the store is scared stiff about something.'

'Any more?' Slade asked evenly.

'Not right now. There's a piece of scandal dope I want to trace. If I get it, I might tell you where. That will be your muscler in.'

'Now would be better,' Slade said. Then he drew his lips back against his teeth and whistled sharply, twice.

I jumped. A car door opened outside. There were steps.

I brought the gun around from behind my body. Slade's face convulsed and his hand snatched for the Luger that lay in front of him, fumbled at the butt.

I said: 'Don't touch it!'

He came to his feet rigid, leaning over, his hand on the gun, but the gun not in his hand. I dodged past him into the hallway and turned as two men came into the room.

One had short red hair, a white, lined face, unsteady eyes. The other was an obvious pug; a good-looking boy except for a flattened nose and one ear as thick as a club steak.

Neither of the newcomers had a gun in sight. They stopped, stared.

I stood behind Slade in the doorway. Slade leaned over the desk in front of me, didn't stir.

The pug's mouth opened in a wide snarl, showing sharp, white teeth. The redhead looked shaky and scared.

Slade had plenty of guts. In a smooth, low, but very clear voice he said: 'This heel gunned Steiner, boys. Take him!'

The redhead took hold of his lower lip with his teeth and snatched for something under his left arm. He didn't get it. I was all set and braced. I shot him through the right shoulder, hating to do it. The gun made a lot of noise in the closed room. It seemed to me that it would be heard all over the city. The redhead went down on the floor and writhed and threshed about as if I had shot him in the belly.

The pug didn't move. He probably knew there wasn't enough speed in his arm. Slade grabbed his Luger up and started to whirl. I took a step and slammed him behind the ear. He sprawled forward over the desk and the Luger shot against a row of books.

Slade didn't hear me say: 'I hate to hit a one-armed man from behind, Slade. And I'm not crazy about the show-off. You made me do it.'

The pug grinned at me and said: 'Okay, pal. What next?'

'I'd like to get out of here, if I can do it without any more shooting. Or I can stick around for some law. It's all one to me.'

He thought it over calmly. The redhead was making moaning noises on the floor. Slade was very still.

The pug put his hands up slowly and clasped them behind his neck. He said coolly:

'I don't know what it's all about, but I don't give a good —— damn where you go or what you do when you get there. And this ain't my idea of a spot for a lead party. Drift!'

'Wise boy. You've more sense than your boss.'

I edged around the desk, edged over towards the open door. The pug turned slowly, facing me, keeping his hands behind his neck. There was a wry but almost good-natured grin on his face.

I skinned through the door and made a fast break through the gap in the hedge and up the hill, half expecting lead to fly after me. None came.

I jumped into the Chrysler and chased it up over the brow of the hill and away from that neighbourhood.

X

It was after five when I stopped opposite the apartment house on Randall Place. A few windows were lit up already and radios bleated discordantly on different programmes. I rode the automatic elevator to the fourth floor. Apartment 405 was at the end of a long hall that was carpeted in green and panelled in ivory. A cool breeze blew through the hall from open doors to the fire escape.

There was a small ivory push-button beside the door marked '405'. I pushed it.

After a long time a man opened the door a foot or so. He was a long-legged, thin man with dark brown eyes in a very brown face. Wiry hair grew far back on his head, giving him a great deal of domed brown forehead. His brown eyes probed at me impersonally.

I said: 'Steiner?'

Nothing in the man's face changed. He brought a cigarette from behind the door and put it slowly between tight brown lips. A puff of smoke came towards me, and behind it words in a cool, unhurried voice, without inflexion. 'You said what?'

'Steiner. Harold Hardwicke Steiner. The guy that has the books.'

The man nodded. He considered my remark without haste. He glanced at the tip of his cigarette, said:

'I think I know him. But he doesn't visit here. Who sent you?'

I smiled. He didn't like that. I said:

'You're Marty?'

The brown face got harder. 'So what? Got a grift – or just amusin' yourself?'

I moved my left foot casually, enough so that he couldn't slam the door.

'You got the books,' I said. 'I got the sucker list. How's to talk it over?'

Marty didn't shift his eyes from my face. His right hand went behind the panel of the door again, and his shoulder had a look as if he was making motions with a hand. There was a faint sound in the room behind him – very faint. A curtain ring clicked lightly on a rod.

Then he opened the door wide. 'Why not? If you think you've got something,' he said coolly.

I went past him into the room. It was a cheerful room, with good furniture and not too much of it. French windows in the end wall looked across a stone porch at the foothills, already getting purple in the dusk. Near the windows a door was shut. Another door in the same wall at the near end of the room had curtains drawn across it, on a brass rod below the lintel.

I sat down on a davenport against the wall in which there were no doors. Marty shut the door and walked sideways to a tall oak writing-desk studded with square nails. A cedarwood cigar box with gilt hinges rested on the lowered leaf of the desk. Marty picked it up without taking his eyes off me, carried it to a low table beside an easy chair. He sat down in the easy chair.

I put my hat beside me and opened the top button of my coat and smiled at Marty.

'Well – I'm listening,' he said.

He stubbed his cigarette out, lifted the lid of the cigar box and took out a couple of fat cigars.

'Cigar?' he suggested casually, and tossed one at me.

I reached for it and that made me a sap. Marty dropped the other cigar back into the box and came up very swiftly with a gun.

I looked at the gun politely. It was a black police Colt, a .38. I had no argument against it at the moment.

'Stand up a minute,' Marty said. 'Come forward just about two yards. You might grab a little air while you're doing that.' His voice was elaborately casual.

I was mad inside, but I grinned at him. I said:

'You're the second guy I've met today that thinks a gun in the hand means the world by the tail. Put it away, and let's talk.'

Marty's eyebrows came together and he pushed his chin forward a little. His brown eyes were vaguely troubled.

We stared at each other. I didn't look at the pointed black slipper that showed under the curtains across the doorway to my left.

Marty was wearing a dark blue suit, a blue shirt and a black tie. His brown face looked sombre above the dark colours. He said softly, in a lingering voice:

'Don't get me wrong. I'm not a tough guy – just careful. I don't know hell's first thing about you. You might be a life-taker for all I know.'

'You're not careful enough,' I said. 'The play with the books was lousy.'

He drew a long breath and let it out silently. Then he leaned back and crossed his long legs and rested the Colt on his knee.

'Don't kid yourself I won't use this, if I have to. What's your story?'

'Tell your friend with the pointed shoes to come on in,' I said. 'She gets tired holding her breath.'

Without turning his head Marty called out:

'Come on in, Agnes.'

The curtains over the door swung aside and the green-eyed blonde from Steiner's store joined us in the room. I wasn't very much surprised to see her there. She looked at me bitterly.

'I knew damn' well you were trouble,' she told me angrily. 'I told Joe to watch his step.'

'Save it,' Marty snapped. 'Joe's watchin' his step plenty. Put some light on so I can see to pop this guy, if it works out that way.'

The blonde lit a large floor lamp with a square red shade. She sat down under it, in a big velours chair and held a fixed painful smile on her face. She was scared to the point of exhaustion.

I remembered the cigar I was holding and put it in my mouth. Marty's Colt was very steady on me while I got matches out and lit it.

I puffed smoke and said through the smoke: 'The sucker list I spoke of is in code. So I can't read the names yet, but there's about five hundred of them. You got twelve boxes of books, say three hundred. There'll be that many more out on loan. Say five hundred altogether, just to be conservative. If it's a good active list and you could run it around all the books, that would be a quarter of a million rentals. Put the average rental low – say a dollar. That's too low, but say a dollar. That's a lot of money these days. Enough to spot a guy for.'

The blonde yelped sharply: 'You're crazy, if you—'

'Shut up!' Marty swore at her.

The blonde subsided and put her head back against the back of her chair. Her face was tortured with strain.

'It's no racket for bums,' I went on telling them. 'You've got to get confidence and keep it. Personally I think the blackmail angles are a mistake. I'm for shedding all that.'

Marty's dark brown stare held coldly on my face. 'You're a funny guy,' he drawled smoothly. 'Who's got this lovely racket?'

'You have,' I said. 'Almost.'

Marty didn't say anything.

'You shot Steiner to get it,' I said. 'Last night in the rain. It was good shooting weather. The trouble is, he wasn't alone when it happened. Either you didn't see that, or you got scared. You ran out. But you had nerve enough to come back and hide the body somewhere – so you could tidy up on the books before the case broke.'

The blonde made one strangled sound and then turned her face and stared at the wall. Her silvered fingernails dug into her palms. Her teeth bit her lip tightly.

Marty didn't bat an eye. He didn't move and the Colt didn't move in his hand. His brown face was as hard as a piece of carved wood.

'Boy, you take chances,' he said softly, at last. 'It's lucky as all hell for you I didn't kill Steiner.'

I grinned at him, without much cheer. 'You might step off for it just the same,' I said.

Marty's voice was a dry rustle of sound. 'Think you've got me framed for it?'

'Positive.'

'How come?'

'There's somebody who'll tell it that way.'

Marty swore then. 'That – damned little ——! She would – just that – damn her!'

I didn't say anything. I let him chew on it. His face cleared slowly, and he put the Colt down on the table, kept his hand near it.

'You don't sound like chisel as I know chisel,' he said slowly, his eyes a tight shine between dark narrowed lids. 'And I don't see any coppers here. What's your angle?'

I drew on my cigar and watched his gun hand. 'The plate that was in Steiner's camera. All the prints that have been made. Right here and right now. You've got it – because that's the only way you could have known who was there last night.'

Marty turned his head slightly to look at Agnes. Her face was still to the wall and her fingernails were still spearing her palms. Marty looked back at me.

'You're cold as a night watchman's feet on that one, guy,' he told me.

I shook my head. 'No. You're a sap to stall, Marty. You can be pegged for the kill easy. It's a natural. If the girl has to tell her story, the pictures won't matter. But she don't want to tell it.'

'You a shamus?' he asked.

'Yeah.'

'How'd you get to me?'

'I was working on Steiner. He's been workin on Dravec. Dravec leaks money. You had some of it. I tailed the books here from Steiner's store. The rest was easy when I had the girl's story.'

'She say I gunned Steiner?'

I nodded. 'But she could be mistaken.'

Marty sighed. 'She hates my guts,' he said. 'I gave her the gate. I got paid to do it, but I'd have done it anyway. She's too screwy for me.'

I said: 'Get the pictures, Marty.'

He stood up slowly, looked down at the Colt, put it in his side-pocket. His hand moved slowly up to his breast-pocket.

Somebody rang the door buzzer and kept on ringing it.

XI

Marty didn't like that. His lower lip went in under his teeth and his eyebrows drew down at the corners. His whole face got mean.

The buzzer kept on buzzing.

The blonde stood up quickly. Nerve tension made her face old and ugly.

Watching me, Marty jerked a small drawer open in the tall desk and got a small, white-handled automatic out of it. He held it out to the blonde. She went to him and took it gingerly, not liking it.

'Sit down next to the shamus,' he rasped. 'Hold the gun on him. If he gets funny, feed him a few.'

The blonde sat down on the davenport about three feet from me, on the side away from the door. She lined the gun on my leg. I didn't like the jerky look in her green eyes.

The door buzzer stopped and somebody started a quick, light, impatient rapping on the panel. Marty went across and opened the door. He slid his right hand into his coat pocket and opened the door with his left hand, threw it open quickly.

Carmen Dravec pushed him back into the room with the muzzle of a small revolver against his brown face.

Marty backed away from her smoothly, lightly. His mouth was open and an expression of panic was on his face. He knew Carmen pretty well.

Carmen shut the door, then bored ahead with her little gun. She didn't look at anyone but Marty, didn't seem to see anything but Marty. Her face had a dopey look.

The blonde shivered the full length of her body and swung the white-handled automatic up and towards Carmen. I shot my hand out and grabbed her hand, closed my fingers down over it quickly, thumbed the safety to the on position, and held it there. There was a short tussle, which neither Marty nor Carmen paid any attention to. Then I had the gun.

The blonde breathed deeply and stared at Carmen Dravec. Carmen looked at Marty with doped eyes and said:

'I want my pictures.'

Marty swallowed and tried to smile at her. He said: 'Sure, kid, sure,' in a small, flat voice that wasn't like the voice he had used in talking to me.

Carmen looked almost as crazy as she had looked in Steiner's chair. But she had control of her voice and muscles this time. She said:

'You shot Hal Steiner.'

'Wait a minute, Carmen!' I yelped.

Carmen didn't turn her head. The blonde came to life with a rush, ducked her head at me as if she was going to butt me, and sank her teeth in my right hand, the one that had her gun in it.

I yelped some more. Nobody minded that either.

Marty said: 'Listen, kid, I didn't—'

The blonde took her teeth out of my hand and spat my own blood at me. Then she threw herself at my leg and tried to bite that. I cracked her lightly on the head with the barrel of the gun and tried to stand up. She rolled down my legs and wrapped her arms around my ankles. I fell back on the davenport again. The blonde was strong with the madness of fear.

Marty grabbed for Carmen's gun with his left hand, missed. The little revolver made a dull, heavy sound that was not loud. A bullet missed Marty and broke glass in one of the folded-back french windows.

Marty stood perfectly still again. He looked as if all his muscles had gone back on him.

'Duck and knock her off her feet, you damn' fool!' I yelled at him.

Then I hit the blonde on the side of the head again, much harder, and she rolled off my feet. I got loose and slid away from her.

Marty and Carmen were still facing each other like a couple of images.

Something very large and heavy hit the outside of the door and the panel split diagonally from top to bottom.

That brought Marty to life. He jerked the Colt out of his pocket and jumped back. I snapped a shot at his right shoulder and missed, not wanting to hurt him much. The heavy thing hit the door again with a crash that seemed to shake the whole building.

I dropped the little automatic and got my own gun loose as Dravec came in with the smashed door.

He was wild-eyed, raging drunk, beserk. His big arms were flailing. His eyes were glaring and bloodshot and there was froth on his lips.

He hit me very hard on the side of the head without even looking at me. I fell against the wall, between the end of the davenport and the broken door.

I was shaking my head and trying to get level again when Marty began to shoot.

Something lifted Dravec's coat away from his body behind, as if a slug had gone clean through him. He stumbled, straightened immediately, charged like a bull.

I lined my gun and shot Marty through the body. It shook him, but the Colt in his hand continued to leap and roar. Then Dravec was between us and Carmen was knocked out of the way like a dead leaf and there was nothing more that anybody could do about it.

Marty's bullets couldn't stop Dravec. Nothing could. If he had been dead, he would still have got Marty.

He got him by the throat as Marty threw his empty gun in the big man's face. It bounced off like a rubber ball. Marty yelled shrilly, and Dravec took him by the throat and lifted him clean off his feet.

For an instant Marty's brown hands fought for a hold on the big man's wrists. Something cracked sharply, and Marty's hands fell away limply. There was another, duller crack. Just before Dravec let go of Marty's neck I saw that Marty's face was a purple-black colour. I remembered, almost casually, that men whose necks are broken sometimes swallow their tongues before they die.

Then Marty fell down in the corner and Dravec started to back away from him. He backed like a man losing his balance, not able to keep his feet under his centre of gravity. He took four clumsy backward steps like that. Then his big body tipped over backwards and he fell on his back on the floor with his arms flung out wide.

Blood came out of his mouth. His eyes strained upward as if to see through a fog.

Carmen Dravec went down beside him and began to wail like a frightened animal.

There was noise outside in the hall, but nobody showed at the open door. Too much casual lead had been flipped around.

I went quickly over to Marty and leaned over him and got my hand into his breast-pocket. I got out a thick, square envelope that had something stiff and hard in it. I straightened up with it and turned.

Far off the wail of a siren sounded faintly on the evening air, seemed to be getting louder. A white-faced man peeped cautiously in through the doorway. I knelt down beside Dravec.

He tried to say something, but I couldn't hear the words. Then the strained look went out of his eyes and they were aloof and indifferent, like the eyes of a man looking at something a long way off, across a wide plain.

Carmen said stonily: 'He was drunk. He made me tell him where I was going. I didn't know he followed me.'

'You wouldn't,' I said emptily.

I stood up again and broke the envelope open. There were a few prints in it and a glass negative. I dropped the plate on the floor and ground it to pieces with my heel. I began to tear up the prints and let the pieces flutter down out of my hands.

'They'll print plenty of photos of you now, girlie,' I said. 'But they won't print this one.'

'I didn't know he was following me,' she said again, and began to chew on her thumb.

The siren was loud outside the building now. It died to a penetrating drone and then stopped altogether, just about the time I finsihed tearing up the prints.

I stood still in the middle of the room and wondered why I had taken the trouble. It didn't matter any more now.

XII

Leaning his elbow on the end of the big walnut table in Inspector Isham's office, and holding a burning cigarette idly between his fingers, Guy Slade said, without looking at me:

'Thanks for putting me on the pan, shamus. I like to see the boys at Headquarters once in a while.' He crinkled the corners of his eyes in an unpleasant smile.

I was sitting at the long side of the table across from Isham. Isham was lanky and grey and wore nose-glasses. He didn't look, act or talk copper. Violets M'Gee and a merry-eyed Irish dick named Grinnell were in a couple of round-backed chairs against a glass-topped partition wall that cut part of the office off into a reception room.

I said to Slade: 'I figured you found that blood a little too soon. I guess I was wrong. My apologies, Mister Slade.'

'Yeah. That makes it just like it never happened.' He stood up, picked a malacca cane and one glove off the table. 'That all for me, Inspector?'

'That's all tonight, Slade.' Isham's voice was dry, cool, sardonic.

Slade caught the crook of his cane over his wrist to open the door. He smiled around before he strolled out. The last thing his eyes rested on was probably the back of my neck, but I wasn't looking at him.

Isham said: 'I don't have to tell you how a police department looks at that kind of a cover-up on a murder.'

I sighed. 'Gunfire,' I said. 'A dead man on the floor. A naked, doped girl in a chair not knowing what had happened. A killer I couldn't have caught and you couldn't have caught – then. Behind all this a poor old roughneck that was breaking his heart trying to do the right thing in a miserable spot. Go ahead – stick it into me. I'm not sorry.'

Isham waved all that aside. 'Who did kill Steiner?'

'The blonde girl will tell you.'

'I want you to tell me.'

I shrugged. 'If you want me to guess – Dravec's driver, Carl Owen.'

Isham didn't look too surprised. Violets M'Gee grunted loudly.

'What makes you think so?' Isham asked.

'I thought for a while it could be Marty, partly because the girl said so. But that doesn't mean anything. She didn't know, and jumped at the chance to stick a knife into Marty. And she's a type that doesn't let loose of an idea very easily. But Marty didn't act like a killer. And a man as cool as Marty wouldn't have run out that way. I hadn't even banged on the door when the killer started to scram.

'Of course I thought of Slade, too. But Slade's not quite the type either. He packs two gunmen around with him, and they'd have made some kind of a fight of it. And Slade seemed genuinely surprised when he found the blood on the floor this afternoon. Slade was in with Steiner and keeping tabs on

103

him, but he didn't kill him, didn't have any reason to kill him, and wouldn't have killed him that way, in front of a witness, if he had a reason.

'But Carl Owen would. He was in love with the girl once, probably never got over it. He had chances to spy on her, find out where she went and what she did. He lay for Steiner, got in the back way, saw the nude photo stunt and blew his top. He let Steiner have it. Then the panic got him and he just ran.'

'Ran all the way to Lido pier, and then off the end of that,' Isham said dryly. 'Aren't you forgetting that the Owen body had a sap wound on the side of his head?'

I said: 'No. And I'm not forgetting that somehow or other Marty knew what was on that camera plate – or nearly enough to make him go in and get it and then hide a body in Steiner's garage to give him room.'

Isham said: 'Get Agnes Laurel in here, Grinnell.'

Grinnell heaved up out of his chair and strolled the length of the office, disappeared through a door.

Violets M'Gee said: 'Baby, are you a pal!'

I didn't look at him. Isham pulled the loose skin in front of his Adam's apple and looked down at the fingernails of his other hand.

Grinnell came back with the blonde. Her hair was untidy above the collar of her coat. She had taken the jet buttons out of her ears. She looked tired but she didn't look scared any more. She let herself down slowly into the chair at the end of the table where Slade had sat, folded her hands with the silvered nails in front of her.

Isham said quietly: 'All right, Miss Laurel. We'd like to hear from you now.'

The girl looked down at her folded hands and talked without hesitation, in a quiet, even voice.

'I've known Joe Marty about three months. He made friends with me because I was working for Steiner, I guess. I thought it was because he liked me. I told him all I knew about Steiner. He already knew a little. He had been spending money had had got from Carmen Dravec's father, but it was gone and he was down to nickels and dimes, ready for something else. He decided Steiner needed a partner and he was watching him to see if he had any tough friends in the background.

'Last night he was in his car down on the street back of Steiner's house. He heard the shots, saw the kid tear down the steps, jump into a big sedan and take it on the lam. Joe chased him. Half-way to the beach, he caught him and ran him off the road. The kid came up with a gun, but his nerve was bad and Joe sapped him down. While he was out Joe went through him and found out who he was. When he came around Joe played copper and the kid broke and gave him the story. While Joe was wondering what to do about it the kid came to life and knocked him off the car and scrammed again. He drove like a crazy guy and Joe let him go. He went back to Steiner's house. I guess you know the rest. When Joe had the plate developed and saw what he had he went for a quick touch so we could get out of town before the law found Steiner. We were going to take some of Steiner's books and set up shop in another city.'

Agnes Laurel stopped talking. Isham tapped with his fingers, said: 'Marty told you everything, didn't he?'

'Uh-huh.'

'Sure he didn't murder this Carl Owen?'

'I wasn't there. Joe didn't act like he'd killed anybody.'

Isham nodded. 'That's all for now, Miss Laurel. We'll want all that in writing. We'll have to hold you, of course.'

The girl stood up. Grinnell took her out. She went out without looking at anyone.

Isham said: 'Marty couldn't have known Carl Own was dead. But he was sure he'd try to hide out. By the time we got to him Marty would have collected from Dravec and moved on. I think the girl's story sounds reasonable.'

Nobody said anything. After a moment Isham said to me:

'You made one bad mistake. You shouldn't have mentioned Marty to the girl until you were sure he was your man. That got two people killed quite unnecessarily.'

I said: 'Uh-huh. Maybe I better go back and do it over again.'

'Don't get tough.'

'I'm not tough. I was working for Dravec and trying to save him from a little heartbreak. I didn't know the girl was as screwy as all that, or that Dravec would have a brainstorm. I wanted the pictures. I didn't care a lot about trash like Steiner or Joe Marty and his girl friend, and still don't.'

'Okay. Okay,' Isham said impatiently. 'I don't need you any more tonight. You'll probably be panned plenty at the inquest.'

He stood up and I stood up. He held out his hand.

'But that will do you a hell of a lot more good than harm,' he added dryly.

I shook hands with him and went out. M'Gee came out after me. We rode down in the elevator together without speaking to each other. When we got outside the building M'Gee went around to the right side of my Chrysler and got into it.

'Got any liquor at your dump?'

'Plenty,' I said.

'Let's go get some of it.'

I started the car and drove west along First Street, through a long echoing tunnel. When we were out of that, M'Gee said:

'Next time I send you a client I won't expect you to snitch on him, boy.'

We went on through the quiet evening to the Berglund. I felt tired and old and not much use to anybody.

SALLY THE SLEUTH
ADOLPHE BARREAUX

Adolphe Barreaux (1899–1985) studied at the Yale School of Fine Arts and the Grand Central Art School. He created 'Sally the Sleuth' for *Spicy Detective*, one of the sleaziest of the pulp mazagines, in November 1934, with a little two-page strip titled 'A Narrow Escape.' the material published in this pulp was generally produced by the worst writers of the era, mainly when they failed to sell their work to the better-paying, higher-end books. All the stories included illustrations of scantily clad women, frequently in bondage – all so racy that the magazines were kept under the counter at most newsstands and sold only to adults. These illustrations were provided by Majestic studios, a tiny art shop owned by Barreaux from 1936 to 1953, he also was the owner of Trojan Publishing from 1949 to 1955. Although he worked for a few other pulps from the 1930s to the 1950s, most of his work went to *Spicy*, for which he drew the 'Sally the Sleuth' strip until 1942, when other artists took it over. Barreaux went on to work for many of the major comic book publishers, including DC ('The Magic Crystal of History'), Dell ('Enchanted Stone'), Ace ('The Black Spider' and 'The Raven') and Fox ('Flip Falcon' and 'Patty O'Day').

These episodes of 'Sally the Sleuth' appeared in *Spicy Detective*.

Matinee Murder

THERE'S OUR GREAT BASE AT PEARL HARBOR. IT'S ENDANGERED BY A SPY RING DIRECTED BY A MASTER MIND UP IN THE HILLS. TOMORROW, WE START OUT TO LOCATE HIM.

NEXT DAY

WE'LL JUST PRETEND TO BE TOURISTS AND KEEP OUR EYES AND EARS OPEN. IF ANYTHING HAPPENS, I HAVE A WAY TO CONTACT THE ARMY AT ONCE. THEY WILL BE WATCHING...

THAT'S SWELL, ISN'T IT, CHIEF?

I'LL BET YOU COULD DO BETTER, YOURSELF.

BUT ALREADY THEY AROUSE SUSPICION AS A RUNNER STREAKS UP THE SIDE OF AN EXTINCT VOLCANO.

A MILE FURTHER ON — CHIEF AND SALLY ARE TAKEN PRISONERS.

THEY REACH THE MASTER SPY'S HIDEOUT

SO YOU THINK YOU COULD FOOL SANTOS, EH? I KNEW ALL ABOUT YOU TWO AS SOON AS YOU GOT OFF THE BOAT.

TIE HER OUTSIDE. THE NIGHT CHILL WILL COOL HER TEMPER A BIT

BRRRH! IT'S CHILLY. I WONDER WHAT THEY'VE DONE WITH THE CHIEF---

MEANWHILE, THE CHIEF MAKES A ROPE OUT OF HIS BLANKET:...

...AND FASHIONS A SNARE OUTSIDE HIS WINDOW.

THE UNWARY GUARD STEPS INTO THE NOOSE -- IS YANKED OFF HIS FEET AND IS KNOCKED COLD.

AH, THE KEYS -- THIS IS LUCK.

PSST- SALLY!

CHIEF!

SOMEONE'S COMING!

IT'S SANTOS!

A SHOCK FOR THE COUNTESS
C. S. MONTANYE

Carlton Stevens Montanye (1892–1948), an active writer in the early years of pulpwood magazines, appears to have had an exceptional fondness for criminals as protagonists.

Although he wrote for many different periodicals, he achieved the peak of any pulp writer's career by selling numerous stories to *Black Mask*, beginning with the May 1920 issue and continuing through the issue of October 1939. Most were about various crooks, including an old-fashioned Monahan, a yegg, Rider Lott, inventor of the perfect crime, and the Countess d'Yls, an old-fashioned international jewel thief: wealthy, beautiful, brilliant and laconic, the female equivalent of his most famous character, Captain Valentine, who made his *Black Mask* debut on September 1, 1923, with 'The Suite on the Seventh Floor,' and appeared nine more times in two years, concluding with 'The Dice of Destiny' in the July 1925 issue. The gentleman rogue also was the protagonist of the novel *Moons in Gold*, published in 1936, in which the debonair Valentine, accompanied by his amazingly ingenious Chinese servant Tim, is in Paris, where he has his eye on the world's most magnificent collection of opals.

Montanye also was one of the writers of the Phantom Detective series under the house name Robert Wallace.

'A Shock for the Countess' first appeared in the March 1923 issue of *Black Mask*.

A SHOCK FOR THE COUNTESS

C. S. MONTANYE

From the terraces of the Chateau d'Yls, the valley of Var was spread out below Gattiere, threaded with the broad bed of the River Var, swirling over its stony reaches from its cradle in the Hautes-Alpes. The snow-crowned mountains frowned ominously down but in the valley summertime warmth prevailed – quietude disturbed only by the song of birds and the voice of the river.

On the shaded promenade of the Chateau, the pretty Countess d'Yls stared thoughtfully at the unwinding river of the dust-powdered highway, twisting off into the dim distance. Beside her, a tall, well-built young man in tweeds absently flicked the ash from his cigarette and tinkled the ice in the thin glass he held.

Once or twice he surreptitiously considered the woman who reclined so indolently in the padded depths of a black wicker chair. The Countess seemed rarely lovely on this warm, lazy afternoon.

Her ash-blond hair caught what sunshine came in under the sand-colored awning above. Her blue eyes were dreamy and introspective, her red lips meditatively pursed. Yet for all of her abstraction there was something regal and almost imperious in her bearing; a subtle charm and distinction that was entirely her own.

'I do believe,' the Countess remarked at length, 'we are about to entertain visitors.'

She motioned casually with a white hand toward the dust-filled road. The man beside her leaned a little forward. A mile or less distant he observed an approaching motor car that crawled up the road between clouds of dust.

'Visitors?'

The Countess inclined her head.

'So it would appear. And visitors, *mon ami*, who have come a long way to see us. Observe that the machine is travel-stained, that it appears to be weighted down with luggage. Possibly it is our old friend Murgier,' she added almost mischievously.

The face of the man in tweeds paled under its tan.

'Murgier!' he exclaimed under his breath.

The Countess smiled faintly.

'But it is probably only a motoring party up from Georges de Loup who have wandered off the main road, Armand.'

The man in tweeds had torn the cigarette between his fingers into rags. As if held in the spell of some strange fascination he watched the motor grow larger and larger.

'There are men in it!' he muttered, when the dusty car was abreast the lower wall of the Chateau. 'Four men!'

The woman in the wicker chair seemed suddenly to grow animated.

'*Mon Dieu!*' she said in a low voice. 'If it is *he*, that devil!'

The man she addressed made no reply, only the weaving of his fingers betraying his suppressed nervousness. The hum of the sturdy motor was heard from the drive, way among the terraces now.

There was an interlude – voices around a bend in the promenade – finally the appearance of a liveried automaton that was the butler.

'Monsieur Murgier, madame.'

The man in tweeds stifled a groan. The Countess turned slowly in her chair.

'You may direct Monsieur Murgier here, Henri.'

The butler bowed and turned away. The man in tweeds closed his hands until the nails of them bit into the palms.

'God!'

The Countess laid a tense hand on his arm.

'*Smile!*' she commanded.

The Monseiur Murgier who presently sauntered down the shaded promenade of the Chateau was a tall, loose-jointed individual with a melancholy mustache and a deeply wrinkled face. A shabby, dusty suit hung loosely and voluminously about his spare figure. A soft straw hat was in one hand; he was grey at the temples.

When he bowed over the slender fingers of the Countess there was a hidden glow in his somber eyes.

'To be favored by the presence of the great!' the woman murmured softly. 'Monsieur, this is an honor! May I make you acquainted with the Marquis de Remec?'

She introduced the visitor to the man in tweeds, who bowed stiffly. Somewhere back around the corner of the promenade the drone of the voices of those who had been in the car sounded faintly.

'A liqueur, m'sieu?' the Countess asked. 'A cigar?'

Her visitor shook his head, gazed on the peaceful panorama of the valley of the Var.

'Thank you, no. My time is limited. My journey has been a long one and I must make a start for Paris with all due haste. You,' he explained courteously, 'and the Marquis will put yourselves in readiness with as much rapidity as possible. You are both my guests for the return journey!'

The man in tweeds whitened to the lips. His startled glance darted to the

Countess. The woman had settled herself back in the black wicker chair again and had joined her fingers, tip to tip.

'Accompany you to Paris?' she drawled. 'Are you quite serious?'

The wrinkled face of Monsieur Murgier grew inflexible, brass-like!

'Quite serious,' he replied. 'You are both under arrest – for the theft of the de Valois pearls!'

For a week, intermittently, Paris had known rain – the cold, chilly drizzle of early springtime. Because of the weather cafés and theatres were crowded, fiacres and taxis in constant demand, omnibuses jammed and the drenched boulevards deserted by their usual loungers.

From Montmartre to Montparnasse, scudding, gray clouds veiled the reluctant face of the sun by day and hid a knife-edged moon by night.

The steady, monotonous drizzle pattered against the boudoir windows in the house of the Countess d'Yls, mid-way down the Street of the First Shell. Within, all was snug, warm and comfortable. A coal file burned in a filigree basket-grate, the radiance of a deeply shaded floor lamp near the toilette table, where a small maid hovered like a mother pigeon about the Countess, diffused a subdued, mellow glow.

The evening growl of Paris came as if from faraway, a lesser sound in the symphony of the rain.

'Madame, will wear her jewels?'

The Countess turned and lifted her blue eyes.

'My rings only, Marie, if you please.'

The maid brought the jewel casket, laid it beside her mistress, and at the wardrobe selected a luxurious Kolinsky cape which she draped over an arm. The Countess slipped on her rings, one by one – flashing, blue-white diamonds in carved, platinum settings, an odd Egyptian temple ring, a single ruby that burned like a small ball of crimson fire.

When the last ring glinted on her white fingers she dropped the lid of the casket, stood and turned to a full length cheval mirror back of her.

The glass reflected the full perfection of her charms, the sheer wonder of her sequin-spangled evening gown, the creamy luster of her bare, powdered arms, shoulders and rounded, contralto throat. Standing there, the soft light on her hair, she was radiant, incomparable, a reincarnated Diana whose draperies came from the most expert needles of the Rue de la Paix.

'I think,' the Countess said aloud, 'those who go to fashionable affairs to witness and copy will have much to occupy their pencils on the morrow. My gown is clever, is it not, Marie?'

'It is beautiful!' the maid breathed.

With a little laugh the Countess took the Kolinsky cape.

'Now I must hasten below to the Marquis. Poor boy, it is an hour – or more – that I have kept him cooling his heels. Marie, suspense, they say, breeds appreciation but there is such a thing as wearing out the patience of a cavalier. The really intelligent woman knows when not to overdo it. You understand?'

'Perfectly, madame,' the maid replied.

The Countess let herself out and sought the stairs. She moved lightly down steps that were made mute by the weight of their waterfall of gorgeous carpet. Murals looked down upon her progress to the lower floor, tapestries glittered with threads of flame, the very air seemed somnolent with the heaviness of sybaritic luxury.

Humming a snatch of a boulevard *chansonette*, the Countess turned into a lounge room that was to the right of the entry-hall below. The aroma of cigarette smoke drifted to her. When she crossed the threshold the Marquis de Remec stood, a well-made, immaculately groomed individual in his perfectly tailored evening clothes.

'Forgive me, Armand,' the Countess pleaded. 'Marie was so stupid tonight – all thumbs. I thought she would never finish with me.'

The Marquis lifted her fingers to his lips.

'How lovely you are!' he cried softly, 'Ah, dear one, will you never say the word that will make me the happiest man in all France? For two years we have worked together shoulder to shoulder, side by side – for two years you have been a star to me, earth-bound, beautiful beyond all words! Two years of—'

The Countess interrupted with a sigh.

'Of thrills and danger, Armand! Of plots and stratagems, plunder and wealth! I think, *mon ami*,' she said seriously, 'if we are successful tonight I will marry you before April ends. But wait, understand me. It will be a secret. I will still be the Countess d'Yls and you will remain the Marquis de Remec to all the world but me. Then, my friend, if either of us suffers disaster one will not drag the other down. You see?'

She seated herself beside the Marquis, considering him wistfully.

'But *tonight?*' he said in a stifled voice. 'The de Valois affair is the hardest nut we have yet attempted to crack! Tonight we will need all of our cunning, all of our wits!'

The Countess lifted airy brows.

'Indeed?'

The Marquis leaned closer to her.

'There is not,' he explained rapidly, 'only Monsieur Murgier of the Surete to consider – the knowledge that he has been blundering after us for months – but the Wolf as well! An hour ago only, François picked up some gossip across the river, in some dive. The Wolf steals from his lair tonight *questing the de Valois pearls!* Do you understand? We must face double enemies – the net of Murgier, the fangs of the animal who sulks among the Apache brigands of the river front. And this is the task you give to set a crown upon my every hope!'

The Countess d'Yls touched his hand with her pretty fingers.

'Does the threat of Murgier and the presence of the Wolf pack dismay you?' she questioned lightly. 'You, the undaunted! You who have been the hero of so many breathless adventures! Armand, you – you annoy me.'

De Remec stood.

'But this is different!' he cried. 'Here I have something at stake more precious than gold or jewels – your promise! I – I tremble—'

The Countess laughed at his melodrama.

'Silly boy! We shall not fail – we will snatch the famous pearls from under the very noses of those who would thwart and destroy us. *Voilà!* I snap my fingers at them all. Come now, it grows late. Had we not better start?'

The other glanced at his watch.

'Yes. François is waiting with the limousine—'

When they were side by side in the tonneau of the purring motor, the Countess glanced at the streaming windows and shivered.

'Soon it will be late spring,' she said quietly. 'Soon it will be our privilege to rest city-weary eyes on the valley of the Var. I intend to open the Château in six weeks, *mon ami*. It will seem like heaven after the miserable winter and the rain, the rain!'

The car shaped a course west, then south. Paris lifted a gaudy reflection to the canopy of the frowning clouds, flashing past in its nightly pursuit of pleasure. The Countess eyed the traffic tide idly. Her thoughts were like skeins of silk on a loom that was slowly being reversed. She thought of Yesterday – of the little heap of jewels in the boudoir of the villa at Trouville that had been the scene of that week-end party, of herself stealing through the gloom to purloin them – of the Marquis bound on the same errand – of their meeting – surprise – their pact and the bold, triumphant exploits they had both planned and carried out.

The red lips of the Countess were haunted by a smile.

It had all been so easy, so exciting, so simple. True, the dreaded Murgier of the Law had pursued them relentlessly but they had always outwitted him, had always laughed secretly at his discomfiture, rejoicing together over their spoils.

Now, tonight, it was the de Valois pearls – that famous coil the woman had had strung in Amsterdam by experts. Tomorrow Madame de Valois would be bewailing its loss and the necklace – the necklace would be speeding to some foreign port, safe in the possession of the agent who handled all their financial transactions.

'The Wolf!' the Countess thought.

Surely there was nothing to fear from the hulk of the Apache outlaw – a man whose cleverness lay in the curve of a knife, the slippery rope of the garroter, the sandbag of the desperado. How could the Wolf achieve something that required brains, delicate finesse? It was only the chance that Murgier might upturn some carefully hidden clew that was perilous—

'You are silent,' the Marquis observed.

'I am thinking,' the Countess d'Yls replied dreamily.

A dozen more streets and the motor was in the Rue de la Saint Vigne, stopping before a striped canopy that stretched from the door to the curb that fronted the Paris home of Madame de Valois. The windows of the building were brightly painted with light. The whisper of music crept out. Set in the little, unlighted park that surrounded it, the house was like a painted piece of scenery on a stage.

A footman laid a gloved hand on the silver knob of the limousine door and opened it. The Marquis de Remec assisted the Countess to alight. Safe from the rain under the protection of the awning they went up the front steps and entered the house.

'You,' the Countess instructed cautiously, 'watch for Murgier and I will take care of the Wolf whelps! If the unexpected transpires we will meet tomorrow at noon in the basement of the Café of the Three Friends. François has been instructed?'

'He will keep the motor running – around the corner,' the Marquis whispered.

Then, pressing her hand: 'Courage, dear one and a prayer for success!'

To the Countess d'Yls it seemed that all the wealth and beauty of the city had flocked to the ballroom which they entered together.

Under the flare of crystal chandeliers Fashion danced in the arms of Affluence. Everywhere jewels sparkled, eyes laughed back at lips that smiled. Perfumes were like the scents of Araby on a hot, desert breeze. Conversation blended with the swinging lilt of the orchestra on the balcony – the shuffle of feet and the whisper of silks and satins filled the room with a queer dissonance.

Separating from the Marquis, the Countess, greeting those who addressed her with a friendly word, a smile or bow, promptly lost herself in the crush. Murgier's assistants she left to the attention of de Remec. She decided, first, to mark the presence of Madame de Valois and the pearls – after that she would seek the Wolf or his agents in the throng.

After some manoeuvering the Countess discovered the location of Madame de Valois. The woman was dancing with a gray-bearded Senator – an ample, overdressed burden from whose fat neck the famous rope of pearls swayed with every step. The Countess watched the woman drift past and then turned to seek the footprints of the Wolf.

In and out among the crowd she circulated, disregarding those she knew, scanning anxiously the faces and appearance of those she had never before seen. An hour sped past before she believed she had at last discovered the man she sought. This was a beardless youth in shabby evening attire who lingered alone in a foyer that adjoined the south end of the ballroom.

Watching, the Countess touched the elbow of a woman she knew, discreetly indicated the youth and asked a question.

'That,' her friend replied, 'is a Monsieur Fernier. He is a young composer of music from the Latin Quarter. Madame de Valois invited him tonight so that he might hear the orchestra play one of his own dance compositions. He is so melancholy, do you not think?'

'From the Latin Quarter,' the Countess told herself when she was alone again. 'I will continue to watch you, Monsieur Fernier!'

A few minutes later the Marquis de Remec approached.

'Three agents of Murgier present!' he breathed, drifting past. 'The doors are guarded. Be cautious, dear one!'

Another sixty minutes passed.

It was midnight precisely when the Countess saw the putative student from the Latin Quarter make his first move. The youth took a note from his pocket and handed it to a footman, with a word of instruction. The servant threaded a way among the crowd and delivered the message to Madame de Valois. The woman excused herself to those about her, opened the note, read it, and after several more minutes began to move slowly toward the ballroom doors. The Countess, tingling, tightened her lips. A glance over her shoulder showed her that Fernier had left the foyer.

What was the game?

A minute or two after Madame de Valois had disappeared through the doors of the ballroom the Countess had reached them. She looked out in time to behold the other woman crossing the entry-hall and disappearing through the portieres of the receptionroom beyond. There was no one in evidence. Certain she was on the right trail and filled with a growing anticipation, the Countess waited until the portieres opposite ceased to flutter before moving swiftly toward them.

The metallic jar of bolts being drawn, a scraping sound and then a damp, cool current of air told the Countess that without question the long, French windows in the receptionroom, opening out on a balcony that overlooked one side of the park, had been pushed wide. She parted the portieres cautiously and looked between them.

The chamber was in darkness – Madame de Valois was a bulky silhouette on the balcony outside – voices mingled faintly.

On noiseless feet the Countess picked a stealthy way down the room. Close to the open windows she drew back into a nest of shadows, leaned a little forward and strained her ears.

There came to her the perplexed query of Madame de Valois:

'But why do you ask me to come out here? Who are you? What is the secret you mention in your note?'

A pause – the suave, silky tones of a man:

'A thousand pardons, Madame. This was the only way possible under the circumstances. My secret is a warning – unscrupulous people are within who would prey upon you!'

'You mean?' Madame de Valois stammered.

'I mean,' the man replied, 'your pearls!'

Another pause – plainly one of agitation for the woman on the balcony – then the man again:

'Madame, allow me to introduce myself. Possibly you have heard of me. Paris knows me as the Wolf! Madame will kindly make neither outcry nor move – my revolver covers you steadily and my finger is on the trigger! I will take care of your pearls and see that no one takes them. Madame will be so kind as to remove the necklace immediately!'

Madame de Valois's gasp of dismay followed hard on the heels of a throaty chuckle. Came unexplainable sounds, the words:

'*Thank you. Adieu!*'

– then the woman tottering in through the open windows, a quivering mountain of disconcerted flesh, making strange, whimpering sounds.

Madame de Valois had hardly reached the middle of the reception room before the Countess was out on the balcony and was over its rail. A single glance showed her the shadowy figure of the Wolf hastening toward the gates at the far end of the park that opened on the avenue beyond.

With all the speed at her command the Countess ran to the other door in the street wall that was to the right of the house. The door was unlocked. She flung it open and surged out onto the wet pavement, heading toward the avenue, running with all speed while her fingers found and gripped the tiny revolver she had hidden under the overskirt of her evening creation.

She reached the gates at the northern end of the park at the same minute footsteps sounded on the other side of them. They gave slowly, allowing a stout, bearded man to pass between them. The Countess drew back and waited until he turned to close the gates after him.

Then she took two steps forward and sank the muzzle of her weapon into the small of his back.

'Do not trouble yourself to move, Monsieur Wolf,' she said sweetly. 'Just keep facing the way you are and I will help myself to the pearls without bothering you.'

She could feel the quiver of the man's back under the nose of the gun.

'You will die for this!' the Wolf vowed.

The Countess found the smooth, lustrous coil of Madame de Valois's necklace in his side pocket and stuffed it hastily into her bodice.

'Possibly,' she agreed amiably. 'But this is no time to discuss the question. Pay attention to what I say. If you move before two minutes elapse I will shoot you down in your tracks! Continue to keep your face glued to the – gates – and—'

Dropping her weaponed hand, the Countess surged around the turn of the wall where the avenue joined the side street and raced across the petrol-polished asphalt toward François and the waiting limousine. Hazily aware of the growing tumult in the house itself, the Countess was stunned by the sudden crack of a revolver, the whistle of a bullet flying past her, the hoarse bellow of the Wolf's voice:

'Police! . . . Police! . . . Thieves! There she goes! . . . In that car . . .'

Pausing only to fire twice at the howling Apache, the Countess, sensitive to the fact that a machine was rolling down the street toward her, climbed into the limousine.

'Quick!' she cried breathlessly. 'Off with you, François!'

Like a nervous thoroughbred, the car sprang toward the junction of the avenue beyond. The Countess pressed her face to the rear window. The other motor was a thousand rods behind, a car with pale, yellow lamps – a police car – one of the machines of the Sureté.

'Across the river!' the Countess directed through the open front glass of the limousine. 'We will shake them off on the other side of the Seine!'

Across a bridge – over the night-painted river – past cafés and then into a district of gaunt, silent warehouses, the limousine panted. Twice more the Countess looked back. The pale, yellow lamps behind followed like an avenging nemesis.

'Round the next corner and slow down,' the Countess commanded crisply. 'The minute I swing off, speed up and head for the open country—'

On two wheels the limousine shot around into the black gully of a narrow, cobble-paved side street. Its brakes screamed as it slowed for a minute before lunging forward again. Shrinking back behind a pile of casks that fronted one of the warehouses, the Countess laughed as the second car whirled past.

'The long arm of Murgier!' she sneered. 'What rubbish!'

Still laughing a little, she moved out from behind the casks – to stiffen suddenly and dart back behind them again. A motorcycle had wheeled into the silent street and a man was jumping off it.

The Countess, frantic fingers clutching the pearls of Madame de Valois, knew it was the Wolf even before his level tones came to her.

'Mademoiselle,' the Apache said. 'I know you are there. I saw the shimmer of your gown before you stepped back behind those casks. You cannot escape me. *Hand the necklace over!*'

'The theft of the de Valois pearls?' the Countess d'Yls cried softly. 'Monsieur is joking!'

Murgier, on the shaded promenade of the Chateau, touched the tips of his disconsolate mustache.

'There is really,' he said almost wearily, 'no use in pretending surprise or indignation. Four days ago we bagged the Wolf – he made a full and complete confession . . .'

The sunlit quiet of the promenade was broken by the throaty cry of the Countess d'Yls. She jumped up, her blue eyes cold, blazing stars.

'Yes, you devil!' she said unsteadily. 'Yes, Monsieur Ferret, we took the pearls – *I* took the pearls! The Wolf did not get them! No one else shall! I have hidden them well! Take me, take us both – jail us – you will never find the necklace – no one ever will!'

Murgier snapped his fingers twice. The men who had come up the dusty road in the travel-stained motor rounded the corner of the walk. The Countess laughed insolently at the man who faced her.

'In a measure,' Murgier said quietly, 'your statement is true. No one will ever reclaim the de Valois pearls. Let me tell you something. When the Wolf made his appearance that night at the warehouse, you saved the necklace from him by dropping it into the mouth of an open cask. Is that not correct? You marked this cask so you might distinguish it again. When you foiled the Wolf your agent began a search for the cask. It had been stored away in the warehouse – there were difficulties – so far your aid has not been able to locate it – but you have hopes. Madame Countess, it is my duty to disillusion both you and—' he nodded toward de Remec— 'your husband. There was one thing you over-looked – the contents of the cask in question—'

The Countess drew a quick breath, leaning forward as if to read the meaning of the other's words.

'The contents?'

Murgier smiled.

'The cask,' he explained, 'we found to be half full of vinegar. The pearls are no more – eaten up like that! Pouf! Let us be going.'

SNOWBOUND

C. B. YORKE

Harold B. Hersey, the publisher who created *Gangster Magazine*, wrote in his memoir, *Pulp Editor* (1937), that this was the magazine 'that enabled me to lose money in that enterprise until the depression wiped out the business.' He had also created *Racketeer Stories*, *Mobs*, *Gun Molls* and *Gangland Stories*. The American public had become enthralled with gangsters and their luxurious lifestyle, so vividly reported in the nation's newspapers. While ordinary people suffered privation as the country plunged into what is now referred to as the Great Depression, they took solace and guilty pleasure from reading about the fun gangsters enjoyed as they partook of music, wine, beautiful women, fast cars, and so on. Little of it was true, but it made for good reading. Tastes change, and soon it was the FBI and the G-Men, those who captured or killed the criminals, who suddenly became the heroes, killing off the gangster publications.

Many of these pulps came to an abrupt end as the Roaring Twenties drew to a close. During their brief lives, they had failed to seduce the top writers into working for them, and most of the by-lines appearing in their pages are unknown today. It is entirely possible that many of the stories were produced by popular writers using pseudonyms on their lesser work that appeared in less prestigious publications. Nothing could be discovered about C. B. Yorke.

'Snowbound' was first published in the October 1931 issue of *Gangster Stories*.

SNOWBOUND
C. B. YORKE

CHAPTER I

OVER HER HEAD

She was nervous from the moment she entered my apartment. I didn't blame her much. Suds Garland had given her a tough job.

'Here's the money,' she said, fumbling in her purse with trembling hands. 'Five grand, cash.'

I laughed softly. The girl looked up at me with wide eyes. Something in her gaze told me she feared more than what I might do to her.

'Chicken feed,' I said, still smiling.

'Seven thousand?' she countered.

'That's funny!'

'Ten grand? That's a lot of money.'

Perhaps ten thousand was a lot to her. She looked like a kid who wasn't accustomed to dealing in big figures when it came to cold cash. But as for me, ten thousand dollars didn't even get me interested in her proposition, and I told her so.

'Well,' she went on, her thin voice shaking slightly from excitement and nervousness, 'I'll give you fifteen thousand. Suds will go that high just to get you—'

'Make it fifty grand,' I told her sharply.

A little gasp escaped her. I knew she didn't have fifty grand with her, and in all probability Suds wouldn't consider that price. It made no difference to me. So when she got over the shock of the figure I'd named I gave it to her straight.

'Listen, kid,' I explained quietly. 'I was just kidding about that fifty grand limit. No matter what—'

'Then you'll take fifteen grand?' she interrupted.

'No. Now listen closely. No matter what Suds Garland offers I'm not accepting it. See? Not even fifty grand in cash could tempt me to tie up with him in the dope racket. And that's final. What's your name?'

*

The girl looked at me with troubled eyes. She had come to my apartment that afternoon to try to get me to change my mind. I'd already told Suds that I wasn't interested in dope, wouldn't be interested, and couldn't be interested. He had sent the girl over to my place to see if money talked louder than words.

That had been a smart move on his part, but not smart enough. Had he known the real Queen Sue he wouldn't have wasted his time. Sure, I could probably supply much needed brains in his racket, but dope is one thing I don't touch, not even the racket angle of it.

Apparently the girl hadn't heard much about me, either. The kid figured I needed cash and would take anything she offered, gladly. Now when I asked for her name she snapped her purse shut and started to get up.

'Sit still,' I told her gently. 'There's nothing to get excited about. You've done your part, and you can't help it if I refuse the offer you've made. So now, just as one woman to another, let's have a little talk. Smoke?'

When we had cigarettes going she seemed to forget her nervousness. But she still watched me with sort of a sidewise glance as though she expected a couple of guns to appear around the corners of the rug and begin shooting. Perhaps she had heard something about me.

'Tell me your name,' I went on presently.

'Kate Travers,' she said softly.

'All right, Kate,' I continued. 'You know who I am, and now that we're acquainted I'm going to tell you something. You look like a nice sort of girl to be mixed up in this dope business. Just how—'

'Oh, I don't use it myself,' she broke in quickly.

'I didn't think so,' I responded, smiling faintly. 'You're just playing along with Suds for what you can get out of it. That right?'

Kate Travers nodded and dragged at her cigarette. I framed my next speech carefully.

'I'm going to tell you something, Kate. Maybe you know it already, and maybe you don't. It doesn't matter much. I just want you to know that I'm not the least bit interested in Suds Garland, personally or financially. Feel better now?'

'But you—'

'Sure,' I broke in swiftly. 'Suds and I teamed up against Buzz Mallon. That was business, but I didn't take a cent from Suds. Partners in a business arrangement aren't necessarily friends. Suds and I worked together to protect ourselves. But that's all over now.'

'Then you won't consider my proposition at all?'

I pitied the kid. She asked that question out of sheer ignorance. She was in the middle of something she didn't know a thing about, just acting as a cat's paw for Garland.

'No,' I answered, moving my head slowly from left to right. 'The proposition doesn't interest me. We're talking as friends now.'

'But what will I tell—'

She stopped suddenly and stared at the cigarette in her hand with frightened eyes. She knew she had said too much, but it was too late to take back her words.

'You've got an out, Kate,' I explained. 'A good out. Suds can't blame you if I won't agree to throw in with him. I'll put it in writing if you want me to. I don't want to get you into trouble.'

'Kind of you,' she murmured.

I paused a moment and during the brief silence I wondered why I was being so lenient with the kid. I should have tossed her out the minute she tried to bribe me to join Suds Garland's mob. But I didn't.

Perhaps I saw in her a vision of myself a few years ago – young, slightly innocent of certain phases of gang life, and a little fearful of everybody and everything. Well, I was still young, but no longer innocent. And I was entirely without fear of physical forces. I'd managed to take care of myself, had fought my way up to the top of a big mob, and had seen it crumble under me.

Now I was lone-wolfing it, freelancing in crime for what I could get out of it. But I wasn't taking part in a dope racket, and anything Suds Garland had to offer was connected with dope. I had the Club Bijou, and was making money. For the moment that was all I wanted.

Later, perhaps, I would start building another mob. If I could find the right men to work with I'd do that. But it was all in the future. The loss of Dan Reilly, Biff Brons and Blimp Sampson, who had died in my fight with the cops, was still too recent to raise my hopes of ever finding men who could take their places.

So while I looked at the pathetic, frightened figure of Kate Travers I felt sorry for her. I did the best I could, but it wasn't much. Her troubles were not mine. She was sitting in with Suds Garland and there was nothing I could do about it. But I told her something I thought she should know.

'I'll be frank with you, Kate,' I said finally. 'You've probably heard that Queen Sue, Sue Carlton, was the toughest mob leader that ever pulled a rod. Well, I am hard sometimes. You've got to be in this life. But there's a time and place for everything. So you've got nothing to worry about now. How long have you been with Suds?'

'Two weeks, but I've known him—'

'No matter about that, Kate,' I interrupted. I didn't want her life history. 'He expecting you back right away?'

'I'm seeing him tonight to give him your answer.'

'Fine. Now, I'll tell you what you do. Got a boy friend?'

Kate looked up, then nodded slowly. I went on.

'Well, run around and see him for awhile. I'll get in touch with Suds myself and deliver my message in person. Then when you see him tonight there won't be a chance for him to get sore at you. Okay?'

'That's awfully kind of you, Queen,' the girl said tremulously, 'but Suds said I'd have to arrange things with you or—'

'Don't worry about that. Suds won't have anything to say, won't do anything to you.' I smiled my assurance and she brightened. I honestly believed at that moment I was telling the truth. 'So just run along now. It's not quite three o'clock. Have dinner with the boy friend and I'll fix everything with Suds.'

After again thanking me, the kid moved to the door. I saw her to the elevator and then went back to my apartment and watched her leave the front entrance of the building a few minutes later. Suds should have known better than to pick a kid like her to talk to me about joining a racket.

When the kid passed out of sight along the street I turned away from the window, went over to the telephone, and called Suds Garland's number. There was no answer, so I made a mental note to call him later and dismissed the frightened little Kate Travers from my mind.

I had other work to do, what with managing a night club, arranging for liquor deliveries, entertainment, and a lot of other details and it wasn't until almost an hour later that I remembered I had to call Garland and arrange for a meeting with him.

I'd just lifted the receiver when the door-bell rang. I got up, moved across the room, opened the door and got a real surprise.

Standing in the doorway, his soft felt hat pushed back off his brow, was Sid Lang, the big detective from the District Attorney's office who had broken me as a mob leader. I hadn't seen him since that night in Cincinnati when I had trapped him in my room and had purchased my freedom by sparing his life.

Since then the indictments against me had been quashed. So I put a big smile on my face, knowing full well there was nothing to fear.

'Come in, Sid,' I said, not stopping to wonder why he was calling on me. 'Certainly is nice to see you again. How's the D. A. and all your flat-footed playmates?'

The broad face of Sid Lang didn't relax in a smile. His cold eyes held mine steadily as he stepped into the room. He kept his hands in plain sight so I didn't make any moves toward the gun on my right leg.

"Lo, Queen,' he said laconically when the door was closed. 'Heard the news?'

'The D. A. after me again?' I laughed.

'No. I'm not with the District Attorney's office any more. I'm working for an agency now – private dick.'

'Trying to drum up business with me?'

132

'Cut it, Queen!' he said sharply. 'I just heard something I thought you ought to know.'

'Nice of you, Sid,' I nodded, wiping the smile from my face. 'When did you start playing on my side of the fence?'

'Don't be funny,' he continued. 'A kid by the name of Kate Travers was gunned out awhile ago, a half dozen blocks from here.'

My heart stopped.

'I got it straight,' Sid Lang went on slowly, his voice sounding strangely hollow, 'that she left you a few minutes before she got it. She was running with Suds Garland's mob. I happen to know that he wants you to join up with him.'

Lang paused. I wasn't telling him anything, so I merely said, 'Yes?' and waited. A moment later Lang added:

'The cops found fifteen thousand in marked bills in her purse. I'm interested because Kate Travers was – my girl friend!'

CHAPTER II

CLEVER – BUT NOT ENOUGH

Red rage gripped me as I heard Sid Lang's words. For a moment I didn't think about him or his feelings. I saw only the clever plot that Suds Garland had tried to trap me with.

It was all plain enough now. Perhaps Garland had really wanted me to join his mob at first, but my refusal had angered him. So when I wouldn't change my mind he wanted me out of the way. Perhaps it wasn't just business that was on his mind, and in turning down his business proposition I had unconsciously insulted his amorous intentions.

Well, it was too late to worry about what had brought on all the trouble. Kate Travers was dead. But I saw his whole plan.

Not for a minute had Garland expected me to refuse the money that Kate had offered. He had taken it for granted that I had taken the money. Then he had the girl killed so I would get into a pile of trouble.

And trouble it would have been. The cops would have swarmed all over me, for Suds Garland would have tipped them quietly that I'd taken money from the kid and then had had her killed so it wouldn't become known that Queen Sue could be bought.

Yes, it might have worked out that way. Suds Garland had planned carefully. The only hitch in his plans had been the fact that Queen Sue is her own boss. I never sell out to the side with the most money.

In the midst of my thoughts I was suddenly brought back to the present. Sid Lang stepped in close to me and gripped me hard with a big hand on either shoulder.

'What d'you know about the kill, Queen?' he demanded, icy points of cold rage appearing in his blue eyes. 'Better talk fast because I'm going—'

'You're going to do – nothing!' I snapped.

'I'm going to kill you just as sure as I'm standing here! You put Kate on the spot and—'

My harsh laugh brought back his common sense. Looking him in the eye, every muscle in my small body steeled against the pain of that iron grip on my shoulders, I gave him glare for glare. Physically I didn't have a chance against him, but I won that silent clash of wills.

'Sorry, Queen,' he muttered brokenly a moment later, taking his hands from my shoulders and flopping into a chair. 'I guess I – lost my head.'

'Forget it, Sid,' I said quietly. 'We all think we're pretty tough until something comes along that hits right at our hearts.'

He nodded slowly. 'Kate meant a lot to me. You wouldn't know how much.'

A bitter smile curled my lips. In a low voice I said:

'I know exactly how you feel. Remember Chick Wilson and Dan Reilly? Well, you can't tell me a thing about sorrow. I've been there myself. You're just getting a dose of what I felt when you helped gun out Dan and Blimp and—'

'But I had to do—'

'Sure,' I broke in quickly. 'There was nothing personal in it. I know that. You just happened to be on the side of the law. I wasn't. If it would have done me any good I'd have killed you long before this. But that wouldn't bring Dan or Chick back. Neither will killing me give Kate a new lease on life. How did she happen to tie up with Suds?'

'Don't know – unless it was the money in it. We were going to be married as soon as I got enough money saved. But you don't put aside much in my work and—'

'Yes, she was just the type that would try to help her man. I'd have done the same myself. She probably thought she could step out of it after she'd made a couple of thousand. What did you let her do it for?'

'I couldn't stop her, Queen. She was in with Suds before I knew it. Then when I found out about it I didn't know how to go about telling her that she was making a mistake. You see—'

'Of course I see,' I answered in a tired voice. 'You men are all the same; great big stone brutes who can lick their weight in wildcats, but you're afraid of a little woman who might get angry with you. Kate didn't know what it was all about – didn't realize what she was doing. Listen.'

I told Sid Lang how the kid had tried to buy me. That part of it I told quickly so he wouldn't get another idea that I'd had anything to do with the killing. Then I explained what had been behind her murder.

When I finished, Sid Lang took off his hat, ran broad fingers through his thin blonde hair, and looked at me with bleak eyes.

'God only knows why, Queen, but I believe you. See you later.'

He got up and moved quickly toward the door. But I was quicker. 'Calm down, bright guy,' I ordered, turning the key in the lock and slipping the piece of metal down the neck of my dress. 'You're not leaving here until you cool off.'

'Give me that key before—'

He never finished that sentence. As his big hands reached for me again I sidestepped away from in front of the door. At the same instant my right hand shot under the hem of my dress and came out with my gun in my fingers.

'Back up, Sid!' I snapped. 'You're not such a bad guy for being a dick, and you're not going to make a damned fool of yourself. Sit down – before I send you to the hospital with a slug in your leg. You'll be safe there.'

For a moment I thought my argument wasn't going to work. I've never seen a guy with more nerve than Sid Lang has, but he knew I meant every word I said. He'd learned by experience that Queen Sue doesn't bluff.

When he was seated in the chair again I gave him some advice.

'I didn't want to do this, Sid, but I had to. You don't mean a thing in my young life, but listen anyway. If anything happens to Suds Garland now, the cops will come looking for you. You aren't on the force now. You're just an agency man – a private dick. And you might end up in the electric chair. Get it?'

He got it all right, but he didn't nod immediately. Behind his cold eyes I could see that his brain was working again.

'That's fine,' I continued. 'Perhaps in a way I was partly responsible for what happened to Kate, but you can't go around shooting a guy just because you know he's guilty of a dirty trick. You've got to have proof.'

'I'll get it, and then I'll—'

'You listen to me! Get yourself a good alibi and sit tight. Remember, the cops will look you up if anything happens to Suds Garland.'

'You mean you are going to—' Lang half rose to his feet in his eagerness.

'Sit down, Sid. That's better. I'm saying nothing about what I'm going to do or not going to do. I'm just giving you some good pointers. You happen to be a dick and I happen to be – well, a gang girl. We've always been enemies, but we're calling a truce for the next few days or weeks.'

'I guess we are,' nodded Lang resignedly. 'But I'm not letting you fight my battles. I see the point in what you've been talking about, and I'll take it easy. Think I'll go now.'

There was no use of talking to him any longer, so I went over, unlocked the door, and then stepped aside as I put my gun back on my leg. Sid Lang paused at the threshold and looked down at me with a faint smile.

'Thanks, Queen, for not letting me go off half-cocked,' he said quietly. 'I'll remember that.'

Yes, he would remember that I'd done him a favor, but he didn't fool me. I knew as well as though he'd told me in so many words that he was going to kill Suds Garland, regardless of what I had said. And after I'd closed the door behind him I did some fast brain work.

Then a few minutes later I stepped to the telephone and called Suds Garland's number again. This time I got him on the wire. After that I didn't waste time.

'Don't ask who's calling,' I said quickly. 'this is just a friendly tip. You're on the spot!'

Before Suds could say a word I hung up. He had been clever in trying to frame me for the killing of Kate Travers, but not clever enough to outwit Queen Sue. My telephone message would give him something to worry about.

CHAPTER III

Straight Talk

Don't get the idea I was playing stoolie for anybody. No, nothing like that. I just didn't like the way things were shaping up.

There was a lot more to this whole business than surface indications showed. In the first place, Sid Lang's explanation of how Kate Travers happened to be in with Suds Garland's mob was very weak. But right at the moment I wasn't arguing the point.

My best bet was to play a waiting game, and I did just that. With Sid Lang thinking that I believed his story I figured something would break. Of course, I was taking a big chance that I wouldn't get in a jam, but I can usually take care of myself.

So far as Lang wanting to kill Suds Garland was concerned, I knew it was true. Garland had gunned out the girl and ought to pay for it. But for no reason at all both Garland and Sid Lang were trying to get me into the fight.

That's why I tipped Garland that he was on the spot. I didn't want anything happening to him until I found out just why and how I figured in his plans. I knew something would happen if I let things run their course. And it happened, but not as I'd expected.

I was sitting in my private office at the Club Bijou two nights later when there was the sound of scuffling outside my door. It was long past midnight and with a big crowd in the dining room I thought it was just a couple of drunks who'd found their way back into the corridor that led past my office.

A moment later I discovered what it was all about. The door opened and Francis, my head waiter, and one of the bouncers dragged in a small man who was sniveling and begging for mercy. I took one look at the three of them, then got up and closed the door behind them, locking it.

'What's up, Francis?' I demanded, frowning at the little man who suddenly became silent when he saw me.

Francis was nothing like his name sounded. He was more than two hundred pounds of bone and muscle packed into six feet of height. In the dining room, bowing and smiling to the patrons of the club, he looked and spoke like a gentleman. Out of character, he was the best muscle man I had.

So when I asked that question Francis scowled, jerked the little man around in front of him and snapped:

'Caught this guy peddling dope – snowbird himself.'

I took a moment to think that over. The Club Bijou is on the lower East Side and in that district nobody but Suds Garland sells the stuff that makes old men out of younger men quicker than anything else in the world. So I figured this was another of Garland's bright ideas.

'What's your name, buddy?' I asked.

The little man cringed and looked up at Francis and the bouncer like a whipped dog. Then he babbled:

'I ain't done nothing! These birds just framed me—'

'Search him,' I ordered, not wanting to hear his sob story.

'Already did it, Queen,' replied Francis. 'Here's what he had left.'

He took a number of small folded papers from a side pocket of his tuxedo jacket and tossed them on my desk. I gave them only a glance and then looked back at the little man.

'So they framed you, eh?' I said quietly.

The little man nodded vigorously.

'Like to sniff a deck? Fix you up – steady your nerves,' I continued, and almost smiled at the little man's reaction.

He looked at the folded papers on the desk, licked his lips with a nervous tongue, and frowned with indecision. He didn't know whether I was kidding him or not. I didn't wait for him to make up his mind.

'Sock him once, Francis,' I instructed, 'and toss the rat out into the alley. He won't come back.'

Francis and the bouncer dragged the little guy out before he could squeal. A few minutes later I picked up the bindles of coke, went into the ladies' room, and washed them down a toilet. Then I went out to the main room and looked over the crowd.

Had the guy really been peddling the stuff in the club, or was he just

137

trying to hide it? I didn't know, but I wouldn't have been surprised if Suds Garland had made a plant and then tipped the narcotic agents to raid me.

But there was nothing to gain by trying to figure things out by mere headwork. Francis had spotted the fellow before he could do any harm. So I dismissed the incident from my mind and sat down at one of the tables with some friends.

An hour later I was still there, laughing and chatting after the floor show had played its last turn of the night, when Francis gave me the high sign from the side of the room. I excused myself and went over to him.

'Suds Garland just went back to your office,' he whispered rapidly. 'I couldn't stop him without raising a row and that would have been bad for business.'

'Anybody with him?' I inquired. Things were beginning to move faster. I like speed.

'Two bodyguards. What'll I do?'

'Get a couple of the boys and hang around the corridor. No gunplay unless I give the word. Don't want to ruin business. See?'

Francis nodded and I started to move toward the corridor that led to my office in the rear of the building. I'd taken two steps when Francis caught me by the arm.

'Where are you going?'

'To my office,' I answered quietly. 'Any objections?'

'No – but I don't want you to get hurt.'

I smiled. 'Thanks, Francis. Save your sympathy for Suds.'

With that I moved on. It seemed like old times again to have somebody worrying about my safety. But it wasn't unusual. I pride myself on picking men who are loyal to me through thick and thin. And Francis was proving me right.

Once out of sight of the crowd in the main room I got the gun from the holster on my leg. Then with the comforting feel of steel in my palm I moved quickly down the corridor.

At the door of my office I paused for a moment and listened. Little sounds of movement came from the room, but there was no talking. Suds was apparently looking over the place before he settled down to wait for me. I didn't give him time to get impatient.

Turning the knob with my left hand, I opened the door a few inches, and slipped silently into the room. The next moment I had the door closed again, my gun up at my hip, and my back to the wall.

'Looking for me, Suds?'

The three men whirled at the sound of my voice. At the moment I had entered the room they had been crowded around my desk with their backs to the door.

None of them had their guns out. But as I spoke one of the bodyguards, a young fellow with a smooth, beardless face, raised his right hand toward an armpit holster.

'I wouldn't!' I snapped, and the youngster froze.

'What's the meaning of this?' demanded Suds.

I narrowed my eyes slightly while I smiled at his weak attempt to bluff my play. His tall, thin body was stooped in a half-crouch as though he was going to leap across the room at me. His black eyes were expressionless, but the sight of my gun had caused the blood to drain from his ruddy face, leaving his skin the color of dirty milk.

'Sit down, all of you,' I ordered. 'You, Garland, squat at the desk, hands on the glass where I can see them. Snap into it!'

Suds Garland didn't argue. He seated himself in the chair in front of the desk and flattened his hands, palm downward, on the top like I'd ordered. The two bodyguards flopped into a couple of chairs along the wall at the right of the desk.

'Hands on your knees – and keep them there!' I continued.

They didn't need to be told twice. My smile broadened as I looked at each of the three men for a moment in silence. Then abruptly I wiped the smile from my face, bent slightly, replaced my gun in the holster on my leg, and then straightened.

'Think you're pretty tough, eh?' I sneered as the three held their poses. 'Dealing with a woman is usually soft pickings for hard guys like you. Well, here's your chance to prove how tough you are. Reach for your gats!'

For perhaps all of ten seconds none of the three men moved a muscle. Maybe they knew I wasn't bluffing when I put my gat back on my leg. I knew I could beat them to the draw and none of them wanted to take the chance. Where I only had inches to move my hand they had feet, and covering distance in split seconds counts on the draw.

Finally Suds Garland shifted his eyes to the men along the wall and shook his head slightly. I laughed harshly.

'Bright guy, Suds,' I snorted. 'Telling the boys not to draw when they've already made up their minds to be good. I guess my reputation isn't so bad!'

Suds spread his lips in a sickly smile. 'We're just making a friendly call, Queen. You beat up Johnny's brother and—'

'Who's Johnny?' I wanted to know.

Garland nodded toward the beardless fellow who looked like a kid alongside the other muscle man who had a scarred lip and a broken nose.

'Okay,' I said. 'Go on with your song and dance.'

'Well, you beat up Johnny's brother and – well, I just wanted to know what the idea was,' Suds finished lamely.

'And I'll tell you,' I returned in a harsh voice. 'Dope peddling – or planting – is out at the Club Bijou. Get that straight! The next time I catch one of your punks around here you pick him up at the morgue. See?'

'But, Queen, I thought we were friends?' whined Garland.

*

For a moment I didn't know whether to laugh or call Francis and the boys and have the three of them thrown out. But I did neither. I just nodded slowly.

'I'm going to talk straight,' I said quietly. 'I think I was right when I guessed that you thought you were going to have an easy time fighting a woman. Now, I'm going to tell you something, Suds, and your two trained seals can listen in for future reference.'

I paused a moment, but Garland had nothing to say. So I went on.

'A month ago when we were both fighting Buzz Mallon we played ball together. But if you got the idea we were friends you were mistaken. I told you then I didn't like dope and wouldn't join your racket. You, Suds, came into power after the cops wrecked my old mob and I had to leave town. You only know Queen Sue from what you've heard about her. If you were bright, you'd have learned something from what I did to Mallon.'

'Didn't I help you get rid of Mallon?' Suds asked in a thin voice.

'You did, but I also helped you and that squared our account,' I shot back quickly. 'And from now on you'd better watch your step, or you'll think Mallon had an easy time of it. Maybe I'm not running a big mob like I used to, but I'm still Queen Sue. That's not boasting. That's a fact. Remember it.'

'Ah, you're just nervous about something, Queen,' shrugged Garland.

'Not half as nervous as you,' I pointed out, smiling at the way Suds and his henchmen were holding the pose I'd given them. 'You're walking out of here like good little boys, unless you want a skinful of lead. Move!'

The three of them got slowly to their feet. Keeping their arms at the sides they moved slowly towards the door. I backed off to one side, kept my back to the wall, ready for anything. But nothing happened that time.

Suds paused at the door and the other two crowded around him.

'Sorry we can't be friends, Queen,' he said.

'I'm not,' I replied. 'Just because you had an easy time of rubbing out one woman you don't have to think all of them are that easy. And don't try to plant any more kills on me.'

Suds arched thin eyebrows in feigned surprise. 'Me – tried to plant a kill?'

I laughed again. 'Forget it, Suds. It didn't work. But don't make the same mistake twice. By the way, better get a couple of guys with nerve. Bodyguards that let a woman bluff them don't amount to much.'

Garland didn't reply to my taunt. He swung open the door and ran smack into Francis in the corridor. The other two crowded out after him and I smiled at my head waiter who looked at me for instructions.

'Take them out the front way,' I said. 'Just a little friendly call, but give them the works if there's any funny business. Scram.'

Suds gave me a parting glare. My little talk hadn't accomplished much, but I knew it would serve to bring matters to a head. And it did, even sooner than I expected.

CHAPTER IV

Foolish Business

Dawn was breaking when I finally left the night club. I hadn't given Suds Garland and his mob a second thought since I'd seen him go down the corridor with Francis and the boys.

There had been no trouble at all about their leaving. But the moment I stepped out of the Club Bijou into the first faint light of a new day I had the uneasy feeling that something was going to happen. Perhaps it was just the eery half-light between night and day that affected me that way, but I was taking no chances.

A slight fog had settled over the city and now hung in shifting ribbons that swirled along the street like ghosts hurrying to escape the rising sun. I noticed those little details unconsciously because I wasn't interested in the beauties of a new day at the moment.

Across the pavement from the entrance of the club a cab waited. There was nothing unusual in that because the doorman or Francis always ordered a cab for me when I left in the morning, and any cab they ordered was safe.

So with scarcely a glance to either side I walked across the sidewalk and stepped into the cab. Then just as I seated myself I caught a glimpse of moving figures in the fog beyond the entrance of the club.

Before I could say a word the doorman, who was on duty late that morning, slammed the door and the driver let in the clutch. The figures in the fog grew plainer as they approached the cab, heads down, hands sunk deep in the side pockets of their coats.

I didn't wait to see more. The cab started to move as I opened the door on the far side and stepped out into the street. Shielded by the slowly moving cab from the figures on the sidewalk, I slipped across the street and was partly concealed by the fog.

I hadn't acted too soon, for as I reached the opposite curb guns crashed across the street. A man cursed, and the cab stopped with a sudden squeal of brakes. I counted five quick shots. Then the slap of running feet on pavement came to me.

Straining my ears to keep the running men within earshot, I started along the street after them. A moment later the fog parted and I got a brief view of two men. Instantly my gun was in my hand, but even as I raised it the fog closed in again and the men were lost in the half-light.

Then as I started to cross the street again I heard the low purr of a powerful motor behind me. At the same time there was a chorus of shouts from the Club Bijou as Francis and some of the late diners and drinkers piled out on the street.

Almost before I knew it a long sedan slid past me in the fog and swung in toward the curb. The sound of running stopped.

Thinking fast, I sprinted across the few yards that separated me from the big car and swung up on the trunk rack that jutted out over the gas tank in the rear as the car gathered speed.

Minutes passed while the car swung around several corners, putting plenty of distance between it and the Club Bijou. I had all I could do to keep my balance on my precarious perch during the first few moments of that ride, but finally the car settled down to a steady run.

A few minutes later the protecting wisps of fog became thinner and finally vanished. But the hour was early and the few persons that were on the street didn't give me a look.

Then after about ten minutes of fast riding the car slowed down and slid in alongside the curb on one of the side streets uptown. I watched my chance and slipped off the trunk rack just before the car stopped.

I'd just gained the shelter of the doorway of a small apartment house when a rear door of the car opened and two men hit the sidewalk, moving fast. I raised my gun, then changed my mind.

They thought they'd got me in the taxicab. It wouldn't hurt anything to let them continue to think that for awhile.

The house before which the car had stopped was a two story brick structure. The first floor was vacant, so I figured the boys were to meet Suds Garland on the second floor. He had lost no time in repaying the courtesy I'd shown him at the Club Bijou.

But I couldn't tip my hand in broad daylight with no means for a getaway. So I put my gun back on my leg and watched the men go into the house. A moment later the car pulled away from the curb and disappeared around the next corner.

Five minutes later I was walking fast across town. I'd recognized one of the men who had tried to get me as the young fellow who'd been with Garland, but after being up all night I needed sleep more than anything else. I was going to have a lot of work to do that night.

Presently I caught a cab and twenty minutes later I was at my apartment. I had the driver wait for me while I packed a bag, and then went up to a hotel in the theatrical district.

It was almost three o'clock in the afternoon when I got up, bathed, dressed, and had breakfast sent up to my room. Then I phoned Francis at his apartment.

'God, Queen!' he exclaimed when he heard my voice. 'I thought they'd taken you for a ride.'

'Almost did,' I admitted, 'but I'm still alive and kicking. Get a couple of the boys and meet me at the club at five-thirty sharp. I've got work for you.'

Well, that was that, I thought while I ate breakfast and then took a cab across town to Simon Grundish's office. I was going to need some airtight protection, and perhaps an alibi, and Grundish was the man who could fix it for me.

The political power behind the throne at City Hall didn't keep me waiting. He met me at the door of his private office right after I'd sent in my name. His wizened face and pale eyes seemed almost joyful when I greeted him and closed the door.

'What have you been up to now?' he asked quietly, knowing that I didn't waste time with social visits during business hours.

'Nothing much,' I smiled. 'Suds Garland tried to gun me out this morning. That was foolish business on his part. Understand?'

'I think I do,' returned the little old man who had been instrumental in seeing that the old indictments against me had been dismissed. 'Remember what I told you about Garland a month ago? Well, I still think he's bad company. It won't be any great loss if he—'

'Think you can fix it for me if there's a flareback after I get done with him?'

Grundish frowned for a moment, then nodded.

'Good,' I smiled. 'Seems like a lady can't even run a night club around this city any more without having some guy think he owns her. I don't like it. I think I'll have to branch out into something bigger just to keep the small timers away from me.'

'Suds Garland isn't a small timer.'

'No, and he's not so big, either. He thinks he's tough just because he makes a lot of money out of the racket. Maybe he was tough once, but money and good living have made him soft. It's ruined more than one good man, and dope doesn't draw good men.'

'Well, Queen,' Grundish shrugged, 'you branch out any way you want to. I'd be careful of Garland, though.'

'From now on I'm going to be,' I admitted. 'Just pass the word along to the cops that I know nothing about the dope business. See?'

Grundish smiled his thin smile which was as near as he ever came to genuine mirth. I left him a few minutes after that, knowing that even if some bright cop did want to ask questions he wouldn't get far. Grundish would see to that.

It was almost five-thirty when I reached the Club Bijou. Francis and four of the bouncers at the club were already there, waiting for me to give them the office. I did, starting first with the address of the house where the two men from the car had holed up.

'Drop out there after it gets dark,' I ordered, 'and smoke the boys out. It's a fairly quiet neighborhood so don't make too much noise.'

'Leave it to us, Queen,' promised Francis. 'Anything else?'

'I think that will be enough for one night,' I replied, and didn't smile when I said it. That business wasn't any joking matter, but I knew those two punks would never squeeze another trigger.

And they didn't. Francis and the boys returned to the club around ten o'clock that night. I listened quietly while Francis told me how they'd trapped the pair in the upper apartment. Maxim-silenced guns had done the rest.

I figured that incident would make Suds Garland think twice before he tried any more funny stuff with me. The killing of Kate Travers had ceased to be of importance in my mind, because to me the quarrel with Suds Garland was nothing but a personal grudge fight.

So I paid off on that job and when the club opened for business at midnight Francis and the boys were on deck as usual.

Everything went along quietly that night for the first hour or so, and then in the midst of the floor show, shortly after one-thirty, Suds Garland pulled the most foolish stunt of his career.

I was standing at the doorway of the corridor that led back to my office when it happened. The orchestra was playing a snappy little number and the chorus was cavorting across the floor when suddenly there was a stunning roar of an explosion.

Instantly the lights went out. Glass crashed at the front of the club and was lost in the crescendo of splintered wood, hurtling bricks and falling plaster. One guess was enough to know what had happened.

Suds Garland's mob had tossed a pineapple into the entrance hall!

CHAPTER V

The Queen Acts

Fighting my way blindly through the darkness and the crush of the mob that tried to rush the front entrance, I finally gained the main door. By that time tiny flames were crackling in the wreckage of what had been a hall, and were gaining headway fast.

The crowd of diners and dancers didn't get far. The whole front corridor was a shambles. Then over the shouts of the crowd sounded the bellowing voice of Francis, directing them to the rear corridor which led to an alley in the back.

With one accord the crowd rushed the narrow hall. It didn't take five minutes for them to jam themselves out of the main room. By that time I'd found a fire extinguisher in the darkness and was trying vainly to stem the tide of the flames.

Francis and some of the boys were lighting the place as best they could with flashlights. Other waiters were working more fire extinguishers and making no progress. Then suddenly in the distance I heard the clang of fire bells and the wail of police sirens.

'No talking boys,' I ordered, shouting to make myself heard. 'I'll deal with the cops.'

A chorus of agreement came to me out of the semi-darkness of what a few minutes before had been a brilliantly lighted spot of night life. I thought of the checkroom girl and wondered whether any guests had been caught by the blast.

For the first few minutes the battalion chief and the sergeant in charge of the emergency squad of cops had their hands full with the fire and the crowds that gathered in the street. Then when the flames were under control both the chief and the sergeant looked me up.

'Well, young lady,' began the grizzled fire fighter, 'what have you got to say for yourself?'

'Who tossed the bomb?' shot in the sergeant, another veteran of bulldozing tactics which were usually effective.

'One at a time,' I said quietly. 'Suppose we go back to my office. It's still in one piece.'

When I had a cigarette going in the back room and had rubbed most of the sweat and grime from my face and hands, I looked the two men in the eyes. They'd been firing questions at me continually, but they hadn't been able to break down my pose of ignorance.

'Listen,' I said finally. 'If I knew who did this, I'd tell you. Right at the moment this night club happens to be my only means of making a living. It's going to cost money to make repairs, but that's my worry. That's all I know. The blast get anybody?'

The two men exchanged a quick glance. Then the sergeant cleared his throat and said:

'Killed the checkroom girl and injured a man. That's all we've found so far.'

'Who was the man?'

Why I asked that question, I don't know. Right at the minute I really wasn't interested in who the man might be, but the question popped out before I could stop it. A moment later I was glad I'd asked.

'The man was a private detective,' said the sergeant. 'Name of Sid Lang.'

I didn't move a muscle as I heard those words, but my brain was

145

working hard. What had Sid Lang been doing at the Club Bijou? Had he suspected that I'd had the two men, Suds Garland's bodyguards, rubbed out? I didn't know.

So I kept my face expressionless while I said:

'That's tough. Tell the guy I'll stand good for his hospital expenses and those of anybody else who was hurt. I don't want to have it said that Queen Sue doesn't take care of her friends. Tough about the checkroom girl. She was a nice kid.'

'And you don't have any idea of who might have tossed that bomb?' persisted the battalion chief.

'None at all. You might scout around and see whether any of the neighbors saw anybody they'd recognize just before it happened. I wasn't paying anybody protection and wasn't asked to. I just don't know who might have wanted to ruin my business.'

'That's a lie, Queen Sue!'

I opened my mouth to deny that accusation, but I didn't speak. The voice had sounded strangely familiar, but had not come from the sergeant or the fire chief. Suddenly I caught my breath as I looked past them.

Swaying in the doorway, big hands braced doggedly against the jambs, his head swathed in bloody bandages, was Sid Lang!

'What are you doing here?' demanded the sergeant. 'You ought to be—'

'That's – all right,' gasped Lang, waving the sergeant's objections down while he crossed the room unsteadily and stopped in front of me.

For a moment none of us spoke. Hovering outside the door, I could see the dim form of Francis. Then I looked up and met Sid Lang's boring gaze.

'Get out you,' mumbled Lang. 'I want to talk – to the girl – alone.'

Slowly the two older men moved to the door and closed it after them. In the light of the flash that was propped up on one corner of the desk Lang's blood-streaked face was ghastly. I expected him to collapse any moment, but when I placed a chair for him he merely shook his head and remained standing.

'Sorry, Queen,' he said slowly with a great effort, his voice nothing but a hollow whisper. 'Didn't mean – to spoil your play.'

'You didn't,' I assured him. 'You ought to be in the hospital.'

'Going there – soon.' He paused, laboring for breath. Finally he went on. 'Listen, Queen. I'm out of this – for awhile. I'm going to tell you something. I didn't give it to you straight – on Kate Travers.'

'I know you didn't,' I responded. 'Come clean this time.'

'Yes, do that. Kate was an undercover agent. Wasn't working for the agency – just for me. She thought she could get more than I could. I told you straight about – what she meant to me. I'm hired to bust Suds for

some rich guy. Garland made a snowbird out of his son. And so far Suds
has made a bum – out of you. Get it?'

'Better rest up in the hospital,' I said quietly. 'You're off your head.'

'Want me to – tip your play to the cops?'

'Spill and be damned!' I snapped. 'I'm taking orders from no dick – not
even a private flattie! Beat it!'

My heart stopped as Sid Lang turned slowly, laboriously toward the
door. I wasn't fighting his battles, and he knew it. He had hoped to enlist
my aid against Garland by giving me the straight story on Kate Travers.

Perhaps under ordinary circumstances I might have been impressed. As
it was, I was fighting my own battles. I had a lot to settle with Suds
Garland and his dope racket, but I wasn't giving Sid Lang any definite
indication of what I was going to do to Garland. After all, Sid Lang was on
the side of the law. I wasn't.

I'd played a lone hand this far, but as Lang started towards the door I
thought sure he was going to spoil my play. Then I sighed with relief as he
opened the door and said:

'I was wrong, sarge. The girl's okay. God – I'm tired.'

As he finished speaking in a hoarse whisper, Sid Lang stumbled. Only
the strong arms of the sergeant and the battalion chief kept him from
crashing to the floor. Instantly I was at his side.

He opened his eyes for a moment. A faint smile wreathed his pallid lips
as he looked up at me. Then he relaxed and lay still.

'Just fainted,' grunted the sergeant. 'Hey, somebody! Give us a light!'

I caught up the flash from the desk and led the way down the corridor to
the alley. Silently I paid tribute to the sheer nerve that had kept Sid Lang
on his feet until he had set me straight on the Kate Travers business.
Perhaps that was what he had come to the club to do in the first place. It
didn't make much difference now.

When Lang had been carted away in an ambulance the sergeant turned
to me.

'A real man, that one,' he said with genuine admiration. 'He did great
work while he was with the D. A.'s office.'

'I know it,' I said softly, and let it go at that.

The sergeant looked at me hard for a moment. Then he nodded.

'I guess you do,' he agreed, remembering how Sid Lang had smashed
my old mob. Then he added, 'Well, I'll leave a police guard here, young
lady, till morning. If you hear anything about who did this, let us know.'

Thanking him quickly, I made my way back into the club and found
Francis. By some strange means he had managed to avoid ruffling even a
hair of his shiny head, and his dinner clothes were still as immaculate as
though he had just come on duty. That suited me fine.

I'd been doing a lot of headwork in the spare moments I'd had between arguing with the sergeant and the battalion chief. I meant to pay my debt to Suds Garland in no uncertain way, but first I was going to play havoc with certain parts of his racket. So I gave Francis his instructions quickly.

'Get four or five of the boys who are still presentable. I'll meet you a couple of blocks away, corner of Severn and Leistner, in twenty minutes. We've got a lot to do, so make it fast.'

Watching my chance, I slipped out the back way again. A few minutes later I was at an all night garage, renting a sedan. I drove the car myself and picked up Francis and the boys right on schedule.

During the time Suds and I had been fighting Buzz Mallon, Suds had made the mistake of showing me what he called 'spots of gold.' In reality they were nothing but high-class apartments in the swankier districts of town where those who could afford to pay plenty were privileged to indulge their dope habits unmolested.

Suds furnished protection for the places and maintained them for his high class clientele. I meant to smash at least three of the places that I knew existed.

Perhaps this bit of sabotage sounds like a childish prank, but it wasn't. Suds had struck at my pocket-book through bombing the Club Bijou. I meant to cut into his bankroll by smashing his expensive joints. Loss of money in a racket hurts worse than having a couple of punk gunmen killed.

So when I picked up Francis and the boys I explained the situation to them rapidly. They were all for the idea immediately and were in high spirits as I started uptown.

For my part, I wasn't exactly light-hearted. Anything can happen when you start out on a job like that, and right at the moment I didn't want anything to happen to me before I got to see Suds Garland personally.

He had a lot to answer for, and I meant to make him do it. Still, I've never been able to send my men into a place that was too tight for me to go myself. And I always lead the way when there's work to be done.

This time was no exception. When I pulled up at the corner above a tall apartment house twenty minutes later I cautioned the boys to go easy with the gats, and then piled out of the car.

Francis had a gun equipped with a silencer so I had him follow close behind me while we walked down to the entrance of the building, a half block away. The four other men paired off behind us.

Only one mug was on duty in the lobby. I gave him a bright smile as I walked towards the elevators, and then as I passed him I turned quickly, slipped out my gun, and jammed it against his back.

'Quiet!' I warned, and the guy wilted. Suds didn't seem to have luck in picking gunmen.

Francis pushed the signal bell at the elevator and a moment later the car stopped at the ground floor. It was one of those automatic affairs and it crowded us considerably as we all piled into it. I didn't take my gun from the mug's back for a moment.

On the way up to the tenth floor Francis relieved the guy of his rod and turned him over to the boys. Then as the elevator stopped, Francis and I stepped out while the rest of the boys held back. So long as the door was open the elevator couldn't be called to any other floor.

Walking towards the rear of the building, we didn't see anybody in the corridor. When I came to the door of apartment 1014 I pushed a bell button.

Almost immediately the door opened. Francis jammed his foot in the opening and followed it with a massive shoulder as he dug his gun into the belly of a guy with a long, thin face. After that there was no trouble at all.

I signaled the boys in the elevator and they came trooping back to the apartment. Half a dozen couples and two unattached men were lounging around the lavishly furnished rooms in various stages of helplessness. There had been a larger crowd earlier in the evening, I knew, because of the heavy reek of opium smoke that was still in the air.

We had a little trouble herding the people into one of the back rooms with the guards. Two of the women had to be carried, but after that the boys had the place to themselves. In less than ten minutes it was one sweet wreck. Then we left.

We visited the other two places before we called it a night. At the third one Francis had to put a bullet through one guard's belly before he'd listen to reason, but there was no other trouble. Then I felt better.

Back in the car again, I told the boys to call at my hotel the next day for their pay, and then promised them a vacation while the Club Bijou was being remodeled. I let them out at one of the better hot spots, and then returned the car to the garage.

It was only a few minutes past three when I left the garage. I had intended to return to the hotel and catch up on some sleep, but after I'd caught a cab I decided to drop around to my apartment and get another dress. Crawling through that wreckage hadn't helped the looks of my evening gown much.

After that bit of work I figured Suds Garland would be plenty busy for a few hours, listening to the stories his guards would tell. I didn't know then that he still had another card up his sleeve.

I'd been dragging on a cigarette, very much pleased with myself, but when the cab came in sight of my apartment house I got a shock. Several cars were parked along the curb and a large crowd was gathered around the entrance of the building.

A crowd at that time of night meant just one thing. The cops were staging a raid, and something told me they were looking for me.

149

CHAPTER VI

In The Bag

Quickly I leaned forward in the seat, rapped on the glass partition, and told the driver to swing around the next corner and stop. While he followed those instructions I did some fast headwork.

By the time the cab halted alongside the curb I'd decided to see for myself what all the excitement was about. So I paid the driver and let him go. Then I started down the street towards the crowd.

If the cops were looking for me, I knew it wouldn't be a bad idea to find out what I was wanted for before they found me. There was enough of a crowd in the street to give me a chance to look around and ask some questions without being too conspicuous. And that's just what I did.

At first I tried to piece together the comments of the spectators that I overheard, but except for a lot of excited chatter about nothing in particular nobody was volunteering real information. Finally I moved in beside a man at the edge of the crowd.

'What happened, buddy?' I inquired, smiling my sweetest. 'Raid a disorderly house?'

The man smiled at my sally. Then he became very blasé.

'Maybe that's what it is,' he answered. 'There's nothing to see here. I'm going home and get some sleep.'

I was all set to crack wise at him when suddenly I felt a hand close over my left arm. Turning my head, I looked into the pale eyes of Simon Grundish. So I didn't say a word, just responded to the pressure on my arm and followed him down the street, away from the crowd.

When we were alone he took his hand from my arm. Grundish wasn't much of a night owl, and at his age when he was on the street at that hour I knew it was serious. But I waited for him to open the conversation.

'I just heard about it, Queen,' he said a moment later, 'and came right down to see what I could do. Lucky I found you.'

'Yes, it is lucky,' I admitted, 'but I don't know what it's all about. What do the cops want me for now?'

'You don't know?'

'I don't. I just arrived before you found me.'

'Well, Queen, this is pretty serious. The men who raided your place were Federal narcot agents.'

'What!' I stopped and looked hard at Grundish.

'That's right, Queen,' he continued. 'They found a large quantity of dope – cocaine, I think it was – in your apartment. We're going to have a devil of a time beating the rap on that charge. I'll do what I can, but I can't promise—'

150

'Jeeze, what a lousy break that is!' I interrupted. 'Snowbound, and no way of explaining that dope in my apartment!'

'No way at all that I know of. Looks like Suds Garland has played his ace.'

'Yeah, but I'll beat the rap.' I said that impulsively, not having the faintest idea of how I was going to do it. Then I got an idea. 'Let's walk.'

We walked, and I did some hard thinking. Presently I thought I had things doped out enough to give Grundish my idea.

'Listen,' I began, speaking slowly in a low voice, 'remember Sid Lang, the big detective who used to work for the district attorney? You know, the guy who smashed my liquor mob.'

'Yes, I know who you mean. I don't think I ever met him, but—'

'Well, you're going to meet him. He's in the Mercy Hospital with a cracked head. That blast at the club caught him – killed my checkroom girl at the same time. He's a private dick now and has been working quietly on breaking Suds Garland's racket.'

'Did he put the Federal agents on you?'

I shook my head. 'No, nothing like that. Suds thinks he's clever, but he isn't. He planted that dope in my place – not Lang – and then passed along the tip for the raid. Remember the girl who was killed several days ago shortly after leaving my place?'

Grundish nodded.

'Well,' I continued, 'she was Sid Lang's sweetheart. That's something he's got to settle with Suds himself. So I want you to see Lang as early as you can. Explain the situation to him. Tell him I'm going to do him a favor and expect one in return.'

'But what can he do that I can't, Queen?'

'Just this. He's been on the prod against this dope racket. He knows who's at the head of it and probably was all set to make the pinch when he got smacked by that blast. I could use his testimony if the Feds get me and bring me to trial. See?'

'Bright idea, Queen,' said Grundish admiringly. 'I could probably fix the case, but it would take time and might cause a lot of questions to be asked. It isn't as though it were merely a liquor charge.'

'Okay, then. You do that for me. Also see my lawyer and send him around to the hotel later today. You might drop around yourself and tell me what Sid Lang says. I think he'll come through. He's a pretty white guy for a dick. And thanks a lot for showing up when I needed you most. See you later.'

'Where are you going now?'

'Me?' I put on a good act of being surprised. Then I smiled slightly and added, 'I'm getting under cover where it's safe.'

'Do that,' said Grundish in parting.

My smile became bigger while I turned and watched Grundish walk off down the street, his short, thin body looking very frail in the darkness. And I had good reason to smile.

I wasn't going under cover just yet. I was going to settle the score with Suds Garland in the only way he seemed to be able to understand – with guns.

It was still more than an hour before daylight, and I figured I had time enough to call upon Garland in person that night. The weight of the gun on my leg gave me added confidence as I hailed a cab a few minutes after Grundish left me.

Giving the driver an address that would bring me within a block of Suds Garland's place, I lighted a butt and settled back to enjoy the ride. Fifteen minutes later I left the cab and waited until the car moved away again getting down to the business at hand.

The apartment house where Garland was living was a six story structure, situated on a corner. Along one side ran an alley that showed the faint outline of fire escapes up the side of the building in the darkness. The other side of the building was adjoined by a small brownstone front.

I didn't waste any time trying to climb up the fire escape. Suds lived on the fourth floor and that was too much of a climb for the time I had to spare. I went right to the main entrance and looked over the array of bell buttons and name cards, among which was one plainly labeled Garland.

But I didn't push the bell under that card. I selected two apartments on the sixth floor and held down the buttons for a full minute of steady ringing.

The street door was one of those safety latch things that can be opened from any apartment in the building. Somebody in one of the two apartments I was ringing would almost certainly release the latch, late though it was. And they did.

With the first click of the latch I was in the building. The main corridor was dimly lighted by widely spaced bulbs. I found the stairs and climbed fast, ignoring the automatic electric elevator opposite the steps. Too much noise might warn Suds of my visit.

At the fourth floor landing I paused. Not a sound came to me. As yet the people at the top floor didn't suspect they were receiving no visitors and had not opened their doors to investigate.

Silently I moved along the corridor until I stopped at the door of Suds Garland's apartment. Then after a final glance along the hall I got my gun in my right hand and pressed the doorbell with my left forefinger.

I was taking a big chance, and I knew it. I wasn't certain that Garland was home, and if he was I wanted to be ready for anything. I was.

After a couple of minutes there was the sound of a key turning in the lock. Then several bolts were shot back. Keeping off to one side of the door, my back flattened against the wall so that I was out of sight, I waited.

I felt rather than saw the door swing open on silent hinges. For a long breathless moment I thought my plan wasn't going to work. Then, curiosity aroused, Suds Garland himself put one foot over the threshold and looked out along the corridor.

My gun hit his belly and stayed there.

'Inside!' I breathed, increasing the pressure of the gun as Garland recoiled from its touch. 'Keep your hands high!'

His eyes went wide with sudden terror, but he raised his hands without a murmur. The next moment I was on the other side of the door and had kicked it shut and locked it.

'Got company?' I asked.

Suds shook his head. I didn't believe him.

'You lead the way. I want to talk to you, but if you're lying I'll give you the business pronto. Move!'

He walked steadily enough into the living room. There I found a couple of softly shaded lights burning. Garland was in his shirt sleeves, and had apparently come in only a few minutes before I arrived. His hat and coat were lying on a chair as though he had just taken them off.

So far as I could see he hadn't been lying after all about not having company. From the living room I could see into a small dining room. Beyond that I knew was a bedroom, and both rooms were in darkness.

But I didn't take any chances with Garland. The boy was tricky, and before I faced him again I relieved him of a snub-nosed .38 revolver that bulged plainly in his hip pocket. Then with a gun in each hand I backed around in front of him and made him sit down on a divan. I remained standing.

'Suppose we cut the talk short,' I opened, noticing that Suds had regained his composure. If I hadn't been so mad I might have known that his confidence spelled trouble.

'Just as you say, Queen,' he answered evenly. 'You didn't have to come busting in here like that. I'd have let you in.'

'Yes, you would!' I jeered. 'I'm finished with playing nice with you, Suds. I'm going to show you how tough a lady can be.'

'You and who else?'

'We won't argue the point,' I went on. 'I want a signed confession from you that you planted that snow in my apartment.'

'What snow?'

His pose of innocence was funny. But I didn't laugh.

'You've got a pencil in your vest pocket,' I continued. 'Get that newspaper off the floor in front of you. Write the confession on the margin. I'll dictate it.'

153

'I'm a hard man to deal with, Queen,' he stated with a great show of nerve. 'A hard man. You just think I'm soft because I've been easy with you. Now I'm going to show you just how tough I am.'

'Can the chatter!' I snapped. 'Get that pencil in your hand!'

I gestured with the gun in my left hand. Suds Garland laughed softly, derisively.

'You little fool!' he blazed, leaning forward while he looked up at me with flashing black eyes. 'You've been covered ever since I sat down. Give it to her, Gus, if she moves a muscle!'

For a moment I didn't know whether he was merely bluffing or really meant that speech. The business of getting you to look behind you for an attack from the rear was old stuff. So I hefted the guns in my hands and watched Garland closely.

Suddenly I froze.

'Right,' drawled a voice behind me.

Suds Garland had not been bluffing. The single word told me that a gunman was concealed in the darkness of the dining room. Just when I thought I had Garland in the bag I had been trapped myself!

CHAPTER VII

Not So Tough

For a full minute I remained perfectly motionless. Not a sound could be heard, save the hoarse breathing of Suds Garland and the man behind me.

The strain was terrific, but I've been in a lot of tight places and my nerves can stand plenty. This time was no exception. If I could prolong the suspense either Garland or the fellow called Gus would break under the nervous torture. But I wasn't doing nothing while I waited.

I was thinking – hard!

Finally as Suds moistened his lips with the darting point of his tongue I raised my left thumb and slowly pulled back the hammer of the .38. There was a sharp click as the hammer settled into the full cock position.

That slight sound only served to increase the tension. Garland's black eyes narrowed to slits. The muscles of his lean face became rigid as he sought to control his features. I might be in a tight place, but he certainly wasn't having a picnic.

'Well?' I said softly, and in that intense silence it sounded as though I had shouted at the top of my voice.

I wasn't making a grandstand play. Pulling back the hammer of the .38 had been straight business. I figured that if it came to a showdown with the man behind me I could get in at least one shot that would keep Garland with me when I went down under a bullet.

But I really didn't want to kill Suds Garland – yet. I wanted him to live long enough to write that confession and sign it. After that I would kill him with his own gun and make it look like suicide. That would give him the best out he could get.

When there was no answer to my single question I knew Garland and the guy behind me were uncertain about their next move. They had expected me to drop my guns and be a good girl, but they didn't know Queen Sue.

After another minute or so of silence I got tired of waiting. It was evident enough that both men knew what would happen if the guy in the dark took a shot at me. But waiting was getting me nothing. I wanted action.

'Take plenty of time to think it over, Suds,' I advised in a sneering voice. 'If you're the hard mug you think you are, tell your buddy to squeeze lead or drop the gun.'

'You – you don't have a chance, Queen,' he stammered after a moment. Little beads of sweat oozed from his face and formed bigger drops that ran down his cheeks and the sides of his nose unheeded. 'You can't get out of here alive.'

'Speaking for yourself?' I threw back coolly.

But I wasn't as cool as I sounded. I'm only human after all and with a guy like Garland I couldn't tell how this battle of wills was going to turn out.

My last crack floored Garland for a moment. Then he looked past me and did things with his eyes.

I guessed what he meant, and raised the gun in my right hand slightly. Then I shifted the .38 slightly to the left where it would be handier for a quick shot without interfering with the movement of my right arm.

Suds' work with his eyes had meant only one thing. The man behind me was to close in and overpower me without risking the chance of Garland getting shot.

The next moment soft-soled shoes slithered over the floor behind me. But I didn't turn immediately. I waited until I figured the man behind me was almost within reach. Then I went into action.

Raising my right hand swiftly, I brought the nose of my automatic down hard on Suds Garland's mouth. Simultaneously I whirled towards the left, brought the .38 in the open away from my body, and squeezed the trigger once.

I hadn't been a moment too soon. The guy behind me had raised the gun in his right hand to club me down. The bullet from Garland's gun caught him in the center of the throat under the chin, passed upward through his head, and knocked plaster from the ceiling.

The impact of the bullet lifted him up on his toes. Then while the roar of the shot still seemed to fill the room he started to fall.

I shot a quick glance at Garland. The guy who claimed he was so tough was grovelling on the divan from the blow on the mouth that had brought blood spurting to his smashed lips. I started to talk fast, but something that wasn't on the schedule took the words out of my mouth.

The guy who'd tried to slug me hit the floor with his face. At the same instant his gun exploded as his right hand thumped the rug, throwing the muzzle of the gun upward.

He wasn't six feet from the divan when he fell. The bullet plucked at the skirt of my dress and slammed into Suds Garland's chest. The guy called Gus must have used hollow-nosed slugs, for that hunk of lead made a gaping hole as it tore through flesh and bone.

I didn't wait to see more.

Slipping my automatic back into the holster on my leg, I quickly wiped the butt of the .38 with a corner of my dress and tossed the gun down beside Suds. I didn't try to remove all traces of fingerprints. It would look more natural if they were only smeared so they couldn't be recognised.

One look was enough to know that trying to get a confession from Garland was useless. He was still alive, but that slug had ripped a lung wide open. Already bloody froth bubbled to his lips.

I didn't wait to see the end. Less than a minute had passed since I'd fired that first shot, but voices in the corridor told me that I didn't have a moment to spare.

Moving swiftly, I passed through the dining room and into the bedroom. Another moment and I had the window up, and stepped out on the fire escape. A police siren moaned plainly as my feet touched pavement again, and I was a block away when the cops rushed into the building.

Yes, Suds Garland thought he was pretty tough. Maybe he was. But all men – and women, for that matter – look alike to a hunk of lead.

The cops put Suds Garland's death and that of Gus down as a duel over gang affairs, and I didn't tell them any different. On the advice of my lawyer I gave myself up and stood trial on the dope charge.

But I didn't stay snowbound long. Sid Lang's testimony about the dope ring resulted in my acquittal, and I wondered what Suds thought of me beating the rap with the aid of a dick.

THE GIRL WHO KNEW TOO MUCH
RANDOLPH BARR

Not too surprisingly, the author of this rather formulaic story is unknown, as Randolph Barr was a house name, used by many of the hacks willing to work for one of the *Spicy* publications. Published by Culture House (perhaps named ironically), the minor empire included *Spicy Detective*, which was issued from April 1934 to December 1942; *Spicy Adventure* (July 1934–December 1942); *Spicy Mystery* (July 1934–December 1942); *Spicy Western* (November 1936–December 1942) and *Spicy Movie Tales* (one issue only in October 1935). Because of the racy covers and interior illustrations, plus the content of the stories, public pressure caused the publisher, now Trojan Publishing Co., to change titles to *Speed Detective*, *Speed Mystery*, etc., and reduce the provocative nature of its contents. But don't get your expectations too high. What was racy, spicy, snappy and saucy in the 1930s will seem rather tepid today. 'The Girl Who Knew Too Much' is one of the better stories to be found behind the garish covers of the *Spicy* books, which does not make it Shakespeare, or Chandler, either, since the magazine paid much less than its contemporaries. While *Black Mask* and *Dime Detective* were paying two cents a word, and lesser periodicals half that, *Spicy* paid only a half-cent a word – the bottom of the barrel for writers struggling to pay the rent. As is true of most of the stories in *Spicy*, we meet our heroine with her dress ripped down to her waist. This is what passed for titillation in April 1941, when 'The Girl Who Knew Too Much' was first published.

THE GIRL WHO KNEW TOO MUCH
RANDOLPH BARR

There wasn't any particular reason for my being way down on the East Side. It was a warm Spring night, and I was taking a walk, not paying much attention where my feet strayed. It was nearly two o'clock when I looked at my watch, wondering if I shouldn't be turning back and thinking again about going to bed.

I looked around. Deep in thought, I'd wandered all the way to Second Avenue and Second Street. That part of town was, curiously, almost deserted.

Then from up a side alley I heard the clicking heels of a running girl. I turned. She came like a miracle of beauty out of that dingy cul-de-sac of warehouses and manufacturing lofts. Her skirt was bunched in her hand above her knees to facilitate her speed, and white flesh gleamed in the dim light.

I stood stock still, just around the corner of the building where she'd come out on the avenue. Her black dress had been ripped to her waist, and the remnants of a pink silk slip barely held together at one shoulder.

She reached the mouth of the alley and I stepped suddenly in front of her, blocking her way. I studied her in the winking lights of the Little Albania, Louis Russo's third-rate night club. I said, 'What's the hurry? Something scare you?'

Her breasts were heaving from her running, and she fairly panted when she spoke. 'Let me alone! Look out! For God's sake!' She darted suddenly to the side and tried to compress herself into a doorway.

I didn't know what it was all about, but she hadn't been fooling when she spoke. I squeezed in beside her and followed suit in trying to keep out of sight.

Then there were other footsteps coming up the unlighted alley. This time they were made by a man, a man who was trying to move soundlessly.

I chanced a look.

There was a black shape creeping around the corner of the building to the street. It hugged the wall.

*

Out of the alley came a flash of orange flame. There was the report of a gun that was like a sharp cough, and the crouching figure tumbled in a heap, legs in the alley, head and outflung arms on the sidewalk of the avenue.

The girl and I remained flattened in the doorway – even when unseen hands caught the ankles of the fallen man, and we heard the gruesome sound of his body being dragged over the rough cobblestones back into the darkness.

My forehead had an uncomfortable clammy feeling as I peered out again and saw the little pool of blood and the man's hat near the curbstone. As a newspaper man, I'd seen my share of violent death, but this was giving me the jitters.

The street itself had become morgue-quiet. The only sound was the faint sobbing of violin strings, the occasional pulse of a drum, and the wail of a saxophone from the Little Albania's shuttered windows.

The girl came to life. She said, 'You'd better scram fast, mister!' She caught up her skirt again and started to run north up Second Avenue, sticking closely to the shadows. Automatically I followed.

A couple of blocks up, she halted in a vestibule and confronted me. 'Will you keep out of this? Haven't you seen enough? Do you want to be laid out on a slab beside that other man back in the alley?'

I caught her arm. 'I'm a newspaperman, sister. Give!'

Her eyes widened. 'You'd better not print anything you've seen tonight! Russo's mob doesn't like reporters. Anyway, I'm in a hurry!'

'That's okay with me,' I told her. 'I've got a lot of time. And I'm sticking with you.'

She smiled wanly. It looked as if she were going to lose the slip when she shrugged, but she caught it and pulled the tatters of her clothes together. 'If I can't shake you, let's go. The farther we get away from here, the better!'

At the next corner I whistled for a cab. I asked, 'Where do you live?'

'Not far away. But I'm not going home tonight! It might not be healthy.'

She shivered against me as I helped her into the cab. I slid an arm around her, and she didn't object. Speculatively, I gave the driver the address of my own Grove Street apartment.

She didn't demur, even when we pulled up at my place and I asked her in for a drink.

The first sip of her highball went far in helping her to relax. We sat side by side on my divan, and she smiled when I put an arm around her shoulders. 'Feel like loosening up?' I asked her.

She misunderstood me and snuggled closer, but I didn't mind. I kissed her warm, moist, inviting mouth. But a minute later I laughed. I said, 'I really meant do you feel like telling me what it's all about?'

She reddened prettily. 'You mean about Dick Tobin's shooting. He wasn't really a bad guy—' She stared straight ahead as if deciding how much to tell me. 'Both Dick and the big fellow—'

'You mean Russo?'

'Yes. They both wanted me. The mob considered me Dick's girl. Louis intended to bump Dick anyway. I'm not sure just why he had it in for Dick, but he used me as an excuse to get rid of him.'

I pointed to the silk dress which hung in jagged strips. Through the tatters her flesh was pink and smooth and warm-looking.

She colored again, and tried to cover herself better. 'Russo did that. He had me in his office, and was getting rough. I managed to fight him off, and slipped out the back way. He sent Dick Tobin after me—'

I nodded. 'And then he himself came out—'

'Yes. And I'm scared! I know he wants me now, but he'll kill me when he tires of me! I know too much about his mob.'

She seemed as pitiful as she was lovely, sitting there in my living room. I looked into her great dark eyes, and wondered what I could do for her. I said, 'You've got a hell of a good story, but it would be dynamite to handle. At least, without a lot of substantiation.' She was cuddled against me so that I could feel the vibrancy of her slender, exquisite form. I hugged her against me so tightly that her breasts flattened on my chest, but she strained even harder . . . .

Breathless, she pushed away. She said, 'Now that you've got me here, what are you going to do with me? I don't dare go home.'

'What about a hotel?'

'At this time in the morning? And looking like this?' She indicated her ruined dress.

I said, 'Well—?'

'You haven't even thought of inviting me to stay here?'

I grinned. 'It's okay with me. It ought to be safe enough.'

She caught my arm when I picked up the telephone. 'What are you going to do?'

'My job, baby.' I brushed her arm off and dialed the *Courier*. I talked to the desk briefly, then turned back to the girl. 'That's that,' I said. 'Tomorrow the paper will carry a short paragraph saying that a gangster named Dick Tobin was killed near the Little Albania. By the way, you haven't told me your name.'

'Polly Knight. And where can I sleep?'

I pointed to the bed. 'Such as it is, it's all yours. I'll see if I can find you a pair of pajamas.'

When I turned back from the bureau, she was seated on the edge of the bed, peeling off her stockings. The picture was tempting, but I forced myself to think of my job. I should be reporting at the office. I picked up my topcoat.

'Where are you going?' Polly asked, her eyes showing panic again. I told her, and she caught at my arm. 'No! No! You can't leave me! You've already called in. If there was anything important for you, they would have told you!'

I studied her. And her terror wasn't faked.

She said, 'I didn't like the way that taxi-driver stared at me. He might be one of Russo's men. Please don't go!'

I hung up my coat. While she watched me, I got my automatic from my desk and put it in a hip pocket. I saw that the key in the lock was turned so that it wouldn't easily fall out. For extra precaution I wedged a chair under the knob. I said, 'That ought to cover everything.'

Much calmer, Polly slipped out of her torn dress. While she got into the pajama jacket, I fought to keep from sweeping her into my arms. All that saved her, I think, was her atmosphere of utter helplessness.

She said, 'You're being awfully decent. And me, I'm just a gangster's girl! Funny, isn't it?'

I took off my coat and vest and shoes and sprawled in the morris-chair. When I looked at Polly again, she was under the covers.

Her voice was a gentle murmur. 'I feel like a heel – chasing you out of your bed.'

I knew how I felt, but I didn't tell her. I said, 'Don't worry. In case we should have visitors—' I switched off the lights, and tried to make myself comfortable.

It seemed like a long while, but couldn't have been more than half an hour when I heard the shuffling footsteps outside down the corridor. I was wide awake in an instant. I got silently to my feet. I tiptoed to the bed.

A small soft hand caught mine. Polly was sitting up in bed, trembling.

The steps came nearer. I took out my automatic, and stared through the gloom toward the door. But the footsteps shuffled past and grew fainter.

Relieved, I stuck the gun back in my pocket. 'It was a drunk, trying to find his room,' I whispered. I patted Polly's shoulder.

'Stay here beside me for a little while,' she pleaded. 'When I can't see you or touch you, I get the willies.'

Tired and sleepy, I leaned back. . . .

It seemed like ten seconds, but it was daylight when I opened my eyes. Dressed in my over-size pajamas, Polly was seated in the morris-chair, examining her ruined dress. She smiled ruefully. 'I don't suppose you'd have a needle and thread?'

I wouldn't and I told her so. I had a better idea. 'Tell me where you live, give me your key, and I'll get you something to wear. None of Russo's crowd knows me.'

She assented. 'Before you go,' she said, 'I'd like to tell you that, in spite

162

of what they all said, I never really was Dick Tobin's sweetheart. None of Russo's crowd ever actually touched me.'

She was a little wistful, and I don't think she really expected me to believe her. Curiously, I did, and my heart was strangely light as I fitted her key into her door.

The apartment was nicely furnished, done with restraint and in good taste – not at all the sort of place you would have expected a gang girl to have.

I headed for a closet, had a sudden apprehension of danger, turned, and caught the full weight of whatever it was that hit me squarely on the head. . . .

Coming back to consciousness was an agonizing experience. My head had bells in it, and was all but cleft in two, anyway. Then I discovered that my hands were tied behind me and that my ankles were roped together. I was in Polly's apartment. Louis Russo sat in a chair across from me.

He leered at me. 'So you tried to butt in!' he sneered. 'I was waiting for Polly. If I keep on waiting, she should be along anyway. I'm in no hurry.' He blew smoke in my face.

I recognized the truth of what he said, but there was nothing I could do about it.

He grinned. 'I'll take care of you later,' he said. 'When I get through with Polly, I'm not going to leave you where you can talk about it.'

There were icicles in my blood.

Russo must have heard the step outside before I did, for he jumped up suddenly, caught me by the collar, and literally dragged me across the floor to the bathroom. He left the door open a crack – probably due to his haste – and I could see into the other room without being easily seen.

The knob of the door to the corridor turned, and the door opened. It was Polly Knight. Her mouth made an explosive gasp as Russo suddenly appeared from behind the door. He jammed the muzzle of a gun into her side.

Without a word he reached out, caught her torn dress at the neckline and ripped it all the way down. Then he stood off and surveyed her. He said, 'Get into another rig! That thing might attract too much attention where I'm going to take you.'

While she, helplessly, took another dress from a hook and slipped it over her shoulders, he said, 'I thought you'd be along when your boy-friend didn't come back to you.' All the time, his eyes were licking at her alluring loveliness.

When she had dressed, he flung the door to the bathroom wide. I glared at him and tried to flash some sort of encouragement to Polly. I'm afraid that, bound up as I was, I couldn't have helped much.

Louis Russo grinned unpleasantly. 'We'll have to leave this one. If we took him in the car, it might attract too much attention. We'll send some one to take care of him soon.' He turned to the girl. 'You walk ahead of me. And don't forget the gun in my pocket!'

When they had gone, I continued my struggle against my bonds. The only result was to make them bite more deeply and painfully into my flesh. Nevertheless, realizing that Russo's men might arrive at any moment, I didn't relax my efforts.

My eye lingered on the glass shelf over the wash bowl. One end had been splintered and looked as if it might provide a cutting edge.

Sweating, I edged across the floor, nudged a stool along with me. After half a dozen tries I got onto the stool and worked my wrists up to the jagged edge of the shelf.

My wrists were lacerated and bloody before my hands were free. It was a matter of seconds then to release my ankles.

My muscles still felt cramped and my head was dizzy when I reached the street. A long black sedan was edging in to the curb. Certain that the car was driven by Russo's men, I kept my head down and hurried my steps to the drugstore on the corner.

I stumbled in to a phone booth and dialed police headquarters. My pal, Inspector Daly, wouldn't be in for a couple of hours. I cursed. But, knowing pretty well what my answer would be, I talked to his relief, Lieutenant Finger. He said, '*What?* You want us to raid the Little Albania! And the only reason you can give us is your word that a girl is being held prisoner!

'Listen, newshound! Louis Russo's too smart to be playing with that kind of stuff. Before we tangle with him, we're going to need a little more to go on. Besides, the police department wasn't established to build up the circulation of your lousy paper. Better lay off the pipe, and tell your boss the same thing!' He hung up.

It had been about what I'd expected, but that didn't make me feel any better. Whatever I did, I'd have to do alone – and in a hurry.

I flagged a taxi and gave an address a block away from the Little Albania. The alley that led to the back entrance was deserted. I edged down it and found that the door was locked. There was an open window on the third floor.

The alley was only a few feet wide and the open window gave me an idea. Across from Russo's place was an abandoned warehouse, most of its windows shattered.

I slid into the warehouse and picked my way up stairs jammed with refuse. On the third floor I found a long plank lying among dust-covered heaps of rusty, outmoded machinery. I dragged the plank to the window and eased it across the alley. It reached the sill on the other side with a foot to spare.

Cautiously, giddy with fear, I worked my weight out on the sagging plank. I had reached the other side when the thing canted sideways. I caught at the open sash as the far end of the plank slipped clear, slapped at me, and crashed thirty feet down to the cobbled court. Weak as water, I half fell over the window sill.

The room I was in was evidently a storeroom. Cases of all sizes, crates, and boxes crowded all but an aisle to a door. I open it noiselessly and looked into a private banquet room. A thug-like porter was mopping the floor.

I kept back behind the door until he had worked around to where I waited. Then I leaped. Both my hands got him around the throat. He was gasping for breath when I released him a second and swung my Sunday punch to the point of his jaw. He went limp.

I devoted precious minutes to knotting a twisted table-cloth about his wrists and ankles, and gagging him with a napkin. By the time I'd dragged him under a table, I was sure that he wouldn't be able to bother me for a while.

There was the sound of voices from a door that I took to be Russo's office. I tried the knob silently and found the door locked. Now I could make out the words. It was Russo speaking. 'You can yell your head off, sweetheart. Nobody will hear you. Up here we are very safe.'

I tiptoed toward the front of the place, entered a cloakroom, and followed it through to a door on the other side. I came out on the landing of a stair-case. And, as luck would have it, there was another entrance to Russo's office! Prayerfully I tried the knob. Thank God, Russo hadn't thought it necessary to lock this door!

I had it open a fraction of an inch when I froze. Voices came from the banquet room. Hands rattled the door I had found bolted. 'You there, boss? We went to the dame's apartment, and the guy wasn't there.'

'He wasn't there?' It was Russo's unbelieving bellow. 'I will be with you in ten minutes. You mugs wait downstairs until I call you.'

Feet shuffled away.

And I made my move. I opened the door wide.

Louis Russo was bending Polly back over a table. The dress she had changed to was now more tattered than the one in which I had first seen her. The gangster ran his tongue over thick lips—

He hadn't even looked around when I started my charge. But the man was quick. Before I was half way across the floor, he'd whirled and snatched for his shoulder holster. The flame of the gun seared my shoulder as I tackled him. My hand clamped down on his wrist.

For a little while it was touch and go. I threw my weight into bending his arm back in an attempt to get the gun. Russo was plenty husky. The gun exploded again and its lead ploughed a furrow in my ankle.

I redoubled my pressure and heard the crack of a bone. The gun dropped. Russo writhed like an eel. His teeth closed in one of my wrists as he lunged for the gun with his good arm. I kicked it out of his reach, wrenched free, and leaped for it myself.

Coming up with the gun, I found that Russo had been as quick as I. He held Polly in front of him as a shield. 'Shoot if you dare!' he gritted. Then, 'Tony! Joe! Smash the door down! Come in!'

The door shook as powerful bodies lunged against it. I fired twice as the lock gave way, then snapped the trigger and heard the hammer click on an empty cylinder.

Two guns bored into my kidneys. I was backed against the wall and held in impotence. Once again my hands and wrists were tied expertly.

Russo grinned. 'Now leave him here, and you boys go outside until I call you.'

Leering like a madman, Russo waited until his men had left. Then once more he turned to Polly who cringed away from him. His brutal hand reached out and snatched even more of her few remaining garments from her.

A red film of hate and rage blinded me. Bound as I was, I tried to dive for the man. He turned from the girl and began methodically to beat me with his revolver. Blood poured from my lacerated scalp, from my torn face, but still he raised the gun and brought it down. At any moment he could have knocked me out, but that was not his intention. In cold blood he hacked and cut, and I could do nothing but take it.

Eventually he tired of his sport. He slipped a cartridge into the gun. 'You've been asking for it,' he said. 'You're going to get it!'

I could actually see his finger grow white as it tightened on the trigger.

At that instant Polly Knight came out of her semi-conscious state. Half-naked, she hurled herself in front of Russo. 'Stop! Don't kill him!' she begged.

Russo shoved her away, slapped her face brutally. He brought up the gun again toward me. . . .

A fusillade of shots hammered in from the banquet room. One of Russo's men lurched over the threshold and fell, blood gushing from his throat.

Russo fired once toward the door, then squealed and pitched to the floor under a hail of lead.

The film cleared from my eyes and I saw Inspector Daly come into the room followed by two men in uniform. Polly Knight, ignoring her state of nudity, knelt beside me, loosening the knots that held me.

Daly grinned at me. 'That fathead Finger, my relief, told me about your call. Technically, he may have been within his rights, but I thought I'd better look into the matter!' He smiled down at Polly. 'I'll take the boys and wait outside until the young lady has had a chance to cover herself up a little.'

I gave her my coat and sat patiently while she wiped blood from my face. 'Was it worth it – all for a gangster's girl?' she whispered.

I put an arm around her, not caring how much the effort hurt. 'I don't care what kind of girl you are,' I told her. 'It was worth it!'

There was a devil dancing in her eyes. 'As a matter of fact, I'm not a gangster's girl. And my name isn't Polly Knight. Don't you remember "God's Good to the Irish"?'

I stared at her in amazement. 'You're Polly Day!' I gasped. 'You played the lead in the show!'

She nodded. 'But the show folded. I was broke and I got a job for a private detective agency. I was sent down here because there were indications that Russo's mob was behind a series of hold-ups. I went to work in the Little Albania as a hostess. I was trying to get something on the gang—'

I stopped her explanations with a kiss. 'That'll be enough for now,' I said. 'You can give me installment two of your story when we get back to my apartment.'

THE CORPSE IN THE CRYSTAL
&
HE GOT WHAT HE ASKED FOR

D. B. McCANDLESS

An element of a great deal of pulp fiction that correctly prevents it from being regarded as serious literature is the absurd reliance on the reader to accept virtually any far-fetched coincidence or series of events. The suspension of disbelief is often pushed to the very brink of fantasy.

The Sarah Watson stories of D. B. McCandless are a case in point. They are humorous and charming, and the protagonist runs against stereotypes. She is not a sexy red-head in tight, low-cut sweaters who has every man she encounters eating out of her hand. She is, instead, middle-aged, heavy, dowdy and relatively charmless. This element of originality, as well as a fast-paced narrative, combine to make the stories among the most readable of their kind – so much so that two tales of 'The Female She-Devil' have been included in this collection. Do not, however, judge the stories based on credibility, as they will fall somewhat short. Even allowing for the difference of era between the 1930s and the present day, railroad and airplane travel had little in common with the events related in the second of these adventures.

'The Corpse in the Crystal' and 'He Got What He Asked For' were originally published in *Detective Fiction Weekly*.

THE CORPSE IN THE CRYSTAL
D. B. McCANDLESS

A massive individual in blue and brass marched resoundingly down a tiled corridor and halted before a door. Scabby gilt letters on the door said: 'Watson Detective Agency.' The massive individual pounced upon the door knob, wrenched it and swung himself into the office beyond.

A long, languid young man with red hair let his feet thump from his desk to the floor, sat upright, said: 'Cheese it, the cops!' and relaxed again, grinning.

The massive individual, standing spread-legged and stroking a black eyebrow thick enough to have served as a mustache for a daintier man, greeted the young man.

''Lo, Ben Todd. Where's your boss?''

''Lo, Sergeant. Sarah Watson has gone out.'

'I can see that, even if I am a cop. Where's she gone?'

'Crazy, I guess. She said she was going to consult a crystal gazer.'

Sergeant O'Reilly cried out and shook his fists at the ceiling.

'Damn Sarah Watson!' he exclaimed. 'A crystal gazer, eh! I might have known she'd get ahead of me!'

O'Reilly sat down heavily in the chair beside Sarah Watson's roll-top desk. He reached a thick arm and laid heavy fingers upon a newspaper lying there. He lifted the paper and stared at a square hole cut neatly therein. He took a square clipping from his pocket and fitted it into the hole in the newspaper.

'Read this, Ben Todd.'

Ben Todd shambled across, lounged over the Sergeant's shoulder and read. The clipping fitted into the empty space in Sarah's newspaper, under 'Letters from Readers.' It read:

Dear Editor: People say all fortune tellers, mediums and crystal gazers are fakes. Two weeks ago, I sat before a crystal ball and the most wonderful seer in the world looked into the crystal and saw the body of a certain well known wealthy young man laying dead in a marsh, with cat-tails drooping over him and a bone-handled knife in his heart. That was two weeks ago, and the next day, the body of that same well known, wealthy young man

171

was found dead, laying in a marsh, just exactly as the wonderful seer had seen it in the crystal. Now that young man lays in his grave and the police can't find his murderer. And then people say crystal gazers are fakes! Yours respectfully, Lily Tarrant.

'A certain, well-known, wealthy young man,' Ben Todd whistled, went on. 'Found in a swamp ... with a bone handled knife in his heart ... *Alexander Courtwell!*'

'The same!' O'Reilly agreed. 'I wonder if this wonderful seer saw the ring when he saw the corpse in the crystal?'

'Ring?'

'The ring we found under the corpse. The big onyx ring with the two big diamonds in it. The ring we knew belonged to Honest Jim Carson.'

'Well, for Pete's sake, O'Reilly, if you knew, why isn't Honest Jim Carson in jail for the Courtwell killing?'

'Honest Jim Carson,' said O'Reilly, 'is in his grave. He was there, of unnatural causes, three days before Courtwell was killed.'

'Oh!,' said Ben Todd.

O'Reilly got to his feet, cast the crumpled newspaper from him, and shook his fist again at Sarah's roll-top desk. Ben Todd said, thoughtfully:

'So ... a crystal gazer saw Alexander Courtwell dead before he was found dead ... and Sarah's gone to consult a crystal gazer!'

'Damn her brains! There's ten thousand dollars reward for the apprehension of Courtwell's murderer, Ben Todd, and that Watson woman had to set her eagle eye on that clipping before I ... Wait!'

O'Reilly grabbed the 'phone on top of the roll-top desk. He shouted a number, glared at Ben Todd.

'Evening Star? O'Reilly. Yeah, the cop. Gimme Watkins. You, Watkins? Listen, you made one bad boner, letting that Tarrant woman's letter get into print. You made another bad boner not calling the papers off the street quick enough after I ordered you to. Let's see, now if you've made another boner? Anybody get the Tarrant woman's address out of you since that paper went on the streets? What? They did? *She* did? I might have known! I might have ... Oh, God!'

O'Reilly slammed up the 'phone and whirled on Ben Todd.

'That Watson woman is a liar and a thief,' he roared. 'She called up the Star and told 'em she was assisting me on the Courtwell case. She asked for that Tarrant woman's address and she got it.'

'She would.'

'She got it. Which means she's probably with the crystal gazer now, picking his brains dry, and she'll have that ten thousand dollars reward in her damn, thieving fists before I ...'

'Listen,' said Ben Todd. 'I don't allow anybody to damn Sarah Watson.

She may be an old battle-axe and an old liar but she's not a damn old thief.'

'She is a damn old thief!' shouted O'Reilly, thrusting his blue jaw close to Ben Todd's: 'I came here with every intention of sharing that reward with her if she'd help me by going to that crystal gazer and picking his brains dry before we closed in on him. Now she's got the jump on me, and she'll cop the whole reward!'

Ben Todd yawned and said:

'Well, you're giving her a good start, anyway, O'Reilly, while you stand here, sizzling in your own grease. Listen, O'Reilly! I just thought of something! If the crystal gazer knew about the murder before the murder was done, then he's involved, and if he's involved . . .'

'*If* he's involved! Of course he's involved! What else do you think I've been thinking? What I should have done was to close in on him first and sweat him after, instead of thinking of conniving with Sarah to pick his brains first . . .'

Ben Todd reached for his hat and took a long stride toward the door.

'The old girl may be with him now!' he cried. 'If he gets wise to what she's after, then Sarah's in . . .'

O'Reilly reached over Ben Todd's shoulder and opened the door.

'Of course she's in danger!' he admitted. 'What else do you think I've been thinking? If you don't move quicker, Ben Todd, I'll grind down your heels.'

At just about the moment that Sergeant O'Reilly first made his entrance into the office of the Watson Detective Agency, Sarah Watson herself was leaning upon the rickety stoop railing of a certain flathouse, conversing with a janitress perfumed with gin.

The thick shaft of Sarah's sturdily corseted body was wrapped in nondescript, rusty black garments. Her antique headgear was set at a hurried angle on her straggling gray hair. There was a slight, unaccustomed tinge of hectic red on the high cheek bones under her grey, bristling-browed eyes. There was, however, no hint of excitement in the hoarse, downright voice with which she fired questions at the vague and wavery target of the janitress.

'She left in a hurry, eh? In a big, black car with red wheels? Walking between two men, eh? Did you get a look at those two men?'

'Well, now.' The janitress ran a soiled hand over her mouth. 'Well, I tried to get a look, because it seemed kind of queer, Mrs. Tarrant going off with two strange men like that and her a new widow woman that's always trying to communicate with her dead husband through the spirits and such, but the men walked awful fast. Seems to me they was both dark and one of 'em had his lip puckered down at the side by a scar, sort of, and the car was the swellest thing on four wheels I ever seen, four red wheels . . .'

'What time? Think, woman! Remember I'm paying you to think.'

'Am thinking. Fifty cents will buy . . . Well, don't glare at me that way, missus. They left right before twelve, because I remember, I was wiping up the halls right after and I smelled something in Mrs. Tarrant's kitchen and her door was open and I edged in and the smell was beans – burnt to a crisp.'

'Burnt to a crisp, eh? Mrs. Tarrant must have left in a hurry! Well, here's your fifty cents and take my advice and put it in the bank and not down your gullet.'

Sarah Watson started briskly down the stoop, wheeled abruptly and transfixed the janitress with a glinting eye.

'By the way, what's the name of the crystal gazer Mrs. Tarrant goes to?' she asked. 'I might find her there . . .'

'You might. She's been running there enough, trying to see her dead husband in heaven, but it's my opinion she's been looking in the wrong place for him . . . Don't growl, missus. It's Charlot she goes to. Charlot, his name is, and his place is on Green Street, Number . . .'

Sarah took a little black notebook from her capacious handbag and noted down the address.

A ramshackle vehicle which faintly resembled an automobile chugged to a stop at a corner on Green Street. Sarah Watson stepped out and strode down the street.

Halfway down the block, she passed a dirty first-floor window with a sign in it which said: 'Charlot.' She strode by the window, about-faced suddenly, and disappeared down an odorous alley which led to a backyard.

Five minutes later, she mounted the first flight of an iron fire escape ladder and was sitting, bolt upright, on the top step of the ladder, gazing calmly through a rift in the dirty curtains on the open back window of Charlot's flat.

There was no one in the kitchen beyond the curtains but something was sizzling on the stove. The nostrils of Sarah's beak quivered appreciatively as a little breeze blew the fragrance out.

Presently, a door in the kitchen opened. For a moment, the aroma of cooking was diluted by the heavy odor of incense and the room beyond the kitchen showed dimly. Then, a swarthy man in a white robe and white turban closed himself into the kitchen, ripped off his white wrappings, flung them on the floor, yanked off his dark, pointed beard, slung it at a chair, kicked at the discarded robe and turban and bent over the sink. Outside on the fire escape, Sarah Watson nodded grimly.

The man turned from the sink suddenly, facing the window. Sarah edged closer to the wall of the building. The man was clothed in dark trousers and undershirt. He was towelling vigorously. His face was no longer swarthy. It was white, very white – and young.

A fuzzy grey kitten rolled out from under the kitchen table and dabbed at the fringes of black beard protruding from the edge of the chair. The man threw down his towel, picked the kitten up by its scruff, grinned at it, and thrust its soft body under his chin. With the kitten cuddled between his collar bone and his jaw, the man bent over a pan on the stove and expertly flipped over a sizzling steak. He bent over another pan, stirring . . .

A square door in the wall between the man at the stove and the window where Sarah Watson watched began to open, very slowly, very silently. Sarah edged closer to the curtain. The stubby fingers of her right hand began to slide into her handbag . . .

Suddenly the opening door flew wide, revealing the black hole of a dumbwaiter shaft. A man leaped noiselessly through the door and into the kitchen. He was dark and his profile showed a mouth drawn down by a puckered scar. Before his feet hit the oilcloth, he had placed a gun between the shoulder blades of the man bending over the stove.

The man at the stove stiffened but did not move. The kitten clawed at his shoulder and dropped to the floor, squealing.

'Take it now, snitcher—!' the man with the gun snarled.

A gun blasted. The man with the scar dropped his gun, clawed at his back, slid slowly to the floor. The man at the stove bent over the prostrate man, straightened and looked up at the billowing curtains at the back window. There was smoke still wreathing out of the rift in those curtains, but nothing else.

A few minutes later, a brilliant female in rusty black strode along Green Street and climbed into the ancient automobile parked at the corner. For a moment or so, she sat behind the wheel, her hard bosom rising and falling hurriedly, her stubby fingers wiping away the moisture that beaded the incipient mustache upon her upper lip.

Then the old car coughed and chugged down Green Street. Halfway down the block, it slowed. There was a car parked opposite the window in which Charlot's sign appeared. It was a fine car, black, with red wheels.

Sarah Watson's car snorted on a few more yards and stopped. Sarah got out.

The man sitting behind the wheel of the black car sat up suddenly, taking his eyes off the dingy entrance to Charlot's flathouse and transferring them to the woman standing with her elbow resting on the edge of the open window at his left.

'No use waiting,' she said. 'He's not coming out.' She jabbed her elbow viciously into his neck just below the chin. Something in her right hand cracked down upon the back of his head. His slid, his lids fluttering down over amazed eyes.

Sarah Watson drew a hairpin from the knob of grey hair under her hat.

She thrust the pin into the button in the center of the steering wheel. The horn began to blow.

Sarah leaned over the man slumped under the wheel and peered into the back of the car.

'It's all right, Mrs. Tarrant,' she soothed the frightened woman. 'The cop will come running when he hears the horn and the cop will take the ropes and bandages off you. I haven't time.'

Sarah withdrew her head, gazed sternly for a moment at the unconscious man behind the wheel, then strode away.

As she mounted the steps of the tenement which housed Charlot, a horn was still blowing behind her, and a ruddy cop was tearing around the corner and down Green Street toward the black car with red wheels. Sarah stepped into the vestibule of the tenement, opened a door into the hall, pressed a firm finger on the bell under Charlot's name and kept the finger there.

The horn of the black car ceased blowing suddenly. Sarah took her finger off Charlot's bell. A smell of burned steak permeated the hall.

The door opened two inches. A man's voice said: 'Charlot is not receiving.'

Sarah leaned on the door and said, hoarsely:

'Charlot's receiving me, if he knows what's good for him,' and she wedged her commonsense shoe into the two inch opening.

'Madam, if you wish a reading, you must return later. The crystal is clouded. Charlot cannot . . .'

'Listen,' Sarah interrupted fiercely, wedging her foot farther in, 'the crystal may be clouded, but it ain't too clouded for me to see that there's a corpse in Charlot's kitchen . . .'

The voice behind the door gasped. Sarah pushed through, stepped into the dimly lit room beyond, slammed the door shut behind her, locked it, and faced a white robed man whose white turban was over one ear and whose dark, pointed beard was slightly askew.

'Charlot,' Sarah declared, 'I got a premonition we ain't got much time. Now talk. I want to know how you were able to tell that fool Tarrant woman just where and how the body of Alexander Courtwell would be found, and I want to know quick.'

The man in the tipsy turban looked down at the gun in Sarah's stubby fingers.

'Who . . . ? What . . . ?' he stuttered.

'And what have you done with the man shot down in your kitchen?' Sarah asked.

'My God! You know about that . . . You think I killed him?'

'Young feller, you're in a mess and if you want to get out of it, you'd better talk. Sit down here by your glass ball. I'll sit here on the other side, where your fool clients sit. I'll look into the crystal myself, young feller, and see what I see. I see you, Charlot, without that brown stain on your skin and without that beard. You're peaked and white . . . prison white . . .'

'Prison! How did you know . . . ?'

'I saw it in the crystal, young man. Yes, you've been in jail. Maybe you didn't belong there . . .'

'I didn't. I was . . .'

'Half of 'em don't belong there – so they say. You've been in jail, Charlot, and somehow, either there or after you got outside, you found out just how and why Alexander Courtwell was going to be killed, and you blabbed it to one of your gullible woman customers. Why?'

'I had to. I had to tell her something. She kept tormenting me, kept coming here every day, begging me to see something in the crystal. I kept seeing things, of course, things I thought she wanted me to see. But I kept thinking of that poor fellow, Courtwell. I kept thinking of how I'd heard those two planning in the next cell, planning to stick him in the heart with the bone handled knife one of 'em owned, and planning to throw his body in the swamp.

'I kept thinking how I'd heard them whispering about what Courtwell had done to 'em, how he'd cheated 'em out of some big gambling debt. I kept thinking about it, I tell you, and when the Tarrant woman kept nagging me to see something, I kept seeing Courtwell's body in a swamp with a bone handled knife sticking out of the heart, and one night, before I knew I'd done it, I blabbed. I didn't mean to. I didn't think she'd ever tell anybody, 'till I saw that letter in the paper today, and then I knew something was going to happen – something like that dead man in the kitchen – something like you . . .'

'Young man,' said Sarah, 'worse things could happen to you than me. Now, I'm looking in the crystal I see two men, planning and plotting in a cell. What do they look like?'

'I don't know.'

'What?'

'I was released the morning after they came in. I never saw them. I only heard their voices.'

'Damn,' said Sarah and leaned over the crystal. 'Wait! I'm beginning to see . . . One of them had a scar on his chin . . .'

'No,' Charlot shivered, twisted in his chair. 'That one spoke to me before he fell down with a bullet in his back. I'd have known the voice, if he'd been one of them.'

'Drat it, man,' Sarah explained. 'You can't hang a murderer on a voice. Think, now! You must have heard those two say something definite, something that would identify them?'

'I heard their names.'

Sarah Watson stood up. She waved her gun under Charlot's nose.

'At last we're getting some place,' she said, hoarsely. 'Their names, young feller! What were their names?'

A bell shrilled suddenly, went on ringing, filling the dim room with clamor. Charlot sat erect, staring into Sarah's glinting eyes. Someone began to bang lustily upon the flimsy door to the hall.

'The cops!' Sarah cried. 'You've got one chance, Charlot. Scuttle down the fire-escape. Take my car outside – License 4738. In the side pocket, you'll find the keys to my flat and the address. Get there quick – and stay there 'til I come. It's your one chance, Charlot. There's a dead man in your kitchen and your fingerprints are all over the place and you've been to jail . . .'

Charlot got up, still staring at Sarah.

'Leave that white nightgown in the kitchen,' she said, 'and take the kitten with you. It might starve before you get back here again.'

Charlot looked into her grim eyes a moment longer, then turned and fled. Sarah got up and opened the door. O'Reilly and Ben Todd stood outside.

'Too late, boys,' she lied. 'The swami's evaporated . . . climbed up a rope and disappeared . . . magicked himself into thin air or something. There's a man in the kitchen and you might ask him, but I don't think he'll answer. He's dead.'

The police car sped through the night, O'Reilly at the wheel, Sarah Watson bolt upright beside him, Ben Todd lounging in the rear.

'A little speed, please, Sergeant,' Sarah urged. 'I'm used to speed.'

'You'll have to get unused to it, then,' O'Reilly chuckled. 'Your racing car is gone and Charlot, alias Eddie Danville, has gone with it.'

'You know, Sergeant,' said Sarah, dreamily, 'Charlot – Eddie Danville, I mean – didn't look like a boy that would steal a poor old woman's car.'

'Whadya know about how he looked?'

'I saw his prison picture, didn't I? A nice looking feller. Didn't look like he belonged in jail.'

'He don't,' admitted O'Reilly. 'He belongs in a nice comfortable chair, wired for electricity.'

'All men are alike,' said Sarah. 'They jump to conclusions. Just because Eddie left a dead man in his kitchen and just because Eddie's fingerprints showed he'd been in jail . . . Listen, O'Reilly. Anybody could have shot that man. I could have shot him.'

'You!' O'Reilly laughed. 'You couldn't hit a clay pigeon in a shooting gallery, woman.'

'No, but men make better targets than clay pigeons – bigger targets, I mean. Now, O'Reilly, you can let me off at this next corner. I've got to . . .'

'I'm taking you right to your door, Sarah Watson. You're tired, woman, hanging around with a bunch of cops all afternoon. It must have been a shock to you, too, woman, when you came on that dead body in Charlot's kitchen.'

'It would have been a greater shock if the body hadn't been dead. You slow up, O'Reilly. Stop at the next corner. Stop, I say! Let me off here. I've got to . . .'

The car swept past the corner with Sarah grabbing the door handle beside her. It swung into Sarah's street, slid halfway down the block. O'Reilly shouted:

'Glory be! Look what's out in front of your door, Sarah Watson. Look! Your car!'

'Stop!' Sarah shouted. 'Don't run into it. My car! What a coincidence! O'Reilly, I told you that Eddie Danville wasn't all bad. Maybe he stole my car to make a getaway in, but he found my name and address in it, and left it here for me, before he went wherever he was going . . .'

O'Reilly put on the brakes. He turned slowly in his seat and stared hard at Sarah.

'Woman, I'm beginning to understand why you were so anxious to stop at that corner . . .'

Ben Todd poked his head out of the open rear window and twisted his neck to look up.

'Sarah,' he yelled, 'somebody's in your flat. There's a light . . .'

'Of course there's a light,' Sarah agreed. 'There's always a light. You know that Ben Todd, you crazy squirt. You know I always turn a light on in the morning, so I won't have to come home to a dark place. You know . . . O'Reilly, turn this car around!'

O'Reilly did not stir. His black brows were gathered, his eyes glaring at Sarah's craggy countenance.

'Woman,' he began, but choked suddenly, as Sarah reached across him, put one foot on the starter, and kicked his shins viciously in an effort to put her other foot on the clutch.

'Woman,' O'Reilly repeated, giving her a dig with his elbow which sent her bouncing back to her own side. 'I'm taking you to that corner, but if you was a man, I'd . . .'

The car whirled into a U-turn and sped back toward the corner.

'Thank you, Sergeant. I have to stop at the corner to buy milk. I've got a new cat in my flat.'

Sarah Watson sat on the edge of her bed. The bed was in a cubbyhole between the front room and the rear room of her railroad flat. The window of the cubbyhole looked out on a dark, narrow airshaft. Both doors of the cubbyhole were closed.

On a straight chair, facing the bed, sat Charlot, whose real name was

179

Eddie Danville. He was still in trousers and undershirt and his face was whiter, if possible, than it had been when Sarah first saw it.

'Now, Eddie, we're safe here for a few minutes,' Sarah began. 'I've got a premonition there will be a big mick cop stamping through the premises soon. Let's have them now, Eddie, the names I've been waiting all afternoon to hear.'

Eddie Danville looked around the room. He wet his lips and whispered:

'One of 'em was named Jake.'

'Jake what?'

'Jake. That's all I know.'

'Jake! There are ten thousand Jakes. What was the other one's name. Come now, Eddie. Hurry!'

'Tony. That's all I know. Tony.'

'You're a big help. Tony! Ten thousand Tonys! Wait a minute . . . that man with the scar who died in your kitchen . . . you ever see him before this time?'

'No.'

'His name was Chinny Downs. A killer, according to the cops. Now, Eddie. We know that Chinny Downs was mixed up with Jake and Tony somehow, because he came to your place to do their dirty work for them, and get you before the cops got you. If we could find out who else Chinny Downs was mixed up with . . . Drat it! There's the bell! Remember what I told you, Eddie, about the fire escape . . .'

The bell in Sarah's kitchen went on ringing. It rang furiously, first in frenzied spurts, then long, loud, and insistently. Presently, Sarah swished into the kitchen, silencing the bell by the simple method of jabbing a button in the kitchen wall. As she jabbed, her eyes roved over the kitchen. Suddenly, she ceased jabbing, dashed to the table, grabbed one of the two used coffee cups there, rinsed it and set it back in the cupboard. A moment later, she was at the door which opened from her parlor to the main hall.

'Sergeant,' she greeted the man puffing up the last flight, 'why, I never expected to see you . . .'

Sergeant O'Reilly did not answer. He came on up the stairs, rounded the banister, pushed past Sarah, strode into the little parlor, strode into the cubbyhole bedroom, peered under the bed, jerked open a closet door, yanked at a yellow rubber raincoat and some dangling black garments, then strode back into the kitchen.

'What is this? A raid?' Sarah asked.

'You know what it is. Where is he?'

'Where's who?'

'Charlot. Eddie Danville.'

'Heavens, O'Reilly! You don't mean you think that jail bird . . . that . . . er . . . murderer . . . is here?'

'You know I think he's here and you know why. Ten thousand dollars is why, Sarah Watson. You'd do anything for ten thousand.' His eyes shifted to the window. 'What's that outside that window? Glory be! She's got him on the fire escape!'

O'Reilly dashed to the kitchen window, his gun ready. The shade flew up revealing a dark form on the fire escape.

'Don't shoot, Sergeant,' the fellow pleaded. 'It's Ben Todd. I'm here for the same reason you are. I came back because I got a hunch the old gal was up to something . . .'

Ben Todd jumped down into the kitchen. Sarah Watson stepped between him and O'Reilly, her hands on her broad hips, her bristling brows tied in a knot.

'O'Reilly,' she said, hoarsely, 'I might have expected this from you, but you, Ben Todd . . .' she whirled on the long-legged, red headed young man standing just inside the open window. 'You, you young addlepate. Who do you think you're working for, anyway? Me, or O'Reilly?'

'I'm working for you, Sarah.'

'Not any more, you ain't.'

'I'm working for you, Sarah, and when I got a hunch that jail bird might be here with you . . . Well, I just had to come back to protect you, old girl.'

'Any time I need protection from any man, I'll ask for it! Now, git! No, you stay, Ben Todd. You and me are going to have a talk. O'Reilly, you git! And next time you come here to go through my personal belongings and look under my bed, you bring a search warrant.'

The door banged on O'Reilly's broad back. Before the echoes died away, Sarah was at her front window, peering down. A few moments later, she returned to the kitchen.

'Now,' she said to the young man sitting on the window sill, 'we can talk, Ben Todd. We can talk about what's going to become of you, poor soul, now that you're out of a job.'

Ben Todd grinned. He twisted about on the window sill, reached out a long arm, and dragged into the kitchen a white faced young man in undershirt and dark pants.

'Sarah,' Ben chuckled, 'what do you think would have become of you, poor soul, if I hadn't been out on that fire escape to create a little diversion for Sergeant O'Reilly?'

Sarah Watson looked at Eddie Danville then grinned at Ben Todd.

'Bennie, I wouldn't have given you credit for that much brains!' she said. 'Bennie, meet Eddie – a nice feller, even if he has been in jail, and he's kind to animals and knows how to cook. Drat it! I let the Sergeant get away without asking him . . .' Sarah wheeled and charged out of the kitchen door.

Sarah barked a number into the 'phone on her parlor table.

'O'Reilly back yet?' she asked. 'Good. O'Reilly? Listen. That dead feller in Charlot's kitchen. You said you recognized him – that he was called Chinny Downs. Now listen, O'Reilly. Chinny Downs was a gangster. What gang was he mixed up in?'

'I thought of that, too, you old war horse,' boomed O'Reilly's voice. 'But it's no soap. Chinny was a punk in Big Smiley's gang, just joined up recent. There are a hundred punks just like him lined up with Smiley . . .'

'What's a hundred punks to a bull like you? Get the whole hundred rounded up. Take 'em under the light . . . Listen, O'Reilly. What about the man you found unconscious in the car with that fool Tarrant woman? Maybe he'd spill something?'

'Maybe he would, if he knew something. He says he don't, and I believe him. He says Chinny Downs knew something, but Chinny Downs is dead.'

'Somebody made a mistake,' said Sarah. 'If Chinny had been allowed to live, he might have talked. Oh, well, sometimes it ain't good to be too impulsive.'

'What's that?'

'Nothing, Sergeant. I was just thinking you've made some headway, anyway, toward collecting that ten thousand reward. You know the Courtwell murderer is connected somehow with the Smiley mob. Now, you'd really have that ten thousand reward cinched, Sergeant, if you just knew the name of the murderer, even the first name . . .'

The 'phone clanked in Sarah's ear. She hung up, smiling grimly.

Sarah Watson stalked back into her kitchen. She found Ben Todd with a gun pointed at Eddie Danville, who stood with his back to the wall.

'Bennie, you're being childish,' Sarah said.

'I ain't. This guy is trying to tell me that you put that bullet in Chinny Downs.'

'He's trying to tell you the truth.'

'Sarah! What the devil? Why—'

'If I hadn't, Chinny would have put a bullet in Eddie. I didn't want to see murder done, Bennie, especially when the murderer was liable to be worth ten thousand to you and me.'

Ben Todd sank into his chair, his gun and his mouth both slack. Sarah shoved Eddie Danville into a chair.

'Now, Eddie, tell us,' she asked. 'Do you know the Smiley outfit?'

'Do I know it? Smiley's the guy who framed me into the pen, because I . . .'

'Never mind what you did to him, Eddie. Whatever it was, he deserved it. Now, when you knew the Smiley mob, Eddie, was there maybe a Jake connected with it – a Tony?'

Eddie Danville jumped to his feet and held on to the edge of the table.

'Jake Benner and Tony Corelli!' he cried. 'Why didn't I think of them before? What a blasted fool I am!'

'Of course,' agreed Sarah. 'Sit down, Eddie. You need food. We all need food. We've got work to do before morning, bloody work, maybe. We need red meat.'

Sarah Watson stepped out on her front stoop and peered up and down the dark, sleeping block. She made a dash down the steps, across the sidewalk, and into the battered wreck waiting at the curb.

Two young men ran after her, one of them hatless and enveloped in a voluminous yellow raincoat. The car door slammed. The machine snorted away from the curb.

'Sarah, for Pete's sake, tell us what we're up against,' Ben Todd pleaded. 'If you're planning to break into Smiley's roadhouse hangout, we wouldn't have a chance, the three of us . . .'

'If we break into Smiley's roadhouse,' said Sarah, swerving the car around a corner, 'we'll break in because I know we have a chance.'

'Sarah, for Pete's sake, stop being cryptic . . .'

Sarah Watson slowed the car, stopped it in front of an all night drug store.

'Cryptic? What's that mean?' she asked, then got out of the car and stalked into the drug store.

Sarah Watson stood wedged into a telephone booth, the receiver clamped to her car.

'Hello? This Smiley's roadhouse? Want to speak to Jake. Jake or Tony.'

Sarah waited. She waited a long time. She heard some one step into the booth next to hers. She put out a tentative hand to pull open her door and peer out. Just then, a voice spoke into her ear.

'Yeah? This is Jake.'

'Tony there, too?'

'Who wants to know?'

'Listen, Jake. Smiley don't know it yet but Chinny Downs got his today. He got it in Green Street. Yes, Green Street. And the cops found Jim Corker knocked-out in a car with the Tarrant skirt tied up in the back. They found Jim Corker on Green Street, too. Jim's down at Headquarters now, sweating. Yes, I said sweating. Now listen, Jake. The feller Chinny Downs was after is sneaking back to-night to Green Street. Never mind who I am, Jake. I'm no fool, and neither are you.'

Sarah hung up, tore open the door and peered into the adjoining booth. A red headed young man peered back at her, through smudged glass, then opened the door and stepped out.

'Dumb-ox!' she cried. 'Suppose Eddie's got nervous and skeedaddled while you've been in here, spying on me?'

'Double-crosser,' muttered Ben Todd. 'You never had a job yet that you didn't double-cross somebody. You've double-crossed O'Reilly and now you're going to double-cross Eddie. You old female snake! If Eddie has made a getaway, so much the better for Eddie . . .'

Sarah did not answer, but stalked out of the drug store. Ben Todd followed. At the curb, Sarah peered into the rear of her car and gave a satisfied grunt. She slid in under the wheel, reached out and yanked Ben Todd in by his long arm.

'Bennie,' she said, 'you had one bright flash of intelligence to-night when you stalled off O'Reilly. I suppose I oughtn't to expect anything more of you. Shut up, now. I'm going to talk to Eddie. Eddie, we're going back to your crystal gazing den right now . . .'

'No,' shouted Ben Todd. 'We can't. There'll be at least one cop on duty there. Maybe two.'

'If there's three,' said Sarah, 'there's three of us.'

'Eddie,' Ben Todd warned, 'you take my advice and get out of this car now, while you can.'

'Be quiet,' commanded Sarah. 'Eddie, we're going back to Green Street because if Jake and Tony are as dumb as I think they are, we're going to have callers there.'

'Sarah,' apologized Ben Todd, 'forgive me. But I still don't . . .'

'You ought to apologize,' said Sarah, complacently. 'You ought to grovel.'

'I will,' Ben Todd agreed, 'if I'm able to, after the cops at Eddie's place get through with us.'

'Don't worry about a few paltry policemen,' Sarah insisted. 'The thing to worry about now is whether we can beat Jake and Tony to Green Street.'

The old car plunged around a corner and rattled into amazing speed.

'But, Sarah,' Ben Todd asked, 'even if you get this Jake and this Tony, how are you going to hang the Courtwell murder on 'em so it sticks? You've only got Eddie's word, and Eddie's word . . .'

'Ain't worth a hoot,' Sarah finished for him. 'I know. But there's no use worrying about more than one thing at one time. You leave things to me, Ben Todd.'

Three figures stole down an odorous alley at the side of a tenement in Green Street and stopped in deep shadows. One figure whispered:

'Look's like our company ain't here yet, but we can't be sure. Eddie, you go back into this alley and wait 'til I call you. Cops are too dangerous for you.'

'Listen, old girl,' whispered another one of the figures, 'if you're going to mess up with cops . . .'

'Who said I was going to mess up with cops? Come along, Ben Todd. Keep your hand off that gun and don't get any bright ideas of your own.'

Sarah Watson moved down to the mouth of the alley. She surveyed the street, then charged swiftly out of the alley and up the front stoop of the tenement, with Ben Todd behind her. A long, sleek car was just turning the corner.

Sarah and Ben went through the vestibule door and into the hall. A cop sitting on the bottom step of the stairs roused suddenly, stood up.

'Quick, officer!' Sarah yelled. 'Get inside and turn the lights off in that flat. Eddie Danville's on his way here. Sergeant O'Reilly sent us . . .'

'The hell he did!' roared the cop, reaching for his holster. 'Sergeant O'Reilly is inside that flat . . .'

Sarah Watson lurched suddenly. The cop staggered under the onslaught and sat down again on the bottom step with Sarah on his lap. Sarah's stubby fingers gripped the cop's right wrist.

'Move, Bennie. Take his gun,' she ordered.

Ben Todd snatched at the gun, backed with it in his hand. The cop heaved suddenly, throwing Sarah back, sprawling. The cop charged at Ben Todd. Sarah got to her knees, straightening her hat.

'Officer, she warned, 'if you don't behave, I'll tell Sergeant O'Reilly a woman disarmed you.'

The door to Eddie Danville's flat swung out. Sergeant O'Reilly stood framed in the dim light from the swinging lanterns beyond.

'What's this?' he asked.

'Misunderstanding,' Sarah answered. 'Get those lights off in there, O'Reilly, and get this competent cop stowed away somewhere where he won't be seen. Eddie's coming home.'

Sarah pushed by O'Reilly and into the room beyond, reaching up and switching off the hanging lanterns as she went. O'Reilly remained rigid a moment, then crooked a hairy finger at Ben Todd and the cop and followed Sarah.

Sarah was at the window, the heavy curtains parted in her stubby fingers.

'Two,' she whispered. 'One of 'em coming up the stoop. One of 'em going around the back way. Lord! Eddie's out back, I've got to . . .'

She wheeled, saw the dim forms of the three men.

'All of you hide,' she commanded. 'Somewhere . . . anywhere, and don't move, whatever happens . . . Get in back of those curtains hanging on the wall, the three of you . . .'

'Say!' O'Reilly's voice was husky. 'Who's giving the orders around here, anyway?'

'I am,' said Sarah. 'And if you know what's good for you, O'Reilly, you're taking 'em.'

Sarah strode out of the room and through the kitchen, which was dark. She poked her head out of the window and called softly:

'Eddie!'

No answer. A faint scuffling, a deep groan. Sarah got on the fire escape, peered down.

'Eddie!'

Two forms in the shadows below, struggling. Sarah went down swiftly. The two wrestling figures fell, rolled on the asphalt at her feet.

'Eddie! Which is you?'

A groan answered her. She bent, caught hold of a slippery garment which gleamed faintly yellow in the darkness.

'I'd like to watch a good battle, but there ain't time,' she said, smashing the butt-end of her gun down on the skull of the man straddling Eddie.

Sarah and Eddie dragged a recumbent figure through the kitchen window, laid it on the floor in the darkness. Sarah whispered:

'Which one, Eddie?'

'Jake, I think.'

'Leave Jake lay. I've got to see what Tony is up to . . .'

Sarah stole to the door which led into the front room, and inched the door open. The room on the other side was dark and still. Dimly, Sarah could discern bulges in the dark stuff which curtained the walls, three bulges. In the silence there came a faint clicking of metal against metal. It seemed to come from the door to the hall.

Sarah turned back into the kitchen.

She whispered a warning. 'Eddie, you stay here.'

'No. That's Jake at that door, Sarah. He's a killer.'

'You stay. No nonsense. Wait a minute! Where's that white nightgown of yours . . . ?'

Sarah stepped into the front room and closed the kitchen door firmly behind her. She moved silently in the darkness, reached up and switched on a lantern which hung directly over the crystal ball. The dim rays of the lantern revealed her swathed in a white robe and wearing a white turban well down over her bushy brows. A snort came from one of the bulges in the curtains. Sarah looked at the bulge.

'O'Reilly,' she whispered, 'I've got one of the Courtwell killers in the kitchen and the other one is coming through that door. You stay put and don't snort . . .'

Sarah walked to the hall door and threw it open. The man outside straightened suddenly, reached for his hip.

'Why didn't you ring the bell?' Sarah asked. 'I don't often look into the crystal this late, but if you want a consultation . . .'

Sarah backed into the room. The man followed, shutting the door with his foot. He kept his hand on his hip.

'Where's this guy Charlot?' he rasped.

'Charlot? I don't know. At least, my conscious mind don't know, mister.

Maybe if I looked in the crystal I might see him. Of course, it's late, and my fee would be double . . .'

The man shoved his face close to Sarah's, stared at her under the eerie rays of the lantern.

'So that's it? How much?' he asked.

'Twenty,' Sarah replied. She stalked to the table which held the crystal globe and sat down.

The man hesitated, then lowered himself into the seat opposite.

'Come on now,' he ordered. 'No use stallin' with the fortune tellin' stuff. You know where Charlot is and you're willin' to spill for twenty. Spill, or . . .'

He drew his hand from his hip and showed the gun in it to Sarah. Sarah glanced at it, then bent her head over the crystal globe.

'Charlot!' she muttered. 'I can almost see him. I can see him! He's near, very near. Wait! There's something else swimming into the crystal . . .'

'Can that stuff! Where's Charlot?'

'In a minute. It's coming clear. I see a man's figure . . . lying down . . . very still . . . there are cat-tails swaying over him . . . there's a dark stain on his breast . . . there's something in his breast . . .'

The man with the gun jumped out of his chair, then sat down again. He ran his left hand over his forehead. 'You can't pull that. That's a lot of . . .'

'Ah!' Sarah went on. 'I see it now. It's sticking out of his heart. It's still quivering in his heart. It's a knife, a bone handled knife. . . .'

'Hey!' cried the man on the other side of the table.

'Wait! It's going. Charlot! I see Charlot. Something is between his face and mine. Something black with two sparkling circles in it. Ah! A ring, an onyx ring with two diamonds . . .'

The man with the gun leaped up again. His gun arm came up. He said:

'O. K. You know everything. I don't know whether you see it in that ball, or whether you don't. You know it. You know about the ring I took off Honest Jim Carson's stiff and lost the night I croaked Courtwell. You know it, and it's just too bad for you! Look into your damned crystal and see if you see yourself with wings, lady, because you're going . . .'

Two guns spurted fire – one from the curtained wall, one from the gun in front of Sarah Watson. At the same moment, Sarah pitched the crystal ball through the air. It struck, splintered, crashed. The man who had shot at Sarah crashed with it.

Lights flashed on. Three men – O'Reilly, Ben Todd and the cop, dashed to the writhing figure on the floor. He was surrounded by jagged, bloody glass.

Sarah Watson clasped stubby fingers over an arm which was beginning to seep red into the white of her robe.

'Meet Tony, boys,' she said. 'Too bad I had to break Eddie's crystal.'

O'Reilly straightened, turned and faced Sarah.

'Eddie! Eddie Danville!' he bellowed. 'You said he was coming . . . ?'

'He's come,' said Sarah. 'He's in the kitchen, guarding Jake – Tony's helper in the Courtwell killing. When Jake and Tony are able to talk some more, O'Reilly, you might get 'em to talk a little about how Eddie was railroaded to jail. I'd like to see Eddie cleared, because I want him to buy a new crystal. I want to look into a crystal, O'Reilly, and see future events. I want to see myself handing part of the ten thousand dollars reward for Courtwell's murderers to Ben Todd and part to Eddie Danville . . .'

'Part!' shouted O'Reilly. 'It will be a small part indeed you'll hand out to anybody, Sarah Watson.'

'And part,' said Sarah, 'to Sergeant O'Reilly. It will have to be a small part, of course, because I'll have to divide the ten thousand dollars four ways.'

HE GOT WHAT HE ASKED FOR
D. B. McCANDLESS

I

The heavy front doors of the Citizens' Saving Bank swung in. A woman in rusty black entered the cloistered silence of the main banking room, strode purposefully across the tiled floor and halted at one of the depositors' windows. The woman had a savings bank book in her black-gloved fingers, with some soiled bills folded inside it. The outside of the savings book said, 'Sarah Watson.'

She shoved the book and the money under the elaborate wicket, put an elbow on the marble shelf of the window and swung the thick, rigidly corseted column of her body around, waiting and staring from under bristling iron gray eyebrows.

The clerk behind the wicket made haste to enter her deposit, murmuring polite nothings. She paid no attention to the nothings. She was watching the door. The armed guard stalking from marble column to marble column bowed respectfully to her. Her gray eyes glinted on him a moment, and returned to the door.

The door swung in. A long, lank young man with red hair and ginger-snap freckles entered. The woman's craggy chin grew a trifle more prominent. She reached around, took her savings book from the clerk, thrust it into her shabby, capacious black handbag, and bore down upon the young man.

'Ben Todd!' she said in a voice which echoed hoarsely back from the vaulted ceiling. 'Thought you'd be along, feller. Which are you going to do – put or take?'

The young man grinned sheepishly. He said: 'Whadya think?'

'How much you got left, squirt?'

'Nine dollars and two cents. Not that it's any of your damn business. Just because I'm a ground down underling in your measly detective agency is no reason . . .'

Sarah Watson adjusted her ancient black headgear more firmly upon her hard knob of gray hair. She said: 'You put your bank book back in your pants, young man.

'We're going to see the President of the bank.'

189

'Good Lord! You don't think the President of this mausoleum is going to take pity on my plight?'

'From what I know of him, he never took pity on anything,' said Sarah, grasping the young man's arm firmly, 'but we're going to see him, because he telephoned and asked us to see him. After we've seen him, maybe you won't need your piddling nine dollars. Come on.'

Two minutes later, Sarah Watson and Ben Todd were behind the door which said, in gold letters, 'Adolph A. Hecker, President,' and Sarah was being bowed into a chair by Mr. Adolph A Hecker himself.

'Mr. Hecker,' said Sarah, leaning forward stiffly from the waist, 'meet Mr. Todd, my assistant. We came as soon as possible. Of course we have a great press of work at the office . . .'

'Quite,' said Mr. Hecker, nodding grudgingly at Ben Todd and settling himself behind his large mahogany desk. Mr. Hecker had some difficulty settling himself, because the distance between the edge of the desk and the edge of Mr. Hecker's pot belly had to be nicely judged.

Mr. Hecker made a steeple of his thin white hands and turned his bleak eyes upon Mrs. Watson. He said: 'Quite! Mrs. Watson, I will state the case frankly and concisely. I find myself in need of an agent upon whose discretion I may rely. I make it a practice, as you know, to be informed regarding each and every depositor in my bank . . .'

'The case, please,' said Sarah.

'And so,' said Mr. Hecker, 'knowing you, Mrs. Watson, and your excellent reputation, I – ah – that is to say – Mrs. Watson, what would your fee be for recovering a stolen diamond necklace belonging to my wife?'

'Ten per cent of the value of the necklace,' said Sarah promptly.

'Ten per cent? I had no idea! Does that not seem excessive, my dear lady?'

'Ten per cent,' said Sarah, firmly.

'Ten per cent. Well – ah – perhaps in that case, you would not care to undertake my – ah – job. The necklace I wish recovered is, you see, only paste. A very clever imitation, but paste. The value is relatively small – not more than two thousand dollars.'

'Ten per cent,' said Sarah, '*and* expenses, of course.'

'Ah? The expense would be slight in this case. I happen to know the – ah – young person who stole the necklace. I happen to know where – ah – she will be at a certain time this evening.'

Sarah Watson got to her feet, stood looking down at the square toes of her black shoes. She said: 'A case for the police, Mr. Hecker. Too simple for us.'

'Sit down, Mrs. Watson, pray. It is not simple at all. I – ah – wish it were. Let me explain. I will be frank. This is confidential, of course. Quite!

The necklace – the paste necklace, Mrs. Watson – was taken under peculiar circumstances. The young lady who took it was calling on me at the time at my apartment.

'My wife – ah – happened to be travelling abroad.'

'Quite,' said Sarah.

'What? Oh! Yes, yes. Well, Mrs. Watson, I was showing the young lady my wife's collection of jewels, among them the imitation diamond necklace which my wife keeps for most functions. The real one, which is the famous Gautier necklace, remains in our safe deposit box practically all the time. Now, the – ah – young lady managed to abstract the necklace – the imitation necklace, Mrs. Watson, and shortly afterward, she departed with it, believing that I would be in no position to accuse her of theft . . .'

'Was she right?' said Sarah.

Mr. Hecker's pale eyes wandered away from Sarah's. After a moment, he said: 'She was.'

'Quite,' said Sarah. 'Well now, Mr. Hecker, while I never object to picking up a bit of small change even so small a bit as I would pick up on this job, it doesn't seem to me that it's worth it to you to hire us. If the necklace the young lady removed was simply an imitation, it would be simpler and easier for you to have another imitation made, and . . .'

'Ah, Mrs. Watson, there you have me. I cannot have an imitation made, for this reason. It was yesterday morning that I discovered the theft of the paste necklace and it was yesterday morning that my wife returned from abroad. I had just time to go to our safe deposit box, remove the real necklace and place it in my wife's safe at home, where the imitation had been. It is there now, and there isn't a chance in the world of my extracting it again in order to have an imitation made without my wife's knowing, so . . .'

'I see,' said Sarah, staring intently at Mr. Hecker, 'and of course, there's the fact, too, Mr. Hecker, that if we steal back this necklace for you . . .'

'Mrs. Watson! I beg you – not steal – *recover!*'

'Steal,' said Sarah, firmly. 'If we steal back this necklace for you, Mr. Hecker, it will cost you only two hundred dollars, plus expenses, whereas, if you were to have an imitation made, it would cost you two thousand dollars. Eh, Mr. Hecker?'

'Quite,' said Mr. Hecker. 'I have considered that angle, naturally. A banker always considers . . .'

'Let's get down to brass tacks,' said Sarah. 'What's the young lady's name? What's she look like? Where is this place that you know she'll be this evening? How have you any guarantee that she'll have the necklace with her?'

'She will be on the eight o'clock train to Chicago tonight. She has lower berth number 3, car Number 654,' said Mr. Hecker. 'I am sure she will have the necklace with her, because I have information that she has quit the theatrical production with which she was connected and has – ah – closed her books definitely in this city.'

'Mr. Hecker,' said Sarah, 'did you get all that data yourself?'

'I did.'

'You'd make a good detective,' said Sarah. 'What's the young female's name?'

Mr. Hecker's thin lips writhed a trifle as though he were about to swallow a dose of astringent. He said: 'Her name is Dolores Flores.'

'That describes her,' said Sarah. 'Now, if you'll advance some expense money, Mr. Hecker, about two hundred dollars to start with, we'll get ready to steal your necklace.'

Sarah Watson and Ben Todd stepped out of the bank and into the sunshine. Sarah said: 'You've got two hundred dollars in your pants, Bennie, and all afternoon. You might get the tickets. Be sure to get in Car 654, and be sure you get me a lower, young feller. You might drop my ticket at the office. Then you might check up on this Dolores Flores female and make sure she is taking that train. You might get a look at her, if you can, but not too long a look, Bennie. I know men! Then you might interview somebody that knows jewels and find out what the Gautier necklace looks like and how much the real one is worth, and then you might . . .'

'Listen, slave driver,' said Ben Todd, 'after I do all that, there won't be any *then*. What are you doing in the way of work yourself this afternoon, old girl?'

'Bennie,' said Sarah solemnly, 'I'm going to a tea – a Republican tea.'

'Republican? I thought you were a Democrat?'

'What if I am? It ain't branded on my forehead, is it? I'm going to a Republican tea, Bennie, because Mrs. Adolph A. Hecker is giving the tea, in her own apartment.

'Listen, you old wench! You're not beginning your double-crossing tricks already?'

'Fiddlesticks! I'm merely interested to see the woman who could bear Adolph as a husband. Bennie, do ladies wear diamond necklaces at tea parties?'

'Not ladies,' said Ben Todd. 'Sarah, you're up to something. Now listen, you stalking tigress, Adolph may only be going to pay us a coupla hundred . . .'

'And expenses . . .'

'But a coupla hundred would pay my salary for four weeks, Sarah, so for hell's sake, stick to Adolph.'

'Bennie, you know me. I have yet to betray the confidence of a client. Good-by. I'll see you on the train.'

II

Sarah Watson stalked down the ramp beside which the Chicago train waited. She was dressed as she had been dressed that morning. She held firmly a large yellow suitcase of the cardboard variety and ignored, as she stalked, the three pestiferous red caps who pursued her.

Halfway down the long train, her steps slackened. There was a young man lounging there, with one foot on the lowest step of a car. He was a red-headed young man and he was deep in converse with a slinky young person who was aggressively female from the black velvet hat perched on her platinum curls to the black velvet bows on her spike heeled slippers.

Sarah took longer strides. She stopped abruptly beside the conversing couple. She said:

'Young man, is this car 654?'

The young man stared blankly at her a moment, then his wide mouth grew wider. He said: 'Well, if it ain't Aunt Sarah! Auntie, you're early. I want you to meet my friend, Miss Dolores Flores.'

Miss Flores extended a drooping hand which dripped ruby red at the fingernails. She said: 'Charmed!'

Sarah Watson grunted. She gave a nod which set her ancient headgear to quivering. She turned her back and mounted the steps. At the top of the steps, she paused. Ben Todd's red head was close to the platinum blonde curls. Ben Todd was whispering and the young lady was giggling. Sarah peered down at them and made a horrible face.

The conductor was bawling his last warning when Miss Dolores Flores made her entrance into car 654, followed by Ben Todd. The young lady's progress down the aisle was marked by a small flurry among the seated passengers, particularly the males. Only the woman in Section 4 remained oblivious, and she kept her rugged countenance bent over a printed circular until the pair passed. The circular said: 'Twenty Reasons why American Ladies Should Vote Republican.' One sheet of the circular was devoted to the photograph of a lady whose nose and bosom were both prominent. The photograph was inscribed in flowing ink, 'With regards to Mrs. Sarah Watson, from Mrs. Adolph A Hecker.'

Ben Todd slid into seat 4, beside Sarah. Sarah lifted her eyes from the circular and fixed them on the elaborate curls which covered the back of Miss Flores' head. Sarah said: 'If you've got the necklace, Bennie, we've still time to get off?'

'Got the—! Whatya think I am, woman, a professional dip?'

'I think you're a damn fool,' said Sarah. 'If you ain't got the necklace, what was the idea of all the billing and cooing?'

'Listen, horse-face,' whispered Ben Todd, leaning closer, 'I – er – happened to scrape an acquaintance with the charmer in the course of my investigations this afternoon and . . .'

'I'll bet you didn't have to scrape very hard!'

'No. She likes auburn hair. Now listen, and no more cracks, old lady. This is biz. The charmer's afraid. She's asked me to protect her. There's a naughty, bad man with dark hair and slimey eyes and a wart on his chin . . .'

'And two hairs growing out of the wart,' said Sarah. 'I know. I saw him on the observation platform as I came by. And I've seen him somewhere before, but I can't think where. He looks like a bad 'un. Now, I wonder who sicked him on Dolores?'

'Hell knows. You say he was on the observation . . . ?'

'He was, but he ain't now. Look!'

Ben Todd followed the lift of Sarah's gray eyes. A dark individual was sliding into the seat directly opposite theirs.

'Bennie,' said Sarah, 'I've got a premonition we have competition. We've got to look spry. It might not be a bad idea for you to go and bill and coo some more with Dolores. Buy her new magazines and things and charge 'em to Mr. Hecker. Stick with her – No! Wait—'

Sarah had risen abruptly. The young lady with the platinum tresses was making her way forward toward the door marked 'Ladies.' Sarah stepped over Ben Todd's long legs and into the aisle. The train began to move. Sarah lurched forward toward the door marked, 'Ladies.'

Five minutes later, Miss Flores was back in her seat and Sarah was back in hers.

'Ben,' whispered Sarah, 'when that girl bleached her hair, she bleached out all her brains. She's got that necklace in her handbag, crammed in with all the face paint and lip paint and the cigarettes and the rest of it. I saw it – the Gautier necklace!'

'The imitation of the Gautier necklace.'

'I was forgetting,' said Sarah. 'Well, the imitation's worth two thousand, ain't it? The girl's an imbecile. Go on up, now, Bennie, and sparkle for her. Keep your eye on her purse but don't put your hand in it. When the time comes for snitching, I'll snitch.'

'Well, when is the time coming for snitching? That's a little detail we ain't worked out, yet, old girl.'

'*We* ain't but *I* have. It won't be until after dinner anyway, Bennie. I never steal except on a full stomach.'

The train sped on. Sarah sat with her head back against the green plush, her hands folded over her prominent abdomen. Two hours passed. A black man with a white smile and a white coat came down the aisle, beating a musical gong. Sarah stirred. Ben Todd came down the aisle, behind him, Miss Dolores Flores. They stopped at Sarah's seat.

'If you don't object, Auntie,' said Ben Todd, 'Miss Flores and I are going to dine togeth—'

'Delighted,' said Sarah, rising. 'Love to eat on trains. Lead the way, nephew.'

After dinner was over, Ben Todd squired Dolores into the club car at the end of the train for a cigarette. Sarah returned to car 654, and was occupying the seat opposite her own, while the porter made up her lower and the upper above it – reserved for Ben Todd. Sarah wore the complacent and reminiscent look of one who has relished good food.

A long-legged young man charged suddenly into the almost empty car and gripped Sarah by the shoulder. He said: 'Listen. There's a stop in five minutes. I saw you fingering the girl's purse. If you've got the goods, let's hop off and . . .'

Sarah shook his fingers off. She half rose from the seat and pushed her face close to his. She said: 'You go back and stick with the fool girl, Ben Todd. She's in danger as long as she's got that thing in her bag. I've just remembered where I saw the gent with the wart last – Go!'

Ben Todd waited a moment, staring. Then he wheeled and charged back down the aisle. In the doorway he collided with a gentleman who also seemed in haste. The gentleman had a wart on his chin.

Sarah settled back in her seat and closed her eyes. A few moments passed. Someone again laid a hand on her shoulder. She started, looked up into a pair of slimey, dark eyes. She said: 'Mercy! I'm afraid I'm sitting in your place, mister. The porter's making up my bed. If you don't mind, I'll just—' she slid over to make room for the owner of the seat.

The gentleman with the wart sat down.

Sarah said: 'You know, I've seen you some place before, mister.'

The gentleman with the wart looked her over. He said:

'Old stuff! You ain't.'

'Maybe it was a picture of you I saw,' said Sarah thoughtfully. 'I see a lot of pictures of people—'

The porter said: 'All ready, Madam.'

Sarah rose. She glanced down at the face with the wart. She crossed the aisle and disappeared between the green curtains of her berth.

For five minutes thereafter, Sarah's hoarse voice grunted and groaned behind her curtains. Then, she emerged, swathed in a purple crêpe robe, and lurched up the aisle toward the Ladies' Room. When she returned, the gentleman with the wart had vanished. There was no one in the car to notice that Sarah was still thoroughly corseted and shod under her kimono.

An hour passed – two hours – three hours. The berths were all made up and the car dark, except for the dim lights at either end. Someone fell against the curtains of Sarah's berth. She opened them with a gun in her hand. She saw a ladder and a pair of long legs ascending the ladder, and she lay back. She kept the curtains slightly parted with one hand, and her eye fixed to the opening.

More hours passed, hours filled with the hooting of the train's whistle and the rattling of the train's wheels. Sarah opened her curtains wide and surveyed the empty aisle. She drew back into her cubicle and tapped smartly on the ceiling above her.

'Huh?' said a sleepy voice. Sarah tapped again. She put her feet into the aisle and stood up. She was still wrapped in her purple kimono.

The curtains of the upper berth parted. A rumpled red-head appeared in the opening. Sarah said, very softly:

'Time! Ring for the porter. Keep him busy this end.'

The red head nodded. Its eyes blinked. Sarah strode up the aisle. At the other end of the car, the porter's bell began to ring, insistently. It was then three A.M.

Two minutes later, Sarah thrust her head out of the Ladies' Room door and peered down the car. Deserted. Not a sound but the faint wailing of the train.

Sarah began to walk down the aisle toward her own section. She paused before she got there, her hand gripping the curtains of the lower occupied by Miss Dolores Flores.

III

In the men's washroom, Ben Todd took his head out of his hands and looked up into the anxious face of the porter. Ben Todd said:

'I feel better now, George. What time is it?'

'Three fifteen, suh.'

'Um. So we been in here ten minutes, huh? Well, George, that was sure nifty liquor you gave me. It did the trick. Here!'

Ben Todd thrust a bill into the porter's ready fingers and stood up.

He said: 'Don't bother any more about me, now, George. Just stay and finish up that bottle.'

Ben Todd swayed down the aisle toward section 4. The car was dark, silent. The ladder was still in place in front of his berth.

Ben Todd climbed up. Someone had switched the light on over his bed. Someone had left a slip of paper stuck into his pillow with a large safety pin. The determined script on the paper was Sarah Watson's. It said: 'Next stop 3:25. Get ready. The girl is dead.'

There was no signature. There was a smudge of red near the ragged lower edge of the note.

Ben Todd sat hunched up, staring. His freckles began to take on a darker hue against the whitening of his face. Presently, the paper began to shake a little in his hand.

It was sixty seconds before he began frenziedly adjusting the few garments he had removed that night. He was badly handicapped by the jerkiness of his breathing and the fumbling of his fingers.

At 3:24, he was sitting cross legged on his berth, gripping his valise. There was no sound from the berth beneath him.

At 3:25, the train stopped. Still no sound from below.

At $3:25\frac{1}{2}$, there was a stir in the aisle. Ben Todd peered down, saw a man dashing into the vestibule of the car.

At 3:26, the conductor's whistle blew from the platform outside the train, and the train gave a preliminary lurch.

Sarah Watson erupted from her berth, charged down the aisle. Ben Todd swung his long legs over at the same instant, ignored the ladder, leaped, followed her, caught up with her in the vestibule. The conductor was just mounting the steps. Sarah put a hand on his chest and shoved. She went by him like a blast.

The conductor leaped back on the moving train, cursing. Ben Todd slid into the next vestibule and jumped. He landed sitting down on the dark platform, the few scattered lights of the town beyond the station pinwheeling in his head.

A firm hand hauled him up. A hoarse voice said: 'Stop resting, feller. I've got a car waiting.'

Together, they dashed around the dark bulk of the station, dived into the lone car waiting in the dreary street beyond. The taxi began to move. There was only one other car in sight, its tail light rapidly diminishing. Ben Todd said: 'Sarah! That poor girl! How—?'

Sarah lifted her black gloved hands. She crooked the fingers suggestively. She said: 'This is the way it happened, Bennie.'

'God!' breathed Ben Todd. 'Strangled! Sarah, what in the name of hell are we going to do now?'

'We're going to keep quiet if you know what's good for you,' said Sarah, with a glance at the driver's back. 'This is no place to discuss—'

Sarah broke off and leaned toward the driver. She said:

'This flying field, young man. It is the only one hereabouts? You're sure? Good! Now, listen, young feller, a lot depends on this. You sure there ain't a single solitary private plane to rent at that field, for love nor money?'

The taxi driver kept his head over the wheel and nodded. They were making speed. The tail light of the single car ahead was growing larger.

Sarah said: 'Then you're damn sure, young man, that there ain't a plane of any kind or description flying out of this place until the regular passenger plane comes through at four A.M. and takes off again?'

The driver nodded. He said, 'You can stake your life on it.'

'Maybe I am,' said Sarah, quietly, and leaned back against the cushions.

Ben Todd spent the next ten flying minutes hunched in his corner, staring at Sarah Watson's rugged profile, which looked white in the flash of occasional street lamps, dark and brooding in the intervals between.

The taxi swerved on to a dirt road, bumped to a stop in front of a fenced field. There was a gate in the fence, and beyond the fence, a square, box-like structure.

Ben Todd reached for the door handle on his side of the car. Sarah gripped his arm. She said: 'Wait!'

The man standing just inside the gate of the flying field moved on, passed into shadows, emerged again and walked through the door of the square building beyond the gate.

Sarah said: 'All right, now,' thrust a crumpled bill into their driver's hand and got out. They passed through the gate and halted, Sarah's fingers digging into Ben Todd's arm, in their ears, the diminishing sound of the car they had come in. Sarah Watson said: 'We've got about fifteen minutes to wait, if the plane's on time. Don't spend any of 'em in the light, Ben Todd, and don't go near that waiting room, until the last minute, and then get our tickets. If you can change your appearance any while you're hanging around in the dark, do it. And give me your valise. I need the duds in it.'

'Sarah!' Ben Todd's voice sounded as though rust had attacked his vocal chords, 'Sarah, you're not going to try to get into my clothes? They won't fit you and you couldn't get away with it anyway, old girl. Listen! I'd do anything to get you clear of this terrible thing, Sarah, but . . .'

'Idiot! Give me that bag. Remember, keep out of sight 'til the last minute. I'll meet you just before the plane leaves the ground.'

Sarah Watson grabbed Ben Todd's valise from his nerveless hand and strode away and was lost in the shadows at the far side of the field.

Ben Todd located the spot where the plane would settle down to discharge and admit passengers. Thereafter, he skulked in shadows, his forehead beaded with perspiration in spite of the cool wind of approaching dawn. Once or twice, he thought he saw the dark bulk of Sarah's figure melt into the darker bulk of the shadowed side of the waiting room structure. Several times, he was sure he saw a flashlight darting there, close to the ground. Then, the distant drone of a big plane came to his ears and he lifted anxious eyes. The stars were fading out and gray was washing into the ceiling above him.

Like a monstrous, murmuring white bird, the plane rested in the white path of the runway. The trim stewardess stood at one side of the rear door, the collar-ad co-pilot at the other side, watch in hand. Faces peered out of the windows of the plane, waiting.

The co-pilot snapped his watch shut, grinned at the stewardess, put his foot on the first of the two little steps up to the plane's door.

A woman ran out from behind the waiting room, carrying a man's valise in one hand, a yellow cardboard suitcase in the other. An enveloping, bright yellow rain coat flapped as she ran. The bags smacked against her thighs as she came on.

She slowed. She lifted the hand with the valise in it and straightened the exotic creation of black velvet and nodding violets which had slid forward off her grey hair and was threatening to blind her. She came to a full stop, set the valise down, and adjusted the polka-dotted veil which hung from the hat, drawing it well down and over her prominent chin.

A long legged young man shot out from the waiting room door and joined her. She thrust the bags into his hands.

'Here,' she said. 'You handle it. Tell 'em we know the suitcase weighs too much, but your valise don't weigh anything, because it's empty now. Tell 'em to divide the weight of the suitcase between us, because we're travelling together. Don't bollix it, feller. It's important—'

Sarah Watson charged on, thrust a ticket under the co-pilot's handsome nose and entered the plane. She went in with no more sound than the rattling of her stiff yellow raincoat, and she took a seat at the rear.

The seats were brown leather, four seats on each side of the aisle. A man and woman sat on one side, rather white and tense. In front of them, an elderly gentleman, evidently a person of means, read a book.

On the other side, Ben Todd sat in the last seat, with his back against a walled-off cubicle labelled 'Stewardess.' In front of him, sat Sarah Watson. In the front seat on that side of the aisle, just behind the glass partition which separated the passengers from the pilots, a man sat. All that was visible of the man from the rear was a section of dark hair and a soft felt hat.

The plane soared. The squares of dark and light on the earth beneath grew smaller, then began to take form in the growing light. Here and there, sunlight glinted on a steeple.

Sarah Watson turned in her seat. Ben Todd leaned forward. Sarah said, through her veil: 'Well, we made it. But I can't say I think much of your ideas of disguise. Any fool can turn up his coat collar and pull down his hat. Couldn't you have rustled a false mustache or something, Bennie? Not that it matters now. We're on and nobody can get off this thing until—'

'Sarah, listen! You can't get away with it, old girl! The cops will be waiting for you at the next stop.'

'Waiting for me?' Sarah thrust her proboscis close to Ben's, 'Waiting for *me?* Ben Todd, do you mean to say you've been thinking that I – do you mean to say that you've been thinking that poor girl is dead because I—?'

Ben Todd stared into the eyes behind Sarah's dotted veil. For a long time, neither of them moved, except to sway slightly with the swaying of the plane. Ben Todd said, slowly: 'I've been a damn fool, old girl. But you've got to admit you acted like you had something damn unpleasant to run away from.'

'Not from,' said Sarah, hoarsely. 'After! Look ahead, Bennie. Ain't there something familiar about the back of that head?'

Ben Todd stared at the dark hair resting on the leather cushions of the seat up the aisle. He stared at the soft felt hat on top of the hair. Presently, Ben Todd said, very quietly:

'Wart face!'

'Exactly,' said Sarah.

'But listen – if you mean you think he killed—'

'I know he killed her.'

'Well, then, why the hell all the dramatics? Why the hell didn't we get him at the landing field?'

'You're forgetting we also want to get the necklace.'

'What of it? If he killed her, he's got the necklace. We'd have got it. You could simply have claimed it for old Hecker.'

'And had the cops hold it as evidence for months? Listen, Bennie. I set out to steal that necklace, and I'm going to steal it, for reasons of my own. Bennie, in which of a man's pockets do you think he'd be likely to hide a diamond – a necklace he thought was diamonds?'

'Listen, you damn fool woman. If that guy has the necklace, let him keep it. He's dangerous!'

'Bennie,' said Sarah, 'don't worry about me. Now, think! Where'd he be likely to put that necklace?'

'God knows. The Gautier necklace is pretty bulky, so the imitation must be, too. He might hide it in his luggage, far as that goes.'

'He has no luggage. He must have hopped that train in a hurry, must have learned at the last minute that the necklace was on board. Think, now, Bennie! Which pocket?'

'Wait a mo,' said Ben Todd, slowly. 'I'm remembering something – in the dining car, while you were shovelling in grub, I was watching. I saw that guy take his wallet out to pay. He took it out of an inside coat pocket, left hand side. The pocket seemed to have some special kind of zipper arrangement on it.'

'Bennie, you're worth your wages, sometimes! Let's see, now. The next landing is in three quarters of an hour. In about half an hour, Bennie, I'm going to be sick.'

'Sick? Whad'ya mean, sick?'

'Sick. Lots of people get sick on planes. I never rode on a plane before, and I'm a sensitive nature, Bennie. I'm not only going to be sick, but I'm going to get hysterical. I'm going to do some staggering and some screeching. I'm going to stagger up front and then I'm going to stagger back.'

'Listen, Sarah, for hell's sake! That fellow's a killer. He's dangerous.'

'After I stagger back, Bennie, I'm going to stagger into that little cubbyhole right behind you. Your job is to see that that little snip of a stewardess don't follow me in there. After I'm in, Bennie, just let things take their course . . . just let things take their course.'

Sarah turned squarely around. She became absorbed in peering out of her window. Ben Todd regarded the grey, rocky knob of hair on the back of her head for a long time. His lips moved silently. A lip reader reading those lips would have blushed.

Presently, Ben Todd relaxed and stared down from his window. Below, the earth revolved, slowly. Above, the thin, pink tinted clouds raced.

Sarah Watson stirred. She glanced at the small, plump watch pinned on her bosom. She rose.

Sarah gulped dangerously as she stood up. She gulped again and lurched into the aisle. She made some loud, unintelligible noises. She began to sway up the aisle.

The alert stewardess started down the aisle to meet her. Sarah stumbled, knocked the stewardess sidewise, went on with a rush. Sarah was screeching now, loud, thin screeches from which words were beginning to emerge.

'Stop the plane! I'm scared! I'm scared stiff! Something's going to happen—'

Ben Todd was in the aisle, racing after the stewardess. The stewardess was racing after Sarah. Sarah was now at the glass partition which separated the pilots from the passengers. Sarah was banging on the glass with clenched fists. She was yelling her terror.

The stewardess reached Sarah, clawed at the yellow rubber which covered Sarah's broad back. Sarah went on yelling, went on pounding.

Ben Todd reached the stewardess. He put firm hands on the stewardess. He said: 'The old lady's scared into a fit. You can't handle her. Let me.'

Sarah Watson wheeled suddenly. She staggered. One of her thick arms went out in a wild, wide sweep. The fist at the end of the arm struck Ben Todd on the point of the chin. Ben Todd staggered. His long arms sawed the air. One of the arms struck the stewardess.

With a last weird yell, Sarah Watson collapsed. She collapsed over the dark gentleman sitting directly behind the glass partition. The dark gentleman and Sarah became a conglomerate, moving mass of waving arms and legs, a mass slipping and sliding over the leather seat, a mass vocal with grunts and gasps.

The stewardess recovered. She leaped into the fray. She clawed indiscriminately at portions of Sarah's anatomy and portions of the dark gentleman.

Ben Todd gripped the edge of the dark gentleman's seat. Ben Todd swung out a long arm and curved it about the slender waist of the stewardess. Ben Todd lifted the stewardess up and out into the aisle. He said:

'I told you I could handle her. Lay off!'

Suddenly, Sarah Watson was on her feet. She was sagging against Ben Todd. She was pulling down her veil as she sagged. She was moving rapidly toward the rear of the plane, moaning as she moved, and taking Ben Todd with her.

The dark-haired gentleman was straightening himself. He was gulping in deep breaths. He was putting his hand to his left side. He was rising from his seat.

Sarah reached the door of the little cubicle marked 'Stewardess.' She opened the door. She said, loudly:

'No! Leave me alone! I want to be alone! Oh, I'm so ashamed!' and she slammed the door of the little cubicle shut in Ben Todd's face.

The stewardess was at Ben Todd's shoulder. The stewardess was reaching past Ben Todd, trying to open the door of the little cubicle.

Ben Todd closed his fingers about the wrist of the stewardess. He said: 'Leave the poor old thing alone. She just got scared, and now she's ashamed.'

A new voice rose over the tumult, the voice of the dark haired gentleman:

'I've been robbed!' he screamed. 'Robbed!' The dark haired gentleman was in the aisle now, facing the rear, his arms raised, his wart revealed to all who cared to look. 'Robbed!' he screamed again.

The door of the little cubicle burst open. Sarah Watson came out of the cubicle with a rush, covering her veiled face with her hands.

'A man in there!' she howled. 'A man! He hit me. Oh, my! He hit me and he jumped out of the window in there. He jumped and he's going down with one of those parasol things!'

The passengers were all on their feet now, swaying and jerking, momentarily in danger of entangling with each other in the centre of the aisle. As Sarah's screech reached them each followed with his eyes the direction of Sarah's stubby, pointing finger, and each scrambled into a seat, peered out a window.

'Look! A man – she's right – his parachute's stuck – no, it's unfolding – he hit her – he must have been hid in there all the time!'

The dark haired man got back into the aisle again. He raised an arm and pointed it at Sarah. He yelled:

'I've been robbed! That woman robbed me!'

'What?' Sarah's answering yell was hoarse, 'You've been robbed? You're accusing me – me? Look down there, man. Look! There goes your thief!'

'I've been robbed!' yelled the dark haired man. 'She took them. She took the diamonds – my diamonds! She . . . that woman . . .'

'Diamonds?' said Sarah hoarsely. 'My dear man! Just look out of the windows, as everybody else is looking!'

The passengers ceased staring with popping eyes at Sarah and the man with the wart. The passengers pressed their faces again against the windows:

'Look! He said diamonds – wait – the wind is carrying the parachute this way. What's that shining down there in the man's hand? Diamonds – he said diamonds – there's something shining in that man's hand. He's got away with the diamonds – he must have been hiding in there all the time. It's a blessing we're not all dead!'

The man with the wart got out into the aisle again. He raised his arms and shook his fists. He cried:

'That man's got my diamonds! That man! Stop the plane! That thief has my diamonds. He's going to land any minute! Stop the—'

And suddenly the man with the wart ceased yelling and crowded to a window and fixed his eyes avidly on the figure slowly drifting down, drifting now very close to earth, near the wide spread of a red factory's roofs!

The plane tilted, began to point its nose toward the earth. The man with the wart lost his balance on the slippery seat upon which he had been kneeling. He slid, he clawed at the seat, he banged his head against the back of the seat in front, and he fell.

The stewardess ran to him and said, 'The plane's stopping very soon now, anyway, sir – the regular stop. And you must have seen where that thief landed with your diamonds—'

Sarah Watson settled in her seat and folded her hands complacently. She turned her head and Ben Todd leaned toward her.

'Bennie,' she said, close to Ben Todd's ear, 'Bennie, I've always said that all men were alike, but the one that just landed under that parachute is different, Bennie, because I made him myself. I had a hell of a time finding enough scrap iron about that airport to weigh him down, and a hell of a time stealing a parachute there, too, and, of course, there's a good suit of yours gone to pot to clothe him, but we can charge the suit to Mr. Heckcr.'

A hand touched Sarah on the shoulder. She turned, looked up through her veil at the face of the gentleman with the wart.

'Madam,' said the gentleman, 'I wish to apologize for accusing you of stealing my diamonds. I was wrong!'

'That,' said Sarah, 'is perfectly all right, perfectly all right.'

The man with the wart leaned closer. He stared down into the face behind the polka dots of Sarah's veil. He said: 'Madam, I—' and suddenly wrenched the veil away, brushing aside the clutch of Ben Todd's fingers.

The man with the wart stared down into the eyes under Sarah Watson's bristling brows. He said, very slowly, and lingeringly:

'Ah!'

Sarah said nothing. The thin lips under her incipient mustache curved slightly.

The gentleman with the wart began to talk with a rush of words. He said:

'I see! I remember you! I know you now! You took them and you passed them over to him back here and he jumped with them. What a dummy I've been! – A *dummy!* I see it all now! A *dummy!* Not a man, but a—'

The plane bumped. Dust fanned past its windows from the whirring propeller. There was another bump.

The man with the wart took one more moment to glare balefully into Sarah's eyes. He said: 'You think you're damn smart, yes, but I'll outsmart you yet, you old harridan.'

And then he rushed to the door at the rear of the plane, wrenched it open, and leaped while the plane was still gliding down the runway. In the silence which followed the cessation of movement and sound, Sarah Watson's voice said hoarsely: 'The gent who lost his diamonds seems to be in a hurry to get some place.'

The car carrying Sarah Watson and Ben Todd away from the airport sped along the wide, white boulevard. Ahead of it, another car sped – far ahead.

Ben Todd took his clenched hands off his knees for a moment and turned to Sarah. He said:

'He may make it yet. If he's as smart as I am, he knows just about where that dummy landed.'

Sarah Watson unfolded her hands, opened her capacious handbag, stared at herself in the bag's mirror. She said: 'Becoming hat, this. It's my Sunday hat.'

'Sarah, for the love of – listen, that guy with the wart is gaining. He's going to get there long before we do. He's going to get there and he's going to find that dummy, and he's going to get that necklace. Sarah, you've got to think of something!'

'I am thinking of something,' said Sarah, snapping her bag shut. 'I'm thinking we'd better tell the driver to slow up a bit.'

'Listen, you! You gone batty? Can't you see that guy is eating up the road?'

'Bennie,' said Sarah calmly, 'some day you're going to have a nervous breakdown. Now listen. You may think you know just where that dummy landed and probably the gent with the wart thinks he knows, too, but things look different from the air, Bennie, and I'm betting the gent with the wart is going to spend a long time searching for that necklace . . .' Sarah broke off and leaned forward to the driver.

'Driver,' she said. 'Take the next turning, please. And don't go so fast. My partner's a bit nervous.'

'Who wouldn't be nervous!' yelled Ben Todd, 'with an idiot woman like you! Slow up and let me out of here, driver. I'm going to get another car and go after that guy . . .'

'You're going to stay right in this car,' said Sarah firmly. 'Take the next crossing, driver – the one that leads to the police station.'

IV

Sarah Watson strode into police headquarters, her fingers on Ben Todd's arm. Ben Todd's pallor was excessive and his forehead was dewed with sweat.

'Captain,' said Sarah to the man behind the desk, 'I'm Sarah Watson. Here's my card. This is my assistant. We're here to put you on the trail of the murderer of Dolores Flores.'

'Already?' said the man behind the desk. 'We just got it over the wire that they'd found that dame dead on the train to Chi.'

'Let me talk, Captain. I'm in a hurry. I was on that train. I had the berth opposite the murderer's. I meant to keep my eyes on him all night because I knew who he was. I'd seen his photo in the police files at home. Wait, let me talk, Captain.

'I meant to watch him, but my eyes got stuck together for a few minutes and when I opened them, I saw the murderer sneaking back into his berth from somewhere. He was in his shirt sleeves. He had something red on his cuff, his right cuff. It'll be there yet, when you get him.'

'Blood, eh? Where is this guy?'

'Not blood, captain. There was no blood. The girl was strangled to death. When I found her, dead, in her berth, her handbag was lying open beside her. There was a lipstick in it, blood red, and uncapped. The metal case of the lipstick had printing on it that said the lipstick was made special for Dolores Flores. Your chemists will be able to match that lipstick up with the red smudge on the murderer's cuff, Captain, when you get him.'

'Say listen, where is this guy? Where do we get him?'

'Let me talk, Captain. The murderer got that smudge on his cuff, of course, when he put his thieving hand in the girl's purse to steal her valuables. I would have got the same smudge on my own – er – hand, if I had put it in. But of course, I didn't. Fingerprints, you know, Captain. Now, Captain, if you'll just send a squad car out with a half dozen men with guns. There's a big red brick factory about ten miles southwest of the airport here.'

'The Furness factory,' said the Captain.

'The name don't matter,' said Sarah. 'The point is, you'll probably have to beat the woods that lie south of the factory. The murderer will be in those woods, doing some beating himself, for something he lost. You'll catch him easy, Captain. Those woods are big and they're thick, and the murderer don't know just where to look. He's a dark man, the murderer, with black eyes, and a wart on his chin with two hairs sprouting out of it and—'

'Warty Capruccio! He's been up for murder before, and slipped clear.'

'The same, Captain. Well, Captain, you've got my card and you can reach me if you want to, though you won't have a smidgin of trouble convicting Warty without me, I'm sure. I'm in a hurry now, Captain, because I'm on a job, and it ain't finished yet.'

Sarah Watson and Ben Todd emerged from the building which housed the local police. Ben Todd was not only perspiring, he was gnawing his nails.

'Sarah, here comes a cab. I don't know what in hell's name you were up to in there, wasting time, setting the cops on that guy's trail.'

'Time,' said Sarah, sententiously, 'is never wasted when it's used to bring a criminal to justice.'

'You should talk about criminals! Listen, you imbecilic old battle-axe, we may have time yet to repair the damage you've done. If we hire a plane, we can get there before the cops get there . . . Sarah, stir your stumps! We've got to get that necklace . . .'

'Bennie,' said Sarah, 'you can go hire a plane if you want to. But it ain't worth it, especially as we couldn't charge it to Mr. Hecker's expense. The necklace that dummy took down to earth came from the five and ten, Bennie, and it cost me a dollar. It ain't worth retrieving, because it's already charged to Mr. Hecker, anyway. I had it ready to drop in that poor girl's purse, in case I managed to steal the string she had.'

'Sarah! Do you mean to say you fumbled getting the imitation string from the murderer?'

'I never fumble anything, young man,' said Sarah, and opened her purse.

Ben Todd stared down at the coiled, glittering thing in the bottom of Sarah's purse. He had put his hand out toward the purse. Sarah snapped the purse shut. She advanced to the curb and signalled a taxi. She said: 'The thing to do now, Bennie, is to get the first train out of here for home. I've got a date with Mrs. Adolph A. Hecker.'

'Mrs. Hecker! Why you damn, double-crossing old . . .'

'Mrs. Hecker,' said Sarah, 'is a very fine woman, even if she is married to Mr. Hecker. Mrs. Hecker has promised me ten thousand dollars for this necklace, Ben Todd.'

Sarah Watson stepped into the cab. Ben Todd stepped after her and flopped on the seat. Ben Todd took his head in his hands. He said:

'My head, my poor, poor head! I knew before this thing was over you'd have us tied up in a mess of double-crossing, triple-crossing knots!'

'Bennie,' said Sarah, firmly. 'You wrong me. I engaged to do a job for Mr. Hecker and I intend to do it. Of course, Mr. Hecker shouldn't have lied to me. If you had eyes in your head, Bennie, you'd have seen him lying. Ten per cent seemed excessive to him, Bennie, until he happened to remember that the necklace he wanted to recover was paste, nothing but paste. Oh, well, all men are alike! Let's see now . . . Ten thousand from Mrs. Hecker, and two hundred from Mr. Hecker, and expenses from both of them.'

'Sarah Watson! How in hell are you going to collect two hundred from Mr. Hecker when you haven't got a necklace to turn over to him – when you're turning the necklace over to his wife?'

'Simple,' said Sarah. 'Mrs. Hecker is turning the imitation over to me, Bennie, when she pays me the ten thousand. The imitation has been in Mrs. Hecker's wall safe ever since Mr. Hecker put it there, after Dolores Flores – poor girl – stole the real necklace under Mr. Hecker's eyes. Let's see now . . . ten thousand and two hundred and . . .'

The doors of the Citizens Savings Bank swung open, letting in morning sunshine. A woman in rusty black strode across the tiled floor and halted at a depositors' window. A long legged young man entered behind her and strode to another depositors' window. With perfect timing the two shoved bank books and sizeable wads of bills under the wickets of their respective windows.

A door at the side of the banking room slammed. The slam echoed against the vaulted ceiling. Sarah Watson turned, leaning her elbow on the sill of the window. Her bristling brows lowered over her eyes as she watched the pompous figure of the bank's president come toward her across the tile floor.

The president came very close. His pale eyes lifted and regarded Sarah bleakly. He said:

'Mrs. Watson, that necklace you returned to me an hour ago – that necklace for which I've already paid you two hundred dollars and an exorbitant expense account – that necklace, Madam, is nothing but—'

'Nothing but paste,' said Sarah. 'A clever imitation, but paste. Well, Mr. Hecker, that's what you asked for, and that's what you got.'

The clerk shoved Sarah's bank book through the wicket.

He peered around Sarah's bulky figure and addressed himself, in a loud and cheery voice, to the president of the bank.

'Mr. Hecker,' he said, 'I thought you'd like to know. Mrs. Watson has just made a very nice deposit, very nice indeed. Mrs. Watson must have put over a very shrewd piece of business this time, I think.'

GANGSTER'S BRAND

P. T. LUMAN

Like most of the authors who worked for *Gun Molls Magazine*, nothing is known of P. T. Luman, except in the negative. He never published a novel, his name appears in no reference book and no information could be gleaned from the Internet, where there were numerous references to P. T. Barnum, with whom it seems unlikely that there was a connection.

His pulp publisher did think enough of his story to feature it on the cover of the magazine, where it also is first in the table of contents.

While it would be untrue to compare its literary quality to that of Hammett, Chandler, Woolrich or the other great pulp writers of the era, 'Gangster's Brand' has a narrative that never slows for an instant. Since the author presumably was paid the standard rate for this lower-rung magazine, which was a quarter-of-a-cent a word, he may have been tempted to do a little padding to earn just a little more (as Charles Dickens, in another era, was famous for doing) but, if so, he obviously resisted the temptation.

'Gangster's Brand' was first published in the August, 1931, edition of *Gun Molls Magazine*.

GANGSTER'S BRAND

P. T. LUMAN

Two small, trim feet, then shapely legs in sheer silk, swung below the fire-escape in the dim light of the areaway. They swung only for an instant and then dropped, ten feet to the concrete pavement below. The girl staggered from the shock, and then, picking herself up, swung back into the shadow of the big apartment building, hugging the wall as she regained her breath.

A wicked-looking gat glistened in her right hand as her snapping black eyes riveted on the iron door above her through which she had reached the fire-escape and safety.

Carlotta Wynn, active member of 'Mort' Mitchell's mob, waited expectantly for the opportunity to plug the guy or guys who had spoiled one of the prettiest lays the gang had had for many a month.

A shadow moved behind her, far back in the areaway in which she stood. The gat in the girl's hand swung around like lightning.

'Stick 'em up,' she said through gritted teeth, or I'll—!'

'Out of here, quick, kid,' responded a guarded, but agitated voice, and Mort Mitchell himself motioned the girl to his side. With Mort leading, the rod and the moll stole through the shadows to a doorway in the wall surrounding the court and slipped through as Mitchell threw the door open cautiously.

They were in the alley behind the big apartment. A half-block away was their getaway car, planted there a half-hour before with 'Needle' Sam Schwartz at the wheel and with the engine running. They hustled to the corner of the alley and looked around the protecting wall cautiously. The car was there, and Barry Crandall, the fourth of the mob, was stepping into the front seat with the driver.

'Take the right-hand side of the street and hit for that car as fast as you can make it,' whispered Mort, 'I'll take the left hand side – and watch!'

The girl's gat was hidden under her light coat now and she walked quickly to the car. Mort hopped into the seat beside her just as Needle Sam stepped on it and the big car jumped away from there.

There was cursing a-plenty as the car dashed through side streets where traffic cops would not bother them. For the third time in two weeks Mort

211

Mitchell's mob had been within an inch of grabbing off some of the softest-looking hauls in their history. And for the third time, just as everything was right for the heist, something had gone wrong. The fall guy was wised up – and Mort and his mob had gotten nothing for their carefully laid plans.

Mort and his mob were being double-crossed and every one of them knew it. After the curses came silence as the minds of the four recalled the mysterious jinx which seemed to have fastened itself upon the mob. Three times – and every one the same. Even as the roaring car sped toward their hideaway the four looked at each other curiously and askance. Suspicion, even between members of the mob against each other, was growing. The same thought came to all. Somebody in the mob – or somebody in a position to know their movements – was a rat!

Mort Mitchell, thinking deeply, was puffing feverishly on his cigarette as the car pulled into the garage in back of 'Dapper' Dan's speakie, where the gang hung out.

'In the back room,' Mort said curtly as they climbed from the car, and the four slipped through the passageway between the garage and the farthest back room of Dan's. Mort Mitchell was going to find out, and that very night, too, if he could, just who was putting his mob over the jumps of failure. He sat at the end of the table and nodded to Dapper Dan, who appeared at the signal which came with their entrance.

'Send a bottle of rye and some soda, Dan,' said Mort grimly, 'and then go out and forget we're here. Don't let anybody disturb us, for this ain't no mass meeting. This is a secret party that may end seriously for somebody!' His dark eyes snapped as he looked into the faces of his mobsters. The bottles were brought and the door snapped shut behind Dapper Dan. Mort poured himself a stiff shot of rye and shoved the bottle down the table to the others. They poured and drank and Mort, throwing his hat on the near-by desk, faced them again.

Mort didn't look the part of the mobster any more than Carlotta Wynn looked the rôle of a moll. He was tall and thin, but of a deceptive thinness which concealed his tremendous strength. His hair was dark brown and his eyes almost black, with a particular snap and keenness. His clothes were of expensive material and conservative cut; clothes such as a broker might select.

The girl could have walked into the Ritz on his arm and seemed perfectly in place. She was of medium height and slender, but sinuous figure. Her features were small and regular, set in skin of marked smoothness and whiteness. The whiteness of her skin was emphasized by her silky black hair and eyebrows and black flashing eyes, which were large, almost round, giving her an appearance of innocence, of surprise.

Needle Sam and Barry Crandall, the other two at the table, however, looked their parts. Sam's face was fat, with close-set eyes. His suit was flashy, of extreme cut. The first and second fingers of his right hand were stained deeply by the cigarettes he smoked in every waking moment. Sam was a chauffeur par excellence – nothing else. He thought he was a hard rod, but he wasn't. He just was about the best driver in the city, for he knew every short cut in traffic, he drove like a charioteer and he never had accidents. They didn't pay in his business.

And Barry Crandall was a rod who had graduated from a lowlier beginning. There had been days when he did not scoff an opportunity to lift a wallet or even bend a lead pipe over an unsuspecting head. Now, however, he was in faster company and was Mort Mitchell's right hand – and Mort wasn't a piker.

Mort's handsome face was turned on the other three.

'Well,' he asked, sarcastically, 'who spilled it?'

None answered.

Mort's expression grew hard and ominous, as he went on:

'One slip-up can happen. Two *might* happen, but three times means—' He looked intently into the faces of the moll and the two other rods. 'Three slips – and each one almost spelling curtains for me – mean *a rat!*'

The moll's eyes flashed dangerously.

'Don't insinuate that I'm a rat, Mort,' she said evenly, but the tiny muscles at the corners of her mouth tightened and her small hands clenched. 'I'm no rat and you know it. I'd go to hell for you, and the boys, would, too. Maybe *you've* talked too much in your off moments. Remember, you're mingling in *society* now!' Her voice was bitter and jealousy showed in the tone of that word 'society.'

'Never mind what I'm doing,' retorted Mort, angrily, 'I'm not monkey enough to talk where there's going to be a comeback at me.'

He turned to face the girl squarely.

'Let's start from the beginning,' he said grimly, 'and maybe we can find the leak. You got the tip-off from the Hag didn't you?'

'Yes.'

'When?'

'The night "Carmen" was sung at the Metropolitan,' answered the moll. 'She was doing her usual stuff, whining around the automobiles near the entrance, with that tooth sticking down on her lower lip and that mole on her cheek sticking out over her coat collar. She slipped me the signal and I watched my chance to step up to her and drop four-bits into her tin-cup.

' "The Vanderpools on Wednesday night, girlie," she said in that whine of hers. "It's a pipe. I heard 'em talkin' as they dropped me a dime from the carriage window. All of 'em will be away Wednesday night, except the old dame, herself, and she'll be home taking a backgammon lesson from a girl sharp. And the old woman wears her diamonds for dinner every night, even in her home. It's a pipe, girlie. Tell Mort – an' I want my cut." '

'Anybody see you getting the info from her?' asked Mort.

'What if they did see me talking to her?' retorted the moll. 'Who'd think she was tipping us to a job? I was just an opera-goer to the crowd on the pavement. Everybody talks to her – she's the Hag of the Opera to everybody. Never misses the carriage door on opera nights. All the society folk know her whining story; she was Dolores, the dancer, she tells them as she begs. Dolores the famous ballet dancer. How she gets away with it with that fang sticking out over her lower lip from her upper jaw and that mole, I don't know. Figure her as a dancer! But they listen to her and slip her change – and she's the best lookout and tipster *this* mob ever had, until now!'

'Yes,' agreed Mort, reluctantly, 'but she gave us the bum steer on the Stickney job, too, didn't she? And she sent us out on Hark Island for that bust in the Longman's home that pretty near put me back of the walls.'

'She's tipped us to plenty. She doesn't get her cut unless we click.'

'Yes,' responded Mort grimly, 'but maybe she's changed her racket. Anyway—' he paused and looked into the anxious faces before him. 'Anyway, either the Hag – or somebody here in this room – tipped off the Vanderpools tonight and we came damned near to dissolving this mob when that roomful of private dicks stepped on our feet. Now, suppose some one of you tries to answer that!'

'She's playin' with the Orange mob, maybe,' suggested Barry, ' "Blackie" Rango and his gorillas been knockin' off some sweet jack without no trouble while we're sticking our throats out for the knife.'

'Yes,' added Carlotta vengefully, 'and Blackie Rango is a hog so greedy that he'd send us to hell in a minute, if he could. It gives him violent cramps if he hears any other mob's grabbed a few dollars. He wants it all himself.'

'Yes,' responded Mort, grimly. 'Some day Blackie and I are going to argue that little matter out – especially if I find he's back of this business of steering us into jams!'

Mort Mitchell straightened himself in his chair. He turned to the moll, who now was watching him admiringly.

'Baby,' he said, 'this looks like your job. The Hag has been playing with us – and getting plenty for it. But, maybe she's *getting more* to double-cross us now. You find out – and maybe when you do find out it'll have some bearing on your private grudge.'

As he spoke the moll's hand went involuntarily to her right shoulder and a spasm of hatred crossed her face.

'If it does,' she answered grimly, 'I'll want no more of any mob's takings. I'll be happy.'

'Watch the Hag,' warned Mort earnestly. 'When's the next opera?'

'Friday night. It's "Lucia" with Stephanie and Bendi in the cast. All the box-holders will be there.'

'You go, as usual with that music hound from the Village – and watch the Hag for her signal. And watch her close, *before and after you talk to her* Maybe she's spilling her chatter for Blackie and his rats, and if she is, she's trying to put the finger on us!'

Mort pushed back his chair and rang for Dapper Ben again.

'Mort,' interrupted the moll anxiously, 'are you coming over to my place with me?'

'No!' His tone was abrupt and he avoided looking the moll in the eyes.

'Society man again!' The girl snapped the words. 'I guess—'

'Never mind about my business, baby,' Mort replied menacingly. 'I'll go with who I please. Your job is to watch the Hag, and bring the dope to me. I'm running this mob yet!'

The moll stifled her anger. She threw down another generous drink and stepped to the door. Her voice was cold now, despite the glitter in her eyes.

'I'll see the Hag Friday night,' she said, 'and if she's got any stuff I'll get it and bring it here to the Big Society Man – if he's not too busy drinking tea and eating lady-fingers to accept it!'

She stepped through the door and slammed it behind her before Mort could reply. Barry and Sam grinned, for they knew the reason for her anger. Deeply in love with the handsome Mort, Carlotta knew that a mysterious woman, a strikingly beautiful woman with flaming hair and star-like eyes who haunted the better supper clubs and mingled freely with Park Avenue pleasure-lovers, was claiming every spare moment that the handsome Mort could give her. Their grins, however, were wiped from their faces by the grave words of Mitchell.

'Lay low for a few days,' he cautioned them. 'That moll is smart and she may be able to smell out the rat who's trying to put the finger on us. And, if she doesn't, well— Then, it looks to me as though this mob is through. Blackie Rango is trying to hog every racket in the city, and he'll do it, too, unless the jane spoils his plans before they work any further.'

Mort Mitchell left them abruptly. He hurried to his rooms to dress, for he was going to step out that night to one of the city's snootiest supper clubs where he knew he would meet and have at least a few words with the woman whose flaming beauty had fascinated him, the red-haired, glorious Vi Carroll, mystery woman of the night clubs and associate of those who moved in the faster set of Society with the capital S.

Perhaps Mort Mitchell would not have been so eager for the smiles of the flashing Vi had he known of the scene which was being enacted at the time he was dressing for his night's pleasure. For the dazzling Vivian, her face unsmiling now and her musical voice harsh in emphasis, was talking angrily and excitedly, not with one of her society friends, but with Blackie Rango himself, the greedy mob leader, who seemed perfectly at home amid the luxuries of Vi's apartment.

And Blackie Rango was no sheik. He puffed from the exertion of crossing one fat leg over the other and his language seemed very much out of place in the tasteful surroundings. His beady eyes peered from beneath thick, bushy brows in a beetling forehead that wrinkled as he talked. Vi's anger he passed unnoticed.

'You messed it up again, didn't you, broad?' he asked, interrupting her. 'Everything set to give the works to Mort Mitchell, his frail with him an' all his mob an' instead o' him getting' his'n he's still around, getting' in my hair.'

'Yes! He's still around because you and your gorillas didn't have the guts to take him when I put him right in your hands!'

'Maybe,' answered Blackie, evenly, 'an' then again, maybe not. Now, see here, broad.' His gimlet eyes glowed as he thrust his ugly face closer to hers. 'It's got to be me or Mort Mitchell. They ain't room in this town for his mob an' mine, an' mine ain't goin' to be the one to go out.'

He reached over and grabbed the red-haired moll by the wrist.

'Get this,' he said, and there was murder in his tone. 'I'm puttin' up for you. There ain't no limit. You can play this society gag an' you sock away plenty of jack. Yes, I know you're doin' it, but I don't care, so long as you're on the level with me. Your job is to frame Mort Mitchell – he's got to go. An' don't think I don't know how friendly you are with him, too!'

The moll started as Blackie's eyes bored into hers. She started to speak, but he went on:

'An' when Mort goes, you'd better see to it that his frail goes, too. Maybe you don't know her. An' maybe you do. Anyhow, she's with him on all his jobs an' she's a fightin' fool. Carlotta Wynn, that's what they call her. But that ain't her name. She ain't no ordinary moll. Nobody knows where she come from, but she's a moll for a reason – and nobody but her knows why.'

'What do I care about his moll?' asked Vi angrily.

'Maybe you don't, but you're monkeyin' with her man, an' she looks like poison to me. Anyway, get this through your skull. Three times now you've slipped info to the Hag to send Mort Mitchell and his mob into a jam. An' three times you've made a fine mess of it. Now, dame—'

Blackie's manner was menacing and he twisted the moll's wrist to emphasize his words.

'*Get that guy!* Tell the Hag to slip him a certain one, a tip he won't pass up – an' leave the rest to me. I'll see they's a load o' hot lead waitin' for him when he steps into it. An', broad, don't miss *this time!* Make it right, so Mort and his whole mob will go, includin' the moll, for if you don't—'

'Well, if I don't?' challenged the girl defiantly.

'Here's your answer,' replied Blackie ominously, 'that moll Carlotta, in swimmin' suit or evenin' clothes, *never was known to bare her right shoulder!* Does that mean anythin' to you?'

Vi Carroll cried out hoarsely. There was terror in her eyes.

'What's her name?' she screamed. 'Tell me, you big ape – what's her name?'

'You guess it,' replied Blackie brutally, with a half-smile. 'She come from Chi, too.'

Horror was written on the white face of Vivian Carroll. Her hands shook and the words she tried to speak would not come. Blackie laughed loudly.

'Maybe you'll follow orders now, eh, kid?' he asked. He wheezed from the deep chair and balanced his fat body on his feet. 'Better forget your yen for that pretty boy, Morton,' he added, 'an' play along with the guy who's been right with you. Get me, frail?'

The girl nodded. Finally she regained her composure.

'I'll frame him, Blackie,' she said with visible effort. 'I'll frame him *if you promise me you'll get that moll, too.* My life isn't worth a nickel if that girl ever recognized me. Don't worry. I'll play a hundred per cent with you now!'

'Atta baby, Vi,' answered Blackie, and he pulled on his coat with the help of the girl and waddled from the room. His soul was at peace as he waited for the elevator which took him to the street, and, as he rode away in his armored car with his gat bodyguard, Blackie Rango saw himself seated soon on the throne of gangdom. With the menacing Mort Mitchell and his mob out of the way, none in the underworld would dare dispute his leadership.

'An' that there Vi,' Blackie said, half audibly, as he mused, 'I'll keep her around. She's pretty easy on the eyes – an' besides, I got the deadwood on her. She oughta pay dividends!'

Despite her valiant efforts to appear natural Vi Carroll plainly was suffering from some repressed emotion that night. Her companions in the gay party which went to the ultra-fashionable Club Meta to see the new floor show and hear the reigning tenor noticed it. They joked with her; in mock solicitude they inquired gravely whether her dampened spirits were due to Wall Street, to a love affair, to the loss of a dear friend, or what else?

Then the floor show engaged their attention and she had a moment's peace from their banter. She fingered the thin-stemmed glass before her and looked through the crowd anxiously. She was looking for the handsome Mort Mitchell, the striking-looking, mysterious Mort, who held such a subtle attraction for her and the man she was pledged to frame. Her usual complacency was gone when she saw his tall figure appear. She was agitated when he bowed to her and exchanged a greeting.

'Let's dance,' she said as the orchestra struck up a number. 'I'm blue tonight, I'm depressed.'

They danced silently for a round of the small floor and then the girl said abruptly:

'Morton, I want to talk to you. Let's walk out on the balcony, so we can be alone. Try to cheer me up. I feel morbid, almost afraid.'

The mob chieftain laughed. What in the world, he thought, could this glorious girl, with wealth, social position and beauty, have to worry about? They leaned over the balcony rail together, looking out on the lights of the city. When Vivian spoke, she tried to conceal the eagerness in her voice.

'I've been hearing things about you, Morton,' she said.

'What were they, Vi?'

'You're the man of mystery to all my friends,' she went on. 'They like you, but they do not know your antecedents – and, as a matter of fact, neither do I.'

'Just a fellow lucky to have a little bit of money,' Mort said, 'and a business which takes care of itself. I'm a consulting engineer, if you must know, but my duties are not confining.'

Vi turned to him with an air of frankness.

'I'm not questioning you, Mort,' she said, 'and I don't care what the crowd thinks of you. But—' She hesitated, and then went on with a burst of apparent frankness. 'Mort, who is the beautiful girl, the beautiful black-eyed girl I've heard is in your company pretty often? Frankly, I'm a bit jealous of her.'

Mort laughed heartily.

'You jealous?' she scoffed. 'I just wish you cared enough about me to be jealous. The other girl? Just an employee, Vi, a girl who has worked in my office, an efficient stenographer, that's all. We have no social contact. She's been in my car, of course, but only in the line of her duties.'

'Who is she, Morton?'

'Just a girl who came here from Chicago a year ago. I really don't know her first name. Miss Wynn, that's all the name I know.'

Vi's voice was strained as she persisted in her questioning.

'This girl, Morton. Has she particularly large, black eyes?'

'Yes, she has.'

'Did she—' Vi hesitated, then she went on, speaking almost desperately. 'Morton, did this girl ever have an accident? Was she ever hurt badly, was—?'

Mort looked at the agitated Vivian curiously.

'Why all this interest in an office working girl, Vi?' he asked. 'I don't know anything more about her. How would I know whether she ever suffered injury?'

'Forgive me, Morton,' said Vi. 'I've heard this girl described, and – and the description fitted a girl I once knew in the West. I thought, maybe—'

She broke off with a laugh, a relieved laugh. 'Let's forget about the girl and rejoin the party,' and she led the way back to the dining-room with the attentive, but slightly puzzled Mort behind her.

From that moment Vi Carroll's manner changed. Her spirits rose, she laughed gayly, she seemed determined to still any disquieting thoughts with an excess of gaiety. 'It can't be the same girl,' she said to herself as she tripped through a dance with Mort. 'Only a chance in a million it's the same, and my luck is good.'

Mort left the party comparatively early, for he had troublesome things on his mind. That matter, that vital matter of Blackie Rango, wouldn't be brushed from his recollection by the bright lights and gaiety. He left before the party broke up, managing a few whispered words again with Vi before leaving.

'Shall I see you tomorrow night, Vi?' he asked anxiously.

'Tomorrow,' replied the flushed girl – 'let's see, tomorrow's Friday. No, Morton, but I'll see you Saturday. Tomorrow night's the opera, you know, and I'm going with the Elberts, and then out to the island for the night.'

She smiled fondly at Mort's disappointment and squeezed his hand tightly as he said adieu. A qualm came to her heart as she watched his tall figure moving toward the door. God, but he was a fine looking fellow to be marked for Death! Why did he have to be the one?

Friday night and the opera, with favorites singing the principal roles and the diamond horseshoe ablaze with celebrities and color. Outside the forbidding opera house the stream of automobiles, the crowds of curious, fascinated by the jewels and scintilating frocks of society. And along the line of crawling automobiles, slowly approaching the entrance to disgorge their cargoes of dressed-up and bejeweled folks, croaked the Hag of the Opera, the bunchy figure of that wreck of a woman who whined for her alms at the automobile windows. Her slovenly body was swathed in the ground-length, dingy coat which came high on her neck, to her chin. Over her head the inevitable dirty shawl. Beneath the shawl peered the beady eyes, the gnarled sallow skin of the Hag, whining and showing the long discolored tooth, more like a fang, which reached from the front of her upper jaw down over her lower lip as she pleaded with the richly-gowned opera patrons for alms. Adding to her hideousness was a blemish – a huge, hairy mole – on her right cheek, which moved up and down as she whined.

Dirty, hideous, repulsive was the Hag of the Opera, yet she had her clientele. Women in shining automobiles shrank from her dirty extended paws, yet they besought their escorts to help her.

'Help Dolores,' the Hag cried, 'help the old woman who once knew so well the plaudits of the crowd. Dolores of the Imperial ballet – I, Dolores, who danced for kings. Now I need crusts. Help me, good people.'

And, as she begged her acute ears were attuned, not for words of

219

sympathy, but for the intimate talk inside the vehicles, the chatter about social engagements, anything that might mean an unguarded mansion, a particularly fine display of gems at some social gathering – some target for the mob's arrows!

Receiver of their largess, the Hag of the Opera was betraying their secrets to the banditti! Long had it been her trade, with no suspicion directed at her. She had played into the hands of Mort Mitchell and to those who had gone before him in command of the same mob. Now, however, the Hag had extended the scope of her double-crossing. Her greed aroused by the calculating Blackie Rango, the Hag was getting the heist info for Blackie while purporting to be co-operating with Mort, and was acting as the go-between to arrange the frame-ups against Mort's mob which Blackie engineered!

The Hag was watching closely the faces in the cars as they approached the entrance. She was looking for the flaming hair and the face of Vi Carroll, the bearer of instructions, and she wandered up and down the row of cars until she saw Vi's signal. She hobbled to the side of the handsome limousine and approached the window through which Vivian's brilliant opera cape showed.

'Alms, good folks,' the Hag cried, leaning close to the window, and Vi lowered it, compassionately, turning to her escort as she did so.

'Give me some money for this miserable creature,' Vivian said, and a man of the party thrust a bill in her hand. Vi's daintily gloved hand stretched through the auto's window as the Hag whined her thanks. Her mumbled words, however, merely were a cover for the whispered words which Vi directed to her.

'The Horton Place on the Sound, Monday night!' Vi said, and the Hag winked acknowledgment of the words.

The shiny limousine moved forward toward the opera house entrance with Vi Carroll chatting laughingly with her companions as the Hag moved away. The first step in the trap set for Mort Mitchell and his mob had been taken. Within a half-hour the deceiving message would be on its way to pave the road for destruction. The Hag would relay the false information to Carlotta Wynn, emissary of the Mitchell mob!

The Hag moved down the line of carriages, ready to relay the frame-up message. She now was looking for Carlotta, the moll from Mitchell's mob. She did not know that Carlotta, hidden in the milling throng on the sidewalk, had been almost at her elbow when Vi Carroll whispered her message – and further than that, the keen-eyed Carlotta, seeing through a changed appearance in the beautiful Vivian, had recognized the society-minded moll as the enemy she was stalking so desperately!

*

Carlotta Wynn, her teeth clenched and her hands doubled into small fists, gloried in the triumph she foresaw over the woman who had sent her into the underworld on her adventure into vengeance. That smiling beauty with the flaming hair now, apparently, a society favorite, only two years before had done the irreparable wrong to the black-eyed girl who stood in the opera crowd and planned her revenge!

The moll forgot the presence of the 'music-loving kid' who always accompanied her to the opera performances. He was a harmless sort; he did not know that he was a pawn in the machinations of a mob. He went to the opera with the pretty girl who seemed pleased to enjoy the music with him.

Everything except revenge was forgotten by the black-haired moll. She moved forward as Vi's auto moved toward the entrance.

'I could kill her now—!' she spoke aloud and the music-loving kid startled.

'Who could you kill, Carlotta?' he asked in astonishment. The girl recovered her poise.

'No one, Robbie,' she replied, 'I was just joking.' She saw the Hag approaching and she knew the crone sought her, to relay the death-trap message to Mort Mitchell.

'There's the Hag,' Carlotta said, pushing toward her. 'I always give her a little change. Isn't she horrible looking? I feel as though I had to help her.'

She drew a few coins from her small purse and stepped to the side of the Hag, dropping the coins into the outstretched tin cup. The Hag leaned close to her, the repulsive, hairy mole almost touching the girl's face.

'The Horton Place, on the Sound – on Monday night, girlie,' the Hag whispered. 'Tell Mort it's a pipe – and not to forget me.'

She turned from the girl, whining her plea for alms to others as Carlotta and her escort walked to the entrance.

Blackie Rango's message to trap Mort Mitchell and his mob to death was delivered – but it was delivered through a moll who knew that the Hag had turned on her former benefactors and was plotting with their enemies for their deaths!

The beautiful strains of 'Lucia' meant nothing to Carlotta that night. She sat through the performance with the lad because she did not know where to reach Mort until late in the night. And before her eyes, instead of the singers and the brilliant audience, was the picture of Vi Carroll, the woman the moll was determined should feel the weight of her vengeance.

The moll dismissed her escort quickly as the throng poured from the house of music. She raced to a taxicab and hurried to Dapper Dan's, where she felt sure she would find Mort at midnight. She entered the speakie through the garage and the rear door, and waited for Mort in the secret chamber.

The moll was on her feet, pacing the room, when Mort entered.

'I've got the works, Mort,' she cried, 'It's a cold frame, set up by Blackie Rango. Here's the message from the Hag; "The Horton Place, on the Sound – Monday night!" It's phony! It's—'

'How do you know it's phony?' demanded Mort.

'Because I overheard the message slipped to her, Mort, I heard it slipped to her by the very woman I've been hunting, the jane I've sworn to find and to repay a certain debt.'

'And who,' asked Mort, eagerly, 'was Rango's messenger? Did you spot her?'

'Yes, I spotted *her!*' responded the moll, and her eyes were blazing. 'And maybe you'll be interested to know just who she is! You've been playing around with your society friends – with a red-headed woman who's got you dizzy, haven't you?'

'Never mind that. It's my business where I go and—'

The moll blazed at him angrily:

'Well, maybe this is your business, too. The red-headed moll who gave the Hag the tip that's set to put you under the grass went to the opera with the Elberts, your society friends, and is the crookedest snake that ever wore woman's clothes!'

Mort Mitchell's amazement held him speechless.

'Not Vi, not Vi Carroll!' he ejaculated. 'It can't be—'

'Fall for the tip, then, sap,' retorted the moll, 'but I won't. If you go near the Horton Place Monday night, Mort, you'll die from hot lead poisoning. I know!'

Mort grabbed the moll by the wrist and swung her around until she was looking up right into his eyes. His voice was low, but it was full of menace.

'Damn you,' he snarled, 'are you on the level, or are you framing Vi Carroll, just to—'

The moll twisted away from him furiously.

'Take it or leave it, you sap,' she snapped, 'but I'm going to get HER! And I'll make you believe it. Listen, Mort, will you believe your red-headed vamp is crossing you before it's too late? Will you believe me if I prove it to you?'

'Yes,' he answered sullenly, 'if you prove it. But, how are you going to do it?'

An inspiration came to the moll.

'I've got it, Mort,' she cried excitedly. 'You'd kidnap the Hag of the Opera, wouldn't you – to save yourself?'

'No, but why?'

'Because,' replied Carlotta, 'I want her out of my way on the next opera night – because that night I'LL BE THE HAG OF THE OPERA!'

'What?' asked Mort, bewildered.

'Just that,' replied the moll. 'Act just as though we're falling for that bum tip on the Horton Place, but stay away from there. Then, on the next opera night, grab the Hag, so I can get her clothes. I'll do her whining act and I'll get the tip-off from your red-headed friend who's trying to put the finger on you!'

'You can't do it, kid,' responded Mort, 'you can't impersonate the Hag. There's no other like her. Look at that fang which hangs down her lip – that mole!' He almost shuddered when he recalled the evil face of the Hag.

'I'll do it, Mort,' cried the moll, her eyes snapping. 'I'm entitled to a chance this time, for I've got a score to even and then, maybe—' Her voice caught, but she went on. 'Maybe, Mort, you won't think so badly of me. Does my scheme go?'

'Yes,' he replied. 'We'll stay just about a thousand miles away from that Horton Place and, then—' His eyes gleamed ominously. 'Then, if your dope is right, we'll see how Mr. Blackie Rango likes lead for supper! It's up to you, kid!'

He squeezed her arm and the girl stepped closer to him, expectantly. But his mind wasn't on the moll. He was wondering whether he could successfully fight against the power of Blackie Rango. He left her absently, and walked to the front of the speakie. The girl, her face showing her disappointment, walked from the speakie and went to her room. She slept little, for she was laying her plans, not only to thwart Blackie Rango's plot against the Mitchell mob, but also to satisfy her ancient feud against the brilliant Vi Carroll.

Mort Mitchell and his mob stayed severely away from the country place of the Hortons on the Sound that Monday night. It was well they did, for hidden in the shrubbery a quarter-mile up the private road which lead to the estate was a band of a dozen rods in the employ of Blackie Rango, ready to mow them down. And Blackie Rango was a sadly disappointed vice king when he got the word of the failure. He called Vi Carroll on the telephone and told her in no uncertain words that her job was in peril – that she must make good on her next attempt.

So it was a perturbed Vi who rode with friends slowly toward the opera house entrance on the next opera night. She had her instructions from Blackie and they were explicit. She was to tell the Hag to lure the Mitchell mob to an uptown apartment building with an exciting story of unguarded jewels and an absent family and the following Friday night was to be the time for the massacre.

Again, on this occasion, Vi was a guest of the Elberts. She chatted nervously with Elbert and his wife and another guest as their car approached the glittering opera house. But her mind was not on the small talk. She was watching anxiously for the Hag of the Opera – for she simply had to make good now. Morton Mitchell had to be sacrificed. Her eyes wandered through the crowd as the car approached the entrance. God!

Would that damnable Hag never appear? At last she saw the tottering, repulsive figure. It hurried to the side of the Elberts auto and Vi lowered the window, coins in her hand to cover the few words she must exchange with the repulsive croon.

The Elberts and their guests looked in wonder as Vi leaned nervously from the car window. Why did Vivian pay so much attention to that pest, that wreck of a woman with the revolting face? But Vi was oblivious to them.

'Dolores,' she whispered vehemently, 'they've *got* to fall for this; tell them the Donaghan jewels, a half-million dollars worth, will be absolutely unguarded Friday night. The approach is through the areaway beside the apartment. *Make* them fall for it.'

She peered intently into the wrinkled face before her. She saw the loathsome fang denting the Hag's lower lip. She shuddered as she looked at that horrible mole on the crone's right cheek.

'Yes, dearie,' whined the Hag, accepting the coins Vi handed to her. 'They'll go, all right. I'll fix that. Now, here's something for Blackie, and tell him it's a chance of a lifetime. Mrs. Alex Wilson's pearls, the great Wilson pearls, will be delivered to their country place Thursday night by automobile, a car with only the Wilson butler and one guard in it. The car will get there at seven o'clock in the night – and if Blackie don't get them he'll never get another such a chance at them.'

The Hag was creeping alongside the slowly moving car. Vi heard the message leaning from the window. The Elberts and their other guests wondered at the whispering between the glittering Vi and the loathsome Hag. The Hag, however, leaned close to Vi again.

'Tell Blackie it won't be easy; tell him to have the whole mob, but for God's sake not to miss this one!'

She fell back into the crowd as Vi turned back to her hosts apologetically.

'I'm sorry,' she said as their car neared the opera entrance, 'but the Hag insists upon my hearing her troubles. I've tried to help her; to get her off the street in this pitiful begging, but she insists upon haunting the opera.'

Vi accepted the arm of an escort and the Elbert party moved under the marque to the foyer of the opera house, Vi in possession of two things she cherished – belief that she had set the trap for Mort Mitchell's mob, and information that would make her even more solid with Blackie Rango.

Hardly had the Elbert party disappeared into the interior of the opera house, however, when the Hag of the Opera House, for the first time in a decade, lost all interest in the opera-going crowd. With surprising quickness for one of her age and dumpy figure, she slipped through the crowd on the pavement, and away from the opera. Ignoring her former benefactors who might still be mulcted, she disappeared down a cross street and boarded an automobile which waited there.

'Quick, Sam,' she snapped to the chauffeur, and Needle Sam did his stuff, taking the short cuts to Dapper Dan's speak. At the garage, she left the car and traversed the secret way to Dan's furthest back room and entered. Mort Mitchell was waiting there. He jumped from his chair as the Hag entered. It MUST be the Hag, that dumpy, uncouth figure, that revolting fang which dented her lower lip; that mouse-like mole which blemished the right side of her face.

'Hell!' Mort ejaculated, 'I thought—'

The dumpy figure of the Hag straightened and a quick hand pulled the dirty shawl from the head. Another quick motion and Carlotta Wynn, the fake Hag of the Opera, pulled from her mouth an odd dental plate to which was attached the fang which protruded from her mouth. Another pull wrenched from her face the 'mole', the imitation such as marked the face of the real Hag. Quickly she wiped the grease paint from her face – and Carlotta, the moll, stood before the mob leader in the Hag's habiliments. With an expression of disgust, she ripped the Hag's rags from her body and stood before Mort in her undies.

'Had to get that filth off me before I could think or talk,' she said calmly. She slipped into a suit which she had left in the speakie room, ordered a drink by pressing a button and turned to face Mort, the mob leader and more than that to Carlotta.

'The trap's set, Mort,' she said quietly. 'Blackie Rango's greed will not let him pass up a chance at the Alex Wilson's pearls. If you don't get him and his gorillas Thursday night, you'd better knuckle to Blackie's orders – for you'll never again get such a chance.'

Carlotta explained the set-up 'tip' she got from Vivian – and her face contorted with hate as she told it.

'You get Blackie and his apes, Mort,' she said, vindictively, 'and while you're doing it, I'll pay off my score.'

'You'll lay off that dame,' Mort replied, angrily, 'I'm not satisfied that she's not regular. Hands off – till I give the word!'

Carlotta laughed – a bitter laugh.

'All right, Mr. Society-Man-About-Town,' she said sarcastically. 'I'll promise you this; I won't harm a red hair of her head – until I tell you about it first.'

The moll gathered up the discarded clothing of the Hag and threw them into a suitcase. She turned to Mort.

'What'll you do with the Hag?'

'Keep her prisoner until I decide,' he responded shortly. 'Anyway, I'll hold her till after Thursday. Don't worry about her.'

'Good night, Mort,' said the moll, moving toward the speakie door, 'don't you want to come over to my place for awhile and have a nightcap with me? I'm tired and I've got some Scotch such as Dapper Dan never dreamed of.' The moll's voice was pleading, but it drew no response from the handsome mob leader. His thoughts, despite Carlotta's expose of Vi's perfidy, still were on the red-haired siren.

'No, kid,' he answered absently. 'See you some other time.'

Carlotta slammed the door and went out into the night. More than ever she was determined to 'get' the red-haired Vivian Carroll.

Thursday night in that secret back room of Dapper Dan's speakie. There was an air of tenseness as Mort Mitchell explained for the last time the plans for the night.

'We'll reach the Wilson place road a half-hour before Blackie's gang,' Mort said slowly, 'and Sam, you'll hide the car in the cross-road, pointed for a quick getaway. The big tree at the proper spot has been cut so deeply that a push will sent it across the road. That's your job, Barry. When you get the signal, you and Sammy give the tree a shove. It can't fall, except across the road.

'Our Tommy-guns will be beside that same tree trunk. When the tree falls, you, Barry, and Sam grab them and step to the side, where you can rake Blackie's car. If his car withstands your fire – I'll have a surprise package for him. That's my part of the job. I'll attend to that and you attend to yours. But, above all else, *don't go near Blackie's car* until I give the word!' Mort turned to Carlotta.

'And you,' he said emphatically, 'you're going along! You'll sit in the car and wait for us until—'

'But,' interrupted the moll heatedly, 'I won't do anything of the kind – for I won't be there!'

'Where will you be?' The question came in a snarl from Mort.

'I'll be calling on your red-haired society girl friend,' mocked Carlotta, 'and I'll be waiting for you in her apartment.' Her voice grew biting with scorn, as she continued:

'You still think she's on the level, don't you? You poor sap! You believe her, but you won't believe me. Do this, then. Settle your score with Blackie Rango. I was smart enough to plant that job for you and to save your neck! Then, when you've done your job, drive back to your red-head's place. I'll be waiting for you there. I won't hurt her before you come. I'll merely set the stage for the show which is going to make you see that one of us is crooked and the other straight. Are you game for that?'

The moll's eyes were snapping in her challenge.

'I won't hurt the dear thing before you come,' she mocked as he hesitated. 'You've my promise. Answer, big boy, are you game?'

'Yes,' he snapped angrily. 'Remember, no fireworks till I get back!'

The mobsters rose from the table and prepared to go to the garage for their car.

'Happy trip, boys,' said the moll. 'I hope, when you return, there'll be fewer snakes in the world.'

*

As the gorillas passed from the room, the moll helped herself to a man-sized drink from the bottle on the table. She had stern work before her and she welcomed the scorching liquor as it warmed her throat. The moll walked swiftly from the rear door of the speakie, just as Mort Mitchell's big black car slid away from the garage door on its errand of death.

Silently through the twilight the big car swept, through the outskirts of the city and into the fashionable residence area. Hardly a word was spoken, for the route was well-mapped and the trip timed to the minute. Finally it drew up in the shadows of the small cross-road outside the Wilson estate and the gangsters took up their stations.

Ten minutes before the time they looked for the car of Blackie Rango and his apes, its dimmed lights appeared far down the smooth road leading to the Wilson country mansion. Smoothly and menacingly the armored car of Rango approached through the semi-darkness. They recognized its lines, even at a distance.

Mort gave his last order.

'When they get opposite the big pine on the right,' he whispered, 'over with the tree – and then grab your Tommy-guns and open up on the car. And, remember, STAY AWAY FROM THAT CAR if you fail to penetrate his armor!'

Closer came the Rango car as Mort and Sam and Barry crouched in the protecting foliage at the roadside. Sweeping up the road, the big car approached almost before they were hidden. It seemed right upon them when the shoulders of Sam and Barry leaned against the big tree which already was cut for falling. With a muffled roar, the tree plunged across the road, hardly a dozen feet in front of the rival gangsters' auto!

There was a screeching of brakes – but not in time. Blackie Rango's automobile, carrying the eager Blackie and three of his gorillas, plunged into the tree's foliage just as the Tommy-guns of Mort Mitchell's gorillas spat flames!

The lead hail played a tattoo against the sides of the heavy armed car, and in a minute Rango and his rod men had picked themselves from the floor and were replying to the fire through slits in the body of the car.

Despite his trap, Mort Mitchell found Rango, his enemy, apparently safe in his fort-like automobile embedded in the foliage of the felled tree.

'Back!' yelled Mort, and there was a momentary silence as the Tommy-guns of Sam and Barry stopped. 'Back into the woods,' yelled Mort – and he dived to a depression beneath a distant tree. As he dived, his hand stretched out and struck a plunger – a plunger such as is used in dynamiting. The pressure on the plunger completed the electric contact he had set.

There was a flash and a roar – and the road beneath Blackie Rango's enmeshed automobile opened up in a devastating blast.

The mine which Mort Mitchell had set in the road had done the work the Tommy-guns could not do through the thick armor of the Rango car. Struck from below, its vulnerable spot, the big armored car flew apart as though the explosion came from within itself. As the echoes of the blast died away, a heavy pall of smoke hung over the spot. And as it cleared, nothing remained except a huge crater in the once smooth road, a few broken and twisted bits of metal.

The stunned Sam and Barry rushed for their car as Mort joined them.

'Out of here, quick,' Mort commanded. 'That blast will bring every dick and every motorcycle cop from miles around. Back to the city, Sam – and by the back road.'

The car leaped ahead under the skilled hands of Sammy, with Mort urging him to more speed. A gripping fear came to Mort as the car swept on. Carlotta! Would she keep her promise not to molest the rival moll, Vi Carroll, until Mort returned? Through gritted teeth, Mort ordered Sammy to drive to Vi's apartment. As they swept into the city proper, he said:

'Drop me at the corner and you three hit it for Danny's. I'll join you there as soon as I can.'

The car merely slowed for him. He leaped to the street and the car swept away, leaving Mort a scant half-block from the imposing apartment building on fashionable Park Avenue where Vi Carroll lived among her friends of society. Mort entered the elevator, scorning the suspicious looks of the attendant at his dusty and disheveled clothing. He left the car and hurried down the quiet corridor on the fifth floor, reaching the door of Vi's home.

No sound came through the door and Mort tried the door knob. The door opened to his touch and he stepped inside, peering through the dim light of the reception room. He saw no one. Silently he walked to a door on his left. That door, he knew, led to Vi's sumptuous boudoir. That door, too, was closed. He turned the knob softly and the door half opened. He peered into the room.

There, facing him in negligée, sat Vivian Carroll, a look of horror on her face, facing someone else in the room, directly opposite her. A look showed Mort the reason for the fright of the red-haired beauty. Her 'caller' was Carlotta Wynn, the gun moll, who sat quietly toying with a shiny gat pointed toward Vi's body!

'Drop that gat!' Mort's voice brought a subdued scream from Vi and Carlotta sprang to her feet. 'What's this stuff?' he demanded.

'Hands off, Mort,' retorted Carlotta quietly, but her eyes were snapping dangerously. 'You've had your party and this is MINE! Come in and shut the door.' She waved the gat toward the red-haired siren and said elaborately:

'Mr. Mitchell, let me introduce Miss Vivian Carroll, alias "Chicago Red" Hardy, the red-haired Siren of The Loop and a few other names!

And, also, Mr. Mitchell, the moll who has been trying to put the finger on you for weeks as a small favor for her good friend, the late Mr. Blackie Rango!'

'You lie!' snapped Vi, looking to Mort for protection, 'I've never been in Chi—'

'Put that gat down, moll,' snapped Mort, 'I know this girl and you're all wrong about her!'

Carlotta laughed sardonically. She threw the gat from her and it clattered on the polished floor, as she faced Mort.

'Mort, you poor fool,' she said, bitingly, 'will you never be convinced? That red-headed moll was head of one of the most cruel, savage mobs that Chi ever knew. She blew here because Chi got too hot for her – and she's making saps out of people here just as she did before. But, I KNOW HER!'

The moll's eyes flashed with bitter hatred as she spoke and her voice rose shrilly. 'I know her – and I'll never forget her, the snake that she is.'

She turned again passionately to the confused Mort.

'You won't believe? Then I'll show you!'

With a quick gesture she seized the right sleeve of her dress and tore it away, exposing her arm. Again she tore at the dress, ripping it open at the shoulder. As the fabric tore she pointed dramatically to the white skin of her upper arm and body.

'Look there,' she cried vengefully, 'there's the mark put on me by that hell-car, that vampire!'

And as Mort looked and Vi stifled the involuntary sob which came, Carlotta bared to them an angry-looking fiery-red brand on her white shoulder – a vivid brand of the *fleur de lis*, the ancient French brand for a thief!

'Look at that Mr. Mitchell,' cried the moll. 'That's what your society girl-friend did for me. She laughed while her gorillas put the hot electric needle to my flesh and drew that design there, drew it because that red-headed bum thought I'd stolen the dirty little hop-head she claimed as her "Man"! That's what I owe her.'

She turned on Mort vengefully.

'And you want to save her, to protect her, the moll who put the finger on you! All right, then, take my gat – and I hope the two of you will be happy. I won't drill her. She'd poison a decent bullet!'

She stopped and looked from the disconcerted Mort to the now relieved Vi. Her voice was lowered and she apparently had expended her anger.

'I'll go,' she said sadly. She wiped her eyes with her handkerchief and took from her bag a small, silver vanity case. 'Might as well go,' she went on monotonously to the two silent ones, and she dabbed at her face with a small powder puff from the compact. She turned to Vi as she used the puff.

'Before I go,' she went on, stepping closer to Vi's side, 'there's one thing I want to say—' She put the small powder puff back into the vanity case and absently took another small puff from the receptacle, holding it poised in her hand. 'Just one thing—!'

She stood facing the now reassured Vivian, the little puff half way to her face.

'You branded me, Vi Carroll,' she cried, quietly, 'and I've spent time and money to track you down to punish you.' She paused again. Then her voice came like a whip lash.

'AND I'M GOING TO DO IT!'

There was a flash of a bared white arm, and the small powder puff from Carlotta's compact smacked firmly against the left cheek of the red-haired woman. Vi screamed and Mort Mitchell grabbed the now violent Carlotta.

'We're even!' Carlotta Wynn's voice was triumphant now. She looked without pity at the suffering and horrified Vi, who was clawing at the left side of her face, which was turning a blotchy red and then purple.

'I've branded you, you hell-cat,' she went on. 'Branded you with acid – you rat!'

She turned to the astonished Mort and asked:

'Do you want her or do you want me? She branded me and she double-crossed you. Look at her and see whether I speak the truth!'

They looked, and the sobbing, hysterical Vi answered for Mort.

'Yes,' she said, 'I branded you because I hated you – and I hate you, too,' she blazed at the confused mobster. 'I'll get the pair of you. I'll get you—'

Mort Mitchell interrupted her. He seemed to come to himself, as though recovering from the influence of some insidious drug. He reached out to the little black-eyed moll, Carlotta, and pulled her close to him. He held her coat as she slipped it over her scarred, exposed arm and the two of them, the rod and his moll, moved toward the door. At the threshold Mort turned to the acid-marked Vivian. There was nothing lover-like in the tone of his voice now. It was cold as steel.

As Carlotta hung on his arm, he said:

'Get out of town in two hours, red-head! If you don't – I'll be back here to put MY mark on the OTHER cheek – and I don't want to have to bother to do that, for I'm going to be busy, squaring myself with my own moll. Eh, baby?'

He smiled at Carlotta as he asked the question – and the smile he got in return indicated the answer.

DANCE MACABRE
ROBERT REEVES

One of the forgotten authors of the pulp era is Robert Reeves (1911 or 1912–1945), largely because he came to the game late and because his career was cut short by World War II. His first short story was not published in *Black Mask* until 1942, his last in 1945. Altogether, there were nine stories in *Black Mask*, two others in *Dime Detective*, and three novels. His major creation was Cellini Smith, a private eye who appeared in all three of his novels: *Dead and Done For* (1939), *No Love Lost* (1941) and *Cellini Smith: Detective* (1943), as well as in seven of his eleven short stories. Three additional stories featured Bookie Barnes who got his nickname, not for making books, but because he attended college and actually read books – rare for pulp characters. 'Dance Macabre,' Reeves's second story, is the only one he wrote that did not feature one of his series heroes. It is darker than his other tales since none of his principal characters fall into the standard pulp mode of being tougher or smarter or funnier than everyone with whom they come into contact. The mousey Firpo Cole, a former petty thief and pickpocket, hangs around a nightclub because of a crush he has on one of the dime-a-dance girls, the All-American seeming Ruth Bailey.

The author served in WWII in the 500th Bombardment Squadron in the Army Air Corps and it is believed he died in action only a month before the war ended. He was buried in a common grave with four other GIs, probably having been in the same plane.

'Dance Macabre' was first published in the April 1941 issue of *Black Mask*.

DANCE MACABRE
ROBERT REEVES

CHAPTER ONE

Swollen Feet

Outside, the neon sign styled Jugger Callahan as the *King of Swing* but since Jugger owned the Tango Palace and had conferred the title on himself, not many people believed it. The sign also described the forty-eight hostesses as glorious, glittering, glamorous, and *that*, absolutely nobody believed – not even the girls.

Inside, Jugger Callahan kicked off the beat to the *Smiling Troubadours*. They played mechanically, with that automatic, pounding, unvarying rhythm that experienced jazz bands acquire, and, belying their name, they were unsmiling. It was nearing the closing hour of one A.M. and they were tired.

The tinted baby spots that were set in the ceiling revolved and played amber, red and blue over the dance floor. The place was large and ramshackle – the kind of second-story loft where you get natty, credit clothing – and it was just as much a fire trap as the taxi joint that had burned down on Jugger two months before. Nevertheless, the Tango Palace was a thriving enterprise aiming at that thin item of change known as the 'dime.' The dances were three for a dime and most of the customers stayed on a dime through all three of them.

The hostesses who waited for trade, chatted behind the frayed velvet rope that encircled the dance floor. Their low-cut evening gowns were creased and soiled, their eyes heavy-lidded with mascara and no sleep. Yet when a customer seemed inclined to switch partners, smiles appeared on vermilion lips, hips undulated sensuously and swollen, tired feet sugges-tively beat time to the music. Out of every dime ticket theirs was two and a half cents.

Ephraim Tuttle, who served as business manager, accountant and general factotum for Jugger Callahan, wandered back and forth, keeping a nervous eye on the girls and the ticket chopper. He was a tall, gaunt man with a bony, skeleton-face. His treatment of the girls was always scrupulously fair and they respected him. They could not even accuse him of showing favoritism to Evelyn Dorn, his flame of the moment.

He made a mental calculation of the swaying couples on the dance floor and found that business was only fair for a Friday night. He decided that they'd better pass out some more handbills on Spring and Main streets and approached a man quietly sitting on one of the settees that lined a wall.

'Firpo, have you been messing around in my office?'

Firpo Cole looked up at Ephraim Tuttle. 'No. Why should I?'

'Someone stole my letter opener,' responded Tuttle.

'That's bad,' said Firpo. 'If you get a letter now you'll have to open it with your fingers.'

Ephraim Tuttle pulled a five cent stogie out of his vest, carefully split the end and lit it before replying. 'It's funny,' he mused, 'how the squirts always act the toughest. If I'd spit at you you'd drown, yet you like to throw your weight around.'

'Just leave me alone,' said Firpo. 'When somebody loses a night's sleep around here they right away think I took it.'

'Firpo, you don't appreciate the break we're giving you. We let you mooch a few bucks around here instead of letting you go back to picking pockets on the street. But remember, it's only because Ruth Bailey's a nice girl and she wants us to give you a break.'

'Thanks.'

'I don't know what you want from the Bailey kid anyway, Firpo. You'll never get to first base and—'

Ephraim Tuttle broke off as he noticed Firpo Cole's face. He didn't like what he saw there. 'God, but you're touchy about that skirt,' he muttered and walked away.

With expressionless eyes, Firpo Cole watched the business manager retreat. He didn't know that his face, which always showed an unhealthy pallor, was now even whiter and more strained than usual. He was a youngish, frail man with spindle-legs, chicken-breast and sunken cheeks and he had once been facetiously dubbed 'Firpo' by someone who was supposed to be as funny as a card.

He found a loose cigarette in his pocket and lit it. As he did so, he forgot to make his customary salute to the medical profession by thumbing his nose. The medicos had told him that each cigarette took one month of his life. Like oil and water, cigarettes and lungers don't mix.

Jugger Callahan and his boys wound up the quickie trio of dances and immediately started on another set of three. The hostesses collected tickets from the men and slipped into their arms for another few minutes of those curious, swaying gyrations that passed for dancing.

Firpo Cole took a pad out of his pocket and marked down the figure *8*. Then he leaned back to watch a man and a girl sitting and talking on a sofa in a far corner. He didn't like to have Ruth Bailey sitting out dances. It was a funny thing, he reflected, but he didn't at all mind when Ruth Bailey was being pawed by some ten dollar millionaire out on the floor. It was her job. At first, his stomach used to tighten up from jealousy but even that had stopped. You get used to those things. What he did mind, though, was to have her talking with some man through eight dances and not get the tickets for them. She was an easy mark for chiselers. But he'd see to it that this baby got away with nothing. He could do nothing if Ruth preferred some other guy to him, but at least he'd see to it she wasn't rooked out of her rights.

On the band platform, Jugger Callahan broke into *Ain't Misbehavin'* and Mona Leeds, the outfit's torch singer, took over the mile. A hush settled over the place. The voice was rich and husky and, like her face and figure, possessed a torrid beauty. She sang into the mike but faced Jugger Callahan – as if to let the world know who her man was.

Mona Leeds finished her number and the dance hall echoed with appreciative whistles and stomping feet. Next to Firpo Cole, a voice said: 'That's the kind of chicken they should have in every pot.'

Firpo looked up to find Rocco Pace standing beside him. Rocco was one of the city's moderately successful racketeers. He dressed according to color charts, seemed pleasant and mild-mannered, but, if occasion demanded, could be dangerous.

Firpo said: 'Yeah, Mona's all right.'

Rocco nodded toward Ruth Bailey who still talked with the stranger. 'But nothing like her, eh?'

'Nobody's like her,' said Firpo in a flat, emotionless voice.

'Has she still got that yen for Jugger?'

Firpo Cole nodded.

'How come you take it laying down, Firpo? Me, I'd blow a fuse.'

'Jugger's a good-looking guy. I don't blame her. I'm just going to see she gets them dealt from the top of the deck.'

Rocco Pace shrugged. Certain things were beyond his Latin comprehension. He slipped a flat .32 automatic out of a shoulder holster and handed it to Firpo Cole who dropped it in his pocket. It was a service for which Firpo usually made four bits. Rocco had long ago discovered that he couldn't hold the girls the way he liked if he sported an eighteen ounce piece of metal over his chest.

Rocco Pace waved to Firpo and walked toward the barrier. The hostesses made a beeline for him. They liked this smiling, pleasant racketeer who gave big tips and who really came to dance.

Firpo Cole saw the stranger in the corner stand up and nod a farewell to Ruth Bailey. He didn't hand her any tickets. Firpo waited till the man got near him, then stood up and blocked his path.

'Well?' asked the stranger. He was middle-aged and asthmatic.

Firpo Cole said: 'What are you trying to get away with?'

'Anything I can,' replied the stranger pleasantly.

'Well, I'm here to see that you don't, mister.'

'Get out of my way, son.'

'Not till you pay her, chiseler.'

'Pay Miss Bailey?' The stranger sounded puzzled. 'Maybe you got me mixed up with Santa Claus.'

'You owe her ten tickets,' said Firpo, figuring the extra two as a tip. 'That'll be one buck.'

'For the last time, get out of my way.'

Firpo Cole knew it was coming but he did nothing to prevent it. Ruth Bailey was worth a beating any day in the week. It never occurred to him to draw the flat automatic in his pocket.

The stranger's arm came around in a wide arc that sent the frail Firpo spinning over the floor for fifteen feet. Firpo saw the stranger leave with unhurried steps, then a sudden attack of vertigo seized him and he passed out.

Firpo Cole came to on a couch in Ephraim Tuttle's office. Mona Leeds, the torch singer, was swabbing his forehead with a damp rag and, from behind his desk, the business manager regarded them sourly.

Tuttle said: 'Firpo, for a guy who couldn't lick a butterfly you certainly like to throw your weight around.'

'Stop riding him,' snapped Mona Leeds.

The door opened and Ruth Bailey came in. 'Firpo, they told me you were in a fight. Are you all right?'

Firpo Cole struggled into a sitting posture. 'Nothing happened. I'm fine.'

Ruth seemed to notice the torch singer for the first time. The corners of her mouth twisted. 'Well, well, if it isn't our little thrush trying to cut in on Firpo.'

'Now, Ruth,' said Firpo weakly. 'She was just trying to help me.'

Mona Leeds stood up and walked over to the hostess. The two women faced each other: Mona Leeds, in all her beautiful, slithering, scented allure, and Ruth Bailey, refreshing and young in a simple gown with a gold brooch at the neck. The one, a night life beauty with a duco finish, the other, a breath of fresh air too rare in a taxi-joint.

Ruth Bailey's voice had a faint hint of hysteria. 'Why aren't you satisfied with Jugger? You got him solid – why do you want more? Firpo would be a pretty miserable addition to your collection. Why don't you leave him alone?'

'You ——,' said the torch singer.

Ruth's hand snapped out and slapped Mona Leeds squarely over the face.

Ephraim Tuttle's warning shout was lost as the torch singer sprang for Ruth Bailey, her claws spread like a cat's. Mona's hands tore into Ruth's face and hair and the hostess clutched at the singer's dress. In a moment they were on the floor, scrabbling in mute fury. Paralyzed with the fascination of the spectacle, the two men simply watched.

With a yank, Ruth ripped apart the front of Mona's dress and the torch singer sank sharp, white, translucent teeth into the hostess's shoulder. Long, lacquered nails clawed, fists pummeled, slipper-shod feet kicked. The wildcats rolled over the floor and, with squeals of rage, tore at hair, face, clothing.

The door opened and Rocco Pace appeared. He said, 'What the hell,' and leaped to separate the fighting girls.

Their fury subsided as suddenly as it rose and they stood up, appraising the damage they had done each other.

'That's a lousy way to act in my office,' complained Ephraim Tuttle.

'Oh go add up some numbers,' said Mona Leeds calmly. She pulled her torn dress together and left.

Ruth Bailey anxiously scanned her face in a compact mirror.

'Girls will be girls,' philosophized the racketeer. 'I used to have one who tried to kill me every time I went to sleep.'

Ruth Bailey picked up the brooch that had been ripped from her gown. It was a simple item of jewelry, with what seemed to be a pale-blue piece of glass set in the center.

'Say, don't that belong to Mona?' asked Tuttle.

'Even if it did,' replied Ruth Bailey smoothly, 'I wouldn't give it to her.' Then she walked out.

'There's life in those girls,' said Rocco Pace. He turned to Firpo Cole. 'I came for my persuader.'

Firpo returned the automatic. The racketeer tossed him a half dollar and bade them good-bye.

Tuttle snorted and hunted for a cigar. 'This place is getting to be a regular nuthouse. First somebody steals my letter opener and now this. Did you hook that opener, Firpo?'

Firpo Cole was feeling a little better. The stranger hadn't hit him very hard. He said: 'Don't bother me.'

Ephraim Tuttle's Adam's apple bobbed up and down. 'Listen, you lousy pickpocket, I'm just asking nicely if you took it. It was pretty valuable. It had an onyx handle with silver edging.'

Firpo said, 'The hell with you and your letter opener,' got up and left.

It was after one already and the customers had gone. On the bandstand, Jugger Callahan and his boys were putting away their instruments, though Monkey Harris, a drummer, still banged on the skins as if to relieve his pent-up weariness.

Firpo Cole made his way to the back, entered a large dressing-room and sat down in a corner to wait for Ruth Bailey. The hostesses were hanging their gowns in a closet and changing into street clothes. Some sat quietly and rested their swollen feet in pans of hot water. None paid the slightest attention to Firpo.

Ruth Bailey changed her stockings, which had snagged during the fight, and touched up a blackened eye with powder. Ephraim Tuttle came in and asked whether anyone had seen his letter opener. No one had and he left. Ruth Bailey finished making up and she and Firpo Cole quit the dressing-room and went out to the street.

These nightly walks, when he took her home, were usually full with the talk and gossip of the Tango Palace, but tonight, it was some time before Ruth Bailey finally broke the heavy silence between them.

'Firpo, I'm afraid.'

'Forget it, Ruth. Mona won't get you fired. She's too white for that.'

'I'm not talking about the fight,' she said. 'I just forgot myself when I saw her by you and she was mad about this.' She touched the brooch at her throat.

'What has that got to do with it?'

'Well, you remember the night the old ballroom burned down? I went back for my purse which I'd forgotten and there was a light in Jugger's office. I went inside and there was no one there but I saw a jewel case on his desk. It had this inside of it.'

'You shouldn't of taken it.'

'Maybe, but all I knew was that Jugger bought it for Mona and I guess I got jealous. I started wearing it a few days ago. Jugger's seen it but he's too much of a gentleman to say anything. But Mona knows it belongs to her and that's what she was really fighting about with me.'

'You've got to give it to her, Ruth.'

'I will. Tomorrow. She's beautiful – I don't blame Jugger for preferring her to me.'

'Jugger may be a nice guy but he's a damned fool for wanting Mona Leeds instead of you.'

They reached her rooming house and halted.

'You know, Firpo, it's funny how I'm sick about Jugger and you about me. It seems like such a damned shame that life never—'

'I know all about it,' he cut in harshly. 'You didn't tell me what you're afraid of.'

'Firpo, someone – I don't know who – put five hundred dollars in my purse tonight.'

He whistled. 'That's a lot of money.'

She reached into her coat pocket. 'This is what the money came in.'

He took a plain, white envelope from her hand and read the typewritten line on it: *This better be enough.*

Under a lamplight, Firpo Cole's prematurely weazened face was lost in thought. After a while he returned the envelope to her and said: 'You better hold on to this and the dough. You didn't see anyone messing around with your purse tonight?'

'No – but of course anyone could have gotten at it in the dressing-room.'

'Has anything like this happened before?'

'No.'

'Well all I can figure, Ruth, is that someone's mixing you up with somebody else. I'll try and check tmorrow.'

'There's another thing, Firpo. You know that man you had a fight with today?'

'What about him?'

'He said not to tell anybody but he's a detective from an insurance company. They think that fire wasn't an accident. He knows I came back that night after everyone was gone and he asked me a lot of questions about it.'

Firpo Cole shrugged. 'If that fire's faked it's Jugger's worry – not yours. He got the insurance dough from it.'

'I know Jugger wouldn't do a thing like that. Something's wrong, Firpo. I'm afraid.'

'Forget it, Ruth.'

She leaned over and kissed him full on the lips. 'You're swell, Firpo. I'm sorry we don't hit it off together.'

'Sure,' said Firpo Cole. 'I'm swell.' He turned abruptly and made for his own lodgings.

CHAPTER TWO

Dead Feet

There was hard and insistent rapping on the door panel. After some time, the steady pounding had its effect. Firpo Cole stirred uneasily in his sleep, then awoke with a start.

He groped for the light chain above his bed and the light revealed a small, unkempt, five-dollar-a-week room. He knuckled his eyes, then peered at a clock on the dresser but found that he had forgotten to wind it. Through the window he could see the first streaks of dawn. The pounding on the door did not let up.

Firpo Cole disentangled himself from the bed covers, worked his feet into straw slippers and opened the door. Two men entered. He knew one – a plainclothes police dick named Simms. The other was a uniformed cop.

Simms said, 'Go to it, Max,' and the uniformed cop began a somewhat perfunctory search of the room. The dick sat down on the bed. 'How you getting along, Firpo?'

'Fine,' replied Firpo Cole. 'And you?'

'Just dandy, thanks. Have you been picking pockets lately, Firpo?'

'No.'

'That's swell. Your record ain't so good on the blotter, is it?'

'I lost once.'

'I remember, Firpo. Meatball rap. Two years in college, wasn't it?'

'One year. What is this, Simms – a frame?'

The police dick shook his head. 'Nope. I've just been checking on you, Firpo. I'm glad you're going straight. What time did you check in last night?'

'I came home around two or a little after.'

'Go out again?'

'No.'

'How do you pay for your room and grits, Firpo?'

'I do odd jobs around the Tango Palace.'

Simms nodded sagely. 'So I hear. I also hear you're carrying a torch for one of the dames that works there – a Ruth Bailey – and that she won't give you a tumble because she got a yen for Jugger Callahan.'

'What are you driving at, Simms?'

Max was finished with his cursory examination of the room. 'Nothing,' he grunted.

Simms shrugged. 'There's nothing to find anyway. It's open and shut.' He turned to Firpo again. 'I'll tell you what I'm driving at. That Ruth Bailey of yours was murdered a couple of hours ago.'

'If you're being funny,' said Firpo Cole tonelessly, 'I'll kill you, Simms.'

Simms said: 'Sure I'm being funny. Me and Max come here only to have tea and crumpets.'

Firpo's eyes searched the police dick's face. He saw that Simms was speaking the truth. Suddenly he felt sick. He got up and stumbled through the door, across the hallway, to the washroom. He kneeled over the bowl and the fleshless body shook and strained convulsively.

Simms cautioned, 'Don't let the guy pull any fast one,' and Max walked over to the open door and watched till Firpo returned.

Simms said: 'I figure it this way, Firpo. Tell me if I get the details wrong. You were after Ruth Bailey but there was no sale because she was hot for this Jugger Callahan. So you got fed up with the whole business and went and killed her.'

'I didn't kill her.' He began to tremble and a fit of coughing seized him. He covered his mouth with a towel and when he took it away there were flecks of blood on it. 'I didn't kill her,' he repeated.

Simms said: 'It probably just slipped your mind, Firpo. I guess we can make you remember again. Get some duds on that gorgeous torso of yours and come along.'

The prowl car stopped at the rooming house of the late Ruth Bailey. The sun was already showing itself and supplanting the coolness of a Los Angeles night with a dry desert heat.

Simms, Max and Firpo Cole went up the two flights of groaning steps and entered Ruth Bailey's small apartment. The place had already been dusted and photoed and the few department men who remained, sat around yawning and wishing they were home in bed. A couple of bored reporters were handicapping the Caliente races and exhibiting a complete disinterest in this murder of a taxi dance hall hostess.

The body lay on the floor where it had fallen. Simms yanked off the bed sheet that covered it and said: 'Come here.'

Firpo Cole walked over and stared down on Ruth Bailey. He thought he would be sick again but the feeling passed. She wore the same dress, and the brooch that Jugger had bought for Mona Leeds was still clasped at her neck. The steel point of Ephraim Tuttle's stolen letter opener was buried deep in her heart.

But Firpo was looking neither at the brooch nor the murder weapon. His eyes were fastened on the dead lips and the heavy coloring of lipstick over them – and on the strange shading of tangerine.

As if from a great distance, Firpo heard Simms' matter-of-fact voice saying: 'Take a good look at what you done and then see if you still got the crust to deny it.'

Firpo Cole gave a queer, strangled gasp and sank down on his knees beside the body. His hand went out and caressed Ruth Bailey's neck and he bent over and kissed her on the forehead. Behind him, a flashlight bulb exploded.

After a while, Firpo stood up. His eyes were dry and had a strange glint of understanding in them and the white, unhealthy face was set with rocky determination.

Simms said: 'You did a pretty messy job, didn't you? Do you feel like talking about it now?'

'I didn't do it.'

'No? Then who did?'

Firpo Cole was sure he knew. Jugger Callahan! It couldn't be anyone else. But his face gave no inkling of his thought. He would get at the truth – and when he did, no one but he would have the pleasure of dealing with the murderer. He said: 'I didn't do this, Simms. I would of killed myself for even thinking of doing it.'

Max gave a yell and pointed at the body. 'It's gone!'

They followed the cop's fingers. The brooch that had been clasped at Ruth Bailey's neck was missing.

'Kee-rist!' roared Simms. 'You lousy pickpocket, what the hell do you think you're pulling off here?'

The police dick grabbed at Firpo Cole and began to bounce him up and down like a cocktail shaker. 'You wouldn't kill her!' he shouted. 'Why you even rob her dead body to get a two buck hunk of jewelry!'

'I didn't take it,' Firpo gasped as well as he could.

'No one else was near her,' snorted Simms. His hands plunged into Firpo's pockets – and came up empty. Bewilderment spread over his beet-face as he ran his hands over Firpo's clothes. 'What the hell did you do with it?'

'I didn't touch it,' said Firpo.

'Take your duds off!'

Firpo Cole shed his clothes till he stood completely naked. Simms carefully felt and looked over each item of clothing and even ran his hands through Firpo's hair and looked in his mouth. The brooch was not on him. Simms gave the shivering Firpo permission to dress.

Then the department men carefully combed the room for any possible hiding place. The search did not reveal the missing jewel. Simms scratched at his chin, puzzled.

'Sure as hell that thing was on her neck when we come in here,' he said.

Max asked: 'Are you sure it was there when Firpo touched her?'

They looked at each other uncertainly, even suspiciously. Finally, Simms said: 'Well we know that Firpo hasn't got it.' He jerked a finger at the reporters. 'Search those crumbs down to their drawers. If it ain't on them you better take this room apart till you find it!'

Simms grabbed Firpo by the arm and pushed him toward the door. He never felt Firpo's sensitive, experienced fingers as they dipped into his jacket pocket to retrieve the missing brooch.

Alone in a small cell in the city jail, Firpo Cole hid the brooch in one of his shoes, then lay down on the iron cot and waited. He tried not to think of the dead body. It would just make him sick again and he couldn't afford that now. Afterwards it would be all right but first there was work to do.

Several hours passed and it was nearing ten before a guard came along and roused Firpo out of his dull, lethargic sleep. He blinked as he was taken into a sunlit, cheerful room. Simms sat behind a desk talking with Jugger Callahan and Ephraim Tuttle. There were a few cops there, including Max, and a male secretary was taking notes on a stenotype. The guard pushed Firpo into a chair and left.

Jugger was saying: 'I didn't see her after she left with Firpo. Firpo used to walk her home every night so it was nothing out of the ordinary. Lots of crumbs hang out in front of every dance hall and she never liked to go home alone.'

Simms asked: 'Didn't you have another joint which burned down a couple of months ago?'

'Yes. I have a new place now. What of it?'

'Nothing. I just remembered. Was Ruth Bailey on the weed?'

'Not that I know of.'

'The autopsy'll show anyway.' Simms absently tore at a blotter. 'It still looks like Firpo did it. He was nuts about Ruth Bailey but she passed him up for you.'

Jugger's words came clipped and precise. 'Ruth Bailey and I were friends and nothing more. Understand?'

Simms shrugged. 'It makes no difference what you call it. Any way you slice it the motive is still jealousy. Last night Firpo got particularly jealous when he saw some guy talking to her through a few dances. Afterwards he picked a fight with the guy and got poked. He was mad clear through so he stole the letter opener and took her home and let her have it.'

'That don't hold water,' Ephraim Tuttle intruded. 'My letter opener was missing *before* Firpo had that fight.'

Simms carefully dropped the shreds of the blotter into a waste basket. 'Before-after-sooner-later. What's the difference so long as he hangs for it?'

'I still think you're all wet about Firpo,' said Jugger Callahan. 'I'll be glad to stand the bail for him if he's held.'

Simms pushed his chair back. 'There ain't no bail in a first degree homicide charge.'

Jugger Callahan and Ephraim Tuttle moved for the door. The band leader said to Firpo, 'Take it easy,' and they left.

Simms came from behind the desk and planted himself in front of Firpo. Max and one of the other cops moved in closer.

Simms spoke persuasively, almost with a note of regret: 'It's open and shut, Firpo. If you get a good shyster you'll probably be able to beat it with an insanity plea. Sick guys like you who don't rate with the dames often get violent about it. You suddenly got tired of playing second fiddle to Jugger Callahan with the Bailey frill so you stole the letter opener. You had a chance to steal it any time because you were always around the Tango Palace. You walked her home, went up to her room and killed her.'

Simms went over to a water cooler and drank three times from a lily cup.

Max said: 'Firpo thought he wiped his prints off that letter opener but we'll bring 'em up with a special process.'

Simms returned. 'It had to be you, Firpo,' he continued, 'because anyone coming along later would have found Bailey in bed and she was wearing her street clothes when she was killed. What makes the whole thing worse is that you stole the letter opener beforehand so that makes it premeditated murder. Why don't you plead guilty, Firpo, and we'll let you cop an insanity plea?'

Firpo Cole didn't reply. The dick's words made him wonder why Ruth was still wearing her clothes when she was murdered. Ordinarily, she would have gone to bed right away. She was tired enough. Did she stay up to wait for Jugger? Did she go out to visit him and then come back?'

Simms sighed. He said: 'I hate to do this.' He slapped Firpo squarely over the mouth and someone behind Firpo hit him over the ear. 'Are you gonna look at this sensibly?' asked Simms.

The stenotypist left. The brooch was cutting into the sole of Firpo's foot but he was glad to feel it there. That cheap piece of jewelry which Jugger Callahan had bought for Mona Leeds would yet prove his guilt.

Simms hit Firpo over the mouth again and repeated his question. Blood from a broken tooth choked Firpo and he could only shake his head in reply. Somebody gave him a sharp, clipping blow over the nape of his neck, the chair tilted and the broadloom rug seemed to rush up at him.

'Like hitting an old woman,' commented Max disgustedly.

When Firpo Cole regained consciousness, he found himself lying on the cot in his cell. The tooth socket had stopped bleeding. He did not know how long he stayed there. Somebody brought him a tin platter full of some mush but he didn't touch it. A drunk in the next cell tried to find out from Firpo what had caused the Yankees to slump.

After a while, the guard came along and he was taken up to that cheerful room again. Simms, Max and the other shams were there but this time the outsider was the stranger who had sat through eight dances with Ruth and who had subsequently biffed Firpo.

'Sit down, Firpo.' Simms sounded friendly. He indicated the stranger. 'This is Mickey Hymer.'

'I met him,' responded Firpo through bruised lips.

'So you did. How come you tried to step on Mr. Hymer last night?'

'He wouldn't pay Ruth Bailey her tickets.'

'As it turned out, Firpo, she didn't need them. Mr. Hymer is an investigator for Easternstates Insurance and he wants to ask you a few questions.'

Mr. Hymer reached over and extended a hand to Firpo Cole. 'First how about letting bygones be bygones?'

Firpo ignored the outstretched hand.

'Have it your way,' shrugged the insurance dick. 'Firpo, I'll be frank with you. We think that was no accidental fire that burned down the Tango Palace. Jugger Callahan had a pretty heavy policy on it and the whole business stinks.'

Firpo Cole felt a sudden surge of panic. Jugger Callahan in jail for incendiarism and insurance fraud was the last thing he wanted. Jugger had to be kept free – and very accessible. He said: 'That fire was on the level.'

'What makes you think so, Firpo?'

'Jugger had over twelve hundred bucks in his desk when the place burned down. It was the take for three days and he was going to deposit it the next morning. If he would have started that fire he wouldn't have left that much dough there.'

Mr. Hymer nodded. 'That's the story I heard, Firpo, but Callahan had a heavy property policy on the place and that more than made up for the money that burned. Besides,' he added with careful emphasis, 'outside of Jugger Callahan's business manager, we have no proof that the money was really left there.'

'What stinks about the fire?' asked Firpo.

'We found what looks like the remains of a few empty oil cans in the basement. In addition, it was a very profitable fire for Callahan. But what I'd like to know from you is where Ruth Bailey came in on it.'

'Don't think you can frame her because she's dead,' said Firpo tensely.

'Keep cool,' soothed Mr. Hymer. 'I got as much respect for the dead as the next man. Only I know she was the last one in the dance hall before it burned down and I thought maybe she told you something she forgot to say to me.'

'She told me nothing you don't know. When she got home that night she found out that she forgot her purse at the dance hall so she had to go back.'

'Why couldn't she get it the next day?'

'Because the key to her apartment was in it,' said Firpo.

'I see. What's the rest of her story?'

'When she got back the place was empty and outside of a couple of lights someone left on, she saw nothing suspicious. She got her purse and went home. That's all she had to do with it.'

Firpo wondered what the insurance dick would say if he knew that Ruth had taken that brooch from Jugger's office. Did it prove that Jugger Callahan had also come back after the others were gone and forgotten it on his desk?

Mr. Hymes picked at his nose thoughtfully. 'That's the same story she – the deceased – told me last night.' He stood up. 'I guess I'll mosey along.'

When the door was closed behind the insurance dick, Simms turned to Firpo. 'It still looks like you're the murderer,' he informed him cozily.

'I didn't do it,' said Firpo Cole for the sake of the secretary's record.

'My men have been checking all morning and they can't find anyone who saw Ruth Bailey go out after you took her home last night. So you must have gone up to the apartment with her and killed her before she had a chance to get her clothes off and go to bed.'

Suddenly, Firpo Cole knew the meaning of the lipstick on the dead woman's mouth. It was something no one could have noticed but he. He knew the kind of lipstick she always used – a deep carmine brand named *Machavelli*. On those rare occasions that Ruth had kissed him, he had never wiped it off. But the lipstick on her, when she was murdered, had a tangerine coloring – the kind that Mona Leeds, the torch singer, used. It could mean only that Ruth had gone out again to see Mona.

Firpo hadn't been listening to Simms' persuasive arguments for appointing him the murderer. He said: 'Go jump in a sewer.'

Simms and Max came around to where Firpo sat. The stenotypist left the room. Firpo braced himself.

Simms sighed. 'This is a hell of a case. I wish I knew what happened to that jewelry that was on Bailey's neck.' Then he began to hit Firpo methodically, with semi-clenched fists.

A spasm of coughing shook Firpo's spare body. The contents were heavy and deep from the lungs.

Max moved away. 'Watch those damned germs,' he complained. 'You oughta learn enough to cover your mouth.'

Firpo knew he was going to faint again. He struggled against it, for a few moments, then gave way.

When Firpo Cole came around, he found himself lying on a cot in the dispensary. He could see through an unshaded window ahead of him. It was dark outside. He must have been out for several hours.

The doctor who was bending over Firpo stood up and faced Simms and Max. 'He's all right now but if you give him another shellacking I'm not responsible.'

'Shellacking!' exclaimed Simms. 'We hardly touched the guy. We just gave him a few slaps to help his memory and—'

'I'm not interested,' cut in the doctor. 'All I say is that another memory course might bring on a much worse hemorrhage, so don't try it.' He snapped his bag shut and stalked over to a desk to fill in a report.

'And that's what you call cooperation,' muttered Max.

Firpo sat up on the edge of the cot and buttoned his shirt. The telephone jangled and Max took it. He listened a moment, then tendered the receiver to Simms. 'It's for you. The autopsy report on the Bailey woman.'

'Yes?' said Simms. He glanced covertly toward Firpo. 'You say that Ruth Bailey was opened by the usual mid-line incision? . . . You're some cut-up, ha, ha, ha . . . Now forget that scientific bull – tell me in plain, everyday American . . . I see . . . And how about her guts? . . . I see . . . Aha – the liver and spleen . . . and the markings on the body? . . . Good-looking, eh? . . . O.K., send up the report.'

Simms cradled the receiver and turned to Firpo. 'That sawbones just hasn't got any feelings.'

'I know,' said Firpo. 'It's the psychological angle, so forget it.'

'Wise guy. Well, what do you think about this? Ruth Bailey was gonna have a kid.'

Firpo found some kind of medicine bottle within his reach and threw it.

Simms ducked. 'A lie like that,' he said darkly, 'don't give you the right to throw things at me. Watch your step or I'll forget myself and give you the shellacking of your life. Now beat it.'

'Beat it?' said Firpo stupidly.

'Yeah. Get out of here. We know damned well you did the murder but we can't prove it – yet. We're just giving you rope, Firpo.'

Max emitted a sudden guffaw. 'Maybe,' he explained, 'we'll give him more rope later – around the neck!'

CHAPTER THREE

Requiem in Jazz

Leaving the Hall of Justice, Firpo Cole cut across to old Chinatown. He dodged into a dark alley and pressed himself against the wall. He waited thus for fifteen minutes before he felt assured that he was not being followed. The cops didn't even have enough on him to put a shadow on his tail.

He removed his shoe and took out the brooch. The sole of his foot was criss-crossed with cuts and his cotton sock was caked with blood. He bound the foot with a soiled handkerchief and proceeded up Main Street.

Some ten minutes later he reached a pawn shop just as the owner was closing up for the night. He put the brooch on the counter.

'I want you to look at this, Saul.'

'Firpo, when will you guys learn I don't handle hot stuff?'

'I only asked you to look at it.'

The short, bald-headed man picked up the brooch and studied it. Finally, he said: 'I wouldn't touch it, Firpo, but it's worth two or three hundred dollars.'

Firpo started. 'For that little gold and a little piece of glass? Are you sure?'

'Not for the gold, Firpo. It's for what you think is a piece of glass.' Saul held it back to let the light of a lamp fall on it. Small white rays seemed to radiate from a flaw in its sparkling sky-blue center.

'It's a fair example of a star sapphire,' continued Saul, 'and if it wasn't hot you'd even be able to get up to four and a half hundred for it.'

Firpo took the brooch from Saul's hand and walked out. This gave Jugger Callahan an even stronger motive to murder Ruth Bailey. The brooch was worth real dough – all the more reason for Jugger to be thoroughly enraged over its theft.

Firpo saw a clock over a bus depot. It was already after ten. He wasn't at all hungry but he hadn't eaten since the previous evening and he knew that he should have something. He found some loose change in his pockets and entered a cafeteria. With swollen lips he sipped a glass of buttermilk through a straw, and then he headed straight for the Tango Palace.

The taxi dance hall was going full blast. On the platform, Mona Leeds was giving her all to the *Basin Street Blues* and extra hostesses were on the floor to take care of the large, Saturday night trade.

Firpo Cole sank into the settee and his eyes automatically searched among the dancers for Ruth Bailey. Then he remembered. Some of the girls walked over to tell him that Ruth had been a good kid and that if they could do anything . . .

To one side, Simms was grilling the hostesses by turns. He saw Firpo and came over to him.

'I hope there's no hard feelings, Firpo.'

'Who found the body, Simms?'

'The apartment door was left open and some tenant who came in at three thirty saw her on the floor.'

'O.K.'

'You don't look so good, Firpo. You're as white as a baby's behind. Why don't you go home?'

'Why don't you leave me alone?'

'Now don't take it that way, Firpo. Just regard me as a plainclothes dick who has to do his job.'

Firpo said: 'I love you with an overwhelming passion.'

Simms snorted. 'If you didn't do the murder a guy would think you'd try to help me find who did. But everybody in this stinkhole thinks I'm their enemy.' He stalked off.

Mona finished her number and left the stand. Ephraim Tuttle scurried back and forth settling arguments when he found them and creating them when he didn't. He stopped by Firpo Cole.

'I heard you were out, Firpo. I tried to tell those dopes that you couldn't have done a thing like that to her.'

'Thanks.'

The business manager regarded Firpo's battered face and clucked sympathetically. 'That's a hell of a way to treat you. As if you would have touched a hair of her head.'

'We won't talk about it, Tuttle.'

'Sure. She'd want us to forget it.'

'That's right. Shut up.'

Ephraim Tuttle muttered something under his breath and left. Firpo buried his face in his hands and sobs seemed to rack his body, but when his hands dropped away, his eyes were dry. Rocco Pace, dressed to the hilt, came by and sat beside him.

The racketeer asked: 'Are you still a checking-room?'

'Sure.'

Rocco Pace slipped his gun out of the shoulder holster and handed it to Firpo. 'I see that the shams gave you the lumps, pal.'

Firpo Cole nodded.

'Don't let it worry you, Firpo. You'll get used to it – after a while.' He patted Firpo's back and went out on the dance floor. In a moment, he was dancing a wild waltz, to the beat of a fox trot, whirling in and out among the unmoving couples.

Firpo Cole ran fingers over the automatic in his pocket. He caressed its smoothness and put down the safety. He stood up and pushed his way through the dancers and idlers, down the length of the hall. He went through a curtained archway, that led backstage to the band platform and knocked on the dressing-room off the right wings.

Mona Leeds said: 'Come in.'

He entered the small dressing-room. The torch singer was buffing her nails before the mirror.

'I'm glad they let you go, Firpo.' The rich, husky voice sounded strained.

He took a cigarette from a case on a table and sat down. 'They had to. They didn't have anything on me.'

'You shouldn't smoke cigarettes, Firpo. They're not good for you.'

He laughed.

'I know,' she said rapidly. 'You feel you don't give a damn any more. I'd feel that way if something happened to Jugger but its wrong, Firpo. I don't know how to tell you but—' She floundered for the right words. 'You can't know how sorry I am about the quarrel I had with Ruth last night. It was just a crazy fit of jealousy.'

'Don't let it worry you, Mona. You couldn't help it and even Ruth wasn't mad about it.'

'Firpo, if only we could find out who did it.'

'Don't let that worry you either, Mona. What'd you tell the cops?'

'Just what happened,' she replied. 'I had that argument with Ruth and I never saw her again.'

'That's a lie,' said Firpo Cole deliberately. 'I took Ruth home about one thirty. She probably went right out again and visited you. She didn't bring her purse along and before she left you she probably said that she looked like the wrath of God and—'

'Those were her exact words,' uttered Mona Leeds softly.

He gave a wry grin. 'Don't be surprised. I know Ruth. Anyway, you loaned her your powder and lipstick and she came home. That couldn't have been later than three in the morning. Somebody was either waiting for her at the apartment or followed her home and killed her. What I want to know is why you keep that visit to you a secret.'

'You won't like it, Firpo. That's why I kept it to myself.'

'I'm not a very sensitive plant. Go on.'

'Well she came to tell me she was sorry about our fight – and that she was a thief. She said she went back to the dance hall the night the old place burned down and found a piece of jewelry that Jugger had bought for me.'

Firpo produced the brooch and showed it to the torch singer. 'Is this what Ruth was talking about?'

'Yes – but she was wearing it on her dress. How did you get it?'

'That's a trade secret. Go on.'

'Ruth took it from Jugger's desk,' continued the torch singer, 'and she came over last night to give it to me. I wouldn't take it.'

'Why not?' he asked.

'Because it wasn't mine. Jugger might have bought it for me but he never mentioned it, so I told her to keep it – a sort of peace offering for that fight we had. I guess Jugger thinks it got lost in the fire.'

Firpo Cole shook his head. 'Jugger must have seen her wearing it.'

'I guess so,' replied Mona Leeds. 'That's the way Jugger is. If he figured that she wanted it enough to steal it, he'd let her keep it.'

'It's worth four or five hundred bucks, Mona, so I doubt it. You know, the Easternstates Insurance thinks the fire wasn't an accident.'

The torch singer's hand went to her mouth in a frightened gesture. 'No. Jugger wouldn't do a thing like that.'

'How do you know?'

'But it's crazy, Firpo. He had a lot of money in his office – the receipts of a couple of days – that burned down, too.'

'The insurance money more than made up for it. Besides, they're not so sure the money was there in the first place. They only have Jugger's and Tuttle's word for it.'

'But why should he take such a chance for a few dollars, Firpo? He's doing fine the way he is.'

'I don't know but I'll damned well find out.' He stood up. 'You're O.K., Mona. Don't take it too hard if I find out that Jugger killed Ruth.'

He left her staring after him with wide-eyed apprehension.

Firpo Cole entered on the right wings of the band platform, found a meeting chair and sat down. From where he was, he could watch Jugger Callahan fronting the band.

Jugger caught sight of Firpo, snapped his fingers to the boys and the music trailed off. He spoke into the mike.

'Ladies and gentlemen, last night one of our beloved hostesses met a tragic end and out of respect to her I'd like everybody to keep thirty seconds of real silence.'

He bowed his head and checked his wristwatch. Throughout the semi-dark hall, couples waited with their arms twined around each other. Some girl in the back giggled and said: 'No.'

The thirty seconds were up. Jugger Callahan's toes beat a tattoo and he snapped his fingers. 'All right boys. A one-a, a two-a, a three-a, scratch!' The band began *Potato Head Blues* and the couples started to sway again like puppets whose wires had suddenly been jerked.

Jugger walked over to Firpo. He patted his greased-back hair, obviously pleased that he had done the right thing by Ruth.

'Firpo,' said the band leader, 'we already got sixty-two bucks collected. How much can you chip in?'

'For what?'

'Ruth's funeral, of course,' replied Jugger.

'I'm not interested in Ruth's funeral. There's somebody else's funeral I want to see about.'

'Uh-huh. I get you, Firpo, but you ought to leave that to the cops. You probably never even met the guy who did it.'

Firpo's bloodshot eyes fixed themselves on the band leader's face. 'I won't have far to go. That letter opener was stolen from here.'

'Say, that's right, isn't it? Ephraim come to me around eleven thirty last night and asked me if I'd taken it so it must have been stolen earlier.'

Firpo's hands were in his pockets. There was something friendly and comforting about the feel of the automatic. He said: 'We'll talk about it later.'

'Sure, Firpo,' said Jugger, not too heartily. 'Sure.'

The band leader returned to his post. The music ground on. Twenty sets, of three melodies each, every hour. Sixty dances in as many minutes with only an occasional break to give the customers a chance to buy more tickets.

The *Smiling Troubadours* never stopped playing, though every once in a while a musician left the stand. And, as the hours wore on and they became more tired, the music became faster and more frenzied.

Firpo stayed in his chair, watching the band leader. He didn't intend letting Jugger out of his sight – not till he could trap him some way and prove to himself that here was the murderer of Ruth Bailey.

Simms reached backstage in the course of his investigations. He seemed as much in a fog as ever. He asked Firpo whether Ruth had had any jewelry on her dress when he'd seen the body. Firpo couldn't remember and the police dick left.

The time went by and Firpo sat unmoving, watching Jugger Callahan with lackluster eyes. He tried to think of the murder of the only person he had ever cared for. What had Ruth said? That she was afraid? Of what?

251

Suddenly, it hit Firpo Cole like a ton of dynamite. Where was the five hundred dollars that had found its way into Ruth Bailey's purse and where the envelope that read: *This better be enough?*

The police hadn't said anything about the money or envelope so the murderer must have stolen both. There was no reason why the killer shouldn't have taken the money but the envelope was a different matter. That typewritten sentence on it meant something to the murderer. Someone in the Tango Palace had probably thought that Ruth Bailey was blackmailing him. That very envelope had probably been written on one of the office typewriters.

Firpo frowned and the swollen lips pursed in thought. His job was to find out who had typed that envelope.

At two in the morning, the *Smiling Troubadours* gradually, almost reluctantly, stopped playing. There seemed to be a kind of weary excitement among them after the long grind. Customers filed out, spotlights went off and hostesses sat down to nurse their feet.

Firpo Cole fell into step beside Jugger Callahan as the band leader talked to friends, visited the washroom and finally went to his office. Jugger did not object. He imagined that Firpo felt lost – that he needed friendship. Firpo was like a dog that had lost its master and was trying to attach itself to someone else.

After Jugger had finished checking the night's receipts with the business manager, he turned to Firpo. 'We're having a tea party tonight. How about coming along? A couple of reefers might do you good.'

Tea parties were a custom of long standing on every Saturday night at Jugger Callahan's apartment. Any other time, Firpo Cole would have felt highly honored by the invitation, for these parties were attended only by the elite of the Tango Palace.

'I wouldn't miss it for the world,' said Firpo.

Ephraim Tuttle locked up the books, said he'd see them later and went to pay off the girls. Firpo and the band leader left the dance hall. They walked down Main, then turned up Sixth.

'Jugger,' asked Firpo Cole, 'can you typewrite?'

'One finger stuff. Why?'

'It's not important. Is there a file up in the office listing the girls' addresses?'

'Of course.'

'Then anyone at the Tango could find out where Ruth lived.'

'I guess so, Firpo, but—'

'You could find out, too, couldn't you?' cut in Firpo.

'What the hell are you getting at?'

'Forget it, Jugger.'

The band leader started to say something but stayed his reply. They turned into an all-night drugstore. Here, for a fiver, the clerk forgot the narcotic laws and gave Jugger a twelve ounce bottle of *cannabis indica*. The band leader then bought a carton of cigarettes and some brown cigarette paper.

They went outside and hailed a taxi.

CHAPTER FOUR

Paid in Full

Jugger Callahan's apartment was large and comfortable. Most of the boys from the band were already there. Mona Leeds and Evelyn Dorn, Ephraim Tuttle's current doll, were making and serving sandwiches to the guests. Jugger lolled in an overstuffed chair and Firpo sat right beside him watching the preparations.

Monkey Harris and a few of the other boys had sliced open the cigarettes from the carton and emptied the tobacco into a wide, shallow pan. Now they took the bottle of *cannabis indica* and poured the greenish-brown liquid into the pan. They allowed the tobacco to soak in the poisonous drug for several minutes, then put a match to it – which served both to burn up the excess alcohol and to dry the tobacco. This done, they began to wrap the residue in the brown cigarette paper. They worked diligently and the heap of these homemade marihuana cigarettes grew steadily.

Jugger said to Firpo Cole: 'These give a much better kick than the ready made kind.'

'I never tried them,' replied Firpo. 'When did you first start?' He wanted to hear Jugger talk – to wait for that mistake, that slip of the tongue which would point the finger of guilt at him.

Jugger Callahan was in an expansive mood. He said: 'Back in Chi, in the Capone days. A bunch of us muggle-hounds would get together and play hot music long before the word "swing" was ever invented. Today the high school punks have taken over. They call themselves jitterbugs and if we send good we're out of this world. They call the clarinet a licorice stick, a trombone a grunt iron, the bass fiddle a doghouse – and most of the time I don't know what the hell they're talking about.'

'Yeah,' said Firpo. 'Those sure were the good old days, all right, in Chi.'

'The only thing that flowed freer than money,' continued the band leader reminiscently, 'was blood. We used to have classy apartments and buy a lot of jewelry for our women.'

Firpo suddenly reached into his pocket and held the brooch out. 'You mean like this thing you bought for Mona?'

253

Jugger Callahan didn't bite. 'I bought that for Mona? What you getting at, Firpo?'

'Haven't you ever seen it before?' asked Firpo Cole.

'No – yes, I think Ruth Bailey wore something like that.'

Firpo frowned. Jugger was too old a hand to be caught that crudely. He said: 'This is a star sapphire. It's pretty valuable.'

Evelyn Dorn was hovering over them with a sandwich tray. Her doe eyes bulged. 'Geeze! A star sapphire.' She took it and examined it reverently. 'That's what I always wanted to get – a star sapphire.' She sighed. 'But I guess I ain't got what it takes. Nobody's given me any – not even one yet.'

'I'd still like to know what you were getting at, Firpo,' said the band leader.

Firpo retrieved the brooch. 'Let's drop it.'

Evelyn Dorn suddenly snapped her fingers. 'Hell, Firpo, I forgot to tell you!'

'What?'

'That gangster – that Rocco Pace is on the warpath after you. You better watch out.'

'What's the matter now?' asked Jugger.

'That's all right,' said Firpo. 'It's nothing to worry about. I just stole Rocco's gun.'

Jugger Callahan looked at him queerly but made no comment. Evelyn Dorn wandered off. Firpo leaned back and closed his eyes. An idea was stirring within him.

Turnip Billings, who played tenor horn, called out: 'All finished, boys. Jugger Callahan and his Twelve Shtoonks will now get high.'

He tossed a few reefers to Firpo Cole and Jugger Callahan.

Jugger Callahan was a breather and it was not long before a quiet contentment seemed to come over him. After a while, he fixed glazed eyes on Firpo and said: 'You're not running after me because you like my mustache. You think I killed Ruth Bailey.'

Firpo Cole, who was bluffing his smoke, nodded.

'What'll you do about it?'

'When I make sure, I'll kill you.' Firpo's voice was dispassionate but as certain of itself as a pile driver.

Jugger Callahan laughed. His good humor was not even ruffled. 'You two-bit grifter, you talk big. How come you think I killed your Ruth Bailey?'

'She was in love with you, Jugger – really in love – the way a bum like you couldn't understand.'

'I liked Ruth, but that's all, Firpo. I never two-timed on Mona.'

'I know,' replied Firpo. 'I would of made you marry Ruth if you had.'

The band leader laughed again. 'Pickpocket to marriage broker. That's good. But you haven't told me how you think I come to kill Ruth.'

They were talking in low tones. The others around them still laughed and shouted boisterously. The drug had not yet begun to take effect.

Firpo said: 'I figure it this way. You put a lot of insurance on the old Tango Palace and then faked a fire by soaking the drapes and everything else in oil and gasoline.'

'You better keep those ideas to yourself,' said Jugger Callahan a little more seriously.

'I don't have to. An insurance dick thinks that. He found what used to be oil cans in the ruins. You also forgot that stone I showed you, on your desk because Ruth had to go back to the Palace that night and she saw it there. You must have been fixing for the fire about that time and you probably saw her take it.'

'So now you're calling Ruth Bailey a crook.'

Firpo's hands began to tremble and he waited a few moments before replying. 'She took it because she knew you bought it for Mona and she was jealous. She started wearing it every day after that, Jugger, just to get Mona's goat but you thought it was her way of saying that she knew you started that fire.'

'Not so fast, Firpo. I lost over twelve hundred dollars in cold cash during the fire and you don't think I'd be crazy enough to leave it up there if I burned the place down.'

'I know that angle too, Jugger, but there's no proof you left the dough to burn and that it isn't in your pocket right now.'

'Well, I'll be damned,' the band leader uttered softly. 'And what do you think I did after the fire?'

'Ruth was wearing that thing and you thought she was blackmailing you so you tried to buy her off. You slipped five hundred bucks into her purse with a note saying that it better be enough. But she kept wearing the brooch and you thought she wanted more sugar so you stole Tuttle's letter opener, figuring that anyone at the Palace could be blamed. Then you killed her with it. It had a sharp point. It must have been easy.'

'That's a lot of shtush, Firpo, and you know it. You're just excited about the killing. When you have a good night's sleep you'll decide you couldn't prove a thing.'

'That's the only reason you're still alive, Jugger.'

Ephraim Tuttle had come in and walked over to them in time to hear the last sentence. 'What's going on?' he asked.

'Firpo's puking about some kind of star sapphire and that I killed Ruth Bailey,' responded Jugger.

'Oh, he's just weed-wacky,' pronounced the business manager. 'I don't know why the hell we let him louse up the place around here.' He walked away.

*

The doorbell to the apartment rang. Mona Leeds came in from the kitchen and said: 'See who it is, Firpo.' He went through the vestibule. It was Rocco Pace standing at the door.

'I thought I'd find you here,' said the racketeer.

'Do you want to come in?'

'That ain't what I'm here for. I get a plenty good jag with dago-red.'

'Then what did you want?' asked Firpo.

'Why'd you hook my gat?'

'I want to borrow it for a while, Rocco.'

Rocco Pace gave a vague smile. 'You liked that jane a lot, didn't you, Firpo?'

'Yes.'

'I see. And you have to go gunning with my rod.'

'I'll give it back to you after, Rocco.'

'Let's have it now.'

'I said I want to keep it for a while.'

Rocco Pace's voice was silken. 'You know better than to give me any backtalk, Firpo. Let's have it.'

Firpo Cole hesitated a moment, then surrendered. 'O.K.,' he said bleakly and handed the automatic to the racketeer.

Rocco Pace whipped a polka-dotted handkerchief out of his breast pocket and carefully wiped the gun. Then he returned it to Firpo. 'You ought to know better than to sport a rod with my prints on it.' He started off, then paused. 'I don't know if it'll help you, Firpo, but one of the guys up at the Tango Palace has been plunging pretty heavily with a bookie I know. It's practically bankrupted him. You can have it for what it's worth.'

'Who is it?'

'I blowed my whistle plenty. It ought to satisfy you.'

'Thanks, Rocco. You're white.'

'Think nothing of it,' said the racketeer breezily.

Firpo Cole returned to the living-room.

The tea party was in full session. All the lights were out but for a small, red bulb in a floor lamp. Firpo could distinguish the figures as they moved only to lift the reefers to their mouth for short, quick puffs. Mona Leeds reclined next to Jugger, in the easy chair that Firpo had vacated.

An expensive phonograph was playing repeats of a swing record as slowly as it was able. The record was Armstrong's version of *Knockin' a Jug* and in one corner Monkey Harris was beating an accompaniment on a tom-tom. His slim, yellowed fingers beat rapidly. The test of a good musician, on these occasions, was the number of beats and variations the player could get in, between two chords – and Monkey Harris was rated highly.

The effect was weird as the disk revolved and the tom-tom beat. The record was played slowly and the reefers themselves tended to slow and dull everything – thereby providing for a full appreciation of the music. And every so often a musician grunted or delivered an 'Oh' or an 'Ah' as he caught some new nuance in the music that he'd never before heard.

The air was heavy with those pungent, cloying fumes and Firpo Cole began to cough. He didn't have to look at his handkerchief to know it was becoming smeared with red. But he didn't care. At last he knew what was what. That small item of information from Rocco Pace had done the trick. The coughing became worse and he walked into the kitchen.

Evelyn Dorn was wolfing minced ham sandwiches. 'I'd rather eat here than get sick in there,' she explained.

Firpo Cole said: 'Inside you were raving about star sapphires. Did you ever ask Tuttle to give you one?'

'Sure. It don't harm to ask – but I never got it.'

'That's what I thought. Tuttle did buy it for you, Evelyn, only he forgot it at the old place when it burned down.'

'No kiddin'?'

'He's bought you a lot of stuff, hasn't he?'

'Some,' she said coyly. 'Ephraim ain't a tightwad.'

'That's what I figured – and on top of that he's been playing the horses. That's why he set that fire and later killed Ruth.'

Evelyn Dorn stopped eating for a moment. 'You mean it?'

Firpo nodded. 'He stole twelve hundred bucks in receipts from Jugger and then burned the joint down. He figured rightly that Jugger would think the money burned with the building and that he was making enough profit on insurance not to investigate too much.'

'Well, what do you know?' marveled Evelyn.

Firpo's voice became bitter. 'When Tuttle stole that dough from Jugger's office he accidentlly left that brooch which he bought for you on Jugger's desk – and that's where Ruth found it. He made a too-big stink about losing his letter opener and then killed Ruth with it. He thought she was blackmailing him about the fire and wasn't satisfied with a five hundred buck payoff.'

'You can never tell about someone,' she commented. 'Can you?'

The double-hinge door swung open and Simms, the police detective, Max and Ephraim Tuttle came in.

'All right, Firpo,' said Simms. 'I know you got that jewelry you stole from Bailey's body. Let's have it.'

The automatic appeared in Firpo's hand. The safety catch was still off – the way he wanted it. 'Stick your mitts up and line against the wall.'

The three men did as they were bid. Evelyn Dorn gave a squeal and fled. They could hear the apartment door slam shut.

'Now look here, Firpo,' Simms' voice was hoarse. 'This ain't gonna help. If you just take it easy—'

'Can it,' interrupted Firpo. 'I suppose Tuttle told you I had the brooch.'
Simms nodded.

Tuttle said quickly: 'I didn't mean anything, Firpo. I just heard it was stolen and then when Jugger said you was talking about it I thought I better call the cops.

Firpo's voice was as calm and as steady as the hand that held the gun. 'Tuttle, all you figured was that you'd pin the killing on me and get out of it yourself. But there's no chance of that because you're paying for it now.' He took a bead on the pit of Ephraim Tuttle's stomach.

'Now watch it,' said Simms rapidly. 'Let us take care of it, Firpo. If he did the killing he's entitled to a trial but sure as hell you'll swing if you try it yourself.'

'I know I will,' said Firpo Cole, 'and this'll be one condemned man that'll really eat a damned hearty breakfast.'

Then he sighted carefully and pulled the trigger six times.

THE GIRL WITH THE SILVER EYES
DASHIELL HAMMETT

'The Girl with the Silver Eyes' seems to be a story about the Continental Op, the unnamed private eye who stars in most of Hammett's best short fiction as well as in his first two novels, *Red Harvest* and *The Dain Curse*. It is actually the story of the very beautiful young woman with long, lush brown hair who calls herself Jeanne Delano; in a previous adventure, 'The House in Turk Street,' she was Elvira, with bobbed red hair. A lot of people died in the first story, and more deaths followed in the second. It is Jeanne and her scheme which sets into motion the events that bring about the involvement of the Continental Detective Agency and its fat but very tough operative. Like many of the women in the stories by Hammett (1894–1961), she is young, very pretty, feminine, an inveterate liar and utterly without conscience. She is a chameleon, changing from a desirable kitten to a someone so cold-blooded that she will allow, even encourage, the slaughter of innocent people for her own selfish and greedy ends. Think of Brigid O'Shaughnessy in *The Maltese Falcon* and you know all you need to know about Hammett's *femmes fatales*, and, in fact, just about every sexy girl in every noir book and motion picture.

'The Girl with the Silver Eyes' is connected to 'The House in Turk Street' in that it features Jeanne/Elvira as the catalyst for the ensuing action. It was originally published in the June 1924 issue of *Black Mask*. 'The House in Turk Street' had been in the April 1924 issue.

THE GIRL WITH THE SILVER EYES
DASHIELL HAMMETT

A bell jangled me into wakefulness. I rolled to the edge of my bed and
reached for the telephone. The neat voice of the Old Man – the
Continental Detective Agency's San Francisco manager – came to my ears:

'Sorry to disturb you, but you'll have to go up to the Glenton
Apartments on Leavenworth Street. A man named Burke Pangburn, who
lives there, phoned me a few minutes ago asking to have someone sent up
to see him at once. He seemed rather excited. Will you take care of it? See
what he wants.' I said I would and, yawning, stretching and cursing
Pangburn – whoever he was – got my fat body out of pajamas into street
clothes.

The man who had disturbed my Sunday morning sleep – I found when
I reached the Glenton – was a slim, white-faced person of about twenty-
five, with big brown eyes that were red-rimmed just now from either
sleeplessness or crying, or both. His long brown hair was rumpled when he
opened the door to admit me; and he wore a mauve dressing-robe spotted
with big jade parrots over wine-colored silk pajamas.

The room into which he led me resembled an auctioneer's establishment
just before the sale – or maybe one of these alley tea rooms. Fat blue vases,
crooked red vases, vases of various shapes and colors; marble statuettes,
ebony statuettes, statuettes of any material; lanterns, lamps and candlesticks; draperies, hangings and rugs of all sorts; odds and ends of furniture
that were all somehow queerly designed; peculiar pictures hung here and
there in unexpected places. A hard room to feel comfortable in.

'My fiancée,' he began immediately in a high-pitched voice that was
within a notch of hysteria, 'has disappeared! Something has happened to
her! Foul play of some horrible sort! I want you to find her – to save her
from this terrible thing that . . .'

I followed him this far and then gave it up. A jumble of words came out
of his mouth – 'spirited away . . . mysterious something . . . lured into a
trap' – but they were too disconnected for me to make anything out of
them. So I stopped trying to understand him, and waited for him to babble
himself empty of words.

I have heard ordinarily reasonable men, under stress of excitement, run

261

on even more crazily than this wild-eyed youth; but his dress – the parroted robe and gay pajamas – and his surroundings – this deliriously furnished room – gave him too theatrical a setting; made his words sound utterly unreal.

He himself, when normal, should have been a rather nice-looking lad: his features were well spaced and, though his mouth and chin were a little uncertain, his broad forehead was good. But standing there listening to the occasional melodramatic phrase that I could pick out of the jumbled noises he was throwing at me, I thought that instead of parrots on his robe he should have had cuckoos.

Presently he ran out of language and was holding his long, thin hands out to me in an appealing gesture, saying:

'Will you?' over and over. 'Will you? Will you?'

I nodded soothingly, and noticed that tears were on his thin cheeks.

'Suppose we begin at the beginning,' I suggested, sitting down carefully on a carved bench affair that didn't look any too strong.

'Yes! Yes!' He was standing legs apart in front of me, running his fingers through his hair. 'The beginning. I had a letter from her every day until—'

'That's not the beginning,' I objected. 'Who is she? What is she?'

'She's Jeanne Delano!' he exclaimed in surprise at my ignorance. 'And she is my fiancée. And now she is gone, and I know that—'

The phrases '*victim of foul play*,' '*into a trap*' and so on began to flow hysterically out again.

Finally I got him quieted down and, sandwiched in between occasional emotional outbursts, got a story out of him that amounted to this:

This Burke Pangburn was a poet. About two months before, he had received a note from a Jeanne Delano – forwarded from his publishers – praising his latest book of rhymes. Jeanne Delano happened to live in San Francisco, too, though she hadn't known that he did. He had answered her note, and had received another. After a little of this they met. If she really was as beautiful as he claimed, then he wasn't to be blamed for falling in love with her. But whether or not she was really beautiful, he thought she was, and he had fallen hard.

This Delano girl had been living in San Francisco for only a little while, and when the poet met her she was living alone in an Ashbury Avenue apartment. He did not know where she came from or anything about her former life. He suspected – from certain indefinite suggestions and peculiarities of conduct which he couldn't put in words – that there was a cloud of some sort hanging over the girl; that neither her past nor her present were free from difficulties. But he hadn't the least idea what those difficulties might be. He hadn't cared. He knew absolutely nothing about her, except that she was beautiful, and he loved her, and she had promised to marry him. Then, on the third of the month – exactly twenty-one days before this Sunday morning – the girl had suddenly left San Francisco. He had received a note from her, by messenger.

This note, which he showed me after I had insisted point blank on seeing it, read:

Burkelove:

Have just received a wire, and must go East on next train. Tried to get you on the phone, but couldn't. Will write you as soon as I know what my address will be. If anything. [These two words were erased and could be read only with great difficulty.] *Love me until I'm back with you forever.*

Your Jeanne

Nine days later he had received another letter from her, from Baltimore, Maryland. This one, which I had a still harder time getting a look at, read:

Dearest Poet:

It seems like two years since I have seen you, and I have a fear that it's going to be between one and two months before I see you again.

I can't tell you now, beloved, about what brought me here. There are things that can't be written. But as soon as I'm back with you, I shall tell you the whole wretched story.

If anything should happen – I mean to me – you'll go on loving me forever, won't you, beloved? But that's foolish. Nothing is going to happen. I'm just off the train, and tired from traveling.

Tomorrow I shall write you a long, long letter to make up for this.

My address here is 215 N. Stricker St. Please, Mister, at least one letter a day!

Your own Jeanne

For nine days he had had a letter from her each day – with two on Monday to make up for the none on Sunday. And then her letters had stopped. And the daily letters he had sent to the address she gave – 215 N. Stricker Street – had begun to come back to him, marked 'Not known.' He had sent a telegram, and the telegraph company had informed him that its Baltimore office had been unable to find a Jeanne Delano at the North Stricker Street address.

For three days he had waited, expecting hourly to hear from the girl, and no word had come. Then he had bought a ticket for Baltimore.

'But,' he wound up, 'I was afraid to go. I know she's in some sort of trouble – I can feel that – but I'm a silly poet. I can't deal with mysteries. Either I would find nothing at all or, if by luck I did stumble on the right track, the probabilities are that I would only muddle things; add fresh complications, perhaps endanger her life still further. I can't go blundering at it in that fashion, without knowing whether I am helping or harming her. It's a task for an expert in that sort of thing. So I thought of your agency. You'll be careful, won't you? It may be – I don't know – that she won't want assistance. It may be that you can help her without her knowing anything about it. You are accustomed to that sort of thing; you can do it, can't you?'

I turned the job over and over in my mind before answering him. The two great bugaboos of a reputable detective agency are the persons who bring in a crooked plan or a piece of divorce work all dressed up in the garb of a legitimate operation, and the irresponsible person who is laboring under wild and fanciful delusions – who wants a dream run out.

This poet – sitting opposite me now twining his long, white fingers nervously – was, I thought, sincere; but I wasn't so sure of his sanity.

'Mr. Pangburn,' I said after a while, 'I'd like to handle this thing for you, but I'm not sure that I can. The Continental is rather strict, and, while I believe this thing is on the level, still I am only a hired man and have to go by the rules. Now if you could give us the endorsement of some firm or person of standing – a reputable lawyer, for instance, or any legally responsible party – we'd be glad to go ahead with the work. Otherwise, I am afraid—'

'But I know she's in danger!' he broke out. 'I know that— And I can't be advertising her plight – airing her affairs – to everyone.'

'I'm sorry, but I can't touch it unless you can give me some such endorsement.' I stood up. 'But you can find plenty of detective agencies that aren't so particular.'

His mouth worked like a small boy's, and he caught his lower lip between his teeth. For a moment I thought he was going to burst into tears. But instead he said slowly: 'I dare say you are right. Suppose I refer you to my brother-in-law, Roy Axford. Will his word be sufficient?'

'Yes.'

Roy Axford – R. F. Axford – was a mining man who had a finger in at least half of the big business enterprises of the Pacific Coast; and his word on anything was commonly considered good enough for anybody.

'If you can get in touch with him now,' I said, 'and arrange for me to see him today, I can get started without much delay.'

Pangburn crossed the room and dug a telephone out from among a heap of his ornaments. Within a minute or two he was talking to someone whom he called 'Rita.'

'Is Roy home? . . . Will he be home this afternoon? . . . No, you can give him a message for me, though . . . Tell him I'm sending a gentleman up to see him this afternoon on a personal matter – personal from me – and that I'll be very grateful if he'll do what I want . . . Yes . . . You'll find out, Rita . . . It isn't a thing to talk about over the phone . . . Yes, thanks!'

He pushed the telephone back into its hiding place and turned to me.

'He'll be at home until two o'clock. Tell him what I told you and if he seems doubtful, have him call me up. You'll have to tell him the whole thing; he doesn't know anything at all about Miss Delano.'

'All right. Before I go, I want a description of her.'

'She's beautiful! The most beautiful woman in the world!'

That would look nice on a reward circular.

'That isn't exactly what I want,' I told him. 'How old is she?'

'Twenty-two.'

'Height?'

'About five feet eight inches, or possibly nine.'

'Slender, medium or plump?'

'She's inclined toward slenderness, but she—'

There was a note of enthusiasm in his voice that made me fear he was about to make a speech, so I cut him off with another question.

'What color hair?'

'Brown – so dark it's almost black – and it's soft and thick and—'

'Yes, yes. Long or bobbed?'

'Long and thick and—'

'What color eyes?'

'You've seen shadows on polished silver when—'

I wrote down *gray eyes* and hurried on with the interrogation.

'Complexion?'

'Perfect!'

'Uh-huh. But is it light, or dark, or florid, or sallow, or what?'

'Fair.'

'Face oval, or square, or long and thin, or what shape?'

'Oval.'

'What shaped nose? Large, small, turned-up—'

'Small and regular!' There was a touch of indignation in his voice.

'How did she dress? Fashionably? Did she favor bright or quiet colors?'

'Beaut—' And then as I opened my mouth to head him off he came down to earth with: 'Very quietly – usually dark blues and browns.'

'What jewelry did she wear?'

'I've never seen her wear any.'

'Any scars, or moles?' The horrified look on his white face urged me to give him a full shot. 'Or warts, or deformities that you know?'

He was speechless, but he managed to shake his head.

'Have you a photograph of her?'

'Yes, I'll show you.'

He bounded to his feet, wound his way through the room's excessive furnishings and out through a curtained doorway. Immediately he was back with a large photograph in a carved ivory frame. It was one of these artistic photographs – a thing of shadows and hazy outlines – not much good for identification purposes. She was beautiful – right enough – but that meant nothing; that's the purpose of an artistic photograph.

'This the only one you have?'

'Yes.'

'I'll have to borrow it, but I'll get it back to you as soon as I have my copies made.'

'No! No!' he protested against having his lady love's face given to a lot of gumshoes. 'That would be terrible!'

I finally got it, but it cost me more words than I like to waste on an incidental.

'I want to borrow a couple of her letters, or something in her writing, too,' I said.

'For what?'

'To have photostatic copies made. Handwriting specimens come in handy – give you something to go over hotel registers with. Then, even if going under fictitious names, people now and then write notes and make memorandums.'

We had another battle, out of which I came with three envelopes and two meaningless sheets of paper, all bearing the girl's angular writing.

'She have much money?' I asked, when the disputed photograph and handwriting specimens were safely tucked away in my pocket.

'I don't know. It's not the sort of thing that one would pry into. She wasn't poor; that is, she didn't have to practice any petty economies; but I haven't the faintest idea either as to the amount of her income or its source. She had an account at the Golden Gate Trust Company, but naturally I don't know anything about its size.'

'Many friends here?'

'That's another thing I don't know. I think she knew a few people here, but I don't know who they were. You see, when we were together we never talked about anything but ourselves. There was nothing we were interested in but each other. We were simply—'

'Can't you even make a guess at where she came from, who she was?'

'No. Those things didn't matter to me. She was Jeanne Delano, and that was enough for me.'

'Did you and she ever have any financial interests in common? I mean, was there ever any transaction in money or other valuables in which both of you were interested?'

What I meant, of course, was had she got into him for a loan, or had she sold him something, or got money out of him in any other way.

He jumped to his feet, and his face went fog-gray. Then he sat down – slumped down – and blushed scarlet.

'Pardon me,' he said thickly. 'You didn't know her, and of course you must look at the thing from all angles. No, there was nothing like that. I'm afraid you are going to waste time if you are going to work on the theory that she was an adventuress. There was nothing like that! She was a girl with something terrible hanging over her; something that called her to Baltimore suddenly; something that has taken her away from me. Money? What could money have to do with it? I love her!'

R. F. Axford received me in an office-like room in his Russian Hill residence: a big blond man, whose forty-eight or -nine years had not blurred the outlines of an athlete's body. A big, full-blooded man with the manner of one whose self-confidence is complete and not altogether unjustified. 'What's our Burke been up to now?' he asked amusedly when I told him who I was. His voice was a pleasant vibrant bass.

I didn't give him all the details.

'He was engaged to marry a Jeanne Delano, who went East about three weeks ago and then suddenly disappeared. He knows very little about her; thinks something has happened to her; and wants her found.'

'Again?' His shrewd blue eyes twinkled. 'And to a Jeanne this time! She's the fifth within a year, to my knowledge, and no doubt I missed one or two while I was in Hawaii. But where do I come in?'

'I asked him for responsible endorsement. I think he's all right, but he isn't, in the strictest sense, a responsible person. He referred me to you.'

'You're right about his not being, in the strictest sense, a responsible person.' The big man screwed up his eyes and mouth in thought for a moment. Then: 'Do you think that something has really happened to the girl? Or is Burke imagining things?'

'I don't know. I thought it was a dream at first. But in a couple of her letters there are hints that something was wrong.'

'You might go ahead and find her then,' Axford said. 'I don't suppose any harm will come from letting him have his Jeanne back. It will at least give him something to think about for a while.'

'I have your word for it then, Mr. Axford, that there will be no scandal or anything of the sort connected with the affair?'

'Assuredly! Burke is all right, you know. It's simply that he is spoiled. He has been in rather delicate health all his life; and then he has an income that suffices to keep him modestly, with a little over to bring out books of verse and buy doo-daws for his rooms. He takes himself a little too solemnly – is too much the poet – but he's sound at bottom.'

'I'll go ahead with it, then,' I said, getting up. 'By the way, the girl has an account at the Golden Gate Trust Company, and I'd like to find out as much about it as possible, especially where her money came from. Clement, the cashier, is a model of caution when it comes to giving out information about depositors. If you could put in a word for me it would make my way smoother.'

'Be glad to.'

He wrote a couple of lines across the back of a card and gave it to me; and, promising to call on him if I needed further assistance, I left.

I telephoned Pangburn that his brother-in-law had given the job his approval. I sent a wire to the agency's Baltimore branch, giving what information I had. Then I went up to Ashbury Avenue, to the apartment house in which the girl had lived.

The manager – an immense Mrs. Clute in rustling black – knew little, if any, more about the girl than Pangburn. The girl had lived there for two and a half months; she had had occasional callers, but Pangburn was the only one that the manager could describe to me. The girl had given up the apartment on the third of the month, saying that she had been called East, and she had asked the manager to hold her mail until she sent her new address. Ten days later Mrs. Clute had received a card from the girl instructing her to forward her mail to 215 N. Stricker Street, Baltimore, Maryland. There had been no mail to forward.

The single thing of importance that I learned at the apartment house was that the girl's two trunks had been taken away by a green transfer truck. Green was the color used by one of the city's largest companies.

I went then to the office of this transfer company, and found a friendly clerk on duty. (A detective, if he is wise, takes pains to make and keep as many friends as possible among transfer company, express company and railroad employees.) I left the office with a memorandum of the transfer company's check numbers and the Ferry baggageroom to which the two trunks had been taken.

At the Ferry Building, with this information, it didn't take me many minutes to learn that the trunks had been checked to Baltimore. I sent another wire to the Baltimore branch, giving the railroad check numbers.

Sunday was well into night by now, so I knocked off and went home.

Half an hour before the Golden Gate Trust Company opened for business the next morning I was inside, talking to Clement, the cashier. All the traditional caution and conservatism of bankers rolled together would but be one-two-three to the amount usually displayed by this plump, white-haired old man. But one look at Axford's card, with '*Please give the bearer all possible assistance*' inked across the back of it, made Clement even eager to help me.

'You have, or have had, an account here in the name of Jeanne Delano,' I said. 'I'd like to know as much as possible about it: to whom she drew checks, and to what amounts; but especially all you can tell me about where her money came from.'

He stabbed one of the pearl buttons on his desk with a pink finger, and a lad with polished yellow hair oozed silently into the room. The cashier scribbled with a pencil on a piece of paper and gave it to the noiseless youth, who disappeared. Presently he was back, laying a handful of papers on the cashier's desk.

Clement looked through the papers and then up at me.

'Miss Delano was introduced here by Mr. Burke Pangburn on the sixth of last month, and opened an account with eight hundred and fifty dollars in cash. She made the following deposits after that: four hundred dollars on the tenth; two hundred and fifty on the twenty-first; three hundred on the twenty-sixth; two hundred on the thirtieth; and twenty thousand dollars on the second of this month. All of these deposits except the last were made with cash. The last one was a check.'

He handed it to me: a Golden Gate Trust Company check.

Pay to the order of Jeanne Delano, twenty thousand dollars.
   (Signed) *Burke Pangburn*

It was dated the second of the month.

'Burke Pangburn!' I exclaimed, a little stupidly. 'Was it usual for him to draw checks to that amount?'

'I think not. But we shall see.'

He stabbed the pearl button again, ran his pencil across another slip of paper, and the youth with the polished yellow hair made a noiseless entrance, exit, entrance, and exit. The cashier looked through the fresh batch of papers that had been brought to him.

'On the first of the month, Mr. Pangburn deposited twenty thousand dollars – a check against Mr. Axford's account here.'

'Now how about Miss Delano's withdrawals?' I asked.

He picked up the papers that had to do with her account again.

'Her statement and canceled checks for last month haven't been delivered to her yet. Everything is here. A check for eighty-five dollars to the order of H. K. Clute on the fifteenth of last month; one "to cash" for three hundred dollars on the twentieth, and another of the same kind for one hundred dollars on the twenty-fifth. Both of these checks were apparently cashed here by her. On the third of this month she closed out her account, with a check to her own order for twenty-one thousand, five hundred and fifteen dollars.'

'And that check?'

'Was cashed here by her.'

I lighted a cigarette, and let these figures drift around in my head. None of them – except those that were fixed to Pangburn's and Axford's signatures – seemed to be of any value to me. The Clute check – the only one the girl had drawn in anyone else's favor – had almost certainly been for rent.

'This is the way of it,' I summed up aloud. 'On the first of the month, Pangburn deposited Axford's check for twenty thousand dollars. The next day he gave a check to that amount to Miss Delano, which she deposited.

On the following day she closed her account, taking between twenty-one and twenty-two thousand dollars in currency.'

'Exactly,' the cashier said.

Before going up to the Glenton Apartments to find out why Pangburn hadn't come clean with me about the twenty thousand dollars, I dropped in at the agency, to see if any word had come from Baltimore. One of the clerks had just finished decoding a telegram. It read:

BAGGAGE ARRIVED MT. ROYAL STATION ON EIGHTH. TAKEN AWAY SAME DAY. UNABLE TO TRACE. 215 NORTH STRICKER STREET IS BALTIMORE ORPHAN ASYLUM. GIRL NOT KNOWN THERE. CONTINUING OUR EFFORTS TO FIND HER.

The Old Man came in from luncheon as I was leaving. I went back into his office with him for a couple of minutes.

'Did you see Pangburn?' he asked.

'Yes. I'm working on his job now – but I think it's a bust.'

'What is it?'

'Pangburn is R. F. Axford's brother-in-law. He met a girl a couple of months ago, and fell for her. She sizes up as a worker. He doesn't know anything about her. The first of the month he got twenty thousand dollars from his brother-in-law and passed it over to the girl. She blew, telling him she had been called to Baltimore, and giving him a phony address that turns out to be an orphan asylum. She sent her trunks to Baltimore, and sent him some letters from there – but a friend could have taken care of the baggage and could have remailed her letters for her. Of course, she would have needed a ticket to check the trunks on, but in a twenty-thousand-dollar game that would be a small expense. Pangburn held out on me; he didn't tell me a word about the money. Ashamed of being easy pickings, I reckon. I'm going to the bat with him on it now.'

The Old Man smiled his mild smile that might mean anything, and I left.

Ten minutes of ringing Pangburn's bell brought no answer. The elevator boy told me he thought Pangburn hadn't been in all night. I put a note in his box and went down to the railroad company's offices, where I arranged to be notified if an unused Baltimore–San Francisco ticket was turned in for redemption.

That done, I went up to the *Chronicle* office and searched the files for weather conditions during the past month, making a memorandum of four dates upon which it had rained steadily day and night. I carried my memorandum to the offices of the three largest taxicab companies.

That was a trick that had worked well for me before. The girl's apartment was some distance from the street car line, and I was counting upon her having gone out – or having had a caller – on one of those rainy dates. In either case, it was very likely that she – or her caller – had left in a taxi in preference to walking through the rain to the car line. The taxicab companies' daily records would show any calls from her address, and the fares' destinations.

The ideal trick, of course, would have been to have the records searched for the full extent of the girl's occupancy of the apartment; but no taxicab company would stand for having that amount of work thrust upon them, unless it was a matter of life and death. It was difficult enough for me to persuade them to turn clerks loose on the four days I had selected.

I called up Pangburn again after I left that last taxicab office, but he was not at home. I called up Axford's residence, thinking that the poet might have spent the night there, but was told that he had not.

Late that afternoon I got my copies of the girl's photograph and handwriting, and put one of each in the mail for Baltimore. Then I went around to the three taxicab companies' offices and got my reports. Two of them had nothing for me. The third's records showed two calls from the girl's apartment.

On one rainy afternoon a taxi had been called, and one passenger had been taken to the Glenton Apartments. That passenger, obviously, was either the girl or Pangburn. At half past twelve one night another call had come in, and this passenger had been taken to the Marquis Hotel.

The driver who had answered this second call remembered it indistinctly when I questioned him, but he thought that his fare had been a man. I let the matter rest there for the time; the Marquis isn't a large hotel as San Francisco hotels go, but it is too large to make canvassing its guests for the one I wanted practicable.

I spent the evening trying to reach Pangburn, with no success. At eleven o'clock I called up Axford, and asked him if he had any idea where I might find his brother-in-law.

'Haven't seen him for several days,' the millionaire said. 'He was supposed to come up for dinner last night, but didn't. My wife tried to reach him by phone a couple times today, but couldn't.'

The next morning I called Pangburn's apartment before I got out of bed, and got no answer.

Then I telephoned Axford and made an appointment for ten o'clock at his office.

'I don't know what he's up to now,' Axford said good-naturedly when I told him that Pangburn had apparently been away from his apartment since Sunday, 'and I suppose there's small chance of guessing. Our Burke is nothing if not erratic. How are you progressing with your search for the damsel in distress?'

'Far enough to convince me that she isn't in a whole lot of distress. She got twenty thousand dollars from your brother-in-law the day before she vanished.'

'Twenty thousand dollars from Burke? She must be a wonderful girl! But wherever did he get that much money?'

'From you.'

Axford's muscular body straightened in his chair. 'From me?'

'Yes – your check.'

'He did not.'

There was nothing argumentative in his voice; it simply stated a fact.

'You didn't give him a check for twenty thousand dollars on the first of the month?'

'No.'

'Then,' I suggested, 'perhaps we'd better take a run over to the Golden Gate Trust Company.'

Ten minutes later we were in Clement's office.

'I'd like to see my canceled checks,' Axford told the cashier.

The youth with the polished yellow hair brought them in presently – a thick wad of them – and Axford ran rapidly through them until he found the one he wanted. He studied that one for a long while, and when he looked up at me he shook his head slowly but with finality.

'I've never seen it before.'

Clement mopped his head with a white handkerchief, and tried to pretend that he wasn't burning up with curiosity and fears that his bank had been gypped.

The millionaire turned the check over and looked at the endorsement.

'Deposited by Burke,' he said in the voice of one who talks while he thinks of something entirely different, 'on the first.'

'Could we talk to the teller who took in the twenty-thousand-dollar check that Miss Delano deposited?' I asked Clement.

He pressed one of his desk's pearl buttons with a fumbling pink finger, and in a minute or two a little sallow man with a hairless head came in.

'Do you remember taking a check for twenty thousand from Miss Jeanne Delano a few weeks ago?' I asked him.

'Yes, sir! Yes, sir! Perfectly.'

'Just what do you remember about it?'

'Well, sir, Miss Delano came to my window with Mr. Burke Pangburn. It was his check. I thought it was a large check for him to be drawing, but the bookkeepers said he had enough money in his account to cover it. They stood there – Miss Delano and Mr. Pangburn – talking and laughing while I entered the deposit in her book, and then they left, and that was all.'

'This check,' Axford said slowly, after the teller had gone back to his cage, 'is a forgery. But I shall make it good, of course. That ends the matter, Mr. Clement, and there must be no more to-do about it.'

'Certainly, Mr. Axford. Certainly.'

Clement was all enormously relieved smiles and head-noddings, with this twenty-thousand-dollar load lifted from his bank's shoulders.

Axford and I left the bank then and got into his coupé, in which we had come from his office. But he did not immediately start the engine. He sat for a while staring at the traffic of Montgomery Street with unseeing eyes.

'I want you to find Burke,' he said presently, and there was no emotion of any sort in his bass voice. 'I want you to find him without risking the least whisper of scandal. If my wife knew of all this— She mustn't know. She thinks her brother is a choice morsel. I want you to find him for me. The girl doesn't matter any more, but I suppose that where you find one you will find the other. I'm not interested in the money, and I don't want you to make any special attempt to recover that; it could hardly be done, I'm afraid, without publicity. I want you to find Burke before he does something else.'

'If you want to avoid the wrong kind of publicity,' I said, 'your best bet is to spread the right kind first. Let's advertise him as missing, fill the papers up with his pictures and so forth. They'll play him up strong. He's your brother-in-law and he's a poet. We can say that he has been ill – you told me that he had been in delicate health all his life – and that we fear he has dropped dead somewhere or is suffering under some mental derangement. There will be no necessity of mentioning the girl or the money, and our explanation may keep people – especially your wife – from guessing the truth when the fact that he is missing leaks out. It's bound to leak out somehow.'

He didn't like my idea at first, but I finally won him over.

We went up to Pangburn's apartment then, easily securing admittance on Axford's explanation that we had an engagement with him and would wait there for him. I went through the rooms inch by inch, prying into each hole and hollow and crack; reading everything that was written anywhere, even down to his manuscripts; and I found nothing that threw any light on his disappearance.

I helped myself to his photographs – pocketing five of the dozen or more that were there. Axford did not think that any of the poet's bags or trunks were missing from the pack-room. I did not find his Golden Gate Trust Company deposit book.

I spent the rest of the day loading the newspapers up with what we wished them to have; and they gave my ex-client one grand spread: first-page stuff with photographs and all possible trimmings. Anyone in San Francisco who didn't know that Burke Pangburn – brother-in-law of R. F. Axford and author of *Sand-patches and Other Verse* – was missing, either couldn't read or wouldn't.

This advertising brought results. By the following morning, reports were rolling in from all directions, from dozens of people who had seen the missing poet in dozens of places. A few of these reports looked promising – or at least possible – but the majority were ridiculous on their faces.

I came back to the agency from running out one that had – until run out – looked good, to find a note asking me to call up Axford.

'Can you come down to my office now?' he asked when I got him on the wire.

There was a lad of twenty-one or -two with Axford when I was ushered into his office: a narrow-chested, dandified lad of the sporting clerk type.

'This is Mr. Fall, one of my employees,' Axford told me. 'He said he saw Burke Sunday night.'

'Where?' I asked Fall.

'Going into a roadhouse near Halfmoon Bay.'

'Sure it was him?'

'Absolutely! I've seen him come in here to Mr. Axford's office often enough to know him. It was him all right.'

'How'd you come to see him?'

'I was coming up from further down the shore with some friends, and we stopped in at the roadhouse to get something to eat. As we were leaving, a car drove up and Mr. Pangburn and a girl or woman – I didn't notice her particularly – got out and went inside. I didn't think anything of it until I saw in the paper last night that he hadn't been seen since Sunday. So then I thought to myself that—'

'What roadhouse was this?' I cut in.

'The White Shack.'

'About what time?'

'Somewhere between eleven-thirty and midnight, I guess.'

'He see you?'

'No. I was already in our car when he drove up.'

'What did the woman look like?'

'I don't know. I didn't see her face, and I can't remember how she was dressed or even if she was short or tall.'

That was all Fall could tell me. We shooed him out of the office, and I used Axford's telephone to call up 'Wop' Healey's dive in North Beach and leave word that when 'Porky' Grout came in he was to call up 'Jack.' That was a standing arrangement by which I got word to Porky whenever I wanted to see him, without giving anybody a chance to tumble to the connection between us.

'Know the White Shack?' I asked Axford, when I was through.

'I know where it is, but I don't know anything about it.'

'Well, it's a tough hole. Run by "Tin-Star" Joplin, an ex-yegg who invested his winnings in the place when Prohibition made the roadhouse game good. He makes more money now than he ever heard of in his piking safe-ripping days. Retailing liquor is a sideline with him; his real profit comes from acting as a relay station for the booze that comes through Halfmoon Bay for points beyond; and the dope is that half the booze put ashore by the Pacific rum fleet is put ashore in Halfmoon Bay.

'The White Shack is a tough hole, and it's no place for your brother-in-law to be hanging around. I can't go down there myself without stirring things up; Joplin and I are old friends. But I've got a man I can put in there for a few nights. Pangburn may be a regular visitor, or he may even be staying there. He wouldn't be the first one Joplin had ever let hide out there. I'll put this man of mine in the place for a week, anyway, and see what he can find.'

'It's all in your hands,' Axford said.

From Axford's office I went straight to my rooms, left the outer door unlocked, and sat down to wait for Porky Grout. I had waited an hour and a half when he pushed the door open and came in. ''Lo! How's tricks?'' He swaggered to a chair, leaned back in it, put his feet on the table and reached for a pack of cigarettes that lay there.

That was Porky Grout. A pasty-faced man in his thirties, neither large nor small, always dressed flashily – even if sometimes dirtily – and trying to hide an enormous cowardice behind a swaggering carriage, a blustering habit of speech, and an exaggerated pretense of self-assurance.

But I had known him for three years; so now I crossed the room and pushed his feet roughly off the table, almost sending him over backward.

'What's the idea?' He came to his feet, crouching and snarling. 'Where do you get that stuff? Do you want a smack in the—'

I took a step toward him. He sprang away, across the room.

'Aw, I didn't mean nothin'. I was only kiddin'!'

'Shut up and sit down,' I advised him.

I had known this Porky Grout for three years, and had been using him for nearly that long, and I didn't know a single thing that could be said in his favor. He was a coward. He was a liar. He was a thief, and a hop-head. He was a traitor to his kind and, if not watched, to his employers. A nice bird to deal with! But detecting is a hard business, and you use whatever tools come to hand. This Porky was an effective tool if handled right, which meant keeping your hand on his throat all the time and checking up every piece of information he brought in.

His cowardice was – for my purpose – his greatest asset. It was notorious throughout the criminal Coast; and though nobody – crook or not – could possibly think him a man to be trusted, nevertheless he was not actually distrusted. Most of his fellows thought him too much the coward to be dangerous; they thought he would be afraid to betray them; afraid of the summary vengeance that crookdom visits upon the squealer. But they didn't take into account Porky's gift for convincing himself that he was a lion-hearted fellow, when no danger was near. So he went freely where he desired and where I sent him, and brought me otherwise unobtainable bits of information.

For nearly three years I had used him with considerable success, paying him well, and keeping him under my heel. *Informant* was the polite word that designated him in my reports; the underworld has even less lovely names than the common *stool-pigeon* to denote his kind.

'I have a job for you,' I told him, now that he was seated again, with his feet on the floor. His loose mouth twitched up at the left corner, pushing that eye into a knowing squint. 'I thought so.' He always says something like that.

'I want you to go down to Halfmoon Bay and stick around Tin-Star Joplin's joint for a few nights. Here are two photos' – sliding one of Pangburn and one of the girl across the table. 'Their names and descriptions are written on the backs. I want to know if either of them shows up down there, what they're doing, and where they're hanging out. It may be that Tin-Star is covering them up.'

Porky was looking knowingly from one picture to the other. 'I think I know this guy,' he said out of the corner of his mouth that twitches. That's another thing about Porky. You can't mention a name or give a description that won't bring that same remark, even though you make them up.

'Here's some money.' I slid some bills across the table. 'If you're down there more than a couple of nights, I'll get some more to you. Keep in touch with me, either over this phone or the under-cover one at the office. And – remember this – lay off the stuff! If I come down there and find you all snowed up, I promise that I'll tip Joplin off to you.'

He had finished counting the money by now – there wasn't a whole lot to count – and he threw it contemptuously back on the table.

'Save that for newspapers,' he sneered. 'How am I goin' to get anywheres if I can't spend no money in the joint?'

'That's plenty for a couple of days' expenses; you'll probably knock back half of it. If you stay longer than a couple of days, I'll get more to you. And you get your pay when the job is done, and not before.'

He shook his head and got up. 'I'm tired of pikin' along with you. You can turn your own jobs. I'm through!'

'If you don't get down to Halfmoon Bay tonight, you *are* through,' I assured him, letting him get out of the threat whatever he liked.

After a little while, of course, he took the money and left. The dispute over expense money was simply a preliminary that went with every job I sent him out on.

After Porky had cleared out, I leaned back in my chair and burned half a dozen Fatimas over the job. The girl had gone first with the twenty thousand dollars, and then the poet had gone; and both had gone, whether permanently or not, to the White Shack. On its face, the job was an obvious affair. The girl had given Pangburn the *work* to the extent of having him forge a check against his brother-in-law's account; and then, after various moves whose value I couldn't determine at the time, they had gone into hiding together.

There were two loose ends to be taken care of. One of them – the

finding of the confederate who had mailed the letters to Pangburn and who
had taken care of the girl's baggage – was in the Baltimore branch's hands.
The other was: Who had ridden in the taxicab that I had traced from the
girl's apartment to the Marquis Hotel?

That might not have any bearing upon the job, or it might. Suppose I
could find a connection between the Marquis Hotel and the White Shack.
That would make a completed chain of some sort. I searched the back of
the telephone directory and found the roadhouse number. Then I went up
to the Marquis Hotel. The girl on duty at the hotel switchboard, when I
got there, was one with whom I had done business before. 'Who's been
calling Halfmoon Bay numbers?' I asked her.

'My God!' She leaned back in her chair and ran a pink hand gently over
the front of her rigidly waved red hair. 'I got enough to do without
remembering every call that goes through. This ain't a boarding-house.
We have more'n one call a week.'

'You don't have many Halfmoon Bay calls,' I insisted, leaning an elbow
on the counter and letting a folded five-spot peep out between the fingers
of one hand. 'You ought to remember any you've had lately.'

'I'll see,' she sighed, as if willing to do her best on a hopeless task.
She ran through her tickets.

'Here's one – from room 522, a couple weeks ago.'

'What number was called?'

'Halfmoon Bay 51.'

That was the roadhouse number. I passed over the five-spot.

'Is 522 a permanent guest?'

'Yes. Mr. Kilcourse. He's been here three or four months.'

'What is he?'

'I don't know. A perfect gentleman, if you ask me.'

'That's nice. What does he look like?'

'He's a young man, but his hair is turning gray. He's dark and
handsome. Looks like a movie actor.'

'Bull Montana?' I asked, as I moved off toward the desk.

The key to 522 was in its place in the rack. I sat down where I could
keep an eye on it. Perhaps an hour later a clerk took it out and gave it to a
man who did look somewhat like an actor. He was a man of thirty or so,
with dark skin, and dark hair that showed gray around the ears. He stood a
good six feet of fashionably dressed slenderness.

Carrying the key, he disappeared into an elevator.

I called up the agency then and asked the Old Man to send Dick Foley
over. Ten minutes later Dick arrived. He's a little shrimp of a Canadian –
there isn't a hundred and ten pounds of him – who is the smoothest
shadow I've ever seen, and I've seen most of them.

'I have a bird in here I want tailed,' I told Dick. 'His name is Kilcourse and he's in room 522. Stick around outside, and I'll give you the spot on him.' I went back to the lobby and waited some more.

At eight o'clock Kilcourse came down and left the hotel. I went after him for half a block – far enough to turn him over to Dick – and then went home, so that I would be within reach of a telephone if Porky Grout tried to get in touch with me. No call came from him that night.

When I arrived at the agency the next morning, Dick was waiting for me. 'What luck?' I asked.

'Damnedest!' The little Canadian talks like a telegram when his peace of mind is disturbed, and just now he was decidedly peevish. 'Took me two blocks. Shook me. Only taxi in sight.'

'Think he made you?'

'No. Wise head. Playing safe.'

'Try him again, then. Better have a car handy, in case he tries the same trick again.'

My telephone jingled as Dick was going out. It was Porky Grout, talking over the agency's unlisted line. 'Turn up anything?' I asked.

'Plenty,' he bragged.

'Good! Are you in town?'

'Yes.'

'I'll meet you in my rooms in twenty minutes,' I said.

The pasty-faced informant was fairly bloated with pride in himself when he came through the door I had left unlocked for him. His swagger was almost a cakewalk; and the side of his mouth that twitches was twisted into a knowing leer that would have fit a Solomon.

'I knocked it over for you, kid,' he boasted. 'Nothin' to it – for me! I went down there and talked to ever'body that knowed anything, seen ever'thing there was to see, and put the X-rays on the whole dump. I made a—'

'Uh-huh,' I interrupted. 'Congratulations and so forth. But just what did you turn up?'

'Now le'me tell you.' He raised a dirty hand in a traffic-cop sort of gesture. 'Don't crowd me. I'll give you all the dope.'

'Sure,' I said. 'I know. You're great, and I'm lucky to have you to knock off my jobs for me, and all that! But is Pangburn down there?'

'I'm getting' around to that. I went down there and—'

'Did you see Pangburn?'

'As I was sayin', I went down there and—'

'Porky,' I said, 'I don't give a damn what you did! Did you see Pangburn?'

'Yes. I seen him.'

'Fine! Now what did you see?'

'He's camping down there with Tin-Star. Him and the broad that you give me a picture of are both there. She's been there a month. I didn't see her, but one of the waiters told me about her. I seen Pangburn myself. They don't show themselves much – stick back in Tin-Star's part of the joint – where he lives – most of the time. Pangburn's been there since Sunday. I went down there and—'

'Learn who the girl is? Or anything about what they're up to?'

'No. I went down there and—'

'All right! *Went down there* again tonight. Call me up as soon as you know positively Pangburn is there – that he hasn't gone out. Don't make any mistakes. I don't want to come down there and scare them up on a false alarm. Use the agency's under-cover line, and just tell whoever answers that you won't be in town until late. That'll mean that Pangburn is there; and it'll let you call up from Joplin's without giving the play away.'

'I got to have more dough,' he said, as he got up. 'It costs—'

'I'll file your application,' I promised. 'Now beat it, and let me hear from you tonight, the minute you're sure Pangburn is there.'

Then I went up to Axford's office. 'I think I have a line on him,' I told the millionaire. 'I hope to have him where you can talk to him tonight. My man says he was at the White Shack last night, and is probably living there. If he's there tonight, I'll take you down, if you want.'

'Why can't we go now?'

'No. The place is too dead in the daytime for my man to hang around without making himself conspicuous, and I don't want to take any chances on either you or me showing ourselves there until we're sure we're coming face to face with Pangburn.'

'What do you want me to do then?'

'Have a fast car ready tonight, and be ready to start as soon as I get word to you.'

'Righto. I'll be at home after five-thirty. Phone me as soon as you're ready to go, and I'll pick you up.'

At nine-thirty that evening I was sitting beside Axford on the front seat of a powerfully engined foreign car, and we were roaring down a road that led to Halfmoon Bay. Porky's telephone call had come.

Neither of us talked much during that ride, and the imported monster under us made it a short ride. Axford sat comfortable and relaxed at the wheel, but I noticed for the first time that he had a rather heavy jaw.

The White Shack is a large building, square-built of imitation stone. It is set away back from the road, and is approached by two curving driveways, which, together, make a semi-circle whose diameter is the public road. The center of this semi-circle is occupied by sheds under which Joplin's patrons stow their cars, and here and there around the sheds are flower-beds and clumps of shrubbery. We were still going at a fair clip when we turned into one end of this semi-circular driveway, and—

Axford slammed on his brakes, and the big machine threw us into the windshield as it jolted into an abrupt stop – barely in time to avoid smashing into a cluster of people who had suddenly loomed up.

In the glow of our headlights faces stood sharply out; white, horrified faces, furtive faces, faces that were callously curious. Below the faces, white arms and shoulders showed, and bright gowns and jewelry, against the duller background of masculine clothing.

This was the first impression I got, and then, by the time I had removed my face from the windshield, I realized that this cluster of people had a core, a thing about which it centered. I stood up, trying to look over the crowd's heads, but I could see nothing.

Jumping down to the driveway, I pushed through the crowd.

Face down on the white gravel a man sprawled – a thin man in dark clothes – and just above his collar, where the head and neck join, was a hole. I knelt to peer into his face. Then I pushed through the crowd again, back to where Axford was just getting out of the car, the engine of which was still running. 'Pangburn is dead – shot!'

Methodically, Axford took off his gloves, folded them and put them in a pocket. Then he nodded his understanding of what I had told him, and walked toward where the crowd stood around the dead poet. I looked after him until he had vanished in the throng. Then I went winding through the outskirts of the crowd, hunting for Porky Grout.

I found him standing on the porch, leaning against a pillar. I passed where he could see me, and went on around to the side of the roadhouse that afforded most shadow.

In the shadows Porky joined me. The night wasn't cool, but his teeth were chattering. 'Who got him?' I demanded.

'I don't know,' he whined, and that was the first thing of which I had ever known him to confess complete ignorance. 'I was inside, keepin' an eye on the others.'

'What others?'

'Tin-Star, and some guy I never seen before, and the broad. I didn't think the kid was going out. He didn't have no hat.'

'What *do* you know about it?'

'A little while after I phoned you, the girl and Pangburn came out from Joplin's part of the joint and sat down at a table around on the other side of the porch, where it's fairly dark. They eat for a while and then this other guy comes over and sits down with 'em. I don't know his name, but I think I've saw him around town. He's a tall guy, in fancy rags.'

That would be Kilcourse.

'They talk for a while and then Joplin joins 'em. They sit around the table laughin' and talkin' for maybe a quarter of an hour. Then Pangburn gets up and goes indoors. I got a table that I can watch 'em from, and the place is crowded, and I'm afraid I'll lose my table if I leave it, so I don't follow the kid. He ain't got no hat; I figure he ain't goin' nowhere. But he must of gone through the house and out front, because pretty soon there's a noise that I thought was a auto backfire, and then the sound of a car getting' away quick. And then some guy squawks that there's a dead man outside. Ever'body runs out here, and it's Pangburn.'

'You dead sure that Joplin, Kilcourse and the girl were all at the table when Pangburn was killed?'

'Absolutely,' Porky said, 'if this dark guy's name is Kilcourse.'

'Where are they now?'

'Back in Joplin's hang-out. They went up there as soon as they seen Pangburn had been croaked.'

I had no illusions about Porky. I knew he was capable of selling me out and furnishing the poet's murderer with an alibi. But there was this about it: if Joplin, Kilcourse or the girl had fixed him, and had fixed my informant, then it was hopeless for me to try to prove that they weren't on the rear porch when the shot was fired. Joplin had a crowd of hangers-on who would swear to anything he told them without batting an eye. There would be a dozen supposed witnesses to their presence on the rear porch.

Thus the only thing for me to do was to take it for granted that Porky was coming clean with me. 'Have you seen Dick Foley?' I asked, since Dick had been shadowing Kilcourse.

'No.'

'Hunt around and see if you can find him. Tell him I've gone up to talk to Joplin, and tell him to come on up. Then you can stick around where I can get hold of you if I want you.'

I went in through a French window, crossed an empty dance-floor and went up the stairs that led to Tin-Star Joplin's living quarters in the rear second story. I knew the way, having been up there before. Joplin and I were old friends.

I was going up now to give him and his friends a shake-down on the off-chance that some good might come of it, though I knew that I had nothing on any of them. I could have tied something on the girl, of course, but not without advertising the fact that the dead poet had forged his brother-in-law's signature to a check. And that was no go.

'Come in,' a heavy, familiar voice called when I rapped on Joplin's living-room door. I pushed the door open and went in.

Tin-Star Joplin was standing in the middle of the floor: a big-bodied ex-yegg with inordinately thick shoulders and an expressionless horse face. Beyond him Kilcourse sat dangling one leg from the corner of a table, alertness hiding behind an amused half-smile on his handsome dark face. On the other side of the room a girl whom I knew for Jeanne Delano sat on the arm of a big leather chair. And the poet hadn't exaggerated when he told me she was beautiful.

'You!' Joplin grunted disgustedly as soon as he recognized me. 'What the hell do *you* want?'

'What've you got?'

My mind wasn't on this sort of repartee, however; I was studying the girl. There was something vaguely familiar about her – but I couldn't place her. Perhaps I hadn't see her before; perhaps much looking at the picture Pangburn had given me was responsible for my feeling of recognition. Pictures will do that.

Meanwhile, Joplin had said: 'Time to waste is one thing I ain't got.'

And I had said: 'If you'd saved up all the time different judges have given you, you'd have plenty.'

I had seen the girl somewhere before. She was a slender girl in a glistening blue gown that exhibited a generous spread of front, back and arms that were worth showing. She had a mass of dark brown hair above an oval face of the color that pink ought to be. Her eyes were wide-set and a gray shade that wasn't altogether unlike the shadows on polished silver that the poet had compared them to. I studied the girl, and she looked back at me with level eyes, and still I couldn't place her. Kilcourse still sat dangling a leg from the table corner.

Joplin grew impatient: 'Will you stop gandering at the girl, and tell me what you want of me?' he growled.

The girl smiled then, a mocking smile that bared the edges of razor-sharp little animal-teeth. And with the smile I knew her!

Her hair and skin had fooled me. The last time I had seen her – the only time I had seen her before – her face had been marble-white, and her hair had been short and the color of fire. She and an older woman and three men and I had played hide-and-seek one evening in a house in Turk Street over a matter of the murder of a bank messenger and the theft of a hundred thousand dollars' worth of Liberty Bonds. Through her intriguing three of her accomplices had died that evening, and the fourth – the Chinese – had eventually gone to the gallows at Folsom Prison. Her name had been Elvira then, and since her escape from the house that night we had been fruitlessly hunting her from border to border, and beyond.

Recognition must have shown in my eyes in spite of the effort I made to keep them blank, for, as swift as a snake, she had left the arm of the chair and was coming forward, her eyes more steel than silver.

I put my gun in sight.

Joplin took a half-step toward me. 'What's the idea?' he barked.

Kilcourse slid off the table, and one of his thin dark hands hovered over his necktie.

'This is the idea,' I told them. 'I want the girl for a murder a couple of months back, and maybe – I'm not sure – for tonight's. Anyway, I'm—'

The snapping of a light-switch behind me, and the room went black.

I moved, not caring where I went so long as I got away from where I had been when the lights went out.

My back touched a wall and I stopped, crouching low.

'Quick, kid!' A hoarse whisper that came from where I thought the door should be.

But both of the room's doors, I thought, were closed, and could hardly be opened without showing gray rectangles. People moved in the blackness, but none got between me and the lighter square of windows.

Something clicked softly in front of me – too thin a click for the cocking of a gun – but it could have been the opening of a spring-knife, and I remembered that Tin-Star Joplin had a fondness for that weapon.

'Let's go!' A harsh whisper that cut through the dark like a blow.

Sounds of motion, muffled, indistinguishable . . . one sound not far away . . .

Abruptly a strong hand clamped one of my shoulders, a hard-muscled body strained against me. I stabbed out with my gun, and heard a grunt.

The hand moved up my shoulder toward my throat.

I snapped up a knee, and heard another grunt.

A burning point ran down my side.

I stabbed again with my gun – pulled it back until the muzzle was free of the soft obstacle that had stopped it, and squeezed the trigger. The crash of the shot. Joplin's voice in my ear, a curiously matter-of-fact voice: 'God damn! That got me.'

I spun away from him then, toward where I saw the dim yellow of an open door. I had heard no sounds of departure. I had been too busy. But I knew that Joplin had tied into me while the others made their get-away.

Nobody was in sight as I jumped, slid, tumbled down the steps – any number at a time. A waiter got in my path as I plunged toward the dance-floor. I don't know whether his interference was intentional or not. I didn't ask. I slammed the flat of my gun in his face and went on. Once I jumped a leg that came out to trip me; and at the outer door I had to smear another face.

Then I was out in the semi-circular driveway, from one end of which a red tail-light was turning east into the country road.

While I sprinted for Axford's car I noticed that Pangburn's body had been removed. A few people still stood around the spot where he had lain, and they gaped at me now with open mouths.

The car was as Axford had left it, with idling engine. I swung it through a flower-bed and pointed it east on the public road. Five minutes later I picked up the red point of a tail-light again.

The car under me had more power than I would ever need, more than I would have known how to handle. I don't know how fast the one ahead was going, but I closed in as if it had been standing still.

A mile and a half, or perhaps two—

Suddenly a man was in the road ahead – a little beyond the reach of my lights. The lights caught him, and I saw that it was Porky Grout!

Porky Grout standing facing me in the middle of the road, the dull metal of an automatic in each hand.

The guns in his hands seemed to glow dimly red and then go dark in the glare of my headlights – glow and then go dark, like two bulbs in an automatic electric sign.

The windshield fell apart around me.

Porky Grout – the informant whose name was a synonym for cowardice the full length of the Pacific Coast – stood in the center of the road shooting at a metal comet that rushed down upon him. . . .

I didn't see the end.

I confess frankly that I shut my eyes when his set white face showed close over my radiator. The metal monster under me trembled – not very much – and the road ahead was empty except for the fleeing red light. My windshield was gone. The wind tore at my uncovered hair and brought tears to my squinted-up eyes.

Presently I found that I was talking to myself, saying, 'That was Porky. That was Porky.' It was an amazing fact. It was no surprise that he had double-crossed me. That was to be expected. And for him to have crept up the stairs behind me and turned off the lights wasn't astonishing. But for him to have stood straight up and died—

An orange streak from the car ahead cut off my wonderment. The bullet didn't come near me – it isn't easy to shoot accurately from one moving car into another – but at the pace I was going it wouldn't be long before I was close enough for good shooting.

I turned on the searchlight above the dashboard. It didn't quite reach the car ahead, but it enabled me to see that the girl was driving. While Kilcourse sat screwed around beside her, facing me. The car was a yellow roadster.

I eased up a little. In a duel with Kilcourse here I would have been at a disadvantage, since I would have had to drive as well as shoot. My best play seemed to be to hold my distance until we reached a town, as we inevitably must. It wasn't midnight yet. There would be people on the streets of any town, and policemen. Then I could close in with a better chance of coming off on top.

A few miles of this and my prey tumbled to my plan. The yellow roadster slowed down, wavered, and came to rest with its length across the road. Kilcourse and the girl were out immediately and crouching in the road on the far side of their barricade.

I was tempted to dive pell-mell into them, but it was a weak temptation, and when its short life had passed I put on the brakes and stopped. Then I fiddled with my searchlight until it bore full upon the roadster.

A flash came from somewhere near the roadster's wheels, and the searchlight shook violently, but the glass wasn't touched. It would be their first target, of course, and . . .

Crouching in my car, waiting for the bullet that would smash the lens, I took off my shoes and overcoat.

The third bullet ruined the light.

I switched off the other lights, jumped to the road, and when I stopped running I was squatting down against the near side of the yellow roadster. As easy and safe a trick as can be imagined.

The girl and Kilcourse had been looking into the glare of a powerful light. When that light suddenly died, and the weaker ones around it went, too, they were left in pitch unseeing blackness, which must last for the minute or longer that their eyes would need to readjust themselves to the gray-black of the night. My stockinged feet had made no sound on the macadam road, and now there was only a roadster between us; and I knew it and they didn't.

From near the radiator Kilcourse spoke softly:

'I'm going to try to knock him off from the ditch. Take a shot at him now and then to keep him busy.'

'I can't see him,' the girl protested.

'Your eyes'll be all right in a second. Take a shot at the car anyway.'

I moved toward the radiator as the girl's pistol barked at the empty touring car.

Kilcourse, on hands and knees, was working his way toward the ditch that ran along the south side of the road. I gathered my legs under me, intent upon a spring and a blow with my gun upon the back of his head. I didn't want to kill him, but I wanted to put him out of the way quick. I'd have the girl to take care of, and she was at least as dangerous as he.

As I tensed for the spring, Kilcourse, guided perhaps by some instinct of the hunted, turned his head and saw me – saw a threatening shadow.

Instead of jumping I fired.

I didn't look to see whether I had hit him or not. At that range there was little likelihood of missing. I bent double and slipped back to the rear of the roadster, keeping on my side of it. Then I waited.

The girl did what I would perhaps have done in her place. She didn't shoot or move toward the place the shot had come from. She thought I had forestalled Kilcourse in using the ditch and that my next play would be to circle around behind her. To offset this, she moved around the rear of the roadster, so that she could ambush me from the side nearest Axford's car.

Thus it was that she came creeping around the corner and poked her delicately chiseled nose plunk into the muzzle of the gun that I held ready for her.

She gave a little scream.

Women aren't always reasonable: they are prone to disregard trifles like guns held upon them. So I grabbed her gun hand, which was fortunate for me. As my hand closed around the weapon, she pulled the trigger, catching a chunk of my forefinger between hammer and frame. I twisted the gun out of her hand; released my finger.

But she wasn't done yet. With me standing there holding a gun not four inches from her body, she turned and bolted off toward where a clump of trees made a jet-black blot to the north.

When I recovered from my surprise at this amateurish procedure, I stuck both her gun and mine in my pockets, and set out after her, tearing the soles of my feet at every step.

She was trying to get over a wire fence when I caught her.

'Stop playing, will you?' I said crossly, as I set the fingers of my left hand around her wrist and started to lead her back to the roadster. 'This is a serious business. Don't be so childish!'

'You are hurting my arm.'

I knew I wasn't hurting her arm, and I knew this girl for the direct cause of four, or perhaps five, deaths; yet I loosened my grip on her wrist until it wasn't much more than a friendly clasp. She went back willingly enough to the roadster, where, still holding her wrist, I switched on the lights. Kilcourse lay just beneath the headlight's glare, huddled on his face, with one knee drawn up under him.

I put the girl squarely in the line of light.

'Now stand there,' I said, 'and behave. The first break you make, I'm going to shoot a leg out from under you,' and I meant it.

I found Kilcourse's gun, pocketed it, and knelt beside him.

He was dead, with a bullet-hole above his collar-bone.

'Is he—' her mouth trembled.

'Yes.'

She looked down at him, and shivered a little.

'Poor Fag,' she whispered.

I've gone on record as saying that this girl was beautiful, and, standing there in the dazzling white of the headlights, she was more than that. She was the thing to start crazy thoughts even in the head of an unimaginative middle-aged thief-catcher. She was—

Anyhow, I suppose that is why I scowled at her and said:

'Yes, poor Fag, and poor Hook, and poor Tai, and poor kid of a Los Angeles bank messenger, and poor Burke,' calling the roll, as far as I knew it, of men who had died loving her.

She didn't flare up. Her big gray eyes lifted, and she looked at me with a gaze that I couldn't fathom, and her lovely oval face under the mass of brown hair – which I knew was phony – was sad.

'I suppose you do think—' she began.

But I had had enough of this; I was uncomfortable along the spine.

'Come on,' I said. 'We'll leave Kilcourse and the roadster here for now.'

She said nothing, but went with me to Axford's big machine, and sat in silence while I laced my shoes. I found a robe on the back seat for her.

'Better wrap this around your shoulders. The windshield is gone. It'll be cool.'

She followed my suggestion without a word, but when I had edged our vehicle around the rear of the roadster, and had straightened out in the road again, going east, she laid a hand on my arm.

'Aren't we going back to the White Shack?'

'No. Redwood City – the county jail.'

A mile perhaps, during which, without looking at her, I knew she was studying my rather lumpy profile. Then her hand was on my forearm again and she was leaning toward me so that her breath was warm against my cheek. 'Will you stop for a minute? There's something – some things I want to tell you.'

I brought the car to a halt in a cleared space of hard soil off to one side of the road, and screwed myself a little around in the seat to face her more directly.

'Before you start,' I told her, 'I want you to understand that we stay here for just so long as you talk about the Pangburn affair. When you get off on any other line – then we finish our trip to Redwood City.'

'Aren't you even interested in the Los Angeles affair?'

'No. That's closed. You and Hook Riordan and Tai Choon Tau and the Quarres were equally responsible for the messenger's death, even if Hook did the actual killing. Hook and the Quarres passed out the night we had our party in Turk Street. Tai was hanged last month. Now I've got you. We had enough evidence to swing the Chinese, and we've even more against you. That is done – finished – completed. If you want to tell me anything about Pangburn's death, I'll listen. Otherwise—'

I reached for the self-starter.

A pressure of her fingers on my arm stopped me.

'I do want to tell you about it,' she said earnestly. 'I want you to know the truth about it. You'll take me to Redwood City, I know. Don't think that I expect – that I have any foolish hopes. But I'd like you to know the truth about this thing. I don't know why I should care especially what you think, but—'

Her voice dwindled off to nothing.

Then she began to talk very rapidly – as people talk when they fear interruptions before their stories are told – and she sat leaning slightly forward, so that her beautiful oval face was very close to mine.

'After I ran out of the Turk Street house that night – while you were struggling with Tai – my intention was to get away from San Francisco. I had a couple of thousand dollars, enough to carry me any place. Then I thought that going away would be what you people would expect me to do, and that the safest thing for me to do would be to stay right here. It isn't

287

hard for a woman to change her appearance. I had bobbed red hair, white skin, and wore gay clothes. I simply dyed my hair, bought these transformations to make it look long, put color on my face, and bought some dark clothes. Then I took an apartment on Ashbury Avenue under the name of Jeanne Delano, and I was an altogether different person.

'But, while I knew I was perfectly safe from recognition anywhere, I felt more comfortable staying indoors for a while, and, to pass the time, I read a good deal. That's how I happened to run across Burke's book. Do you read poetry?'

I shook my head. An automobile going toward Halfmoon Bay came into sight just then – the first one we'd seen since we left the White Shack. She waited until it had passed before she went on, still talking rapidly.

'Burke wasn't a genius, of course, but there was something about some of his things that – something that got inside me. I wrote him a little note, telling him how much I had enjoyed these things, and sent it to his publishers. A few days later I had a note from Burke, and I learned that he lived in San Francisco. I hadn't known that.

'We exchanged several notes, and then he asked if he could call, and we met. I don't know whether I was in love with him or not, even at first. I did like him, and, between the ardor of his love for me and the flattery of having a fairly well-known poet for a suitor, I really thought that I loved him. I promised to marry him.

'I hadn't told him anything about myself, though now I know that it wouldn't have made any difference to him. But I was afraid to tell him the truth, and I wouldn't lie to him, so I told him nothing.

'Then Fag Kilcourse saw me one day on the street, and knew me in spite of my new hair, complexion and clothes. Fag hadn't much brains, but he had eyes that could see through anything. I don't blame Fag. He acted according to his code. He came up to my apartment, having followed me home; and I told him that I was going to marry Burke and be a respectable housewife. That was dumb of me. Fag was square. If I had told him that I was ribbing Burke up for a trimming, Fag would have let me alone, would have kept his hands off. But when I told him that I was through with the graft, had "gone queer," that made me his meat. You know how crooks are: everyone in the world is either a fellow crook or a prospective victim. So if I was no longer a crook, than Fag considered me fair game.

'He learned about Burke's family connections, and then he put it up to me – twenty thousand dollars, or he'd turn me up. He knew about the Los Angeles job, and he knew how badly I was wanted. I was up against it then. I knew I couldn't hide from Fag or run away from him. I told Burke I had to have twenty thousand dollars. I didn't think he had that much, but I thought he could get it. Three days later he gave me a check for it. I didn't know at the time how he had raised it, but it wouldn't have mattered if I had known. I had to have it.

'But that night he told me where he got the money; that he had forged his brother-in-law's signature. He told me because, after thinking it over, he was afraid that when the forgery was discovered I would be caught with him and considered equally guilty. I'm rotten in spots, but I wasn't rotten enough to let him put himself in the pen for me, without knowing what it was all about. I told him the whole story. He didn't bat an eye. He insisted that the money be paid Kilcourse, so that I would be safe, and began to plan for my further safety.

'Burke was confident that his brother-in-law wouldn't sent him over for forgery, but, to be on the safe side, he insisted that I move and change my name again and lay low until we knew how Axford was going to take it. But that night, after he had gone, I made some plans of my own. I did like Burke – I liked him too much to let him be the goat without trying to save him, and I didn't have a great deal of faith in Axford's kindness. This was the second of the month. Barring accidents, Axford wouldn't discover the forgery until he got his canceled checks early the following month. That gave me practically a month to work in.

'The next day I drew all my money out of the bank, and sent Burke a letter, saying that I had been called to Baltimore, and I laid a clear trail to Baltimore, with baggage and letters and all, which a pal there took care of for me. Then I went down to Joplin's and got him to put me up. I let Fag know I was there, and when he came down I told him I expected to have the money for him in a day or two.

'He came down nearly every day after that, and I stalled him from day to day, and each time it got easier. But my time was getting short. Pretty soon Burke's letters would be coming back from the phony address I had given him, and I wanted to be on hand to keep him from doing anything foolish. And I didn't want to get in touch with him until I could give him the twenty thousand, so he could square the forgery before Axford learned of it from his canceled checks.

'Fag was getting easier and easier to handle, but I still didn't have him where I wanted him. He wasn't willing to give up the twenty thousand dollars – which I was, of course, holding all this time — unless I'd promise to stick with him for good. And I still thought I was in love with Burke, and I didn't want to tie myself up with Fag, even for a little while.

'Then Burke saw me on the street one Sunday night. I was careless, and drove into the city in Joplin's roadster – the one back there. And, as luck would have it, Burke saw me. I told him the truth, the whole truth. And he told me that he had just hired a private detective to find me. He was like a child in some ways: it hadn't occurred to him that the sleuth would dig up anything about the money. But I knew the forged check would be found in a day or two at the most. I knew it!

'When I told Burke that he went to pieces. All his faith in his brother-in-law's forgiveness went. I couldn't leave him the way he was. He'd have babbled the whole thing to the first person he met. So I brought him back to Joplin's with me. My idea was to hold him there for a few days, until we could see how things were going. If nothing appeared in the papers about the check, then we could take it for granted that Axford had hushed the matter up, and Burke could go home and try to square himself. On the other hand, if the papers got the whole story, then Burke would have to look for a permanent hiding-place, and so would I.

'Tuesday evening's and Wednesday morning's papers were full of the news of his disappearance, but nothing was said about the check. That looked good, but we waited another day for good measure. Fag Kilcourse was in on the game by this time, of course, and I had had to pass over the twenty thousand dollars, but I still had hopes of getting it – or most of it – back, so I continued to string him along. I had a hard time keeping off Burke, though, because he had begun to think he had some sort of right to me, and jealousy made him wicked. But I got Tin-Star to throw a scare into him, and I thought Burke was safe.

'Tonight one of Tin-Star's men came up and told us that a man named Porky Grout, who had been hanging around the place for a couple of nights, had made a couple of cracks that might mean he was interested in us. Grout was pointed out to me, and I took a chance on showing myself in the public part of the place, and sat at a table close to his. He was plain rat – as I guess you know – and in less than five minutes I had him at my table, and half an hour later I knew that he had tipped you off that Burke and I were in the White Shack. He didn't tell me all this right out, but he told me more than enough for me to guess the rest.

'I went up and told the others. Fag was for killing both Grout and Burke right away. But I talked him out of it. That wouldn't help us any, and I had Grout where he would jump in the ocean for me. I thought I had Fag convinced, but— We finally decided that Burke and I would take the roadster and leave, and that when you got here Porky Grout was to pretend he was hopped up, and point out a man and a woman – any who happened to be handy – as the ones he had taken for us. I stopped to get a cloak and gloves, and Burke went on out to the car alone – and Fag shot him. I didn't know he was going to! I wouldn't have let him! Please believe that! I wasn't as much in love with Burke as I had thought, but please believe that after all he had done for me I wouldn't have let them hurt him!

'After that it was a case of stick with the others whether I liked it or not, and I stuck. We ribbed Grout to tell you that all three of us were on the back porch when Burke was killed, and we had any number of others primed with the same story. Then you came up and recognized me. Just my luck that it had to be you – the only detective in San Francisco who knew me!

'You know the rest: how Porky Grout came up behind you and turned off the lights, and Joplin held you while we ran for the car; and then, when you closed in on us, Grout offered to stand you off while we got clear, and now . . .'

Her voice died, and she shivered a little. The robe I had given her had fallen away from her white shoulders. Whether or not it was because she was so close against my shoulder, I shivered, too. And my fingers, fumbling in my pocket for a cigarette, brought it out twisted and mashed.

'That's all there is to the part you promised to listen to,' she said softly, her face turned half away. 'I wanted you to know. You're a hard man, but somehow I—'

I cleared my throat, and the hand that held the mangled cigarette was suddenly steady.

'Now don't be crude, sister,' I said. 'Your work has been too smooth so far to be spoiled by rough stuff now.'

She laughed – a brief laugh that was bitter and reckless and just a little weary, and she thrust her face still closer to mine, and the gray eyes were soft and placid.

'Little fat detective whose name I don't know' – her voice had a tired huskiness in it, and a tired mockery – 'you think I am playing a part, don't you? You think I am playing for liberty. Perhaps I am. I certainly would take it if it were offered me. But – Men have thought me beautiful, and I have played with them. Women are like that. Men have loved me and, doing what I liked with them, I have found men contemptible. And then comes this little fat detective whose name I don't know, and he acts as if I were a hag – an old squaw. Can I help then being piqued into some sort of feeling for him? Women are like that. Am I so homely that any man has a right to look at me without even interest? Am I ugly?'

I shook my head. 'You're quite pretty,' I said, struggling to keep my voice as casual as the words.

'You beast!' she spat, and then her smile grew gentle again. 'And yet it is because of that attitude that I sit here and turn myself inside out for you. If you were to take me in your arms and hold me close to the chest that I am already leaning against, and if you were to tell me that there is no jail ahead for me just now, I would be glad, of course. But, though for a while you might hold me, you would then be only one of the men with which I am familiar: men who love and are used and are succeeded by other men. But because you do none of these things, because you are a wooden block of a man, I find myself wanting you. Would I tell you this, little fat detective, if I were playing a game?'

I grunted non-committally, and forcibly restrained my tongue from running out to moisten my dry lips.

'I'm going to this jail tonight if you are the same hard man who has goaded me into whining love into his uncaring ears, but before that, can't I have one whole-hearted assurance that you think me a little more than "quite pretty"? Or at least a hint that if I were not a prisoner your pulse might beat a little faster when I touch you? I'm going to this jail for a long while – perhaps to the gallows. Can't I take my vanity there not quite in tatters to keep me company? Can't you do some slight thing to keep me from the afterthought of having bleated all this out to a man who was simply bored?'

Her lids had come down half over the silver-gray eyes, her head had tilted back so far that a little pulse showed throbbing in her white throat; her lips were motionless over slightly parted teeth, as the last word had left them. My fingers went deep into the soft white flesh of her shoulders. Her head went further back, her eyes closed, one hand came up to my shoulder.

'You're beautiful as all hell!' I shouted crazily into her face, and flung her against the door.

It seemed an hour that I fumbled with starter and gears before I had the car back in the road and thundering toward the San Mateo County jail. The girl had straightened herself up in the seat again, and sat huddled within the robe I had given her. I squinted straight ahead into the wind that tore at my hair and face, and the absence of the windshield took my thoughts back to Porky Grout.

Porky Grout, whose yellowness was notorious from Seattle to San Diego, standing rigidly in the path of a charging metal monster, with an inadequate pistol in each hand. She had done that to Porky Grout – this woman beside me! She had done that to Porky Grout, and he hadn't even been human! A slimy reptile whose highest thought had been a skinful of dope had gone grimly to death that she might get away – she – this woman whose shoulders I had gripped, whose mouth had been close under mine!

I let the car out another notch, holding the road somehow.

We went through a town: a scurrying of pedestrians for safety, surprised faces staring at us, street lights glistening on the moisture the wind had whipped from my eyes. I passed blindly by the road I wanted, circled back to it, and we were out in the country again.

At the foot of a long, shallow hill I applied the brakes and we snapped to motionless.

I thrust my face close to the girl's.

'Furthermore, you are a liar!' I knew I was shouting foolishly, but I was powerless to lower my voice. 'Pangburn never put Axford's name on that check. He never knew anything about it. You got in with him because you knew his brother-in-law was a millionaire. You pumped him, finding out everything he knew about his brother-in-law's account at the Golden Gate Trust. You stole Pangburn's bank book – it wasn't in his room when I searched it – and deposited the forged Axford check to his credit, knowing that under those circumstances the check wouldn't be questioned. The next day you took Pangburn into the bank, saying you were going to make a deposit. You took him in because with him standing beside you the check to which *his* signature had been forged wouldn't be questioned. You knew that, being a gentleman, he'd take pains not to see what you were depositing.

'Then you framed the Baltimore trip. He told the truth to me – the truth so far as he knew it. Then you met him Sunday night – maybe accidentally, maybe not. Anyway, you took him down to Joplin's, giving him some wild yarn that he would swallow and that would persuade him to stay there for a few days. That wasn't hard, since he didn't know anything about either of the twenty-thousand-dollar checks. You and your pal Kilcourse knew that if Pangburn disappeared nobody would ever know that he hadn't forged the Axford check, and nobody would ever suspect that the second check was phony. You'd have killed him quietly, but when Porky tipped you off that I was on my way down you had to move quick – so you shot him down. That's the truth of it!' I yelled.

All this while she watched me with wide gray eyes that were calm and tender, but now they clouded a little and a pucker of pain drew her brows together.

I yanked my head away and got the car in motion.

Just before we swept into Redwood City one of her hands came up to my forearm, rested there for a second, patted the arm twice, and withdrew.

I didn't look at her, nor, I think, did she look at me, while she was being booked. She gave her name as Jeanne Delano, and refused to make any statement until she had seen an attorney. It all took a very few minutes.

As she was being led away, she stopped and asked if she might speak privately with me.

We went together to a far corner of the room.

She put her mouth close to my ear so that her breath was warm again on my cheek, as it had been in the car, and whispered the vilest epithet of which the English language is capable.

Then she walked out to her cell.

THE JANE FROM HELL'S KITCHEN
PERRY PAUL

While the better pulps offered a pretty good living to those writers who could work fast and produce hundreds of thousands of words a year, there was a definite hierarchy, well known to the top guns of the fiction world – as well as to the least of the hacks, the beginners and the wannabes.

Black Mask was the gold standard, but a few other magazines, like *Argosy* and *Dime Detective*, as well as such 'hero' pulps as *The Shadow* and *Doc Savage*, paid equally well. Down at the bargain basement level were such trashy publications as *Gun Molls Magazine*. Literary quality was pretty much non-existent, though stories usually galloped along at a blazing pace, substituting action and violence for subtlety and characterization.

Major writers would send them stories only when they had been rejected by the better pulps. Lesser writers never could crack the top publications and generally failed to earn a living at their chosen profession. They vanished as quickly as they appeared, and they are largely unremembered today. Perry Paul is such a figure. A former crime reporter who created two series for *Gun Molls*, the other being 'Madame,' a mystery moll of the underworld, nothing else could be discovered about him.

'The Jane from Hell's Kitchen' first appeared in the October 1930 issue of *Gun Molls*.

THE JANE FROM HELL'S KITCHEN

PERRY PAUL

CHAPTER I

Dizzy Malone

The grizzled district attorney stood over a newspaper spread out on his desk, scare heads staring up at him in crude challenge.

CHICAGO PROSECUTOR
VANISHES IN NEW YORK
Mysterious Kidnaper Demands
Huge Ransom
Local District Attorney Scouts
Gangster Vengeance Motive

The district attorney, scourge of New York's underworld, glanced nervously from the headlines to the watch on his wrist and showed his teeth in a smile of cynical satisfaction.

Behind him the door opened noiselessly – a flash of chiffon and silk – the door closed and a girl backed her quivering body against it, her mouth open, panting.

Her high, pointed heels ground into the heavy rug as she struggled for self-control. Her lithe, supple body tautened. Her lips hardened into a thin scarlet line. The grey eyes, shadowed by a tight-fitting crimson bit of a hat, tempered to the glitter of new steel.

Sensing an alien presence, the district attorney's head came up sharply.

' "Local D.A. scouts gangster vengeance motive!" ' the scarlet lips jeered.

The man sprang round to face the door with the agility of a jungle beast of prey.

'Dizzy Malone,' he gasped, 'the same, gorgeous body and all!'

The girl swung her slender hips across the room until she faced the man.

James Mitchell, veteran district attorney of New York, looked down at

297

her lovely blonde bravado with the expression of a man charmed against his will by some exotic yet poisonous serpent.

Dizzy Malone was like that. She went to men's heads. Her moniker was a stall. They called her Dizzy because she most decidedly wasn't any way you looked at it.

'Well, when did you get back to your purple paradise in Hell's Kitchen?' the district attorney demanded. He was a tough baby. He knew all the dodges. He talked gangster talk and every crook in New York feared him. 'I thought you lammed it to Europe with the Ghost when he finished his rap up the river.'

The girl's sensitive nostrils quivered.

'Yeah? You *thought* so!' she sneered. 'Well, I didn't. The Ghost saw to it that I missed the boat. He'd decided to change his luck, I guess. Anyway Spanish Lil went with him. Her hair is black, mine's blonde. And that's why—'

'Say, wait a minute!' Mitchell interrupted. 'I'm not running any lovelorn bureau. What's the idea? How did you get in here, anyway?'

'That's my business!' she flared. 'Now collapse, stuffed-shirt, while I put on the loud speaker!'

The D.A. opened his mouth – and closed it again. When Dizzy made up her mind to talk, she talked, and everyone else listened.

'Now, get a load of this,' Dizzy snapped. 'It's about that guy Burke, the D.A. from Chicago, that's disappeared. I gotta hunch who lifted him.'

It was Mitchell's turn to sneer.

'So you want to squeal, huh, Dizzy?'

'Squeal?' Dizzy panted. 'You – you—!'

She crouched like a feline killer ready to spring. Coral-tipped fingers that could tear a man's face to ribbons, tensed. Her lips curled back from her teeth in a fighting snarl of defiance.

'Now calm down, Dizzy. Calm down.'

The girl's rage did a quick fade-out, leaving in its place a cold, calculating grimness that was a sure danger signal.

'No more cracks like that then, big boy.' Her voice grated slightly on a note of savage restraint. 'Get this through your smart legal mind – I came here to make you a proposition, not to turn anyone up. Get that straight!'

'All right, Dizzy,' the D.A. growled, glancing hastily at his watch. 'Shoot.'

'You gotta job to do, Mitchell. I gotta job to do. You help me. I help you. See?'

The district attorney waited.

'Now about this D.A. from Chicago. His disappearing act puts you in a tough spot, doesn't it? Looks like a smart game to me. He gets a phoney wire to come see you. He hops the Century and walks into this office the next morning. You don't know what it's all about. You didn't send any wire. Burke walks outa here and disappears. You get a letter demanding a big ransom for his return. Your job is to get Burke back and turn up the guy that pulled the job. Right?'

'Right, Dizzy.'

'My job's a little different. A guy – yes, it was the Ghost – put the double-x on me. I was his moll. We worked a good racket. We piled up a stake, a big one. We were all set to beat it for the sticks, get married and settle down respectable, and forget about rackets. My man was clever, he never let the coppers get anything on us. Then some fly dick framed a rap on him.'

'Oh, yeah?'

'*Yeah!* I said *framed.* My man went stir-bugs up there in the Big House, and no wonder. Baldy Ross, his partner, and a straight-shooting guy, gets lit out in Chi with a cokie that's a rat. A copper gets bumped off and the rat turns states evidence to save his stinking hide. Baldy swings because my man's in stir and can't spring him.'

Her pink fists clenched.

'The cokie that *shot* the copper's dead now – they put him on the spot for the rat he was.'

The girl's grey eyes narrowed.

'Then what happens? Well, if there's one guy the Ghost's crazy about, it's his kid brother. The Kid's a wild one but my man can hold him. He keeps him outa the racket, sends him to college. While the Ghost's in the "Can" some wise yegg gets the Kid coked up and they pull a job. A watchman gets knocked off. You got nothing on the Kid but circumstantial evidence, but you send him up the river and he fries, across the court from where the Ghost is raving in a strait-jacket.

'The Ghost's already a little nuts from the bullets he gets in his head when that German ace shoots him down in France – but he's a genius just the same. He comes outa the Big House completely bugs. What they did to Baldy and the Kid turns him into a mad killer.

'I been waiting for him, not touching our stake. I figure if I can get him to Europe I can nurse that killer streak outa him.

'Then what happens? That black-haired flossie, Spanish Lil gets her hooks into him and he takes the stake I'd helped him make, and lams it with her. She takes him for the wad and the Ghost is flat, and more bugs than ever.'

'Well, what of it, Dizzy?' the D.A. cut in impatiently, shooting a hurried look at his watch.

'Just this, big boy. The Ghost taught me all he knows. He taught me how to fly, among other things, and how to work rackets the flatties never heard of. And I can spot the Ghost's technique through a flock of stone walls. Just about now he's got two things on his mind – dough and revenge.

'Listen! Someone will pay handsome to get this D.A. from Chi back. And don't forget – he prosecuted Baldey Ross – *he's the guy that swung Baldy!*'

She paused a moment to let her words sink in.

'This is the Ghost's work all right. You'll never find him but I think I can. And I can spring this bozo Burke for you, and *get* the guy that double-crossed me. But I want to do it legal. All I ask is a plane, a fast one, with a machine-gun on it, and your say so to go ahead.'

The district attorney's laugh grated through the silence of the room.

'For once I think you're really dizzy,' he said.

His sarcasm cut the girl like the flick of a whip. Her face went white. 'Then you won't—'

'Take it easy for a minute, Dizzy, and let me talk,' the big man interrupted not unkindly. The beaten look in the girl's eyes touched him in spite of himself. 'In the first place the Ghost is still in Europe. I'd have been tipped-off the moment he stepped off a boat.'

'I think you're wrong there, big boy, but – go on.'

The man took another surreptitious glance at his watch.

'It won't be long now, Dizzy, so I don't mind telling you a few things,' he went on. 'We've got this Burke business on ice.'

He took an envelope from his pocket and drew out a soiled sheet of paper.

'Here is the ransom letter. For once we outsmarted the newspaper boys. They know it exists but they *don't* know what it says. Listen!'

He read:

' "UNLESS HALF A MILLION DOLLARS IS FORTHCOMING BURKE WILL NEVER BE SEEN ALIVE AGAIN. FOLLOW THESE DIRECTIONS. THE MONEY, IN GRAND NOTES, IS TO BE TIED SECURELY IN A MARKET BASKET PAINTED WHITE. PLACE MONEY AND BASKET IN THE EXACT CENTER OF VAN CORTLANDT PARK PARADE GROUND AT 7:30 P. M. TODAY AND CLEAR A SPACE FOR A QUARTER OF A MILE AROUND IT. IF THERE IS A PERSON WITHIN THAT AREA BURKE WILL BE PUT ON THE SPOT AT ONCE. THE MONEY WILL BE CALLED FOR AT 7:55 AND BURKE WILL BE DELIVERED AT THE CITY HALL ALIVE AT 8:00 IF DIRECTIONS ARE FOLLOWED IMPLICITLY. ONE FALSE MOVE QUEERS THE GAME." '

Mitchell looked up and grinned.

'We followed the directions all right, but there's a cordon of police around the park that a midget louse couldn't get through. They wait for a flash from us and make the pinch, exactly at the moment Burke is being returned to City Hall. Furthermore, the money in the basket is phoney and there's a ring of plainclothesmen for five blocks each way around City Hall. Whoever made way with Burke won't stand a show. We'll nab them sure.'

'Clever, all right,' Dizzy admitted, 'but you can't outsmart the Ghost. He's a genius, I tell you, a crazy genius. And there's only one person can put the skids under him, and I'm that baby.'

'Okay, okay, Dizzy,' the man replied genially, 'but whoever pulled this Burke coup is going to get it in the neck in a few minutes.'

The girl hunched her shoulders.

'*Somebody'll* get it in the neck, all right,' she said cryptically. 'And don't forget I told you to keep your eyes off the ground.'

Her remark went unheeded, however, for a rap sounded on the door and the next instant it was flung open admitting the slick, dark head of Tom Louden, the D.A.'s shrewd young assistant.

'Seven forty-five, Chief,' he reminded Mitchell. 'Most time for the show to start.'

'All right, Tom. Is the car ready?'

'Yes, sir.'

'Good. Come on, Dizzy. You offered to help us so we'll let you in on the pay-off.'

The girl followed them to a low, black police car that waited at the curb in front of the Tombs. She took her place in the back seat between Mitchell and the assistant D.A. without a word.

A sign from the district attorney and the car purred down Centre Street.

Mitchell rubbed his hands with keen anticipation. A suspicion of doubt drew Louden's lips down in a faint frown. Dizzy's face was a blank.

The car swung into Chambers Street and stopped opposite the rear entrance to City Hall. They were out and hurrying around the grimy, outmoded building.

The plaza in front wore a peculiarly deserted appearance. Walks and benches were empty. The statue of Civic Virtue thrust its marble chest upward, unwatched by newsboy or tattered bench-warmer.

Broadway and Park Row were still literally sprinkled with homeward-bound workers, but they shunned the plaza as though it bore a curse. An atmosphere of tense expectancy hung over it, brooding, sinister, almost palpable in the gathering summer dusk.

Dizzy found herself on the broad steps before City Hall in the midst of a group of grim, tight-lipped men.

The district attorney held his watch in his hand.

'Seven fifty-five,' he muttered. 'Five minutes to go.'

The familiar sounds of traffic came to them in a muted murmur as though muffled by the wall of silence that ringed them in.

'Fifty-seven.'

Bodies tautened.

'Fifty-nine.'

Keen eyes swept the approaches to the plaza – right hands flicked furtively to bulging pockets.

Dizzy's shoulders slumped forward in a nonchalant slouch, her eyes rose in slow boredom toward the darkening heavens.

A low rumble impinged upon the silence, like the growl of distant thunder. Into it burst the first booming note of the clock in the tower.

The rumble increased to a roar, filled the air with a howl of sound, snuffed out the metallic clang of the clock's second note. The screaming drone of wind through wires.

Eyes snapped upward.

Then it came.

Sweeping in low over the Municipal building hurtled a black shadow – a low wing, streamline racing monoplane. It banked sharply as though to give its pilot a view of the square below him, then disappeared behind the Woolworth building.

The watchers stood petrified.

Once more the black ship swung into their range of vision, lower this time, banked, and circled the cramped area like a hovering eagle.

No one moved.

Suddenly the pilot pulled his somber-hued bus into a steep zoom above the Municipal Building, fluttered up into a graceful reversement and hurled his crate across the plaza again directly at the grey Woolworth tower. Swooping down he pulled the screaming ship up into a sharp inside loop that almost scraped the walls and reached its apex directly above the huddled group on the steps.

As it hung there for an instant, upside down, a black shape dropped like a plummet from the auxiliary cockpit. The pilot brought his plane out of the loop and scudded out of sight toward the south.

The black object fell writhing. A flutter of black sprang from it, mushroomed out, breaking the swift descent with a jerk.

'A parachute!'

The cry broke like a single word from the lips of the stunned watchers, a moan of mingled surprise and relief.

The thud, thud of running feet as the nucleus of a crowd closed in.

Slowly, silently the 'chute floated down through the windless dusk, the figure suspended beneath it swinging back and forth in an ever-lessening arc.

The group on the steps scattered from beneath it.

A flash of sudden enlightenment burst upon the district attorney. His cry split the silence like the shrill of a siren.

'Burke!'

The kidnaper had kept his word.

A ragged cheer rose. It changed to a gasp of horror, an instant later, as the 'chute deposited its burden with a dull crash on the stone plaza and its black silken folds crumpled slowly over it.

There it lay in a huddled heap, unmoving.

The D.A. sprang toward it, followed closely by his men. Hands tore eagerly at the enveloping silk. A cordon of police appeared as if from nowhere to hold back the milling crowd.

Dizzy Malone stood unnoticed in the excitement, watching slit-eyed.

The black silk came away disclosing the still figure of a man crumpled on the pavement.

It was Burke, district attorney of the city of Chicago.

'He's stunned by the fall!' Louden cried. 'Broken bones, maybe! Call an ambulance!'

Mitchell bent over the huddled body, fingers probing deftly.

He straightened up again.

'No need,' he said, simply. 'Burke is dead – hung.'

A spasm of rage swept him. He shook his fists at the sky overhead and cursed the vanishing plane and its pilot with blasting, withering oaths.

'Hung him, the carrion!' he shrilled. 'Burke was alive when he dropped. His body's still warm. The parachute was attached to a noose around his neck. When it opened it hung him – hung him by the neck until he was dead!'

He covered his face with his hands.

An examination of the corpse proved that he was right.

It was a clever job and timed to the second.

The shrouds of the 'chute had been fastened to a rope which ended in a noose. The noose circled the dead man's neck, a knot like a hangman's protruding from beneath one ear. His hands were wired together.

When the plane went into a loop and hung there bottom side up, the man had been catapulted downward from his seat. The 'chute opened automatically and snapped his neck with the dispatch of a hangman's sprung trap.

An ambulance jangled up.

From Centre Street came the roar of a motorcycle. A police-runner elbowed his way to the district attorney.

'Flash from Van Cortlandt Park, Chief. At 7:55, a black plane swooped down over the parade ground and scooped up the basket with the ransom. Got into the air again before anyone could get near him.'

The D.A.'s big shoulders drooped.

'And then he got wise to how we'd tried to frame him,' the big man mumbled. 'Poor Burke. My God! Oh, my God!'

His shoulders quivered spasmodically.

In the confusion, Dizzy Malone edged her way in until she stood beside him.

Her words dripped across his numbed mind – measured, stinging, calculated to cut with the bite of a steel-tipped lash.

'Yes, hung by the neck until he was dead – *like he hung Baldy Ross on a frame-up!*' The voice went on, its words searing themselves across the district attorney's soul. 'And remember, big boy, *you sealed the death warrant that sent the Kid to the Big House to fry!*'

CHAPTER II

THE MOLL PAYS A VISIT

Dizzy Malone nodded her way between the huddle of tables that shouldered each other for space around the El Dorado's gleaming dance floor. With a crooked grin and a toss of her smoothly-waved blonde hair she dismissed half a dozen offers of parking space at as many tables.

She wanted to be alone – to think – and it was in the strident, blaring heart of a night club that her mind worked best. About her beat waves of flesh-tingling, erotic sounds – rising and falling rhythmically from brazen throats, from tense, stretched strings, from the quivering bellies of drums – the swirling, clamoring pulse of Broadway's night life.

Dizzy loved it.

She chose a table in the corner and sat down facing the writhing mass of lights and color.

Against its bizarre background the scene in the district attorney's office and the mad happenings in front of the City Hall that afternoon passed rapidly in review.

The job had all the ear-marks of the Ghost. She snarled the name hatefully into the drunken medley of sound. The Ghost must be back then, and broke.

Yes, it all fitted in perfectly. A quick recoup of the stake – part of it hers – that he'd thrown away on that flossie, Spanish Lil – and – revenge. A double-barreled goal that would eat into his twisted mind like acid.

It was like the Ghost to combine business with – revenge.

First this bird Burke who had convicted Baldy, and then—

A waiter with a broken nose and a livid scar that stretched from lip to ear bent over her solicitously, yet with an air of being in the know, of belonging.

'Scotch,' Dizzy said, automatically.

The waiter disappeared.

Dizzy's shrewd mind pieced together the scattered bits of the puzzle. With Burke out of the way who would be next? Who, but—

The waiter again.

He placed the drink before her, bent close to her ear as he smoothed the rumpled tablecloth.

'I hear Spanish Lil is back.'

Dizzy stiffened.

'Where?'

The words seemed to slip out of the corner of her mouth. Her lips did not move.

'At Sugar Foot's in Harlem, throwin' coin around like a coked-up bootlegger.'

'Thanks.'

The grapevine! System of underworld news.

The waiter moved away.

Dizzy made a pretense of drinking, smiled woodenly at a shrill-voiced entertainer, and rose.

Where Spanish Lil was, there the Ghost would be.

Outside the El Dorado, Dizzy climbed into a low, nondescript hulk of a roadster. There was class about the roadster. Its dull, grey finish gleamed in the lamp light. Its nickle fittings were spotless.

When she stepped on the starter, the car's real class became apparent, for under her hand pulsed the steady flow of a V-16 Cadillac. The long, grey hood covered a sixteen cylinder motor mounted on the very latest in chassis.

The gears meshed and the iron brute rolled away with scarcely a sound.

Dizzy swung the wheel and they turned south into Seventh Avenue, then west to skirt the uppermost extremity of Times Square, south on Ninth, then west again and the grey snout of the roadster buried itself deep into the heart of the sink of gangland – Hell's Kitchen.

Before an inconspicuous brownstone front in the odd Forties the car drew up. The motor hissed into silence.

Dizzy climbed the battered stone steps and let herself into an ill-lit hallway. Two steep flights of stairs – another door. It yielded to her key and she stepped into her purple paradise and snapped on the lights. Behind her the door swung to with the solid clang of steel meeting steel and the snap of a double lock.

The room was a perfect foil for Dizzy Malone's blonde, gaming beauty, and truly a purple paradise. It ran the gamut of shades of that royal color, from the light orchid of the silk-draped walls to the almost-violet of the deep, cushion-drenched divans that lined three walls. Into the fourth was built a miniature bar whose dark, blood-purple mahogany gleamed dully in the subdued light of innumerable silken-covered lamps.

Cigarette tables on tall, slender legs flanked the divans; a massive radio was half-concealed by an exquisite Spanish shawl, worked with intricate mauve embroidery and surmounted by a silver vase holding a gigantic spotted orchid. There was not a book to be seen – not even 'Indian Love Lyrics,' acme of chorine literary taste and attainment; or Nietzsche's 'Thus Spake Zarathustra' which is now considered passé by Broadway beauties; or Durant's 'History of Philosophy,' displayed, but never read.

Dizzy's purple paradise was, indeed, an institution.

She crossed its thick, soft carpet with a hurried step and entered the bedroom.

It was done entirely in the same color-scheme as the outer room, but, unlike it, was strictly private.

Dizzy tossed her hat on the square, purple bed that stood on a raised dias in the center of the room. From two wardrobes that squatted against the wall she took the flimsy garments she figured to need and spread them in readiness on the chaise-lounge stretching in luxurious abandon beneath the heavily-shaded casement window.

Then the clothes Dizzy had on fell at her feet in a crumpled shower and she stood, stretching her arms above her head, in provocative marble-pink nakedness.

But not for long. There was work to be done.

Throwing a smock about her slender shoulders, she sat down before a make-up table that would have done credit to the current reigning dramatic favorite, and switched on the blinding frame of electrics that threw its mirror into a pool of dazzling brilliance.

For several minutes her gaze concentrated on the reflected image of herself, then she rubbed the make-up off with cold cream and set to work.

Dark shadows blended in skillfully around her eyes, made their grey depths even deeper, faint penciled lines gave them a slanting oval appearance. She blocked her eyebrows out with grease paint and drew fine, arching ones over them. Deft dabs of rouge close up under the eyes and flanking her nose aided in completely changing the round, youthful contour of her face. It was the long, smouldering, passionate countenance of the Slav. She clinched the impression by drawing out her lips in two, thin crimson lines.

Dizzy gazed at the reflection and grinned. Even she failed to recognize herself. The make-up was perfect.

To complete the illusion, she combed the smooth waves of her blonde bobbed hair flatly down on her little head, then searched through the drawers until she found a flaming red wig.

It was a work of art, that wig, and so expertly made as to defy discovery of its artificiality.

Carefully Dizzy fitted it into place.

An exclamation of delight slipped between her lips.

Perfect, indeed!

Satisfied, Dizzy dressed slowly, choosing a scanty gown that hinted broadly at the palpitating curves beneath. Its vivid, jealous-eyed green threw into hot relief the flaming flower of her hair.

Throwing a light wrap about her, she descended the stairs to her roadster, eased in behind the wheel and gunned the grey hulk toward the river. She swung north on deserted lower West End Avenue, breezing along easily. There was no hurry and she had no desire to run into the drunken crush that marked the three o'clock closing hour of most of Broadway's night clubs.

The blocks slipped past.

At Cathedral Parkway she turned right, passed Morningside Park, and left into Lenox Avenue, the great pulsing artery of Harlem.

Into the maze of side streets the roadster nosed and came to a stop at last before a row of lightless, grimy stone fronts.

Dizzy climbed out and walked around the corner to where an awning stretched across the sidewalk.

In its shadow, towered an ebony doorman.

He scrutinized her closely but at the mention of the name she snarled into his ear, he began to bow and scrape frantically. Flinging the locked doors behind him open, he admitted her to deep-carpeted stairs.

Down them she went, and at the bottom there rushed to meet her the hot music, the din, the flashing movement and color that was the underworld's basement-haven – Sugar Foot's.

Her eyes swept the crowded room in the split second before it was plunged into darkness punctured by a spotlight that picked out a brown-skinned girl in the center of the dance floor. The orchestra throbbed into a barbaric African rhythm and the girl flung herself into a writhing, shuddering dance.

Under cover of it, Dizzy threaded her way to an empty corner-table near the door, which she had spotted in that brief instant, before the lights went out.

When the lights flooded on again she was seated behind the table facing the room. She leaned one elbow negligently on its checked calico-top and joined in the applause. To all appearances she had been there for hours.

A boisterous waiter came and hung over her shoulder.

'Scotch!' Dizzy snapped.

There was that in her tone which sent him away on the jump, respectful, in spite of the aura of flaunted lure that clung about her.

In a moment he was on his way back, skipping, sliding, weaving his way across the dance floor in perfect time to the music. He lowered his tray and placed the drink before her, a tall glass, soda, ginger ale, a bowl of cracked ice, and melted away again.

Slowly, lingeringly, Dizzy mixed the drink, sipped it and settled to the business of looking over the crowd that jammed the stifling room to capacity.

Everyone was there – sporting gents flush from the race-track; sinister underworld figures, suave, shifty-eyed; a heavyweight contender with his wizened-faced manager; a florid police sergeant from the tenderloin; the principals of a smash colored review; a sprinkling of tight-lipped gamblers and individuals who fitted into no particular category. All their women – good, bad, and so-so.

But nowhere on the dance floor could Dizzy find the sunken, grey, cadaverous face of the Ghost, or the long, gangling stretch of his emaciated limbs. He would surely be there. He loved to dance, almost as much as Dizzy herself.

The saxophones sobbed their quivering 'That's All!' and the dancers made for their tables.

The lights went out – the spotlight fell upon a black Amazon in a glittering, skin-tight gown. Swaying sensuously to the beat of the music, she broke into a wailing, throbbing blues. Wild applause.

Lights again – the beat of the music quickened – couples left the tables for the dance floor and locked themselves in shuddering embraces to the fervent tempo of the band.

Dizzy's eyes swept the tables.

There – ah! Dizzy's fists clenched. The pink nails went white.

At the ringside table sat Spanish Lil, high-bosomed, languorous, drunk.

The shimmer of new steel gleamed out from the slits that were Dizzy's eyes. They probed at each of the faces that swarmed around Spanish Lil, each one a worthless hanger-on scenting dough. For an instant they paused at a bloated face faintly reminiscent of the Ghost.

Her heart flopped over and beat wildly.

But no! The man's nose was small and straight, nothing like the Ghost's colorless, almost transparent hooked beak. His shoulders were square, not round and sloping; his eyes puffed and bleary.

A keen stab of disappointment tore at her throat.

Her eyes passed on.

Everywhere she met hot stares, pleading, offering, suggesting unmentionable things. Her own swept them coldly.

A pie-eyed newspaper reporter slouched over her table and began to talk. Dizzy knew him, but to add authenticity to her changed character she sent him away with a stinging rebuff that made even his calloused sensibilities writhe.

Darkness and the spotlight again. A dusky chorus hurled itself into an abysmal jungle dance. A roar of applause.

Lights.

Dizzy rose and made her way toward the ladies' room, taking care to pass close to the table where Spanish Lil and her satelites clustered.

The man with the bloated face looked up and caught her eye for an instant as she went past.

On the way back he was waiting for her. When she came abreast of the table he swayed to his feet.

'Dance, kid?' he mumbled thickly.

Something made Dizzy hesitate instead of brushing quickly by him. Misinterpreting it for assent he insinuated his hand under her elbow.

Spanish Lil leaped to her feet.

'Lay off that, you – you—!' she shrilled.

Her eyes burned with anger and liquor as she seized the man's arm and dragged him away.

'Come on, we're going home.'

Dizzy eased out of the jam and returned to her table. She sat down watching every move of Spanish Lil and the man with the bloated face as they stumbled toward the door.

Suddenly, with a half-stifled cry, Dizzy sprang upright.

There was no mistaking that shuffling gait, that gangling length of limb. A plastic surgeon could chisel away the hooked beak, booze and coke could bloat the sunken, cadaverous face, a tailor could pad the round sloping shoulders; but nothing could disguise that shuffling, long-legged gait.

It was the Ghost.

Dizzy flung a bill down on the table and plunged after them, fighting her way through the crowd, taking the stairs two at a time.

As she burst through the outer door to the sidewalk faint streaks of dawn were silvering the sky.

Spanish Lil and the Ghost were in the back of a waiting taxi. The driver slammed the door and spurted away.

Dizzy dashed round the corner, wrap trailing – scrambled into the grey roadster without opening the door – clawed the ignition switch – kicked the starter.

The iron brute leaped ahead – swung – backed into the curb – hurtled ahead once more – bumped over the opposite curb – and took the corner into the avenue with a screaming skid.

A red tail-light was just visible in the distance.

Dizzy booted the accelerator to the floor and the sixteen cylinders responded with a lurching burst of speed.

The red light drew rapidly nearer and she eased off the terrific pace.

A slit-lipped grin broke across her face, mirthless, cruel.

She was on the trail of the Ghost at last, the only man who had ever double-crossed her.

'There's only one person that can put the skids under him,' she muttered through clenched teeth. *'And I'm that baby!'*

CHAPTER III
In the District Attorney's Office

It was well into the afternoon before Dizzy finally slid her roadster to the curb before the brownstone front in the Forties that masked her purple paradise.

A drizzling summer rain fell steadily.

She climbed out and looked the iron-gutted monster over affectionately. It was spattered with mud and one of the rear tires was flat, cut to ribbons. Like its owner it seemed to droop with the fatigue of a sleepless night and almost continuous driving.

As Dizzy turned wearily toward the house a smile of grim satisfaction creased the corners of her mouth.

She knew all that she needed to know – now! It *was* the Ghost!

Stiffly she plodded up the stairs and let herself into the purple salon. Slamming the door behind her, she crossed to the bedroom leaving a trail of sodden garments in her wake. Her white body disappeared into the bathroom to be followed almost instantly by the hiss of a shower.

She came out in a few minutes, fresh, almost radiant, all traced of her character of the night before completely removed.

It was a 100 per cent Dizzy Malone again who chose a quietly expensive street dress from a wardrobe and drew it on over her head.

When she stepped into the purple salon once more she was as modishly dressed, as cool and collected, as any millionaire broker's private secretary. And probably infinitely more beautiful. She looked, indeed, as though she had stepped out of the proverbial bandbox.

But then, Dizzy was Dizzy, and just at the moment she was ravenously hungry.

From the refrigerator behind the bar she salvaged half a grapefruit; set a percolator brewing coffee and made toast in a complicated electrical gadget.

When breakfast was ready she disposed of it with neatness and dispatch. Into the second cup of coffee she poured a generous slug of cognac and sipped it leisurely. Then she lit a cigarette.

At last Dizzy Malone was herself again and ready for whatever the day would bring, which, she figured, would be plenty.

And in that she was right, as she usually was, although things did not begin to happen as soon as she expected.

Calmly, at first, she sat smoking cigarettes and waiting while the rain dripped dolefully outside. Then she got up and began pacing the room, smoking with short nervous puffs.

Finally the break came.

An ominous rapping on the door.

Dizzy started, pulled herself together and ground the cigarette into an over-full ash-tray.

'Who is it?' she called.

'Horowitz and Rourke from Headquarters. The D.A. says you should take a walk to see him.'

'Just a second, boys.'

The expected had happened.

Dizzy straightened her hat in front of a mirror and opened the door. Outside were two plainclothes men.

'Hello, Dizzy.'

Dizzy grinned.

Together they descended the stairs and made a dash through the rain for the black sedan with the P.D. shield on its radiator that was parked behind her roadster.

Instantly the police chauffeur was on his way, siren shrieking.

'What's the big idea of the ride?' the girl asked.

The dicks shrugged.

'We don't know ourselves.'

And it was obvious to her that they didn't, although it was evident, too, that they were laboring under an over-dose of suppressed excitement. But they offered nothing and Dizzy asked no questions.

The remainder of the ride to the grim building on Centre Street was accomplished in silence. Once there she was conducted immediately to the office where she had had the futile conference exactly twenty-four hours before.

The district attorney sat at his desk, Tom Louden beside him.

'Fade!' the D.A. snapped at the plainclothes men and they backed out, closing the door behind them.

Dizzy stood in the middle of the room, waiting, watching.

Mitchell looked up at her out of eyes deep-sunken and blood-shot. His face showed lines of worry and strain. Even his grizzled hair seemed a trifle greyer. It was a cinch that his nerves were keyed close to the breaking point.

What had happened to the big boy, Dizzy wondered. It would surely take more than that business in front of the City Hall to throw a veteran like himself so completely haywire.

His eyes bored into her and a flush slowly rose to his cheekbones.

'You damned little punk!' he roared, suddenly, springing to his feet.

311

'But, Chief—'

'Shut up!' he snarled at his assistant. 'Let me handle this!'

Seizing the girl's arm he twisted it savagely.

'Now come clean! What do you know about that Burke job?'

Dizzy looked him in the eye.

'I told you what I knew yesterday,' she said coldly. 'I made you a proposition purely on a hunch. The offer still holds. Give me a plane, a fast one, with a machine-gun on it, and your say-so to go ahead, and maybe I can get the Ghost for you. And when I say "get" I mean *"get"!* That's all.'

'It is, huh?'

The D.A. dragged her roughly to the desk.

'Well, what about *this?*'

He snatched a sheet of paper from its top and thrust it in front of her eyes.

It was in the same handwriting as the Burke ransom letter and on the same type paper.

Dizzy read it hurriedly.

'You see what happens when you try to double-cross us, Mitchell! Don't try to chisel again. Unless you announce through the papers that you will comply with our demand for $500,000 as we shall direct, you will be dead by midnight!'

'Well?'

The district attorney pointed to a newspaper scare head.

DISTRICT ATTORNEY DEFIES
BURKE KILLERS

'Now what have you got to say?' he asked fiercely.

'My proposition is still open. And remember, big boy, you prosecuted The Ghost's kid brother. *You sent him up to fry in the chair.*'

'Is that all?'

'Yes.'

The D.A. stood over the girl threateningly.

'Listen, baby, you know plenty and you're going to spill it. Now are you ready to talk nice?'

Dizzy shrugged.

'You heard me the first time, big boy.'

Mitchell's big hand shot out and clamped over her slim arm.

'You're gonna come clean with what you know, see, baby!' he snarled. 'Or else I'll give you the works!'

'I'm no squealer!' Dizzy spit the words in his face.

The D.A. flung her savagely into a chair.

'All right, then, you little punk, *I'll just sweat it out of you!*'

'Good Heavens, Chief! Can't you see she'd had enough?' Tom Louden's voice quivered. 'Lay off her. She won't talk.'

The D.A. turned his back on the crumpled heap that lay whimpering piteously in the chair.

'All right, Tom. Jug her then for safe keeping. She's dangerous.'

'Oh, go easy, Chief! Don't do that. I'll be personally responsible for her. I don't think she's in the know anyway.'

Dizzy looked up gratefully at the young assistant D.A. out of a face that had become pinched and drawn. Racking sobs shook her, but she bit her lips to keep them back.

Mitchell gave tacit consent to his assistant's plea by ignoring it.

'Well, guess I'll call it a day,' he said gruffly, pulling out his watch. 'Eleven-thirty. The buzzards have got half an hour yet to keep their promise, *but they won't get me!*'

Mitchell turned abruptly on his heel and left the room.

When the door closed Louden crossed to the shuddering heap in the chair.

'I'm sorry, kid,' he said with real emotion. 'Feeling better?'

Dizzy nodded and tried to smile.

'Good kid. Now promise that you won't take it on the lam and I'll run you home in my car.'

'I won't lam it – now!'

'Let's go then, Dizzy,' Tom urged as he helped her gently to her feet. 'We'll just trail along behind the Chief to see that *he* gets home all right, then I'll chance Hell's Kitchen and drop you at your door.'

Dizzy gulped her thanks and clung to his arm for support as they hurried to the street.

What amounted to a riot squad had been called out to escort the D.A. to his home. It roared away from the big grey building while Dizzy and Tom climbed into his modest sedan. An armored motorcycle preceded and followed Mitchell's limousine. On the seat beside him sat a pair of plainclothes men.

Mitchell had boasted that the buzzards who knocked off his colleague from Chicago wouldn't get him, but he was taking no chances.

Tom Louden's sedan stuck its nose into the drizzle of rain and scampered after the cavalcade as it streaked away northward.

Into Fifth Avenue they raced, sirens shrieking; past red lights and green alike, the smooth wet asphalt flowing behind them like a black ribbon.

Forty-second Street slid by and the rain-drenched statue of General Sherman dripping in its tiny park at Fifty-ninth.

A few blocks further on they turned right, bumped across the car tracks at Madison Avenue, past the great church on the corner of the Park. It was dark except for the illuminated dial of the clock on its steeple whose hands quivered on the edge of midnight.

Half way up the block the cavalcade stopped before the private residence of the D.A.

Louden pulled in behind the limousine. The coppers leaped to their stations, guns drawn. The D.A. stepped out, chuckling, and headed for his door, waving aside the proffered umbrella of the plainclothes men who walked beside him.

'The buzzards won't get me,' he gloated. 'Not tonight they won't.'

He reached the door and stood on the mat, regardless of the pelting rain, drawing out his key.

The first stroke of midnight clanged hollowly from the church on the corner.

'I fooled 'em this time,' the D.A. laughed.

He thrust the wet key in the lock.

As it touched, a point of blue flame appeared, sputtered into a glow that ran hissing across his hand and up his arm. The D.A.'s body stiffened. Blue sparks cascaded from his feet. His bulky frame writhed in spasmodic jerks, thin spirals of smoke rising from his seared flesh. His features convulsed in agony.

Then, its work done, the burning wave of electricity flung the charred body of New York's district attorney shuddering to the sidewalk.

When his bodyguard bent over him, Mitchell was dead.

In Tom Louden's sedan Dizzy's white lips framed scarcely audible words – 'He fried – just like the Ghost's kid brother!'

CHAPTER IV

ANOTHER DEMAND

Dizzy Malone threw off the purple coverlet of her bed and reached for the morning papers. There was one thing she wanted to find out – how the trick had been turned.

The papers exposed the ingenious device in detail. She lapped them up as she munched rolls and drank coffee prepared by her cleaning woman.

A man had called at the D.A.'s house with the forged identification card of an inspector for the Electric Light Company. He wished to inspect the meter. He was admitted without question by an unsuspecting servant.

The meter was out of order, he said. He would fix it. As well as the servant could remember he had mentioned something about the wiring of the doorbell fouling the house current.

The bogus inspector set to work.

What he really did was to install a transformer which stepped-up the house current to a deadly degree. Ingenious wiring of the metal door frame and the steel door mat completed the trap, which was set by simply connecting a wire outside the door. An apparently innocent passerby could stoop over and make the connection. That done the victim stepped on the mat, inserted the key and completed the circuit that electrocuted him. The rain, of course, aided the design materially.

Dizzy shuddered at its utter hellishness.

It smacked lustily of the Ghost, but a Ghost goaded by homicidal mania, a Ghost stooping to the exhibitionism born of illusions of grandeur, a Ghost whose twisted mind was disintegrating in a final burst of fiendish bravado.

If it *was* The Ghost he had gone stark mad. And as such he was doubly dangerous.

But even Dizzy had no real evidence to pin the two killings on her former partner. From long experience with his methods she sensed, however, that he would have executed them in practically the same manner as the unknown. And then, too, there was the element of poetic justice in the two slayings that she had hunched in the very beginning.

She was two points up on the police any way you looked at it – she knew the Ghost was in New York and she knew his hideaway. And those two bits of information she intended to keep to herself, to be used to bring to a successful ending her vendetta of hate.

She would put the bee on the Ghost, and she would do it herself – that was her right – but she was smart enough to realize there must be a semblance of legality about it or it would be bars, and possibly the chair, for her.

The next move was up to the Ghost.

It came even as she wondered what it would be.

The faint buzz of the telephone.

Dizzy snatched for the French phone in its recess under the bed.

Tom Louden, acting district attorney for the city of New York, was on the wire. Mr. Louden's compliments and would Miss Malone be so kind as to come to Headquarters immediately?

Miss Malone would.

She held the hook down for a few seconds, then called the garage around the corner for her car. Tumbling out of bed she made a hurried toilette and dashed down the stairs. The grey roadster was waiting at the curb, motor running.

Dizzy craved action and she got plenty of it from the crowds of early bargain-shoppers on the drive to the big grim building on Centre Street.

*

It was the third time in three days that she had crossed the threshold of the district attorney's office, but this time she entered with a perky smile and a jaunty step, for she realized that she was master of the situation. It was her turn to dictate.

Tom Louden greeted her with a harassed smile.

'There's hell to pay, Dizzy,' he said, running his hand wearily through his hair. 'Look!'

She took the extended sheet of paper, recognizing with an ominous shiver the soiled foolscap of the two previous ransom letters.

'This just queers everything,' Tom Louden groaned. 'Read it.'

Dizzy's eyes swept back and forth across the paper.

'You see we mean business! The ante is raised to $1,000,000. Follow these instructions exactly. Wrap the dough (grand notes only) in a bundle and attach same to an automatically opening parachute. A pilot is to take a single-seater up from Roosevelt Flying Field with the dough and parachute today at 2 P. M. and head due east out over the ocean, flying 100 miles an hour at 5,000 feet. Plane is to be plainly marked with alternating black and white stripes. When pilot sees a yacht whose decks are similarly painted he is to descend, drop the parachute and return. Bets are off if any attempt is made to follow plane or discover yacht. No tricks this time! We see all, know all!

'If these directions are not followed to the letter within twenty-four hours we will bump off Jake Levine!'

A cry of horror burst from Dizzy's lips at sight of the sinister name.

Jake Levine – Boss Fixer of gangland, human octopus in whose tentacles danced dip and judge alike, maker and breaker of politicians, super-fence, master blackmailer, banker for anything from petty larceny to murder if the return was not less than fifty per cent, chiseler and double-crosser feared from the lowest sink in the tenderloin to the highest holder of the public trust.

'You see what I'm up against on my first job, Dizzy,' Tom growled hopelessly. 'Levine got a duplicate of this letter. He's been down here already – he's here yet. Says he'll blow the lid off, knock the legs out from under the administration – and he will, too – if something isn't done. The party leaders have been on my neck since daylight, and I'm half crazy.'

He looked up to the girl appealingly.

'What I heard of that dope of yours about the Ghost sounded pretty sensible and I'd like—'

The door of the office burst open and an undersized, rat-faced man burst into the room.

'What the hell you going to do about this, Louden?' he demanded, his voice high pitched with panic.

He was trembling violently. The sickly sallow pallor of fear showed through his natural swarthiness. His eyes, beady and set close together, jerked furtively about the room. The aggressive loudness of his clothes even had lost their swagger and he stood revealed as the yellow rat he was.

'You've gotta do something, I say!' he almost screamed. 'Listen, you heel! When I got that letter I fixed it so there'll be hell to pay for *certain parties*' – he emphasized the words slyly – 'if anything happens to me, and they know it. Have they come through with the dough that bum wants?'

'Why – a – not yet, Mr. Levine,' Louden stalled. 'You see—'

'The hell I see! That guy means business. Look who he's bumped off already. He ain't fooling, and if you don't do something for me damn soon I'll start talking and break every punk in this administration.'

His yellow teeth showed in a snarl.

'And don't make a false play either, boy. Remember – if I go on the spot, I wreck the grafters just the same. Nobody ever made a heel outa Jake Levine. Now what kinda protection you givin' me?'

'I can lock you up in a cell, Mr. Levine,' Louden suggested. 'You would be safe there.'

'In a cell – a cell!' the man shrieked. 'Listen to him! Maybe that bum's got somebody planted to get me there – some lousy screw maybe. I don't trust nobody.'

He paused a moment.

'I know where I'll go!' he burst out again. 'I'll stick to one of those *certain parties* until he gets me out of this.'

Turning abruptly he flung himself through the door.

'Well, it won't be long now before the axe falls,' Tom muttered.

'And it won't be long before the time set by that letter is up, too,' Dizzy cut in from where she had flattened herself against the wall. 'It's almost noon now.'

The acting D.A.'s eyes lit up hopefully.

'Oh, yes. That dope of yours about the Ghost – what was it?'

Dizzy gave him the same story she had Mitchell. It was all good hunching, she knew, but not tangible enough evidence on which to make a pinch. She even told Louden that she had positively seen the Ghost the night before, but she carefully refrained from any mention of having trailed him. It was too late to nail him at his hideaway, and even if she *had* been a squealer.

'And my proposition remains practically the same,' she finished. 'Let me fly that striped ransom plane from Roosevelt's Field at two o'clock this afternoon. Be sure it's a fast one and have a machine-gun mounted on it – and *I'll get the Ghost* for you.'

Suspicion flashed squint-eyed across Louden's face.

'Say!' he demanded sharply. 'How do I know *you're* not in on this game too? You were his moll.'

Hot hate flushed Dizzy's face which changed, gradually, to the amused expression she might have worn when watching the helpless squirming of a newborn puppy.

'Listen, stupid,' she laughed. 'I don't carry any dough. You weigh the 'chute with a flock of bricks. Everything's like it should be except for that, and the machine-gun, and Dizzy Malone flying the ship.'

Louden considered.

'No, no, Dizzy,' he burst out petulantly. 'It's impossible. I can't take upon myself the responsibility of sending you of all people. It's a job for the police. Your proposition is absurd. I've a Boeing pursuit plane out at the field ready and waiting. It's camouflaged to look like an old crate that's about ready to fall to pieces, and it's striped black and white. The parachute is waiting for its load of a million dollars.'

He laughed harshly.

'A million dollars! And I'm sitting here doing nothing. Why, look here! The thing to do is to lay a trap for the boat that's to pick up all that money.'

'Don't be dumb!' Dizzy snapped. 'I know the way the Ghost's mind works. He's a racketeer and a flier. He don't play with rowboats. I know him like a book and I'm the only one who can get him. Give me a chance!'

The peremptory jangling of the telephone cut in on the voice that had become low and pleading.

Louden picked up the receiver. His face went white as he listened.

'Yes, sir. Yes, sir . . . I'm doing the best I can . . . No, nothing definite yet . . . I'll give you a ring . . . Yes.'

His hands trembled violently as he replaced the receiver.

'Come on, Tom.' Dizzy was at him again. 'Take a chance. Stall those certain parties off. Tell them someone's come through with the dough and you've sent it out. Call the field about the machine-gun. It's the Ghost – I know it's the Ghost and I'll get him so he won't bother anyone again. If I don't get him I won't come back,' she finished simply.

Louden's eyes fixed themselves despairingly on hers and slowly a look almost of relief came into them.

He stood up and squared his shoulders with decision.

'I'll do it!'

Dizzy was across the room. Her arms went around his neck and she pressed a red kiss full on his lips. Before he knew what had happened she was half-way through the door. There she turned.

'Plenty gas in the Boeing and two motorcycle cops to shoot me through traffic,' she shouted with a wave of the hand.

Then she tore.

Louden stood there, stunned, his mouth open.

'Gas – cops—' he mumbled, nodding his head dumbly.

But when Dizzy reached her grey roadster, two red motorcycles were coughing impatiently beside it. Their drivers were looking with some disdain at the unpromising hulk, but before they had gone two blocks they were pleasantly disillusioned.

Then, sirens shrieking, they proceeded to do their stuff and, for the first time in her life, Dizzy looked at a copper with favor. The baby in front of her could ride, and he did so.

Through traffic they wailed their way, screamed across crowded Queensborough Bridge and on to Long Island.

There, Dizzy gunned the V-16, worrying the heels of the man in front. In the mirror she could see the man behind grin as he hung on doggedly.

Then all three went raving speed-mad.

It was with fifteen minutes still to spare that they whined through the entrance to Roosevelt Field.

The coppers flung wearily off their busses and kicked them into their rests. But they stood to attention and brought their fingers to their caps with real admiration when Dizzy stepped jauntily to the ground and hurried to where she saw a battered looking crate, striped black and white, being warmed up on the line.

A field official stepped forward.

'The ship is ready,' he said, waving his hand.

'Gas?' Dizzy snapped.

'Full tanks.'

'Cruising radius?'

'A thousand miles.'

'Good!'

Dizzy stepped into the flying suit he held toward her and adjusted helmet and goggles.

She waved aside the parachute straps he started to buckle about her with a grim: 'That won't do *me* any good!'

It was to be a battle to the death.

Dizzy climbed aboard and the man explained the manipulation of the machine-gun that had been hastily geared to the motor and camouflaged and showed her where the auxiliary belts of ammunition were nested in the cockpit.

'This is a regulation army pursuit ship,' he said, 'with complete equipment Very pistol and lights, earth inductor compass—'

'Okay, okay!'

The girl checked the details as he pointed them out and shot a glance at her wrist watch.

Two o'clock!

She revved the motor, thrilling to the smooth precision of its whining roar as the man snapped the buckles of the safety-belt.

'Money 'chute!' she cried.

The man brought it and stowed it away within easy reach.

'Bricks!' he shouted with a grin.

Dizzy nodded.

'Let's go!'

The chocks were pulled from the wheels. She gave it the gun and the crate rolled into the runway, hurtled forward. A slight pull on the stick and it catapulted into the air.

Climbing in a tight spiral she watched the altimeter – a thousand feet, two, three, four, five. Then she leveled off and threw the ship into a series of intricate maneuvers. She had been taught by a master – the Ghost – and had proved a more than apt pupil. The Boeing responded to the slightest touch on rudder and stick. Never had she flown such a ship.

She leveled off again and, putting the blazing disc of the sun at her back, set her course by the compass dead into the east. Full gun she watched the speed indicator climb to its maximum, then throttled down to an easy hundred miles an hour. No need to figure drift – not a breath of air stirred.

Long Island slid out from under her and the Boeing nosed out over the Atlantic.

Dizzy dipped her left wing and scanned the smooth blue expanse of water. No yacht with striped deck met her eager gaze; in fact, there was no boat of any sort to be seen, no smudge of black smoke, even, on the horizon ahead. She wormed round in the cockpit as far as the safety-straps would permit and scanned the air.

Nothing.

The scorching sun beat blindingly into her eyes.

A sense of utter loneliness settled depressingly about her.

She shot the moon to warm her guns, quivering with a throb of power at their chattering death-talk.

An hour spun round on the dial of her watch.

The sea below her was a round blue waste circled by a shimmering heat haze.

Another hour—

She dispelled a growing uneasiness with a screaming burst of the guns.

The sun settled slowly behind her. The Boeing roared on into the east.

Another hour—

The ship, perceptibly lightened of its load of gas, floated easily in the air. She flew left-wing low, now, searching the water for a striped-deck yacht.

Still nothing. The sea was as barren as a deserted mill-pond. She searched the sky above and behind. Nothing but the red round of the sun, slowly sinking.

The vague restlessness of fear shuddered along her nerves that the staccato of the guns failed to dispel. The gas was almost half gone and still the bare, tenantless reach of water stretched below her.

Where was the yacht?

The suspicion born in the D.A.'s office that it was only a stall grew into a certainty. Real fear gripped her. What was this all about? Should she turn back?

No! She remembered her boast and screamed it into the surrounding void.

'Damn the Ghost! I'll get him or I won't come back!'

As if in answer to her screamed challenge a black shadow seemed to sweep out of the sun.

Her eyes jerked to the side, her body went rigid.

Beside her floated a low-winged black Lockheed Sirius monoplane.

Her gaze probed through the pilot's goggles, locked with the pale smoldering eyes of – the Ghost!

He waggled his wings and motioned over the side with a long-armed gesture.

Dizzy held up the readied 'chute.

The Ghost nodded and she flung it clear.

A cold dash of warning from some seventh sense sent her up in a steep zoom and she fell off on one wing.

And none too soon for a spatter of holes ripped through the doped linen of one wing. The Ghost was heeled too.

She banked to see the man pull his ship out of a zoom that had been intended to rake her bus from prop to tail assembly, and dive for the opened 'chute. He caught it deftly on a hook suspended from the undercarriage and hauled it rapidly aboard.

Dizzy rammed forward on the stick, the wind droned through the wires as she dropped down and threw a burst of steel into the Sirius. It dropped off clumsily on one wing and pulled itself up heavily.

With that maneuver the insane daring of the Ghost's final gesture came clear. The Sirius with its cruising radius of 4,300 miles was fueled to capacity. The Ghost gambled to blast the ransom plane out of the sky with a single burst, pick up the money 'chute and head for Europe.

Dizzy thrilled in spite of herself at the very audacity of the thing, its colossal bluff.

Then the red mantle of hate dropped over her.

She dropped the Boeing down out of the sky and swept alongside the black ship. This would be a fair fight and to the death. She would get him, if she could, and on the level.

Dizzy tore off goggles and helmet, noting with satisfaction the cringe of recognition that swept across the Ghost's face.

She shook her fist at him and motioned him to dump his gas.

He accepted the challenge and a sheet of spray gushed downward. The black ship, lightened of its load, leaped upward.

They were on even terms now.

*

Dizzy tripped her guns and the man answered the salute – the salute of death, for one of them at least and perhaps both.

They flung their ships at each other, guns flaming.

Steel seared Dizzy's cockpit, rocking the Boeing. She dove, zoomed up in a loop and stood on her head pumping chattering hail into the Sirius.

The Ghost wing-slipped out of the way and they clawed down the sky to get at each other's bellies, then roared upward, guns raving.

Dizzy's instrument-board went to pieces. Stunned, the Boeing slipped into a spin, the Ghost on its heels waiting to rip in the coup de grace.

The girl threw the stick into neutral and when her crate steadied, sat on her tail and clawed for altitude.

Sirius steel tore into the Boeing. Dizzy pulled into a reversement and for an instant the black crate was glued to her ring-sights. She pressed the trips. Steel gutted the black ship.

It wabbled. She was under it, ripping, tearing.

The Sirius nosed over into a spin, flame streaming behind.

The Boeing nosed in for the kill, wires screaming, guns raving.

A black wing collapsed and the Sirius spun faster, down, down.

Dizzy leveled off, banked and leaned over the side.

Below her a flaming ball cometed down through the dusk to be extinguished, suddenly, in a mighty geyser of spray—

Dizzy was limp and trembling when she pulled back on the stick and gunned the Boeing into a staggering climb. The motor missed, caught again and roared on as she leveled off and stuck its nose into the faint afterglow that streaked upward into the gathering darkness.

She rode the air alone, sky-victor in a riddled ship. Ominous metallic growlings broke the smooth beat of the motor from time to time. The instrument-board was shot away, but she realized that her gas must be running low.

The compass needle wabbled perilously on its luminous dial.

She nursed the game crate on – on.

The motor began to miss badly. Her eyes strained into the blackness below, but she remembered the deserted sea and gave up hope of distinguishing a light. A thin, complaining whine from the iron guts of the motor.

Bullet through the oil tanks, she thought. This can't last much longer.

But she kept on, content to take death as it should come, but still fighting. The score was even – victory hers even though she would never enjoy its spoils.

The whine of the motor was rising in a screaming crescendo – she felt the Boeing settle.

Her hands unloosed the buckles of the safety-belt, grazed the butt of a Very pistol. Her fingers closed about it and tore it out of its holster.

Pointing the Very gun over her head a rocket of light shot upward, burst in a shower of colored stars.

With a final shrill of protest the motor clanked into silence.

She nosed the ship down in a long easy glide.

The face of Spanish Lil sneered up out of her mind. Dizzy gritted her teeth. That score would have to go unsettled.

The Very pistol spurted another streamer of light that rocketed into twinkling stars.

The ship nosed down, a darker blackness rising to meet it. Wave crests slapped at the undercarriage, a spurt of spray dashed upward from the dead prop and the Boeing settled gently in the arms of the sea.

Uncomprehendingly, at first, Dizzy Malone's eyes took in the little white room, the stiffly-uniformed nurse, the white iron bed; came to rest on the face of the man bending over her – Tom Louden.

Realization filtered gradually into her mind.

Tom grinned.

'Feeling better?'

Dizzy nodded feebly.

'I may get myself into a jam for – ah – commandeering that sea sled but – it was worth the chance. And I was just in time.'

'Thanks,' she whispered. 'You took a chance for me, huh? Well, I'm just dizzy enough to take one myself – now. I'll chance the straight and narrow, if you – think—'

Tom Louden's face bent closer – closer—.

THE DUCHESS PULLS A FAST ONE
WHITMAN CHAMBERS

The author of more than twenty crime and mystery novels, as well as an active screenwriter, Whitman Chambers (1898–1968) is surprisingly neglected today. He created several private eye characters for the pulps and novels; perhaps the failure to produce an especially engaging series character has militated against his continuing popularity.

Among his most successful works are *The Come-On* (1953), which was filmed in 1955; he was the co-writer of the screenplay with Warren Douglas. A good and complex film noir, it starred Anne Baxter and Sterling Hayden; Russell Birdwell was the director. Hayden also starred in *Manhandled*, filmed in 1949, which also featured Dan Duryea as the quintessential small-time hood and Dorothy Lamour; Lewis R. Foster directed the Paramount feature. In 1960, Chambers wrote a novelization based on his own screenplay.

Among the many pulp stories Chambers wrote in the 1930s, he created Katie Blayne, known as 'the Duchess,' for *Detective Fiction Weekly*. Unlike many of her contemporaries, Katie was no one's assistant, wife, secretary or partner. A reporter for *The Sun* who dated a man on a rival newspaper, she investigated crimes while digging out facts for her articles. She is good looking and aggressive but often relies on intuition to solve a mystery; it was said that she could 'produce hunches faster than a cigarette machine turns out coffin nails.'

'The Duchess Pulls a Fast One' first appeared in the September 19, 1936, issue of *DFW*.

THE DUCHESS PULLS A FAST ONE
WHITMAN CHAMBERS

The three of us, Spike and Katie Blayne and I, were alone in the City Hall press room. It was six thirty of a dark and rainy evening. I'd just taken over the beat from Spike, for the *Telegram*, and Katie was waiting for the *Sun's* night police reporter to come on the job.

'Duchess,' Spike Kaylor beefed, 'why don't you scram out of here and go home?'

'Spike, why don't you give yourself up?' the Duchess retorted, smiling.

'Pinky, doesn't she get in your hair the way she hangs around and hangs around, all the time?' Spike persisted.

I didn't say anything. I didn't want to be drawn into their quarrel which, for seven months, had kept the press room on pins and needles. In the first place, Spike Kaylor is my best friend. And in the second place, Katie Blayne – well, never mind about Katie Blayne.

The fire alarm gong tapped out 236. Spike strode over to the card tacked on the bulletin board. 'Fifth and Chesnut.' He looked more cheerful. 'Our City Hall apparatus will roll on the deuce.'

'And you, dear little boys, I suppose, will take a ride on the big old fire engine,' Katie jeered. 'Won't that be just ducky!'

'Well,' I said, 'it's some consolation to be able to do something that you can't do.'

Katie's blue eyes twinkled. 'Maybe you think I can't.'

'Skip it,' I said. 'You're not going kiting around on any fire truck. Not the way these lunatics drive.'

At that instant the second alarm clanged in. 'There's the deuce!' Spike shouted, and leaped toward the door.

I was on his heels and I realized, unhappily, that Katie was on mine. We tore down the corridor and into the fire house. The big pumper was just starting to roll. The three of us caught the hand rail and swung onto the running board. Two firemen up beside the driver looked back and yelled at Katie. The roar of the powerful engines drowned their words and the Duchess looked the other way.

As the pumper turned into the street with a breath-taking skid and

327

roared away with bell clanging and siren wailing, Katie swayed toward me and shouted happily: 'I've always wanted to do this.'

'It's just the little girl in you,' I growled.

We saw the red glow in the sky while we were still blocks away from the fire. Huge clouds of yellow smoke were rolling upward.

'Kurt Bergstrom's chemical plant is at Fourth and Chesnut,' I yelled.

'Fine!' Spike shouted. 'And if Bergstrom is going up in smoke with his chemicals, I'll buy the drinks.'

Which is the way most newspaper men feel about Kurt Bergstrom. The head of the Bergstrom Chemical Company is an inventor, a nationally known chemist, a man of wealth and substance. But! He'll stool to any gag, short of murder, to get his name in the papers. And reporters do not like publicity hounds.

The pumper pulled up a block from the fire. Katie and Spike and I piled off and started down the street as one of the firemen yelled: 'Hey, Duchess! Next time you want to go to a fire, hire a cab!'

'Thanks for the buggy ride,' Katie called sweetly, and blew him a kiss.

The fire, we discovered with some disappointment, was confined to the north wing of the two-story brick building. It was evidently already under control, despite the billowing clouds of acrid smoke which rolled out of the shattered windows.

'Not much to this,' I remarked.

Then we saw an elderly man talking excitedly to Battalion Chief Murphy. We pegged him for the night watchman and ran over.

'He was in the chem lab in the north wing when I come on at six,' the old man was saying. 'He was alone, workin' on some experiment. I goes over the plant and I'm down in my room makin' some coffee, when I smell smoke. That's about a half hour later. I runs upstairs and the whole chem lab is in flames. I never seen him go out. His car's right there in front of the office where he parked it, but he ain't nowheres around.'

'Who?' Spike bellowed. 'Who?'

The watchman blinked at us. 'Mr. Hamlin. Mr. John Hamlin. He's Mr. Bergstrom's assistant in the lab.'

Chief Murphy grunted. 'Well, we'll find out if he's in there in a few minutes. I'll send in a couple of men with gas masks.'

A little later they found the body, or what was left of it. They didn't even try to carry it out. They left that grisly job to the coroner. In the confined space of the laboratory the heat had been intense.

We cleaned up as many angles of the story as we could and then Spike called a cab. The Duchess, as usual, was right on our heels. She climbed into the taxi with us and sat down calmly between Spike and me.

Spike stared straight ahead as the cab pulled away from the curb. 'My nose tells me it's still with us,' he commented acidly.

'My Christmas Night perfume,' Katie said blandly. 'Don't you adore it?'

'I'd adore to drop you down a manhole,' Spike groused.

She let that pass. 'Are you by any chance going to the Hotel Drake?' she asked. 'Because if you are, I'll go with you and we'll interview Kurt Bergstrom together.'

Spike groaned, but didn't argue.

The clerk at the Drake directed us to the dining room and the head waiter told us Bergstrom was eating alone in the south alcove. Spike started off, then checked himself. A cagey look came into his eyes as he asked casually: 'How long has Mr. Bergstrom in the dining room?'

'Since a little after six, sir.'

As we paraded through the room, a bit damp and sooty and bedraggled, Katie asked:

'Now what was the occasion for that question?'

'Did you ever hear, my little cabbage, of the crime called arson?'

'Yes,' Katie said promptly, 'and I've also heard of the crime called murder. But if you're thinking of them in connection with Kurt Bergstrom, you'd best forget them. Mr. Bergstrom is a wealthy man. He had no reason to stoop to arson, much less to murder.'

'That mugg would stoop to anything to get his name in the papers.'

Bergstrom rose when he saw us coming. He's a heavy-set chap of fifty, with very pink cheeks, keen blue eyes and close-clipped blond hair.

'Goot evening, gentlemen. Goot evening, Miss Blayne.' He knew every reporter in the city. 'There is something I can do for you?'

'There sure is,' Spike said. 'Who is John Hamlin?'

'Hamlin is my assistant in the laboratory.'

'Not any more he isn't your assistant.' Spike never beat around the bush. 'The north wing of your plant was just gutted by fire. Hamlin was burned to death, or so the watchman believes. Anyway, the firemen found a body in the lab. Hamlin's car is out in front but Hamlin is missing.'

Bergstrom took it calmly but that didn't prove anything. He's the type who never shows emotion.

'Now about this man Hamlin,' Spike hurried on. 'Was he married?'

'Yes. He lived with his wife at 17 Bay Terrace.'

'Why was he down there after hours?'

'An experimental chemist,' Bergstrom proclaimed, 'has no hours. He was working nights on an experiment of his own. Only during the day did he help me with one of my inventions.'

'Which is?'

Bergstrom brightened. 'An inexpensive device for recording sound on motion picture film. An attachment for the home movie camera, selling for only a few dollars, which—'

'Give the details to the advertising department,' Spike broke in. 'We're not handing out any free publicity for your invention.' He paused, looked the big German straight in the eye. 'Do you believe, Mr. Bergstrom, that the body found was John Hamlin's?'

Bergstrom shrugged, said cautiously: 'You say Hamlin iss missing und a body was found in the laboratory. Surely you, as a brilliant young newspaper man, should be able to draw the obvious conclusion.'

'But perhaps,' Spike said slowly, 'the conclusion is too *damned* obvious!' He glared at the bristling Bergstrom. 'Have you stopped to think of that?'

'I haff hardly had time,' Bergstrom retorted stiffly, 'to think of anything. Und now if you excuse me please, I run oud to the plant.'

We followed him out of the dining room. In the lobby Katie asked: 'Are you going out to see Mrs. Hamlin?'

'Yes, *darling!*' Spike shot back. 'And I suppose you'd like to tag along.'

'Yes, *dear*! I'd love it. You know how I enjoy your company.'

We found Mrs. Hamlin dry-eyed and calm, though we knew immediately we saw her that she had been informed of her husband's death. She was a tall, big-boned woman with black hair that looked dyed and dark, close-set eyes.

She invited us into the living room and asked us to sit down. 'I knew that those experiments would end in tragedy,' she told us calmly. 'You see, my husband was developing a high explosive.'

'So far as anyone knows,' Spike pointed out, 'there was no explosion.'

'The chemicals he used were highly inflammable.'

'I see.' Spike didn't look as though he saw at all. 'Did your husband come home for dinner tonight, Mrs. Hamlin?'

'He came home, yes. He ate an early dinner, as always, and rushed back to the laboratory. He must have got there a little before six. I did my dishes and sat down and tried to read. I had planned to go to a movie. But, somehow, I didn't dare leave the house. I was sitting here on the Chesterfield when the coroner phoned. I was neither surprised nor shocked. You see, I have been expecting this.' She wiped her dry eyes with a folded handkerchief. 'I suppose you will want pictures?'

She turned to a table, picked up three large snapshots and handed them to me. 'They were taken a year ago today. Our wedding day.'

Well, it should have been pretty pathetic, but somehow it wasn't. I looked at the pictures. Mr. and Mrs. John Hamlin on somebody's lawn. A little guy with a head too big for his stooped shoulders, his thin arm held in the possessive grip of a smirking, over-dressed Amazon.

Spike asked quietly: 'Did Mr. Hamlin carry any insurance?'

'Yes. He took it out before we were married.'

'A large amount?'

'Eighty thousand dollars.'

Spike peered around the room.

'Quite a sizable policy for a man in his circumstances, wouldn't you say?'

I could see her stiffen as she glared at Spike. 'Considering the dangers of his work, no. He wished me to be provided for if anything happened.'

'Well, we'll hope his wish is granted,' Spike said, rubbing a smile off his lips. 'Although insurance companies sometimes get tough about things like this. Any further questions, – children? If not, that will be all, Mrs. Hamlin. Sorry to trouble you, and thanks for the pictures.'

We filed out, climbed into our cab and started back to the Hall.

'What a story, what a story!' Spike chortled. 'If we can only crack it!'

'You mean this poor woman's losing her husband on their wedding anniversary?' Katie asked.

Spike moaned. 'Brilliance. That's it. Positive brilliance. Duchess, don't you know a Schwartz when one jumps up and spits in your face?'

'A Schwartz?'

'Tell her, Pinky. She was still in kindergarden when the Schwartz case broke.'

'This Schwartz was a chemist and inventor too,' I said. 'He had a laboratory out in Walnut Creek where he was working on a process of manufacturing artificial silk. One night there was an explosion and the joint burned down. They found a man's body in the ashes. Everybody thought, of course, that Schwartz had cashed his checks. His wife put in for the hundred grand insurance he carried.

'Then it developed that the body wasn't Schwartz's at all. The dead guy was an itinerant preacher whom the chemist had lured into the laboratory and knocked over the head. Schwartz, in the meantime, had holed up in an apartment he'd rented weeks before he pulled the hoax. The dicks got on his trail and were closing in on him when Schwartz put a .45 slug between his eyes. Since then, Katie, an insurance hoax of that type has been known as a Schwartz.'

The Duchess took one of my cigarettes and lit it with hands that weren't very steady. 'And you think this is an insurance hoax?'

'Cinch,' Spike declared flatly.

'Why?'

'Because it's too damned pat and because that guy Hamlin carried too much insurance.'

'And who was the man they found in the laboratory?'

'Some hobo who'll never be missed. Hamlin got him in there on the pretext of giving him a job, slapped him over the conk and fired the joint. Simple, Duchess.'

'And you think Kurt Bergstrom was in on the hoax?' Katie pursued.

'Cinch.' Spike nodded gleefully. 'The way I dope it, the time of the fire was prearranged to put Bergstrom in the clear. John Hamlin is a weak sister and the whole plot was cooked up by Bergstrom and Mrs. Hamlin.

Hamlin is safely holed up somewhere, and when the heat is off he and the dame'll scram to South America with forty grand.'

'And the other forty grand?'

'Into Kurt Bergstrom's sock. Well, what do you think of it, Duchess?'

'I think the whole thing,' Katie promptly retorted, 'is a silly machination of a disordered brain.'

When we got back to the press room I called the beat while Spike and the Duchess phoned their offices. Then, on a hunch, I rang the morgue and by sheer good luck got hold of the coroner himself.

'Pinky Kane,' I said. 'Look, coroner. About that man who was burned to death in the Bergstrom fire. Have you got around to a p.m. yet?'

'We've made a cursory examination at the request of Captain Wallis.'

'What'd you find?'

'Perhaps you'd better ask Wallis. He ordered me not to give out any details.'

Katie and Spike were still in the phone booths as I impatiently jiggled the hook, got the operator and asked for the Captain of Detectives. Wallis came on almost immediately.

'This is Kane, skipper. Understand you ordered a post mortem on Hamlin's body.'

'That's right, Pinky.'

'What'd you find out?'

'Well, his height and build approximate that of John Hamlin. He carried a gold watch on which Hamlin's initials are still discernible. He wore a full denture – not a tooth in his head. Same as Hamlin. And that, Kane, is about the works.'

'Come on, skipper. Kick in.'

'I said that was the works.'

'Now look here. You were on that Schwartz case and so was I. And I haven't forgotten it. Now what else did your medical examiner discover when he went over that body? Tell me everything.'

'Well,' Captain Wallis sighed, 'you'll get it sooner or later, so I might as well give it to you now. The man's skull had been fractured.'

'Uh-huh, I thought you were holding out something like that. Hamlin's skull couldn't have been cracked in the fire, could it?'

'Chief Murphy said nothing fell on him and if he had a fractured skull he must have got it before the fire broke out.'

'Well, what do you think?' I asked.

'I don't know how you spotted it, Pinky, but I think you're on the right track. Another Schwartz.'

'How about Bergstrom? Do you think he's in on it?'

'If I answered that question I'd be guessing. So let's pass it.'

'And Mrs. Hamlin?'

'I've only talked to her on the phone. She may be a party to the hoax and she may not. Probably not. Schwartz's wife wasn't, you know. He planned to contact her after the pay-off and, as the saying goes, tell all. Anyway, I've just sent out an all-state teletype with Hamlin's description. I've ordered him held.'

'On what charge, skipper?'

'Murder, my boy. Murder,' Captain Wallis said cheerfully.

I hung up, a bit breathless all of a sudden.

The Captain certainly had been working fast.

Katie came out of the *Sun* booth. 'You've been talking to Bodie Wallis, haven't you?' she said, smiling.

'Bodie did most of the talking. I listened. He's sent out an all-state teletype to pick up John Hamlin.'

Katie's laugh told me what she thought of Bodie Wallis. 'John Hamlin has already been picked up. In a basket, by a couple of coroner's deputies.'

'Captain Wallis doesn't think so.'

'String with Captain Wallis, Pinky, and you'll sleep in the street,' she said airily.

Spike tumbled out of the telephone booth bellowing:

'Hey, Pink! The office just got a flash from Duke Wayland on the lower beat. Captain Wallis—'

'I know. I was just talking to him.'

'That guy had a fractured skull!' Spike exclaimed excitedly.

'Yeah,' I said.

Katie's jaw dropped as she looked from Spike to me. 'What guy had a fractured skull?' she asked in a small voice.

'The guy they picked up in a basket. The guy you were dumb enough to think was John Hamlin.'

Katie sat down abruptly. Spike and I stood looking at her, gloating a little. It wasn't often that the Duchess put her money on the wrong number.

'Well, muh frand?' Spike grinned at last.

She shrugged. 'It looks bad but it isn't hopeless. I'm banking on one thing: the integrity of Kurt Bergstrom. I've known him for several years and I can't see him getting mixed up in an insurance hoax involving murder. And I can't see that meek and mild person, John Hamlin, hitting a man over the head and burning his body.'

'That's logic for you,' Spike jeered. 'Kurt Bergstrom looks too honest to go in for murder. And John Hamlin looks too meek to kill anybody. Forget, for a minute, the looks of those two guys and where are you? Well, I'll tell you. You're stringing along with Pinky and me and Captain Wallis.'

'Three,' Katie said sarcastically, 'of the most brilliant minds in the city. Well if you three are brilliant, I'm a low moron. Good night.'

Katie breezed, slamming the door.

333

Spike chuckled. 'Did we get the little lady's goat, all right. But I'd much rather get John Hamlin.'

'And maybe you think we won't. Now look. It's a ten to one shot the guy never left the city. His best bet was to establish a residence in some quiet apartment house. He's probably had the apartment for weeks, just like Schwartz did. All right. So what?'

'I'll bite.'

'We smoke him out.'

'You and me?'

'Don't be a sap. We got a staff, haven't we. We got three or four cubs sitting over there in the office wearing out the seats of their pants, haven't we? Oke! Tomorrow morning early we turn 'em loose, along with anybody else Andy can spare. We contact every hotel and apartment and rooming house in the city.'

'The dicks will be doing just that,' I pointed out.

'What of it? We can put as many men on the job as Bodie Wallis. We got just as good a chance as he has of turning up Hamlin. And if we get a break – well, will Katie's face be red? Dunt esk!'

We went to work the next morning. It was house-to-house stuff and it was tiring. But we didn't care. Spike and I felt, the whole *Telegram* staff felt, that we were on the right track.

As we read John Hamlin's mind, he never expected any hue and cry. He thought the corpse would be accepted as his, and the pay-off would be a pushover. He'd made only one mistake. He'd hit the poor devil he'd hired to double for him too hard a blow. The body wasn't wholly consumed, as he'd expected it to be, and the skull fracture showed up in the post mortem. John Hamlin, we reasoned, must have got quite a shock when he read the papers in the morning and learned that every law enforcement officer in the state was looking for him.

It was a long hard day and we found no trace of John Hamlin. Something, however, was in our blood. The thrill of the chase. We felt, Spike and I and the cubs, as though surely we'd locate him in the next apartment house, the next hotel. We kept doggedly at it all day, all the day following, all the day after that.

At five in the afternoon of the third day, dead on my feet, I strolled into the City Hall press room. The reporters on the afternoon papers had gone home and Katie, looking fresh and spruce and more than a little like a million dollars, was all alone.

'You looked dragged out, Pinky,' she smiled. 'Where have you been all day?'

'Hunting John Hamlin,' I said, slumping into a chair.

'Why, don't you read the papers? Hamlin was buried today. I covered the funeral.'

I sighed. 'You don't really think that was Hamlin, do you? I know you're silly, Duchess, and I know your judgment isn't very good. But you're not that silly, are you?'

She looked at me hard for a long minute. Then:

'See here, Pinky Kane. I don't like that. I don't like it even a little bit. You can call me almost anything else, but I draw the line at being called silly. I was going to spare you this, but on second thought I won't. I'll go out of my way, for once, just to show you how silly *you* are. Will you meet me at the Drake Hotel at eight tonight?'

'What for?'

'For the pay-off,' Katie said.

The door had opened and Spike Kaylor stood on the threshold. 'Where's the pay-off?' he demanded.

'At the Drake, tonight,' the Duchess told him. 'You're invited.'

''Thanks,' Spike grinned. 'Will this affair be formal, or shall I—'

'Wear tails, by all means,' Katie shot back, and left the room.

'What's the kid got on her mind?' Spike asked.

'You can't prove anything by me.'

'Do you really think she has a hot lead?'

'I wouldn't put it beyond her.'

'But what is it? She hasn't found John Hamlin, has she?'

'No. She insists Hamlin is dead and buried.'

'But maybe that's just to throw us off the track.' Spike eased into a chair. 'Pay-off, huh? Pay-off,' he mused. 'Pink, there's something screwy about this picture. If she was ready to crack this story, would she invite us to the party? Not any! She'd tell us something was due to pop and let us stew in our own juices until two o'clock tomorrow morning when the final edition of the *Sun* comes out.'

'That's what you'd think, all right. So what?'

'So we take her up. What the hell else can we do?'

We found the Duchess, sitting off by herself, in the lobby of the Drake at eight o'clock.

'Well, keed, when does the curtain go up?' Spike asked.

'Almost any minute,' Katie returned shortly. 'Just keep your shirts on and your mouths shut.'

She lit a fresh cigarette off a glowing butt.

Her hands were shaking and I saw that the palms were moist. Her eyes were bright, feverish, as she kept watching the door.

'Our little pal seems a bit nervous,' Spike grinned.

'We can do without your puerile mouthings for a while, Mr. Kaylor,' the Duchess told him.

*

335

Then Kurt Bergstrom strode into the lobby and Katie rose. The chemist spotted her and came over. He looked keyed up and he didn't smile as he bowed perfunctorily over her hand.

'These are your friends?' he asked, looking at Spike and me with cold and fishy eyes.

'Not my friends, but they'll do as witnesses.'

'Goot! Bring them up in ten minutes.'

Bergstrom turned and walked briskly toward the elevators. Katie sat down and lit another cigarette. She was plenty nervous.

I began to feel restive myself. Even Spike, who is almost irrepressible, didn't have anything to say. We watched ten slow minutes tick off on the clock over the desk. Then Katie stood up.

'When we go up to Bergstrom's room,' she said, 'you two will do as you're told and ask no questions. Have you got that straight?'

'Oke, kid,' Spike nodded. 'Lead the way.'

Bergstrom received us in the living room of his suite. He waved Katie to a chair and then stood for a minute eying Spike and me. You could see he didn't like us. You could see he wished we were a long way from there. Finally he said:

'I hope we can trust them, Miss Blayne.'

'They'll do as they're told and like it,' the Duchess said.

'That all depends,' Spike said, 'on what you tell us to do.'

Bergstrom threw open a door to a clothes closet. 'You will go in there und stay there und keep quiet,' he said crisply. 'You will leaf the door oben two or three inches, joost enough so you can see und hear what goes on. You will nod come oudt until you are told to come oudt. All right?'

'All right,' Spike agreed.

'I will tell you when to go in. In the meantime, please to sit down und be comfortable.'

We sat down diffidently. So help me, I couldn't get the angle. I couldn't make head or tail of the layout. Spike caught my eye, while Bergstrom paced briskly up and down the room, and signalled: 'Watch yourself. I don't trust this guy.' I didn't trust him either.

After a time the telephone rang. Bergstrom took it up, listened a moment, ordered: 'Show him up at once.'

Spike started to rise.

'No, no. Nod yet,' Bergstrom said irritably. 'It iss only Captain Wallis.'

Spike sat down again, looking a bit deflated. Bodie Wallis came in after a few minutes. In his quiet blue serge business suit, he didn't look much like a detective.

He nodded to Katie and Bergstrom, grinned at Spike and me.

'You two boys don't miss anything, do you?' he chuckled.

'Not if we can help it,' Spike admitted, a bit boastfully.

'I might point out,' Katie remarked, 'that they are here at my invitation.

336

And anything they see or hear won't be reported in the *Telegram* until it has appeared exclusively in the *Sun*. Right, Mr. Kaylor?'

'Wrong, Miss Blayne!' Spike bristled. 'That wasn't part of the bargain.'

'It's part of the bargain now.'

'Sister, it takes two to make a bargain. And as long as I have two legs and can run to the nearest telephone—'

The phone buzzed at that instant and Bergstrom raised his hand authoritatively. 'Silence, if you please!' He picked up the instrument, and after a moment: 'Show her up at once.'

He turned and waved us toward the closet. We got up and went in and closed the door to a two-inch crack. Spike jammed his foot against the door and I pulled on the knob, to hold it steady open. Spike, kneeling at the crack, whispered:

'It's a funny one, Pink. You got any ideas?'

'No ideas, but I got a good hunch,' I whispered. 'Bergstrom is on the spot. With Katie's unwitting help, he's trying to slide out from under.'

'Yeah. That's the way I dope it. He's about to pull a fast one. And when it comes down the groove, we'll pole it over the right-field fence for a home run. How's about it?'

'That's okey by me.'

We didn't say any more, because Bergstrom had stepped to the hall door and was admitting – Mrs. John Hamlin! She wore black and she looked tense and watchful and cool. Bergstrom was saying:

'Miss Blayne you haff met, I believe. Und this, Mrs. Hamlin iss Mr. Wallis.'

Mister Wallis! Well, why not? The whole situation was cockeyed anyway.

'Please to sit down, Mrs. Hamlin,' Bergstrom said, helping her to a chair with great solicitude. 'We haff wonderful news for you. Your husband, my dear, iss *alive!*'

Mrs. Hamlin sat on the edge of her chair, stiffly, blinking up at him. She said carefully: 'I buried my husband this afternoon.'

Bergstrom smiled down at her gently, shook his head. 'The man you buried vas nod your husband. John iss alive. He vas badly burned in the fire und he sustained a severe injury to the head. He hass been suffering from amnesia ever since. In fact, even now he iss delirious. But the doctor assures me that his chances for pulling through are excellent.'

The woman never moved but I could see the last of the color in her cheeks fade out.

Spike whispered: 'Amnesia! Did I tell you a fast one was coming down the groove? Amnesia!'

Well, it was easy enough for a couple of smart reporters to dope the play. I saw it this way: When Bergstrom and Hamlin realized their hoax wasn't going over, they got together and devised this amnesia gag. Burned Hamlin with a little acid, probably. Cooked up a good story. 'I don't remember anything that happened till I woke up in the hospital.' That sort of thing – it's pulled every day.

Yes, it was all pretty smart. Just about the type of stuff you'd expect a bright lad like Herr Bergstrom to pull. Having Captain Wallis there on the job was just the right touch. It showed the supreme confidence and egoism of the chemist.

'I feel certain there has been some mistake,' Mrs. Hamlin said slowly, gripping the arms of her chair. 'I did not see John's body. I did not want to look at it. But I knew, as I sat there staring at the coffin this afternoon, that my husband was in it.'

'But,' Bergstrom pointed out calmly, 'there iss no way you *could* know, Mrs. Hamlin. No way in the world, because – John iss in bed in the next room. Alive. Delirious, seriously burned, very ill – but *alive!*'

He shouted that last word in a way that sent a chill down my spine – even though I'd suspected all along that Hamlin wasn't dead.

And then all at once I was conscious of a voice from the room on the far side. Someone in there had been talking for quite a while, talking very softly. And now, as Spike and I and the people in the living room listened, the voice grew louder. We could catch a word or two: 'Valence of three. . . . calcium chloride . . . neutralized . . .'

What a shock to that woman who was sitting there so white and rigid. A voice, literally, from the dead!

I felt my hair standing on end. I heard Spike's fast and unsteady breathing. I could feel his body shaking with the tension of nerves about to snap. Let me tell you, it was electric!

Bergstrom stepped to the other door. He threw it open. The room was dark but we heard that rasping voice going on monotonously: '. . . carbon union in the aliphatic hydrocarbons has apparently the same effect on the boiling point as two hydrogen atoms. But as I was telling you, Kurt, an acetylenic or triple linkage is associated with a rise in the boiling point. However . . .'

Mrs. Hamlin was on her feet, staring into the darkened room. She screamed: 'No! No!'

Bergstrom said patiently, gently: 'But yes, Mrs. Hamlin. Surely you recognize John's voice.'

The woman caught the arm of a chair, steadied herself. 'I tell you,' she cried hysterically, 'John is *dead!*'

'No. John iss very much alive.'

Bergstrom reached inside the door, flipped the switch. The bedroom was bright with light. Looking straight across the living room, I could see a figure in the bed. I caught a glimpse of a head swathed in bandages. I saw lips moving. I heard the deadly monotonous voice going on and on.

'. . . true of the fatty acid series, Kurt, and the corresponding ketones and . . .'

Then the bedroom door was blocked by the angular figure of Mrs. Hamlin. She swayed against the frame, caught herself, screamed: 'No, no, I tell you! It can't be true! He can't be alive! I killed him myself with a hammer. I got into the plant with a key to the back door. I've had it for months. I crept up behind him. I knocked him down. I poured gasoline over him and struck a match. I saw him burn. *I saw him burn!*'

All this in a wild screech that sent icy chills up and down my spine. John Hamlin's voice went on:

'. . . although, Kurt, the correlation of melting point with constitution has not . . .'

The tall woman covered her face with her angular hands. She screamed through her bony fingers: '*I tell you I killed him!*'

Then she dropped in a dead faint.

'. . . symmetry of the resulting molecule may exert such a lowering effect that the final result . . .'

'Westoby!' Bergstrom yelled, 'Ged out uf bed und turn that damn' thing off. If I haff to listen to John Hamlin's voice one minute longer I shall haff hysterics!'

Well, after Mrs. Hamlin had snapped out of her faint and Captain Wallis had taken her away, we were all pretty limp. Bergstrom brought out a bottle and some ice, and we all sat down and tried to come back to earth. The chemist remarked finally:

'Fortunately, Hamlin had been helping me with my sount devize. I suppose I haff a mile or two uf film on which his voice iss recorded.'

Westoby, who is one of the chemist's lab men, added: 'Lucky, too, the film was stored in the physical laboratory in the south wing, which the fire didn't touch.'

The Duchess was smiling. 'And speaking of luck, wasn't it a break that I brushed against Mrs. Hamlin's coat in her hallway the other night?'

'Huh?' Spike grunted. 'What's Mrs. Hamlin's coat got to do with it?'

'It was wet, darling,' Katie said pleasantly. 'There were beads of rain on the fur collar. And Mrs. Hamlin had told us she hadn't left the house that evening.'

'Look here!' Spike snorted. 'Do you mean to tell me you had the play doped from the beginning?'

'I had it doped, as you put it, within an hour or two after I brushed against that wet coat.'

'Well, Duchess, I got to hand it to you. You're the top.' He drained his glass and stood up. 'Bergstrom, you've put on a grand show and we'll give your sound recorder a million dollars' worth of publicity. Now I've got to hit a phone with the story. Okay to use yours?'

'No,' Bergstrom said steadily. 'It iss most decidedly nod okay to use mine.'

'Huh?' Spike gasped. 'Wha-zat?'

Bergstrom, still smiling, bowed to Katie. And the Duchess rose.

'Mrs. Bergstrom has ordered the operator to accept no out-going calls,' she informed us. 'So if you want to give your office the story, Spike, you'll have to find another telephone.'

She moved toward the door, adding over her shoulder: 'If you can, and that will be quite a job!'

'If I can!' Spike bellowed, and started after her. 'While I've got the use of my legs, I guess—'

Katie threw open the door. Lounging in the hall outside I caught a glimpse of half a dozen of the toughest looking punks I ever saw outside of a penitentiary – or a morning paper's circulation department. Spike stopped in his tracks.

'Keep them here, boys, until midnight,' the Duchess ordered cheerfully. 'And try not to hurt them too badly if they make a break.'

'We won't hurt 'em, Miss Katie,' a big bruiser grinned. 'Not *much*!'

Well, they didn't hurt us – because we didn't make a break. We stayed there till midnight, drinking very good whisky with Kurt Bergstrom and wondering where we ever got the idea that the Duchess was silly, and dumb, and slow on the pick-up.

MANSION OF DEATH
&
CONCEALED WEAPON
ROGER TORREY

It was rumored that Roger Torrey's real name was Torres, but he insisted he was of Irish descent and apparently tried to prove it by giving most of his cops and private detectives Irish names. And with so many other pulp writers, famous and not-so-famous, he was a heavy drinker of such mythical stature that he found the perfect woman for him – in a bar. Also a hard-drinking writer, she moved into his hotel room and they established a system of producing fiction that seems to have worked for them. He sat at one desk, she at another, with a bottle of booze nearby. The first person to finish the story on which they were working was permitted to drink while the other had to finish the story before being allowed to have a nip. Torrey, a veteran of the pulps, wrote faster, so generally finished first, then drank and mocked her while getting smashed. A prolific as well as gifted short story writer, Torrey produced fifty stories for *Black Mask* alone, writing for many other publications as well. He wrote only one novel, *42 Days for Murder*, published by the un-prestigious house of Hillman-Curl in 1938. In 'Mansion of Death,' Torrey has produced the most atypical story one could imagine in the pages of a pulp as a little old lady takes a hard-boiled detective and leads him around by the nose. It was originally published in the *Detective Fiction Weekly* issue of May 25, 1940. 'Concealed Weapon' is a more common story of a private eye with an invaluable female assistant, first published in the December 1938 issue of *Black Mask*.

MANSION OF DEATH
ROGER TORREY

I liked the old lady the first time I saw her ... but then, I've always gotten along better with old ladies than with the young ones. Though maybe that's because I've never worried about the old ones as much. Anyway, she came in the office and held out her hand as if she expected me to bow over it, and said:

'I'm Miss Conklin! I talked with you over the telephone, young man.'

I bowed, though I hadn't intended any such foolishness, and told her I was glad to meet her in person. And she twinkled her bright little blue eyes at me and shook her finger at me and said:

'Now young man! You're glad to see me because I'm a customer.'

And then she perched on the edge of the chair I'd bounced around the desk and brought up for her.

She was really cute. She looked like an old-fashioned grandmother dressed up in Fifth Avenue clothes. They fitted her beautifully and undoubtedly had cost her a lot of money. But she didn't seem to belong in them. She should have been wearing a lot of ruffles with lace around her neck and a poke bonnet. And Congress gaiters instead of high-heeled shoes. I sat down on my own side of the desk and asked:

'What was it, Miss Conklin?'

'I've been robbed,' she said calmly. 'And I don't like it. I don't like the feeling of not being able to trust my own household.'

I said that was understandable. She went on: 'There was $1,864 taken from my desk drawer. There was an envelope containing slightly more than $50,000 in negotiable bonds directly beside the money, but that wasn't touched. No one had broken in the house and it's self-evident that some one in the house itself is guilty of the theft. I don't wish to have the police tramping over my house and asking innocent people a lot of silly questions, but I *do* want to catch the thief.'

'Suppose I find the guilty person. Will you turn him – or her, if that's the way it turns out, over to the police?'

She shook her head and said: 'I will not. I have an odd household, Mr. Shay. If you'll ride up to the house with me, I'll explain that remark on our way.'

343

I took my gun from its place in the upper desk drawer and started to slip it in the clip under my arm – and she frowned and said:

'You will not need a weapon, Mr. Shay. I'm sure there'll be no necessity for one.'

So I put the gun back and reached for my hat instead. She hadn't talked about payment for what I was or wasn't going to do, and I thought I'd better look over things before bringing the subject up.

I wasn't worried; people who leave eighteen hundred odd dollars loose in desk drawers can usually pay a private cop's starvation wages.

Her chauffeur was an ugly bird that looked as though he'd just got out of jail. And the funny part of it was he just had. She told me all about it on the way up to the house. She said:

'My house is staffed with people who have been . . . well, let us say in houses of correction. I believe they should be given a helping hand and a chance to earn an honest living, once they have paid their debt to society.'

'And you keep eighteen hundred dollars, loose, in a desk drawer. Along with fifty thousand dollars worth of bonds that could be hocked with any fence.'

She said: 'I have never been robbed, young man. Never.'

'What about now?'

She sounded stiff and old-ladyish now. 'There is some mistake, young man. Of that I am sure. One of my people must have faced a problem that only money could solve. Something he or she couldn't come to me about.'

I told her I faced the same sort of a problem every rent day and listened to more. She had a nephew and niece with her, besides the jail help. And then I got a shock. She said:

'My nephew is George Lawrence, Jr. His sister is Frances Lawrence. I understand they are fairly well-known among the younger set.'

'I know Georgie, Miss Conklin,' I said. 'If you have your driver stop, I'll get out here and go back to my office.'

She asked me what was the matter and I told her. I said: 'I had the pleasure of knocking young Georgie almost over the *Black Cat Club's* bar, just night before last. I'm surprised you didn't hear about it – the newspapers had a lot of fun with the thing.'

'I know all about it,' she said placidly. 'In fact, that's one reason I came to you. George has had that coming to him for some time. He came home with a black eye, after my lawyer bailed him out of jail, and told me all about it.'

'What did he say?'

She twinkled her eyes at me and said: 'You can depend on it not being the truth. But I asked questions and found out the truth. That should happen oftener to the boy.'

'You're not sore about it?'

'My goodness no! I'm grateful to you, Mr. Shay. You'll find George isn't the kind to cherish a grudge, Mr. Shay. . . . Just forget all about the episode.'

Personally I thought young Georgie would carry a grudge until the day he died, but I didn't care a whoop whether he did or not. He was one of those loud-mouthed freshies that grates on me, and I was perfectly willing to knock him over a bar whenever we met. A bar was the logical place to look for young George. The kid was a society swack and they don't come any swackier than that.

And then we pulled into the driveway and up to her house.

It could have been turned into a library without much trouble; it had the lines and the size. An old place and very dignified. I helped her, judging her to weigh not over eighty pounds wringing wet and with lead in her shoes, and as we watched the chauffeur swing the car on and around toward the garage, she cautioned me:

'Now use tact, Mr. Shay! I want none of my people worried. The innocent shouldn't suffer for the thoughtlessness of one.'

Then the butler opened the door and we went in.

I got a break right off the bat. Fresh from the griddle. The butler was Preacher Toomey, who usually did his time for slipping up on some confidence racket. Of course he'd taken one jolt for armed robbery and another for assault with intent to kill, but they were outside of his regular field of endeavor.

'Why hello, Preacher,' I said.

He bowed and looked at me out of mean little eyes.

'Good afternoon, Mr. Shay.'

Little Miss Conklin twinkled her eyes at both of us and marveled: 'Well, isn't this nice. You know each other then?'

'You might say a professional acquaintance, eh, Preacher?' I said.

Preacher said: 'Yes, sir.'

And then Miss Conklin and I went in the library and found the maid.

She hadn't been dead long . . . and her name had been Mary Morse. At least that was one of them. She'd done time for everything from shoplifting on up. Somebody had caved in her right temple with something that hadn't broken the skin at all. The skull bone there is not much thicker than paper and it was crushed in all right, but there was no blood. Just a sort of darkening, where blood vessels below the skin had broken.

Miss Conklin and I had walked in on her together, and I turned to catch the old lady when she fainted, but she just caught the corner of the desk to steady herself.

'My goodness sake!'

'I'll call the police,' I said.

She waved her hand, palm up, in front of her, but didn't speak for a moment. And then she said: 'Not for a little while, please. I ask that, Mr. Shay.'

'It's the law, Miss Conklin. They have to be notified at once.'

'Not for a little while, please. I can handle any trouble resulting from your not calling them at once, I can assure you.'

I thought the moment I got a chance at a phone I'd call, so didn't argue. Just looked at the dead girl.

She'd been pretty. She was maybe twenty-five or twenty-eight, not over that, and she'd been a good-sized wench. Probably around a hundred and thirty, though she didn't look half that big lying there.

Dead people never do look their weight – they seem to shrink.

There was no sign around of anything she could have been hit with; I decided it was probably a shot-filled sap, though it could have been some home-made affair, filled with sand or anything like that. She was right by the desk, and the drawer above her was half open, as though she might have been searching in it. She was dressed in a neat little black and white outfit – the kind that has a little apron all frilled at the edges and a cap to match.

The cap was still on her head, but it was riding a little cock-eyed.

'This is murder, Miss Conklin, and the first thing to do is call the police.'

'I know exactly what to do, Mr. Shay,' she said. 'Please don't ask any questions now. Just come with me.'

We went out in the hall then and found Preacher Toomey still puttering around there. Miss Conklin said:

'Toomey, have there been any visitors?'

'Why no, Miss Conklin,' he told her. 'Mr. Franks is here calling on Miss Lawrence, but that is all that I know of.'

'Is Mr. Lawrence in?'

'Yes, ma'am.'

'You haven't been out, have you, Toomey? You'd surely know if there's strangers here?'

'I've been here all afternoon, ma'am.'

'Noticed anything wrong?'

'Why no, ma'am.'

She told him that was all and we went back to the library. She said then, in a tired voice: 'Well, I wanted to be sure. I'll call the police now. . . . It was possible somebody else had killed poor Mary, but now it's surely someone in the house. Toomey would say if there'd been anybody else here.'

'Would he know for sure?'

She said: 'If he knew this had happened, he'd have said that various unknown people had been in and out. Toomey is no fool, Mr. Shay; he would realize that he and everyone else in the house would be under immediate suspicion. Because of their past lives, you know.'

That made sense. Then there was a knock on the door and Toomey followed it, stopping just inside where he couldn't see the dead girl's body.

'Might I have a few words, Miss Conklin?'

She said he could. He looked at me and said: 'Of course I know Mr. Shay is here investigating the robbery, Miss Conklin. I'd just like to say I know nothing about it. I want to tell both you and Mr. Shay that I'm innocent, that I'm leading a decent life.'

'I'm sure you are, Toomey,' she said. 'But I'd like to know just how you knew about the robbery. I told no one.'

'Morse told me of it, ma'am. I'm sure I don't know how she knew. . . . She informed me it was confidential, but all of us seem to know of it.'

He bowed then and left, and Miss Conklin said: 'I told no one about the robbery but George and his sister. Do you suppose one of them could have told poor Mary?'

I didn't know the sister but I knew George, and the way he chased girls. And I knew that Mary had just adored being chased – and had never run very fast when pursued. And she'd still been a good-looking gal and young George had money. I got the answer right away, but I only said:

'I'm sure I don't know.'

'I'll call the police now,' she sighed. 'I *do* wish this hadn't happened. The police will certainly be most abrupt with my people – there's nothing I can do to prevent it.'

I thought her using 'abrupt' as a description of what the police would be with her collection of jailbirds was a miracle of understatement, but I let that go along with the other. She picked up the telephone and I wandered out in the hall.

Toomey was waiting for me. He beckoned me away from the door, and when I followed he said:

'Look, shamus! That's gospel that I gave in there. I haven't done a thing.'

'I believe you,' I said, 'that's the funny part of it. If it had been you, you'd have taken the bonds along with the dough. You'd have gone hook, line, and sinker – and left the town because you couldn't take that along too. Okay! *Now* what?'

'I didn't want you picking at me all the time, is all. Maybe I'm no lily, but I'm clear on this deal.'

'I get it, Preacher. You were holding off – waiting to get a chance at a *real* killing. Who's this guy Franks you told Miss Conklin was here?'

'He's the gal's sweetie. He tags her all around. He comes here every day.'

'What kind of a guy is he?'

He shrugged. '*She* likes him. She's going to marry him.'

*

347

I went back in the library and Miss Conklin hung up the phone and said: 'The police tell me they will be here at once. Oh my goodness! The trouble my poor people will have.'

I grinned and she saw it. She said sharply: 'Mr. Shay! These poor unfortunate victims of our society are entitled to decent treatment, once they have made penance. There's no reason why they shouldn't be treated as any decent citizen should be. I want you to think of that.'

I thought of Preacher Toomey and the cutthroat that had driven us to the house – and the Lord knows what other specimens she had around – and said:

'You think of it, Miss Conklin. I'd as soon live in a cage with wild tigers as here.'

'That is very unfair,' she said.

I waved toward the desk that shielded the dead Mary Morse and said: 'If Mary could talk, I'll bet she wouldn't agree with you.'

The cops came and there was merry hell to pay. They lined up the help and of all the collection I ever saw they won in a walk. They'd have made the average police line-up look like a meeting of the Ladies Aid. The chauffeur had served time in Dannemora and Joliet. One gardener had taken a course at McAlester, in Oklahoma, and a P.G. at Folsom, in California. The other one had graduated from Leavenworth, which is a Federal pen. The cook was an old gal who'd killed her husband with a frying pan and had done seven years for the trick. The two other maids were about in the dead Mary Morse's class, though they didn't own the looks she'd had.

And then there was young George Lawrence, who was a worthless bum if one ever walked. He was half drunk, and when he saw me wanted to pick up the argument where we'd left it off two nights before.

The cops stopped him quick on that – telling him they'd do all the fighting necessary.

Franks, the Lawrence girl's fiancé, was a thin-faced, dark young fellow. He seemed to be okay. I didn't know anything about him, but I wondered how a honey like the Lawrence girl could go for him. She could have done better, with what she had to work with, which was practically everything it takes.

She was small and blonde, and had that wide-set appealing stare that makes you want to pick 'em up and cuddle 'em and tell 'em everything will be all right.

Nobody had any alibi – the cops found that out right away. Nobody had any notion about who didn't like Mary Morse. Or said they hadn't. And then I got a break. The cops were ganged up, talking to one of the gardeners, and Preacher Toomey caught my eye and beckoned me over to him. He said, so no one else could hear it:

348

'Listen, Shay! I'll do you a favor and maybe you can do one back for me. The kid, young Georgie, was mixed up with the gal. She was clipping him for all the dough he could get his hands on.'

'You sure?'

'Certain. She bragged about it.'

'Did his aunt know about it?'

'Listen, Shay! If there's one single, solitary thing goes on in this house that she don't know about, I'll put in with you. She's so smart it's painful.'

'Nuts!' I said. 'If she was, she'd never have a bunch like she's got here around her. Was the kid still playing around with the Morse dame?'

'Sure. But she was taking him for dough and he was sore about it. He beat hell out of her three weeks ago. . . . His aunt kept her from calling the cops in on it. That'll give you an idea of how much she knows about it. You going to tell the cops?'

'Why don't you?'

He said gloomily: 'That'd make 'em think I was trying to pass the buck to somebody else. The best thing I can do is keep my mouth shut.'

I told him I thought it a very good idea . . . and I did the same. I figured there'd be plenty of time to tell it later.

It ended right there. The Captain in charge, Chick Williams, grumbled to Miss Conklin: 'And what can I do about it? I tell you I'll take your crew down to the station for questioning and you tell me that you'll have 'em out on a writ of habeas corpus as soon as you can get in touch with your lawyer. What can I do, lady? – You tie my hands.'

'I know very well what would happen to them at the station,' Miss Conklin said primly. 'They would be brow-beaten, if not physically beaten. They have told you what they know.'

'Every damned one of them has stood in front of me and lied by the clock.'

'Can you prove that, officer?'

Williams admitted he couldn't. Miss Conklin said: 'Then I certainly wouldn't make the statement. These people look to me for protection and I intend to see they have it.'

Williams went away, growling about making a check on everybody in the place and on the dead girl's past life. And as soon as he left I told Miss Conklin what Toomey had told me. She gave me a queer stare and said:

'But you didn't tell the police?'

I said that I hadn't as yet. . . .

'Give me a couple of days, Mr. Shay. If I don't think of a plan by that time, you and I will go together, taking Toomey with us, and see he tells his story to the police. I naturally don't want my nephew in jail if he's innocent, though if he's guilty that's the place for him.'

I said: 'Will you tell me honestly what you think about it?'

'I don't think George is guilty – I can tell you that much,' she said, pursing her lips and looking like a grandmother making up her mind about how many jars of pickles to put up. 'No, I really don't.'

'Why not?'

'He hasn't the nerve, Mr. Shay. He's too dependent on me to do a thing like that. Rather than kill the girl, he'd have come to me and made a clean breast of the matter.'

'He did – once. When he beat the girl up and you went to the front for him and kept her from calling in the cops.'

'Toomey told you that, too?'

'You bet.'

She smiled then. 'Doesn't that support my theory, Mr. Shay? If he'd had murder in his mind, wouldn't he have committed it then, rather than just abuse the girl? He knew then I'd find it out.'

'People can change,' I told her. 'Sometimes a man can be driven just so far. And then he'll back up.'

She admitted that maybe I was right and that she'd get in touch with me at my office in a day or so. And I left, wondering why I didn't tell the cops what I knew and have them take the young punk down to the station and sweat a confession out of him.

He was my customer for the killing and there wasn't a doubt in my mind about it. And the only thing holding me back from turning him in was the old lady. In my business, a client's always right, at least until proved a mile wrong. She was a client and so I went along with her on the two days of grace she asked for. I couldn't see it, but there was an outside chance of somebody else having done the killing – and it was just possible that she had an idea who it was.

And, after all, the cops could pick up young Lawrence just as well two days later as then.

She came in two days later, looking even smaller and more fragile. She gave me her pretty, anxious smile and said:

'I have thought it all out, Mr. Shay. There is absolutely no way to prove who killed that girl. Nor who took my money.'

'That's ridiculous,' I told her. 'The cops could take the whole bunch down to the station, and they'd have a confession in twenty-four hours. You know that.'

'It wouldn't be fair to the ones that didn't do it,' she said stubbornly. 'I have a deep feeling about such things. Now I have worked out a plan and I'm sure it will be successful. But I need your help.'

I said I was still working for her, as far as I knew.

So then she told me what she wanted – and I finally said I'd do it. I'd argued two hours and hadn't won a point, before I caved.

'Then I'll depend on you,' she finished. 'I'm supposed to be playing bridge this afternoon, and I'm not expected back until around eight. As I told you, I told George and Toomey that I knew who'd killed Mary Morse and that I intended to tell the police about it tomorrow. I can depend on Toomey telling the others about it.'

'They'd think it was funny you not telling the police right then,' I said.

'Oh no! I told them I was waiting for certain proof,' she said. 'And that I'd find that out tomorrow. But that there was no doubt in my mind right then. So you see I've thought of everything.'

'I'm beginning to think you have,' I said.

I got into the house easily enough. . . . She'd given me the key to a side door that opened into the library, and it was just a question of making sure no one was in the room and then walking in. I moved a couch, at the corner of the room, far enough out to climb behind it, then got it back in place. It made a snug little nest. If I sat down naturally, the thing was just low enough for me to see over, and if I ducked my head a little, I was entirely out of sight.

And then I waited.

Miss Conklin came in a little after nine and never even looked toward where I was. She had that much will power. She was humming to herself, as though she hadn't a care in the world. She got a book from a shelf and sat down in a big chair that almost hid her. Her back was to the door. I could hear pages rustle as she turned them. . . . Then there was a knock on the door, and she called 'Come in!' without looking around.

It was young Georgie. And he looked bad with the black eye I'd given him. I slid my gun out of its clip and got ready to go into action. He passed around in front of her and stood.

'Aunt Alice,' he said, 'I've got to talk to you.'

'Go ahead, George.'

And then I got a shock. 'I heard what you told Frances,' he said, 'and she told me you'd told Toomey the same thing. That you knew who killed Mary.'

'That's right,' she said. 'I intend to notify the police tomorrow. As I told Frances, there's one little detail I want cleared up and I can't do that until tomorrow.'

Then came the pay-off. The kid said: 'I'm going to stay right here with you, Aunt Alice. Don't you realize that you're in danger? The same person who killed Mary knows by now that you know who he is. He's liable to try to silence you. I'm going to stay right here with you.'

Miss Conklin said: 'No, George. I'm perfectly all right. But I thank you for the thought. Now run along – don't waste your time talking to an old lady.'

'I'm going to stay, Aunt Alice.'

The old lady didn't raise her voice, but it now had a snap in it. She just said: 'George!'

'All right, Aunt Alice, you know best.'

He marched out of the room, just barely giving me time to duck out of sight. Then the old lady said, as if she were talking to herself:

'Nice boy, George.'

So there was my number one suspect cleared. . . . I was just getting over the shock of that when there was another knock and the niece came in. Looking like a million dollars! She bounced over in front of her auntie and knelt down and said:

'Oh, Aunt Alice! Aren't you afraid? You know this is Toomey's night off.'

Miss Conklin said: 'Yes, I've thought of that.'

'But aren't you frightened, Aunt Alice?'

I didn't hear what Aunt Alice said because I was too busy ducking back out of sight. The hall door was opening – very quietly and softly – and I wanted to be out of sight until whoever it was had passed me.

And he did. It was young Franks, the girl's fiancé. He was walking on his toes and he was swinging a sap in his left hand. The girl looked over her aunt's head at him and said to the aunt:

'I just thought I'd better stay with you, Aunt Alice. Just in case of. . . .'

I shot young Franks then, taking him just below the knee, where I had a lot of brittle shin bone to aim at. A slug from the kind of gun I shoot will wreck bone structure of that kind and leave a man crippled for life . . . and I was thinking of that. The girl stood and screamed. It cut through the roaring thunder the big gun made in the room. And Miss Conklin got up from her big chair and peered down at Franks, who was rolling around on the floor and making a lot of noise.

'It's as I thought,' Miss Conklin said calmly. 'Mr. Shay, will you telephone for the police. I'm going to be very busy for a few minutes.'

She didn't pay any more attention to me, but went over to a drawer built in the bookcase. She pulled out a heavy riding whip. And then she went back to the girl and said:

'Now, you little sneak! I'm going to take the hide right off your damned back. You ungrateful little—!'

And then, by heaven, she did. She had a nice command of language and every time she gave the girl a new title she came down with the whip.

I didn't want to interfere, but finally I had to.

'You don't want to kill her, do you?' I said.

She stopped then.

'Did you call the police?' she asked.

I said I hadn't but would right away. And then somebody said, from the door doorway: 'I did, ma'am!'

We turned and looked that way. And here was the cook, the chauffeur, and the two maids staring in. The chauffeur said:

'I called when I heard the shot, ma'am. Then I came in to help.'

I said to Miss Conklin: 'You going to turn the girl over to the cops?'

'Certainly not,' she snapped. 'I can take care of her very well. The man, the sneak, he will certainly go to prison, if he doesn't hang.'

'He'll limp when he goes down that hall to the scaffold,' I told her. 'Did you think it was him all the time?'

'Of course,' she said.

And then the cops came.

She came down to see me the next afternoon again. Just as nice as though nothing had happened. She even blushed a little when she asked me how much money I wanted. And I blushed even more when I told her – because all I'd done was what she'd told me to do. She'd supposedly hired a detective and then she'd done all the detective work. She gave me a check.

'Miss Conklin,' I said, 'I don't like to appear too dumb, but what made you think it was young Franks who'd killed the maid? You told me you had that idea right along. Of course we know now why he did it – she'd seen him swipe the dough from your desk. She started to blackmail him, the same as she was already blackmailing your nephew. Of course not for the same reason. But I'd like to know why you picked him as the guilty one, instead of George, or Preacher Toomey, or that thug chauffeur or those gardeners?'

She twinkled her eyes at me and said: 'Why it just *had* to be him, Mr. Shay. I knew that none of my people would steal – and of course I knew my nephew wouldn't. Not that I'd put it past the boy, but there was no need for him to steal; all he had to do was ask me for the money and I'd have given it to him. So that left only Frances and her friend. And do you know, I've never trusted that young man since the first time I met him.'

'But you'd trust that collection of jailbirds you've got?'

'Why of course,' she said pensively. 'You see I know their peculiar psychology. And then I had another reason for thinking young Mr. Franks the murderer. You see poor Mary had been struck on the right temple – that showed me a left-handed man had struck the blow. Just try it – you're right-handed, and you'll notice if you strike another person on the temple it will invariably be on the left side. This was just reversed. And, of course, my nephew, and all the others in the house, happen to be right-handed. Young Mr. Franks is the only left-handed one. But I really didn't need that proof – and it isn't the sort of thing that would stand up in court.'

She went out then and left me trying to figure things out. Not the left-handed angle – that's one of the simple things you overlook because it is *so* simple.

It was the old gal herself. Here she'd acted like one of the nicest ladies I'd ever met – up to the time she'd found out for sure her niece was in the plot to kill her. And even then she didn't turn the girl over to the police. Instead she gave her a beating, and kept her where she could keep an eye on her.

And then the language she'd used was hardly the thing a lady knows.

And to top the whole thing off – having that collection of thugs around her and actually protecting them from the police.

It was all by me.

It stayed that way until I met Chick Williams, the police captain, who'd been in charge of the case. I ran into him on the street and he laughed and said:

'You still working for the Conklin woman?'

I told him I'd like to have her for a partner . . . that she'd shown more brains in the thing than either he or I had. He didn't like this so well and told me that if he'd had his way, and taken the whole bunch down to the station and sweated them, that he'd have had the answer before the old lady had it.

I agreed. And then he laughed again and poked me with a finger and said: 'You know who that old gal *is?* I just happened to mention her to one of the old-timers, who dropped in the office . . . and he remembered her.'

I said I didn't know who she was, other than she seemed like a nice, old gal with a lot of money. Then he poked me again and winked and said:

'She's *the* Miss Conklin. The one that scragged her sweetie, over forty years ago, and did sixteen years in the pen for it. Cold-blooded murder it was, according to the old boy. He said it was a wonder they *ever* let her out. She'd fell into a bunch of dough while she was doing time, and that probably had something to do with that angle. Ain't that a kick, Shay?'

I said it was very funny and felt a lot better. It solved the puzzle. Here I'd been wondering why she'd looked after her convict help and claimed to understand 'em. Why shouldn't she?

And it explained the language she'd used to the girl and the whip act. They talk rough and they handle their own problems in the women's wards in jails.

I left Williams. I was thinking that it would be a good bet the jail was glad to see her go. I'm willing to bet the warden slept better.

Because I had the notion that Miss Conklin would be top dog wherever she was. . . . She was one client of mine that had been right on every count.

CONCEALED WEAPON
ROGER TORREY

The man came weaving down the hall of the office building and McCarthy said to Marge Chalmers: 'Jeez! That guy's got seven dollars' worth of start. What a load!'

McCarthy turned and slammed his office door and the spring lock took hold with a click. The stranger in the hall lurched into Marge and would have fallen if she hadn't held him up with a short but sturdy arm. McCarthy said pleasantly enough:

'Hey, guy! Take it some place else. You better go some place and sleep it off.'

The man's face was a dingy white. Even with Marge's support he was standing bent and twisted. He muttered something and McCarthy said tolerantly:

'All right, guy! I didn't hear you. But you ain't the first to get this way.'

Marge said, not tolerantly: '*You* should tell him that! You, of all people!' And then, with a total change in tone: 'Pat! The man's hurt!'

The man proved it by quietly falling on the floor in spite of Marge's attempt at holding him erect. He went down in a loose and sodden pile, and Marge looked up from him and snapped: 'Pat!'

McCarthy was already in action. He was stooping and tearing the man's coat open, and when he saw the blood mottling the white shirt he said:

'Oke, kitten! We won't move him. Call the ambulance and the cops. Quick! If we move him, it might make it worse.'

'What is it, Pat?'

McCarthy pointed out a half-dozen holes in the bloody shirt. 'Maybe an ice pick, I don't know. But they're in his belly, and that means he shouldn't be moved. Get going.'

Marge took his keys and opened the office.

The police came, after a little while, cars full of them, as did the ambulance. McCarthy watched Doctor Solari straighten up from the wounded man, and that smart young man said to him:

'Maybe we're in time. Unless the fellow gets a transfusion inside the next few minutes he'll be shaking hands with Saint Peter.'

'How bad, Doc?' McCarthy asked.

Solari had a smooth and unlined face. He looked to be about twenty –
but he had ten years and a reputation of being an authority on the sort of
violence police are faced with added to the innocent look. He stared up at
the ceiling, as though looking at something new and different, and said:

'Well, he's been pierced, through and through, with something. I'm not
prepared to say exactly just what, but if this had happened down in colored
town I'd say the weapon was an ice pick. They favor that down there; ice
picks don't come under the head of concealed weapons. Now this man has
twelve wounds in his abdomen and has lost some blood. The shock was
slight, owing to the nature of the wound. He will most certainly have
peritonitis as his intestines are most certainly pierced through and through.
He may get through it if he isn't too far along to react to a transfusion.
Now does that answer you, Mr. McCarthy?'

McCarthy said, 'In a big way, Doc. It means the guy's got a chance,
don't it?'

'If he gets a transfusion immediately. I'm having him removed to the
hospital at once.'

Two husky white-coated men came in with a stretcher. They lifted the
now unconscious man on this with Dr. Solari assisting, and then there
came an outraged bellow from the outer office. A voice came out distinctly
with:

'Hey! Miss Marge! I got to see the Chief.'

McCarthy muttered, 'That damn Benny!' and went through the knot of
policemen and into the outer office.

Benny Cohn, McCarthy's pet cabbie, was at the door. He apparently
didn't want to stay there but two policemen, who had him by the arms,
were winning the argument about just where Benny was going. Or staying.
Benny saw McCarthy and stopped struggling and said:

'Hey, Chief! I come up to see you and it seems I can't. They tell me I
got to stay outside, they do, Chief.'

McCarthy said, 'Let him go.'

Marge, who'd been awaiting the doctor's report, said, 'Personally, I
think one of us ought to see about a transfusion for this man. He fell into
our arms in front of your office. How is he?'

'He might make it. . . . What d'ya want, Benny? I'm busy.'

Benny said, 'And so am I busy, Chief. Like I say, these cops won't let
me in and see you. I got to see you, Chief. No fooling, I got to see you.'

'What about?'

Marge broke in with: 'Does the doctor think he'll live if he gets a
transfusion?'

Benny brightened and broke away from the two policemen. He said to
McCarthy, 'Hey now, Chief! If it maybe is the guy needs the same kind of
blood that I got, maybe you can fix it for me. I took the test – they give you

thirty-five bucks for it and I got my name on the list for giving it. Maybe you can fix it for me, Chief; I got to have the dough.'

'What d'ya want to see me about?'

'That's it, Chief. Dough.'

McCarthy said, 'Then I certainly will try to fix it. If you can earn it, it's better than me having to give it to you.'

Marge said, 'But, Lord, what will the harvest be? With the man full of Benny's blood!'

McCarthy fixed it with no trouble. The wounded man's blood was typed, in a hurry, and found to match that of Benny's. McCarthy and Marge left the hospital, McCarthy grinning, and he said:

'That's the easiest thirty-five bucks I ever made in my life. I'd have had to give it to him if he hadn't made it this way.'

'Why?'

McCarthy said uncomfortably, 'Well, you know how Benny is. He never makes any dough out of his hack and now he's jammed.'

'How?'

McCarthy sounded even more uncomfortable. 'Well, he's been running around with some gal. He got in a little argument with her and slapped her. And she says unless he pays for the three teeth he knocked out she'll have him thrown in the sneezer.'

'Swell kid, Benny is.'

'Hell, baby, if Benny thought I wanted somebody's teeth knocked out he'd do it for me just as quick as he would for himself. He's that way.'

'That's just it,' Marge said warmly. 'He's always getting you in trouble over things like that. You know he is.'

McCarthy led the way into a Bar and Grill and changed the subject quite effectually. He fanned out five brand new hundred dollar bills and said nothing. Neither did Marge for a moment. Her blue eyes bulged and she finally gasped:

'Pat! Where did you get that?'

McCarthy said, in a complacent voice, 'From the guy, kitten. Before the cops came – before they took him into my office. He had five hundred and forty bucks in his wallet, beside a few cards, and I left him the forty bucks and the wallet. I told the hospital I'd guarantee his bill, though, so it won't be all clear profit.'

'But, Pat! It isn't your money.'

McCarthy looked injured and dragged out some cards. He held one out to her and she took it and read: Billy Tucker's Roadhouse. She said:

'What has a man named Billy Tucker got to do with you taking the stabbed man's money?'

'Turn it over, kitten.'

Marge did this. The card had McCarthy's name scrawled in pencil on it, as well as his office address. He said:

'See! It's got my name on it. The guy was probably on his way up to see me when he got stabbed. So this is my retainer; I can't be expected to work for nothing. And anyway, he can't use it right now and I can.'

Marge shook her head and said, 'Let's look over the rest of the cards. What d'ya suppose he wanted to see you for?'

'Probably to keep from getting stabbed,' McCarthy said, spreading out the cards.

There was one that read: The Silver Slipper – Dine and Dance. One of a chop suey place and another advertising a particularly poor brand of bourbon and a bar that sold it. The Silver Slipper card had a telephone number written on it and an explanatory note that read: 'Small; blonde; drinks Scotch; Marie.' McCarthy grinned at this and said:

'The guy's got an idea. Card-indexing his women.'

He put the card down by the one bearing his address and name, then frowned. He pointed out: 'Hey, look! The same man didn't write 'em both. Look!'

The writing was decidedly different and Marge agreed that this was so. She said, 'What difference does it make?'

'Probably none. Maybe the blonde wrote her name and number for him.'

'She wouldn't have gone into details about the Scotch if she had, Pat.'

McCarthy shrugged and looked at more cards. One was of Ira. A. Halstead, Attorney-at-Law, and this was new and unsoiled. Another, equally new, was that of James R. S. Wilson. And then there were two more bar cards, which McCarthy discarded after looking them over for more telephone numbers and descriptions of girls. He studied the lawyer's card and that of Wilson and said:

'This Wilson is a big shot broker. Very strict church member and the rest of that stuff. And this lawyer Halstead has something to do with him, but I can't remember just what.'

'Why not ask him?'

McCarthy said, 'Maybe he wouldn't tell me. I'll get a guy from a newspaper and ask *him*.'

Chet Morris was the newspaper man McCarthy picked for an information bureau. He was short, fat, and almost bald, and he had a notorious passion for checked and wildly patterned suits. McCarthy opened up with:

'Hi, Chet! That's new, ain't it?'

Morris looked down at the plaid affairs that made him look even more roly-poly than ever and said, 'It's half paid for, anyway.'

'It looks good.'

Abe Goldstein, who worked the police beat for a rival paper, snickered and said: 'It looks good, hell! It looks just gorgeous. Just too simply gorgeous.'

Morris managed a sickly grin for McCarthy. He gave Goldstein a cold and haughty look and said, 'Yah! Well, it cost me sixty bucks, anyway.'

The unimpressed Goldstein said that the tailor had certainly seen Mr. Morris coming from a distance and recognized him as the chump he was. He also said his brother-in-law, who was in that business, could duplicate the plaid job for not a cent over thirty-five dollars but that the said brother-in-law ran a quality store and would not have a piece of goods with a pattern like that in the shop. Morris gave up the argument and said hastily to McCarthy, sniffing the press room:

'You want to see me, Pat? Let's go outside. I got to get fresh air, every so often around here.'

Goldstein's voice followed him out with: 'That's quite a breeze you got on your back, Chet, and you can't get an argument against it from the next five guys you meet.'

'What d'ya know about Mr. James R. S. Wilson? A big shot, as I remember about him,' McCarthy asked.

Morris took off horn-rimmed glasses and started a polishing job. He said, 'Right. A very big shot. Chairman of the Community Chest drive last year. Selectman of the Trinity Church. President of Wilson, Marks and Linehan, Investment Brokers. A very big shot to be sure.'

'What about a lawyer named Ira A. Halstead?'

'Another big shot. A different kind. He's the people's friend, if you know what I mean.'

'I don't, Chet.'

'Well, he takes damage cases against railroads and such. On contingency, of course. Some people might call it a form of blackmail but as long as it's a big company that's stuck, who cares? The jury always goes for the poor devil who's suing the heartless corporation, don't they? So that makes him the people's friend, because he doesn't ask for a retainer when he takes that kind of a case.'

'What does he get?'

Morris put his glasses back on and wiped his bald spot with the handkerchief he'd used to polish them with. 'Well, usually half the damages the jury gives the victim. Less expenses, of course. But he gets big damages for his clients and very often there's a few bucks left over for them. A very few though, I'd say.'

'A nice guy, I can see.'

'Not in trouble with him, are you, Pat?'

'Not yet, anyway.'

Morris's round, good-natured face showed worry. 'He's got connections, if you know what I mean. We lay off him in the sheet. If that means anything.'

'It does, Chet. Thanks a lot.'

'Is that what you wanted to know?'

McCarthy said, 'Yeah. It made me remember something. It made me remember that Halstead is the lawyer for some guy that's suing Wilson over a car accident. I remembered it when you said he took damage cases.'

'Wilson is the sort of bird he likes to tackle,' Morris agreed. 'I don't keep up with things on this damn police beat. It's all I can do to keep up with the cops.'

'And Goldstein,' McCarthy suggested. 'Abe can take the hide off a man's back with that tongue of his.'

Morris said sadly, 'Worse than that! He just about took this suit off my back a minute ago and the thing is brand new.'

'I still say it looks good,' said McCarthy, and left.

McCarthy went from the police press room to the paper Morris honored with his services. There he looked over the clippings on the car accident James R. S. Wilson was involved in, and he looked these over thoughtfully. He finally grumbled:

'My stabbed man can be either William Bowes or he can be Antonio Giovanni. And he didn't look Italian.'

He left the newspaper morgue for a drugstore phone booth and telephoned the hospital. He said, 'I'm McCarthy. What about the man who was stabbed in my office building?'

He held the phone, far from patiently, for ten long minutes before he got the doctor in charge of the case. The doctor said:

'He's doing as well as might be expected, Mr. McCarthy. The police are here now, waiting for the man to recover enough to make a statement. This in spite of my telling them the man will be in no shape to talk for at least twenty-four hours.'

'They don't know who he is yet?'

'Apparently not. That fact seems to worry them, I might say.'

McCarthy said, disagreeably, 'It always worries the police when a man is stabbed. They're paid to worry about such things.' He consulted the phone book and got Ira A. Halstead's address and telephone number and studied the phone thoughtfully for a moment. Finally he grumbled:

'Might as well go; he wouldn't tell me anything over the phone, anyway.'

And then went hunting for a cab.

Halstead's law offices looked stately and dignified but Halstead looked like a boy barely out of college – like a boy who'd majored in athletics. He shrugged his bulky shoulders, lifted calm brown eyes from McCarthy's card, and said:

'My secretary told me it was about one of my clients, Mr. McCarthy. Will you explain?'

'I'm trying to identify a man,' McCarthy explained. 'He had nothing in his pockets but your card and I thought possibly you might be a help. He's a man of about forty and he weighs around one fifty. He's got sandy hair and eyebrows and when I last saw him he needed a shave. In fact, he'd needed one for the last couple of days. He wears a brown suit and hat and white shoes. The shoes needed cleaning. He has a scar along his jawbone, not very long but still noticeable. Can you think who that might be?'

Halstead studied the problem and then shook his head. 'I don't recall any client who that describes. You say he had my card in his pocket?'

'And that's *all* he had,' McCarthy lied, leaving out all mention of Wilson's card and the five new hundred dollar bills.

'I'm afraid I can't help you, Mr. McCarthy.'

'It wouldn't be Antonio Giovanni, would it?'

Halstead laughed. 'Antonio Giovanni is at least fifty. He isn't over five feet tall and he must weigh at least two hundred pounds. He talks broken English, very broken English. He's been in this country thirty years or more but he acts like an immigrant to this day.'

'What about William Bowes?'

McCarthy was watching Halstead's hands and he thought one of them tightened almost imperceptibly. And when he looked up he noted Halstead's eyes had lost their warm frankness and now looked wary. Halstead said, as though surprised:

'Now I never thought of him. Bowes *does* answer that description to an extent. By George, it might be Bowes at that.'

McCarthy said, 'I thought it might be.'

'Is the man in trouble? He's my witness in a rather important case that's coming to trial shortly. As a matter of fact, the Giovanni case. By George, that's why you spoke of Giovanni! You associated the two in some way! Where is the man now?'

'In the hospital. He was stabbed.'

Halstead shook his head and said, 'Poor fellow. If he dies, it will be too bad for my client, I am afraid. I was depending on his testimony to show negligence on the part of the driver who killed his son.'

'You mean Wilson.'

Halstead nodded and smiled. The warm look was back in his eyes. He leaned forward and said, 'That was an unfortunate thing. Mr. Wilson was driving along and struck young Giovanni, killing him instantly. Two days after that this man you speak of, William Bowes, got in touch with the elder Mr. Giovanni and told him he'd witnessed the accident. I may add that Mr. Wilson got in a panic immediately after the accident and drove around some time before reporting the matter to the police. You understand that makes him technically liable to a hit and run charge. Bowes insisted Mr. Wilson was entirely at fault.'

'How? How was he wrong on it?'

Halstead said, in as friendly a voice, 'Mr. McCarthy, I am a lawyer. I can't ethically answer your question. I don't understand your interest in the matter unless you should be investigating the matter for Mr. Wilson. Mr. Wilson is opposed to my client and I can't very well tell you our case against him. I hope you will understand.'

McCarthy got to his feet. 'I'm not investigating it for anybody but myself. At least not as yet. But this man Bowes was stabbed in front of my office door, and there was a reason back of it. I'm naturally interested in it. Well, thank you, Mr. Halstead.'

Halstead stood also. 'Is the man in bad shape, Mr. McCarthy? Will he recover?'

'The medicos don't know yet. He's at the Sisters of Mercy Hospital; you can keep in touch with them.'

'I'll certainly do that,' Halstead said, following McCarthy to the door. 'And thank you, Mr. McCarthy, for telling me this. As I said, Bowes is the backbone of our case. If he should die, I'm afraid we haven't one.'

McCarthy shook hands and left the office. He stood on the sidewalk for a moment, then headed for another phone booth. He got the Central Station and Detective Lieutenant Shannon, and told that big Irishman:

'I think the guy that got stabbed in front of my place is named Bowes. William Bowes. You might do a little checking on it. He's a witness in a damage case against Mr. James R. S. Wilson, if that means a thing to you.'

Shannon whistled and said, 'He's flying high, Pat. I'll look into it. How'd you get it?'

'From Halstead, the lawyer who's suing Wilson. The lawyer this Bowes is a witness for. And Shan, here's something funny. I didn't crack about where the guy was or what had happened to him or a thing that would tip Halstead off. But I talked as though something had happened to him and Halstead let it go. He seemed to think the guy was dead. Then he caught himself on it and changed it to asking questions. Does that mean anything?'

'What should it mean?' Shannon asked cautiously.

'Well, it should mean you should keep a police guard on this Bowes, if it's him, until he's out where he's got a chance to fight for himself. This Halstead is supposed to be a smart baby, that's why I talked to him the way I did.'

'He's smart, all right.'

'He's too damn smart,' said McCarthy. 'I don't trust these baby-faced boys that don't look as though they'd ever spoken out of turn in their life. They're the kind I watch because they're too good to be true. I'll be seeing you, Shan.'

'Why are you angling around on it, Irish?'

McCarthy said bitterly, 'Well, I think the guy was coming to me for help when he got the shiv in him. I don't like to lose clients that way, even if I haven't really got 'em at the time. And then I'm a Socialist or something – the poor guy didn't have any money and everybody else that seems interested in him has. Wilson and this lawyer Halstead, both. I want to see the guy get a break.'

'What do you get out of it?'

'Well, exercise, at least,' McCarthy said. 'And maybe practice.'

Benny Cohn was waiting for McCarthy by the time he got back to his office. And Benny's nose was swollen out of shape and his left eye was a lovely green and adhesive tape held down a plaster on his left cheekbone. McCarthy stared at him and said:

'What the hell happened?'

'Didja ever see one of these iron things like they press pants with, Chief?' Benny asked, in a plaintive voice. 'Well, I take the thirty-five smackers I get at the hospital and I go down to pay off this gal I was telling you about and, Chief, guess what happens.'

McCarthy said, 'I don't have to guess. I know. She clouted you with the iron.'

'Wrong, Chief, wrong. I dodge the iron, except for it bouncing off the wall and falling against my neck, sort of. But when I duck the iron, Chief, she unbuckles herself and comes at me with the ironing board thing and she lands with it. I run like hell, Chief, and no mistake.'

'Did you give her the thirty-five?'

'I never had a chance. She started in throwing that iron thing when I put my head in the door and say to her "Hi, sweetheart." Right then she starts. I mail that thirty-five to her, Chief, I mail it. And I get another thirty-five from you tomorrow or the next day, the Doc says.'

'From me!'

'The Doc says you're paying the shot, Chief, and that I should come to you for the dough. So I'll be here.'

McCarthy estimated how long five hundred dollars would last if the man in the hospital had a daily transfusion at thirty-five dollars a copy. He groaned. Benny said helpfully:

'He must be a pal of yours for you to pay off like that. The Doc says he may be in there for the next six months, on account of his guts being all cut to hell. I bet it costs you a pretty penny, Chief, a pretty penny.'

'Will you get out?' McCarthy said.

Benny went out. He poked his head around the door a moment later, however, and said, 'Hey! I get thinking about getting smacked in the puss with that iron board arrangement and I forget. You're to call Miss Marge. See, Chief! Your phone it rings and it's her and she says to call her up.'

'How long ago was this?'

'Just now, Chief.'

Benny left for the second time, and McCarthy called Marge's number. She said in a rush, as soon as she heard his voice:

'Oh, Pat! I've been trying to get you. It's Chet Morris. He tried to get you and when he couldn't he called me. He went up to see that Wilson man and told him you were checking on that accident thing or something.'

'I didn't tell him that.'

'He said that after he talked to you he got thinking and remembered that lawyer was suing Wilson. And that he thought there might be a story in it and went up to see about it. He said Wilson was very nice, but that he got telephoned at the paper, almost as soon as he got back from seeing Wilson, and that somebody told him to lay off and keep out of what didn't concern him. He thinks that means you, too. He said he didn't want to see you get in trouble.'

'Little Mother Morris,' said McCarthy, sourly. 'Why did he have to tell Wilson I was looking around?'

'He said he didn't think it made any difference.'

'Well, it probably doesn't,' McCarthy said, and made a dinner date for eight that evening.

Marge said, 'Why not at seven? I'm hungry now.'

'I've got to see this Giovanni guy that's suing Wilson first, hon. It may take me a little time to find him.'

'I see. You be careful, Pat. It worries me about what Chet Morris said.'

McCarthy laughed and said, 'You and Chet would make a good pair. You both worry.'

Antonio Giovanni owned a small and messy vegetable store in the center of Italian town and it was there McCarthy found him. Antonio was on the floor and on his face and he'd apparently been trying to crawl under a long tray-like metal affair that held vegetables beneath a spray-like arrangement. The tray, possibly four feet wide, sloped down toward the front of the store for a display, and Antonio was sprawled partly under this and looking like a large and very dead frog.

Water from the spray had seeped through on him and washed part of the blood around him away, but there was still plenty left. He'd had long sweeping mustaches and one was soaking in blood while the other hung like a brush toward the floor.

McCarthy, without touching anything, knelt and looked – and thought he'd never seen such a pitifully ridiculous corpse. He saw three small, round, and purple holes in the cheek turned toward him, saw another in the part of fat neck in view. He cursed, silently and viciously and stood, and then a voice from behind him said:

'Hey! Where's Tony?'

McCarthy turned fast. He saw a small and dirty boy of around ten with black curly hair and bigger and blacker eyes than McCarthy thought were possible. He gulped and said:

'Tony isn't here right now. You run along and come back by and by.'

The boy said, 'Ma says for him to come to supper. She says she won't wait, that it'll spoil. Where is Tony?'

'He's out right now.'

The boy said reflectively, 'Ma'll raise hell with him when he comes home. She says all he does is run along and talk to lawyers and that the store ain't run right any more.'

'Is he your dad?' asked McCarthy, going a little sick. There was no resemblance between the dead man and the boy but he got the answer he dreaded.

'Sure! I'll go back and tell Ma he ain't here. If you see him, tell him supper's ready.'

McCarthy said he'd surely do that and watched the boy swagger out. He decided that Tony had been an indulgent father and that the children had rather taken things into their own hands – basing this on the good nature still showing in the dead man's face and on knowledge of other decent, kindly, honest Italian people he'd met. He went out of there, head down and deciding he would not be the one that broke the news of Tony's death to his family.

He called the station and told Shannon what he'd found, and Shannon cursed luridly and asked him to go back and stand guard until he could get a radio car on the scene.

And McCarthy did, praying the youngster wouldn't be back looking for his father.

Chet Morris was at Marge's apartment when McCarthy got there. He was again polishing his glasses and his mild, near-sighted eyes peered up at McCarthy as he said:

'I'm sorry, pal! I guess I spoke out of turn to that big, stuffed shirt. How was I to know he'd take it the way he did?'

'You told him I'd talked to you about him? That it?'

'Yeah! I didn't stop to think a thing about it.' He put his glasses back on and this cleared his vision. He looked McCarthy over and said, in a different tone:

'What's the matter with you, Pat? You look sick.'

McCarthy said: 'I *am* sick. Marge, honey, how's about a drink? I thought I could take it but I guess I can't.'

Marge brought the drink and said anxiously, 'What's the matter, Pat? What's the matter with you?'

'I want to kill a man. This bird with the ice pick. Him or the man who hired him. That's all. I didn't know I could get so crazy mad that I'd be sick.'

Morris asked, 'What's happened?' and McCarthy told them both. Morris started toward the phone, saying: 'I'll telephone it in. With the guy in the hospital getting it the same way, it's a story. They may not get the connection.'

McCarthy said, with no inflection: 'You touch that phone, Chet, and I'll beat you to a pulp. I'm praying God that nobody will see there *is* a connection. That other business didn't rate much of a spread and maybe nobody will add 'em together. I'll work it my own way, Chet. Let the other boys handle it. You're off shift.'

Morris said, 'If you say so, Pat! But give me a break when the thing smashes.'

'If it smashes,' McCarthy said bitterly. 'It's going to be hell to lay it on that guy. You don't accuse men like Wilson of having murder done unless you can prove it. And he's got no motive.'

Marge said: 'Chet told me all about it. This Italian man was suing Wilson for damages. If he was dead, he couldn't sue, could he? That's why that other man was stabbed, too. They tried to kill him so he couldn't testify. It stands to reason, Pat.'

McCarthy said wearily, 'Oh, use your head, Marge. Giovanni was asking for twenty-five grand, claiming Wilson was driving carelessly. Wilson is very wealthy and what's twenty-five grand to a man like that? He'd pay it in a second rather than have anybody killed. It ties up some way, but we haven't caught the angle yet.'

The phone burred and Marge answered it and then said, 'It's for you, Pat. It's Lieutenant Shannon.' McCarthy took it and said, 'Yeah, Shan?' and Shannon blurted out:

'You called the turn on it, Irish! You sure did. I had a man on guard up at the hospital and two guys came in and tried to kill that Bowes guy. One of them even got in the room. That's the one that got away, down the fire-escape. I should have seen that they put him some place where he was easier watched.'

'What happened?'

'Well, this man, his name's Dugan, was sitting out in the hall. He admits he was talking to some nurse, or maybe it wouldn't have gone as far as it did. Two men come up the stairs and walk down to Bowes room and Dugan finally gets wise to himself and asks 'em what they want. One of them pulls a gun and starts using it and Dugan kills him. The other ducked in Bowes' room and down the fire-escape and Dugan missed him three times hand running. He's going to put more time in on the range or get off the force and I told him so.'

'Was Bowes hurt?'

'Hell, no! They've got him doped up so he won't roll around and tear himself up any more and he didn't even know anything happened.'

'Has he talked yet?'

'He can't. And the doctors wouldn't let him if he could.'

'Who was the man the cop killed?'

'Some bird named Weeks. Just a hired hand.'

'Did Dugan see the one that got away well enough to identify him?'

'No. He was talking to that nurse, like I said. He wasn't paying any attention to what he was supposed to be working at. I'm going to see he gets a month's suspension without pay if I have to resign to get it. . . . You coming down?'

McCarthy said not that evening and then he asked if the man the policeman had killed had happened to have an ice pick on his person, and found he hadn't. And then he said to Marge and Chet Morris:

'Let's eat! Chet, why don't you come with us?'

Morris said, 'Don't think I'm not. I'm sticking close until this thing's settled. I'm scared, Pat, and I'm not fooling.'

Marge said, 'I'm afraid about Pat.'

And McCarthy said, 'And I'm afraid the cops will get to the ice-pick guy before I do. I want to be first.'

It took McCarthy the best part of a week to find that Mr. James R. S. Wilson was maintaining a small apartment in a discreet apartment house. And a small blond girl who fitted the apartment. The small girl's name was Mrs. Martha Abott, or at least that name was accepted. Her husband was Mr. James Abott, supposedly a traveling man, but his travels only extended from the Wilson brokerage firm or the Wilson house to the apartment.

It took twenty-five dollars of what was left of the five hundred for McCarthy to get details but he thought it money well spent. He said to Marge and to Chet Morris, who was arrayed in something new that shocked the eye:

'The guy's keeping her all right, but in this day and age that's no crime. And I'm damned if I can see that he's doing anything else. I've tagged him back and forth, from his house to his office, from there to this apartment, and I haven't seen him do one thing that would tie him up to any of the rough stuff.

'Of course I can't tell just who he sees in his office, but he's too cagy an old turkey to meet some hoodlum there where the help could spot it. I've got a boy on the day shift and another one on the night shift to tell me if he meets anybody there at this apartment and they say he doesn't.'

Morris asked, 'Does he know you're following him?'

'If he does, he hasn't done anything about it.'

Marge said firmly, 'He's a nasty old man. Or he wouldn't be doing things like that.'

Morris said, 'Did you ever see his wife?'

'No. Why?'

'Well, I did. When I went to see him. I don't blame him a bit. She'd drive a man to drink.'

McCarthy asked what woman wouldn't and Marge slapped half-heartedly at him. She said, 'What are you going to do now, Pat?'

'Keep after him, of course. He's bound to make contact with his hired killers before long and I want to see 'em. He's the only lead to them I've got.'

'I wish you'd drop it. After all, it's none of your business.'

McCarthy said, 'You didn't happen to see old man Giovanni stretched out like I did. You didn't see this poor kid of his. You didn't go to the old man's funeral.'

'Pat! You didn't go to the funeral!'

Chet Morris said, 'Pat and some of the cops, mostly Shannon, and some of the boys on my paper paid for it, Marge. Even Abe Goldstein came in for ten bucks and the guy thinks money is something to hide in a bank. All of them had seen the family the guy left and it seems he'd given Halstead all the money he could raise to prosecute Wilson for running over his oldest boy. He'd mortgaged the shop he had and they took it away from the family before they could even have his funeral.'

Marge said, 'Oh, the poor people.'

There was a knock on the door and Marge opened it for Benny. He came in, grinning, and said, 'Another thirty-five bucks you owe me, Chief. I'm running you into dough – that's five of 'em.'

'You always cost me,' McCarthy said sourly.

'But not any more, Chief. It seems that I'm getting amnesia or something like that and the docs say I'm no good any more and that they're going to get another boy until I get fat again. Jeez, Chief, I lose ten pounds, but it's seventeen and a half a pound the way I figure it and that buys a lot of groceries.'

'I'd rather pay you than some other mugg.'

'Thanks, Chief, thanks. I like that.'

McCarthy explained, 'If I pay you, you don't have to borrow from me. If I pay somebody else I'm stuck with you again.'

'Jeez, Chief, that ain't right. Don't I always kick it back to you?'

'You haven't yet.'

'Well I never had it yet. When I'm in the dough I will.'

McCarthy looked at his watch and asked, 'You got the hack downstairs?'

'Sure.'

'I'll ride with you then.'

He said to Marge and Chet Morris: 'I'll start after Wilson some more.

He gets out of his office in half an hour; he's as regular as the old maid putting the cat out. See you some more.'

Marge went to the door with him. She said earnestly, 'You be careful, Pat! I've got a funny feeling about this.'

'Forget it, kid! He'll lead me to the right guys sooner or later. He has to – they'll contact him some time. And then I'll step in on him and them both.'

Benny said, from where he was waiting in the hall: 'Hey, the guy talked today. When I was doing my stuff with the docs and him. But all he wanted was a priest. He said he wanted to confess.'

'Shannon know this?'

'Sure. But the guy wouldn't talk to him. He wanted a priest is all, Chief.'

McCarthy said, 'I'll put Wilson to bed, either at his house or at his apartment, and then I'll see Shannon and we'll talk to the doctors. If the guy can talk to a priest he can talk to the cops. And he knows things we have to know to get any place.'

'Is he getting along all right?' Marge asked.

'According to the doctors he is.'

He said good-by again and Marge watched him follow Benny down the hall with quick strides. She went inside and said to Chet Morris:

'This has Pat down. I never saw him get upset about anything like that before.'

Morris said slowly, 'Well, here was a case of the innocent bystander being the victim. Worse than that. That killing was so senseless, and there was no reason for the attack on Bowes. Twenty-five thousand dollars means little to Wilson – and the death of his oldest boy hit Giovanni pretty hard. From what his wife said, he only wanted the money for his family. And then he gets killed and leaves five kids, none of them over ten. Twenty-five thousand isn't worth that.'

Marge said, 'Maybe Pat's after the wrong man. Maybe he didn't do it or have it done.'

Morris shrugged his gaily covered shoulders and said, 'Don't be silly. If it wasn't Wilson back of it, why should the one witness against him be almost killed? Why should the man making the charge be killed? It doesn't make too much sense, but he's the only connecting link between the two happenings.'

'I wonder where the man Bowes got the five one hundred dollar bills.'

Morris said, 'I didn't know he had any,' and Marge told of them. She defended Pat with: 'He just took them so he'd have money to care for the man in the hospital. That was all.'

'Sure,' said Morris, with no conviction in his tone.

Marge said, 'Poor Pat! I've got the oddest feeling about him. I'm really worried.'

'If the cops find out Pat took the five hundred you'll have something to worry about,' Morris told her.

McCarthy walked a hundred feet behind the sedate-looking James R. S. Wilson. But Wilson was alone and McCarthy wasn't. A thin, very dark man was on one side of him and a heavy but equally dark man was on the other. The heavy man was saying:

'Go ahead, shamus. You been following him and he didn't know it and we been following you and *you* didn't know it. Now we're all going to get together and get acquainted.'

The heavy man had a hand in a side coat pocket and the pocket lumped out with more than hand. His thin partner was just as close to McCarthy and his pocket bulged in the same manner. He had a high whiny voice and he said:

'You're a stupid, shamus! You might've known we was keeping watch on him. You're stupid.'

McCarthy admitted it with: 'I've been told so before. By better men than you two punks will ever be.'

'Sing high, sing low,' the heavy man said. 'But if you do it out loud I'll smear you all over the town. You guys out here think you know something but you're made to order.'

The thin man said, 'Yeah, tailor-made.'

Wilson turned into the apartment house, first glancing suspiciously up and down the street, and McCarthy said, 'Now what?'

'We go in. Just act right.'

McCarthy acted right. He went inside and to the elevator as though expected, and the clerk looked at him casually and turned away. They rode up to 3C and the heavy man said:

'You know, Mike, I don't blame the guy for going with the gal here. She's a honey. I don't blame him for going for her.'

The thin partner said, 'Why should you? He's paying for it ain't he?'

'And how!' the heavy man agreed. He said to McCarthy: 'Just you knock on his door. When he opens it you just walk in like you owned the place. No funny stuff now.'

The thin man said, 'Hey, wait!' and reached over and snapped McCarthy's heavy gun from its shoulder sling. He stuck this in the waist-band of his trousers and said, 'O.K. now. Go to it.'

McCarthy knocked. He heard fluttering sounds inside and then a girl's voice said, 'What is it?' McCarthy got a warning gun jabbed in his short ribs and held silent.

The heavy man said, 'Electrician, ma'am!'

There was more fluttering and then the door opened. The small and blond and supposedly Mrs. Abott stood framed in it, a black silk negligée

370

wrapped around what appeared to be herself and nothing else. The thin man jammed his gun into McCarthy's ribs and said:

'In!'

McCarthy went in, accompanied by a small shriek from the blond girl. The heavy man said in an approving voice:

'Now that's nice, lady. That's the way to yelp. If you'd made any more noise than that somebody might have heard you and then there'd have been hell to pay for this chump.'

She said, 'Who are you? What do you want?'

Wilson's voice said, from inside: 'What is it, darling?'

The girl didn't answer, just backed into the room where Wilson was, staring at the three men and the two guns that followed her. Wilson jumped to his feet, his face suddenly white, and the heavy man said:

'Don't have kittens, mister. We're friends. And I'll prove it to you.' He said to his partner: 'You watch 'em, Mike,' and headed toward the French phone by the window.

Wilson said, 'Why, what—' and the heavy man grinned back at him over one shoulder and said:

'Don't get in a lather, dad. I'm going to call Halstead. I'll get him to come up and we can sort of talk things over.'

McCarthy said, 'You'd better call the cops, Wilson. This has gone far enough.'

Then the thin man hit him on the back of the head with his gun and McCarthy went ahead and on his face. And completely out.

He came back to life in time to hear Halstead say, 'This is going to complicate things, Wilson. This man possibly has somebody working with him. This is going to cost money to hush up.'

McCarthy opened his eyes just wide enough to take in the room. He saw Halstead sitting composedly in a chair with the heavy man standing back of it and leaning on it. Wilson was standing in front of him and looking very unhappy. The girl was sitting on a couch, swinging and admiring an arched instep that held a high-heeled bedroom slipper. The thin man was at the window and looking directly at McCarthy. He said:

'Hey! Ain't it about time Sleeping Beauty woke up? I didn't rap him hard, Halstead. I just slapped him a little.'

Halstead said to Wilson: 'You're in this too far to back out now, Wilson. If Bowes gets a police guard, which he is very apt to do, there'll be hell to pay all the way around.'

The thin man said, 'We'll take him and his copper guard if we have to, Halstead. I never liked cops anyway.' He walked over to McCarthy and kicked him in the ribs, and McCarthy took it with a lax body and still half-opened eyes. It took what will power he had to do it but the thin man turned and walked back satisfied and McCarthy thought the effort worth it.

Halstead said, 'You didn't do so well at the hospital, Mike. If that cop had been a better shot, you wouldn't have done well at all.'

The thin man spat on the rug and the girl flared at him with: 'Damn you! Don't do that. You're not in a barn now.'

The thin man told her where he was, using good old English words, and the girl glared at him and used language equally strong. Wilson looked even unhappier and Halstead grinned and said to the girl:

'Shut up, Martha. I'll handle this. As I say, Wilson, it will cost you money. It cost money to buy Bowes off. If he'd gotten on the stand with his yarn, you'd have been tarred and feathered and chased out of town.'

The girl said, 'Yes, Daddy! Think of my reputation. It would have ruined me.'

The thin man, who didn't seem to think a great deal of the girl, snapped, 'Hagh! That'd be a day.'

Halstead said thoughtfully, 'There's only one thing to do. Let Mike and Jerry take the fellow out the back way while he's still out. If they meet anybody they can pretend he's drunk and that they're taking care of him.'

'And then what?' Wilson asked.

Halstead said, 'What can we do? He's wise to the setup. You're wrecked if we don't get rid of him for you. That was the reason for taking care of old man Giovanni. Bowes had told him the story and you couldn't afford to have him telling it around, could you?'

Wilson said miserably, 'I – I didn't know what you were going to do.'

Halstead waved his hand and said, 'You're in it just as deep, whether you knew it or not. And I'll never think you didn't know what was going to happen. Now do you pay for us taking this man out or shall we let him stay here with you? Think fast – he won't be out like that very much longer.'

Then Benny said, from the hallway: 'You're damn right he won't.'

Benny was behind McCarthy and the shock of hearing Benny's voice brought his head around. Benny was in the center of the door, crouching a little and holding an iron jack handle in one big hand. Chet Morris crowded up behind him, holding a small gun, and he menaced the room with this and quavered:

'Hands up!'

That started it. The thin man went for the gun he carried under his arm and Benny went for the thin man with the jack handle. The heavy man jerked at his pocket and Morris closed both eyes and pulled the trigger of his little gun three times.

McCarthy was watching the heavy man and lunging to his feet at the same time, but Halstead's head was in his line of vision. He saw a black dot spring out at the side of Halstead's forehead and saw Halstead put his head down on his knees. And then the heavy man got his gun clear of his pocket and McCarthy hit him at the knees.

The man had a big gun and it drowned out the echo of Morris's small one when it exploded. But the man was falling backward when this happened and the slug smashed into the ceiling. The heavy man clubbed the gun at McCarthy, who was hanging stubbornly to his knees, and McCarthy took the blow on the shoulder and let go of knees with an arm gone numb. Then he heard a crunching sound about him and heard Benny say:

'Leave him go, Chief. I bopped the——'

McCarthy released the heavy man, who showed no further interest in the affair and whose face was now oddly shaped. He heard a screeching sound from the door and turned and saw the blonde pounding at Chet Morris with her high-heeled slipper and saw Morris fending her away and not doing well at all. The girl was crying out:

'You shot Ira! You shot Ira!' and her voice was a high thin scream that didn't sound sane.

And then McCarthy looked for Wilson and didn't see him and heard a door slam above the noise of the girl's keening. He got to his feet and went to the thin man and saw he was lying with his head twisted in a line with his shoulder. He got his own gun from where the thin man had put it in his waist-band and when he got to the hallway he reached out and caught the blond girl by the hair and threw her back by it clear across the room.

Then he crowded past Morris and out into the hall in time to see Wilson dancing up and down in front of the elevator opening. He set himself sidewise, as though preparing to shoot at a target, and then called harshly:

'*Wilson!*'

And when Wilson stopped his mad hopping and turned, McCarthy shot him through the knee.

Later McCarthy told Marge: 'We're celebrating tonight, lamb. Chet Morris and Benny have already started it. They were plastered early this afternoon. They're to meet us here.'

Marge said, 'I can see the reason for celebrating but that's about all I see. I haven't seen you since it happened.'

'I had to be with the cops, hon. I couldn't get away. There was a lot to explain – for that matter the cops are still investigating. I asked Shannon to come along, too, and he's too busy.'

'What happened?'

McCarthy told her what had happened, dwelling with emphasis on Benny's work with the jack handle and on Morris's poor marksmanship.

He said, 'At that it was a good thing. The guy was a good enough lawyer to maybe slide out of it. He can't slide off a morgue slab, even if Morris put him there by mistake. You should have seen that little hell cat of a

Martha go for Morris with a slipper, hon, it was really good. Benny and Morris saved the day when they followed me and came in.'

'So Halstead was bleeding Wilson all the time? Halstead was back of it all?' Marge asked.

'In a way. Halstead had found out Wilson was running around with this tart of a Martha. It was his business to find out those things – he made most of his money by blackmailing. When Wilson ran over the young Giovanni kid the girl was with him, and he was afraid of the scandal and ran away. Halstead got to the girl and she told him the truth – she fell hard for him. He was a nice looking guy, honey.'

Marge said automatically, 'Nobody'll ever say that about you, Pat,' and then: 'Go on.'

'That's about all. Halstead hired Bowes to say he saw the thing. He had to have a witness if he was going to shake down Wilson in a big way. Then Bowes got cold feet on the deal and started to back out. Then Halstead put him out of the way. Or had Mike, one of his two thugs, do it. This Mike used a ice pick, because they can be carried wrapped up and they can't be classed as a dangerous weapon if you're stopped by a cop. Get it?'

'I guess so. But why did they kill that poor Mr. Giovanni?'

'They had to tell him Bowes was a witness before the old man would consent to start suit. Bowes, when he got cold feet – he calls it religion, but he finally talked to both the priest and the cops, so you can take your pick – went to Giovanni and confessed it was a frame. So they had to kill Giovanni, too. Now is it all straight?'

'I guess so. I'm glad it's over, Pat.'

McCarthy said gloomily, 'It got over too soon to suit me, hon. I wanted that little thin guy that was so handy with the ice pick all to myself. Benny got to him first. I'll admit Benny did a good job – he broke his neck. The big guy'll hang and Halstead's dead and Wilson will be laughed out of town as soon as he gets out of the hospital.'

'Why did you shoot him? You didn't have to do that.'

McCarthy said indignantly, 'Hell, kid! If he'd been a man and faced the music, none of this would have happened. If he hadn't been drunk and out riding around with that chippy he'd have never run over the Giovanni boy. If he'd have stood the scandal like a man, the old man wouldn't have been killed. I should have aimed center instead of just crippling him a bit. He started the whole thing. . . . I take that Giovanni thing pretty hard, kid.'

Marge said soberly, 'I see what you mean.' And then her eyes widened and she said, 'My heavens! It isn't possible.'

McCarthy turned and saw Benny and Chet Morris almost at the booth. They were both very drunk. Benny had a severe and formal Homburg perched exactly center on his head and this didn't go well with a shabby sweater and grease-stained slacks. He carried a pair of yellow gloves proudly in his right hand. His left held a half-full whiskey bottle.

Morris looked even more spectacular. He wore a cap on the side of his head and the suit he wore had been made for a taller, much thinner man. The green trouser cuffs dragged four inches on his shoes, which were an ugly yellow. The coat hung almost to his knees. He held two glasses and was saying to Benny:

'Le's stop an' have 'ittle drinkie. Thirsty, I am.'

McCarthy said, under his breath to Marge: 'Look at the poor—— face. That's what the gal did with that high heel.'

Morris' face was blotched and lumpy and both eyes were black. He looked as though he'd fallen down several flights of stairs.

Marge gasped, 'And him so fussy!'

Then Morris looked up and saw them. He waved happily, almost falling down while doing so, and came to a halt in front of the booth. He beamed at them and said:

'Hi! What d'ya think of the new outfit?

'Ain't it something, huh?'

Marge said, 'I'd never deny it.'

Benny came to a halt alongside Morris and said, 'I got me a hat at the same place, Chief. Hey, look at me, too, Chief.'

McCarthy said, 'I can't help it.'

Chet Morris said, in a confidential voice: 'Like this, Pat, m' frien'. Benny and I we bust into Abe Goldstein down at the station while you was busy with the cops. Abe's got a brother-in-law who has a clothing store. So Benny and I and Abe take a couple of snorts or so and go down to get a new outfit. Abe says his brother-in-law's got the best stock in the city and he helped us pick this outfit out. Didn't cost us nothin' at all. How's it look, pal?'

McCarthy said, 'Gorgeous! Simply gorgeous! Will you do me a favor, Chet?'

'Sure.'

'Then let me be with you when you see Abe in the morning.'

'Why? He won't take our clothes back. He *gave* 'em to us. S'funny, too, with him so stingy, but—'

McCarthy said, 'Let's not spoil our fun tonight, guy. But there's reasons and you'll realize it tomorrow. Believe me you will.'

Marge giggled and said, 'It would be bad enough to look at that at any time. But with the hangover Chet'll have, it's liable to be fatal.'

McCarthy agreed with: 'Yeah, fatal to Abe.'

THE DEVIL'S BOOKKEEPER

CARLOS MARTINEZ

Gun Molls Magazine had a brief and unexciting life. The first issue was published in October, 1930, and appeared monthly for only eighteen additional months, folding after the issue of April, 1932. Examining the list of contributors fails to elicit a single recognizable name, even to pulp experts who have devoted the major portion of their professional lives to the scholarly study of what was at one time a major element of American literature. Carlos Martinez is such an author – possibly the pseudonym of another hack trying to pay the rent at the rate of a half-a-cent-a-word, which is what this publication paid.

Gun Molls and such sister publications as *Gangland Detective Stories*, *Racketeer Stories*, *Gangster Stories* and others similarly titled did not offer literary prose nor enduring works of fiction. Characterization has no more depth than spray paint, and stylistic nuance is as rare as a humble politician. The villains are utterly odious; they would be loved neither by their mothers nor their dogs. The molls, unless they are working undercover or hopelessly in love with the wrong man, are still more sinister than the thugs with whom they share adventures. Nonetheless, even the worst of these publications offered exactly what their readers demanded: non-stop action, snappy dialogue, blazing guns, automobiles careering around corners with the cops in hot pursuit, and other standard scenes from the cheap B-movies of the era and the least of the pulps.

'The Devil's Bookkeeper' first appeared in the August, 1931, issue of *Gun Molls*.

THE DEVIL'S BOOKKEEPER

CARLOS MARTINEZ

A cross the roof-top, a dim shadow slipped silently to a barred window, like a dull gray wraith that merged perfectly with the curling fingers of fog drifting in from the lake.

It made no sound in its ghost-like approach, and was visible only when the clouds across the crescent moon allowed a faint ghoulish light to filter for a moment upon the roofs of the sleeping city.

A pale hand attached a small piece of cloth to the glass of the window, on which was smeared a bit of fast drying cement. Then the scratch of a diamond cutting a circle on the glass, a snapping tap as the inner oval fell loose and was withdrawn by the attached piece of cloth.

Came a hissing intake of breath, unmistakably a woman's, as the still form of a man was revealed lying on a small bed within the darkened room. Again that pale hand in the shimmer of greenish moonlight; two dull clicks from the blue metal in his fist; a convulsive jerk from the figure on the bed, and when the clouds again cleared across the crescent moon, the dirty roof-top was empty and silent.

Detective Sergeant Dan Conley was talking to his chief. His Irish face was twisted into a puzzled frown as he hitched his shoulder holster to a more comfortable position, and took a chair opposite the captain.

' "Mugs" Brandon was bumped off last night,' he began.

'Where did they get him?' asked Captain Steele.

'In that roof-top apartment of his,' said Conley. 'No fingerprints. The gun that did for Mugs, cut out a circle of the window with a diamond, and let him have it with a .45. Must have used a silencer!'

'Mugs put up a fight?' asked the captain.

'Never knew what hit him,' said Conley. 'Got him while he was asleep!'

'Hell!' blazed the captain. 'Get out of here and bring somebody in. The commissioner has been threatening to fire every man in the precinct the next time there was a killing. We got to make a showing!'

'I got a tall hunch about this killing,' said Conley slowly.

'Sez you!' sneered Steele. 'What's the big idea this time?'

'There was one footprint on the roof under that window,' said Conley. 'It was made by the rubber-sole from a woman's shoe!'

'One of Mugs' old molls,' said Steele. 'Check up on those Clancy Street dames he used to play around with. Some hallway baby, maybe!'

'I got a hunch,' said Conley, stubbornly.

'Mind letting me in on it?' asked the captain with heavy sarcasm.

' "Clerical Clara," ' said Conley. 'It looks like her work!'

The captain looked at the detective for a moment while his heavy face grew red with exasperation. He spat viciously at the brass cuspidor which is a part of every police captain's office furniture.

'You thimble-wit!' he roared. 'Clerical Clara! You know dam' well that dame ain't never been mixed up in this booze racket, and you've made us all look like dam' fools half a dozen times. Now you get out on the East Side, and bring in some of those Clancy Street trollops!'

'Yes, sir!' Detective Sergeant Conley saluted, swung on his heel, and left the room with his great hands clenched to control his rising anger. He stepped into a squad car, jammed in the shifting lever and roared out of the small courtyard with exhaust wide open.

In a neat little office on the fourth floor of a side street building a blonde beauty was carefully sorting a list of accounts receivable, and making figures on a pad with machine-like accuracy.

Her hair was combed straight back in a mannish bob, and the carefully penciled brows were drawn together in a frown of concentration. Her age might have been anything between twenty-five and thirty-five, according to her mood.

Soft and hard by turns; cold and warmly yielding, whichever best suited her purpose and the business at hand. The sign on her door said: 'Clara Beaumont, Accountant. Income Taxes and Collections.'

She looked up as the handle of the door turned, and then smiled as she motioned lazily to a chair.

'Hello, Conley,' she drawled. 'Can I help you with your income tax?'

'Can the comedy,' said Conley. 'You know dam' well I don't have any grafts that make me pay taxes.'

'More fool you,' she answered. 'What's on your mind?'

'Mugs Brandon,' said Conley. 'When did you last see him?'

'Don't know the gent,' said the girl. 'That is, not personally.'

'He was bumped off last night,' said Conley, watching her carefully. 'Some dame did for him.'

'How interesting,' she sneered. 'But then, I specialize in income taxes.'

'And collections,' said Conley.

'And I always collect,' said the girl.

'I know that,' said Conley. 'You either collect – or else—'

'What do you mean – or else?' The girl shot the question at him viciously.

'Just what I said, and Mugs Brandon never paid anything he could get out of,' said Conley.

He looked critically at her well-shaped legs, and then allowed his eyes to drop to her shoes. He noted that the thin slippers she was wearing were at least two sizes smaller than the print of the rubber-soled shoe he had measured on the roof of Brandon's apartment.

'You dicks make me sick,' she said with disgust.

'Pardon my asthma,' he said. 'I'll be moving along.'

'Wait a minute.' She watched him with puzzled eyes. 'You got nothing on me.'

'That's what I said,' he agreed. 'I'll be shoving along.'

For ten minutes after he had taken his abrupt departure she sat motionless, trying to figure out what the detective had meant. Then she returned to her accounts. It took brains to swindle the government out of taxes, and she was one of the best in the game.

'Clerical Clara in the flesh!'

She started as the smooth feminine voice addressed her, and looked up to see a quietly dressed girl standing just inside the door. As though reaching for a paper, her hand started to slide inside an open drawer.

'Hold it!'

The order shot out like the snap of a whip, as the stranger moved her hand out from her side, a wicked little automatic clenched in the tiny fist.

'I ain't on the kill for sugar, but you make a funny pass at me and I'll fan you a heavy dose of lead poisoning,' she articulated slowly. 'You know who I am?'

'I don't go to cheap shows,' sneered Clara. 'But on a bet I'd say you were Chorus, back row!'

For a moment it seemed as though the stranger would turn her rod on her tormentor. She was a dark slender girl of about twenty-two, with the regal high-breasted carriage that speaks of breeding in any language.

'I am Premier Dancer at Brandon's Club, and you know it,' she said quietly. 'And Mugs stopped two slugs last night while he was sound asleep. You are good at figures, so I thought maybe you could figure that one out.'

'Why, you cheap boop boop a doop, I'll burn you down so quick—'

'Stay put!' snapped the dancer. 'I'd like to let you have it right now, but first I want to see you turn yellow like the sneakin' rat that you are!'

'Put up that rod and give me a break,' begged Clara. 'I'll fan a heat on you so dam' fast that you will think you are up against a Baby Thompson.'

For a moment it looked as though the stranger would comply with the request. Then she sighed and backed toward the door. Never for an instant did she take her gun from the other.

'Not this time, old sister,' she drawled. 'But next time we meet, start doing your stuff with your lead atomizer. I'm giving you a break; that's more than you ever gave anyone.'

The door slammed behind her with a bang, and for five minutes Clara sat motionless. She knew the ways of gangdom. They might wait five minutes outside to plug you if you got reckless and followed, or then they might beat it right away, and have five minutes start to the good. Either way, you never could tell for sure.

Two days later, Mugs Brandon was put away in style. His casket was the most expensive that money could buy, and three cars loaded with flowers followed the hearse. His friends sent them because they regretted his demise, and his enemies were as profligate in the expenditures, to signify their satisfaction.

Weeping women were at the church; the girls from Clancy Street. But there were two who did not weep, though the eyes of one were dry with a burning hate that glittered like the fires of hell, as they looked across the casket at another woman who was coolly looking down upon the pale chiseled features of the corpse.

Clerical Clara looked up from her inspection, and glanced insolently at the woman on the other side of the bier.

'He looks so natural,' she sighed. 'As though he had paid all his debts, and had a clear conscience.'

'Yes,' whispered the other as softly. 'He rests content. He knows *all* his debts will be paid.'

The gangsters in line shoved them along with gentle pressure, and they parted one on each side of the casket, and passed down opposite walls of the little church.

From a nearby pew, Detective Sergeant Conley had observed the little by-play between them. As the stranger left the church he was close behind her, and followed until she turned in at the Club Brandon.

'Carmen Ryan!' he whispered to himself. 'I heard that she was Brandon's real moll, but about those Clancy Street dames?'

He sighed heavily as he turned toward Headquarters to make his report to Captain Steele. Sometimes he wished he had listened to the voice of graft. He was not so young any more, and a detective's pay—

Sergeant Conley could not have told you what prompted him to return to the apartment where Mugs Brandon had been killed, and as he stood in the large living-room with its bizarre furnishings, his eyes strayed to a large desk in one corner beneath a massive floor lamp.

He seated himself in the heavy chair behind the desk, and opened the various drawers with the keys taken from the effects of the slain gangster.

In a secret compartment in the rear of the large center drawer, he found a small japanned box, and fitted a tiny key from the ring in his hand.

On top of a small account book were fifty bills of one thousand-dollar denomination, and in the book were accounts that would incriminate many prominent men. Beneath the book were several pages written in a neat feminine hand. The work of Clerical Clara!

'Jake Cling, $5,000.'

'Soapy Taylor, $5,000.'

'Toad Wilson, $3,000.'

Conley's eyes grew wide with understanding as he scanned the three cards. The three men had been enemies of Mugs Brandon, and each had been shot and killed in some mysterious way. Soapy had been killed while he slept. His mind pieced the puzzle together as accurately as if he had seen the killings take place.

Clerical Clara had done her work, and had then rendered her bill for the service. Mugs Brandon had refused to pay her, and he had remembered Clara's boast that she *always* collected – or else—

So absorbed was he in his thoughts that he failed to hear the slight click of the door as it opened on its well-oiled hinges.

'You find anything, Dick?'

He started to jump to his feet, and then sank back again as he looked into the muzzle of the gun held upon him in the steady hand of Clerical Clara. Her blue eyes were fastened upon the tell-tale slips on the desk before him.

'Hold that pose, please, and keep both hands on the desk where I can see them!'

Keeping him covered, she walked slowly to the desk, and reached for the papers. Before her hand could take them up, another soft voice purred gently over her shoulder.

'As you are, and don't move! Now drop that gat on the desk!'

As the automatic clattered to the mahogany desk, Carmen Ryan jammed the muzzle of her own rod into the back of her enemy.

'Hands high, and swing around,' she ordered.

As Clara obeyed her blue eyes were filled with venom that shook her frail body like the ague.

'I'll get you for this, you cheap hussy!' she hissed through clenched teeth.

Like a steel spring the arm of the dancer shot out, and mashed the lips of the killer woman. All the pent-up anger of the past two weeks went into that one blow that made the dancer careless for a moment.

Before Detective Sergeant Conley could interfere, Clara's right foot shot out, and the automatic flew from the hand of the dancer and went spinning across the room. In the same breath the killer snatched up her own heavy automatic from the desk and swung around on the man and woman with the threat of death in her savage eyes.

'Take those papers out of your pocket and hand them to me!'

As she snapped the words, the detective stiffened. He gazed steadily into the hate-filled eyes before him, and slowly shook his head.

'You have fooled me a dozen times,' he said. 'Now I have enough on you to swing you into hell!'

'You must think I'm a fool,' she sneered. 'Thirty seconds, and then I start shooting.'

The dancer made a movement, and the eyes of the killer swept toward her for a brief instant as she swung the muzzle of her rod around with the movement of her body. In that split second, Conley threw his body forward and down against the desk.

Even as he fell, Clerical Clara wheeled and threw a slug across the desk which was overturning. He slid to the floor, the desk falling on top of him. As the dancer started forward, Clara faced her with the smoking rod.

'I never miss,' she said quietly. 'Another move from you and I'll burn you down, too.'

Watching the dancer closely, she leaned over and attempted to reach into the breast pocket of the fallen detective, but the heavy desk covered his chest like a shield. The telephone lay where it had fallen, and a series of sharp clicks warned her that some one was listening in.

'Take hold of that desk and help me move it, or I'll drill you,' she ordered the dancer.

As the girl started to obey, a sharp knock sounded on the hall door. Then a heavy body smashed against the panels. The killer looked quickly about, and backed toward the window. She slid a slender leg over the sill, and climbed onto a fire-escape. There she paused.

'Take that!'

But even as she fired, the dancer had flung herself sideways behind the desk. Then the hall door crashed down, and two uniformed police rushed in with drawn weapons. One of them covered the crouching girl, while the other hurried to the fallen detective.

'They got Sergeant Conley,' he said.

'You're a liar!'

At the drawling words, the policeman bent over and looked into the twinkling eyes of the detective. Then he smiled with relief.

'Don't stand there,' said Conley. 'Lift this dam' dead wood off of my chest.'

The next moment he was on his feet, and as he pressed a hand to his side he winced with pain. The girl ran to him.

'She shot you! I saw her,' she cried. 'Are you hurt bad?'

'Naw! I got a bullet-proof vest on,' grunted Conley. 'Just knocked me out for a while. Where did that dam' killer go?'

'She took it on the lam out the window, just as these cops broke down the door,' said the dancer. 'Threw a shot at me from the sill, but I did a dive behind the desk-top, and she missed. I think she went over the roof.'

'She knows the way,' said Conley. 'She came over that same roof when she did for Brandon.'

At his words the girl began to sob. He patted her shoulder with clumsy gentleness.

'There now,' he comforted. 'We will be catching her soon, and I'll see to it that you have a seat right up in front when they spring the trap under her.'

He picked up the telephone and reported to Headquarters. Ten minutes later the net was set to tighten about the fleeing killer, and the apartment of the slain gangster chief was once more deserted and silent.

A day and a night went by, and Clerical Clara had not been taken. A score of gangsters and politicians had been questioned about their connection with Mugs Brandon, but they denied any knowledge of his activities, and Detective Conley was about ready to throw the little account book away as worthless.

He was idly thumbing its pages when he came upon a notation on the last page which aroused his interest. He looked closer, and then cursed himself silently for not having recognized the significance of those few penciled words before.

'C.C.,' it read. 'Terry T is heavy.'

It came to him like a flash. So far as he could learn, Clerical Clara had no man in her life. Trust a man like Brandon to know, he ruminated. Brandon's notation meant that Terry T. was her man.

That was funny, too. He knew that Terry Train was a gunman, but had never been able to pin anything on the dapper gangster. It was a well-known fact that Train had no moll, and here was Brandon's notation that Train was *heavy* with Clara!

Conley called to Dick Trent, his running mate, and after explaining his latest hunch, they started for the building where Train leased an apartment. He knew that the gangster would not be expecting a call from the police, but once in the squad car he looked carefully at his gun, and advised Trent to do the same.

Arriving at the apartment building, they walked quickly through the ornate lobby and entered the elevator. Conley turned to the colored operator and snapped his number before the other could voice the protest that showed on his ebony face.

'Fifth floor, and keep your mouth shut!'

As the car stopped, he threw open the door and ran quickly to Apartment 36, with Trent close at his heels.

'Take that window, and watch that no one ducks through to the roof,' he told Trent.

As Trent posted himself at the window which commanded the roof, Conley rang the buzzer of Train's apartment. After a brief pause he rang again.

'Open up!' he called.

The knob was turned slowly, and just as the door swung back, a shot sounded from the roof, and Trent fell to the floor. Like a flash Conley stepped in, his service gun in his hand.

'Get 'em up!' he snapped.

The slender, well-dressed man before him raised his hands, and lifted his eyebrows in simulated surprise. He was evidently just about to leave the apartment when Conley rang his bell.

'Well, what's it all about?' he asked in a quiet voice.

Conley stepped in and clicked a pair of cuffs about the upraised wrists.

'Get in there,' he ordered gruffly. 'I want to see who fired that shot.'

Herding the prisoner before him into the back room, he ran to the closed window and quickly raised it. Leaning out, he scanned the roof which ran just under the windows along the entire side of the building. No one was in sight, and as he turned back into the room, Trent entered from the hall.

'Get you?' asked Conley.

'Just a bare scratch,' said the other detective. 'It was a woman,' he added.

'So Clara has been hiding out here,' said Conley.

'I don't know any Clara,' said the prisoner.

'You better come clean,' said Conley. 'We know that Clerical Clara was your moll. You both kept it pretty shady, but Mugs Brandon knew it, and left word where it would do the most good. One of his cards said you were mixed up in that Toad Wilson killing.'

'The dam' double-crossing punk.' The exclamation seemed to explode from the lips of the dapper gangster before he could control himself. Then he bit his lip and turned furiously on the detective.

'Don't kid me,' he snarled. 'I know you bulls, and you haven't got a thing on me.'

Conley was smiling as he turned to Trent.

'Take him down and book him on suspicion,' he said. 'I'll be down in an hour, so wait for me.'

As Trent drove away with the prisoner, Conley hailed a taxi and gave the address of Carmen Ryan. He phoned to her from the house phone in the hall, and she pressed the buzzer that admitted him.

'You working tonight?' he asked without preamble.

She nodded without speaking. Her eyes were swollen as though she had been weeping, and in their sullen depths he could see the same hatred that had been there the day of Brandon's funeral.

'You'd like to see this Clara get hers, wouldn't you?' he asked.

'If the cops don't get her soon, I'll get her on my own,' snapped the girl. 'Mugs Brandon might not have been so much, but he was good to me, and I loved him. She shot him while he was asleep, like the lousy rat that she is!'

'He left fifty grand that comes to you as his common-law wife,' said Conley.

'The Club is in my name,' said the girl. 'I'm going to run it myself.'

'If you will do what I tell you, I think we can land this Clara dame tonight,' said Conley.

'What can I do?' asked the girl. 'I should have burned her down when I had her under my rod.'

'And you'd have got the hot seat,' reminded Conley. 'I got a hunch that she will be paying you a visit tonight, and my hunches have been working lately.'

'What do you want me to do?' asked the girl.

For twenty minutes Conley talked earnestly, coaching the girl in the part she was to play. Then he left her and hurried to Headquarters.

The 'Club Brandon' was having a formal re-opening. The interior had been decorated according to the whims of the new owner, and was a combination of silver and old gold, with panel bands of somber black contrasting the two.

On a raised dais at the far end of the main room, a ten-piece orchestra was playing the latest dance arrangements. Unlike most orchestras, each man was carrying an automatic under the perfectly fitting dinner coats. They were called 'Brandon's Army.' And Carmen Ryan had seen them in action and had decided to keep them.

Huge bouquets of flowers stood along the walls, representing the good wishes of her friends, and those who would like to be. The tables were well filled with guests, and the waiters moved constantly about with silent efficiency.

At the entrance to the main room just inside the grilled iron doors, Detective Conley was sitting behind a small palm, watching each newcomer. Four men were posted in other places around the room, unknown to any one but Conley and Carmen Ryan.

They mingled with the guests, chatting as affably as though they were part of the reception. Messenger boys rushed in with telegrams of congratulations, and new floral pieces were being added to the masses of blossoms along the walls.

At ten minutes to twelve, a glittering truck drew up in front of the entrance, and unloaded a mass of roses built on a small platform mounted on iron casters. Four men carried it carefully up the stairs, wheeled it through the grilled iron doors and placed it in the center along one of the walls.

A gasp of admiration went up from the assembled guests as one of the attendants pushed a wall socket, and a glitter of colored incandescents flashed out from the mass of roses. They were of the deepest red, and were so placed as to make the entire piece resemble a huge blood-red rosebud.

A small card was fastened to one corner. It read:

'Good luck. Hope you get yours. You deserve it!'

A small gong struck the hour of midnight, and with the last stroke the brilliant lights faded out, to be replaced with soft reflections from the coves which ran around the walls just under the ceiling. They were of different colors, changing from rose and lavender to amber and gold in soft lambent waves.

The orchestra started playing softly, and a strange hush came over the crowd which had been so noisy but a moment before. From the four corners of the room shafts of colored lights shot out, and focused on the very center of the polished floor. The beat of the muffled drums sounded like tom-toms from deep in some savage forest, mingling with the barbaric cadences of the muted instruments.

Another gasp went up from the crowd as the center of the floor opened upward and a silver and gold fountain came into view. Streams of water splashed against the sparkling crystal which formed the lesser ornaments, and changed to cascades of leaping fire as the vari-colored lights played upon their revolving facets.

The beat of the tom-toms became louder as the orchestra was heard playing some wild song of the desert. From above a brilliant floodlight of amber suddenly cast its glow upon the large figure in the very center of the fountain, and breaths were held as the semi-nude goddess became a woman of living gold.

For just an instant she poised on the lip of the fountain shell, and then leaped lightly to the floor. As the lights from the four corners followed her, she began a slow dance to the strains of the half-savage music, which seemed to blend with the shades of colored lights, and made them seem like a part of the very air.

The crowd grew tense as the strange witchery of sound and light crept into their blood. Hearts pounded and hands clenched with passion as the desire to become primitive cast its insinuating spell upon them.

Not a sound was heard as the music went on, and that silent, beautiful figure of gold gyrated maddeningly before them; no sounds except the raking intake of breath in bodies reverting to the abysmal.

Like a wild creature of the forests the dancer began to move in a creeping glide that carried her ever nearer to the tinkling fountain, and then, in one crashing crescendo from the orchestra hidden in the shifting shadows, she leaped onto the fountain and froze into statuesque immobility.

Before the crowd could relax a staccato blur of shots rang out from the center of the farthest wall, and as the spitful orange flames cut the semi-lighted shadows of color, the statue toppled from her pedestal and fell into the shallow water with a sodden splash.

At the same instant the lights went on, and from five different places in the crowded room, a fusillade of shots was directed toward the huge bouquet of deep red roses. The hidden lights were shot out, and clipped roses flew from the frame as the bullets from the guns of the detectives chopped their way into the heart of that massive rosebud.

The crowd stood still, holding their breaths with the surprise of it all, wondering whether it were a part of the entertainment, or whether some new debt of gangdom were being paid.

From behind the grilled doors Dan Conley came in at a crouching run, his gun held at his side as he approached that mutilated offering of roses.

From the far end of the room came the orchestra, spread out fan-wise as every man held a rod ready before him. In the center of the room a dripping figure was climbing out of the splashing fountain, and then the fountain sank again below the level of the floor, as the dancer disappeared behind a group of palms.

Conley and his men ripped the large floral rose to shreds, and deep in the heart of that token of love and good wishes they found nothing – except six brass shells from an automatic, and the rubber print of a woman's shoe!

Again the waiters took up their task of serving the crowd, and again the orchestra played the latest number for the dance. The spell had passed, and the crowd was once again occupied with the business of having a good time in their separate ways.

Behind the palm by the grilled doors Conley sat with Trent, trying to figure out where he had slipped. He felt sure that he could not be wrong, and he was glad that he had insisted that Carmen wear the thin suit of gilded chain armor for her dance. It cost plenty to get that costume, but if they had trapped the murderer it would have been worth it. Even at that, her body would wear the bruises of those bullets for weeks.

From behind the orchestra came a brilliant figure clad in a gown of deepest red that accentuated the contours of her flawless figure with artistic perfection. The only relief to that deep rosebud red was a narrow trimming of black around the bodice.

'Carmen!' The crowd shouted the one word.

She held up her hand for silence, as she reached the exact spot where the fountain had been. And strangely enough, she faced the mutilated rosebud of roses.

'Thank you all,' she said simply. 'I hope you liked the show. It is not over yet, but it will soon be finished.'

She crouched as she spoke, her eyes never leaving that emblem of love along the wall. Without warning, the flood-lights from two corners of the room were focused on that shattered token, and the crowd missed the lightning move of the dancer in the center of the room.

Her right hand flashed to her leg, and came away spitting blood-colored flashes of flame into the heart of that huge rosebud. A figure seemed to emerge from the heart of the rose, and sagged through the crushed flower, to drop on the polished floor.

The crowd gasped. A messenger boy!

Detective Conley started as he turned over the still figure, and closed the glazing eyes. Then he pushed back the small uniform cap and disclosed the blond mannish bob of – 'Clerical Clara!'

'I saw a messenger boy when the lights went out!' he muttered half to himself.

'I saw a footprint,' said Carmen. 'I knew she wouldn't resist trying it again. We wouldn't be looking for it. And now the devil has a dam' good bookkeeper to keep his records straight.'

BLACK LEGION
LARS ANDERSON

Costumed heroes in the pulp era were pretty thick on the ground, largely due to the enormous success of the Shadow, who was soon followed by crime fighters using sobriquets that made them sound more villainous than heroic: Doc Savage, The Spider, The Phantom, The Whisperer, The Ghost, The Black Bat. What was decidedly unusual was a female masked avenger. The Domino Lady in her real life was Ellen Patrick, a gorgeous 22-year-old who swore vengeance on criminals after her father was murdered. She has curly blond hair, penetrating brown eyes, is tall and has a stunning figure. Her modus operandi generally finds her at a party or social gathering in a thin, low-cut, backless dress that clings to her every curve. When she discovers the item that she came to steal from her adversary, she slips into a bedroom or closet, peels off her dress and dons another one (both dresses so gossamer that they fit in a small handbag), puts on a mask, and returns to the party. Her disguise apparently works, just as Clark Kent removing his glasses appears to make him unrecognizable. When successful, she leaves a card bearing the inscription: 'Compliments of the Domino Lady.' There were only six stories about her, five of which appeared in *Saucy Romantic Adventures* and one in *Mystery Adventure Magazine*. Little is known of the author, whose career appears to have lasted only about four years (1935–1938), and all of whose stories were published in the second level pulps. 'Black Legion' was first published in the October 1936 issue of *Saucy Romantic Adventures*.

BLACK LEGION

LARS ANDERSON

CHAPTER ONE

THREATENED

Ellen Patrick, radiantly youthful and possessed of that intangible something which lends allure to some fortunate women, rose from the crimson *chaise longue*.

Pink-nailed fingers patted her perfect sun-touched coiffure, and straightened the blue silken kimono that she wore. She smiled up into the dark, good looking features of a man.

'You must be very careful, Paul,' she breathed softly, 'I'm afraid this is more than a mere threat. That Black Legion wouldn't hesitate to kill you, you know.'

She laughed nervously, stepped closer to his side. The man could see the tiny fires of interest blazing deep in her great brown eyes, and he laid a caressing hand upon the heated velvet that was her rounded shoulder.

Paul Cathern flashed white teeth in an engaging grin. He was of medium height, slender, wiry, and possessed more than his share of vibrant magnetism. Astutely fearless, he was known as one of the most successful special investigators working out of the sheriff's office. His deep voice was low, passionate.

'You're sweet, Ellen!' he told her, his gray eyes frankly admiring her sensuous figure, set off as it was by the filmy kimono. Lovely bosom, lithe thighs, slender calves, trim ankles, dainty feet.

His grin widened.

'Of course, I'll be careful, honey. It's part of my job. But they can't scare or bluff me off! I'm out to get the goods on this outfit, and I'm not quitting cold when success is in sight! Why, the information on the Obispo rendezvous alone gives me a swell chance of rounding up some of the ringleaders.'

Ellen quivered within the depths of her being. Paul Cathern had long been an intimate friend, and more. She admired him greatly, loved him not a little. Now, the mysterious Black Legion threatened his life because of his

393

activities as investigator into their atrocities along the Pacific Coast! Theirs was no idle threat.

Already two detectives had been cruelly tortured by black hooded creatures. Another had mysteriously vanished without a trace. And judging from their cowardly ultimatum delivered to Cathern's apartment a few hours previously, the young sleuth was to be next on their list!

Ellen's brown eyes were filmed with worry as she walked to the door with her caller. There, she lifted her moist, red lips for his goodnight kiss. As Cathern bent his dark head to the pale oval of her face, he clasped her in his arms. She laughed softly at his hungry zeal.

'You're sweet, Ellen!' he repeated, huskily, gazing into her eyes. The little adventuress thrilled to the touch of his hands and the caress of his long fingers.

She couldn't resist liking the possessive embrace of his arm about her pliant waist as Cathern drew her close to him. Her ductile curves were flattened against him, and she experienced an emotion that was strangely new to her! She returned the kiss as his lips were pressed to the ripe contours of her cerise mouth.

'I'll be seeing you in a couple of days, Ellen,' he whispered as he reluctantly released her, and opened the door.

'As soon as I've investigated that hide-out a bit further, I'll have some good news for you, I hope. Keep sweet, honey.' And he was gone.

Ellen did not move for a little while. Her agile brain was clicking rapidly over the details of the disclosures concerning the Black Legion which Paul Cathern had given her.

Her piquant face was grim as she moved sensuously over the deep-piled rug, procured a cigarette from a black and silver box which stood on an end table, and lighted it. Filling her lungs with the fragrant smoke, she began to pace back and forth with feline grace, her racing mind sorting and filing the information she had obtained.

Ellen Patrick, known in certain circles through California as The Domino Lady, was nearing twenty-three.

Just tall enough to be majestic, with a figure whose curves set men's pulses hammering, her beautiful rounded features, crowned by a coronet of silky, golden curls, often graced the rotogravure supplements of the Sunday newspapers as one of the Southland's prettiest debs. Yet no one connected Ellen Patrick with the notorious Domino Lady!

Her father, Owen Patrick, had been the czar of California politics at one time.

A murderer's cowardly bullet had cut him down in his prime some three years before. Rumor was that the killer had been an employee of the state political machine. A small trust fund, and a wealth of wit and courage had been his bequeathal to his lovely, orphaned daughter.

Previous to her father's brutal slaying, Ellen had lived a life of comparative ease as befitted the only child of Owen Patrick.

She had graduated at Berkeley, spent several glorious months in the Far East and then an assassin's slug had robbed her of the one who meant more to her than life itself! Small wonder that her life had been dedicated to a campaign of vengeance against the murderers of her parent!

Ruthless, roguish, Ellen at times accepted almost impossible undertakings simply for the sake of friendship and an inordinate craving for adventure! For example, her recent exploits in Santa Anita, in which she had matched wits and daring with the notorious Kilgarlin gang, and emerged victorious.

At other times she was coldly involved in hazardous schemes, aimed at the discomfiture and embarrassment of the authorities whom she blamed for her father's death, at the same time earning a princely income, most of which was donated to a worthy charity.

Oft-times, her adventures were so arranged as to encompass both the friendship and vengeance angles, and those were the ones in which she gloried, particularly.

Only a short time ago, she had retrieved a packet of compromising letters for a friend in a daring raid upon the penthouse apartment of Rob Wyatt, aspirant for political honors, and at the same time had bluffed the big game hunter and politician into a state of oblivion!

A unique black and white, or white and black ensemble was widely recognized as The Domino Lady's costume, and mention of it in certain circles was always productive of inward shudders! No vulpine politician or unscrupulous crook in all California wanted any part of The Domino Lady!

Now, as she moved back and forth about the beautifully-furnished apartment, Ellen was prodding her keen mind, searching for some method by which she could aid Paul Cathern in his struggle with the Black Legion, and perhaps save his life.

The special investigator had confided in Ellen, never dreaming that he was betraying secrets to the formidable Domino Lady! Without a doubt, leading politicians (some of them, Ellen's sworn enemies) were members of the feared organization, according to Cathern, and especially was he convinced that this was true in the case of J. Riggs Saint, the district attorney.

Saint, campaigning for reelection, was loud in his vociferations against the Black Legion. His newspaper editorials were heated protests against their reputed outlawry and murder.

He cried long and loud for some scrap of evidence with which to push prosecutions, knowing full well that there was scant possibility of any such damaging material coming to light. In fact, the very storm of his indignation and threats was the moving factor behind Cathern's conviction of the district attorney's implication!

Two days previously, the special investigator had chanced upon a Black Legion rendezvous in the Obispo country; a wild spot well-suited to their campaign of torture and death.

He had kept the fact strictly to himself, but had called the district attorney for another detective to aid him in his Legion investigation, dropping the hint that he expected results, shortly. Then, he had received the anonymous death threat, commanding him to cease all operations immediately, and get out of the state!

With typical courage, the young sleuth had squared his craggy jaw, and ignored the cowardly ultimatum! All these facts harassed Ellen as she pondered the dilemma. What an opportunity to clean-up the state, expose crooked politics, if Cathern's information was correct! And Ellen felt sure that it was.

A frown puckered her lovely features, and a chain of cigarettes overflowed from the ashtray as she paced the floor. The frown was still there as she peeled the kimono from her shapely body, and stepped into pajamas. And, when Ellen retired for the night, long moments passed before she drifted off to her usual dreamless sleep.

CHAPTER TWO

A DARING VENTURE

The odds and ends closet was small, really nothing more than a locker built into one corner of the garage.

Slightly stooped, Ellen Patrick found it exceedingly uncomfortable. Although the door was open a few inches, it was stuffy and unbearably close within the cramped quarters. Perspiration bedewed her smooth white forehead and pert upper lip. From one beautifully-shaped hand protruded the ominous snout of a small, black automatic.

The upper part of her face was covered by a domino mask of black silk. A form-fitting backless frock of white satin covered her shapely figure, the scanty bodice caught in a halter neck across the creamy expanse of her lovely bosom. The cape of black silk concealed bare, kissable shoulders, and her hands were gloved.

For some hour half, Ellen had been waiting like this.

She was beginning to wonder if she had guessed wrong. Raising a gloved hand, she wiped the perspiration from her forehead with a tiny wisp of lace. Then a tight little smile curved the corners of her red mouth.

'He should be along any minute now!' she reassured herself, silently.

'And I'll get things straightened out, or give him a dose of his own medicine!'

There was no thought of failure in the little adventuress' mind. For two nights, she had checked on J. Riggs Saint and his movements. He always arrived home at the same hour, and alone. It shouldn't prove difficult to get the drop on the district attorney, she mused.

Forty-eight hours before, Paul Cathern had disappeared, vanished from his apartment and usual haunts. The sheriff's office had hunted feverishly for their ace sleuth, but to no avail. The disappearance had spurred Ellen into action.

Cautious inquiries on her part had been in vain. Immediately, she had thought of the Black Legion warning. Was her good friend to vanish as had other victims of the hooded organization?

Not if the Domino Lady could help it, she decided. In consequence, she had decided upon the boldest move of her daring career; the snatching of the unscrupulous district attorney whom she was convinced was a ring leader in Legion affairs!

The hour was nine o'clock, and it was very quiet in the residential section of town. Flattened within the tiny locker, Ellen prayed for quick action to ease the strain on her aching body and quivering nerves.

Abruptly the purr of a powerful engine came to her keen ears, and, the whisper of rubber on concrete.

A yellow glow of headlights shone through the frosted glass panels of the doors, dimly illuminating the inner confines of the spacious garage.

It was impossible for Ellen to be sure that this was J. Riggs Saint, but her nerves snapped taut and her slender fingers tightened about the corrugated butt of the automatic. Her mouth was suddenly dry. This was one of the most crucial moments of her career! An overwhelming desire for a cigarette assailed her, but she dared not risk it. Her presence must not be suspected at this stage of the game.

Came the sound of footsteps outside the garage doors, and a key gritted in the lock. The big doors swung gratingly open a moment later, and Ellen shot a surreptitious glance from her place of concealment. J. Riggs Saint, dapper, slender, was outlined in the glow of the headlights as he walked back to a powerful sedan! Her zero hour was at hand!

The big car purred smoothly as it rolled into the garage. Through the crack in the door, Ellen looked closely at the district attorney.

His features were refined, but hardened, his blue eyes icy, flint-hard. A half sneer played about his thin-lipped mouth, giving him a sinister look.

In the narrow confines of the closet, Ellen caught and held her breath. A feeling of vague apprehension went through her soft body as she thought of the gigantic task that confronted her.

Not only might Saint be a dangerous man to tackle, even with the automatic and other equipment with which she was armed, but subsequent moves would be double perilous! She shook off the apprehension, grimly.

The district attorney slid from the driver's seat. He was carrying a bulky briefcase which he handled carefully, placing it on the running board beside his feet. He reached within the car, drew the ignition key from the dash, prepared to slam the door. Abruptly, he tensed.

'*Reach high!*'

The cold, high-pitched command knifed through the garage as Ellen slid swiftly up behind the unsuspecting politician.

The muzzle of her weapon formed an icy ring of menace against Saint's neck. His hands were trembling as they shot upward over his head.

'Who – who're you?' he managed, struggling for composure, 'and what do you want here?' His tones betrayed a mixture of astonishment and rising rage.

Ellen laughed softly, but there was little of mirth in the sound. 'Do you still desire evidence against the Black Legion, Saint?' she snapped, quickly, 'so that you may prosecute? Or is it all pre-election bluff?'

Saint snorted.

'Everyone knows where I stand on that subject! I'm ready to prosecute whenever I get material evidence, not hearsays! But what has that to do with this high-handed outrage? Don't you know I'll get you a stretch in Tehachipi for this, you fool?'

Again Ellen's mocking laughter. 'I don't bluff worth a peso, Saint!' she gritted. 'So you might as well save yourself the effort! I'm going to see to it that you get the evidence you've been crying for! In fact, unless I'm badly mistaken, you'll wish you'd never heard of the Black Legion before the light of another day shines upon you, my friend!'

'I'm afraid I don't understand,' began the district attorney, weakly. 'You're a member of that Legion, Saint!' snapped Ellen, boldly.

Saint laughed, uglily. 'You're taking a lot for granted!' he said. 'And I wouldn't want the job of proving such an accusation!'

'Well, that's exactly what I'm intending to do before I'm finished, Saint!' she returned, coolly. 'Not only prove it, but see to it that you're put where you belong! You're a traitor to the honest citizens who put you in office!'

Saint edged slowly forward, his crafty eyes riveted on Ellen's automatic. 'The Domino Lady is very much wanted by a great many men in this city.' He sneered. 'I'd advise you to tend to your own business.'

Suddenly he lunged, his hand outstretched. For a moment it seemed as though he'd overpowered her. Her gun hand grasped in his own hand he catapulted with her to the floor.

For once Ellen had been taken unawares. In the uncertain light she had failed to notice his forward movement. In the moment he leaped she fired. Her bullet going, as she thought, wild.

For she had scarce time to aim in that split second.

Springing lithely to her feet Ellen stared at the form of J. Riggs Saint on the stone floor. He lay inert, strangely still . . . dead.

For a moment panic seized her.

Murder. Something she had always steered clear of. Murder. A vision of the gallows flitted across her remorseful mind. She noticed a trickle of blood seep from his temple onto the hard floor.

A feeling of nausea swept over her. She reeled, and had it not been for her nervy will, would have slipped to the floor, unconscious.

A harsh breath escaped the figure on the floor. Ellen bent, her hand retrieving the little automatic which but a moment before had slipped from her nerveless fingers. One little hand slid beneath his shirt front. He lived! His breathing was regular, though rapid.

In another moment her fingers had flecked at the smear of blood on his temple. Only a scalp wound, a crease. But it had been that perhaps, that had saved the Domino Lady from prison.

Swiftly her fingers dipped into a tiny pocket inside her cape, drew forth a small object which glittered in the indirect light. It was a little hypodermic syringe, previously loaded with a quick-acting drug. The drug, though harmless, was sufficiently strong to render the victim unconscious for several hours.

A deft motion and the sharp needle sank home, its fluid finding a place beneath his skin. Ellen Patrick was coolness personified, now. Her movements were precise, and executed with a deftness that was truly amazing.

She picked up the briefcase, opened it, and hurriedly scanned its contents. Her features lit up with an exultant smile as she read, briefly, here and there, before replacing the contents back in the case, which she tossed in the front seat of the car.

Working with incredible speed and precision, she produced a roll of cord from the garage locker and proceeded to bind the hands and feet of the insensible man. Bending, she cut a heavy strip of adhesive from a roll taken from her handy wrist bag. This was carefully applied across Saint's mouth.

It was quite a task for Ellen to get the bound figure into the rear of the sedan.

He was not a large man, but his drugged body was a limp, dead freight, and it required all the strength in her hundred and twenty pound frame to accomplish the task. She was panting softly when she had finished and closed the door.

She backed the big car noiselessly from the garage, consumed precious moments in shutting the garage doors.

Although her heart was churning madly from exertion and excitement, she was as cool as a Winter's breeze as she swung the sedan about in the street, and trod the accelerator. A laugh of triumph burst from her lips as she removed the domino mask, the big car leaped forward into the night.

CHAPTER THREE

DANGER TRAIL

The night was dark, moonless, and wisps of yellow fog had drifted in from the nearby Pacific.

A good night for her venture, mused Ellen, as she throttled the sedan to a higher speed. Paul Cathern's directions emblazoned on her mind, she felt no fear of missing her destination. A moment after she had crossed the city line, a new concrete highway stretched before her.

Along this she roared at sixty miles an hour. After five miles, she slowed the car, went forward more cautiously. Suddenly, she swung the wheel, switched on to a narrower macadam road which ran off to the left into open country.

Driving slowly, a half mile brought a winking eye of light to her attention. She cut off the sedan headlights, idled the engine to a noiseless purr. Moments later, she cut the engine off entirely, braked to a standstill. All was ominously quiet in the blackness of the foggy night.

Ellen climbed from the sedan after a quick glance assured her that her captive still slumbered. She hesitated beside the car, drew the tiny black mask again up about her eyes. The automatic again in hand, she set off in the direction of the light.

She moved soundlessly through the darkness. If this were indeed the Obispo rendezvous of the Black Legion, she might expect a guard lurking in any of the darker spaces, she knew.

And this would hold doubly true if her guess concerning the whereabouts of the missing detective was well-founded. Outwardly, she was calm, but her heart was racing, blood pounding wildly through her veins as her crisis approached.

At closer view, Ellen made out the outlines of a rather ramshackle building. It was but one story in height and possessed three rooms. The room on her left was lighted, the remainder of the structure being darkened.

She crept toward the lighted side, every sense alert to her danger. At the mere cracking of a twig under foot, she paused for precious moments, pulse pounding, and a prayer for safety on her quivering lips.

So much depended upon her this night – she just couldn't fail. It would be tonight or never! Failure now would mean tasting Saint's vengeance.

Abruptly, a dark figure loomed between her and the light which filtered from the window!

A sentry!

The man seemed to be leaning against the wall near the corner of the building, unmoving. Ellen tensed, catching her breath sharply. She hadn't tried to fool herself; these were desperate men, if she were caught, it would mean torture, death, or worse!

Many another might have faltered at the obstacle now confronting her. But the little adventuress was made of sterner stuff. The sight of a guard only added to her determination to follow through with her plans.

To one of her temperament, there was but one means of procedure. She must move directly, court the element of surprise to her favor, overcome the sentry by physical means, and as quietly as possible! She tensed, moving an inch at a time upon the unsuspecting man, the automatic reversed in her fist!

The black-hooded sentinel was half-asleep at his post. He snapped to attention a moment too late to miss the white-clad figure which hurtled upon him from out of the blackness.

A hurried motion toward his left armpit, a sucking intake of breath for a cry of warning and Ellen lunged forward, every ounce of her athletic frame behind the move, her right arm swinging in the arc of a swift half circle as she leaped.

The solid shank of the automatic whammed against the side of the guard's head. The force of her charge carried them both to the ground, this time Ellen atop the heap. She rose immediately, dusting dried grass from her clothing, and smiling grimly at the recumbent figure.

She had come prepared for such an emergency. The large roll of adhesive was put into use, sealing the man's lips, and securing his hands and feet against his possible awakening, she quickly rolled the limp figure into a dark corner near a rickety fence to prevent early discovery.

For a full minute, Ellen paused, tense, brown eyes straining in the direction of the lighted window.

Her great orbs were agleam. Here was the work that she loved, and it was being performed in the cause that meant more to her than life itself.

Adventure was her meat and danger her dessert.

Gone were the hours of planning and fuming. Action loomed ahead on the danger trail! Ellen's adventurous spirit leaped at the thought, confident, exultant!

Swiftly, yet noiseless as a night shadow, she gained the side of the window. A purr of voices came to her keen ears from within the building. A ragged shade was but partly drawn, and a view of the room was easily obtained.

Carefully avoiding the light which filtered through the panes, she looked within. She glimpsed three hooded figures seated at a table a few feet away. They were big fellows, but she could not see their features.

A rough table and several rickety chairs went to make up the furnishings of the bare room. There was a brown bottle and glasses on the table, and the men drank occasionally as they waited, conversing in low tones, inaudible to the watching girl. *The Black Legion!*

One man drinking more freely than the others was quite audible to Ellen's straining ears.

'Say, Chenville,' he bellowed, maudlinly, 'why not get things going and get 'em over with? No use waitin' on the others. Old Gorsh always was a slow poke. He'll hold the others up, and we won't get this job done before daylight! I'm for . . .'

The one addressed as Chenville interrupted with a wave of a gloved hand, but Ellen couldn't make out his words. She imagined he was reasoning with the other man. The latter laughed raucously, and poured another drink which he tossed off at a gulp.

'Yeah?' he sneered, loudly, wiping his loose mouth with the back of a gloved hand. 'That's what you say, Chenville! But I say different. I think we could do with less politics in this outfit. I never did like politics or politicians! They can't be trusted! And when it comes time to do a little job, or a little bump, it ought to be hurried along. Waitin' is only invitin' trouble to come along! Now take this snoopin' Cathern mug. He's been here for hours, waitin' for Gorsh to arrive, and superintend the job. He oughta been taken care of hours ago.'

Ellen tensed in the darkness.

Her hunch had been right!

Paul Cathern was in the hands of these men, awaiting a fate she knew not what, and with no hope of rescue save through her own efforts!

And the man's words confirmed her belief that the politicians of the state machine were behind the depredations of the notorious Black Legion!

She saw no point in waiting and listening to further disclosures. Time was speeding; any moment might be too late! She must locate Paul Cathern, save him, and at the same time keep her true identity from him. There was no time to lose if her plans were to be carried out with half a chance for ultimate success!

She tested the catch of her automatic, gripped it firmly, and moved silently through the darkness toward the other side of the house.

Obviously the thing to do was to get to Cathern as quickly as possible. She found the window on the right side of the house without difficulty, paused and listened intently. She could hear the ticking of her tiny baguette in the stillness of the night.

The little adventuress removed a compact folding jimmy from her wrist bag, opened it into a slender sliver of steel. With this handy implement, she began jimmying the window. Using utmost caution, it required several pries to snap the cast-iron fittings. With the fifth effort, they snapped brittlely, and Ellen slid the window upwards.

'Say!' she called in a sibilant whisper. 'Is anyone there?'

A slight, muffled groan was the only answer, but it sent a quick thrill through Ellen's soft body. At the moment, she realized just how alarmed she had really been about the young special investigator!

It was but the work of an instant for her to swing herself upon the sill, and agilely lower herself into the interior of the darkened room. Then, a pencil flash gave her a glimpse of the bare confines of Cathern's prison, and of the sleuth, himself.

Paul Cathern was tightly bound, a handkerchief mask over the upper part of his face, his mouth tightly sealed by a wide strip of adhesives. He had been tossed into a corner of the room to await torture and possible doom!

With a reassuring whisper, Ellen sank to her knees and labored at the cramping gyves. It required three minutes of concentrated effort to free his hands and feet, and a moment to remove the tape from his mouth. A word of thankfulness seeped from his lips as they were freed from the adhesive.

'You took a devil of a chance,' he whispered, grasping her arm, 'in coming here like this. Those men were going to torture me – lash me – burn me with white-hot irons! I owe my life to you! I'm Paul Cathern, investigator with Sheriff Bonsill. Who're you, anyhow?'

Ellen hesitated, briefly. 'No time for introductions now,' she snapped. 'But I can assure you I'm a friend! We must move fast! Everything's clear at the moment. Let's go!'

Abruptly, the little adventuress tensed in the darkness. Her hand went to Cathern's lips as she caught and held her breath. A chair had scraped within the adjoining room, and heavy footsteps were approaching the connecting door!

Her nerves jerked taut as a hand twisted the knob and swung the portal halfway open, yellow lamplight streaming across the rough flooring of the room! The automatic bristled viciously, as she aimed it at the doorway and waited!

'Get away from that door, Lucas!' snapped someone whom Ellen imagined to be the leader, Chenville. The intruder swung about to face the giver of the command, while Ellen's heart churned, madly. Would the drunken brute ignore the other man, and enter to discover her in the act of freeing her prisoner? What mercy might she expect at his hands if he did?

The queries were answered a moment later when the fellow turned again toward the prison room.

'Aw, nuts, Chenville!' he flung back over his massive shoulder. 'I'm goin' to see if the snooper's okay, that's all!'

Ellen's finger tightened upon the trigger, her heart sinking as the big man lunged forward through the doorway!

CHAPTER FOUR

A FRAMER FRAMED

A coolness settled upon Ellen Patrick as she faced one of the most crucial situations of a lifetime of adventure.

Her lovely bosom rose and fell with her accelerated breathing beneath the black cape which she had tightly drawn about the white frock.

Great eyes were fixed in an unwinking stare upon the doorway. Her slender fingers trembled a little as they contacted the safety catch of the automatic to be sure it was down. She was prepared to shoot it out with the black-hooded devils, no matter what the ultimate outcome!

But the drink-drugged intruder was spared a quick end.

Chenville was evidently the man in charge, and a subordinate's disregard of orders infuriated him. As Lucas came through the doorway, a heavy hand was clamped on his shoulder, and he was roughly jerked back into the other room.

A push sent the big man spinning across the floor.

'Damn you, Lucas!' snarled the leader, harshly.

'You'll obey orders or take the consequences! I'm in charge here, and don't forget it! One more funny move out of you, and you'll get what Gorsh gives the others!' His outburst was cut short as he slammed the door behind him, leaving Ellen and the investigator in darkness again.

Ellen heaved an immense sigh of relief. 'Whew! That was a bit too close for comfort!' she breathed, as she helped Paul Cathern to his feet.

'You said it!' agreed the sleuth, softly. 'I thought for a moment we were goners. You're one nervy little person.'

Paul Cathern staggered and would have fallen but for her steadying arm, so cramped were his limbs from long hours beneath the bindings.

She helped him to the window, across the sill, and joined him a moment later. Outside, she leaned close to him, and he caught his first glimpse of her costume and the identifying mask.

'The Domino Lady!' he exclaimed, wonderingly.

'At your service!' she returned, evenly, her soft voice tempered to a lazy, disguising drawl for Cathern's benefit. 'And having a crack at the Black Legion, and its unscrupulous political backers! I've tried to help you, Paul Cathern; will you help me in return?'

'Name it!' he said, quickly, earnestly, 'and the life you've saved will be risked in its accomplishment if necessary!'

She laughed softly in the darkness.

'The help I ask,' she said, 'will bring about the downfall of the Black

Legion and the complete ruin of the higher-ups in this state, Cathern! We must move fast! Come—'

Without another word, Ellen Patrick set out in the direction of the road, and Paul Cathern followed after her.

As the rear door of the sedan swung open, and Ellen's pencil flash sprayed the interior with white light, Paul Cathern's lips curved in a pleased grin. He stood for a moment looking down upon the bound figure of J. Riggs Saint without a hint of compassion in his gray eyes.

Then he shot a questioning glance at The Domino Lady.

'The Black Legion owes much to this man,' drawled Ellen in explanation. 'He's one of the higher-ups who provide protection! It's my idea that he should pay as they have made other victims pay!'

'Just what is your idea?' whispered Cathern, meaningly.

Ellen laughed, liquidly. 'Have you noticed the similarity in size and coloring between you and Saint?'

The investigator started. 'You're right!' he exclaimed, 'though I'd never noticed it before! Just what—'

'They were going to torture you,' she interrupted, evenly, 'and this scoundrel had assured them of immunity! What could be more appropriate than a quick switch of clothing, plant Saint in your place, and his brutes do as they will with him! By the way they looked tonight, I have a feeling that they'll fail to recognize him. And J. Riggs Saint will get a sound flogging; a dose of his own medicine.'

The special investigator grinned. 'All the way!' he cried, softly, 'and then some! Let's get busy!' He began peeling off his coat.

Ellen busied herself with the bulky briefcase she had taken from the politician.

By the dashlight, she gave its contents closer attention than before. She was astounded by the scope of damaging evidence it contained. Evidently the district attorney had been an active organizer and a charter member of the Black Legion in the state!

His intimate papers went into detail, mentioned prominent names, some of them political figures of highest power!

She turned at the sound of Cathern's voice to find him garbed in the district attorney's natty tweeds, his own rumpled worsted gracing the figure of the politician.

The latter was now conscious, and his eyes rolled in fear from one to the other of his captors. Cathern had again bound him, securely.

The tape prevented him from speaking, but he squirmed frantically about, struggling with his bonds.

The investigator bent, placed the handkerchief mask upon the upper part of the attorney's face. Thus rigged, no one could possibly tell the politician from the young detective!

And, since the Legion usually bound and taped a masked prisoner before torturing him, it looked as though J. Riggs Saint was in for a dose of his own medicine!

It wasn't far to the window. Cathern was small but wiry, with spring steel rippling along shoulders and legs. He had no particular difficulty in lifting the flabby form of the district attorney to his shoulders. Guided by Ellen, he moved noiselessly toward the house with his burden.

Sounds of maudlin singing came from the lighted room as they hefted the figure over the sill, and into the interior of the prison. Evidently, the heavy drinking Lucas had reached a state of inebriation where song alone could express his feelings. Ellen was glad.

The sounds of their movements were masked completely by the off-key bellowing of the drunken Legionaries!

They placed the still squirming form of the politician in the exact spot where Paul Cathern had lain.

A moment later, they were again outside the building, the window closed. They hurried toward Saint's sedan. Ellen would have liked to remain in the vicinity to witness the surprising denouement when Saint's men discovered that their victim was the district attorney himself, but the need for retreat was pressing.

Too much depended upon a quick return to the city, and safe disposal of the incriminating evidence to think of tarrying for the sake of pleasure!

So it was that she backed the car in a noiseless half circle, and allowed it to glide toward the distant concrete highway without engine power.

Once at a distance from the torture house, she throttled the engine to a steady, mile-eating pace, headed for the city.

There was little conversation between them as they hurtled along through the night. Ellen thought she understood why Paul Cathern was so quiet.

He was an employee of the sheriff's office, and the Domino Lady was reputedly outside the law. She had saved his life, and he couldn't very well question her or attempt to establish her identity!

He looked out of the window, away from her, his long fingers testing the toughness of a two-day growth of dark beard on his lean cheeks.

As they crossed the city limits, and neared a cab stand, Ellen laughed swiftly, and slowed the sedan.

'Obviously, you must leave me here,' she told him in the assumed drawl, 'since I must remove the mask before driving farther into the city. And I must ditch Riggs Saint's car, you know! You should have no difficulty in getting a taxi to your apartment.'

For the first time in minutes, he looked at her, intently.

'Certainly!' he returned, quickly.

'I understand! But before we part, let me assure you of my undying gratitude for this night's work! I've heard some pretty awful things about The Domino Lady in the past.'

She interrupted. 'And you believed them, of course?'

Cathern grinned.

'Perhaps I did,' he admitted, 'but never again! You're aces with me! If I can ever help you in any way, please call upon me. I owe a lot to you.'

Again Ellen interrupted, as she drew the sedan to the curb.

'Forget it!'

And then, 'It was all in the night's work. I'm amply repaid if you're convinced that I'm not the creature my enemies would have everyone believe. But there is one favor you can grant me, if you will.'

'Just name it!' he said, eagerly.

Ellen held out the briefcase to him.

'Take this,' she said, 'and see that it gets into the right hands. It contains a lot of vital information which will help to break up the Black Legion in California. It contains dates, rituals and a complete list of political office holders who are secretly members of the clan.'

'But the credit?' interpolated Paul Cathern, soberly.

She gestured with gloved hands, briefly. 'Who cares about that? It was only to defeat the political machine that I became interested. If you will take this evidence I'll be more than satisfied. As an officer, the credit will set well on your shoulders.'

He had climbed from the car, briefcase in hand, but now he leaned through the window, and grasped her hand. Her red lips pursed a charming:

'Goodbye.'

'Till we meet?' he breathed, with an engaging grin.

'*Quien sabe?*'

She meshed the gears, rolled from the curb, pulling the domino from her round cheeks as soon as she was out of range of his vision. It was one o'clock when she parked the sedan, got out and walked away. Twice she looked behind her, fearful that some prowl car might connect the abandoned Saint car with her. But her fears were groundless; the streets were deserted. A short time later, she had descended from a cab and entered the exclusive apartment house which she called home.

CHAPTER FIVE

THE DOMINO LADY TRIUMPHANT

It was evening of the following day when Ellen Patrick moved across the heavy Boukhara of her living room and opened the outside door. Paul Cathern entered the room. He carried a folded newspaper, and he was grinning, widely. He took off his gray felt as he closed the door, then followed Ellen to the center of the room.

The powder-blue negligee she affected set off her shapely rounded body to perfection, and Cathern's eyes were freighted with frank admiration as he followed the intoxicating undulations of her figure as she sank down upon a crimson chaise longue. She smiled, motioned him to sit beside her.

'Suppose you give an account of yourself, big boy?' she said, pertly, brows arched in interrogation. 'Haven't seen you around.'

Paul Cathern had such an engaging grin, and it broadened to show his white teeth as he dropped down beside Ellen. He unfolded a late edition of the Express, handed it to her.

'Perhaps this will explain,' he said.

Ellen feigned complete amazement as she looked at the paper. Little sounds of excitement and pleasure escaped her ripe lips as she read the information emblazoned upon the front page:

BLACK LEGION
DEFINITELY DOOMED!
Charter members fleeing after exposé
by ace sleuth from sheriff's office.
Indictments out for leading political figures;
J. Riggs Saint, District Attorney,
Is mysteriously missing!

June 7. Following a startling exposé of Black Legion activities in the state, by Paul Cathern, special investigator from Sheriff Bonsill's office, indictments have been sworn out for some of the leading politicians, including J. Riggs Saint, District Attorney, and Leo U. Gorsh, State Representative.

Saint has handed in his written resignation, but cannot be reached for a statement. One report has it that he is confined in a private hospital, suffering from mysterious injuries that threaten his life. Another that he is taking an extended sea voyage for his health. Mr. Gorsh is reported as flying to Mexico City on business. In any event, both gentlemen will find a warm welcome awaiting them when they are located and turned over to the newly-appointed District Attorney, Mr. John Smithson. This is one of the most startling exposés in the history of the state, and politicians both big and small are leaving for parts unknown by rail, water and air. Mr. Smithson, interviewed at his office today, promises a thorough clean-up, and in taking every step to apprehend the fleeing higher-ups of the Black Legion . . .

There were columns more of lurid details, but Ellen turned to her visitor without reading them. Her great eyes were gleaming. Her plans had worked out to perfection! This was her most successful and far-reaching master stroke against the state machine which had brought about the death of her father! It all seemed too marvelous to be true and she leaned toward Paul Cathern, lovely bosom tossing with emotion.

'Oh, Paul! It's wonderful!' she cried softly. 'Almost too good to be true! It's simply great to think that you accomplished so much where all others have failed.' She leaned closer, kissed him lightly upon the cheek. He grinned.

'It's great, all right, honey!' he told her, enthusiastically, 'but I'd never have accomplished anything without help. In fact, if it hadn't been for the timely interference of a mysterious lady, I wouldn't be alive now!'

Ellen looked at Cathern, intently. 'A mysterious lady?' she repeated softly, 'I don't understand, Paul. It fails to mention her in the news.'

The investigator's grey eyes focused upon her piquant face, the grin fading. 'Last night,' he said, slowly, 'I was a prisoner of the Black Legion, facing torture, or worse. A fearless woman, The Domino Lady, seized the D.A., rescued me from under the noses of my guards, and substituted Riggs Saint in my place! That no doubt accounts for his "mysterious injuries" referred to in the Express! The Domino Lady likewise turned over to me incriminating documents she had taken from Saint. Those documents furnished the exposé you've been reading about, yet she insisted that I take full credit, and leave her name out of it! Don't you agree that I owe the lady much, Ellen?'

She smiled, 'Why, yes, of course, Paul. But I thought The Domino Lady was wanted by the police? How could you permit her to go free?'

Cathern's eyes softened. 'Ellen,' he said, 'I recognized The Domino Lady!'

The little adventuress' body went rigid. With a great effort she fought down the panic that welled within her slender frame. She raised guileless eyes to meet his probing glance.

'So what?' she managed, precisely.

For a moment his eyes held hers, in an effort to read her calm gaze.

'Don't you see I couldn't betray her, honey?' he murmured, 'after she'd saved my life, and accomplished so much good for the state? Besides,' he went on, grinning again, 'the credit she bestowed upon me has assured me a fancy promotion! If the authorities wait on me to reveal the identity of The Domino Lady, they're going to have a mighty long wait!'

She breathed a deep sigh of relief, leaned against Cathern. She smiled at him, her great eyes filled with admiration for the conquering male.

'You're tops, Paul!' she breathed. 'A grand person! Any woman would be lucky to have you for a friend, I'm so glad of your success and promotion, darling! Shall we drink a toast to them?'

Paul Cathern smiled, understandingly, and manipulated the decanter. He handed a drink to Ellen, then dropped down beside her again, glass in hand. They touched glasses, lifted them high.

409

'To the future!' she toasted, softly, brown eyes starry.

'Of The Domino Lady!' added Paul Cathern, meaningly.

He rose, replaced the glasses upon their taboret without looking at her. Then he turned. Ellen Patrick laughed throatily as she went to his open arms.

THREE WISE MEN OF BABYLON
RICHARD SALE

Strangely forgotten today, Richard Sale (1911–1993) was one of the most successful pulp writers of the 1930s and '40s, known as 'the Dumas of the pulps,' and then enjoyed even greater success in Hollywood. At the peak of the pulp era, his work was in such demand that he averaged a story a week for *Argosy*, *Detective Fiction Weekly*, *Dime Detective* and most other top magazines while also writing novels, producing a million words a year for a decade. His first novel, *Not Too Narrow, Not Too Deep* (1936), about tough prisoners attempting to escape from Devil's Island, was filmed as *Strange Cargo* in 1940 with his screenplay. Two of his best, most enduring and quirkiest novels were set in Hollywood. *Lazarus #7* (1942) involves a movie star with murderous intentions and leprosy, and a studio doctor who raises dogs from the dead. *Passing Strange* (1942) tells the story of a doctor shot dead while performing a Caesarian on a famous movie star.

Sale's most famous pulp creations were Joe 'Daffy' Dill, a tough-talking wiseguy who appeared in *Detective Fiction Weekly* with regularity, and Dinah Mason his outrageously gorgeous colleague at the New York *Chronicle*. She is not one of the boys. She looks like a Petty girl, only better, and is a good reporter but gets sick at the sight of a corpse. In a running sidebar to the mysteries they get involved with, for years Dill asked Dinah to marry him.

'Three Wise Men from Babylon' was first published in the April 1, 1939, issue of *DFW*.

THREE WISE MEN OF BABYLON

RICHARD SALE

It was a Friday when the holocaust began. I remember that because Friday was never a good day for me. I don't like fish, black cats bother me, and the Friday issue of the *Chronicle* is always, for some reason, the kind that runs a guy ragged around the arches. So it was a Friday, and when I say holocaust, I don't mean a casual massacre.

I was sitting at my desk in that dark and dingy corner of the city room which I call home because nobody else will, and I was writing a follow up on the suicide of a guy named Milton Swan, when a Western Union boy popped into the city room and began to call my name. McGinty at the sports desk showed the boy over to me, and I signed for the wire and did not tip him.

'Well, well,' Dinah Mason said, 'wires from Garbo, hah? I knew I never should have let you go cover that screwy case in Hollywood. I don't care if Candid Jones did go with you, he's a pal of yours and if you told him to say that you didn't carry the torch for any—'

'Did Candid say I'd been a good boy? Bless his little heart,' I said. 'And how do you get that way, Angel-Eyes? Don't you trust me?'

'Sure,' Dinah said. 'Like I trust king cobras.'

'You've got a nerve,' I said. 'You won't marry me, so why should you worry what cutie I parade in the Tinsel Town? Confidentially, my hollyhock, time goes on, you get older, silver threads among the gold, and your chances may not be so good. You'd better grab me now while you can still handle a husband. And lay off trying to pump Candid on my movie-town activities . . . Well?'

'Well, what?' Dinah said, preening her platinum hair as she sat there on the edge of my desk. 'If you mean will I marry you, the answer is hmm.'

'Nix,' I snapped, irked. 'I mean, what are you hanging around for? Can't you see I'm busy?'

'Yes, darling,' she said. 'But you also have not opened that telegram and I'm just dying to see what kind of a sap would spend the mazuma to send you a message via the wires when it would only cost three cents to write the same thing. Open up and let's have a look.'

I stared at her. 'You uncommon buzzard,' I said. 'No wonder you got so interested and came over to sling words with me. This wire.'

'From Hollywood,' she said. 'Who sent it? Come on.'

I opened the wire and I looked at the date line. It was Babylon, Iowa, and I told her so. That fixed it. 'Babylon, Iowa,' Dinah snorted. 'Well, personally, I wouldn't care what it said after that name for a town. It's all yours and you can have it.'

Well, as it turned out, Dinah did the right thing. It *was* all mine and I was stuck with it. The telegram said:

DAFFY DILL

N Y CHRONICLE

NEW YORK N Y

   WILBUR PENN PROMINENT BABYLON CITIZEN SHOT AND KILLED BY UNKNOWN ASSAILANT TONIGHT AT TEN PM STOP HAVE ATTEMPTED TO REACH PENNS BROTHER NAMED MARTIN PENN SOMEWHERE IN NEW YORK CITY BUT AM UNABLE TO LOCATE HIM STOP APPRECIATE IT IF YOU COULD FIND HIM AND GET STATEMENT FROM HIM CONCERNING MURDER OF HIS BROTHER STOP WILL SPLIT NEWS ON CASE WITH YOU IF YOU HELP STOP WIRE CHARGES COLLECT

JOHN HARVEY

EDITOR BABYLON GAZETTE

Well, that was a hot one. I was to go out and scour New York looking for some punk named Martin Penn to get a statement out of him about a murder in a hick town in Iowa, and the editor of the town rag, Mr. Harvey, was going to be big about it and split news with me concerning his gigantic murder case. As if the readers of the New York sheets would give two hoots about murder in Babylon (Iowa). The picture of me roaming the wintry streets looking for a statement was not at all appealing.

I would have tossed the telegram in the waste basket, if I hadn't had a conscience. Wilbur Penn shot tonight. That meant the night before and that meant I was holding a night letter, not a straight telegram and that meant Mr. Harvey was a cheap skate.

So I took the telegram in to the Old Man who was sitting forlornly in his doghouse, his green eyeshade hiding his eyes and accentuating the glistening prairie of hairless dome that covered his skull. I dropped the thing on his desk and I said, 'Rural editor asks collaboration. How do you like them berries?'

'Don't bother me,' said the Old Man. 'Can't you see I'm reading?'

He had a copy of *How to Make Friends and Influence People* in his lap, and I tsk-tsked and shook my head. 'Come on, come on,' I said. 'You're too far gone for that book to do you any good. Take a look at this thing and grab a laugh. They're few enough nowadays.'

The Old Man picked up the wire and read it, and he didn't laugh.

When he had finished it, he said, 'What's so funny about it? Just because it's a hick town? A hick paper? There's nothing funny in that. We didn't all begin in New York, Mr. Dill, like yourself. Some of us were small town scribes for years before we got a break and came on here. Do you know where I came from before I hit New York? Wipe that smile off your face. The name of the town was Punxatawney, Pa . . . So go ahead and cover for John Harvey.'

'Go ahead – and cover – for him?' I said. 'You mean you're going to waste me on this guy's Babylon killing?'

'I've always made it a policy,' replied the Old Man severely, 'to cast my bread upon the waters. When a man wires me for help from out of town, I give. Don't be a sap, Daffy. The day might come when you would wind up in Babylon, Iowa, needing a stake, an 'in', or just plain help. And having helped this guy once, he'll help you twice.'

'I have no intention of ever going to Babylon,' I said. 'The Bible told me it was a sinful, wicked place. It should have said that there was a moocher in the place too.'

'Never mind the wisecracks,' said the Old Man wearily. 'Cover for this guy. And just to make sure you do, let me see Milton Penn's—'

'Martin Penn,' I said sarcastically.

'You let me see his statement before you wire it. It would not be unlike you to forge a statement from Daffy Dill, Esk., rather than go out and find this other guy. Snap into it.'

When I came out of the doghouse, Dinah met me and shook her head. 'Boy, you look low.'

'I am low,' I said. 'Out of seven and a half million people in this burg, I've got to find one guy to ask him for a statement.'

'Far be it from me to simplify your existence,' Dinah said, patting my cheek. 'But did you ever think of looking up the lug in a telephone book and asking for his statement via Alexander Bell's marvelous invention?'

I said, 'Wonderful! At rare intervals you show genius.'

'A mere nothing, my dear Watson.'

I went through a Manhattan telephone directory and found one Martin Penn as easily as falling off a log. *Martin Penn*, it said, *107 Beeker Place r. CRawford 2-2399.*

I buzzed the number, but after a few clicks the operator said, 'Sorry, sir, your party does not answer. I will call you again in twenty minutes.'

Well, that was all right. But when five P.M. rolled around and the party still had not answered, I knew that I was going to have to go up there and interview the guy when he got home from work, and that it was all kind of a nuisance. Dinah made a date for dinner, but I agreed only on condition that she went up to Beeker Place with me. She must have been hungry because she accepted the stipulation without a howl.

415

So off we went to cover the man from Babylon, Iowa, little knowing what we were letting ourselves in for . . .

Martin Penn was not home. He lived in a small apartment house in Beeker Place and we rang his doorbell for ten minutes before we gave it up as a bad job. I was just as glad but Dinah, the little nimbus cloud, only said, 'Hi-ho, it only means you have to come back tomorrow and try, try again. Let's eat at the Hideaway Club. I haven't seen Bill Latham since they put Santa Claus' whiskers back among the moth-balls.'

That was all right with me. We took a cab over to Broadway where the Hideaway Club failed to live up to its name by advertising its location in no uncertain neon lights.

Bill Latham greeted us at the door with a broad grin. 'Well, well,' he said, 'the Fourth Estate in person. Are you following Poppa Hanley around or did he tell you to meet him here?'

'Is that galoot here?' Dinah sighed. 'Oh great gouts of blood – now he and Daffy will discuss death and detection all night. It's like going out to dinner with a signal 32 ringing in your ears. I'll bet you five fish, Bill, that they get a call before dessert.'

'I'll take it,' Latham grinned. 'Things have been pretty quiet, Poppa was telling me, so the chances are you'll lose. He's over there in a wall booth, down by the band.'

We wended our way past the jitterbugs on the dance floor and reached the red leather booth where Poppa was sitting, mangling a half a dozen oysters and looking pompously dignified.

When he saw us, he leaped to his feet and looked happier. Poppa is one homely man, when you come right down to it. He was all dressed up, but that didn't keep his long ears from sticking out like an elephant's flappers, and his face, always brick red, was holding its own. 'Golly,' he said, 'this is a pleasure, Dinah. If only you could have left the runt at home. Oh well, a guy can't have everything. Sit down.'

. . . Dinah won the five bucks. We had finished the beefsteaks and were waiting for the salad when Bill Latham came over and slipped a fin in Dinah's bag and said, 'Telephone call for you, Lieutenant. Will you take it here?'

Poppa looked grim and nodded. They brought a telephone to the booth and plugged it in.

'Wow,' I said, 'so you've been to Hollywood, Bill, eh? This is the way they do it in the Brown Derby and Sardi's out there. Guys go to eat in those joints and tell their butlers to give them a ring, just so they'll be paged and get the eye from the other customers.'

Poppa said, 'Hello? This is Hanley . . . Oh, hello, Babcock. I'm eating dinner. I told you not to call unless it was something important . . . eh? . . . Oh . . . Hell . . . All right. What's the address again? . . . I've got it. I'll meet you there. You pick up Claghorn and Louie, and tell Dr. Kyne to come running. I think he's over in Bellevue. I'll see you there.'

He hung up and took a deep breath and sighed and looked at me.

Dinah groaned, 'The march of crime.'

'A guy,' Hanley said to me. 'Bumped off. Want to come?'

'Who is it?' I said. 'Of course I'll come. If I didn't come, the Old Man would beat my pride into the dust, grrr!'

'Guy named Fenwick Hanes,' said Poppa. 'Babcock got the call through Telegraph Bureau. Someone telephoned in and said that this guy had been found in the Hotel Metronome on West 45th. That's not far from you. Let's go see. Just up Broadway a couple of blocks. You heard what I said.'

'Well,' Dinah said sourly, 'I'll be a rootin' tootin' hillbilly if I get left here alone with the check. I'm coming too, boys, and don't argue with a woman. *Garsong! L'addition* for these gentlemen!'

We got out of there and walked north, the three of us, until Dinah got a stitch in her side from the pace. 'Take it easy,' she said. 'That meal is having its troubles. The fellow is dead. Why the rush?'

'Listen, Angel-Eyes,' I said. 'The last time you saw a corpse, you passed out on me. I think you'd better go home.'

'Not me,' Dinah said grimly. 'I've got a date with you and not even a murder is going to make me a wall-flower.'

We reached the Metronome a few minutes later and found Detective Claghorn waiting for us in the lobby downstairs. We shook hands with him and then we went up.

Claghorn said, 'I came right up, Chief, when I heard the news. Did Babcock telephone you? I guess he's on the way with the stuff and the M.E. I happened to be home when he buzzed me and I don't live far from here myself. The manager is upstairs and I don't think we're gonna get a lead from what he said.'

On the seventh floor, we found the manager, a man named Horace Wilson, who was pasty faced and nervous. 'These things are always bad publicity for the hotel,' he groaned, 'but what can we do about them? They always happen.'

'Let's have a look-see,' Hanley grunted noncommittally.

We opened the door and went in. Dinah took one look and opened the door and went out again. 'I'll wait downstairs,' she said. 'I'll tell the other boys where to come. But as for me, I just had dinner and I don't want to waste the money you all spent on it. See you anon.'

Dinah is a sissy, but I like her for it. These women who can look a stiff in the eye without flinching are too hard-boiled for Daffy. It wasn't that Mr. Fenwick Hanes was a mess, for he wasn't. He had been murdered very neatly indeed, and there was little blood.

Fenwick Hanes had been shot to death. One shot. He was lying in his bed with his shoes and his coat and vest off.

'Mr. Hanes left a message at the desk that he was to be awakened at eight o'clock,' the manager explained. 'Apparently he decided to take a nap. He was in from out of town and had been running around quite a bit and was tired. At eight P.M., the elevator boy heard a shot. He called me and I came in and found him like that.'

'Hmm,' said Hanley. 'Looks like a .32 . . .' He stared at the manager. 'You mean that's all there is? You didn't see anyone in here?'

'Yes.'

I went over and picked up a small alarm clock which Hanes had set by his bed. It said eight-thirty. I looked at it sharply and I said, 'Boy, if this could only talk.'

The elevator boy showed up then along with Dr. Kerr Kyne and Babcock and the police fotog. Hanley went to work on the boy and the gist of it was that the boy had been going by the floor when he heard a shot. He instantly came back to the seventh floor and stepped out. He said he heard a bell ringing. Then he went for the manager. He did not see anybody.

Big help. I could see the disappointment in Hanley's face.

Well, it was one of those things. I wasn't particularly interested in the killing and I didn't see where the *Chronicle's* readers would be. Just a hotel knock-off. That is, until I asked for some dope on Fenwick Hanes himself.

'We don't know anything about him,' said the manager. 'He checked in three days ago and signed the register Fenwick Hanes, Babylon, Iowa—' The manager stopped short because of the way I gaped at him.

'Babylon, Iowa!' I said.

'That's right.'

I grabbed the telephone and then set it down again. I was that excited. Then I took up a telephone book and looked up the apartment in Beeker Place and telephoned the superintendent. 'This is the police department,' I growled at the super while Hanley watched me as though he thought me half cracked. 'I want you to go right up to Mr. Penn's apartment and open it and have a look at it. We have a tip that there's been foul play and we're checking on it. You telephone back and tell me what you find.' And I gave him the number. 'Ask for Lieutenant Hanley, room 706.'

'All right,' said the super. 'I'll take a look right away.'

Ten minutes later he telephoned back and I grabbed the handset and listened while he roared shrilly, 'Murder! Murder! Mr. Penn is been murdered!'

I hung up instantly and I turned to Poppa Hanley and said, 'Three wise men, all of Babylon, all dead. Come on, Poppa. The thing is really beginning to get hot.'

*

Wilbur Penn had been killed in Babylon. Martin Penn had been killed the day before we found him. Fenwick Hanes had been killed at eight P.M. this very night.

What had started with a routine inquiry from Iowa had suddenly blossomed into three exceedingly dead corpses. Which goes to show that life is still full of little surprises.

Poppa and I sent Dinah home and we left Babcock and Claghorn over at the Metronome and took Dr. Kerr Kyne with us. 'I want it clearly understood,' Dr. Kyne said to me with sarcasm as we drove to Beeker Place, 'that you never call me Buzzard again. For if anybody ever made me look like an amateur when it comes to hovering over the dead, you are that man, Mr. Dill, and it gives me great pleasure to say that I can practically scent the smell of graveyards all over and around you.'

I let him go on. I couldn't help smiling because it was about time he got a chance to crow a little. We reached Beeker Place in nothing flat and were greeted at the door by the superintendent who was almost hysterical with fright. He took us right up to the apartment where Dinah and I had previously rung the bell to no avail. He unlocked the door and we trooped in.

Dr. Kerr Kyne went right to work. Martin Penn was dead, all right. You didn't have to be the chief M. E. of New York County to gather that much. He was a thin, sharp sort of man with a shrewd face, this corpse which sat comfortably in a chair. No bullet in the head this time, as in the case of Fenwick Hanes. This bullet had struck Martin Penn directly over the heart. From the expression on the dead man's face, it was plain that he had seen his killer, perhaps even talked with him. For there was hate in Martin Penn's face and no fooling.

We had better luck here though. Dr. Kyne said that Penn had been dead for at least thirty-six hours and that the slug was a .32, and undoubtedly the same gun which killed Hanes had killed Penn. I reminded myself to check with John Harvey of the *Babylon Gazette* on the slug which had killed Wilbur Penn. There was an avenging angel on the trail somewhere and it would be a good idea if we stopped him. Murder is a habit when you do too much of it, the killer might easily leave a line of dead behind him, getting scared and more scared on the way. It's fear that makes murder, in one way or another.

Martin Penn had been a shrewd man, so shrewd that even in death he had pointed out a clue to the identity of his killer.

Sitting in that chair, with a bullet in his body, he had not died at once. This isn't strange, for I have seen men shot through the heart with a high-power copper-jacket still stumble on and fire several shots, although they were already dead. In man, there is sometimes an unconquerable will which makes him perform even after a mortal wound has been inflicted. In any case, with his own finger, dipped in the blood of his own wound,

Martin Penn had traced something upon the maple arm of the chair in which he sat.

It was a flat-sided arm, wide enough to take a pad for sketching, and the blood had dried black upon the wood, leaving his handiwork quite plain there by his right hand.

It was the sketch, crude and macabre, of an ear. Just one ear.

But it was enough to start me thinking and I remembered the alarm clock and suddenly I said, 'Poppa, I think I get it.'

'You're a smarter guy than I am if you do,' Poppa said sourly.

'An ear,' I said. 'Well, what about an ear? It would just be guessing if we had this killing alone. But we've got the Fenwick Hanes murder too, and to me, the distinctive thing about that one was the alarm clock. Did you know that the alarm had run down on the thing? And the alarm hand was set for eight o'clock. Now it's my guess – guess, mind you – that Hanes wanted to make an evening performance at eight-thirty in some theater. He told the desk to wake him at eight. He didn't trust them, but set the clock for eight himself. Everything happened at eight. There was a killer in there who shot him. The elevator boy heard the bell ringing even when the shot was fired. Which would mean the alarm went off before Hanes was killed. *And it was allowed to run down!* Now, Poppa – look me in the eye and imagine me a killer. I'm standing here and I'm going to bump you off. Just as I'm getting up nerve, an alarm clock goes off. What do I do?'

'You instinctively turn off the alarm because it's noisy and you're afraid of two things: You're afraid it'll wake up your victim and you're afraid it will attract outside attention.'

'Fine,' I said, 'and right. I never saw a man yet who didn't dive for an alarm clock to turn it off when it started to holler. Yet this killer stood there, heard the alarm, shot Hanes, then scrammed, and the alarm kept going to advertise things. What does that mean to you?'

'It means,' said Hanley heavily, 'that the killer was deaf.'

'It sure does,' I said. 'And Martin Penn didn't sweat out his last seconds drawing this ear for no other reason but that.'

Hanley grunted. 'Well, you don't have to look so pleased about it. I still don't see how it gives us a lead. All we have to do is find a guy with a .32 caliber gun which fits these bullets, the guy being deaf. Huh. That's *all* we have to do.'

'I think,' I said, 'that when you get a line on the Penns and Hanes, it will narrow down your choice considerably. But as for now, I see nothing to keep me from returning to the gay white way. So long, Pater, I'm to pick up Dinah and see the sights. Tomorrow I'll buzz John Harvey in Babylon and see what he has to offer on the murder of Wilbur Penn.'

At the city room of the New York *Chronicle*, next morning at ten A.M., I gladdened the Old Man's heart by pounding out the dope on the stories of the night before, and then I telephoned the *Babylon Gazette* out in Iowa – at the *Chronicle's* expense – and asked to speak with John Harvey. I got a man named Wooley who apparently worked on the sheet and he said, 'Gosh, Mr. Dill, it's funny you should call him. He's not here. He left for New York yesterday morning and he'll be arriving on the Golden Arrow sometime this morning in Pennsylvania Station. This murder out here is raising a lot of fuss, and when he didn't hear from you in answer to his telegram, he decided to go on to New York himself and see Wilbur Penn's brother. There are some folks here think Martin Penn shot his own brother, and John wants to be first on the spot to make sure. He said he'd go see you and maybe you could help him find Martin Penn. I think the train gets in at eleven.'

'I can show him Martin Penn all right,' I said. 'Mr. Penn is now residing in the morgue. There's a headline for your rag. Martin Penn was shot and killed two days ago in his New York apartment. He was killed before his brother Wilbur was, only nobody knew it. I'll meet Harvey at the train. So long.'

How I was going to pick John Harvey out of the welter getting off the Golden Arrow I didn't know, but I made a try. I went up to Pennsy and tipped a porter to page John Harvey when the crowd came off the ramp. But I didn't locate him in the crowd and no one answered the name. I had lunch at a drugstore fountain and then went downtown again.

When I got there, Mr. Harvey was waiting for me.

He was a little man in an old suit, his hair touched with gray, and he smoked cigarettes without touching them. The one I saw just hung in his mouth and he handled it wonderfully with his lips. He had a big mole on the right cheek.

'Sure am glad to meet you, Mr. Dill,' John Harvey said. 'I guess you don't know how out-country editors kind of idolize the way you do things. When that Penn murder broke I said to myself, what a break it would be if Daffy Dill could help us out on the New York end.'

'Well, I was helping you,' I said. 'I didn't wire you but I got out on the rounds and I telephoned you this morning and got Woolsey. Then I went up to the station to meet you.'

'You went up to meet me?' he said. 'I didn't see you, and I'd have recognized you from your pictures, I think. I went out the cab way and got right in a cab. I've still got my luggage with me here.'

I glanced down and saw he had two bags with him.

'Well,' I said, 'I suppose you've heard the news.'

'I just arrived. I've heard nothing.'

'Martin Penn is dead, shot and killed before your friend Wilbur ever was. Did you know a man named Fenwick Hanes?'

'Of Babylon? Certainly I did. Nasty old coot. Used to hang around with

Wilbur and Martin Penn and Maxwell Green. The four of them pulled together quite a while.'

'He's in New York,' I said. 'Dead too.'

Harvey stared at me. 'Dead in New York? I saw him in Babylon on Wednesday.'

'At the morgue,' I persisted grimly. 'With a tag on his toe.'

'My God,' he said huskily.

'Now listen,' I said, 'you're supposed to go over to Police Headquarters. Lieutenant William Hanley wants to talk with you. He thinks you can give him some dope on the backgrounds of these corpses, and I think you can too. We need help. We're stymied.' I watched him light a cigarette and he glanced down at the match as he did so, and I said, 'The little brown fox jumped over the big high fence.'

'Well,' said Harvey looking up, 'I'll run down there then and help them out, and then I want to see you again, and get the story on this for my own paper. Will I find you here?'

'You will,' I said, 'as soon as you come back.'

'May I leave my things here? I'll put up at a hotel when I come back. I don't know New York at all. Never been here before in my life.'

'They'll be right here,' I said.

As soon as he had left, I telephoned TWA airlines and I said, 'Did you have a plane leaving from Babylon, Iowa, yesterday morning at ten A.M.?'

'No,' they said. 'But the Des Moines plane left at ten A.M. and Des Moines is only twenty miles from Babylon. If you wanted to fly to New York, you'd run over to Des Moines and get the plane there.'

'When did that ship come in?'

'Three yesterday afternoon.'

'Thanks very much.' I hung up and Dinah came over. I pointed at the grips and I said, 'A very careless guy, my hollyhock. For instance, how would you get a TWA tag on your luggage if you'd come east on the Pennsy's Golden Arrow?'

'Simple, dolt,' she said. 'It's a tag from a previous trip.'

'Could be,' I said, 'but ain't for one reason. Guy says he's never been to New York before in his life. Tag says *Destination N.Y.* So?'

'You've got something there,' Dinah said. 'And you can have it.'

'The little brown fox jumped over the big high fence,' I said.

'Have you gone crazy?' Dinah said. 'What has the fox got to do with the high cost of living?'

'Not a thing,' I said. 'But when I told John Harvey about the little fox, he didn't seem to worry about it at all. Never even noticed I said it.'

'Maybe he's just polite.'

'And on the other hand, maybe the laddy is deaf. He spoke with me all the time, watching my lips carefully. I gave him the fox business when his

422

eyes were off my face, and he never heard it. He's deaf. He reads the lips. He didn't come in on the Golden Arrow. He came in on the Sky Chief yesterday, in time to bump off Fenwick Hanes last night at eight bells. And I'll bet you dough he's only sticking around to grab off someone else. He knocked off Wilbur Penn himself, and I'll bet you a fin he was in town two days ago on Tuesday to slip the slug into Martin Penn up in Beeker Place. How? We see now.'

I telephoned the *Babylon Gazette* again long distance and got hold of Woolsey once more. 'This is Daffy Dill again,' I said. 'I want some info, my friend, and for it I'll promise to hand you the biggest scoop your rag ever printed, and you'll have it on the streets before the Des Moines papers ever see it. Tell me one thing: where was John Harvey on Tuesday? He wasn't in town was he?'

'Oh no,' Woolsey said. 'John left Sunday afternoon to take a little fishing trip up in Michigan. He likes to go after muskellunge up there. He got back here Wednesday morning.'

'Does a Maxwell Green live in Babylon?'

Woolsey hesitated.

'He used to, but he lives in New York now. Him and Martin Penn are lawyers together, somewhere in New York.'

'That's all I wanted to know,' I said. 'Thanks.' I hung up.

'All right, brainstorm,' Dinah Mason said dryly. 'What's up?'

'Get me a telephone book,' I said, 'and we'll soon see.'

Dinah threw hers over and I looked up Maxwell Green. He was there all right. He lived on West 56th Street and I gave him a ring.

'Hello?' a voice said.

'Maxwell Green?'

'Yes.'

'Of Babylon, Iowa?'

'That's right,' he said. 'Who is this? Harvey?'

'Yes.' I said it on the spur of the moment to see what would come.

'Look here, Harvey,' Maxwell Green said heavily, 'I told you I'd see you at eleven-thirty and it's nearly that now. You said it was important enough for me to remain at home. Now you'd better get here and get here fast with your important matter. I haven't got all day to waste on you.' He slammed up.

Victim number four. And he didn't even know it. 'Hello, Poppa,' I said a few minutes later. 'Is Harvey still there?'

'Still here?' Poppa Hanley said. 'He hasn't been here yet.'

Oh yes, I saw the gag nicely. Never been in New York before. Must have got lost. But meanwhile John Harvey was on his way to 56th Street to kill a man.

'Hanley!' I snapped. 'Get over here fast. Pick me up. Bring a rod. We're going to stop another one! Now make it fast, Poppa, we've got no seconds to lose!' I gasped. 'No – wait a minute, Poppa. No time. You haven't time to pick me up. Meet you there!'

I gave him the address, hung up and called Maxwell Green back. 'Listen, Mr. Green,' I snapped, 'and get it straight the first time. This is Daffy Dill of the *New York Chronicle*—'

'No statement,' he snapped and hung up.

The damned old fool. I rang him again but he wouldn't answer.

I got my faithful old grave-scratcher out of the drawer, tore downstairs and grabbed a cab. I waved a bill under the driver's nose and we went north like a bat out of hell. We took the west side express highway up to Fifty-second and cut off and then doubled back. We made it damned fast. When we pulled up in front of the building I saw that I had beaten Poppa Hanley there and I went in like a Roman ram.

The doorbells said that Maxwell Green lived on the fourth floor. I tried the vestibule door but it was locked, so I broke the glass with my gun butt and opened the door from the inside. I went up the stairs like a madman, and I heard Poppa Hanley's siren approaching down the street. It was a nice thing to hear, believe me.

When I reached the fourth floor I was in a blind panic. I went from door to door looking for the name *Green* and finally found it and tried the knob. The door was locked.

From across the hall I charged at that door and hit it with my shoulder. I weigh one eighty and I was glad of it then because I knocked that lock clean out of its socket, split that door in half and nearly rooked my shoulder.

I didn't fall. I was careful not to fall. I balanced my weight when I hit the door so that I was standing in a fixed position with my gun hand ready when I came to a stop.

I was right.

John Harvey was standing there. He had forced Mr. Maxwell Green into a chair and in Harvey's hand was a .32 caliber Colt revolver with the hammer back and his index finger flexing on the trigger.

I think if John Harvey had ben able to hear, he might have shot me dead when I hit that door. But he couldn't hear. He saw the expression on Maxwell Green's face, and only because of that did he know something was amiss. By the time he turned, he was rattled, and when he saw me, he was more rattled.

He fired twice at me before he had his gun all the way around. He put two bullets through the window, only one of them had an urn in front of it and there was a hell of a crash.

I didn't want to kill that guy because he knew too much that Hanley wanted to know in the way of explanation, but what can you do when someone is throwing lead at you? You don't aim carefully down the barrel and then break a kneecap. You just keep fanning the trigger and aiming low from instinct and hoping your next one will put him down. But he stands there too long; you think he's never going to fall. He stands there and you see the red spit of his gun and a bullet cracks by your ear. Close, that means. They only crack when they're close to your ear. Otherwise, it's a buzz and that means it's away from you.

Harvey went to one knee after my third shot and I was already down, hit in the side. It was as though the dog had bit the hand that fed it, for Harvey had not hit me. Maxwell Green had. He picked up a book end and flung it at Harvey and missed and hit me. He nearly broke a pair of ribs.

The next thing I knew Harvey was limping past me and had reached the door. I couldn't do a thing about it. I was trying to get a breath into my lungs and couldn't. The damned brass book end had knocked the wind clean out of me and I just couldn't manage to get a breath of fresh air.

Harvey made the door at exactly the same time that Poppa Hanley made it. They were both going in opposite directions. I tried to yell to Poppa to stop the lug, but you don't have to tell Poppa what to do. He can scent trouble very easily, and he can scent a killer even more facilely.

Poppo just pulled up without a word and rapped Harvey across the jaw with a gun barrel and then followed it with a lovely left hook which dropped the Babylon editor right in my lap where I rapped him one more for not getting in the way of that book end and getting clipped with it instead of me, who is frail and fragile when it comes to such things.

That was the business. Harvey wasn't out and he made a try at his gun, tried to jam it into his ear and pull the trigger, but Poppa kicked it out of his hand and growled, 'Can't face the Musica, eh?'

Which, I thought later, was really a very good crack, and I told Dinah so when I saw her. Maxwell Green seemed to know what it was all about.

'Yeah,' Poppa Hanley told him, 'the first one he knocked off was Martin Penn. He came to New York on Tuesday instead of taking a fishing trip as he said, and he bumped Martin. Then he went back home and bumped Wilbur Penn, Martin's brother. He telegraphed Daffy mercy to insure his being in Babylon when the body was discovered. Having done that, he told his assistant he was taking the train for this town. Instead, took the plane, got here early, knocked off Fenwick Hanes, and he planned to knock you off this morning.'

'Why he called me last night and made an appointment with me this morning,' Green exploded. 'To kill me!'

'That's right,' I said, 'and you're a lousy shot with a book end, incidentally.'

'Knowing all that,' Poppa Hanley said, 'have you got any ideas on why this deaf plug-ugly was pulling this round robin of homicides? Not just to keep the police department on its toes, certainly.'

Maxwell Green sat back in his chair and sighed. 'Yes,' he said. 'I think I know the answer.'

'Then give, mister. I want to wrap this thing up for the D.A. before this guy thinks up some excuse a dumb jury will like.'

Maxwell Green said slowly, 'Wilbur Penn was the man whom Harvey wanted to get.'

'All right,' I said. 'But you and Martin Penn and Fenwick Hanes were all too smart. I mean, you knew that Harvey would be the one to kill Wilbur. Three wise men of Babylon. So to kill Wilbur Penn, John Harvey had to kill four men.'

Green nodded. 'But I don't doubt he would have enjoyed the extra work involved,' he said bitterly. 'Four years ago, John Harvey and Wilbur Penn were in love with the same woman, but she married Harvey. Well, that was all right. They had a youngster, a little girl, cute little trick. But it seems that Margaret Harvey, John Harvey's wife, came into some money. Her uncle left her nearly one hundred thousand dollars. And Harvey began to run around with other women.

'Next thing, Margaret Harvey was found dead. Gas in the kitchen. Wilbur was county attorney at Babylon then, and when he found Margaret, he also found a live canary in the same kitchen. Now, a canary doesn't live through a gasing that kills a grown woman.

'Wilbur could have put Harvey in the electric chair, but he didn't. He didn't because of Margaret's daughter. Wilbur got quite fond of her. And Margaret's will left her money to her daughter, so John Harvey had outfoxed himself.

'Wilbur told Harvey the truth, told him that if he ever stepped out of line again, or ever tried to regain custody of the daughter – whom, incidentally, Wilbur took over, with Harvey's consent, of course – he, Wilbur, would prosecute Harvey to the full extent of the law. And if anything happened to Wilbur, the rest of us, all former law partners, would take up the task.'

'I get the setup,' I said. 'This little rat without any hearing got desperate for money. He wanted to get his daughter back, contest the will, and get some of the mazuma. To do that, he had to knock off Wilbur, but he also had to knock off the three men Wilbur Penn had put wise to the mess.'

Green nodded.

Well, it was easy to prove. I had to make a trip to Babylon and it wasn't as bad a town as it sounds. Harvey's daughter, little Meg, was a cute trick, and she was too young to know what was going on. She's living now with Uncle Maxwell, as she says, and John Harvey is only a memory.

Dinah still kids me about the allergy I have for book ends, but if you've ever been cracked in the ribs with a well-flung one – or maybe you're happily married – you'll bear with me and understand.

THE ADVENTURE OF THE VOODOO MOON

EUGENE THOMAS

Detective Fiction Weekly, one of the most successful of the mystery pulps, liked to run two or three true crime stories each issue. Easily one of the most popular featured a female spy named Vivian Legrand, who was no sweetheart. Beautiful, intelligent and resourceful, she was also a liar, blackmailer thief who was responsible for her own father's death. Her exploits, which were reported by Eugene Thomas (1894–?), began to appear so regularly that doubt was cast upon their veracity – with good reason. Without apology, *DFW* continued to run stories about the woman dubbed 'The Lady from Hell,' now acknowledging that the tales were fictional. Were any of the stories true? Was there really a woman named Vivian Legrand? There is little evidence either way, but only the most gullible would accept the notion that all the stories published as true had any genesis in reality.

Thomas, the author of five novels, created another series character, Chu-Seng, typical of many other fictional Yellow Peril villains. A Chinese deaf-mute with paranormal abilities, he works with the Japanese in their espionage activities against the United States in *Death Rides the Dragon* (1932), *The Dancing Dead* (1933) and *Yellow Magic* (1934). He is thwarted by Bob Nicholson, an American agent, Lai Chung, a Mongol prince, and a team of lamas who counteract Chu-Seng's powers with their white magic.

'The Adventure of the Voodoo Moon' first appeared in the Feb. 1, 1936 issue of *DFW*.

THE ADVENTURE OF THE VOODOO MOON

EUGENE THOMAS

CHAPTER I

Crooks on Holiday

The Lady from Hell was standing on the upper deck of the little inter-island steamer as it neared the coast of Haiti. Her crown of flaming red hair was beaten back from her smooth forehead and her white dress modeled tightly to her body by the strong trade wind.

She and her companion in crime, Adrian Wylie, had just completed one of the most amazing coups in their whole career, and were now on a vacation. The Lady from Hell had been emphatic on that point before leaving Havana.

'Nothing is to tempt us into mingling business with pleasure,' she had told Wylie. 'Not even if we stumble across the vaults of a bank wide open and unguarded.'

Now, the second day out from Havana, the sun was just rising over the blue bubbles dreaming on the horizon that were the mountains of Haiti, and still she could not account for the vague sense of disquiet, the little feeling of apprehension that had been growing in her ever since the steamer passed between Morro Castle and its smaller counterpart on the other side of Havana harbor.

No one on the little steamer dreamed that she was the notorious Lady from Hell, whose fame had already filtered even to the West Indies. And if they had, it would have seemed incredible that this graceful, beautiful woman could have started her career by poisoning her own father; could have escaped from a Turkish prison – the only time in her career that the net of the law had closed about her – could have held up and robbed the Orient Express, a deed that had filled the press of the world, although her part in it had never even been suspected.

The daring coup in Havana that had added a large sum to the bank account of Adrian Wylie, her chief of staff, and herself had not been brought to the attention of the Cuban police. And, although the police of

429

half a dozen European countries knew her well and swore when her name was mentioned, there was not a single thing with which she could be charged, so cleverly had her tracks been covered, so adroitly her coups planned.

She turned away and began to stride up and down the deck. More than one passenger turned to stare at her as she passed with a rippling grace of motion, a little lithe stride that told of perfect muscles and the agility of a cat.

A sound made her turn as a passenger came up behind her and fell into step with her.

'Good evening, Mrs. Legrand,' he said in English, with the faintest of accents. 'You are up early.'

'I was eager to catch a sight of Haiti,' Vivian responded with a smile. 'The mountains there are lovely.'

'They are lovely,' he responded, 'even though Haiti is my home I never tire of seeing her mountains grow about the horizon line.' Then he added, 'We dock in a few hours. See that headland there,' and he pointed to an amethyst bulk that thrust itself out into the sea. 'That is Cap St. Feral. The port is just beyond it.'

There was an impression of power, perfectly controlled, about Carlos Benedetti that was perfectly evident to Vivian Legrand as she surveyed him for a fleeting instant through narrowed eyes. His face was unhealthily pale, the nose slightly crooked, the black eyes very sharp and alert, beneath the close-cropped and sleek black hair. He had the air of one to whom the world had been kind, and from it he had learned assurance and a kind of affability.

But behind his assurance – this affability – the Lady from Hell sensed something that was foreign to the face he presented to the world, something that made her cautious.

'Do we dock?' she queried. 'I thought that we landed in small boats.'

'The word was incorrectly used,' he admitted. 'I should have said that we arrive. Cap St. Feral is not modern enough to possess a dock for a ship of this size, small as the vessel is.' He hesitated a moment. 'I assume that you are not familiar with Cap St. Feral.'

'No,' Vivian said. 'This is my first visit to Haiti.'

The man's oblique stare was annoying her. Not that she was unaccustomed to the bold stare that men give beautiful women. But this was different. Had the man been wiser he might have taken warning at the hard light that lay in the depths of her geenish eyes.

But he went on suavely:

'To those of us who know the island it offers little in the way of entertainment,' he said, 'but to a stranger it might be interesting. If you care to have me, I should be glad to offer my services as a guide while you are in port.'

A casual enough courtesy offered to a stranger by a native of a place. Vivian thanked him and watched, with a calculating eye, as he bowed and walked on down the deck. The man was sleek, well groomed and obviously wealthy. His spotless Panama was of the type that cannot, ordinarily, even be bought in Equador, where they are woven. A hat so fine and silky that usually they are reserved as gifts to persons in high position. And the white suit that he wore had not come from an ordinary tailor.

It was made of heavy white silk – Habatui silk that in the East sells for its weight in gold, literally.

Adrian Wylie found Vivian on deck. In a few swift words she told him of the invitation and of the intuitive warning she had felt.

Wylie nodded slowly. 'That explains something that had been puzzling me,' he said. 'For an hour last night the purser insisted on buying me drinks in the smoking room and casually asking questions about the two of us. And hardly five minutes after he left me I saw him talking earnestly to Benedetti at the door of the purser's office. Evidently the man hunted you up for the first thing this morning, after his talk with the purser.'

Benedetti, they knew from the ship's gossip, was an exceedingly wealthy sugar planter, who owned the whole of an exceedingly fertile island called Ile de Feral, not far from the port of Cap St. Feral. The Haitian Sugar Centrals – actually the sugar trust, so ship gossip ran – had attempted to drive him out of business, and failed miserably. Despite a price war, he had managed to undersell the trust and still make a profit. Then he had been offered a staggering sum for the island, and had refused. The offer was still open, so she had been told, and any time he cared to sell the sugar trust would be only too eager to buy him out.

A little smile formed on Vivian's lips. Benedetti, she suspected, was accustomed to having his own way where women were concerned. And the Lady from Hell knew full well her own attractiveness as a woman.

But even the Lady from Hell, astute as she was, could not have fathomed the dark reason that lay behind Benedetti's advances.

CHAPTER II

Danger's Warning

The faint sound of drums somewhere in the distance; a regular, rhythmic beat, as though a gigantic heart, the heart of Black Haiti were beating in the stillness of the blazing moon, hung over the little city of Cap St. Feral as the Lady from Hell, Wylie and Benedetti rode through the sun-washed streets.

The heat that hung about them like a tangible thing seemed to be intensified and crystalized by the monotonous beating of the lonely drums.

The Lady from Hell turned to Benedetti with a question, the brilliant sunlight through the trees overarching the road catching her hair and turning it into a halo of flame about her exquisitely lovely face.

'Voodoo drums,' he said. 'The night of the Voodoo Moon is approaching. The drums will keep on sounding until the climax of the Snake Dance. They're beating like this all over the island, even in Port-au-Prince. Worshipers in the cathedral can hear the sound of the drums from the hills outside the city drifting through the intoning of the mass. Then, almost as if they had been silenced by a gigantic hand, they will all stop at the same moment – the climax of the Snake Dance.'

Vivian stole another glance at the people along the roadside as their car passed. Voodoo. It was something out of a book to her, something a little unsettling to come so closely in contact with. And it seemed difficult to believe that the happy, smiling faces were the faces of people who had run mad through the streets of Port-au-Prince, so history said, tearing President Guillaume Sam to bloody bits while he still lived.

Benedetti caught the thought in her mind.

'You have not lived here, Mrs. Legrand,' he said quietly. 'You cannot understand the place that Voodoo holds in these people's lives; the grip it has upon them. And you are not familiar with the effect of rhythms upon the nerve centers. It does strange things to blacks, and to whites things stranger still.'

He leaned forward and flung a few words in Creole French at the driver – words that Vivian Legrand, fluent as her French was, could barely follow. The car stopped before a long, rambling structure, of gleaming white *coquina*, half hidden behind crimson hibiscus bushes.

'I brought you here for lunch,' he said. 'It would be unbearably hot on the ship and there is no hotel at which you would want to eat, even if you could, in the town itself. This is a little house that I maintain, so that I may have a comfortable place to stay when necessity or business compels me to be in town. I took the liberty of assuming that Dr. Wylie and yourself would have lunch with me here.'

Vivian looked about her curiously as their host opened the little gate and ushered them into the flower garden that surrounded the house.

From the whitewashed, angular, stone walls of the old house, almost smothered in pink Flor de Amour, her eyes went to the table set beneath a flowering Y'lang-y'lang tree in the center of the close-cropped lawn. An old woman stood beside it, an ancient crone with more than a trace of white blood in her, one of those incredibly ancient people that only primitive races can produce. Her face was a myriad of tiny wrinkles and her parchment skin had the dull, leathery hue and look that is common in the aged of the Negro race.

*

The woman turned slowly as the trio approached and her eyes fastened on Vivian. In her cold, yellow eyes was a look almost of fear. Something that was like lurking terror coiled in the depths of those alert, flashing eyes and rendered them stony, glassy, shallow.

And then, as Benedetti and Wylie went on past her she made a gesture, an unmistakable gesture for Vivian to halt, and her voice, lowered until it was barely a sibilant whisper, came to Vivian's ears in French.

'Do not stay here,' she said. 'You must not stay.'

There was definite horror in her eyes, and fear also, as her glance flitted from Vivian toward Benedetti. Despite the whisper to which her voice had been lowered there was fear to be distinguished in her tones also.

Her face was impassive as she turned away. Only her eyes seemed alive. They were cold, deadly bits of emerald. The Lady from Hell abhorred the unknown. All through her criminal career the unsolved riddle, the unsolved personality, the unexplained situation, inflamed her imagination. She would worry over it as a dog worries a bone.

And how her mind hovered over this problem with relentless tenacity, her brain working swiftly, with smooth precision. Her intuition had been right, after all. The feeling of danger, of disquiet, of apprehension that had haunted her ever since the coast line of Haiti came in sight over the horizon had not been wrong. She knew now, beyond a shadow of doubt, that danger hovered over her like a vulture.

The fear that she had glimpsed in the old woman's eyes, Vivian reasoned, was fear for herself should she be caught warning the white woman. But what was the danger against which she was warned, and why should this old woman, who had never seen her before, take what was obviously a risk to warn her against it?

Luncheon was just over when a long hoot sounded from the steamer.

'The warning whistle,' Benedetti told her. 'A signal to the passengers that the steamer will sail in an hour.'

He turned to Vivian.

'My roses,' he said, 'are so lovely that I took the liberty of requesting Lucilla to cut an armful of them for you to take back to the ship as a remembrance.'

There was a distinct warning in the old woman's veiled eyes as Vivian stretched out her hands for the big bunch of pale yellow roses that Lucilla brought; not only warning, but that same terror and fear that had stood starkly in them a short time before. Instinctively Vivian stiffened and looked about her, her nerves tense. Was the danger, whatever it was, ready to spring? But the scene seemed peaceful enough.

'How lovely they are!' she exclaimed, and wondered if it could be her imagination that made the old woman seem reluctant to part with the flowers. Then she gave a little exclamation of pain as she took them from

433

Lucilla. 'Like many other lovely things, they are thorns,' she said ruefully, gazing at the long, thorny stems, still slightly damp from standing in water.

'That is true,' Benedetti said, and there seemed to be an expression of relief in his eyes. 'Our Haitian roses are lovely, but they have longer and sharper thorns than any other roses I know.'

'Don't you think we had better be leaving?' Vivian queried, glancing at her watch. The shimmering heat haze that covered everything seemed to have blurred her vision, and she had to peer closely at the little jewelled trinket to make out the time. 'It's a long drive back to the ship.'

'There is still plenty of time,' Benedetti assured her. 'The warning whistle is supposed to sound an hour before sailing time, but it always is nearer two hours.' Then he gave a little exclamation of concern. 'But you are ill,' he said as Vivian swayed a little.

'Just the heat,' she said. 'I am not yet accustomed to it.'

The flowers she had been holding tumbled to the table and thence to the ground. The long-stemmed yellow blossoms gave no hint of the fact that from the moment Benedetti's message had been delivered to the old woman until the moment before they had been placed in Vivian's hands their stems and thorns had been soaking in a scum-covered fluid brewed by Lucilla herself.

'You must go inside for a few moments. You must rest,' Benedetti said sharply. 'I should have realized that you were not accustomed to heat. It might be fatal for you to drive back to the ship in this sun without a rest.'

Wylie, a look of concern on his face, took Vivian's arm and helped her to her feet. Even then, with her vision blurred and an overpowering drowsiness creeping over her, the Lady from Hell did not realize that she had been drugged. It was not until she reached the threshold of the room to which she had been guided that the truth burst upon her dulled senses with the force of a thunderbolt.

Stacked neatly against the whitewashed walls of the room was the baggage she had left in her cabin on the steamer!

Dizzily, clutching at the door for support, she turned . . . just in time to see a short heavy club descend with stunning force on Wylie's head. And then, even as her companion crumpled to the stone flooring, blackness flooded her brain.

CHAPTER III

Vivian Legrand Trapped

Dusk had fallen with tropic swiftness before Vivian awoke. She had not been conscious of her journey, wrapped in coco fiber matting from the house where she had been drugged, to Benedetti's launch, nor of the subsequent trip to the man's home on the Ille de Feral.

Now, anger smoldering in her greenish eyes, she faced him across the dining room table. In the dim room the table floated in a sea of amber candlelight. Barefooted black girls passed in and out, their voices keyed to the soft stillness, a thing of pauses and low voices. The whole thing, to Vivian, seemed to take on a character of unreality – a dream in which anything might happen.

She waited for Benedetti to speak after the slender black girl drew out her chair for her. But the man did not, so finally she broke the silence herself.

'What do you hope to gain by this?' she queried.

'Won't you try your soup?' he said bitterly. 'I am sure that you will find it very good.'

He halted as one of the girls stopped beside his chair and said something in Creole in a low voice. He rose to his feet.

'Will you pardon me?' he said. 'There is someone outside, with a message. I shall be gone only a moment.'

He disappeared through the door beside the staircase, the door that Vivian imagined led to the rear of the house.

Swiftly she beckoned the black maid to her, slipped the glittering diamond from her finger, and folded the girl's hand about it.

'Come to my room tonight,' she whispered tensely, 'when it is safe. No one will ever know. And in Port-au-Prince or Cap St. Feral you can sell that ring for sufficient to live like a *blanc* millionaire for the rest of your days.'

The girl's face paled to a dusky brown, she glanced furtively from the glittering jewel in her hand to the pale face of the woman who had given it to her. Vivian caught the hesitation.

'I have others in my room,' she urged desperately. 'You shall choose from them what you want – two – three – when you sell them there will never have been another girl in Haiti as rich as you will be.'

'I will come,' the girl said in a whisper and stepped back against the wall. A moment later Benedetti returned.

'I regret to have been so poor a host as to leave you alone for even so short a time,' he said.

'Please,' Vivian said shortly, and there was in her manner no indication of the triumph that filled her breast. 'Why dissemble. You've brought me here for a purpose. Why not tell me what it is?'

Already a scheme was forming in that agile mind of hers. When the girl came to her room that night she would persuade her to find weapons – guide Wylie and herself to a boat so that they might escape. But was Wylie still alive?

Benedetti's answer interrupted her thoughts.

'It is not so much what I hope to gain, as what I hope to keep,' he said smoothly. He paused, and through the silence there came to her ears that queer rise and fall of notes from drums that had followed her ever since she arrived in Haiti – the drums of the Voodoo Moon, Benedetti had called it. He leaned forward.

'You might as well know now,' he said abruptly. 'You have until tomorrow midnight to live.'

'Unless?' Vivian queried meaningly. She was very sure that she knew what the man meant.

Benedetti calmly placed the spoon in his plate and pushed it aside.

'There is no proviso. I know nothing of your personal life – of your finances. They are no concern of mine. You may be extremely rich, or completely poor – that does not enter into the matter at all. You have nothing that I care to buy. All I know is that you are young and extremely beautiful.' He studied her with a cold dispassionate interest, then sighed, a bit regretfully, it seemed. 'That is the reason you must die tomorrow night.'

The thing was utterly fantastic. Vivian listened in amazed fascination. She could hardly bring herself to believe that she had heard correctly. So sure had she been that the man's interest in her rose from the fact that he was attracted to her that the thought there might be another, more sinister motive behind the drugging and kidnaping had not occurred to her.

Her green eyes narrowed a trifle – only that, but there was the impression of a steel spring tightening. Then she said quietly:

'Why must I die?'

'Because,' he answered, 'tomorrow night is the night of the Voodoo Moon – the night when the Papaloi and the Mamaloi present Ogoun Badagri, the Bloody One, with the Goat Without Horns.'

'The Goat Without Horns?' Vivian repeated, uncomprehendingly. 'What is that?'

'You,' the man said tersely. 'Tomorrow at midnight, when the Voodoo Moon is fullest, you will be offered as a sacrifice to Ogoun Badagri, the snake god.'

For a moment the Lady from Hell stared at him, a chill feeling clutching at her breast. Then an alert look came into her eyes, a look that she quickly veiled. She was listening intently.

'You're not actually in earnest?' she asked quietly. Every nerve was strained to catch that sound again – the drone of an airplane engine that had come faintly to her ears. It was louder now. 'You are trying to frighten me, to trap me into something. You will find that I am not easily frightened or trapped.'

The sound of the plane was louder now. She shot a furtive glance at Benedetti. Could aid be on the way? Could Benedetti's plans have gone wrong, and a search be underway for them?

'I am very much in earnest,' the man opposite her said. 'You see, that is the secret of my successful defiance of the sugar trust, the secret of why my laborers never leave me, the secret of why I can manufacture sugar at a cost that the sugar trust cannot possibly equal and still make a profit. Once a year I present the Papaloi and the Mamaloi, the high priest and priestess of Voodoo, with a human sacrifice – a white man or woman – and in turn these two guardians of the great snake see to it that my laborers do not leave, and are kept content with the lowest pay scale in the island of Haiti.'

He broke off and smiled.

'You may relax, Mrs. Legrand,' he said. 'That plane that you hear will not land here. It is the marine mail plane that passes over the island every night between eleven thirty and twelve o'clock.'

Vivian looked at him blankly. 'Plane?' she said vaguely. 'Oh, yes, that is a plane, isn't it? Quite honestly, I had not noticed the sound before you spoke.'

It was so well done that it fooled him. She picked up the slender silver fruit knife that lay on the table in front of her, twisting it so that it shone in her fingers, a pale, metallic splinter of light. She regarded him with eyes that had turned mysteriously dark, and leaned forward a little. Her voice, when she spoke, was very soft, and it held a quality of poignancy.

'You seem to live alone here,' she said, and her eyes regarded him warmly. 'Don't you ever become – lonely?'

There was a world of promise and invitation in the soft tone, in the alluring lips.

He looked at her and tightened his lips.

'That is useless,' he said. 'You are beautiful, one of the most beautiful women that I have ever seen, but a dozen such women as you could not make up to me for the loss of my plantation. No, my dear, your charm is useless.'

'But you wouldn't dare,' she said. 'A woman cannot simply disappear from a steamer without inquiries being made. This is not the Haiti of twenty years ago. The Americans are in control – they are the police . . .'

Benedetti shook his head. 'Do not raise false hopes. You sent the purser of the steamer a note saying that you had unexpectedly found friends in Cap St. Feral and were breaking your voyage here. The same man who brought the note took yours and your companion's baggage off the ship. By now he has probably forgotten your existence.

'There is nothing to connect you with me, and if inquiries should be made it will simply be assumed that you either left the island or were murdered by a wandering Caco. And as for an Haitian, who might know something of your disappearance, aside from the fact that the secrets of Voodoo are something that are never discussed, there is an island saying: 'Z affaires negres, pas z'z affaires blancs.' And you will find that the affairs of the Negroes are not the affairs of the whites. And then,' his voice was bland as he made the significant statement, 'there is rarely any proof – left – when the great green snake god has completed his sacrifice.'

'And my companion – Dr. Wylie – what have you done with him?' Vivian queried steadily. A bright spark glowed in her narrowed green eyes for a moment. It died slowly.

'He is safe, quite safe,' Benedetti assured her, 'for the time being. He also will be a sacrifice to Ogoun Badagri.'

He said it with simple, sincere ruthlessness; undisguised, but neither vindictive nor cruel.

'You are quite sure of yourself,' Vivian said softly, and had Wylie been there he would have recognized the meaning of that tone; the threat of that greenish glow at the back of her eyes. He had seen that cold light in her eyes before. But Benedetti, even had he glimpsed it, would not have known that it was like the warning rattle of a snake before it strikes.

Now, with a swift movement she flung the silver fruit knife she held at the gleaming shirt front of the man opposite her. Her aim was deadly, for few people could throw a knife with the skill and precision of the Lady from Hell.

But Benedetti had caught the glitter of the candlelight on the metal a split second before she launched the knife. His agile mind perceived her intention and he flung himself to one side just in time. The knife thudded into the high back of the chair in which he had been sitting and rested there, quivering.

'You are a fool,' the man commented curtly. Striding to the French windows he flung them wide, letting moonlight stream into the room. The sound of the drums came in louder, a barbaric rhythm beating in strange tempo with the pulse in her wrist.

'Look at that,' he said, flinging out an arm.

At the edge of the veranda, which ran along the front of the house, lounged a white cotton-clad Haitian, a three-foot cane knife clasped in his fist. Further along, at the edge of the beach, another man leaned against the bole of a coconut tree, and the glitter of the moonlight on steel betrayed the fact that he also was armed with a cane knife.

'Even if you had killed me,' he said quietly, 'you would have been no better off. You could not escape from the island. There are no boats here. Even the launch on which you arrived has been sent away and will not return until after the ceremony. And if you had attempted to swim, the sea swarms with sharks.'

It was after midnight when Vivian went upstairs to her room again. Benedetti escorted her to the door.

'I am locking you in,' he told her. 'It is really quite useless to do so. You could not escape. There is absolutely no possibility of success. But it is a precaution I always take with my annual – visitors.'

Then he drew from his pocket the diamond ring that Vivian had, earlier in the evening, given to the little black maid.

'You will find,' he said with a smile, 'that it is useless to attempt to bribe my servants. The fear of the Voodoo in them is greater than the greed for money.'

With a slight bow he closed the door, leaving her staring at the blank panels with a sinking feeling in her heart. She was a prisoner in a prison without walls, and yet the sea that girdled the land was a barrier as effective as stone ramparts and iron bars. Instead of one jailer she had dozens – perhaps hundreds – for she realized that every laborer on the island was a potential guard, alert to halt any attempt to escape. She did not attempt to deceive herself by thinking that every native of the place did not know of her presence and the fate for which she was destined.

She wondered what prompted the old woman – Benedetti's servant – to take her life in hand and warn her, back there in Cap St. Feral? The woman had, of course, realized Benedetti's purpose in bringing her here, since it had been she who had prepared the drugged rose stems. It was not for a long time, and then only by accident, that Vivian was to discover that in a Haitian the desire for revenge can transcend even the fear of Voodoo, and that it was to avenge what she considered a wrong that the old woman had warned her.

Vivian turned her thoughts back to her position. She believed she knew where Wylie was being held. On her way down to the dining room a little earlier she had encountered one of the black maids with a tray; had noted the door through which the girl had passed. That, she reasoned, must be the room in which Wylie was held prisoner, unless there were other prisoners in the house of whom she knew nothing.

She smiled a trifle grimly at the thought of being locked in her room. If Benedetti only knew of how little importance a lock – particularly an old-fashioned one such as this – was to her. Opening her suitcase she took out a hand mirror with a long handle. Unscrewing the handle, she removed from the hollow interior a long slender rod of thin steel. This she forced slowly into the thin opening between door and jamb. The rod scraped on metal. She worked it up and down, slowly pressing inward. Bit by bit the sloping tongue of the lock was forced back into its sheath, until the blade slipped through. A twist of the door handle and Vivian was peering out into the corridor.

Darkness hung before her eyes. It was as if a curtain of some impenetrable texture hung before her. She knew nothing of the floor plan of the big, rambling house, but she knew that the room she had seen the girl entering was the last on her side of the corridor, and accordingly she made her way cautiously in that direction, feeling her way, finger-tips trailing the wall, listening intently every step or so for some sound that might warn her of the presence of another person.

Her hand trailing along the wall touched a door – the fifth one she had passed. This was the door she sought. Gently she tried the knob. It was locked. A few minutes' work with the thin steel rod and the door swung inward with only the faintest of sounds. But even that was sufficient to betray her presence to Wylie's alert ears.

'Who is it?' he queried.

'Shhh,' she whispered warningly, and, closing the door, crossed swiftly toward the chair where he sat beside the window.

In low, tense whispers she told him of her conversation with Benedetti and of the fate that was in store for both of them.

'We've got to get away tonight,' she finished. 'It's our only chance. There must be some way – perhaps we can make a raft. At least we can try.'

CHAPTER IV

The First Victim

With Wylie by her side she made her way to the door; peered cautiously outside. By diligent practice the Lady from Hell had long ago acquired the chatoyant eye – the cat's – good for prowling about and seeing things in the dark, but here in the corridor the blackness was intense, with a tangible quality that was numbing to the senses. The utter opacity was tactile, half fluid, like fog. She crept down the hallway with feline assurance, passing her fingers delicately over objects that came into her path with a touch light enough to stroke a butterfly's wing. The house was a sea of silence, and on its waves the slightest noise made long and screeching journeys.

To Vivian's hearing, sandpapered by suspense, the slight give of the polished boards of the staircase beneath their slow steps produced a terrific noise. By making each step a thing of infinite slowness, they crept forward safely. Each downward step was a desperate and long-drawn-out achievement, involving an exactly calculated expenditure of muscular energy, an unceasing, muscular alertness.

Once, as they reached the bottom of the stairs, there came from the dining room in which they stood the rattle of a clock preparing to ring out a quarter hour. It struck Vivian's tense nerves as a thing of abominable violence – like countless, swift hammer strokes on the innumerable frayed ends of her nerves. She had the sensation of being driven into the woodwork of the floor upon which she stood, of being crushed under an immense and lightning-like pressure.

After what seemed an eternity they reached the further side of the dining room. Under her careful manipulation the latch of the door slipped slowly back. The door moved silently, slowly. A brilliant line of moonlight appeared. Vivian caught her breath sharply.

Standing there in the open ground in front of the veranda stood a Haitian, alert, watchful, armed with a machete.

There was no escape that way. Weaponless, they were helpless before the menace of that shining three-foot length of steel, even if they could cross the moonlit space that lay between the veranda and the man without being detected.

'The back of the house,' Vivian whispered to Wylie, her voice barely perceptible.

She knew that the door to the kitchen was beside the staircase they had descended. That much she had observed during her interview with Benedetti earlier in the evening. By locating the staircase first in the blackness, she found the door she sought and opened it. A passageway opened before them, dimly illuminated by a shaft of silver that poured through a half opened door at its further end.

Silently they made their way down the passage and cautiously peered through the partly opened door. Another disappointment.

It was a small room, one wall covered with shelves, boxes and bags stacked high on the other side with a single window, half way up the wall, through which moonlight poured. A storeroom of some sort.

Vivian reached out and caught Wylie's arm, drew him silently into the little room and closed the door.

'There may be weapons here,' she said. But she was mistaken. The nearest approach was a broken kitchen knife used, probably, to slash open the burlap bags which stood against the wall.

It was a poor substitute for a weapon, but Vivian took it thankfully. And then she gave a gasp. Her hand, exploring a shelf, had come in contact with something clammy and sticky that clung and would not be shaken off. Her first thought was that it was some monstrous tropical insect. It seemed alive, it clung so persistently, despite her efforts to shake it loose.

Then, as Wylie snapped his cigarette lighter into flame, the tiny glow illuminated an oblong of sticky fly paper fastened to her hand. There was a pile of the sheets upon the shelf. Despite the tenseness of the situation she almost laughed at the uncanny feeling the thing had given her there in the darkness.

In the dim flame of Wylie's lighter they searched again for anything that might prove of assistance to them in their predicament. Bags of flour. Bags of potatoes. Kegs of pig tails and pig snouts in brine – evidently food for the laborers. A half-emptied case of bacale – dried codfish, a staple article

441

of diet in the West Indies – and a can of phosphorescent paint. Also row after row of canned food. But nothing that might be of assistance to them.

Climbing upon a box Vivian peered through the window, then turned back to Wylie, excitement in her voice.

'We can get out this way,' she whispered. 'There is the limb of a tree almost against the window and shrubbery around the tree.'

'Anybody in sight?' Wylie queried.

'No one,' Vivian said, and pried the latch of the window with her broken knife blade. It came open with a tearing shriek that sounded like thunder in the silence. Disregarding the noise Vivian slipped through the window and swung on to the limb of the tree. Wylie followed her, and in a moment they stood on the ground in the midst of dense shrubbery.

'We will have to keep in the shadow,' she said as they crept silently through the bushes, only an occasional rustling leaf marking their passage. 'The moment we step in the moonlight we'll be seen, if anyone is watching.'

Even there in the bushes the brilliant moonlight illuminated the ground about them. A faint drumming ebbed to them through the brilliance, faintly touching the dark membrane of the night as they emerged on what seemed to be a well-defined path leading toward the beach.

A sudden opening in the trail, a burst of moonlight, and they stood on a strip of white sand with breakers creaming softly in front of them.

'There,' Vivian said, still keeping her voice low. 'See that pile of driftwood. We'll make a raft of that. Drag it to the water's edge while I cut vines to lash it together.'

Feverishly they worked, Wylie dragging the heavy logs into position, lashing them firmly together with the vines that Vivian cut from the jungle's edge, until at last a crazy-looking affair bobbed up and down in the ripple at the edge of the beach. Makeshift, clumsy, but it would float and it was an avenue of escape, the only avenue that had presented itself.

Vivian returned from a final trip to the jungle, dragging behind her three bamboo poles.

'We can use two of these to shove the thing with, until we get into deep water,' she said. 'The other we can lash upright as a mast and use my dress as a sail.'

At that instant, from the path behind them, came the sound of voices. Vivian flashed a frantic glance at the jungle rearing up behind them, and then leaped on board the raft. Wylie followed. It dipped and swayed, but held their weight. The voices came nearer. Desperately Vivian braced her pole against the sandy bottom and shoved. Wylie followed suit. Sluggishly the clumsy craft moved away from the shore – five feet – ten feet – and than half a dozen men poured through the opening in the jungle and raced across the sand, splashed through the shallow water and surrounded the little craft, gleaming machetes raised threateningly.

*

Vivian did not see Benedetti when they returned to the house with their captors that night, nor was he visible when she awoke the next morning after a night spent in futile speculation and planning, and descended to the dining room.

A black girl served them breakfast. Golden sunlight poured through the wide French windows, beyond which they could see the beach and the green cove. Nowhere was there evidence of the fate that hung over them. But both knew, and the fact of that knowledge was evident in their eyes, in their short jerky words, that Death's wings were already casting their shadows across them.

The sun was well up when they went on to the veranda. There should have been the click of machetes in the cane fields and the low, lazy laughter of the workers. But everything was still, and that stillness held an ominous meaning.

Wylie was frankly without hope – more so as the day wore on, and Vivian, although she had never admitted defeat, admitted to herself that she saw no way out of the impasse. Benedetti, she saw now, had made no mistake when he told her that escape was impossible.

The day wore on, and still Benedetti did not put in an appearance. Once Vivian asked one of the maids where he could be found and received in answer a queer jumble of Creole French that held no meaning. Later, they essayed a walk to the Sugar Central, whose smokestacks rose on the other side of the cane fields, but one of the ever-present natives stepped slowly in their path, his machete openly in evidence. From the corner of her eyes Vivian could see others, alert, ready, at the edge of the jungle. Their captors were taking no chances.

On the far side of the cleared space Vivian could see a break in the jungle where a path ended. From this path men kept coming and going, and this, she surmised, must lead to the place where they were scheduled to die that night.

It was after dinner when Benedetti made his appearance, and with him stalked tragedy.

Vivian and Wylie were on the broad veranda, walking up and down. Something – some sixth sense – warned Vivian of danger, even before she heard the quick, catlike tread behind her. She made an attempt to swing around an instant too late. Someone leapt on her. A strong arm was locked about her throat. A hand was clamped over her mouth. A knee dug into the small of her back. She wrenched, tore at the gripping hands, even as she saw other hands seizing Wylie; she was aware of Benedetti's face, his features hard as stone. In the same second something dropped over her head and blotted the world into darkness.

How long she was held there motionless on the veranda she did not know. Then came a quick gabble of Creole in Benedetti's voice and the smothering hand was removed.

She flashed a glance around. The place was deserted save for herself, Benedetti and one tall native who stood beside the veranda steps, the ever-present machete in evidence. Obviously a guard.

The man interpreted her look.

'Your companion is gone. You will never see him again,' he said, and his voice was indifferent. He might have been speaking of some trivial object that had disappeared. He turned back toward the dining room, where candlelight made a soft glow. Vivian followed. The house seemed curiously still, as if all life had departed from it save these two.

'Gone – you mean—' she could not finish the sentence.

Benedetti nodded and selected a cigarette from a box on a little side table; lit it at one of the candles.

'He will be the first sacrifice to Ogoun Badagri. When the great green snake god has finished with him they will come for you. You will be the climax of the ceremony,' he told her brutally.

'You mean that you – a white man – will actually permit these men to make a sacrifice of us?' she queried. She knew, before she said it, that any appeal to him would be useless, but her mind was going around frantically, seeking a method of warding off the death that was imminent.

'What is your life and that of your companion to me?' he asked. 'Nothing – not so much as the ash from the cigarette – compared with the fact that your death means that I keep my plantation a year longer. I refused close to half a million dollars from the sugar trust for the island. Do you think, then, that I would permit a little thing like your life to rob me of it?'

CHAPTER V

Voodoo Death

Vivian did not answer. Her eyes roamed around the room, although already every article in it had been photographed indelibly on her retina. A fly had alighted on the border of the sticky fly paper that lay in the center of the mahogany table. It tugged and buzzed, but the sticky mess held it too firmly.

'You may comfort yourself with the thought,' Benedetti went on, 'if the fact is any comfort, that you are not the first. There have been others. The little dancing girl from the Port-au-Prince cabaret, a Spanish girl from Santo Domingo . . .'

He was not boastful, purely meditative as he sat there and smoked and talked, telling Vivian of the victims whose lives had paid for his hold on his sugar plantation. Vivian's eyes were fastened on the feebly fluttering fly on the sticky paper. They, too, were caught like flies in a trap, and unless she could do something immediately – she faced the fact calmly; it would be the end.

Abruptly she leaned forward. There was a stillness in her pose, a stillness in her opaque eyes. Her hands coiled like springs. She found it difficult to keep her detached poise as the scheme began to unfold and take shape in her brain.

She smiled thinly. The air was suddenly electrical, filled with the portent of danger. Benedetti caught the feel of it, and peered at her suspiciously for a moment. The Lady from Hell knew that it was a thousand to one that she would lose. But, if her scheme worked, she could save Wylie's live and her own, and Benedetti might be made to pay for the thing he had attempted – pay as he had never dreamed that he would have to pay.

Reaching out one hand she moved the candle in front of her, so that its glow fell more on Benedetti's face than her own. Her voice, as she spoke, was quiet, almost meditative. But her eyes told a different story.

'How much time have I to live?' she said.

The man glanced at his watch.

'Roughly, two hours,' he said. He might have been estimating the departure time of a steamer, his voice was so calm. 'It might be a trifle more or less – the time of my workers is not accurate. When the drums stop they will come for you. And when they start again – well, you will be there then.'

She rose to her feet, leaning lightly on the table.

'If I am to die,' she said hysterically, 'I will die beautiful.' Then she added as an explanation, 'My makeup is in my room.'

But he was on his feet too, alert, wary. 'You must not leave my presence,' he said. 'I cannot permit it. The sacrifice must go to the arms of Ogoun Badagri alive, not a corpse.'

His dark eyes held no recognition of the fact that she was a very beautiful woman. Vivian sensed, and rightly, that to him she was merely a woman who might thwart his plans. But she caught the implication in his last sentence.

'I shall not take poison,' she said. 'You may come with me – watch me, if you wish.'

She took a step or two and groped blindly at the table for support. Instinctively he stretched out a hand to steady her.

That was the moment for which she had planned, the instant for which she had been waiting. Benedetti made the fatal mistake that many men had made with the Lady from Hell as an opponent – of underestimating her as an adversary.

Like a striking snake her hand darted to the table, seized one of the heavy candlesticks. Before Benedetti could interfere, had even divined her purpose, the heavy metal fell across his forehead with stunning force. He crumpled to the floor without a murmur.

Leaving him where he had fallen, Vivian ran to the door and peered out. The gigantic black on guard at the veranda steps had heard nothing. He was still standing there, unaware of the drama being enacted within the dining room.

Swiftly she turned back and her slender fingers searched the drawers of the carved mahogany sideboard against the wall until she found what she sought – a heavy, sharp carving knife. She balanced it speculatively in her hand. It would do, she decided.

The man was still standing there when she peered out the door again. He never saw the slender blade as it flew through the air, sped by a hand that had learned its cunning from the most expert knife thrower in Shanghai. The blade went through, sinking into the flesh at the base of his throat as though it had been butter. He died without an outcry.

Now she must work fast, if she were to escape and save Wylie too. Benedetti she bound and gagged and rolled against the sideboard where he was out of the way. But first she had taken his revolver from his side pocket.

Trip after trip she made, first to the flat tin roof of the house, and then to the front of the house. Finally she was satisfied with what she had done, and, snatching up a flashlight from the sideboard fled toward the path in the jungle that she knew led to the place of sacrifice.

A tropical squall was rising out of the sea beyond the little cove. A cloud, black in the light of the moon, was rising above the horizon. She glanced at it anxiously. Then she plunged into the jungle.

The valences of the palms were motionless against the moonlit sky. The atmosphere, as she pushed her way along, seemed saturated with mystery, dew dripping, bars of green moonlight between the trunks of the trees; the cry of night birds, the patter of something in the dark mystery of the tree roof overhead, the thudding of the drums that had never ceased. Out of that familiar hollow rhythm of drums that had begun to emerge a thread of actual melody – an untraditional rise and fall of notes – a tentative attack, as it were, on the chromatic scale of the beat. A tentative abandonment of Africa. It was a night of abandonment, anyhow, a night of betrayal and the peeling off of blanketing layers down to the raw.

Once she stopped short with a sudden emptiness in her chest at sight of what she thought was a man in the path ahead. But it was only a paint-daubed, grinning skull on a bamboo stake planted in the ground – a voodoo *ouanga*. Then she went ahead again. Evidently there were no guards posted. With every inhabitant of the island concerned in the ceremony in one way or another there would be no need for guards to be posted now.

*

The rapid sequence of events had edged Vivian's nerves, and the boom of the drums – heavy, maddening, relentless, did nothing to soothe them. That passage through the jungle was galling, fraying the nerve ends like an approaching execution.

A red glow came to her through the trees, and seemed to spread and spread until it included the whole world about her in its malignancy. The drums, with that queer rise and fall of notes that it seemed impossible to achieve with taut skins stretched over drum heads, beat upon her senses, pounded until the air was filled with sounds that seemed to come from the earth, the sky, the forest; dominated the flow of blood with strange excitations.

She had formulated no plan for rescuing Wylie. She could not, until she reached the spot and saw what she had to contend with. She had the gun she had taken from Benedetti, but six cartridges against a horde of drum-maddened blacks – that was only a last resort.

And then she stood on the edge of a clearing that seemed sunk to the bottom of a translucent sea of opalescent flame.

Something that was age-old was happening in that crimson-bathed clearing, something old and dark, buried so deeply under the subtleties of civilization that most men go through life without ever knowing it is there, was blossoming and flowering under the stark madness of those thudding drums.

Coconut fibre torches, soaked in palm oil, flaring red in the blackness of the night lit up the space in front of her like a stage, the torchlight weaving strange scarlet and mauve shadows. Tall trees, lining the clearing opposite her, seemed to shelter masses of people, darker shadows against the red glow of the burning torches.

Two enormous drums, taut skins booming under the frenzied pounding of the palms of two drummers, stood on one side. A dozen, two dozen dancing black figures, male and female, spun and danced in the center of the clearing, movements graceful and obscene – animal gestures that were identical with similar dances of their ancestors hundreds of years before in Moko or the Congo.

And then she saw Wylie. He was tied to a post in the center of the clearing, and the dancers were milling about him. Beside him stood a woman whom Vivian instinctively knew must be the Mamaloi, the priestess of whom Benedetti had spoken.

Now and then the priestess gave vent to a sound that seemed to stir the dancers to greater activity – to spur the slowly humming throng of watchers to a point of frenzy; a sound such as Vivian had never heard before and never hoped to hear again. When she stopped, it would hang, incredibly high-pitched, small, like a black thrill in the shadow. It was shocking and upsetting out of that ancient thin figure.

Her eyes shifted from the aged figure to the sky line above the trees.

447

The black cloud that, a short time before had been no larger than the palm of her hand on the horizon, was visible through the branches of the trees now. Even as she looked a faint flicker of heat lightning laced through it.

And then, as if at a conductor's signal, more torches flowered on the edge of the clearing, and in their light the Lady from Hell saw half a dozen men staggering forward with an enormous thing of bamboo – a cage – and in that cage was a great snake; a boa constrictor, perhaps, or a python, although neither of them, she seemed to remember, was native to Haiti.

CHAPTER VI

White Man's Voodoo

They placed the cage in the center of the clearing, and Vivian saw that it had been placed so that a small door in the cage was directly opposite Wylie's bound figure. The significance of that fact went through her like a breath of cold wind. If she failed, she also would be bound to that stake. Mentally she could see the little door in the cage opening, the great triangular head of the snake gliding slowly . . .

Swiftly she bent over and caught up a handful of the black leaf mold underfoot, smeared it over her face, her arms, her neck, her shoulders. A section of the dress she was wearing was ripped off and made into a turban that hid the flaming crown of her hair. More earth was rubbed onto the white of her dress.

Then, with swift leaps, she was on the outer fringe of the dancers, and the chaos of moving arms and legs caught her up and swallowed her as a breaking wave on the beach swallows a grain of sand.

It was a mad thing to do, a desperate thing. She knew that, normally, her crude disguise would not have fooled the natives. The Haitian black seems to have the ability to almost smell the presence of a *blanc*, much as an animal can smell the presence of another. But, in that flickering torchlight, the crudeness of disguise would not be so apparent, and in that unceasing madness of drums that went on like a black echo of something reborn, she hoped that her alien presence would pass unnoticed long enough for her to accomplish her object.

Slowly she worked her way through the writhing, dancing mass of figures toward the center. She knew that her time was short – that the lesser ceremony was approaching its height. Even as she reached the inner ring of dancers she saw the ancient Mamaloi joining in the dance, while the others kept a respectful distance from her. Monotonously, maddeningly, the priestess twisted and turned and shivered, holding aloft a protesting fowl. Faster and faster she went, and while all eyes were fastened on that whirling figure Vivian managed to reach Wylie's bound figure.

A swift slash with the knife she had hidden beneath her dress and his hands were free.

'Keep still . . . don't let them see that you're not bound,' she whispered. Another motion and the bonds that fastened his ankles to the post were free.

Vivian moved about Wylie with graceful motions, imitating the movements of the blacks about her, and her voice came to him in broken, desperate whispers:

'Signal . . . you'll recognize it . . . don't move until then . . . dead tree by the edge of the clearing . . . that's the path . . . I'll be waiting there . . . it's only chance . . .'

Then she was gone, breasting her way through the black figures that danced like dead souls come back from Hell in the evil glow of the sputtering torches. And then came a great shout as the Mamaloi caught the chicken she held by the head and whirled it around and around.

Throom . . . throom . . . throom. The drums were like coalescing madness. A moan went up from the onlookers and a chill went through Vivian.

She knew from what Benedetti had told her that the chicken was the prelude of what would happen to Wylie. Next, the old woman would slash Wylie's throat . . . let his life blood spurt into a bowl with which the dancers would be sprinkled. Then would come the lesser ceremony, while the guard at the house would start with her for the ceremony that would end with the door in the great snake's cage being opened . . .

Vivian snatched a torch from the hands of one of the dancers. The man did not even seem to be aware of the fact that it had been taken away. From beneath her dress she took a stick of dynamite with fuse attached – part of her loot from the storeroom – and touched the fuse to the flame of the torch.

It sputtered and she hurled it with all her strength at her command toward the overhanging tree beneath which the drummers sat, then fled for the bare naked branches of the dead tree that stood where the path entered the clearing – the spot where she had told Wylie she would meet him.

She had barely reached the spot when there came a tremendous concussion that shook the earth, and a gush of flame. The thing was as startling, as hideously unexpected to the drum maddened Haitians as a striking snake. Scream after scream – long, jagged screams that ripped red gashes through the dark, were followed by a swift clacking of tongues, a terrified roar as dancers and onlookers milled about, black bodies writhing in the light of the remaining torches. A black tide, rising, filled the clearing with terrified clamor. A moment later there was the sound of running feet and Wylie was at her side.

'This way,' she whispered, and guided him into the path.

Both of them knew that it would be only a moment before the startled natives recovered their wits and discovered that their victim was gone. Then they would take up their trail again immediately.

'Where are we going?' Wylie asked her as he ran behind her along the winding jungle trail.

'The house,' she answered tersely.

'The house?' He almost halted in his amazement. 'But Vivian – that's the first place they'll make for. Even if you've found weapons we can't hold them off forever.'

'Wait,' she said. 'No time to explain now . . . But if things work out, we'll be off this island before morning, safe and sound.'

From behind them a quavering yell rose on the air and the two fugitives knew that Wylie's escape had been discovered. It was a matter of yards and of minutes now. Then they burst from the shadow of the jungle into the moonlight clearing.

'Follow me,' she said quickly. 'Don't take the path,' and he followed her footsteps as she twisted and twined about the space toward the steps.

At the steps he halted a moment in wonder at what he saw there, and then, in spite of the gravity of the situation, a chuckle broke from his panting lips.

'So that's it,' he said, and Vivian nodded.

'That's it. Be careful. It's a slim enough chance, but there is just a chance it'll work – the only chance we've got.'

'But even that,' he said, a thought striking him, as he threaded his way carefully up the steps to the veranda, 'will only be temporary. Even if it holds them at bay until dawn – when daylight comes . . .'

'I know,' she said a trifle impatiently, 'but long before then . . .' She broke off suddenly as their pursuers appeared, breaking out from under the palms, just as a flash of lightning came.

'They're here,' he whispered. If the scheme won't work, then it's all up with us.'

'It will work,' Vivian said confidently.

But, although her tone was cool, confident, there was anxiety in her eyes as she watched the black figures pouring out of the jungle. Vivian knew that her own and Wylie's lives were hanging by the slenderest margin in their criminal career.

The Papaloi, the giant negro with the white lines and scar ridges criss-crossing his muscular torso, was the first to see them as another flash of lightning illuminated the veranda where they stood. He uttered a single bellow, a stentorian cry, which seemed to shake the house, and bounded toward the stairs. Behind him came part of his followers, while others rushed for the other pair of stairs.

The Papaloi leaped for the steps, his men close behind him. His feet landed in something that slid quickly under him, that clung to his soles. He lost his balance, fell asprawl, his followers in a momentary confusion that quickly increased to panic – the panic of the primitive mind confronted with something unseen that it cannot understand.

The hands of the gigantic black Papaloi were glued now to squares of sticky fly paper that he could not shake off – the fly paper that The Lady from Hell had taken from the storeroom and spent so much precious time placing upon the steps and around the veranda without encountering it, save along the narrow, tortuous trail along which Vivian had led Wylie.

There was a square of fly paper on the Papaloi's face now, clinging there, flapping a little as if alive, persistent as a vampire bat. There were more on the side of his body where he had slipped. He struck at them and accumulated more.

The Mamaloi, that ancient crone, was in trouble also. She had slipped and in falling, had a sheet of fly paper plastered squarely across her eyes. She was uttering shrill cries of distress as she pawed at her face with hands that were covered with sticky fly paper and glue. All about the two men and women were struggling, shouting in alarm. The silent attack had materialized out of nothing with such appalling swiftness, and continued with such devastating persistence that it robbed them of every thought save alarm.

Robbed of their spiritual leaders, terror was striking at the hearts of the voodoo worshipers. At the edge of the veranda, black men writhed in horror, snatching at one another for support, tearing at the horrible things that clung as if with a million tiny sucking mouths. Their machetes, covered with glue and flapping fly paper, had been dropped, forgotten in the confusion. Torches had dropped underfoot, forgotten, so that the struggle was in darkness, illuminated only by the light of the moon through the clouds and the flashes of lightning. Flypaper in their hair, across their eyes, clinging, hampering, maddening them with the knowledge that some frightful voodoo, stronger than their Papaloi or Mamaloi, had laid hands upon them.

A flare of lightning slashed from the very center of the storm cloud that was now hanging overhead. Its brilliance illuminated, for a moment, the figure of The Lady from Hell, standing at the edge of the veranda, her arms uplifted as if calling down the wrath of the heavens upon them. A shattering blast of thunder followed and a gust of wind swept across the clearing.

That gust of wind was the crowning touch, the straw that was needed to break the camel's back of resistance in that struggling, milling black throng. It set all the loose ends of the fly paper fluttering, where it was not fastened to bodies. And, more than that, it caught up the sticky squares that were still unattached and sent them dancing through the air.

*

451

There rose a howl of fear. The demons of these *blancs*, not content with lying in wait and springing out upon them, were now flying through the air; attacking them from the heavens, sucking from their bodies all their strength.

What use to resist when even the magic of the Papaloi and the Mamaloi was not sufficient to fight off the demons.

They bolted headlong, flypaper sticking to every part of their anatomy. They fell, scaled with the awful things, and promptly acquired more. Women fell and shrieked as they were trampled upon, not from the pain of the trampling feet, but from the fear that they might be left behind at the mercy of the demons. Men, blinded by the sticky things, ran in circles and clutched at whatever they came in contact with.

Then came the low drone of an airplane engine in the distance, flying low because of the storm. Turning, Vivian ran back into the dining room, where Benedetti still lay, bound upon the floor, his eyes glaring hatred at her. Calmly she sat down and wrote upon one of his letterheads which she found in the desk there. Then she snatched off the gag that muffled his mouth.

'The danger is all over,' she told the man, 'for us. But for you trouble is just beginning.'

'You can't escape,' he raved at her viciously. 'I don't know what you've done, but you won't be able to leave the island. In an hour, two hours – by daylight at least – they will return, and what they will do to you won't be pleasant.'

Vivian smiled. The invisible plane seemed to be circling the house now. She waved the paper she had written to dry the ink.

'What the American authorities in Port-au-Prince do to you will not be pleasant, either,' she told Benedetti. 'Voodoo is forbidden by law. You have not only aided and abetted voodoo ceremonies, but you have also procured human sacrifices for the ceremonial. There was the little French girl from the Port-au-Prince cabaret, and the girl from Santo Domingo – you should not have boasted. For you murdered them as surely as if you had driven a knife in their hearts, and the law will agree with me.'

'You'll never live to tell the Americans, even if they believed the tale,' he scoffed.

'Oh, yes I will,' she mocked. Her voice was as dry and keen as a new ground sword. 'Within an hour I shall be on my way to Cape Hatien. Hear that,' and she raised an admonitory hand. In the silence the plane could be heard. She threw open the French windows. From where he lay Benedetti could see a Marine plane slanting down toward the comparatively sheltered waters of the little cove.

'In less than ten minutes,' she said, 'the plane will have taxied up to the beach and the Marine pilot and his observer will be in this room, asking if we need aid. You see,' and her smile was completely mocking and scornful

452

now, 'you yourself brought about your own downfall – planted the idea in my brain when you told me that the plane passed overhead every night at about this time. There was a can of luminous paint in your storeroom. I saw it, and there he is coming to see what it's all about – and to take you to Cape Hatien – unless . . .'

'Unless what?' he queried eagerly.

'Unless you sign this memorandum. It deposes that I have purchased this plantation from you – that you have received the purchase price – and that proper legal transfer to it will be made later.'

There was a calculating gleam in the man's eyes as he made assent. His gaze flickered out through the open door to where the plane had already landed on the surface of the cove.

Vivian had caught that gleam. 'Of course,' she went on smoothly, 'we will have the Marine officers sign it as witnesses in your presence. Then you can accompany us back to Cape Hatien in the plane, and the lawyers of the Haitian Sugar Central will be glad to see that memorandum is put in proper legal form before I, in turn, resell the plantation to them. I shall not refuse the price they are willing to pay – and it will not matter to the sugar trust whether you or I are the owner.' She gazed at him for a moment. 'Well, do you agree? – or do you go to Cape Hatien a prisoner?'

Benedetti shot a glance at the trim, uniformed figure coming cautiously up from the beach. Feverishly he scribbled his name at the bottom of the memorandum.

BROTHER MURDER

T. T. FLYNN

More famous as a writer of western fiction for the pulps, the prestigious *Saturday Evening Post*, and in book form, Thomas Theodore Flynn (1902–1978) was also a prolific author of mystery fiction, producing a story, 'The Pullman Murder,' for the very first issue of *Dime Detective* (November 1931).

He led the type of macho life that many male writers thought helpful in learning about the world, spending time as a hobo and working as a carpenter, door-to-door salesman, clerk, traveling salesman and in a ship yard, steel mills, on ships in the engine and fire room, and in a railroad shop, inspecting locomotives.

He published five western novels with Dell between 1954 and 1961, one of which, *The Man from Laramie*, was filmed starring James Stewart and directed by Anthony Mann.

Flynn's only two mystery novels were paperback originals published in Great Britain by Hector Kelly, *It's Murder* (1950) and *Murder Caravan* (1951).

His mystery pulp stories tended to be humorous and cheerful, as exemplified by the series featuring Mike Harris and Trixie Meehan, both of whom work for the Blaine International Agency. Mike is tough, red-headed and wise-cracking; Trixie is cute and pert and, while depending upon her partner if a fight breaks out, is also smart and inventive when necessary.

'Brother Murder' first appeared in the December 2, 1939, issue of *DFW*.

BROTHER MURDER

T. T. FLYNN

CHAPTER I

Girl In a Coffin

I was doing sixty-eight on the Ventura highway, north of Los Angeles, when the siren wailed behind me – and you could have had all the fun for a kippered herring.

Sixty-eight on that smooth open highway through the orange groves – and when I heard the siren and looked in the rear-view mirror, the motorcycle cop was coming like a bee to a flower.

'Whoa, Mike,' says I, and stood the long fast coupé halfway on its nose at the edge of the pavement.

He rolled alongside, killed the engine and wanted to know sarcastically: 'Going somewhere?'

'Points east,' says I. 'Did the sunshine make me reckless for a moment?'

'It made you murderous at that speed!' he snapped. 'Name, please!'

'Harris,' says I.

'First name?'

'Michael Harris.'

'Red hair,' says he, peering in at me. 'Sawed-off and wisecracking.'

'Is this a beauty contest?' I gave him.

'It's a pinch,' he informed me coldly. 'We'll go down the road and get it over with. I came out here looking for you.'

'Not me,' I told him. 'No one knew I'd be along this stretch of road.'

He was glancing in a small notebook.

'Blue Packard coupé,' he read off. 'New York tags. Sawed-off redhead named Mike Harris driving.' He pocketed the book and grinned nastily. 'If I hadn't been out this way looking for you, I wouldn't have caught you splitting the road open. Which makes us even for my trouble. Over sixty-five – and that'll cost you huckleberries, young feller.'

'Okay,' I said sourly. 'Huckleberries it is. But why look for me?'

'The Los Angeles office of the Blaine International Agency want you to telephone,' he said. 'Drive on.'

So I drove on – and they took huckleberries away from me. When I put a call through to Lew Ryster, manager of our Hollywood office I was fit to tie.

Lew sounded relieved when he heard my voice. 'So they got you, Mike! I wasn't sure what road you were taking out of the state, and your next address being New York, I put out a general call for you.'

'They *got* me all right,' I said through my teeth. 'And try to explain my fine on your expense sheet, wise guy! *I'm* not taking the rap for it!'

'What fine?' says Lew.

'The cop who came out looking for me slapped a speed charge on me!'

Lew haw-hawed.

'Cackle like a Death Valley jackass!' I said. 'I'm heading on to New York. We'll settle my fine from there.'

'Wait, Mike!' Lew yelled. 'Your vacation's canceled! I telephoned New York. And now you've been formally notified!'

'You Judas!' I howled. '*You* had my vacation *canceled?*'

'I've got a job for you,' says Lew. 'It's important, Mike. Murder, I think.'

'There'll be murder if I get near you!'

Lew said: 'Get back here fast. I'm waiting for you, Mike.'

I slammed the receiver down and blistered the phone booth. But when you worked for the Blaine Agency you were in harness. The Agency had discipline and a tradition of breaking cases fast. An assignment to a case put you to work fast or else.

So I drove back to Los Angeles to meet murder.

There's a cold-blooded touch to murder. Crooks, thieves and swindlers are mostly ordinary people with ordinary weaknesses. A lot of us would like to collect from life the easy way.

But we're all born knowing murder is out of bounds. And you never know what angles a murder case will turn up. Dangerous angles sometimes. Two murders can't draw much worse penalty than one murder. Long ago I'd decided that after the first murder, a second one comes easier – so look out for murder, Mike.

Lew Ryster was waiting in the Hollywood office, big and pink-faced as ever, with the usual striped collar, natty suit and expansive confidence that clicked with the Hollywood trade, which was mostly theft, blackmail and body-guarding.

'What's on your mind, Rat?' I asked as I shoved a paper cup under the water cooler.

Lew grinned. 'I had to do it, Mike. No hard feelings, I hope.'

'Later,' I said, 'we'll settle that. Who murdered whom?'

Lew stood up and took his Panama from the desk.

'I've an appointment, Mike, and I was hoping you'd get here in time to come along. Let's shove off.'

So we shoved off from Hollywood and Vine in my car – and over on Sunset

Boulevard, Lew ordered me to stop before the Greek-colonnaded front of J. Conwell Smythe's Sons, Morticians.

'Did you read my mind?' I growled as we got out. 'A funeral parlor is exactly where I'd like to leave you!'

Lew chuckled. 'Kid, you'll thank me for this before you're through. Did I tell you there was a two grand reward for anyone who broke this case?'

'You wouldn't,' I said, 'if you could figure a way to collar the dough . . . And what does the score have to read before the reward is paid?'

We were inside by then. A long, lean, lugubrious lassie of some forty winters met us.

'Yes?' she said, and thawed visibly as Lew grinned.

'I have an appointment here with Mr. Farnson,' Lew beamed in his best Hollywood manner. 'Ryster is the name.'

A faint flush appeared in her pallid cheeks.

'Mr. Farnson is in Room Three, with two other gentlemen. He is expecting you, Mr. Ryster. If this other gentleman will have a seat, I will show you to Room Three.'

'He's here to meet Farnson also,' says Lew carelessly, and when he grinned again her doubtful look vanished and we all went back to Room Three.

The heavy scent of flowers filled the small room into which we walked. Three men in there had been talking in low tones; and one of them – the tallest said: 'I was wondering if you'd come.'

'Sorry if I'm late, Mr. Farnson,' says Lew – and I saw the old Hollywood chuckle start and freeze off as Lew realized where he was.

Two floor lamps in the back corners of the room dusted indirect light against the ceiling and down in subdued dimness, down over the flower sprays and the pinkish coffin resting just beyond the men . . .

She might have been sleeping in the coffin – that girl whose peaceful, life-like face rested there on a satin pillow surrounded by a chaste froth of lace.

They had dressed her in what might have been a wedding gown of white satin, and she was heart-stoppingly natural, even to the little splash of good-natured freckles still luring along the bridge of a small tippity nose. Her mouth had once been built for laughter – and now it never would again smile.

But the spell of her was there in the room, even on the mortician's lean lady, who lingered inside the door eyeing the coffin for a moment, and whispered: '*So* lovely – and we have *never* brought out a face so well.'

Farnson, whose mustache was a white military line against his heavy, full-blooded face, snapped: 'Enough, Madam! This meeting is *not* an exhibit of your skill!'

She faded out in pallid silence and closed the door and the stocky-chested man on Farnson's left speared me with a disagreeable stare, jerked his head at me and grunted: 'Who's this guy?'

*

459

A cop. He was smeared with copper from sparse, sandy hair to thick-soled shoes – and he didn't like us. He didn't like Lew Ryster who could handle a tight spot coolly when he had to. And who did now.

'This,' said Lew suavely, nodding at me, 'is Mike Harris, one of our best operatives. Mike, this is Jake Dennis, from Homicide – *and* Larry Sweet, who helps Jake think.'

'Never mind the cracks,' Jake Dennis put in belligerently.

'Hold it, Jake,' said Larry Sweet mildly. His light-blue eyes were amused.

I liked this Larry Sweet, who was small, slim and almost too good-looking in a careless way to be a homicide cop. Sweet belonged over on the other side of the Hollywood fence, under the Kleig lights.

And Jake Dennis held it, biting down on his lower lip as he scowled at Lew.

'What,' said Farnson, 'is all this about? I was not expecting these gentlemen from the police again, Mr. Ryster. They will be going soon.'

He was a fine figure of an old gentleman, all of six feet, prosperous and a little on the stern side, now trying not be be angry. And behind all of it showing a bewilderment and hurt which left him almost childishly helpless.

Jake Dennis took a deep breath and spoke through throttled emotions.

'Maybe we'll be going an' maybe we maybe we won't. You didn't tell us you'd called the Blaine Agency in on this.'

Farnson's face hardened.

'You did not ask me. I did what I thought was proper. I am not interested in your opinions of what I do.'

'Now listen,' said Jake Dennis, getting red.

'Hold it, Jake,' Larry Sweet said mildly, and automatically, as if it were a habit with him.

Sweet smiled apologetically at Farnson. 'We understand that Mr. Farnson. No offense meant. Dennis is trying to suggest that he's surprised you aren't satisfied with our investigation of this matter.'

I caught Lew's sour grin. So did Jake Dennis. It was meant for Dennis, and he got redder above the collar.

Sweet must have had eyes in the side of his head. 'Hold it, Jake,' he suggested casually, without looking around.

Farnson missed all that. His high forehead had furrowed with emotion. He looked at the girl in the coffin, swallowed and was husky as he answered Sweet.

'I will not be satisfied until I know exactly why my niece is dead. You tell me it was suicide or an accident. I don't believe you. Why should such a sweet girl want to kill herself? She was happy. Only last week she wrote my wife in Boston, saying how happy she was in her work here, and how much she was enjoying the visit of Nancy Cudahy, who used to be her best friend. And – and the next word we had was the telegram saying she was dead.'

Farnson shook his head emphatically. 'No! I do not believe it!'

Jake Dennis opened his mouth to say something, and Larry Sweet beat him to it, soothingly and argumentatively.

'We only suggested suicide, Mr. Farnson. These carbon monoxide cases are hard to pin down. Folks drive into small garages and stay in there for some reason or other with the motor running and the doors closed – and before they know what's happening it's all over.'

'No,' said Farnson flatly. 'Frances was not so careless. She was always careful. How could she have done so well as a script girl in the moving pictures if she was careless? She has written us how careful she must always be in her work. Every little detail must be considered. And now you tell me she did something that everyone who drives a car knows must not be done.'

Jake Dennis muttered under his breath and rolled his eyes helplessly. Larry Sweet gave him a warning look and went on in the same patient manner.

'We've thought of all that. But we've checked on your niece at NGN, and among her friends outside. She had no love troubles. She was getting ahead at NGN and on the verge of moving into the writing end on a contract. They tell us her voice didn't register well or she'd have had a chance at the acting end. No troubles – and more important, she had no enemies. Doesn't leave much choice but accidental death, does it?'

'This Cudahy girl who was visiting her from the East says it couldn't have been anything else but an accident,' Jake Dennis grunted, and his look at Lew Ryster and me was a scowl. 'So you're wasting any money you pay the Blaine Agency. They'll charge you plenty, an' tell you in the end just what we've told you.'

'That,' said Farnson stiffly, 'is my business, gentlemen.'

Jake Dennis lifted his hands helplessly. Larry Sweet asked patiently: 'Is there anything you've forgotten to suggest to us? Anything we may have overlooked before you leave for the East with your niece's body?'

Farnson was hurt and helpless, but he was stubborn too.

'I am not taking Frances back East until I know why she was murdered,' he stated heavily.

I thought Jake Dennis was going to explode. Larry Sweet stared at him for a moment, and then nodded smoothly.

'You understand, Mr. Farnson, that we're anxious to do everything we can. Perhaps it would be better if we worked with the Blaine people too. No objections to that, I suppose.'

Lew Ryster grinned.

'Glad to have you help, Sweet – for what it's worth – and as long as we get credit for what we do. Jake, that's agreeable, I suppose?'

'What do you think?' Jake Dennis growled. 'And now you've got that settled, what are you going to do that we ain't done?'

Lew looked solemn.

'We're going to bring all the facilities of our organization to bear on this, Dennis. With our usual success, I hope. Suppose you two drop around to the office late this afternoon for a conference. Mr. Harris has some matters to check, and then we'll be in a position to collaborate on any steps that we may be taking.'

Larry Sweet's lip curled slightly in amusement. Jake Dennis looked his disgust at the smear of Hollywood oil Lew had given them. But Farnson was pleased.

'Just what I want, gentlemen,' he said eagerly. 'I will be at the Ambassador waiting for any word from you.'

So that was our interview. I took a last look at the dead girl as we all went out. She made our cross-talk seem poison and useless. And I was scathing when I drove Lew away.

'So you dragged me back for a carbon monoxide case that probably was an accident like the police have decided. Any mug on your payroll could handle this.'

'But not satisfy Farnson,' said Lew cheerfully. 'He's a Boston investment banker and lousy with money. He'll spend high to prove he's right about this. That girl meant more to him than a daughter. He and his wife reared her. And if he thinks it's murder, we might as well try to prove that it's murder.'

'Maybe you *are* a rat!' I snapped. 'You've been around Hollywood too long. You know damn well the Blaine Agency never chisels for money if they're sure there's not a case. And to think I let you scramble my vacation on a play like this!'

Lew chuckled.

'Jake Dennis is a headline hog, Mike. Never give that guy a break or he'll break you. I've done business with him before. And Larry Sweet is so smooth he'll be around you before you know it.' Lew pursed his lips. 'I only hope Larry really believes it is suicide and thinks we're giving Farnson a run-around for his money.'

'Aren't you?' I said disgustedly.

'Maybe,' said Lew. 'You saw the dead girl and heard most of the fact. She made a try for pictures, and when her voice didn't click, she tossed society life back in Boston overboard, rolled up her sleeves out here and went to work with the lower third. Was making good on it too, and then yesterday morning she was found dead in her coupé at the bungalow court where she lived. Garage doors closed, car windows open, the girl behind the steering wheel with her hat on, cigarette between her first and second fingers, just as if she'd driven in and sat there smoking and thinking and forgetting to cut the motor off.

'I guess, Mike, you didn't notice it there in the coffin, and I didn't want to point it out with Dennis and Sweet around. There was a mark on her finger where the cigarette had burned down against the flesh.'

'I didn't notice it,' I said. 'So what?'

Lew grinned.

'If you'd looked close, Mike, you'd have seen that there was the slightest sign of cigarette stain on the other side of her second finger, and on the inside of her third finger. She had an awkward way of holding a cigarette, between her second and third fingers, instead of the usual first and second fingers. And yet she died, holding a cigarette the usual way. As near as I can figure it, Kid, that little fact is going to turn you into a screwball and make you a disciple of the Great Truth, Father Orion.'

CHAPTER II

Peace, Brother

A truck cut over in front of me and I stood the coupé on its nose, and shaved a wreck and said violently:

'Somebody around here is a screwball – and it's not me! What kind of tripe is this about the Great Truth, Father Orion? And how do you know so much about cigarette stains on that girl's fingers?'

'I'm good,' says Lew smugly. 'The body was found by the girl friend, Nan Cudahy – who's due to inherit a couple of million one of these days, if that makes her any more attractive.'

'It doesn't,' I said. 'What's the dope on the cigarette stains?'

'You know me,' says Lew. 'Always on the spot at the right time. When Farnson retained me, I ducked around for a talk with this Nan Cudahy. She was taking it hard and didn't have any more to tell me than Sweet and Dennis know. But she let slip one thing. She'd been thinking, she said, how terribly symbolic it was that her friend should have been holding a cigarette between the first and second fingers when all the girl friends had teased her so much about the awkward way she had always smoked. Wasn't it symbolic, the Cudahy gal asked, with her eyes big and round, that Miss Farnson should have changed an old habit that way just when she died? Crossing the threads of the subconsious like that just as the threads of life got all tragically mixed. The Great Truths of existence, Miss Cudahy said tearfully, get all tangled up like that unless they are interpreted right. And maybe if the dead girl had been a little more of a believer in some things, the terrible accident wouldn't have happened.'

'I'm dizzy but able to stand more,' I said. 'What kind of a screwball is this female?'

'Tut-tut,' says Lew. 'You're talking about two million bucks. She's a poor little girl who came out to Hollywood on a visit and got on the track of the Great Truths of Life.'

'Yeah?'

'Heaven knows,' said Lew more seriously, 'I'd have thought two million dollars could keep its head. But I've seen bigger ones tumble. Miss Cudahy never saw anything like this village, Mike, and before she could catch her breath she went Hollywood nuts. That's the only explanation I can make.

Not that I gave a damn after her crack about the dead girl holding a cigarette between the wrong fingers. And the cigarette staying there until it burned into the skin! Get it?'

'It can't be kosher,' I said. 'The cops would be howling bloody murder. If true, it means that someone shoved a lighted cigarette between the wrong fingers after the girl was dead, and left her there in the car with the motor running to cover up.'

'Now,' says Lew brightly, 'we see all, know all. So it gets murder and I thought fast and hauled you back here. Miss Two Million Bucks didn't tumble she'd said anything that mattered. She had just thought of the cigarette while talking to me. I'm the only one who knows about it. She's been questioned by the police and newspaper men, and has testified at the inquest, and had her picture taken, and her soul is harrowed with grief, and all she wants now is to Get Away From It All, and let the Great Truths of Life assuage the tragedy of losing her best friend.'

I had the car parked near Hollywood and Vine by then, and I sat there with a hand on the door eyeing Lew warily.

'Are you nuts?' I wondered. 'Or was Miss Millions feeding you a line? It's been a long time since I'v heard such addled talk. And that brings me back to your crack about screwballs and someone called The Great Truth, Father Orion.'

Lew was enjoying himself.

'Name your brand of nut and I'll pick it off the Hollywood tree,' he offered. 'Father Orion hangs up on one of the top branches, out near the tip. He doesn't go in for publicity, but I run across his name now and then. His Shrine of Truth is located away out in the hills beyond Laurel Canyon. He's got plenty of acres inside a burglar-proof fence out there, and his buildings and land are worth money. Some of the people who go for his line would rate headlines in any newspaper. And they're not all local folks. Disciples make pilgrimages here. He's got guest houses on the place for the ones who rate lodging while they're hanging around getting injections from the fountain of wisdom itself.'

'What is it, a yoga racket?'

'Heaven knows,' said Lew. 'But it's profitable. You can tell me more about it after you come back from the joint.'

'Say that again.'

'You've going to be a disciple of The Great Truth, Father Orion,' Lew informed me.

'Like hell I am!'

Lew was in fine fettle as he lighted a cigarette and sat there grinning at me.

'You'll arrive from the East with a pocketful of money, Mike. And if we're lucky, you'll get into the inner circle around Father Orion and inspect the skeletons in the closet. I've got it all figured out.'

'When you figure anything out, it's time to run,' I cracked back. 'Why should I get next to this Father Orion?'

And for the first time Lew grew serious.

'That girl was murdered, Mike. Her contacts and life around Hollywood don't offer a reason. It wasn't even robbery. Her purse with money in it was beside her on the seat. I don't think this Cudahy girl knows anything. But from the way she talked, I gathered the dead girl wasn't in favor of her interest in Father Orion. Is that a motive for murder?'

'Is it?'

'You'll have to find out,' says Lew, still serious. 'And don't think if we pin this murder on someone after the police have called it accidental death or suicide, that it won't mean plenty of local business for the Blaine Agency.'

'*If*,' I repeated sarcastically. 'And you had to plaster the job on me. All right – how do I become a disciple of this Father Orion?'

Lew grinned broadly again. 'That's why I wanted you on this, Mike. I've done my share. The rest is up to you.'

So I thought it over, grabbed an east-bound plane, and in the morning was at Chicago Police Headquarters with Brophy, one of the Blaine vice-presidents.

I framed the telegram that went out from the Missing Person's Bureau to Father Orion, Los Angeles.

AMNESIA VICTIM CARRYING LOS ANGELES AIRLINE TICKET AND CONSIDERABLE SUM OF MONEY ON PERSON IN CUSTODY OF THIS BUREAU AND UNABLE TO REMEMBER ANYTHING BUT DESIRE TO SEE FATHER ORION AT LOS ANGELES. PERSON UNABLE TO REMEMBER WHETHER CATHOLIC OR NOT. PLEASE ADVISE COLLECT TELEGRAM ANY KNOWLEDGE YOU MAY HAVE OF PARTY. LIEUTENANT HOWELL

And in less than two hours the Lieutenant had a wire back.

PLACE AMNESIA VICTIM ON LOS ANGELES PLANE AND WIRE HOUR OF ARRIVAL. FATHER ORION WILL ASSUME RESPONSIBILITY.
JOHN PAIGE, SECRETARY TO FATHER ORION.

'Hook, line and sinker,' says I, in Lieutenant Howell's ofice. 'Who could resist an amnesia victim with a pocketfull of cash?'

The Lieutenant, a gray-haired fatherly looking man, scratched his head.

'It ain't according to the rules,' he informed Brophy and me. 'We'd usually investigate further before we let an amnesia case go off to strangers.'

Brophy was more than dubious. He was worried. 'Take good care of that money, Harris. I don't like to see so much of the Agency's cash being exposed to risk. I don't know why I let you talk me into this.'

'You never can tell what'll happen in an amnesia case,' I cracked, and back

I went to the airport and headed west again with eight thousand dollars and some extra bills in my pocket and amnesia on my mind.

How does amnesia feel? I wouldn't know. L.A. was a vast blanket of sparkling lights when the big silver plane eased out of the late evening sky and settled on the airport. And the pretty little stewardess who gave me a parting smile and I walked down the portable steps into the blaze of light beside the plane.

Nine of us left the plane. Three were movie stars, and they walked into waiting photographers, flash bulbs and friends surging to greet them. And I walked past all that with a glassy look, wondering who was going to meet me and could I put this over.

A hand touched my arm. A smooth voice intoned: 'Father Orion sends his greeting, Brother.'

I said, 'Ahhhh . . .' and then almost strangled as I caught sight of two men well off to one side who had stopped and were staring at me.

Jake Dennis and Larry Sweet if I never had a bad dream. Sweet's hand was on his stocky companion's arms. I could almost hear him saying: 'Hold it, Jake.'

Meanwhile Father Orion had sent his greetings.

Sweet and Dennis had caught me offguard. I didn't know what my face had revealed to the man who had touched my arm.

He was a head taller than I, a jolly, well-fed young man with pink smiling cheeks and a stare that took me apart.

'I'm John Paige, Father Orion's secretary, Brother. I've never seen you before, have I?'

I shook my head and mumbled: 'I was hoping you'd know me. Will Father Orion know me?'

The hand he put to my elbow wore a curious jade ring. His manner was cheerfully confident. 'This way, Brother. Father Orion knows all Truth.'

Dennis and Sweet were still watching as we walked away. I was in a sweat as to whether they'd hail me, and in another sweat as to whether they'd follow us.

'Everything went blank . . .' I mumbled to Paige.

'Yes, yes,' he said soothingly. 'But Father Orion has the light. Here's the car, Brother.'

At least Father Orion gave the faithful good taxi service. Paige stowed me into the front seat of a big blue Cadillac sedan and we rolled away. I tried to see if we were being followed and had no luck. But those two flat-feet from Headquarters would at least get the license number.

'How long have you followed the Master?' Paige inquired.

'There's a – a wall in my mind,' I said forlornly. 'In Chicago all I could remember was the name of Father Orion. I asked the police and – and they put me on the airplane.'

'Quite right,' Paige approved. 'Strangers might have taken advantage of you. Remember any more now?'

'No.' And I groaned: 'It's terrible being like this!'

Paige dropped his hand on my arm. 'You're with friends, Brother. Perhaps we'd better make sure you haven't any identifying papers on you. Let's see your billfold.'

He parked at the curb, and I let him have the billfold and watched closely while he looked inside. Paige whistled softly at the hundreds and five hundreds Brophy had reluctantly turned over to me.

'A lot of money to be carrying around, Brother.'

'There was more,' says I vaguely. 'The safe deposit box was almost full. I think I always keep money ready in the deposit box. But I – I can't remember where the box is. Will Father Orion tell me?'

'The Master knows all Truth,' Paige stated. 'Were you bringing this money, Brother, as a Love Offering?'

'I can't remember,' I told him helplessly as I reached for the billfold.

So there we were without any secrets, as we rolled into the high wooded hills beyond Hollywood . . .

Lew Ryster had prepared me for Orion's Shrine. But Lew hadn't told all. Maybe Lew wouldn't have believed it himself. A side road led us to stone gate towers flanked by a high, close-meshed fence topped by strands of barbed wire.

'The top wire is electrified,' Paige remarked casually as we paused in the glare of floodlights on the gate posts.

A guard unchained the gates, and as we rolled through, called: 'Welcome, Brothers!'

And I gandered at the fellow and moved up another notch on the Hollywood nut tree. That big guard wore sandals on bare feet and a white cloak resembling a Roman toga. He had a curly brown beard and the bulging muscles and build of a ham wrestler. And the air of a wild-eyed fanatic.

The whole lay-out was getting a little more unbelievable as I came closer to Father Orion.

'Electricity?' I mumbled.

'Lots of electricity, Brother,' Paige assured me cheerfully.

'But – but—'

'The Shrine, Brother, is guarded from desecration by all unbelievers and scoffers.' Paige delivered the statement with a solemn manner and a deeper voice.

I said: 'Ahhhh . . .'

Paige said nothing. The silhouette of his face was sterner, as if his manner at the station had been for the outside world.

There was nothing screwball about the muscles of that guard at the gate and the electrified fence. It made you wonder what would happen if Father Orion decided not to like a pilgrim. The eight grand cash inside my coat was folding money in any language. And if there did just happen to be murder in the background and Mike Harris stubbed his toe and got in bad – then what?

I'd have felt better with a gun tucked under my armpit or inside my shirt. But it wouldn't have looked kosher for Brother Amnesia to show up packing a rod. So I sat watchful and wary as we rolled up the winding driveway to the Shrine.

Here were broad smooth lawns and narrow paths to small rustic outbuildings haphazardly scattered back against the trees. A few dim bulbs on poles showed the paths and the driveway, and made clear and startling the big white, temple-like building that dominated the center of the broad lawns.

They called it a shrine and it looked like a pillared temple, with softly lighted windows and a wide flag-stone terrace all around. Our headlights picked out several figures on the terrace clad in the flowing white togas.

Paige turned the big car into a narrow side drive that skirted the trees and the small outbuildings. We stopped before one of the small buildings.

'You will live here, Brother,' Paige said, getting out.

Not so bad. It was a snug little cabin built of peeled cedar logs, with screened windows, flower beds and a trellised vine.

'Is Father Orion here?' I wanted to know doubtfully.

'Father Orion,' Paige said as he entered the cabin and switched on a light, 'is now supervising the Evening Circle of Felicity. After you change into your robe and sandals, I'll take you into the Circle.'

'Robe?' says I, eyeing the white garment Paige took from a hook and tossed on a narrow bed.

'I'll change also and come back for you,' Paige nodded.

'B-but I'm dressed,' I protested weakly.

Paige was stern. 'Father Orion only sees those who put aside all things of the world. I'll return in fifteen minutes, Brother.'

CHAPTER III

The Woman in Black

He drove off and under my breath I damned Lew Ryster again. Mike Harris in one of those Roman nightgowns! If someone I knew ever caught me out in that harness I'd never live it down.

But if I balked, I'd probably get no closer to Father Orion.

Outside in the night something was softly throbbing, throbbing.

It sounded like a drum, muted, beating a lazy irregular rhythm. I switched off the light, opened the door and traced the sound to the looming mass of the Shrine off there across the lawns.

More hocus-pocus. It stopped as I buckled on the sandals and stood up in the white toga, feeling like a fool.

They'd saved the day with a roomy inside pocket where I could carry the billfold. Brophy, back in Chicago, would have had a spasm if he'd known the company his eight grand was keeping now.

I lighted a cigarette and was wondering what gives next when Paige returned. He had changed into a white toga. One look and he snatched my cigarette and stamped it under a sandaled foot.

'Tobacco would desecrate the Shrine, Brother,' he reproved. 'This way.'

So I smothered an impulse to slug brother Paige and slap-slapped after him in the leather sandals.

Dew got on my feet. The cold night air blew up my bare legs under the toga. We looked like a couple of lost ghosts as we moved toward the Shrine, crossed the terrace and passed inside.

The lazy drumming had started again, and the soft rhythm was there at the other end of a big crowded patio which we had entered.

Shaded wall lamps filled the place with soft light. Men and women were moving about and sitting on couches, backless chairs and benches. Long ones, short ones, fat and thin, young and old, talking, laughing. All wore white togas and robes. Incense curled from small braziers toward the open sky and stars overhead.

Paige led me toward a dais at the far end. A thin, mystic-faced Oriental was seated cross-legged at one corner of the dais, head thrown slightly back, eyes closed as his hand beat out that lazy, irregular rhythm from a small drum.

And then the huge, white-bearded, patriarchal old man who stood up on the dais caught all my attention.

He had been sitting on a backless couch talking to a small group of men and women. They remained seated as he drew a flowing white toga close and stepped off the dais to meet Paige. His voice was a dreamy rumble.

'Brother, we have been waiting for you. Is this the troubled one you went to greet?'

Paige gestured solemnly toward me. 'Come from the shadows to seek the Truth, Master.' And to me Paige said: 'Where there is truth, there is peace. Father Orion greets you.'

So I mumbled: 'Ahhhhh . . .'

The drummer had paused. Voices had lowered as those near us took a gander at the newcomer. And I stood there in my bare gams and wondered what one did next.

He looked older than the hills and wiser than the Encyclopedia. A big arched nose like a beak came out of the center of the beard and his eyes had a dreamy fixed stare.

He held out a hand as if expecting it to be kissed. I shook it. The big fingers were long and supple, and they returned to toy slowly with the fringes of the beard.

In that dreamy rumble which made you wonder what his shout was like, Father Orion said: 'Welcome, Brother, to the House of Truth.'

'Truth,' I breathed, half-closing my eyes.

He rumbled: 'Your name is?'

'The name hasn't been remembered yet,' Paige answered for me.

A big hand lifted in a benign gesture.

'Wordly names are put aside here anyway. We shall call him Brother Rudolph.'

I started to protest and he cut me off in a dreamy chant.

'Brother Rudolph, you come seeking the great Truths of the past. The old forbidden secrets of the sacred lamas of Lhasa and the teachings of the sages long lost amid the blindness and ignorance of men. You have been seeking that which could not be found. What is it, Brother, for which you grope?'

I looked away for a moment. His manner had almost made me dizzy. I should have known that anyone who could run a show like this had something on the ball.

'My name,' I told him meekly. 'I want to know my name and where can I find my deposit box?'

Father Orion looked at me like a sleepwalker. 'The Truth will be opened up to you. In your heart will be peace. Join our Circle of Felicity now, Brother, and open your heart to Peace.'

Neat, eh, but not obvious. Paige didn't help it any by turning to the crowd and saying:

'I give you Brother Rudolph, a new seeker of Truth. Surround him with Felicity.'

The drumming started again. They surrounded me, long ones, and fat ones, old ones and young ones, pushing heads at me from the togas and robes, clapping me on the shoulder, beaming, smiling, calling me Brother, giving me great bunches of Felicity as I edged through and kept a hand of Brophy's eight grand inside my toga.

And suddenly I gritted my teeth and swore under my breath as a foot kicked my bare shin bone. Then I froze as a voice cooed sweetly at my elbow.

'Welcome, Brother. Welcome, Brother Rudolph.'

You can't guess! But I knew. Only one soft cooing little voice in all the world could set my nerves quivering like this. I looked and I was right.

Trixie Meehan stood at my elbow with a leer on her lovely little face. The others probably thought Trixie was smiling. They didn't know the gal. They didn't know Trixie Meehan.

And who is Trixie Meehan? Brother, Trixie Meehan also works for the Blaine Agency. Pert and sweet, soft and cuddly, harmless as a kitten and luscious-looking to all big strong men – that's Trixie if you don't know her.

But I knew her. Trixie was smart, shrewd, fearless and tireless on a case. And her temper would make a scorpion blush and her little tongue could peel the hide off a brass-bound monkey. And when Trixie and I crossed trails on a case, it was usually *my* hide that took the peeling.

Under her breath Trixie said: 'Brother! Oh, *Brother!*' And behind her hands she giggled: 'If I could only get your picture, Brother!'

A fat lady was pouring garlic-scented Felicity in my ear and inviting me to sit on a couch.

'Madam,' I said, 'the young lady will tell me about Truth – and nothing but the Truth.'

She forgot Felicity and Father Orion long enough to give Trixie a dirty look and crack back: 'Where I come from, they don't call it Truth!'

But I already had Trixie's arm and was shoving her toward the other end of the patio.

'Listen, Ape, you're twisting my arm off!' Trixie said angrily under her breath. 'And someone will see that we know each other!'

'I'd like to twist your little neck off!' I gritted. 'Where did you come from?'

'We're on the same case, Mike.'

'Who said so?'

'Lew Ryster sent me.'

'I'll kill that doublecrossing so-and-so! He didn't say anything about you.'

'And why should he? Let go my arm or I'll scream.'

She would have too. The things Trixie Meehan would do if pushed hard enough would curdle your blood. I released her arm.

Trixie snapped: 'Lew didn't say anything because he knew you'd have a spasm. And if you think *I* cried for the chance to work with the world's greatest ego, they haven't slipped you the proper dose of truth yet!'

Trixie glared at me – and in the midst of it suddenly began to giggle again. 'Mike, have you looked in a mirror yet?'

'I have not,' I said. 'You'd fit in a Roman bath scene yourself. How long have you been here?'

'Since yesterday,' says Trixie, ducking over to a couch where we could have a little privacy. 'And Mike, I'm scared.'

Trixie looked at me soberly. And I looked back, thinking that she was one of the few women in the place who looked appealing and sweet in the graveyard uniforms they issued.

'Afraid of what?' I asked.

Trixie shrugged slightly. 'Nothing – and everything. This place is guarded like a prison farm.'

'So I noticed.'

'Look at them,' said Trixie. 'They're fanatical. They've turned their minds over to that old man.'

'How many of them had a mind to start with?'

'Scratch deep enough,' said Trixie, 'and you'll find that most of them have a bank account. They weren't swept up out of the gutter to be loaded with truth and felicity.'

'Somebody has to pay for the overhead,' I said. 'Look at me. I brought

471

eight grand cash money along, and I've got more in a safe deposit box if I can ever recover from my attack of amnesia and think where it is.'

'Does Father Orion know about the money?' Trixie asked quickly.

'Sister, the Master – knows all!'

'I'm trying to be serious, Mike!'

'Eight grand is always serious,' I grinned. 'What's wrong with the Master?'

'I'm afraid of him,' Trixie said without hesitation. 'Mike, these people *believe* in him!'

'Does Paige?'

'I don't know.'

'Both of us are foggy then,' I admitted. 'The more I see of all this, the less sure I am—' I broke off, staring across the patio, and whistled softly in amazement.

'Don't mug,' I said under my breath. 'But get a load of that thin fellow with the black hair moving along the wall over there? He was looking at us.'

'I knew talking to me this way was a fool stunt!' Trixie snapped.

'He's easing up for a gab fest with Father Time,' I said. 'Know him?'

'I'm not the local directory,' says Trixie nastily. 'I've only been here a day myself.'

'He's dropped some weight,' I said. 'But four-five years ago in Philly he was a con-man just paroled. Eddy Voss was his name. Haggerty, who was in our Philadelphia office then, had helped send him up several years before.'

'Did he see you with Haggerty?'

'I wish I knew.'

'A stir-bird,' says Trixie under her breath. 'And now he's a crackpot with the rest of them. I don't believe it.'

'They bait a mean hook around here for suckers, Baby.'

'Nuts,' says Trixie. 'Do you see any more familiar faces?'

I was looking, and I was more uneasy about Voss than I let Trixie see. If he remembered me, what then? At the least I'd be tossed out on my ear. And I wondered what kind of dice he was throwing in this crowd.

'I can't spot anyone else,' I told Trixie. 'If you see Lew Ryster before I do, have him get Voss' record since the parole.'

Trixie nodded.

'How did you crash the gate here?' I asked.

'I pretended I worked at the studio with Nancy Cudahy's dead friend,' Trixie said wryly. 'Nancy was loaded with Father Orion, and was telling me about him before we'd been together fifteen minutes. I asked for more. It wasn't hard to get her to bring me here.'

'Where is the Cudahy girl?'

'Up there on the platform with Father Time,' says Trixie. 'That lumpy brunette with too much weight.'

'That?' I said. '*That* worth two million bucks?'

'That,' Trixie said.

I decided: 'For a million bucks and a pair of smoked glasses I'd take a chance on her myself. Is she as big a fool as I hear?'

'Not as big a fool as most men who'd do anything for a pretty face or a bank account,' Trixie said acidly. 'She's bad enough. Tutors, guardians, servants and guards have insulated her from a lot she ought to know. That dumb looking face hasn't helped her any. In a way I'm sorry for her.'

'Poor kid.'

'Like hell,' says Trixie. 'Not with millions. And don't make any passes at her. She tells me she's secetly engaged.'

'Who's the lucky speculator?'

'She wouldn't say. It's a great big breathless secret. What are you going to do now, Mike?'

'Keep away from you and keep my fingers crossed.'

'We'll both be happy then!' Trixie snapped. 'Keeping away from you is one of life's pleasures!'

Trixie flounced away with a swirl of her white robe.

And I sat there trying to make two and two into five. How could you tie all this into a slick murder? The dead girl hadn't been one of this bunch. Father Orion had a neat enough racket. Why should he want anyone killed? And to add a little frosting to the cake, why was Eddy Voss here?

Meanwhile I had eight grand inside my robe and Felicity all around. And as I got up from the couch, the woman in black came in out of the night.

I was near the entrance to that big roofless patio. I was one of the first who saw that her pale face was molded in tragedy. I think I was the first to sense that her spirit was feeding on inner fires of suffering.

'Here's trouble, Mike!' I decided – and I drifted across the patio after her to see what would happen.

She wore the somber black of mourning. She was in her thirties, plain looking, uninteresting. Probably like the others for she seemed to be at home here.

But now she stood out sharply from the rest of the gathering. She came in slowly, one hand clutching a black purse to her bosom. She traversed the long patio toward Father Orion with the same heavy steps.

Those who became aware of her stopped talking and watched as I was watching.

A few moved toward the dais after her as I did.

Father Orion saw her. He stood up, hesitated, and stepped slowly off the dais and waited for her.

By now most of the talk had died away. You could feel the quick tenseness, like the quiet before a storm. Eddy Voss left the side of the dais in a stealthy manner.

Father Orion toyed with his beard in that dreamy manner as the woman stopped before him. She did not speak loudly, but in the quiet her brittle voice sounded loud.

'He killed himself,' she said. 'He killed himself after they took the last of his money and kept on threatening him. He's dead. *You* know why he's dead. No one but *you* could have known. I've come all the way back here to settle with you.'

Her voice gave no further warning. She was still talking when she snatched a gun from her black purse. The first blasting shot broke the tension.

Women screamed, men yelled. They fled in all directions and became a milling, helpless mob. And the woman stood there and emptied her gun at Father Orion.

I had leaped on a couch to see better. Her black-clad figure did not move as the small automatic in her hand blasted shots directly into Father Orion's chest.

There wasn't anything I could do. He didn't have a chance. It wasn't pretty to watch. A bloody execution never is particularly pretty.

Father Orion did not try to save himself. I saw it. He stood there with that big white beard over his chest and his arms half-lifted as if he might be blessing her while she poured bullets into his body.

The ripping roar of explosions was over in seconds. All the patio was in an uproar. And I stood frozen on a couch waiting for Father Orion to fall.

Eddy Voss dived in from one side, caught her gun hand and jerked her around to him. He hit her in the jaw. She dropped. And I jumped off the couch and pushed and shoved toward the spot.

Voss was trying to lift the woman's limp figure when I reached them. I caught her feet to help. And once more froze as the unbelievable happened.

Father Orion had stepped back on the dais and lifted his arms. His big hooked nose and half-closed eyes, his bushy white beard and uplifted arms made him like a prophet out of the old books. His voice came in a dreamy, awesome boom above the panic and the noise.

'Peace! Peace, Brothers! The Truth lives. The Great Truth lives undying.'

A woman screamed. 'It didn't hurt him! Master, they can't kill you!'

Guess who! Miss Two Million Bucks screamed that.

Other voices caught her up. 'Master, they can't kill you!'

'Praise the Truth! Praise the Master!'

I almost shivered. They were like animals yapping with fanatical joy. And so help me that huge old man stood there on the dais, unharmed, unhurt.

I was close. I could see two of the bullet holes in the outer cloth of his robes. The holes were over his chest. He should have been dead, dying at least. And I could see no blood, no hurt, no break in the dreamy, unearthly manner.

Voss' eyes were black slits as he snarled: 'Pick her up! Pick her up! Toward that door back of you!'

The crowd was surging toward the dais as we started to carry the woman away. They weren't even thinking of her. Voss had slipped the gun into his pocket. I thought of her purse and didn't see it.

John Paige appeared beside me and snapped: 'I'll take her!'

'She isn't heavy,' I panted.

'I'll take her!' he snapped again, and elbowed me aside.

So I let him have her and started to follow them.

Paige was excited. His voice broke at me. 'We don't need you. Go on back!'

'Scram!' Eddy Voss threw at me. His eyes were black coals. He looked like he might start shooting himself.

So I turned back. Starting a fight with those two wouldn't get Mike Harris any information.

I pushed back toward the dais hoping to find the woman's purse. No sign of it. I looked again to make certain Father Orion was all right. He was.

By now I was thinking again. You don't do tricks with bullets from modern automatics, even if it is small. But you can stop 'em with bullet-proof vests.

And bullet-proof vests mean that someone expects to get shot at now and then. People don't shoot because they're taught the Great Truth of Life.

Trixie Meehan hauled at my elbow.

'I've got her purse, Mike!'

'Slip me!' I said quickly. 'Find out where Paige and Voss are taking that woman. See what they do with her. They ran me away. It'll look suspicious for me to watch them now!'

Trixie gave me the black purse and hurried off like the little trouper she was in a pinch. And for once I was thankful for the bedsheet I was wearing. Under cover of the robe I emptied the purse into the pocket where my money was. Back in the crowd again I dropped the purse on the floor.

As near as I could tell from a quick look, my haul was some paper money and coins, a Pullman check, vanity, nailfile, a little memorandum book, a crumpled envelope and a small handkerchief.

She had spoken of a man who had killed himself, had charged Father Orion with the responsibility. The idea was hot enough to sizzle. A plain trail of death pointed to Orion! And if once, why not twice? Like, say, Frances Farnson? Well, why not?

So we had more mystery. Ideas began to rattle in my mind. A nebulous thought took form, so startling that I almost shrugged it off.

The woman in black could have settled the idea in a few minutes. But would I have a chance to talk with her? I would not. Paige and Voss' manner had left no doubt that I wasn't wanted around her.

I wondered if they suspected me? But why should they? What cop would turn up carrying eight thousand dollars?

Would they turn her over to the police? Don't be silly. By now I could see that this guarded estate in the hills north of Hollywood could settle its own troubles.

I smiled at the thought of Larry Sweet and Jake Dennis. They'd give something to be in on this. Chances were that Jake Dennis was still profanely wondering why I'd appeared on that Chicago plane.

Trixie came back. 'They took her through that door, Mike. It's locked.'

'What's beyond the door?'

Trixie shrugged.

'Will the Cudahy girl know?' I asked.

'Maybe.'

'Ask her. But first, you'd better get outside and see if they're taking her away.'

Trixie nodded. 'Where are you staying, Mike?'

'Fourth – no, fifth cabin – to the right of the driveway.'

'We're two cabins from the eating pavilion. Sometimes Nancy spends the night. And the more I see of this the less I like it,' Trixie said as she turned away.

CHAPTER IV

Hitting the Pipe

Paige was back on the dais a moment later, leaning close as he spoke to Father Orion. The old man nodded. Pate lifted his voice for quiet.

And when he had quiet, Paige called: 'The woman dropped her purse. Who has it?'

'Here, Brother.' A reedy eager little man pushed forward with the purse. Paige solemnly lifted his hand.

'You have seen. The woman is mad. The Master orders that there be no mention of this.'

'No mention,' Father Orion boomed dreamily.

'Another day ends,' Paige told them. 'There will be no ceremonies tonight. The Master gives you Peace and Truth.'

'Peace and Truth!' Father Orion intoned.

So we were eased out, and I had to leave also. Voss hadn't appeared. Outside I made a circuit of the big white building. Trixie wasn't in sight.

The woman had fainted, Paige had said. Fooey. I wondered what Paige would think when he found the purse empty.

The brethren and sistern were scattering. I headed for my cabin to shuck out of the white sheet. I'd left my suit over the foot of the bed with a few flakes of cigarette ash scattered where they'd do the most good. The little gray flakes had vanished from the suit fabric.

So my clothes had been frisked. I lighted a cigarette and was reaching for the loot inside my robe when Paige knocked and entered hurriedly.

'I'll lock your money in the safe tonight,' he told me.

476

'Don't bother,' I said. 'It's safe with all that electricity around and Father Orion near.' And I added: 'Brother, I'm afraid I'll forget where *this* money is if I lock it up anywhere.'

'Nonsense,' Paige said.

'Tomorrow, Brother, I'll look for the Truth about it.'

'Take my advice in this,' Paige insisted.

'Tomorrow,' I promised. 'Tomorrow, Brother.'

Paige looked as if he were not sure whether he was being kidded or not. A slight smile followed.

'Tomorrow,' he agreed. 'We'll settle everything tomorrow. Remember, Brother, no smoking near the Master.'

He left as abruptly as he entered – and I hadn't been so near a chill in years.

Father Orion, Paige and the disciples were funny on the surface. The guarded estate and fantastic Shrine of Truth were good for a laugh. But some crackpots are only a hair-line from an asylum. And a madhouse can have its horrors.

Paige had just called me 'Brother.' His changed manner had suggested 'Sucker.' I switched off the light and got into my clothes fast.

And when the money went back inside my coat I damned myself for thinking of such a stunt. But then I hadn't thought it possible to walk into a situation like this.

The purse loot was next. I drew the curtains before I switched on the light to take inventory.

The money came to fourteen dollars and some coins. The Pullman check didn't tell me much at the moment. A Philadelphia pawnshop ticket made out to Mrs. H. Mossman dropped out of the memorandum book. The crumpled letter was postmarked Bridgeport, Connecticut and was addressed to Mrs. Harry Mossman, at a North Side address in Philadelphia.

Dear Mae:

I can't loan you any more. And I don't see how you and Harry can need so much cash. Last year when you folks came back from Los Angeles and bought the garage, you were well fixed. For that matter I never could see why Harry sold out and came back. He was doing well and liked the Coast. If business is so bad, Harry had better sell out and take a job somewhere. We're all well here. We'd like you two to come up and visit us.

Your Affct. Brother,

Sam

The memorandum book held bridge scores, a housewife's small notation, some addresses, mostly in the East, several in Los Angeles.

But I had my information. She'd come from Philly. She'd been to a pawn shop just before she left, evidently to get rail-road fare.

Fourteen dollars wouldn't take her back. She hadn't been thinking of going back. I had seen her, heard her. There wasn't any doubt in my mind that the woman had been obsessed with the one idea of getting to L.A. and emptying a gun into old Orion. After that it didn't matter.

She'd lived in Los Angeles. She'd been one of the disciples. For some reason her husband had moved to Philadelphia. If you asked Mike Harris, the husband might have gone to Philly to get his wife away from these lunatics.

Suddenly the husband had begun to need cash money. His wife had borrowed from her brother. When the money was all gone, the husband had shot himself. Only a hockshop had gotten the woman back to Father Orion.

All that I knew now. But I didn't know why the husband had bankrupted himself without a squawk and finally shot himself.

The woman could tell me. But could I talk to her in the privacy I had to have? Would she be alive that long? Would I be alive that long?

Sounds jittery, doesn't it? Well, I had Brophy's eight grand, and Father Orion's madhouse all around, and a dead girl down the hill in Hollywood and a dead man in Philadelphia. I'd witnessed an automatic spitting bullets at Father Orion.

A little cool thought about the situation was enough to lift the hair on a sane man's head.

So I tucked the contents of the purse under the mattress, switched the light off again and opened the door quietly.

The local diciples had been driving automobiles off the estate. When I stepped outside, the grounds seemed pretty well deserted. The Shrine was dark. Most of the overhead lights along the paths had been turned off. Here and there I could see the dim-lit windows of occupied cabins. The white shape that suddenly appeared at the corner of my cabin made me jump and swear violently.

'Iss forbidden,' I was sternly informed.

'Forbidden hell!' I said, mad because he'd surprised me out of a week's growth. I needed growth at the moment. This toga-clad fellow was almost as big as the guard at the gate. 'What's forbidden?' I asked.

'Go out,' he said in an accent thick enough to slice.

'Yeah?' I said. 'Who's forbidden and who said so?'

'Everyone – you,' he told me. 'Father Orion orders.'

'The hell with Father Orion,' I started to say – and didn't. Such talk wouldn't do me any good around here. 'Where's Paige?' I snapped.

'Don' know.'

'Where's Father Orion?'

'Don' know. You sleep now, huh?'

'Yeah?' I said. 'Oh, sure, I'll sleep.'

He was big and the white toga made him look bigger. He was carrying a stick. I couldn't see whether he had a gun.

'You go back,' he said.

'Sure,' I said.

What else? His yell would have brought others. I might have ducked into the woods, reached the fence and gotten outside the guarded gate some way. But I didn't think so. Back inside the dark cabin I began to fumble around as quietly as I could.

Ten minutes it took me, maybe a little more. When I finally looked past the edge of the window shade, the white toga was still out there a few feet from the front door. And for once I could have said a kind word for the sheet-wrapped brigade. They were easy to see at night.

The door hinge creaked. He was turning around when I started out, so I talked fast.

'Look,' I said. 'I've got to see Father Orion.'

'Tomorrow,' he said stolidly.

'Tonight,' I said, walking up to him.

'What iss?' he asked suspiciously, looking down at my left hand.

'Money,' says I, holding it out. 'I found it in the cabin. Look, Brother, look.'

He took the money instinctively. Maybe I'd have done the same. And I slugged him with the twisted pillow cases in my right hand and he went down with a funny grunting sound.

I forgot to say that the two pillow covers, one inside the other for strength, had a heavy doorknob knotted in the end. I'd used my knife point for a screwdriver to get the knob off. It was almost as good as a blackjack. For a moment I was afraid I'd caved his skull.

But I hadn't. He was breathing heavily when I dragged him inside, turned the light on and began to tear sheets to tie and gag him. When I was through, he was through too, bound, gagged, helpless on the floor.

His eyes opened. He struggled, made sounds behind the gag and glared up at me.

I hefted the wooden club, which felt like it was loaded with lead in the end, and grinned at him.

'Brother,' I said, 'it's forbidden. You sleep now, huh – or I'll bust you one with this bat you were carrying.'

He was silent and glaring when I turned the light off again and slipped out.

The estate was weird now in its quiet. Many of the cabins had gone dark. I wondered if more of the guards were creeping around. And I wondered where the woman in black was, and where Trixie Meehan was, and would it be safe to go to the cabin that Trixie was occupying with the Cudahy girl.

I decided to take a chance. Second cabin from the eating pavillion Trixie had said.

The cabin was lighted. A small radio was playing softly inside. When I knocked cautiously the light went out, the music stopped.

'That's Trixie all right,' I thought. 'And she doesn't know anything or she'd have looked me up. So what now?'

And the door opened, a girl slipped out and threw her arms around me, crying softly: 'Darling! Sweetheart!'

'Wrong number, sister,' I said, trying to untangle her from my neck.

She'd already discovered that. She uttered a little scream as she jumped back.

'I thought you were John!' she stammered.

Lightning does strike now and then. Miss Two Millions made a bull's-eye with her confused comment – and I knew something I'd been wondering about. I thought fast before I spoke.

'Paige is busy just now,' I said. 'He wanted me to tell you to – er – wait for him.'

'I didn't think he could get back from town so quickly,' she babbled. 'Who – who are you?'

'I've a message for Miss Meehan.'

'She isn't here.'

'Where is she?'

'I don't know. She – she didn't come back from the Felicity Circle.'

'That's funny,' I said calmly. 'I wonder where she could be?'

Inside I wasn't calm. I was suddenly afraid for Trixie. The night was too quiet, too ominously quiet. Paige had made a quick night trip into town for some reason – and Trixie was the first reason I thought of. Could she have been carried helplessly off the estate? And would Trixie's body be found tomorrow somewhere down in the city, accidentally dead?

'Paige didn't tell me where he was going,' I said. 'Do you know any way I could get hold of him quickly?'

She said, 'No,' and it sounded suspicious. So did the question that followed. 'Who are you? I don't believe I know you.'

'I'm Mike Harris,' I said. 'Hasn't John told you about me?'

'No.'

'He will, Miss Cudahy,' I promised, chuckling. 'He'll have a lot to say about me. I'll look around for Miss Meehan. If she comes back, tell her I'm looking for her.'

I left before she could think to turn on the light. One look and she'd have me spotted as Brother Amnesia. And she wouldn't be dumb enough not to smell a rat about my sudden familiarity with Paige's secrets.

And so Paige was her sweetheart, her darling. Smooth, eh? Smoother than I had thought. Sweetheart and darling to millions! Who said there wasn't any profit in being a crackpot?

But there wasn't any profit in Mike Harris wandering around Father Orion's zoo. Everything that happened was making the situation worse. And what about Trixie?

I was afraid – afraid for Trixie Meehan as I walked toward the big white shrine, the loaded club swinging in my hand and growing anger seething inside. Crackpots or no crackpots, if any harm came to Trixie I'd take the whole place apart.

The building was dark and seemed deserted. I skirted the terrace on the damp grass and made a circle of the shrine. Not a light, not a sound.

The patio entrance was open. I slipped inside and felt my way to the door through which Eddy Voss and Paige had carried the woman.

The door was unlocked. A dark hall was on the other side. Dark? It was an inky solid, with a tiled floor underfoot and rough plastered walls on either side. And the silence of a tomb.

I was wasting time. This wasn't finding Trixie, wasn't getting anywhere. I was sniffing unconsciously before I realized what I was doing.

The sickly pungent odor that tainted the air was familiar. Then I got it. Marijuana. So I wasn't alone. Somebody was dragging on the weed close by. A slight draft was moving against my face and I followed it up, and almost walked into a blank wall as the passage made a sudden left-hand turn.

The marijuana fumes were stronger. A partly opened door around the passage turn let out a beam of sickly light, and a voice was mumbling in a dreamy, monotonous monotone. Hefting the club, I crept to the door and looked in.

You could have knocked me over with a marijuana weed. Father Orion was doing the mumbling. Across the room he sat cross-legged with his back to a heap of gay silk pillows. The white toga had been put aside, sandals and bullet-proof vest were gone. He wore a white loin cloth, sat cross-legged like an Oriental, holding the mouthpiece of a water pipe.

A shaded lamp on the floor showed his eyes set in a fixed dull stare. His dreamy monotone was directed into space, and the words were strange and unfamiliar.

A thousand years ago the Egyptians had smoked marijuana like this bony, rather terrible old man across the room. Only the Egyptians had called it hashish.

They too had had their fantastic dreams swirling lazily through drugged minds. And so had Father Orion. You could see it on his face. He'd been partly doped out there in the patio. Hashish gave him that piercing, dreamy stare, that remote manner.

Now he half-turned to suck at the mouthpiece. His back and chest were criss-crossed by livid weals that seemed to be scars left by whips. You could only wonder what gruesome experiences he had lived through far back in the past.

He began to mumble again as I pushed the door open.

I was inside the room before I saw the thin Oriental who had been beating the drum out in the patio. He sat back in the shadows to the right, cross-legged on the floor also, watching, listening as if in a trance.

But he wasn't in a trance. He turned his head. For a long moment we stared at each other. His eyes were like dark bright buttons. He seemed to shrink in on himself and tense as I took a step toward him.

'What's the idea?' I asked, jerking my head toward the old man.

The fellow was dark-skinned, wiry, middle-aged. He might have been thirty or fifty. His thin-lipped face held no expression as he stared.

Father Orion mumbled into space without noticing us.

I wanted to swear. My pulses were jumping. The white loin cloth looked brilliant against the dark, oily skin. His torso muscles had tightened, ridged, until he seemed poised with threat as he sat there cross-legged and silent to my question.

A master mind might have bluffed it out easily. But tonight I wasn't master-minding. I was only Mike Harris, with a club in my hand and seething anger suddenly wild and reckless as I faced discovery, alarm, and the blow-up of everything I was trying to do.

'Which one of you talks first?' I said.

I had started toward him when he jumped at me. One instant he was sitting cross-legged; the next he was flying through the air in an uncanny leap, white teeth gleaming and his hand flashing up from the loin cloth with a knife.

No time to talk, to dodge. I didn't want to dodge anyway. I swung at his knife hand, hit it, smashed the hand aside. He landed like a cat, fighting and clawing. And the biggest claw was the knife which he had grabbed with the other hand.

The blade slashed my arm as I tried to parry the blow. I dropped the club and slugged him in the face with my fist. He staggered back on his heels and I jumped after him and hit him again.

He could use a knife but he didn't savvy fists. He tried to dodge, but I'd softened him into stumbling awkwardness. His chin turned just right. I hooked one to the button – and he dropped the knife and went down, glassy-eyed and cold.

Panting, I snatched the knife and club and turned to Father Orion. And still he hadn't noticed us, hadn't stopped mumbling. It was enough to give you the creeps.

He started to suck on the mouthpiece of the water pipe again, and I shoved the end of the club through the middle of the beard and pushed him back against the pillows.

'Come out of it, you dope!' I panted. 'Can you understand me?'

He shook his head dazedly and his eyes cleared a trifle. 'Truth,' he mumbled. 'Truth, Brother.'

'Truth hell!' says I. 'Where did John Paige go? What did he do with that woman who shot at you?'

'Brother,' he said vaguely. 'What do you desire, Brother?'

'Absolutely nuts!' I said through my teeth. 'And people who ought to be sane are looney because of you! Come out of the clouds, damn you!'

His eyes had already closed. He mumbled inaudibly as he sank back on the pillows. I knew it wasn't any use. He was off on a nod and man nor beast couldn't get sense out of him. I swore at him, wondering what I could do now.

Trixie Meehan's cry of warning took care of that.

'*Look out, Mike!*' Trixie's faint cry sounded somewhere outside the room.

CHAPTER V

Cat O'Nine Tails

I whirled around with the club and knife – and saw the man inside a doorway across the room. He was in the shadows. I saw the gun before I recognized the face behind it.

He thought I was coming at him. Maybe I was. Trixie's voice had set me wild for the moment, and I'd gone too far now to back out.

The lick of fire from the gun muzzle, the roaring reverberations of the report, the numbing shock that paralyzed my left shoulder and arm and side, all seemed to come at once.

I staggered back and couldn't help it. Father Orion's companion was sprawled on the floor behind me. His hand clamped on my ankle and jerked me in a sprawling fall such as I had given him.

The floor didn't seem hard. Maybe my mind was numb too. Trying to fight both men off a moment later was like a slow-motion picture. I couldn't do what I wanted to do. And I was waiting for the second shot and wishing I had Father Orion's bullet-proof vest. Eddy Voss was behind the gun and I thought he was going to finish what he had started.

He didn't. The gun muzzle tapped my head and made me foggier – and then they both yanked me to my feet.

'You want another?' Eddy Voss was snarling. 'Keep quiet or I'll blow your damn face off!'

So I kept quiet as they held me. Warm blood was crawling sluggishly down my left arm. I was dizzy, gasping for breath, sick and weak with the shock and the pain that was beginning to replace the numbness.

'Bring him in here!' Eddy gritted.

Beyond the door was a short, windowless corridor, dimly lit by a single bulb. The floor was carpeted, the walls seemed to be covered with leather over some kind of padding. There were five doors on each side of the corridor. I counted them. Ten doors, covered as the walls were. One stood partly open, and it was as thick and massive as an icebox door.

The little cell-like room inside was padded also; and as Eddy Voss jerked the door wide I saw Trixie sitting on an iron-framed couch in the center of the tiny room.

'Mike!' Trixie said, and then gasped as she saw the blood that had smeared down over my wrist and hand. 'Oh, Mike, what did he do to you?'

Eddy Voss sneered at her. 'I oughta finished him off in there. So you two know each other? Ain't that interesting?'

Trixie was pale, tiny and pretty in her helplessness as she sat there in the white robe with one of her wrists fastened to a corner of the bed by a short chain.

Chains and handcuffs hung from the other three corners of the beds, so that a person could be spread-eagled there helplessly. The low-ceilinged room seemed to crowd in and smother. Even our voices sounded flat and muted.

I felt cold enough to shiver through the pain as I realized that with the masive door closed all sounds would probably be smothered in the windowless, padded room.

'I met the lady tonight,' I said. 'We talked a little. What the hell's the idea of putting her in here?'

'Just met her tonight?' Voss said.

'That's right.'

'So she lets out a yell when she thinks something is going to happen to you. Just met her – and she knows your voice clear from the other room. And she's ready to faint when she gets a look at you.'

'He's bleeding!' Trixie said unsteadily. 'Why don't you stop it before he's lost too much?'

'Look at her,' Voss said to me. 'A hard-boiled little tramp like she's been the last half hour, getting all washy about you. Do I look dumb?'

'Damn dumb,' I said. 'How much of this do you think you can get by with?'

'Plenty,' Voss told me, and he spoke to Trixie. 'Maybe if we hold him here until he bleeds long enough, you'll talk.'

'I doubt it,' said Trixie, and I could have patted her on the back for the way her chin went up and her eyes flashed at him.

We weren't talking like crackpots now. Eddy Voss didn't look like one, although he still wore the toga and sandals. His thin face was hard, sneering, intent as he looked from Trixie to me and back to Trixie.

'She was snooping around here trying to see what she could discover,' Voss said. 'And now you show up doing the same thing. I heard you asking about that fool woman who popped off tonight. And you're the guy who lost his memory and didn't know what it was all about.'

'I'm learning,' says I, seeing that the amnesia role was washed up.

'Hold him, Ali,' he said.

Ali could understand English all right. He nodded and clung to my right arm while Voss frisked me and found the fat billfold.

'Christ!' Voss said under his breath when he got a look at the money. 'No wonder Paige said you were his private sucker.' Voss spat and grinned as he put the billfold inside his toga. 'This'll teach him a lesson.'

Blood was dripping off my finger tips. I caught Trixie's eyes watching it. 'I'm all right,' I said.

But I wasn't. Trixie knew it. So did Voss. He grinned again as he looked at the arm.

'You won't last long if that isn't fixed,' he said.

'So what?' I said.

He hit me in the face. Ali held my good arm while Voss knocked me reeling against the padded wall with blow after blow. I heard Trixie cry out, but Voss was yelling at me in a sudden fury.

'I'll fix you, you red-headed little squirt! I'll have you chained in a cell and let Ali work on you with one of his whips! Who else is with you? What are you here for? I'll find out who you are and what the money's for! Will you talk? *Will you talk?*'

His nerves weren't any better than mine had been before I found Father Orion. He had me, but he was afraid of what he didn't know. He spoke of whips – and I thought of Father Orion's whip-scarred body and these sound-proofed cells fitted up to chain people helplesly for any kind of torture.

Father Orion and his cultists were grotesque, unreal – but this was a look into depths more horrible than I could have suspected. And if I'd get what Voss was shouting, what would Trixie get? What would happen to us both if Voss was sure we were detectives?

I knew. I guess Trixie knew too. Voss probably already had his mind made up. We'd seen too much, we knew too much. There wasn't a chance even now of either one of us getting down into Hollywood to tell our stories.

So I fainted. It's always a good gag, whether the girls use it or Mike Harris tries it in a tight spot. Back against the padded wall I slumped with Ali still holding my arm. Eddy Voss dropped his fist.

'Damn him!' he gasped. 'I—'

My foot caught him in the stomach when he got that far. Never mind Ali, never mind Eddy's gun; braced against the wall I had the leverage I needed. The shoe went deep in his middle and hurled him back over the bed where Trixie was held.

'The gun!' I yelled. 'Get the gun, Trixie!'

She didn't need the order. Little Trixie could think faster than most men. She had the whipcord muscles of an adagio dancer. She was already grabbing at Voss as he tumbled off the bed on the other side.

Trixie had the full length of her arm and the short chain to move in. Voss' coat ripped as she caught it and yanked. He had hardly struck the floor when Trixie was off the bed and down on her knees catching at him.

Ali uttered a gobbling, unearthly cry as he released my arm and dived toward her. I tripped him and grabbed at him. His slippery arm went out of my fingers as he fell on all fours.

I couldn't see what Trixie was doing as I lurched down on Ali. He bounced up from under me like a ball of buttered muscles – and in the same instant Trixie raised up with the gun in her hand.

It was good to see the business-like look on Trixie's face and to know that she could handle any gun like an expert. Ali must have sensed it, must have realized that he didn't have a chance with the gun so close. He whirled with the startling rapidity which had surprised me in the other room and darted toward the door.

Trixie fired at him, high deliberately and he streaked out the door and vanished.

'Hurry, Mike!'

Trixie crouched at the foot of the bed with the gun covering Eddy Voss. When I staggered to her side, Voss was holding his middle and weakly trying to sit up. He looked sick, dazed.

'Keys are in his right trousers pocket, Mike!'

I had them a moment later.

'That littlest one, Mike!'

A moment later Trixie was free and on her feet. She handed me the gun, caught Voss' wrist, and had it in the steel bracelet before Voss could resist.

'Good work, Sweetness,' I told her.

And only then did Trixie's voice break, quaver as she came to me.

'Mike, dear, are you badly hurt? Here, let me see!'

My lip was bleeding. My face felt like it had been jumped on. The pain had been there in my shoulder but I'd been too busy to notice it. Now I did. With clenched teeth I let Trixie get my coat off, jerk my shirt off.

The arm wasn't pretty to look at. Trixie used the shirt for a swab.

'Can you use the arm, Mike?'

'Yes – fingers too,' I groaned after trying.

'Not as bad as I thought,' says little Trixie briskly. 'The bleeding is slowing up too. I'll wrap it quickly.'

'We've got to get out of here, Baby! That bird in the breech clout will have the whole place around our ears!'

Trixie ripped half of Voss' toga off with one pull and tore strips off the edge.

'Only a minute, Mike. And that woman's in the room across the hall. We can't leave her. They'll kill her.'

'I'd like to take Voss,' I said as Trixie hastily bandaged the shoulder.

Voss' head jerked up in surprise at hearing me mention his name.

'Yes, you louse, I know you,' I said. 'And the next time you won't draw a parole. What's the racket here?'

His face had gone pasty. He was afraid, and defiant too, like a rat in a corner.

'That'll do for a little,' said Trixie. 'Hurry, Mike. Maybe we've waited too long now.'

I stopped and grabbed my billfold back from the remnant of Voss' toga.

'If we turn up without *this*,' I said, 'we might as well keep going.'

'That damn money!' Trixie exclaimed. 'If you ever do a trick like that again, I'll – I'll—'

'I'll do it for you,' I promised.

We were across the hall by then and I was trying keys in the door. The third one made it. The door swung out.

'Come on, lady,' I said. 'We're taking you out of here.'

She was on the floor by the bed, as if she'd rolled off and hadn't moved after she landed. I had a premonition. Trixie beat me to it. She was pale and shaken as she looked up from the woman.

'Dead, Mike!' Trixie exclaimed.

'Murdered?' I said.

Trixie picked a little pill box off the floor and held it up so I could see the poison label.

'She killed herself, Mike.'

'I'd call it murder, anyway,' I said. 'Hell, what a joint they've been running here right under the noses of all Hollywood. Let's get out of here while the getting is good.'

I was afraid again, mostly for Trixie. What chance would she have if they caught her now? For that matter what chance had she had chained in that padded cell. At least we had a gun now, with a few cartridges left.

I lingered long enough to lock Eddy Voss in, and the woman too. If no more keys were handy, it would be a long time before anyone beat the police to them. And I wanted the police now. Jake Dennis, Larry Sweet and a squad of big-footed dicks would have looked sweeter than taffy on a stick.

I know! I hadn't solved the murder that Lew Ryster had tossed in my lap. But I'd done something bigger. I'd smashed this whole vicious, gruesome mess wide open. That was enough work for one night.

And there was still more to do. There was Nancy Cudahy. A fool she might be. But also she was a dumb innocent kid with dollars stacking the cards against her.

What chance did she have against men like Eddy Voss, Paige and Father Orion? She'd lost her head in Hollywood, she'd taken a dizzy tumble, she'd fallen in love. Maybe love had thrown her off balance. They say a woman in love is just a woman, or something like that. I wouldn't know.

'Hurry, Mike,' says little Trixie unsteadily.

'Hold it,' I said. 'I want to see what's in a couple of these other rooms. I've got a hunch.'

'You idiot!' says Trixie, half crying. 'Can't you *ever* forget you're a detective? You're half-dead now! Please come on, Mike! I can't have anything more happening to you!'

'What's happening to me – and who cares?' I said as I unlocked another door and opened it.

No soap. Unoccupied.

'One more,' I said to Trixie, who was all but hanging on my bad arm to get me started.

'Mike!' Trixie wailed. 'Can't you see what this is doing to me?'

'You sound worse than a woman in love,' I cracked. 'Buck up, baby. It isn't as bad as that. I'll get you out of here all right.'

'Oh!' says Trixie. 'Why you insufferable—'

'*Holy cow!*' I yelped. '*Now* will you shut up?'

I'd turned across the padded corridor and unlocked a door on the other side. Trixie cried out in pity. I felt a little sick myself as we forgot everything else but the man who was spread-eagled and handcuffed face down on the narrow bed in the center of the room.

A leather cat-o-nine-tails hung on the wall. The man's back was covered with bloody weals. He lay there like dead – but the sound of my voice brought his head up with a convulsive jerk and a whimpering cry of fear.

He was young, unshaven, rough-looking and powerful. He might have been a dock-worker at one time, or a sailor. His arms were tattooed. But he had starved, suffered; ribs showed plainly and his face was haggard, hollow-eyed as he stared at us.

'All right, fellow,' I said. 'We're going to take you out of here. Tell us about it later.'

He wasn't telling anything. He was like a man who'd had fear beaten into his heart and soul and was expecting more. I'll never forget the fearful look of his eyes as he watched me free his hands. And the unbelieving, smoldering look as his hands came free and I moved to his feet.

I saw him eying Trixie and the gun she was holding as I unlocked the last ankle.

'We're detectives,' I said quickly. 'We're taking you down to Hollywood to the police. Don't get us wrong and make a grab for that gun.'

He shuddered and seemed to relax and all but collapse as he swung his feet to the floor. He hadn't spoken; his voice was husky and strained as he stood up.

'Police? You're *police?*'

'That's right,' I said. 'Come on. We may have to fight our way out of here. They're wise to us. Can you run? How'll you be in a scrap?'

He flexed his arms. The muscles bulged.

'God! Can I fight?' he gulped thickly as we started to the door. 'All I want is that brown devil who whipped me every day and that old man who watched and mumbled like it was church service. I'll kill 'em both! I'll kill 'em with my bare hands!'

My club and knife were still on the floor of the room where Father Orion lay back on the pillows breathing stertorously. I was stooping for them when our man saw old Orion and jumped at him with an animal-like cry.

Trixie gasped: 'Mike, he'll kill him!'

And he would have too. His hands had plunged through the white beard and grabbed the throat. He was shaking that bony, drugged old carcass in a frenzy when I reached him.

'The cops'll get him!' I snapped. 'Come on!'

He wouldn't listen. He was in a frenzy. Maybe he didn't even hear me.

'I'll shoot him!' says little Trixie. 'Come on, you big baboon! You're making trouble for us!'

Trixie got to him where I'd have failed. He looked at her angry little face and the gun she was holding on him, and batted his hand across his eyes and laughed sheepishly.

'I shoulda counted ten first,' he mumbled, looking down at the half-strangled heap of beard and bones he had dropped. 'Come on.'

That inky black passage I led them into was like a trip through a macabre nightmare. The breech-clouted brown man had had time enough to call an army. The shrine might have held twenty men by now, waiting for us at any step. And I didn't have much fight left. I was weak, wobbly and beginning to feel light-headed.

But the door at the end was there as I'd shut it. The starlight in the silent patio was bright by comparison. And when we were outside on the terrace I sucked in the cool night air thankfully.

'If we could get an auto,' I said, 'it'd be easier. Paige is in town. Might be we could get the cops back here before he returns – or meet him on the road somewhere. Or if we could find a telephone around the joint. Trixie, know where the phone is?'

'No,' says Trixie. 'In the shrine there somewhere I think. I didn't have a chance to see much. I was looking around outside when that Eddy Voss slipped up on me. He and that gobbling mute who got away from us were looking around out there as if they expected someone to come along.'

'Paige!' the boy with us growled. 'That's the name of the fellow who got me into this! Picked me up on Pershing Square and said he had a job working around his estate. Brought me up here himself – and I was locked up before I knew what was happening.'

'I don't get it,' I said. 'What's the idea?'

'I dunno,' he said. 'I thought they were all crazy – and then I thought I'd go crazy when I found what was happening to me. That old man talking to me by the hour about his dirty heathen gods, and how he'd been to India and Egypt and Tibet and Africa and learned all there was to know about everything. And how the great crystal springs of truth could only come from eternal pain and punishment. And then he'd stand there with his eyes wild and talk and yell stuff I couldn't understand while that brown-skinned devil whipped me! Ten days I'd been there and only fed half the time – and I got the idea from things he said that there'd been others before me and if I died there'd be others after me. I was going nuts. A day or two more was about all I could have lasted. I knew I didn't have a chance. I was just Joe Clark, on the bum and nobody even knowing I'd drifted into California. Mister, what's all this about anyway?'

'Joe,' I said, 'I'm not sure about it all myself. After we get out of here, we can sit down and put the pieces together.'

'We'll get out now! Hell, we're as good as out!'

'There's a fence around here that a monkey would have a hard time climbing over,' I said. 'And the top wire is charged with electricity I was told. Or warned. The gates are chained and guarded. Figure the percentage yourself.'

'What sort of a place is this? Ain't there any law around here?'

'Sure there is,' I said. 'If we can get past that fence and down the mountain to Hollywood. Keep your fingers crossed until then.'

We had been talking under our breath as we hurried across the smooth clipped lawns toward the cabin I'd occupied. The gate was in that direction. I didn't want to get any further away from the gate. And I looked around for a parked automobile that we might have a chance of taking.

It was Trixie who said huskily: 'Over there, Mike! Running towards us!'

I looked over to the left and saw ghosts!

CHAPTER VI

The Great Truth

They looked like ghosts at any rate. Half a dozen of them running across the lawns toward us. They'd evidently been heading for the shrine when they spotted us. They were coming without warning other than their white togas against the night.

'Scram!' I jerked out. 'Toward the gate! It's the only way out I know! If there's only one man there we can handle him very easy! Save the cartridges in the gun!'

We were already running. Thank heaven, Trixie's sharp eyes had spotted them soon enough to give us some start. I expected them to start shooting; but they didn't; and then I remembered the club the guard had carried around my cabin and decided they didn't go armed with guns. Maybe someone thought the brand of fanatics around the place weren't to be trusted with guns. Clubs would do just as well most of the time – and they wouldn't be heard outside the estate by strange curious ears.

We ran. I ran too, weak and wobbly as I was. The idea of being caught and locked up in one of the padded cells was enough to bring double strength.

'Don't leave him!' Trixie panted to Joe Clark. 'He's wounded and almost helpless!'

That to a man who'd been through ten days of hell as had this Joe Clark. But he didn't have any idea of leaving us.

'Gimme that club!' he blurted at me.

So I gave him the club. I had the knife left. Trixie had the gun. That only made the odds two to one against us – if you could forget we were a woman and two half-dead men.

Down through the black, lonesome shadows under the trees, with the crunch of our steps the only sounds.

They made no noise; they didn't even shout; but twice when I looked back the flutter of their white togas was there in grim ghostly pursuit.

Then the gate, with the floodlights glaring from the stone gate posts and the stout iron gates closed. The guard was there, the same big guard with the bulging muscles and curly brown beard.

He had heard us coming or was expecting us. He stood there before the gates in the full glare of the floodlights, holding a club ready for trouble.

'Gun!' I gasped to Trixie.

She shook her head. By the way her eyes had kept turning to me, she expected me to fall any step.

Joe Clark sprinted ahead. It might have been fear or fury; he went ahead anyway despite all he'd been through. He charged that burly guard as if it were all in the day's work.

They came together swinging clubs. I swore helplessly as Joe Clark reeled aside from a blow on the head.

'Don't try it, Mike!' Trixie cried.

But I'd have tried anything. I had the knife. I kept going.

So did Trixie. She darted in front of me and brought the gun up before I realized what she was doing.

He was a bearded, fanatical, challenging figure as Trixie ran in close and pulled the trigger. And he screamed and collapsed like a sawdust dummy that had lost stuffing.

Trixie had shot his knee – little Trixie who went to target practice two and three times a week when she had the chance. I'd kidded her about it – and look now.

The guard was howling, writhing on the ground when I reached him. The gate key on a length of thin chain was attached to his belt. I tore it away.

Trixie had turned and fired a shot as I whirled to the chain and lock that held the gates. Joe Clark had jumped to her side on unsteady feet.

My hand was shaking so that I had to try twice to get the key in. Trixie fired another shot. Maybe it was the last one in the gun. I hadn't looked at the clip. And when we were outside the gate – then what?

Hollywood and help were miles away. What chance did we have after all? I wouldn't be able to stagger another quarter of a mile.

Trixie fired a third shot as I got the lock open . . .

Joe Clark howled: 'Keep back or we'll shoot every damn one of you!'

'Come on!' I yelled as the gates swung open.

And I looked back over my shoulder and saw four of them scattered out and coming after us. And Trixie's voice was agonizing in its helplessness.

'The gun's empty, Mike! What can we *do?*'

'Run!' I said. 'Duck off in the woods beyond the light! Clark and I will hold 'em!'

'No!' Trixie gasped, and I knew she meant it.

One of them yelled in triumph as they burst through the gate after us. We were almost out of the lighted area when Joe Clark's hoarse cry of despair drove sick helplessness right through me.

'More of 'em ahead!'

I saw the two figures charging up the road toward us.

'Get over in the trees!' I cried . . . and a moment later I yelled: 'Wait! They're not trouble!'

Lew Ryster had been wrong. I had been wrong. Jake Dennis and Larry Sweet were the finest fellows in the world. I loved them – I'd always love them after that moment when I recognized them running up the road toward us, guns in their hands and looking for trouble.

Jake Dennis fired a shot in the air and waved the gun threateningly as they came close.

'What the hell's going on here? Hands up!' And then Dennis recognized me and bawled: 'It's that doublecrossing little Blaine guy! Look at him! So help me I never seen—'

'Hold it, Jake!' Larry Sweet snapped. He turned to me. 'What's all this about? Who are those comics who ran back through the gate?'

'Turn in a riot call and collar the whole bunch!' I panted. 'It's murder and torture, kidnapping, blackmail and God only knows what! It's big – and you'll have to move fast to get everyone!'

'It's a laugh by the way you three look!' Jake Dennis sneered. 'I knew Ryster was stalling when he said he'd work with us. I knew he had a slick trick up his sleeve. And when you flew to Chicago I had a buddy in the department there pick you up and keep an eye on you. What d'you think of that?'

'Fast work,' I grinned, breathing easier and wanting to slap that big red-faced dick's back and shake his hand.

'We give you a chance to let us in on it,' Jake Dennis blared indignantly. 'And did you hand Sweet an' me a tumble when you stepped off that plane tonight?'

'I wondered how the hell you happened to be there,' I admitted.

'So we hadda tail you up here in the mountains,' Jake Dennis snorted. 'We had to hang around down there in the bushes slapping at the bugs and wondering what the hell all this was about! All because of a dirty—'

'Hold it, Jake!' Larry Sweet broke in. 'Who are these two, Harris?'

'Miss Meehan, from my agency,' I said. 'And Joe Clark, who was kidnapped and tortured in there. I've got Eddy Voss, an ex-con, locked up, and there's a dead woman who seems to have taken poison, and the old he-goat of the whole outfit was out on a marijuana nod when we left. The guard at the gate there is shot through the knee. I left another fellow tied up. Miss Meehan shot a couple more times. I don't know whether she knocked anyone over or not. It was a close squeak.'

'It sounds like a lunatic party!' Larry Sweet exclaimed.

'It was,' I said. 'And you better get help fast.'

'There's a car coming,' Jake Dennis said, looking down the road.

'Paige!' says I. 'I'll bet it's John Paige, Father Orion's secretary! We want him bad! He's in the center of all this!'

'We'll get him,' Dennis snapped. 'Get back off the road!'

Headlights were flashing beyond the next turn as we faded into the underbrush. The car came into view fast and slowed for the gates.

Jake Dennis waited until it was almost to us and leaped out into the road waving his gun. The car surged ahead. Dennis was expecting it. Give that big cop credit; he knew what to do. He swung on the runningboard with an arm hooked through the front window, and his bellow reached us.

'*You're under arrest! Stop this car!*'

A gun crashed – and it wasn't Jake's. Then his gun blasted twice before he fell off the running board. He stumbled, sprawled, staggered up a moment later as the big Caddy that had brought me from the airport swerved and hit one of the stone gate posts.

Jade Dennis was running unsteadily toward it when we caught up with him.

'He flashed a gun on me! I hope I killed the dirty rat!' Dennis cried hoarsely. 'Shot me in the arm!'

Well, he hadn't killed the man. The smash hadn't either. John Paige was feebly trying to get out from behind the wheel when we pulled him out.

His face was gashed and bleeding, he had a bullet hole through his chest and a line of pink froth was on his lips as he choked and breathed hard.

'What's this?' Larry Sweet said, jerking open the back door.

He dragged out a brown-haired young woman whose head lolled limply and whose eyes were wide and sightless.

'Dead!' Larry Sweet said in a flat voice. 'It must have broken her neck.' He laid her on the ground and turned to Paige. 'Who is she?'

'My wife,' Paige said. His eyes had been rolling at me with a wild, questioning stare. He hesitated before making the admission, and then broke into a fit of coughing that brought more of the bloody froth to his lips.

Then he saw Joe Clark, unshaven, gaunt and menacing and he cowered against the ground.

'His wife,' I said. 'And there's a girl in there who's ready to marry him. And she's lousy with money. What would he do with a wife who stood in his way of getting his hands on that money?'

I was thinking aloud and stooping over the dead girl on the ground at the same time.

'Sweet,' I said, 'did you see this?'

Larry Sweet's handsome face went hard and he cursed under his breath as he followed my pointing finger. She had been a pretty girl with fair delicate skin and a slender neck. The ugly, purple fingerprints on her neck might have been painted there.

'Killed her – murdered her!' Sweet said in a hard voice.

'Murdered her,' I said, 'like he murdered the Farnson girl. Both women were in his way. They would have queered his marriage to a couple of million dollars. Eh, Paige? You wanted the money bad, didn't you? Worse than you wanted my eight grand?'

He coughed, breathing with harsh rattles. 'Damn you – who are you?' he gasped.

'A cop,' I said. 'So is the young lady here who came with Nancy Cudahy. See this fellow you turned over to old Orion? Eddy Voss is locked up. It's all over. I doubt if you'll last until we get you to a doctor. Why did you think you had to kill the Farnson girl?'

I thought he was dying and it didn't matter much. He thought the same. Keeping his mouth shut wouldn't help now.

'She knew I was married,' he got out with an effort. 'She'd known my wife at one of the studios where they worked together. She had me meet her and told me she'd tell Nancy about the wife if I didn't make Nancy forget Orion and me and start back east. Had to get rid of her. She'd have ruined everything.'

'Who runs this joint – Orion or you?'

'Me,' Paige mumbled. 'Good business. They eat it up. He believes in himself and they believe in him. Never was anything like it. He didn't have a dime when I found him. I made him famous. They do anything for him, tell anything . . .'

'Hell, what a story this'll make in the papers tomorrow!' Jake Dennis said prayerfully. 'Watch everything, Larry, while I get the car.' His voice came back to us as he started at a run down the road. 'What a story – *what* a story . . .'

Lew Ryster thought so the next morning, in the Blaine Agency office in Hollywood, after he heard all the details and read the papers.

'But I told you,' Lew yelped, almost purple-faced, 'that those two pirates would steal the shirt off your back when it came to getting credit for a case.'

Lew slapped the papers on his desk. 'Look at 'em! Read it and weep. You have to be a good guesser to find anything about *us* in these papers.'

Little Trixie Meehan, pale and pretty, sweet and soft in a white summer dress and hat, said: 'Nuts, Lew. Mike would have cashed in if those two cops hadn't appeared. Let them have the glory. This man Farnson has promised Mike the two thousand reward, hasn't he?'

'All right,' Lew surrendered. 'Mike takes a thousand, you get a thousand, and I hold the bag. There's just one thing that'll make me happy. What is this Great Truth that was being taught to everyone up there?'

'I never found out,' I confessed; and suddenly I grinned as I stood up and reached for my hat. 'But I've got an idea,' I said. 'Never give a sucker an even break. And when we split Farnson's reward money, I'll keep you in mind. Lew.'

'Swell, Mike – that's decent of you. I didn't expect it.'

'That's right,' I said. 'I've had a shot of the Great Truth myself since you busted up my trip to New York. I'll keep you in mind while this shoulder is healing and I'm spending the reward money.'

I stopped at the door and grinned at Lew.

'So long, Sucker,' I said.

KINDLY OMIT FLOWERS
STEWART STERLING

It was not at all uncommon for pulp writers to be prolific, considering how little they were paid for their work, but some went to extremes, and Prentice Winchell (1895–1976), whose best-known pseudonym was Stewart Sterling, was at the front of that group. In addition to hundreds (about 400 seems the best estimate, as there may have been unrecorded pseudonyms) of short stories, he also wrote and produced more than 500 radio programs, as well as journalism and numerous literary efforts for film and television. Like many other pulp writers, he created detective characters with unusual occupations, most notably a tough fire marshal (Ben Pedley, who appeared in forty stories and nine novels), a hotel dick (Gil Vine, the protagonist in eight novels), and a department store detective (Don Cadee, in nine novels, all written under the Spencer Dean pseudonym). For *Black Mask*, he created an innovative series of nine novelettes headlined as 'Special Squad' stories, covering the activities of the Bomb and Forgery Squad, the Harbor Patrol, the Pickpocket and Confidence Bureau, the Air Police, the Pawnshop Detail, Emergency, Safe-and-Loft, and, twice, Homicide. In the present story, Sergeant Helen Dixon, generally a member of the Policewoman's Bureau, is temporarily assigned to the Homicide Division. Although there were few women cops or private eyes in *Black Mask*, Dixon stood out for, well, not standing out. She was ordinary-looking, a useful characteristic for a policewoman.

'Kindly Omit Flowers' was first published in the March 1942 issue of *Black Mask*.

KINDLY OMIT FLOWERS
STEWART STERLING

CHAPTER ONE

A Gruesome Exhibit

Lieutenant Teccard rocked back in his swivel chair. His fingers gripped the shiny oak arm-pieces tightly. It was an instinctive movement to get as far away as possible from the thing on his desk. Ordinarily, his office in the headquarters building seemed large enough. Now, suddenly, it was oppressively small and close. He kept his eyes away from the long, glass tray on the flat-top, as he reached for the phone.

'O.K. for Sergeant Dixon.'

The woman who came in wouldn't have been noticed in the average Manhattan lunch-hour crowd. She was pretty, but she hadn't worked hard at it. A man might not have paid particular attention to her as he passed her on the street, unless he happened to meet her glance. Her eyes were gray and curiously calm – as if they had seen a lot they hadn't found amusing.

She wrinkled up her nose. 'My God, Jerry! A man can live without food for three weeks and without water for three days! But you can't last three minutes without air!'

Jerry Teccard shoved his brown felt back off a harassed forehead. 'Light a cigarette if it gets you, Helen.' He indicated the roll of checkered oilcloth resting in the photographic tray. 'You don't have to turn yourself inside out, gandering at this. You can take the medical examiner's word for it.'

Acting Detective-sergeant Helen Dixon, second grade, regarded him grimly.

'After that year I put in at the Forty-seventh Street station, it'll take something to turn my stomach,' she declared.

He lifted one corner of the oilcloth cylinder. 'What's left of a woman's thigh. After the wharf rats worked on it a while.'

Her lips compressed a little, but none of the color left her face.

'Where'd it come in?'

'Twenty-third precinct. East Hundred and Fourth.' He consulted a report sheet. 'James Boyle, probationer, found a child trying to salvage the oilcloth

499

that had been tied around it with some string. Boyle's beat takes him along the Harlem docks, foot of Ninety-eighth. This thing was on the tide flat at the side of the Ninety-eighth Street pier.'

'When was this, Jerry?'

'This A.M. Quarter past ten. Doc says it's been lying there, or under the head of the pier, more'n a week. Some *pupae* of flies in the end of the bone. Eggs must've been laid seven, eight days ago, anyway.'

Helen Dixon bent over the tray. She didn't peer at the discolored bone, her finger pointed to brown shreds of fiber which clung to the outside of the oilcloth.

'You said it was tied with string?' she asked.

Teccard pointed to a soggy tangle of frazzled gray in one corner of the tray. 'Was. Doesn't mean a thing, though. Million yards of that stuff used every day.'

'But these look like rope strands to me.'

He squinted at them. 'I noticed those. I'm going to send 'em up to the lab, for a microscopic. But the reason I sent for you—'

'You figure this might be one of the *Happiness* cases?' She moved past his chair to the window, opened it from the bottom a few inches, stood staring down into Centre Street.

'There's better than an even chance. That's why I asked the Policewomen's Bureau to send you up here. I know you've been plugging like hell on that assignment. If Crim. Ident. can help, maybe you and I can work together on it. Like old times, when you were playing Big Sister to the floozies we picked up on Sixth Avenue.' He swung around toward her. 'My office wouldn't want any credit.'

She touched his shoulder lightly for an instant, spoke without turning around.

'Damn the credit! If I could only break the case. I've been running around in circles for three weeks, hoping it's just another flock of old maids forgetting about friends and families because wedding bells are still ringing in their ears. But if this,' she inclined her head toward the tray, 'is one of them, it means the very nastiest kind of murder.'

Teccard nodded. 'Never knew a suicide to cut off her leg. It's pretty obvious.'

'Any special reason to think she was one of this matrimonial agency's customers?'

He lifted his chin, ran a finger around under his collar uncomfortably. 'Remember what you said that day we had lunch at the Savarin. About the kind of heels who have to find their females through an ad? Especially when they pick on dames who've had the lousy luck to be disfigured or crippled?'

Her voice was bitter. 'I'm not likely to forget. Every one of those five appeals for inquiry come from friends or relatives of women who have some physical disability – or some facial blemish that would put them at a disadvantage in the national pastime of husband-hunting. Of course those poor lonely lambs could be led to the slaughter, by some unscrupulous devil who flattered them and promised them . . . whatever he promised.'

Teccard fiddled with pipe and pouch. 'Well, that thigh bone was broken. In two places. While she was living, I mean.'

Helen Dixon turned, perched on the window sill. 'The left leg?'

'Yair. Wasn't there one of those dames . . . ?'

'Ruby Belle Lansing.' The sergeant eyed the oilcloth with repugnance. 'Spinster. Thirty-six. Grade-school teacher in Tannersville. Hip broken in automobile accident, October 1939. Double fracture, set at Catskill Memorial Hospital. Entered into correspondence with the *Herald of Happiness* in August, 1941. Came to New York, October sixth, after being introduced, by mail, to Philip Stanton, then of 4760 Madison Avenue, this city.'

The lieutenant consulted his report sheet. 'Length of femur, 18.1 inches. Let's see – factor for women is three and six-tenths. About sixty-five inches tall. Would this Lansing—'

'She was just five feet, five, Jerry. By the Tannersville Board of Education records. What must have been more important to Stanton, Ruby Belle had a little more than two thousand dollars in the savings bank at Phoenicia. Three days after her arrival, she had this deposit transferred to the Emigrant Bank here. On October tenth, the next day, it was withdrawn, except for ten dollars. Since then, there hasn't been a trace of her. Or of Stanton!'

'Any description of him?'

Helen shrugged. 'Nothing to count. He never went to Tannersville. Her uncle – the one who asked us for a check-up – said he saw a snapshot of Stanton. But all he remembers is, the fellow was good-looking and had a mustache.'

'That's a great big help!' Teccard called for a policeman to take the thigh-bone back to the morgue. 'What about the people where Stanton lived?'

'A rooming house. Man who runs it's nearly blind. Stanton didn't seem to use the room much, anyway. Half the time the bed wasn't disturbed. Best I could get was, he was kind of dark.'

'Ah! Send out an all-borough to pick up dark guys with mustaches! And reserve Central Park to hold 'em in! Yair! How about the other four who're missing? Same skunk, each time?'

Helen bent over the oilcloth, peered at the brown fiber again. 'I wish I could remember what that stuff makes me think of. About the men in the other cases – I'm up against one of those things, Jerry. The disappearances were strangely similar. In every instance, the man resided in New York. The woman involved always lived in some small town, upstate. And every time the man sent the woman a ticket to come to the big city. What's more, flowers were invariably sent. Can you tie that? A bouquet for the unseen bride! Also, every one of the five dropped out of sight within three or four days – after sending for their home-town funds.'

'All cut from the same pattern!'

'I thought so, at first. But the men in each of the cases had different names. Different addresses.'

'What the hell! A crook of that kind could pick out a new alias or a new address as easy as you choose a blue plate!'

'I saw some of the letters these men wrote. In the agency files. The handwritings don't bear any resemblance.'

'He could fake them. Or get someone else to write them for him.'

'Not usual, is it? A murderer taking someone into his confidence? Unless it's a gang. Which it might be, from the varying descriptions of the men – according to the photos. There was always a snapshot, you see. One of the *Happiness* rules. One man had a beard. Another was partly bald. One was around fifty. The fellow in the Schwartz case couldn't have been more than twenty-five, the victim's brother claims. You wonder I've been stymied?'

Teccard spread his hands. 'We'll have to go at it from this end. That oilcloth probably came from the five-and-dime – be tough to trace. But if this killer chopped the Lansing woman up, there'd have been more than a thigh bone to dispose of. Not so easy to get rid of a cadaver. And he slipped up this once. If he was careless again, we'll get somewhere. I've put a crew from the precinct on that. They'll sift that whole damn waterfront through a sieve, if necessary.'

The sergeant sauntered toward the door. 'I hope you beat me to it, Jerry. I haven't been sleeping so well, lately. Thinking about some other poor, lonely fool on her way to meet a murderer. If this guy – or this gang – has gotten away with it five times, there won't be any stop now. It's about time for another one. They've been spaced about a month apart.'

Teccard frowned. 'I thought you said you were up a blind alley on it. What do you mean, beat you to it?'

She smiled, tightly.

'I didn't say I was licked. I still have a card to play.'

'If we're going to work together—'

'That would be all right with me. But this is something you couldn't very well come in on. I'm entered in Cupid's Competition.'

He jumped to his feet. 'Now what in the hell!'

She nodded, calmly. 'Current issue of the *Herald of Happiness*, Meeting Place of the Matrimonial Minded Department. "Miss Mary Lownes, single, thirty-one. Of Malone, New York. Pleasant disposition. Capable housewife, though suffering from slight spinal complaint. Occupation, nurse." I was, you know, before I turned policewoman. "Anxious to meet amiable, sober businessman under fifty." That ought to get him, don't you think?'

'Just because you were assigned to an investigation doesn't mean you're supposed to risk running up against a killer, Helen.'

'After the slimy specimens I've been running up against, a murderer'll be a relief. This chasing up and down subways and elevateds to trap exhibitionists, those hours of stting through double features to nab mashers in the act – that's not only hard work, it kind of gets you to thinking half the world's made up of perverts.'

'Yair. But that's the sort of stuff only a woman can handle. Homicide isn't for the Women's Bureau, it's a man's job.'

'It's my job to put a stop to any matrimonial agency that's doing business like this – to see that love-hungry women don't get murdered when they figure on getting married.'

'You find the man. We'll put a stop to it – without your getting into it.'

'That would suit me swell. But it might not work. I may have to get into it, to find the evidence necessary to convict.'

The lieutenant put his fists on his hips and glared. 'Hey! You don't mean you'd go so far as to marry the murdering so-and-so?'

'I'll go as far as I have to, Jerry. Maybe you've forgotten I had a sister who fell for a slimy snake like this Stanton. Alice turned on the gas one night – without lighting it. I found her body. I hate men like that worse than those phoney abortionists I rounded up this spring. At least those girls knew they were taking a terrible chance. These poor, misguided love-seekers don't even realize their danger until it's too late.' There was a dull, hurt look in the gray eyes. 'But so far, there's been no proof that any of these women wound up with any legal certificates. No record of any licenses at City Hall, even.'

'God's sake, Helen! You know the regulations forbid any infraction of ordinances in attempting to trap a criminal!'

'Nothing criminal about getting married, is there, Jerry?'

He opened his mouth, shut it again, glared at her. When he spoke, it was in the tone of a commanding officer. 'You let me know before you go through with any damn nonsense like that, hear?'

She saluted, stiffly. 'Yes, Lieutenant.'

He wasn't more than a minute behind her in leaving the office. The police clerk by the rail in the outer room spoke out of the corner of his mouth to a plainclothesman one-fingering on a typewriter. 'Geeze! The Lieutenant musta just swallowed a cup of carbolic or something.'

'Teccard? He always looks like that when the Dixon dame gives him "No" for an answer. He's been carryin' the torch for her so long, he sleeps standin' up, like the Statue of Liberty.'

CHAPTER TWO

Herald of Happiness

The detective-lieutenant drove his department sedan up Broadway to Twenty-eighth, studied the directory board in the lobby of a ten-story office building, pushed into the elevator.

The *Herald of Happiness* was housed in a single room at the rear of the third floor. The door was locked, but there was a bulky shadow moving against the ground glass. He rapped.

The man who let him in was fat. Tiny purple veins laced the end of a bulbous nose. The eyes that searched the lieutenant's were slightly bloodshot.

'You the proprietor of this agency, mister?'

'I am, sir. T. Chauncey Helbourne, if I can be of service to you. You are a subscriber?'

'I'm from police headquarters.'

'What, again? I've already put up with a distressing amount of annoyance from a Miss Dixon . . .'

'You'll be putting up with a prison diet, if you're not careful.'

'Prison! You can't frighten me, sir. I run a legitimate business.'

'Nuts! You come close to being a professional panderer. Don't tell me you have a license, it doesn't cover complicity in fraud!'

Helbourne's neck reddened. 'I won't be bulldozed by any such tactics, officer!'

'Lieutenant. Lieutenant Teccard.' He surveyed the cheap furniture, the unpainted rack of pigeonholes along one wall.

'It makes no difference to me if you're the commissioner, himself. I have influential connections at City Hall, too. And my records are always open for inspection by authorized parties.'

'O.K. I'm an authorized party. I'll have a look at any letters that've come in here the last week or so.'

The fat man waved vaguely at the row of green-painted files. 'Help yourself. It would take me a couple of months to locate 'em. I don't file by dates.'

'I'll make a start at it.' Teccard pulled out a steel drawer marked *L*. He ran his thumb along the tabs until he came to one with the letters *LO*, took out all the folders in that section. 'How many letters you rake in, per day, mister?'

'You mean the preliminaries?'

'What the hell is a preliminary?' There was a folder with the name *Mary Lownes* at the top. It was empty, except for an envelope in Helen's handwriting, addressed to *Herald of Happiness* – and a clipped-out advertisement.

Helbourne picked up a proof-sheet of a page. 'Subscribers are allowed one free advertisement to each subscription, plus as many answers to other advertisements as they wish. Our only restriction is, these replies to ads must be addressed to the box-number of the *Herald*.' He pointed to one. 'Any letters coming in, addressed to that box-number, are copied and sent along to the advertiser, no charge. Without the name or address of the sender, naturally.'

Teccard slid the folders back in place. 'The old come-on. What do you tap them for giving out with the address?'

The proprietor of the *Herald* frowned. 'Our fee is five dollars.'

'At each end of the transaction? Five from the snappy skirt who wants the address of some dope who's given her a line of mush? And another five from the dope himself, if he wants to get in touch with her direct?'

'I don't like the way you put it, Lieutenant.'

'Catch them coming and going, don't you! Next thing you know, you'll catch five years in the pen.' Teccard drifted toward the rack of pigeonholes. There were letters and folded carbon copies in most of them. Under each space was pasted a copy of some *Herald* advertisement.

Helbourne watched him sullenly. 'I'm not responsible for what my subscribers do after I've performed an introduction.'

'Hell you aren't! You're wide open for prosecution. You were warned some New York crut has been rooking old maids from upstate, using you as a go-between.' There was a cubbyhole with two letters, over an advertisement reading:

YOUNG LADY OF BREEDING

seeks companionship of amiable, sober businessman, under fifty, with quiet tastes. One who would appreciate a better-than-average table and a comfortable home. Not wishing to be supported, as have slight means of own. Able and active, though slight spinal injury. Brunette, thirty-one, former trained nurse. Box LL27.

Helen was a brunette – the age and the references to the spinal injury and having been a nurse clinched it. Teccard reached for the letters.

The fat man caught his arm. 'You'll have to get a court order, if you're going to ransack my mail, Lieutenant.'

Teccard disengaged the pudgy fingers. 'One side, mister. A minute ago you told me to help myself. I am. You want any trouble, I'll see you get plenty.' He crackled the letters open. The first one read:

Dear Miss Box LL27.

Your ad made a great deal of an appeal to me. I am a farmer, widower five years now, age forty-six. It's a seventy-acre fruit farm, paying good, too. I have

a piano, radio, Chevrolet, nice furniture. The part about better than average cooking appealed to me. Do you play the piano? Hoping to hear from you,
   Very sincerely yours,
   Herman Schichte
   Rural Route Six
   Pathanville. N.Y.

The lieutenant stuck it back in the pigeonhole. 'Park your pants in a chair, mister. It makes me nervous to have anyone reading over my shoulder.'

Helbourne sat down. His mouth was open and he was panting as if he'd been climbing stairs. He kept rubbing his palms on his knees while he watched Teccard run through the other letter.

Your message in the *Herald* was like music heard far off over the water at night. Perhaps I am wrong, dear LL27, but I sense in your heart an aching desire for the finer things which life too often denies those best fitted to enjoy them. If I have understood you rightly, your appeal for companionship strikes a very sympathetic chord in my own soul. I am thirty-five, dark and, though no Adonis, not bad to look upon, I have been told. I have a comfortable business and am fond of travel, theater and books. Possibly you would care to write me so we could exchange photographs and perhaps – *quien sabe* – perhaps, some day, rings to symbolize even more than companionship!
   With eager anticipation,
   Your friend,
   Harold Willard
   971 East 88th Street
   New York City

Teccard put the letter in his pocket. East Eighty-eighth wasn't so far from the pier where that grisly bone had been found.

'This Harold Willard,' he said. 'Let's see the other letters you've had from him.'

Helbourne shook his head quickly. 'That's the only one. I never heard of the man before. I can't keep track—'

'Yair. I heard that one. You recognize his signature?'

'No. Not at all.'

'You sent the copy of this drool along to Box LL27?'

'Not yet. It was going out today,' Helbourne said.

'Don't send it. And don't send out copies of *any* letters that come to you from New York City. Not until I've had a look at them. Understand?'

'Yes, sir.' Helbourne held his head sideways, as if he expected the lieutenant to take a punch at him. 'Is there – ah – any cause for you to believe the writer of that letter – has been involved in these – ah – irregularities you are investigating?'

Teccard stuffed a copy of the *Herald* into his coat pocket. 'Only that he writes phoney as hell. You ought to have your butt booted for handling that kind of sewage. And if I find you've passed on any more of it, I'm coming back and rub your nose in it.'

It was dusk when the sedan reached the Twenty-third Precinct station house. Teccard was glad to get out of the chill wind whistling across Harlem from the river.

'Cap Meyer around?' he inquired of the desk sergeant.

'You'll find him in the muster room, with a couple boys from Homicide, Lieutenant.'

Teccard strode into the back room. Four men stood about the long table under a green-shaded bulb. Three were in plain-clothes, the fourth was in uniform. There was a black rubber body-bag at the one end of the table, at the other a piece of wax paper with as grisly a collection as the Identification man had ever seen.

'What you got, Meyer?'

The captain turned. His face was a curious greenish-yellow in the cone of brilliance. 'I wouldn't know, Teccard. But whatever it is, you can have it.'

One of the Homicide men finished tying a tag to the third finger of a skeleton hand. 'All we're sure of, it was an adult female.'

His partner stripped off a pair of rubber gloves. 'That's all you'll ever establish, for certain. Person who hacked this woman up was pretty tricky.' He indicated the cracked and flattened end of the finger bones. 'Mashed the tips to prevent any print-work.'

Meyer tongued around his stub of cigar. 'Wasn't really necessary, though. The rats took care of that.'

The uniformed man spoke up. 'All this mess had been dumped under the shore end of that Ninety-eighth Street pier, Lieutenant. There was a loose plank there, somebody must of ripped it up. It was near covered by muck, but we shoveled it out and used the hose on it, well as we could.'

'Including that thigh-bone, we got everything but one foot now,' the first Homicide man said. 'But it wouldn't do any good to try a reconstruction. All the teeth were hammered out of that head, before it was dropped in the mud.'

Teccard bent over the yellowish skull, stained with dirty, grayish mold. 'Parts of some fillings left. Jaw still shows where she had some bridgework done. We can check the dentists, up around Tannersville.'

Captain Meyer exclaimed: 'You got a line on her, already?'

'Yair. Schoolteacher who thought she was coming to town for her wedding ceremony. *Till death do ye part.* It parted her, to hell and gone, didn't it?' He turned away. 'How about letting me have one of your men who knows the Eighty-eighth Street beat? In the nine hundreds.'

Meyer and the uniformed man looked at each other. The captain gestured.

'Patrolman Taylor, here, had that beat up to a month ago. How long you need him?'

'Depends. Bird we're after may have flown the coop already.'

'O.K. You're relieved, Taylor. And if you have any trouble when it comes to putting the arm on the crut who did this,' the captain jerked his head toward the table, 'do me one favor.'

The policeman touched the rim of his cap. 'Yuh?'

'Shoot him a couple times where it'll really hurt. All he'll feel, if he goes to the chair, will be a few seconds' jolt. Way I feel, that'd be letting him off easy . . .'

Out in the car, Taylor pulled a folded-up newspaper from his hip pocket. 'That kid who found the leg this morning squawked all over the neighborhood. We warned him to keep his puss shut – but the papers got it just the same.'

Teccard didn't read it. 'They can't print much, if they don't know any more than we do, Taylor. What you know about number 971?' He pulled up half a block away.

The patrolman craned his neck. 'Nine-seven-one? The old brick house? Nothing much. Just four- or five-buck a week furnished rooms. No apartments.'

'Who runs it?'

'Old dodo named Halzer. Him and his wife. They got 969, too – operate 'em together. He's harmless, stewed about half the time.'

'Yair? You ever hear of a guy, name of Harold Willard, in this parish?'

'Harold Willard. Harold Willard. I don't recall it, Lieutenant. What's he look like?'

'Dark, about thirty-five years old. That's all we've got to go on. My guess is he fancies himself for a double of one of the movie stars. Likely to be a flash dresser.'

'I can't seem to place him. Maybe he's just moved in. They keep coming and going in a joint like this.'

'Yair. If he happens to be in now, we'll keep him from going.'

'We can do that, Lieutenant. There's no rear doors on this side of the block.'

'You go on ahead, then. Go into 969. Find out from Halzer what room Willard has. When you know, stand in the door of 969 and wait for me to come past. You can give me the high sign without anyone watching you from one of the windows next door,' Teccard explained.

'Check.'

'And after I go in, nobody comes out. I mean nobody. Until I say so.'

'Got you, Lieutenant.' The patrolman strolled away, idly twisting his night-stick.

Teccard stood on the curb, tamping out his pipe. He gazed curiously up at the lighted windows of 971. What kind of murderer could it be who took such care to hack his victim to pieces – only to attempt to hide all the remains in one spot? There had been other instances of dismembered corpses in the records of the Criminal Identification Bureau but, so far as Teccard could remember, limbs and head and torso had invariably been strewn far and wide, to prevent any reconstruction of the body. Was he up against one of those unpredictable, pathological cases of sadism – where mutilation gives the killer a diabolical satisfaction? That didn't seem to match up with the carefully planned disposition of the victim's funds . . .

Taylor's club showed, in the areaway of 969. The lieutenant walked along, briskly.

'Third floor rear,' the policeman whispered hoarsely. 'Room J.'

Teccard didn't turn his head, or answer. He marched up the steps to 971. The front door was unlatched. There was a row of battered, black-tin mail-boxes. He paused just long enough to make sure one of them bore a piece of paper with the penciled scrawl: *Harold M. Willard.* Then he went in.

The hallway smelled of cooking grease and antiseptic, the carpeting on the stairs was ragged. Somebody was playing a radio. A baby squalled. There was a sound of running water from a bathroom somewhere on the second floor.

Over the sill of room J was a thread of yellow light. Someone was moving about in the room, but Teccard, with his ear to the panel, heard nothing else. He transferred his gun from his left armpit to the right pocket of his coat, kept his grip on the butt.

He knocked and, without waiting, raised his voice.

'Telegram for Mister Willard.'

The movement behind the door ceased. There was a pause, then: 'Slide it under the door.'

Teccard kept his voice high. 'You got to sign a receipt, mister.'

'Shove your receipt book under, too. I'll sign it.' The answer came from halfway down the door – the man inside was evidently trying to look through the keyhole.

'The book won't go under. You want the telegram, or not?'

Another pause.

'Wait a second. I'm not dressed.'

'O.K.' Teccard tried to make it sound weary.

'Where's the wire from?' The man had moved away from the door, but the tone was strangely muffled.

'We ain't allowed to read telegrams, mister. If you don't want to accept it—'

The door opened.

The man was in his underclothes. He stood sideways, so Teccard couldn't get a good look at him. His black hair was rumpled, he held a towel up over his mouth and the side of his face, as if he'd just finished shaving.

'Is there anything due—' He reached out with his other hand.

The lieutenant stepped in, fast.

'Yair. You're due, mister. Put down—'

There was a faint '*Hunh!*' from behind the door, the uncontrollable exhalation of breath when a person exerts himself suddenly.

Teccard whirled.

The blow that caught him across the top of the head knocked him senseless before his knees started to buckle!

CHAPTER THREE

Murder in Room J

Taylor poured a tumbler of water over Teccard's head. 'Take it easy, now. Amby'll be here any second.'

The lieutenant rolled over on his side. 'Quit slopping that on my head.' The floor kept tilting away from him, dizzily. 'Lemme have it to drink.'

The cop filled the glass from a broken-lipped pitcher. 'You been bleeding like a stuck pig.'

Teccard paused with the tumbler at his lips. Was that a pair of shoes lying on the floor behind the patrolman? He shook his head, to clear away the blurriness. 'Who in the hell is that?' he cried.

Taylor's jaw went slack. 'That's the lad you was battling with. You fixed his wagon, all right!'

'I wasn't fighting with anybody! Someone slugged me from behind that door, before I could even get my gun out.' The lieutenant got his elbows under him, propped himself up. The man on his back was T. Chauncey Helbourne – and his skin was a leaden blue.

The officer nodded sympathetically. 'A crack on the conk will do that, sometimes. Make you forget what's been goin' on, when you snap out of it.'

Teccard felt of the back of his neck. His fingers came away wet and sticky, the ache at the top of his skull was nauseating. 'I didn't kill him, you dope!'

'Geeze! You had a right to drop him, didn't you! He was resistin' arrest, wasn't he?'

Teccard crawled on hands and knees to the dead man's side. There was an irregular dark blot on Helbourne's vest, just inside the left lapel; in the center of the blot something gleamed yellow-red, under the naked bulb overhead. The lieutenant touched the fat man's face. It was still close to normal body temperature.

'You got him first clip out of the box.' Taylor pointed to the gun on the floor, by the side of the iron cot.

Teccard stood up shakily, sat down again, suddenly, on the sagging edge of the cot. Taylor, the corpse on the floor, the barren furnishings of the room –

all seemed oddly far away. He bent over to let the blood get to his head again. 'Where's the other gent who was in here? The one in shorts?'

The uniformed man squinted as if the light hurt his eyes. 'The only lug I saw is this stiff, Lieutenant.'

Teccard closed his eyes to stop the bed from shimmying. 'He let me in here. How'd he get downstairs, past you?'

Taylor put up a hand to cover his mouth, his eyes opened wide. 'Now I swear to God there wasn't a soul on them stairs when I come up. If there'd been a guy with his pants off—'

'How'd you happen to come up, anyway?'

'Why, geeze, Lieutenant. When this dame comes scuttling down to the front door, yelling for "Police" naturally I hotfoot over from next door.'

'A woman? What kind of a woman?' Teccard demanded.

'Why, just an ordinary mouse like you'd expect to find in one of these joints. Kind of blond and plump – I don't know.'

'What'd she say?'

'She says, "Officer, come upstairs quick. There's a couple of men fighting and making a terrible racket right over my room." She says, *"Hurry!"* So I figure it's you subduing this Willard and maybe needing a hand. I come up on the jump.'

Teccard started to shake his head, thought better of it. 'Where is she now. Bring her here.'

The policeman pounded out in the hall, downstairs. He left the door open. There was an excited hum of voices from the corridor.

Teccard took a pencil out of his pocket, stuck it in the barrel of the pistol, lifted it off the floor. He wrapped his handkerchief carefully about the butt, broke his weapon. Only one chamber had been fired from the .38. The bullet hole in Helbourne's chest would be about right for that caliber.

Taylor came clumping upstairs. 'She put one over on me. That room underneath ain't even occupied. And she's scrammed, anyway.'

'So has the jerk who was half undressed.' The lieutenant put down the revolver, poured himself another drink of water. 'That's over the dam, don't get gidgety about it. You were right, according to the way you figured it.'

The cop wiped sweat off his forehead. 'It's all balled up in my mind. Was this Willard the one who shot the fat boy, here?'

'Might have been. The gun was still in my pocket when I went down. Somebody took it out and used it on T. Chauncey Helbourne. Somebody else. Not me.' Teccard gazed grimly around the room. 'The worse of it is, I couldn't absolutely identify Willard, even now. He was covering his smush with a towel and he sort of kept his back to me, anyhow.'

He didn't bring up the point that bothered him most – it was a cinch Willard hadn't been the one who crowned Teccard from behind that door. Maybe his unseen assailant had been Helbourne. In any case, what was the proprietor of the *Herald of Happiness* doing up here, when he had claimed complete ignorance of Willard!

A siren wailed, out in the street.

'Holler down to the doc, Taylor. Tell him all he needs to bring up is a few stitches for my scalp.'

'You'd ought to go to the hospital, Lieutenant. Have an X-ray, to be sure there ain't any fracture.'

Teccard went over to the closet door, opened it. 'There's nothing more the matter with my head than's been wrong with it for thirty-seven years. Did you buzz the station, too, Taylor?' he said.

'Yes, sir. Cap Meyer is coming right over, himself, with a couple of the boys.' Taylor went out into the hall, shouted down the stairwell.

The lieutenant sniffed at the empty closet. The only things in it were a few coat hangers and a sweet scent that made him think of church. Queer thing to find in a place like this, probably came from clothing that had been hung up here.

He looked around the room for the weapon with which he had been slugged. There wasn't anything heavier than a cane wastebasket. The wastebasket was empty, too, except for a crumpled piece of cellophane stripped from a pack of cigarettes. He fished it out with the point of his fountain-pen, put it on the bureau.

The interne arrived, went to work with needle and sutures. Meyer and two plainclothesmen came up. While the doctor jabbed the needle through his scalp, Teccard told the captain what was wanted.

'Box up that cellophane, run it down to my office. There might be prints on it. Get a photographer up here from Homicide. Have him powder the knobs, the bureau drawers, the iron part of the bed, those hangers in the closet. Run a vacuum over the floor, ship the dust down to the lab for examination.'

Meyer crouched over the fat man. 'Who's this guy, Lieutenant?'

'Crumb who ran a matrimonial agency. That's what's back of those bones your boys dug up today. Go through his pockets, will you? And mark someone down for going through the house, here, to see what they can get on Willard. Taylor, you learn anything about him from the landlord?'

The patrolman scratched his head. 'Not much. Oh, one funny thing. He must have a night job. Because he only comes here in the daytime. And he must write a lot of letters, because practically the only thing old Halzer remembers his having up here, outside his clothes, is a box of writing paper and a bottle of ink.'

'Yair? See can you find if he threw any of his scribbling in the wastebasket. Maybe some of it is still in the trashcan.'

Meyer said: 'Not much dough, but plenty of unpaid bills, on this fella. He's been hitting the high spots, you ask me. Here's a credit-jewelry store summons for non-payment on a diamond wristwatch. And a bunch of duns from department stores and an automobile company.' He tossed the sheaf of papers on the bed. 'Eleven fish and some chickenfeed, a cheap ticker, two nickel cigars, a silk handkerchief stinking of whiskey, and a bunch of keys.'

'No weapon?'

'Not even a pen-knife, Lieutenant. You're pretty positive he wasn't the fella cut up that girl's body?'

'He'd have been well-padded with folding money, in that case, Cap. No. You rustle around, get a description of Harold Willard.'

Teccard waited until the doctor growled: 'Kind of a patchwork job, Lieutenant. You'd be smart to take a couple days sick leave. That's an ugly gash.'

'If that stuff about the stitch in time is on the up and up, you must have saved about ninety-nine of 'em. Thanks. I'll be around, for you to rip them out again.' He picked up the keys. 'I might use these, Cap.'

'Want Taylor to go with you?'

'No.' Teccard examined his hat. There was a right angle cut where the brim joined the crown. He smoothed the felt thoughtfully. 'You might let me have a gun, though. Mine'll have to go to Ballistics.'

Meyer brought out an automatic. 'You can take Betsy, if you don't mind a big caliber.'

The corners of Teccard's mouth curled up. 'A forty-five is just the ticket.'

'You after big game?'

'Yair.' Teccard checked the magazine to make sure it was loaded. 'You ever go after moose, Cap?'

'Moose? Hell, no. Duck is my limit.'

'Well, when a guy goes after moose, he uses a horn that makes a sound like a female moose. The bull comes a-running – and the hunter does his stuff.'

A puzzled scowl wrinkled Meyer's forehead.

'I'm going to get me a horn, Cap. But there's nothing in the book says for the rest of you to stop hunting.'

He went downstairs.

The night elevator man in the building housing the *Herald of Happiness* regarded Teccard coldly. 'Who you want to see on the third, mister?'

'Just giving the premises the once-over.' The lieutenant held his badge out on his palm. 'Snap it up. I haven't got all night.'

'Ain't anyone up on that floor.'

'That's why I'm going up. Do I push the lever myself?'

The car started. 'I can't have people going in and out alla time. I'll lose my job.'

'Don't worry about it. Everything's strictly copacetic.'

The elevator door clanged loudly. Teccard swung around the corner of the corridor into the ell where Helbourne's office was located – and stopped short. Somewhere ahead of him a light had been suddenly extinguished. He stood still, listening. There were none of the noises to be expected when an office is being closed for the night. No door opened.

He balanced the heavy automatic in his left hand, held the keys in his right, tightly, so they wouldn't rattle. Quietly, on the balls of his feet, he moved to the *Herald's* door. Still he heard nothing, except the faraway roar of Broadway. He tried the key which showed the most signs of use. The latch turned. He stepped aside swiftly to the right, kicked the door open.

If there was anyone inside, the only target would be Teccard's hand, holding the pistol. He snaked his wrist around the jamb of the door, fumbled for the light switch he knew must be there. It clicked. The office flooded with brilliance.

There was a laugh.

'*Kamerad!*'

He swore under his breath, stepped out into the doorway. She was sitting back in Helbourne's chair, her feet cocked upon the desk. There was a pile of letters in her lap, a flashlight in one hand and a short-barreled .32 in the other.

'Imagine meeting you here,' he said dryly. 'I phoned the Policewomen's Bureau for you. They knew from nothing!'

Sergeant Dixon took her high heels off the desk. 'I've been using the super's passkey every night for the last two weeks. How'd *you* get in?'

He jangled the keys. 'Property of T. Chauncey Helbourne. For the evidence clerk.'

She looked at him sharply. 'Evidence? Is Helbourne . . . dead?'

Teccard sat down on the edge of the desk. 'That's what happens when you take a slug under the fourth rib.'

'Who shot him, Jerry?' The sergeant tossed the letters on the desk, stood up.

'There seems to be a general impression I did. The bullet came from my Regulation, all right. But I'd say the killer was the same one who did away with Ruby Belle.'

She saw the bandage on the back of his head. 'Jerry! You were in it! You're hurt!'

'Yair.' He managed a lop-sided grin. 'That was no love-tap. Somebody dropped the boom on me, but good.'

She reached up, lifted his hat off gently. 'That was close, Jerry.'

'They meant to kill me, at first. Changed their minds when they fished through my pockets, found my badge.'

'They? Were there two of them?'

The lieutenant nodded. 'One K. O.'d me while I was putting the gun on the other one. I went bye-bye before I got a square look at either of them. They both scrammed. Now they know we're closing in, they'll be foxier than ever. If they've got anything on fire, they may try to pull it off before they do the vanishing act. But we'll have to move fast, if we're going to catch up with them. That's why I came down here, to see if there might be any other poor boobs readied up for the kill.'

'You might have asked me. Just because I spent two years putting fortune tellers out of business and running around to disorderly dance halls, doesn't mean I've forgotten how to use my mind.' She held up a sheet of pink notepaper. 'I dug this out of Helbourne's private postoffice, there. It has all the earmarks. Box KDD. A Miss Marion Yulett, seamstress of Algers. Thirty-three. Possesses certain means of her own. Has a cheerful, homeloving disposition, yet is full of pep. Miss Yulett encloses five dollars to secure the address of a certain Peter Forst who's apparently been giving her a buildup about his charms.'

'He live in New York City?'

'Can't find any folder for Mr. Forst. Peculiar. Not even any letters to him – or from him.'

Teccard chewed on his pipe-stem. Was Forst another one of Willard's aliases? Had Helbourne been putting one over when he claimed to know nothing about other letters from the mysterious individual who always wrote from Manhattan? 'When did this deluded dame come through with Helbourne's fee?'

'Week ago today.'

The lieutenant reached for the phone. 'Hustle me through to your super, pal. Supervisor? This is Lieutenant Jerome Teccard, New York Police Department, Criminal Identification Bureau. Talking from Bryant 3-2717. Yair. Get me the chief of police of Algers, New York, in a hurry, will you? Algers is up near Whitehall. Yair . . . I'll hang on . . .'

While he was waiting, Teccard tried the only flat key, from Helbourne's bunch, on the locked middle drawer of the desk. It fitted. In the drawer was an empty cigar carton, some paper matchbooks, an overdue bill from one printer and a sheaf of estimates from another, a half-full flask of *Nip-and-Tuck Rye*, and a torn, much-folded plain-paper envelope, addressed to the *Herals of Happiness, Box KDD!*

The envelope was postmarked three weeks ago, from Station U, New York City.

Helen looked up Station U. 'East One Hundred and Sixth Street, Jerry.'

'Same precinct as the bones. And friend Willard. One will get you ten that's where we find brother Forst, too.'

There was a voice in the receiver. Teccard held it to his ear, muttered 'Yair' a few times, added 'Much obliged, chief,' racked the receiver.

'Too late. Sucker Yulett left Algers on the morning train.'

Helen punched the files with her fist, angrily. 'For New York?'

'Didn't know. Southbound, anyway.'

The hurt look came into her eyes again.

Teccard shoved his hands into his pockets, gloomily. 'All he did know – she had her suitcase, and the station agent said she was wearing a corsage.'

She showed teeth that were clenched. 'Those damned flowers again!'

'They'll probably last just long enough to be used on her casket,' Teccard brooded. 'Wait, though. We might still be in time.'

'It wouldn't take her all day to get to New York!'

'It might. Station master didn't tell the chief what time the train left, this A.M. Might have been late morning. And those trains up north of the capital run slower than a glacier. If the Yulett girl had to change at Albany, and wait . . .'

Helen got the phone first, called train information. It was busy. The sergeant kept pounding the desk with her fist until she got her connection.

Before she hung up, Teccard was asking: 'Can we stop her?'

'Only train making connections from Algers to New York arrives at Grand Central, eight forty. Gives us about twenty minutes.'

He caught her arm. 'Hell it does. We'll have to burn rubber to make it. We can't wait until she gets off the train. We'll have to find her, convince her we're on the level, tip her off what she's to do. Chances are, Forst'll be waiting for her. We'd scare him off before we spotted him.'

She was streaking down the corridor toward the elevator. 'We catch the train at a Hundred and Twenty-fifth, come in with her?'

'If she's on it. If we can locate it. And if she'll listen to reason. That's a hell of a lot of "ifs".'

The department sedan zoomed over to Park and Thirty-fourth – went through the red lights with siren screeching. They didn't stop to park at a Hundred and Twenty-fifth, sprinted up the stairs as the conductor gave the 'Boa-r-r-d!'

The sergeant saw the bunch of lilies-of-the-valley first. 'That sweet-faced one, in the dark blue coat and that God-awful hat, Jerry.'

'Yair. You better break the ice. She'll be suspicious of a man.'

Helen dropped into the empty seat beside the woman in the unbecoming hat. The lieutenant stayed a couple of paces in the rear.

'Miss Yulett?' the sergeant inquired, softly. 'You're Miss Marion Yulett, from Algers, aren't you?'

The woman smiled sweetly, opened her bag, produced a small pad and a pencil.

Swiftly she wrote: *Sorry. I am hard of hearing.*

Teccard smothered an oath. It wouldn't have mattered if she'd been crippled or scarred up – Helen would have been able to fix it so the Yulett woman could step into a ladies' room, somewhere, and give her instructions to handle the man she was going to meet. But there wouldn't be time to write everything out in longhand, without arousing 'Forst's' suspicions. And if the killer had an accomplice, as the lieutenant believed, this deaf woman couldn't

516

hear what 'Forst' and the other would be saying to each other – and that might prove to be the most important evidence of all!

Helen scribbled away on the pad. Teccard sidled up along side so he could read.

I am Sergeant Dixon from the N.Y. Policewomen's Bureau. Are you Marion Yulett?

The woman shrank back in her seat.

'Yes. Why do you want me?' Her voice shook.

The pencil raced in Helen's fingers.

Only to save you unhappiness. Maybe worse. You plan to meet a man named Peter Forst?

'Yes. Is anything wrong?'

The sergeant held the pad out, again.

We believe he's a killer who's murdered several women who became acquainted with him through the Herald. Have you a picture of him?

Miss Yulett fumbled nervously in her bag, produced a small, glossy snap-shot. Teccard's forehead puckered up. This couldn't be a photo of Willard, by any possibility! The man in the snap-shot was round-faced and pudgy-cheeked. He had a neatly trimmed goatee and his hair receded at the temples, from a high forehead!

Helen wrote: *How will Forst recognise you?*

'I had my picture taken, too. I sent it to him day before yesterday.' Miss Yulett bit her lip to keep from crying. 'I'm afraid it wasn't a very good likeness – I don't photograph well. But I was wearing this hat and these beads,' she touched a necklace of imitation pink jade, 'and I'm wearing his flowers, too.' Tears began to stream down her cheeks, she turned her face toward the window. 'You must be mistaken about Peter, his letters were so sweet and kind. I can't imagine his . . . hurting anybody.'

The train began to slow for the track intersections in the upper yard. There was no time for softening the blow, with sympathy.

Helen made the pad say: *If he's the man we're after, he doesn't intend to marry you at all. If you have any money, he'll wheedle it away from you and then— Did he mention anything about money?*

The words came out between convulsive sobs: 'Only that he had a small and prosperous business. With a partner who wasn't . . . quite honest, perhaps. If Peter and I . . . got . . . along . . . he said I might want to buy out this other man's interest. So my . . . my husband and I . . . could be partners.'

The pencil moved so swiftly Teccard could hardly follow it.

Brace up now, Marion. We're getting in. Take off your hat. And your beads.

Miss Yulett dried her eyes on a tiny handkerchief, did her best to smile. 'You're going to meet him, with me – so he can have a chance to explain?'

No, I'm going to meet him. As you. Wearing your hat and beads. Unpin those flowers, too.

517

'But, please! Please let me—'

Don't waste time arguing. If he looks all right to me, I'll let you meet him later. I'll take your bag, too. You take mine. And wear my hat.

The disturbed woman unclasped her beads. 'But what on earth am I to *do*? Where will I *go*? I don't know anybody but Peter—'

The gentleman standing behind us is Police Lieutenant Teccard. He'll see that you get to a hotel. Stay where he tells you to until I can get in touch with you.

Teccard gripped Helen's shoulder. 'No you don't. You take Miss Yulett to the hotel. I'll meet pal Peter.'

Sergeant Dixon looked up at him. 'What evidence do you think you'd get out of him, Jerry? He's not the same man you ran into uptown, is he? As things stand, you haven't a thing on him.'

'I'll sweat the evidence out of him, all right.'

'Maybe you couldn't. There's always the possibility this fellow's on the level. If he is, I turn him over to Miss Yulett. If he isn't, I'll be able to give first-hand testimony as to how he operates. This is a job only a policewoman can handle effectively.'

Teccard grimaced. 'Put your gun in her bag, then. And don't be dainty about using it. Another thing: I'm going to turn Miss Yulett over to one of the pick-pocket squad in the terminal and tail you and your intended.'

'All right, as long as he doesn't spot you.' Helen adjusted the ridiculous brim of the hat, snapped the beads around her neck. Hastily, she used the pad once more.

Did Forst tell you where you were to stay in New York? Or how soon you'd get married?

'As soon as we could get the license.' Tears glistened in the woman's eyes again. 'He said I could stay with his family. But I don't know just where they live.'

'I bet Peter doesn't, either,' Teccard muttered, beneath his breath. He watched Helen go through the contents of Miss Yulett's bag – the little leather diary, the packet of envelopes like the one in Helbourne's desk drawer, the savings bank book.

The train slid alongside the concrete platform, redcaps kept pace with the slowing cars.

Helen put her arm around Miss Yulett's shoulders, hugged her lightly. Teccard pulled down the worn, leather suitcase from the overhead rack. 'I'll get a porter for you.'

'Don't be silly.' The sergeant hefted the bag, easily. '*She* wouldn't spend a quarter that way. So I won't.' She nodded cheerfully at the woman, joined the procession in the aisle.

Teccard got out his notebook, penciled: *I'm going to get a detective to take you to the Commodore Hotel. Right here in the station. Register and stay right in your room until Sergeant Dixon comes for you. Don't worry about your bag, or expenses. We'll take care of them. Understand?*

She didn't hide her fear. 'Yes. But I'm afraid.'

He patted her shoulder. 'Nothing to be scared of—' he said before he realized she wasn't reading his lips. He followed her out to the platform, located one of the boys on the Terminal Squad, told him what he wanted done. 'Keep her here on the platform for a while, too. Better take her out through one of the other gates – in case the man we're after is still waiting there. Phone my office and tell them her room number. Notify the desk at the hotel to route all calls to her room through the office of one of the assistant managers.'

He tipped his hat to Miss Yulett, left her staring blankly at the bandage on the back of his head. The poor soul must be scared stiff, he knew. Well, better than *being* a stiff . . .

He had managed to keep sight of Helen's abominable hat, thirty or forty yards ahead. He put on steam to catch up with her. She was playing the part of the timidly anxious woman, to the hilt – searching the faces of the crowd lining the gate-ropes with just the right amount of hesitancy.

Teccard couldn't see anyone who resembled the snapshot. He was completely unprepared for what happened. A young man of thirty or so stepped abruptly out of the thinning crowd and took the suitcase out of the sergeant's hand.

Except for the exaggerated sideburns, his thin, clean-cut features could have been called handsome, in a sinister sort of way. If it hadn't been for the cream-colored necktie against the extravagantly long-pointed soft collar of his mauve shirt, he might have been considered well-dressed. There was no goatee, none of the full roundness of the face in Miss Yulett's snapshot. Yet Teccard was sure he recognized the man. He had only seen those dark eyebrows in side view – the deeply cleft chin had been covered with a towel when the lieutenant had pointed a gun at him. But this would be Harold Willard, beyond much doubt.

Teccard couldn't get too close to them. 'Willard' or 'Forst' or whatever his name was, would be certain to recognize the man who had crashed the room on Eighty-eighth Street! How could the lieutenant shadow them without being spotted himself?

Evidently 'Willard' knew that Miss Yulett was deaf, he showed no surprise when Helen offered him the pad. But apparently there was some difference of opinion going on. The sergeant was shaking her head, as if she were bewildered.

When her escort took her arm and led her across the great central lobby, toward the subway entrance, she evidently protested. She made her way to one of the marble shelves alongside the ticket windows, pointed vehemently to the pad. 'Willard' began to write, furiously . . .

*

Teccard bought a newspaper, unfolded it, kept it in front of his face so he could just see over the top. He edged, unobtrusively, within a dozen feet.

'But I don't understand.' Helen gazed at 'Willard' in obvious fascination. 'You're so much better-looking. Why did you send me the other man's photograph?'

The youth favored her with a dazzling smile, proffered her a sheet from the pad.

She read it, crumpled it, seemed to thrust it into the pocket of her jacket. 'I would have liked you even more, Peter – if you had trusted me – told me the truth.'

They moved on toward the Lexington Avenue subway. Willard was having difficulty holding up his written end of the conversation. He kept setting the bag down, scribbling rapidly, then seizing her arm and rushing her along again.

Teccard followed them through the stile, downstairs to the uptown platform. They boarded the rear of one crowded car. The lieutenant squeezed onto the front platform of the car behind. He saw Helen's hand release the crumpled paper, before she was pushed into the car. People surged in like a mob pressing to the scene of a fire. Teccard struggled through the door over the car-couplings, into the space Helen had just vacated. He stooped, retrieved the paper.

He held it down at his side, unfolded it.

I wanted to be certain you were not attracted to me merely because of my looks, darling. That's why I sent you the other picture. Now I am sure you will love me, for what I really am – not merely what I seem to be. Is that not better, dear one?

Teccard spat out a sibilant, jammed the paper in his pocket. The doors closed, the train rumbled out of the station.

He searched the crowded car aisle, ahead. They must have found seats somehow.

He unfolded the paper again, elbowed his way slowly forward.

They were nowhere in the car. Long before the brakes had screamed for the Eighty-sixth Street stop, he knew they were nowhere on the train.

CHAPTER FIVE

Primrose Path

Teccard was in a cold rage as he shoved through the throng and up to Eighty-sixth Street. 'Willard' had made a sucker of him with the old on-agin, off-agin, Finnegan – gone in the rear door, made his way, with Helen in tow, up by the side door at the middle of the subway car and – at the last instant – stepped off to the platform while the lieutenant was perusing the note Helen had dropped.

Of course, the sergeant couldn't have stopped the man without giving her hand away. Of course, also, 'Willard' must have caught a glimpse of Teccard. Now, the make-love-by-mail guy would be on his guard – and likely to suspect Helen. Teccard had dragged her into this mess, by requesting her assignment from the Policewomen's Bureau. Now she was literally in the hands of a cold-blooded killer!

By force of habit, he called the Telegraph Bureau first, to get the alarm out for the dark-haired youth. The description was complete now. Teccard was good at estimating weight, height, age. Long experience in the Criminal Identification Bureau made him remember points that the average policeman wouldn't have noticed. 'His ears are funny. Kind of pointed, at the top of the helix. He brushes his hair to cover them as much as he can. And his chin looks as if somebody had started to drive a wedge into it. And don't forget, this man is sure to be armed and dangerous.'

Then he called Captain Meyer, repeated the description.

'Send a car around to check every man on beat, will you, Cap? Odds are good he hangs out in this parish somewhere. Have 'em keep an eye out for Sergeant Dixon, she'll be with him.'

He had half expected to find a report from her, waiting for him when he called his office. He was wrong about that. The office didn't have much – there hadn't been any prints on the cellophane, too many on the knobs and furniture in the Eighty-eighth Street room. They hadn't been able to find any of record, though.

Talking with the Telegraph Bureau had given him an idea. He called Western Union, located the night traffic manager. 'There was a bunch of flowers wired from this city to Miss Marion Yulett in Algers, upstate, sometime this A.M. Chances are, they went through Floral Telegraph Delivery. Find out what shop put in the order, will you? Buzz me back.'

He fumed and stewed in the drugstore phone booth for what seemed like an hour. When he passed the clock over the soda fountain, on his way out, he found it had been seven minutes.

The address the telegraph company had given him was only a few blocks away. He didn't bother with a cab, but went on the run. Over to Second, up to Eighty-seventh. There it was, next to the undertaker's place in the middle of the block. *THE REMEMBRANCE SHOP.*

Potted ivy and cactus in the window, flanked by lilies and dried grasses in tin vases – inside, a glass-front icebox with cut flowers, roses and carnations.

Carnations! Now he knew why that fragrance in the closet had reminded him of church, there had always been a big bunch of white carnations in front of the pulpit, when he was a kid. 'Willard' must have had a carnation in the buttonhole of the coat he hung up in the closet . . .

*

521

A girl stood talking to the shirt-sleeved man behind the counter. As Teccard walked in she was saying: 'You'll send those wreaths over to the sexton right away? He's waiting for them.'

The florist nodded impatiently. 'I'll get 'em right over, right away.' He turned inquiringly toward the lieutenant. 'What can I do for you, sir?'

Teccard drew a deep breath. This was the man in the snapshot! Round face, goatee, receding hair! 'You can tell me who ordered some lilies of the valley wired to a lady up in Algers, New York.'

'Was there some complaint?' asked the florist.

'Just checking up on the person who sent them. I'm from the police department.'

The girl paused, on her way out, to stare at him out of stolid blue eyes set deep in a square, pleasant face.

'Police! What's the matter the police should come around?' The man waved his arms, excitedly.

Teccard said softly: 'You have a duplicate record of your F.T.D. orders. Let's see it.'

The florist ran stubby fingers through his hair, dug a flat, yellow book out of the debris on a bookkeeping desk. He ruffled the pages. 'It ain't against the law, sending flowers like this!'

The carbon copy of the wired order wasn't helpful. All it indicated was that Peter Forst had paid two dollars and fifty cents to have a corsage delivered to Miss Marion Yulett at Algers.

'Who took the order?'

'Nobody. The envelope was under the door when I'm opening the shop this morning. With the cash. What's the matter, eh?'

Teccard's hand clamped on the other's wrist. '*You* sent those posies yourself, Mr. Forst.'

'Forst! What's it, Forst?' The man's eyes narrowed. 'I'm George Agousti, I run this business, no nonsense. I pay taxes.'

The lieutenant's grip remained firm. 'Then someone's been framing you, Agousti.'

'Framing me? For what!'

'Murder.' Teccard spoke quietly.

Agousti recoiled as from a blow. 'It's terrible mistake you making. So much as a single flea, I ain't ever hurt.'

'You don't know this Peter Forst?'

'The first time I ever hear his name, so help me!'

'What about Harold Willard? Heard of him?'

The florist shook his head.

'You don't feel like talking, do you? Maybe you'd feel more like it if you came down to headquarters with me.'

Agousti shrugged. 'I'm telling you. There ain't nothing on my conscience. I ain't afraid to go anywhere you like.'

Teccard made one more try. He described the man Helen had gone with. 'Know *him?*'

Recognition crept into the florist's eyes. 'I ain't dead sure. But from how you putting it, this one might be Stefan.'

'Who's Stefan?'

'Stefan Kalvak. He's no good, a low life, sure.'

'Yair, yair. Who is he? What's he do? Where's he live?'

'He's Miss Kalvak's brother, she really owns this shop. I run it for her. She's O.K., fine. But Stefan's a bum, a stinker. Always stealing dough out the cash register when I don't watch. Or getting girls into trouble, you know.'

'He's done his best to get you in trouble. He sent your picture to this girl up in Algers – so she'd come to New York to get married.'

'Holy Mother!'

'Where's he live?'

'You got me. His sister threw him out of her apartment. But you could phone her—'

A freckle-faced boy burst into the shop. 'My pa sent me for the ivy for ma's birthday, Mr. Agousti.'

'All right, Billy. Excuse me, one second.' The florist whisked out of sight, back of the showcase.

The boy jingled seventy-five cents on the counter, an elevated roared overhead – and Teccard began to sweat, thinking of Helen Dixon and Stefan Kalvak.

The youngster called. 'Pa says you needn't bother to wrap it up, Mr. Agousti.'

There was no answer from the rear of the shop, though the sound of the elevated had died away.

Teccard stepped quickly around the glass case.

Agousti was leaning, face down, over a wooden bench – his head under the spreading fronds of a potted palm. There was a dark puddle on the boards of the bench, it widened slowly as drops splashed into it from the gash in the florist's neck.

A sharp-bladed knife that had evidently been used to cut flower stems, lay with its point in the glistening disk of crimson. There was blood on Agousti's right hand, too. Teccard lifted the limp wrist, saw the slash across the base of the fingers.

That settled it! A man didn't cut his hand that way, when he slashed his own throat! The florist had been attacked from behind, while he was putting the ivy in a flowerpot. He had tried to block off the blade that was severing his jugular – and had failed.

Not five feet from the dead man's back was a rear delivery door, with a wire screen nailed over the glass. The door was closed, but not locked.

Teccard tore a piece of green, glazed paper from the roll fixed to the end of the bench, wrapped it around the knob and twisted it. Then he opened the door.

A narrow alley ran behind the two-story building. It was floored with cement. There wouldn't be any footprints on it – and there wasn't anyone in sight.

He came inside, shut the door. He stuck his nailfile through the oval handle of the key, turned it until the bolt shot home.

The boy stuck his head around the corner of the glass case. Teccard stepped quickly between him and the body.

'Is he sick?' the youngster began.

'Yair. You go home, tell your father the ivy will be over later.'

'O.K., mister. Gee, I'm sorry—'

'Wait a minute, son. You seen Stefan Kalvak around tonight?'

The boy made a face. 'Naw. Steve ain't never around, except with girls. I don't like him, anyways—'

'You know where he lives?'

He jerked a thumb toward the ceiling. 'I guess he lives right up over the flower store, here.'

Teccard was startled. 'That so?' Maybe the kid didn't know about the sister tossing Stefan out on his ear . . .

The boy ran. When he'd gone, the lieutenant felt in the pockets of the dead man, without disturbing the position of the body. There was a leather container, with four Yale keys. He took them.

One of the keys fitted the front door. He used it, from the street. Then he stepped into the entrance-way to the second floor stairs.

There was only one mailbox, a big brass one with a mother-of-pearl push button and a neatly engraved card: *Vanya Kalvak, Floriculturist.*

He went up the stairs, noiselessly.

There were two doors opening off the second-floor hall. The one nearest the front of the building had another of the engraved cards tacked to it.

He heard voices. They came from the room behind the door at the head of the stairs.

The tones of the girl who'd asked Agousti to deliver the wreaths, were very distinct.

'Why do you come here, anyway, Miss Yulett?'

'Your brother brought me here,' Helen answered. 'He said it was all right.'

Teccard's heart skipped a couple of beats. What was Helen doing, *talking?* She must have been startled out of her wits by this other woman and been caught off guard. He put his ear to the panel.

'I'm very sorry for you, Miss Yulett.'

'I don't understand! Why should you be?' The sergeant was still playing her part. 'Peter said he would be back in a moment. He'll explain.'

'Peter!' The girl's tone was one of disgust.

'His name is Stefan. Stefan Kalvak.'

'It all seems very queer. I can't imagine why he lied to me about his name. But you ought to know, since you're his sister.'

The girl laughed harshly. 'You stupid idiot! He is my husband.'

'*What!*' The sergeant didn't have to fake that exclamation, Teccard thought.

'It is the truth. I am his wife, God forbid.' The girl spat out the words. 'I know what he told you. The same as he told those others.'

'You're just trying to drive me away from him.'

Teccard decided they were in the kitchen of the apartment. One of them kept moving about restlessly – probably Mrs. Kalvak.

'I'm trying to save your life. You don't know Stefan. He's a fiend, absolutely. After he's taken your money – have you already given it to him?'

'No,' Helen answered. 'Tomorrow after we get the license, we will talk over buying the business.'

'Tomorrow, you will be dead – if you do not let me help you get away.'

'I should think you'd – hate me, Mrs. Kalvak. But honestly, I didn't know Peter – Stefan – was married.'

'I don't care about you one way or the other. The reason I'm praying to God for you to get away quickly is that I don't want him caught.'

'No . . .'

'I know what would happen to him, if the police got him. My eyes haven't been closed all these months. Stefan hasn't earned the money he's been spending. Nevertheless—' she hesitated— 'nevertheless, I love him.'

A phone bell jangled in the front room. Mrs. Kalvak stalked away to answer it. Teccard waited until he heard her answering in monosyllables, then he tried the door. It was locked.

'Helen,' he whispered as loudly as he dared. 'Helen!'

The sergeant didn't hear him.

Mrs. Kalvak was storming back into the kitchen. '*You* talk of lying!' she cried. 'You . . . trickster!' Mrs. Kalvak's voice rose in anger. 'That was Stefan on the phone.'

'He's coming back, then?'

'Sooner than you like, *my fine deaf lady!*'

'Wait—'

'You're no country innocent, Miss Yulett. I know who you are. You're a detective – trying to trap my man. And all the time I was sorry for you, thinking you were caught in his net!'

Helen screamed, once. Teccard heard a thud. He lunged at the panel. 'Helen! Get the door open!'

There was no answer.

He pointed the muzzle of Meyer's automatic an inch from the edge of the jamb, at the lock.

Before he could pull the trigger he felt something, like the end of a piece of pipe, jab painfully into the small of his back. A suave voice murmured: 'Use my key! It will be easier.'

CHAPTER SIX

Cupid Turns Killer

The lieutenant held the pose. A hand came around his side and relieved him of the .45.

'Come on, Vanya! Open up!'

The door swung wide. The girl stared, white-faced. 'I didn't know you were out here, Stefan. I heard him – trying to get in.' She held a heavy, cast-iron skillet at her side.

'I came upstairs while he was bellowing like a bull.' Kalvak prodded Teccard between the shoulder-blades with the muzzle of the automatic. 'Get inside, there.'

Helen sprawled on the floor beside the refrigerator. Her hat lay on the floor beside her, the wide brim crushed by the fall. The sergeant's head rested on a brown-paper shopping bag, her hair over her forehead.

Kalvak whistled, softly. 'You killed her, Vanya!'

'She's only stunned.' The girl lifted the skillet. 'When I found she was a detective, I *could* have killed her.'

'We've enough trouble, without having a cop-murder to worry about. Did you search her?'

Vanya kicked the sergeant sullenly. 'There's no gun on her. What are you going to . . . do with them?'

Kalvak snarled at her. 'I'll take care of them.' He dug a spool of adhesive out his pocket. 'Sit down in that chair. Grab the back with your hands. Close your eyes.'

'Hell! You're not going to tape us, are you?'

'You think I want you to follow us, you ——!'

Teccard saw a peculiar bulge inside the lining of Miss Yulett's hat. He couldn't be certain what it was – but it might be worth a gamble. 'If you don't want to fret about a cop-murder, you better call a doc for her.'

'She'll snap out of it, all right.'

'Damn it! I tell you she's dying!' Slowly and deliberately, so Kalvak couldn't mistake his intention, Teccard moved a step closer to Helen – dropped down on one knee beside her.

The weapon in Kalvak's hand swiveled around to follow the lieutenant's moment. 'Leave her alone.'

Teccard rested his weight on one hand, close to the hat brim. The other he put on Helen's forehead. 'She's like ice – if you don't get her to a doctor, fast—' His hand touched cold metal under the loose lining of the big hat.

Kalvak sensed something wrong. 'Keep away from that hat!'

Teccard fired without drawing the stubby-barreled .32 out from under the hat-lining where Helen had hidden it. It was an angle shot and risky as hell – but the lieutenant knew the risk he and Helen were running, if he didn't shoot. The bullet hit Kalvak about three inches below his belt buckle. It doubled him over and spoiled his aim with that automatic. But the heavy slug ripped across the lieutenant's hip. It felt as if molten metal had been spilled all along the thigh. He lifted the .32 – hat and all – emptied three more chambers. The first bullet missed its mark. The second one caught Kalvak under the V-cleft in his chin. The third wasn't needed.

Vanya sprang, caught him as he fell. She slumped on the floor, held his head in her arms, whimpering.

Helen struggled to sit up. 'You and the U.S. Cavalry, Jerry,' she mumbled.

He helped her to stand. 'I was a sap to lose you, there in the subway.'

Helen pressed her hands on top of her head, winced. 'Peter – I mean Harold – or Stefan – Gone?'

'Thanks to your hiding that .32 in the Yulett dame's bonnet.'

Yanya whined, wretchedly: 'I know you're glad he's dead. I ought to be glad, too. After all the terrible crimes he's committed. But I'm not, I'm not.'

The lieutenant limped over to her. 'It was a good act, while it lasted, Mrs. Kalvak. But it couldn't last forever. You can take off the disguise.'

She stopped rocking. 'You mean I knew about Stefan's having committed murder? Yes, I knew. When it was too late to prevent them.'

'I'll say you knew.' He picked up Meyer's pistol. 'The one who didn't know – for sure, anyway – was Stefan!'

Helen said, 'What?'

The girl sat there, as if stupefied.

'All right. O.K. See what that innocence stuff gets you after patrolman Taylor identifies you as the woman who ran downstairs at Eighty-eighth Street to tell him there was a fight going on over your room. Why'd you chase over there after your husband, anyway? Because you'd read that story in the newspaper about the kid finding the Lansing girl's bones?'

'That'd be my guess. You were up there in the room Stefan had rented as Harold Willard, so he could get his hooks into another dame,' he waved ironically toward Helen, 'and you were packing up the clothes he had in the closet, or maybe just arguing with him so he wouldn't think you knew too much about those bones under the pier. Then who should ride up on his charger but T. Chauncey Heilbourne. When he heard about the disappearing dames and the dough that vanished along with them, he wanted a cut of that, too. And he went to the right place to get it.'

*

Vanya laid her cheek against the bloodless one in her lap. 'You do not really believe such horrible things. No one could believe them.'

Helen was at the sink, using cold water. She held up a small camp hatchet. 'Could it be this Boy Scout meat axe? Somebody's been scouring it with steel wool.'

The head of it would fit the gash in my fedora just ducky.' Teccard answered. 'But it didn't kill Helbourne. It knocked him cold. He was shot after I'd had *my* light put out. *You* shot him, Mrs. Kalvak – so I'd either get blamed for bumping him myself or think Helbourne was the rat responsible for the *Happiness* murders.'

'I was there at Eighty–eighth Street.' Vanya stroked the corpse's forehead. 'I did hear the fight. I told the truth to the policeman. You shot that man yourself.'

'No cop shoots a man lying down, lady. The blood stain on Helbourne's vest was round, with the bullet hole in the center. If he'd died on his feet – the way it would have been if he was shot in a fight – the blood stain would have been tear-shaped – with the point down. How'd you beat it out of the house? Rush your husband down to that bathroom on the second floor – have him wait there, while you murdered Helbourne without Stefan's knowing it? And then take a powder after the patrolman ran up to the third floor?'

The sergeant went over to pick up what was left of Miss Yulett's hat. She picked up the brown-paper market basket at the same time. 'Don't tell me this girl cut up that Lansing woman, all by herself, Jerry!'

'Yair. Probably did it all with her little hatchet.'

'But why?' The sergeant held the bottom of the market bag up to the light. 'If Stefan got the money out of these women, with his honeyed words . . . ?'

'Stefan wheedled it out of them – and turned the cash over to Mrs. Kalvak. She's the sort of skirt who wouldn't mind her husband monkeying with other femmes, if it paid enough.'

Vanya kissed the corpse on the lips. 'Darling! Listen to the hideous lies they make up about me!'

'Talk about lies, Mrs. Kalvak! You must have lied plenty to your husband. You'd probably promised to get the lovelorn out of his way after he'd garnered in the gold.' Teccard turned his back to inspect the wound on his hip. 'Maybe he thought you scared them off by that "he's-a-married-man – I'm-his-wife" line. I don't know. But I'm damned certain *you* thought the easy way to keep the suckers quiet was to plant them. Why you had to hack them to pieces—'

Helen held up the market bag, by its brown-twine handle. 'Recognize those brown fibers that clung to the oil cloth, Jerry? From this twine. Goes through the bottom of the bag to give it strength. She used this to carry . . . them . . . in.'

'Yair. Yair. That's why she had to axe them in small hunks. So she could carry the pieces out of here and down to the wharf, without being conspicuous!' He went over, hauled the girl to her feet. 'Or maybe it's you just like cutting up people. Like Agousti.'

Vanya touched the wound in Stefan's neck, as if she couldn't believe her eyes. 'Stefan went to . . . see Agousti. I know nothing of that.'

'Don't, eh? Then it won't be your prints on that stem-cutter or the door-knob downstairs, eh? You didn't decide Agousti'd have to be shut up before he prevented your getaway, then?'

Mrs. Kalvak looked up at him. There was murder in her eyes.

Helen hurried to the front room. 'I'm going to call the wrecking crew, to take over here.'

'I've had all of this *I* want,' Teccard agreed. 'And I'll sure be glad when you don't have to muck around in this kind of slop.'

'Man works from sun to sun,' the sergeant twiddled the dial, 'but woman's work is never done. In the police department.'

'Far as that goes,' he got out his twisters, 'one cop is enough . . . in any one family. Don't you think?'